Cast the First

Angela Arney

For all my family and friends who put up with the months I spent as a recluse when writing this book. For Judith Murdoch whose constructive criticism and encouragement spurred me on to finish writing the novel.

Table of Contents

PART ONE
1943—1944

Chapter One

1 May 1944

'I do solemnly declare . . .'

When he was speaking Italian, Nicholas managed to sound more English than usual. The very preciseness of his tone was alien to the musical language. Now his clear voice echoed loudly as he repeated the marriage vows.

Liana trembled with nervousness. She wished she didn't feel so sick. To her heightened senses, the walls of the tiny church, already bulging ominously with age, seemed to shudder visibly every time Nicholas spoke.

His voice, so loud in contrast to the mumbling of the priest, made her jump. She looked up fearfully. Common sense told her she was being irrational, but, nevertheless, she half expected to see lumps of mouldy plaster come crashing down from the walls. Like the walls of Jericho. What was it made *them* fall? A voice, a trumpet? She could not remember, and anyway it isn't important, she reminded herself, dragging her wandering attention back to the marriage service.

Nothing so dramatic as tumbling walls happened, and apart from Nicholas's voice repeating the marriage vows, the only sounds were the rustling silk of her dress and the occasional scuffle and cough from the small congregation. Why, oh why, was it so difficult to concentrate, Liana wondered. It was important that she did; more than one life depended on it. But still her mind floated away. Restlessly her fingers smoothed the silk of her skirt, the shiny material slipping beneath her touch. Strange, she thought, this material was a parachute only a short while ago. Some Allied soldier came floating down into my part of Italy, his life dependent on this piece of silk. Now it is my wedding dress, and my life is dependent on it too, because I need this marriage. The gravity of the thought focused her mind, and she concentrated on the service.

'I'm nearly there, *nearly there.*' She repeated the words silently to herself as they clattered through her brain, keeping in time with the regular thud of her heartbeat. She felt impatient. The wedding service was dragging, and Liana was irritated with the old priest. Surely he could hurry it up a little?

9

But at last he finished with the long Liturgy of The Word, and now began the actual Marriage Rite.

'Nearly there.' She relaxed a little, the pent-up tension escaping with a little hissing sigh from her lips. 'But not quite!' The remark exploded painfully somewhere inside her head, and a sudden rush of panic nearly overwhelmed her. I'm going to be sick, she thought. But I can't be sick, not here, not in the church. Not at my wedding, not now! Oh God, I'm not as much in control as I thought.

'But I will get there, I will, I will, *I will.*'

Liana's head jerked up with the effort of reimposing her conscious will over her subconscious. The sheer silk of her wedding dress stuck to her limbs as a fine sheen of perspiration suddenly covered her body. A terrifying thought struck her. Had she spoken the words out loud?

She slid her gaze anxiously past Nicholas and the priest. Biting her bottom lip, she breathed a sigh of relief. It was all right, the words must have been in her head: no-one else had heard. They couldn't have, because no-one was looking in her direction. Nicholas was still repeating the vows after the priest, and Charlie Parsons, the best man standing beside Nicholas, was looking bored, as was Hamish Ross, the officer who had given her away. She had nothing to worry about.

Straightening her back, Liana stared resolutely straight ahead, focusing her gaze on the walls. But no comfort was to be found there. Elongated eyes stared at her from all directions, each one filled with malevolent accusation. The eyes belonged to the faded frescoes of numerous saints. They seemed to jostle for space, as if each one wanted a better view. Liana felt another bout of quickening hysteria spiral in her stomach.

'What do you know? Eight hundred years on a wall doesn't qualify you to denounce me!' The screaming came from far away, shrilling hideously with panic-stricken laughter. She recognized that shrieking voice hurling the words at the silent paintings – it was her voice. Although this time she knew she hadn't spoken.

'Liana,' Nicholas hissing her name broke the nightmare.

Liana nearly wept with relief at the timely interruption, but her response to Nicholas was automatic. Turning towards him, she smiled and presented the serene exterior he knew so well. It was an effort, but somehow she did it. Dragging her mind back to the present, controlling the rigor that threatened to rack her body, she hastily subjugated the menacing thoughts.

I must be vigilant, she thought fiercely. Now is not the time to go to pieces and lose control. Not now that I'm so nearly there.

She concentrated on the gnarled hands of the priest holding the dog-eared missal. He began to speak. 'I do solemnly declare . . .'

Liana spoke after him. 'I do solemnly declare that I know not of any lawful impediment why I, Eleanora Anna Maria, Baroness San Angelo di Magliano e del Monte, may not be joined in holy matrimony to Nicholas Peter Hamilton-Howard.'

There, she had said it, and it was the truth – almost. There was no lawful impediment to their marriage; not unless it counted that Nicholas was not a Catholic, and because of that, they shouldn't be having the full nuptial mass. But what did that matter? The service meant nothing, just a jumble of words. Nothing, nothing mattered, except getting the wedding ceremony over and done with.

'I will.' Once again the voice of Nicholas interrupted her thoughts.

The priest turned to Liana. 'Do you, Eleanora Anna Maria . . .'

Her eyes flickered derisively over the old man standing before them, and her lips curled with thinly veiled scorn. His withered frame was covered in a filthy soutane, stained with food and wine, the droppings of many meals – not all his own by the look of it. The soutane was much too large for him, and flapped loosely around his scraggy body. Probably stolen from some other less fortunate priest. A sham, she thought contemptuously, even you, supposedly a man of God. You don't believe in God any more than I do. How can you? How can you be a priest and take a bribe? She knew Nicholas had paid him well for their wedding. Money bought everything in Naples. Even a civil and church wedding was possible with no questions asked. There was only one question, 'Can you pay?'

But despite her disdain, an unexpected flash of pity caught at her throat. Who am I to judge the poor old devil? He is a walking cadaver underneath that all-enveloping soutane. Suddenly she felt guilty of her pitiless condemnation of the old man. He is no different from me, she thought, or to thousands of other Italians. We are all desperate. Like me, he has long ago jettisoned his principles in order to grasp at any chance to survive. No, I mustn't condemn him, she told herself. Priests have to eat too.

'I will.' Liana's voice gained in confidence.

Nicholas placed the ring on the missal. 'May the Lord bless this ring which you give as a sign of your love and fidelity.'

As if on cue, a shaft of sunlight burst through the narrow chancel window. Like a spear it pierced the pages of the missal. The gold of the ring suddenly came alive, shimmering with living warmth. A good omen, thought Liana, and felt comforted. That shining circle of gold was the tangible evidence of a change in her life. For her, it was like an arrow. It pointed away from Italy, away from the past towards the future, *their* future.

Nicholas picked up the slim, golden band. 'In the name of the Father,' he touched her thumb with the ring, 'in the name of the Son,' the ring touched her forefinger, 'in the name of the Holy Ghost,' now her middle finger. Then he slid the ring slowly on to the fourth finger of her left hand.

Liana heaved a silent sigh of relief, and the inner trembling she'd felt all day began to fade away. It was done at last. They were married. The schemes she had conceived only a few weeks ago were gradually coming to fruition. Allowing herself the luxury of relaxing a little at last, she glanced up at Nicholas. His grey eyes glinted with an urgent expression. A wry, inner smile curled inside her: she understood the urgency of his expression very well. He was impatient to possess her body, and she couldn't blame him for that. These last few weeks she'd led him a merry dance. Playing the seductress one moment, purposely tempting him almost beyond endurance, then closing the shutters snap in his face as she reverted to a virtuous, virginal girl. The plan had worked. She had successfully kept him at bay and kept the flame of passion going at the same time. It hadn't been easy. Sometimes Nicholas seethed with exasperation coupled with frustration.

'You're a prick teaser!'

'Darling, I'm not.'

'Then let's make love.'

'I'm not that sort of girl.'

'What sort are you?'

'The sort that saves herself for her husband.'

How many times, she wondered, had they had that conversation?

But now everything was different. A sense of exhilarating triumph stole over her. Now he was her husband, and tonight they would consummate their marriage. She didn't let herself dwell on thoughts of that. It was a wifely duty, and one she intended to fulfil. Poor Nicholas, she'd make up for his weeks of frustration by giving him a wedding night to remember! After that, everything should be easy. A faint smile curved her lips, floating across the space between them, and Nicholas, misunderstanding, responded eagerly.

Behind what Nicholas fondly thought was a smile of sensual longing, Liana dispassionately observed and analysed her new English husband. Nicholas Hamilton-Howard, Earl of Wessex, was twenty-six years old. He was tall and lean, and had a long face with well-defined features. His thick, fair hair was straight, and had a tendency to fall across the high dome of his brow, and his eyes were a clear grey. His mouth was wide and generous, but betrayed a hint of weakness, a characteristic Liana had been quick to recognize and capitalize on. Every inch of his long-boned form spelled out what he was: an English aristocrat, set apart, physically and mentally, by centuries of inbreeding.

'Happy, darling?'

Nicholas wanted reassurance. Liana's gaze, that a moment ago he'd thought so warm and inviting, had suddenly clouded over and shut him out. He wondered if he would ever understand what was going on behind her enormous dark eyes. At nineteen, Liana possessed a mysterious aura of strange, sensual remoteness that gave hint to a maturity reaching far beyond her years.

'Of course.' She answered automatically.

It was only after she had answered, that she stopped to think. In a way, I suppose I am! The realization surprised her, for it was something she had not thought possible. But then the calculating logic which had served to steady her nerves in the past took over, and Liana knew why she felt the way she did.

She smiled up at Nicholas. 'I've married the man I wanted. That's why I'm happy.'

And, she added silently, our life together will be successful because I shall chart the course. His weakness would be the source and sustenance of her strength. Not that I shall ever let him know that, she told herself, never for a moment even considering how difficult that might prove to be.

The service over, Nicholas offered his arm, and Liana took it. They walked arm-in-arm down the aisle of the small church and emerged outside into the hot spring sunshine of Naples. The sparse congregation, composed mostly of Nicholas's fellow officers, watched him enviously.

Hamish Ross put it into words. 'Some fellows have all the luck,' he muttered.

The creamy silk of her wedding dress emphasized Liana's fragile feminine beauty. She was the ideal woman: beautiful, charming and utterly innocent. Every man present felt his masculinity stirred, bemused by a vague notion that she needed to be protected and cherished from the rough and tumble of life.

The narrow cobbled street outside the church was crowded with curious onlookers. Shabbily dressed women, most with babies balanced in the crook of their hips, craned and jostled for a better view of the bride. A crowd of ragged, barefoot children tumbled at their feet, pickpockets every one of them if they had the chance. But now, even their attention was caught up in the excitement of the wedding, and an explosion of spontaneous gaiety rippled through the crowd at the sight of the wedding party.

Liana felt a conflicting mixture of humility and irritation at their pleasure. They had no right to be happy. How could they laugh? She knew only too well the deprivation of their lives, and it was no laughing matter. The daily grind of the battle merely to survive was wearing and soul-destroying; and yet they were unenvious and genuinely pleased for her. They possessed an innate quality she knew she lacked, the typical Neapolitan ability to rise above misfortune and take pleasure from the moment. But for them, fate had ordained that it would only be a fleeting moment. They were doomed to remain for ever in poverty and hunger; whereas she had meticulously planned her escape to England, and had absolutely no intention of remaining impoverished for a moment longer than necessary. Nicholas might not be rich now, but he would be, and so would she. It was always possible to make money, and Liana knew she would find a way. What had surprised her was the fact that, according to Nicholas, no member of the Hamilton-Howard family appeared to have been bothered by the lack of money.

Nicholas had been very honest with her. His family was of ancient and noble birth, but far from rich. Risky business ventures, drunkenness and gambling by previous male heirs, had virtually wiped out all its wealth.

'People think we're rich because we own so much,' he said. 'But all that's really left is a vast, under-used farming estate in Hampshire and a stately home with a badly leaking roof!'

Liana shrugged gracefully. 'No matter,' she said.

But she knew it did matter. Noble birth meant nothing without the money to back it up. She intended to ensure that Nicholas should become the richest earl in England. Quite how she would achieve this, she was not yet sure, although she had already decided she would start with the farm. Since she had known Nicholas, she had retrieved some of the old geography school books from the cupboard in the chapel. Miss Rose, the English teacher, had left them behind in her haste to quit Italy just before war was declared. From them she had learned that southern England was a lush, arable land with a temperate climate. Liana could think of no reason why a farm in such a climate couldn't be made to pay and show a profit. No need to scratch out a meagre living from arid dusty soil, always praying for rain, the way the mountain peasants did. The fact that she had no practical knowledge of English ways and customs, or of farming for that matter, was not the slightest deterrent. Organization and planning were all that was needed, plus the necessary ruthlessness to do whatever proved to be necessary, even if it met with resistance. Nicholas would have been astonished if he had known what plans and schemes were in her mind, but on their wedding day, he did not. He took the beautiful girl at his side at face value – feminine, mysterious and vulnerable – and felt fiercely protective.

'Naples, May the first nineteen forty-four. Wedding pictures, take one.' Hamish snapped an imaginary clapperboard, and the ritual taking of snapshots began.

'A kiss,' someone shouted.

Nicholas drew her close. 'You arc all mine.' His grey eyes shining with opaque brilliance looked down into hers.

'Nearly, but not quite,' whispered Liana, this time curving her mouth with deliberate sensuality.

She was rewarded by seeing his nostrils flare, and knew she held him in the palm of her hand. Still smiling, Liana drew her veil up teasingly to hide them from the onlookers. Then reaching up she kissed him, purposely darting her tongue between his lips, rubbing it along his teeth and into his mouth in a brief but suggestive movement.

'Hell!' said Nicholas as she drew away.

Liana laughed triumphantly as he pulled her closer. She could feel his erection.

'Come on, break it up you two,' shouted Hamish. 'We don't want to stand in the street all day.'

'You'd better stand here.' Nicholas positioned Liana just in front of him for the final photographs. He was still aroused, and needed the camouflage of her body.

Hamish and Charlie were dragged in for the last photograph, but Charlie, methodical down to his last shiny brass button, was getting agitated. 'We ought to be going along to the reception,' he said.

*

There had been no warning of an air raid, just the familiar high-pitched whistle from above their heads seconds before the first bomb landed at the far end of the esplanade. The wedding party made it just in time to the *palazzo* on the Riviera di Chiaia, where Charlie had rented a room.

'Shall we go to the shelter?' The raids terrified Liana. It was the fear of being buried alive again, although she never mentioned it.

'Hell, no,' Hamish and Charlie answered together. They had no such fear.

The rest of the guests streamed into the room, all seemingly oblivious of the ensuing raid. The men descended on the wine like a herd of thirsty buffaloes, and soon the noise of popping corks vied with the rumble of falling bombs.

Nicholas fetched a bottle of wine and poured Liana a glass. 'Drink this,' he said gently. He had immediately noticed the fear she was so bravely trying to conceal, and wanted to convey some of his own self-confidence to her. Obediently she took a sip, and he smiled. 'Now, go and get changed out of your wedding dress.' He nodded towards one of the Italian girls with an English officer. 'Lola has laid everything out ready for you in the next room.' He brushed a hand tenderly against her cheek. 'Don't worry.'

Gulping back her fear, Liana managed a wan smile. If Nicholas could be brave, then so could she. 'Yes, I'll change,' she said.

When she returned to the main room, the barrage of sound hit Liana like a physical blow. She looked around for Nicholas. He was easy to find, standing as he did a head and shoulders taller than any other man in the room. He was surrounded by Englishmen. Liana noticed they were drinking heavily, and as a result their laughter was over-loud and raucous. Hemmed in as he was, Nicholas could not move, but he caught her gaze, smiled, and shrugged apologetically. Liana smiled back, glad to see that he was not drinking heavily like his friends. She supposed he was too polite to mention the mess they were causing: empty wine bottles lay everywhere. An enormous amount had been consumed in the time she had been changing. Liana tightened her lips in disapproval. What a waste of good wine. She and Charlie had purchased it from a farmer who had had the foresight to bury his best wine before the Germans retreated, thus preventing them from taking it. Now it was being wasted. The English were gulping it down so fast it hardly had time to touch the sides of their throats, let alone linger on the palate. Nicholas made a move to join Liana, but his efforts were in vain; the wall of Englishmen remained solid.

'They drink it like water,' she observed sharply to Charlie, who was standing near.

'Ah, but the effect is different.'

Charlie could not understand her disapproval. In his eyes wine was for drinking, the same as beer. He would have preferred beer; they all would. There was only one problem; the Italians could not make decent beer. At least the wine they made was usually drinkable.

Liana winced as a burst of tracer fire streamed crimson and yellow past one of the windows.

'Firework display, especially for your wedding,' said Charlie.

'I hadn't thought of it like that,' answered Liana, trying not to sound nervous.

There was a muffled roar as a nearby building collapsed, and flakes of plaster drifted down from the ceiling. They eddied and swirled in the smoke-laden air like snow, finally settling in a fine film on the food and drink.

'Christ, that was bloody close.'

Hamish, by now very drunk, lurched unsteadily towards Liana. She tried to hide her distaste as he attempted, but failed, to refill her glass, only succeeding in spilling a puddle of wine on to the floor. She was glad when he gave up the struggle, and putting the bottle to his lips drank the rest of the contents.

Another much louder thud rocked the room, and this time the walls bulged visibly inwards with the blast pressure.

''Nother bugger,' said Hamish, braying with high-pitched laughter.

He sounds like a mad donkey, thought Liana, repulsed by his drunkenness, and glad when he staggered away to find another bottle.

Left alone for a moment, she surveyed the scene. It was unreal. She felt as if she were standing outside looking in on something which had nothing to do with her – the noise of the raid, mingled with the chatter and laughter of the guests. This is my wedding reception, she thought, at the same time feeling coldly divorced from the proceedings. Was it because she had calculated everything with such fine and precise logic? Was it because it was only one, unimportant step towards her final goal, the consummation of her marriage? After that would she be able to relax? She tightened her mouth in a determined line and straightened her shoulders. Of course she would, because then, she and her secret would be safe for ever.

Liana hadn't wanted a party, but Nicholas had insisted. 'We can't have a wedding without a reception,' he said. 'We must have something to remember.'

Without its looking churlish, or strange, Liana had no choice but to agree. Now she wished yet again that she hadn't given in to his wishes, and that the two of them could have just gone away quietly. She felt exhausted physically and mentally. The strain of the last few weeks had taken its toll, and now she knew the emotions boiling beneath the surface were unstable and volatile. But I have kept my sanity so far, she thought fiercely. I mustn't give in to maudlin sentimentality now. But sad, nostalgic thoughts flooded into her mind in spite of her determination to keep them at bay.

The wedding reception was the final straw, because never, never had she imagined her wedding would be anything like the scene unfolding now before her eyes. With a weary sadness Liana knew what she would really have liked. At that moment she would have given anything to have been at a village wedding just like the ones she had been to as a small girl before the war. There, everyone had their plates heaped with pasta. The tables groaned under the weight of fresh bread, plates of home-cured hams and sausages, and the huge wheel of sheep's cheese which always took pride of place. No fancy bottles of wine either, but plenty of earthenware jugs full of strong red wine straight from the barrel. No drunkenness at those weddings, but music, singing and laughter. Most of all Liana remembered the music.

Her mind was dragged back to the present as the level of noise rose. She wished she was somewhere else, anywhere else. But, although she gripped her wine glass a little tighter and an observant person might have noticed the strain in her smile, to all intents and purposes she looked as though she was enjoying herself. But, oh, a despairing thought, everything is so different! These people, they are so different. Will I ever get used to the English?

Immediately she pounced on the traitorous idea, and drowned it straightaway, before she even had time to draw a second breath. Of course

I will get used to the English, and this wedding is different because it's war time, she told herself. As for the English, if this is the English way, and these are the English customs, then these are the ways I will adopt. Her dark intelligent eyes registered everything and stored it away for future use. She would soon become like them, on the surface at least. She would make everyone forget that Nicholas had married a foreign bride. Liana, the Countess of Wessex, would be more English than the English.

At the second bomb blast, Nicholas roughly elbowed his fellow officers aside and pushed his way through the crowd to Liana's side. 'Don't worry, darling.' His voice cut abruptly across her thoughts, and she felt him squeeze her arm affectionately. He was smiling, as unperturbed as the rest of them. The rattle of anti-aircraft guns, the constant drone of planes overhead and the regular thud of bombs might never have existed. 'Everything is going to be all right. You trust me, don't you?'

Liana forced herself to smile. She was not going to admit to fear, not to her new husband, not to anyone. 'Yes, of course.' Her calm voice gave no hint of the tight knot of fear threatening to engulf her, nor did the still expression in her beautiful dark eyes.

Another bomb rocked the building to its already shaky foundations. Liana gripped the stem of her wine glass even tighter and concentrated on ignoring the wildly accelerating beat of her heart.

'Good.' Reassured by her calm appearance, Nicholas drained his glass and grinned. 'Can't have the Jerries frightening you. Here, have another drink, darling.'

Obediently Liana gulped back some of the wine and let Nicholas refill her glass. She knew the English had a reputation for staying cool and calm in any situation, and now she had seen it first hand. She must be like that. She *would* be like that.

Charlie came over to them. 'Do you like my arrangements?' He had organized the reception. Another bomb fell, and for a split second Liana let her guard down. Charlie saw the fear lick across her face and her struggle to control it. He waved at the inebriated wedding party. 'They don't notice the raid because they're all anaesthetized by alcohol,' he said, hoping to cheer her.

'I think they are very brave,' murmured Liana.

She took another sip of wine to disguise her nervousness and carefully composed her face into a smooth mask of tranquillity. Charlie watched her in admiration, having some idea of the effort of will this took. It confirmed his opinion that there was definitely something special about Liana, a kind of inner strength. He had glimpsed it several times when she was off guard. If he had been less of a gentleman, he would have used the word steely, but somehow the thought of steeliness didn't seem to go with Liana's fragile beauty. Now he watched her, demure and smiling, eyes huge and dark, little knowing that this was the impassive mask she would present to the world for many years to come.

The all clear sounded, and a great cheer rose from the assembled guests. Everyone breathed easier now, and the gaiety assumed a more genuine note.

'You like the room I rented?' Charlie asked again. 'I thought a palace was suitable for a princess,' he added shyly. Like all the men, and in spite of being happily married, he was more than a little in love with Liana himself.

Liana laughed, 'I'm not a princess, Charlie. You tease me! But yes, the room and the food, everything. All of it is lovely.'

It was, and even though a few moments ago she had been nostalgically hankering after a village wedding, Liana knew that, considering the war and the shortages, the reception could not have been bettered.

For Liana's sake, Charlie had thrown his scruples overboard and had haggled, bluffed and bullied his way through the underground network of the thriving Neapolitan black market. The hired room in the eighteenth-century *palazzo* was still beautiful. It had an intricately moulded ceiling and baroque wall mirrors heavily encrusted with flaking gilt. A crystal chandelier hanging from the vaulted central ceiling rose, showered a glittering sparkle of light over the assembled company. True, there was a hole in the end wall, caused by a wildly off-target ack-ack gunner. Originally patched over with a makeshift arrangement of cardboard and wood, it had looked ugly and intrusive. However, now even that was disguised. Inspired by an unexpected streak of artistic awakening, Charlie had placed a huge arrangement of wild broom in front of it, so that the ugly patch was almost invisible. He could not resist boasting. 'Do you like my flowers?'

'I noticed them the moment I came in,' Liana said. 'And the food. I don't know how you managed to organize such a quantity. It's quite marvellous.'

'A veritable banquet,' agreed Nicholas, joining in the conversation.

The old chef, who had once worked in one of the most prestigious restaurants in Naples before the war, had attacked his task with enthusiasm and zeal. His food was prepared and arranged with all the artistry of Michelangelo. Quite amazing fare had been concocted with standard packs of army rations, supplemented with a few local delicacies. There were dishes of *cecinciella* – tiny sand eels fried in batter – plates of spicy aubergines and the biggest luxury of all, fresh white bread.

'Courtesy of the United States Army kitchens,' whispered Charlie out of the side of his mouth when he saw Liana's amazed expression.

When everyone had finished eating, Charlie produced his *pièce de resistance*, sugared almonds, smuggled into Naples from Egypt. Any doubts he had entertained concerning the shady dealings involved in obtaining them, were vanquished by Liana's delighted expression. She moved amongst the guests, distributing them in the traditional manner, and Charlie suddenly realized that for the first time he could remember the smile on her lips was truly mirrored in her eyes. 'I hope they bring you luck,' he said gruffly as she handed him a tiny parcel of the almonds.

'Oh, they will. I just know it.'

It was ridiculous to feel happy over something so unimportant, something as trivial as sugared almonds. Liana knew that, but all the same they made her day. The tiny sugar-coated nuts, the height of luxury in wartime, assumed a symbolic significance. Everything was going to be all right, she was sure of it.

'Hey, don't spend all the time talking to the best man while you neglect your husband.' Nicholas caught at her slender waist, impulsively pulling her towards him.

Liana laughed, feigning obedience. 'Sorry, sir.'

Looking up into his adoring face, Liana acknowledged that, whatever his faults, she had married a good man. He was intrinsically honest, and would never let her down. It was a pity she couldn't return his love; another time, another place in another life perhaps she would have loved him. But not now, not in this life. Too many memories intruded, blocked the way. But I will make him a good wife, she vowed, and I'll not defraud him completely. I may not love him as he loves me, but he has my gratitude, and I'll honour him for ever; and later I'll give him a son to carry on his name. No, he'll not regret marrying me. I will make him happy.

Impulsively she raised her glass to Nicholas. 'To us,' she cried, setting a mental seal on her vow.

'To us,' he echoed.

Their glasses touched. The lead crystal rang like a bell and a prism of rainbow light sparkled. Suddenly a tension coiled between them, a taut, expectant, but secret, mutual elation.

I've got her.

I've got him.

Their unspoken thoughts were simultaneous. They stood silently regarding one another, oblivious of everyone else, each wrapped in their own secret triumph. It enveloped them like a protective mantle, holding them together and yet at the same time irrevocably separating them.

Charlie watched them, aware that something unusual existed between them, but unaware of the form it took. A vague doubt fluttered in half-submerged form at the back of his mind. In spite of his fondness for the young and beautiful girl, he could never completely eradicate the nebulous disquiet he felt whenever he thought of his visits to the *castello*. The same question consistently reared its head. Had she always told them the truth?

'Thank you,' Liana smiled, accepting compliments and chatting easily to a group of officers.

At the instigation of Nicholas, who was anxious to leave, they were now moving through the assembled guests. Charlie admired the assured and gracious way Liana thanked them for coming and accepted their good wishes for the future. She was a lady all right; she had all the right airs and graces.

But still the doubts persisted. Although it's too late now, Charlie thought. Nicholas had the wife he wanted. And it would be for better or for worse, as it said in the marriage service.

He lit a cigarette and exhaled, still watching her through the blue haze of smoke. In fact, if he were honest with himself, he could not take his eyes off her. She was undoubtedly the most fascinating woman he was ever likely to come across in his lifetime.

Nicholas thought so as well. His heart swelled with pride as he looked at her. She was wearing a going-away outfit of olive green silk. The dress was pre-war and second hand. Stretched and shiny at the seams from wear, it had definitely seen better days, but Liana wore it as proudly as if it were a *haute couture* model. There was something indefinable about the elegant, fluid movements of her body and the regal tilt of her beautiful head. She was unique, set apart from other women.

'Charlie.'

He jumped, startled out of his daydreaming by her voice. Still in a trance he watched as Liana turned and walked across to him.

She put her arms around him and planted a soft kiss on his cheek. 'Thank you, thank you so much, Charlie.' Her tremulous voice was like a caress. 'All your work has made my wedding day so special.'

She drew back and smiled up at him. The unexpected sight of tears shining in her huge luminous eyes almost demolished Charlie's inbuilt British reserve.

He swallowed the unaccustomed lump in his throat and muttered awkwardly. 'Glad you like it.' What a fool you are, he told himself. How could any man doubt her?

Nicholas, at her side, smiled at Charlie. He was feeling a little crazy, annihilated by love, the wine, and his sense of good fortune. 'I'm a lucky man to have met her, Charlie,' he said. 'Don't you agree?'

'I do indeed.'

Their eyes met across the dark cloud of Liana's hair. I wonder which meeting he's thinking about mused Charlie. The first time, eight months ago? Charlie remembered it vividly – but it could have been eight years, so much had happened since then. It was dark that night, but the city was illuminated by the fires of a living hell. Buildings were falling; bodies were everywhere, some moving, some still, never to move again. In the split second that his eyes met those of Nicholas, Charlie saw it all. So did Nicholas, although it was oddly out of focus, like looking down the wrong end of a telescope. Memory was a strange thing.

Chapter Two

October 1943

The mound of bedclothes on the other side of the cramped room heaved to be followed by a sound of retching which filled the room. A claw of a hand reached out to retrieve a chamber pot from beneath the narrow bed into which the occupant disgorged a mass of vomit before retreating, coughing and choking beneath the pile of filthy blankets and finally lapsing into gurgling silence.

The American soldier abruptly withdrew his hand from inside the girl's bra. The sight and sound he had just witnessed repulsed the wholly American, squeaky clean, deodorized GI. What he'd seen of Italy so far terrified him. Everything was so old and dirty. God help me, I'm going to puke too, he thought, trying not to gag.

Liana watched him with an expression of supercilious cold amusement. She wasn't surprised; they all reacted the same way at first. As for the old woman, she felt sorry for her, but since there was nothing she could do, there was no point in worrying about her. She was old and dying from cold and starvation, but at least she had had her life. Apart from giving her food whenever she could, Liana shut her out of her mind.

'Take no notice,' she told the GI. 'The old woman is bedridden.' She pulled her dress off over her head as she spoke and threw it across the back of a chair, then stepped out of her pants. 'Don't worry, she won't watch us. She always turns her face to the wall. We are civilized here, in spite of the war.'

'Christ!' The soldier exploded into anger. 'For what you charge I expected privacy.'

'For what I charge, you expected sex.'

Liana faced him, hands on hips, eyes narrowed with challenge. She'd never lost a customer yet because of the old woman. Lust always triumphed eventually. It was the nature of soldiers. No matter what the circumstances, they had to have sex. If they could not get it by paying for it, they took it anyway by rape. I'm doing some other poor little kid a favour, thought Liana, contempt spilling openly from her eyes as she held out her hand for the dollars.

The American hesitated, then looked at the girl standing before him. It was true what they said about Italian girls. They were really something. Even in her ragged bra and slip she was beautiful, and as a bonus she spoke good English. Goddamned strange, though, and he asked how.

'I learned at school,' was the abrupt reply.

It was difficult to believe. From what he had seen it was hard to imagine that schools had ever existed in Naples, let alone taught English, and to whores of all people. But what the shit, it sure made his life easier being able to speak to a woman when he needed a fuck, and he sure as hell needed one now. Greed got the better of him. Licking his lips like a hungry animal he looked at her full breasts, narrow hips and long, slender legs. His penis rose up, struggling against the confinement of his army uniform. Swallowing hard he reached in his pocket for the money. Jesus Christ, he had to have her.

Barely disguising her derision, Liana took the wad of dollars he handed her. It was as she had expected, the basic animal need had prevailed. The gluttonous craving for sexual gratification had overcome other considerations. Men wanted sex in the same way as children wanted ice cream – as often as possible.

'Just so long as she isn't looking.'

'She isn't.' Now that she had the money Liana didn't bother to disguise her impatience. 'Do you want me naked? If you do, it will cost more.'

'No, no.' He was still unnerved by the inert heap in the corner, and kept an anxious eye in that direction. 'I just want a quick fuck.'

Liana shrugged. The quicker the better as far as she was concerned. She lay down on her makeshift bed on the opposite side of the room to that of the old woman, and pulled up her slip, exposing her dark bush. The soldier watched, licking his lips in anticipation as she spread her legs invitingly. He had trouble undoing his flies, his big, clumsy hands fumbling and jamming the zip in his haste. Oh God, that's all I need, thought Liana irritably, a soldier who can't get his bloody trousers off. But she need not have worried. He didn't bother with the zip. With one rip he tore his trousers open. The rigid shaft of his penis reared out of the torn opening with a quivering life of its own.

'You do want a fuck!' Liana observed dispassionately.

No problem with this one, thank God. It would all be over in a few minutes, and then she would be free of him. Reaching up, she grasped the throbbing organ with one hand, and pulling him down guided him inside her with the other. A few convulsive thrusts and he was spent.

'Oh, Jesus, that was too quick.' He groaned petulantly, childlike in his disappointment.

Liana thought quickly, her mind ticking like a cash register. Once more with this man, and she could finish for the night and go home.

'You want to come again? I can make you.' Slipping a hand through the gap in his trousers she gently kneaded his testicles, moving them about in their loose pouch of skin. As soon as she felt him shudder with pleasure she removed her hand. 'It will cost you the same again.'

'Mercenary bitch!' He raised his head and glowered down at her.

Unafraid, Liana stared back, her black eyes as cold as stone. 'No money, no fuck,' she said loudly and distinctly so that he understood she meant business. 'Get off me.'

Men, they were all the same, she thought, hatred welling up inside her. American, Italian – all the same; thinking they had a right to a woman's body, that they should have it free. She pushed hard on the GI's chest and brought her knee up ready to kick him if necessary.

'OK, OK, I'll pay.' He reached into his back pocket and pulled out another bundle of dollar bills.

Liana took it without a word. Her practised fingers flicked through the money, mentally counting it. In his haste he had given her far too much, but that was his problem, not hers. She put it away safely under the pillow.

'You'll get your money's worth.'

'You bet I will.' He tried to kiss her, his mouth wet and slimy. Liana turned her head away and concentrated on getting him aroused as quickly as possible.

Slipping a hand back between his legs she began to squeeze and fondle. She was expert, using tricks of the trade taught her by the other prostitutes. The quicker a man was aroused, the quicker he came and the sooner she could push the alien body out of her own. This one shouldn't take too long. The American was already wildly enthusiastic, sucking at her neck and working her breasts like pump handles. Perhaps he thinks I'm a cow to be milked, she thought caustically, trying to ignore the pain his breast-wringing was causing her. But the GI grunted and wrung away even more excitedly, pulling one breast from her bra so that he could suck ferociously at her nipple.

Liana tried to empty her mind of the present, and fixed her eyes on the ornate brass clock which ticked away on a shelf over the old woman's bed. Liana knew it was the old lady's last treasured possession – a wedding present, a memento of the days when she was a girl and had known what it was like to have an eager young man between her legs. Her mind drifted on, wondering what the old woman's life had been like when she was young. Had she been happy? Had she been in love? Had she enjoyed sex? The latter two concepts were beyond Liana's comprehension, having never experienced either herself. I suppose they must exist, she thought, otherwise people wouldn't talk and write about love and sex. But for the life of her she could not imagine it. Sex was a hateful abomination to her, but unfortunately necessary for survival. To actually love a man and want sex – Liana shuddered at the repulsive thought.

The soldier groaned and heaved, sucking more vigorously than ever, and Liana watched the hands of the clock creep round. Good, she'd be finished earlier than she had thought. Eleanora would be pleased to see her back. The pale face of her friend floated past in her mind's eye, a flimsy ghost from another world, and as usual, whenever she thought of Eleanora, she worried. Why, oh why, didn't Eleanora get well? She had more than adequate food now. Liana made sure of that. She got plenty of American army rations as well as money for her services, and Eleanora was never hungry now. But still she was ill. Still she coughed her heart out, day after day. She ought to be seen by a doctor. Liana had the money: hundreds of dollars hidden safely away, the proceeds of nearly a year's prostitution. The problem was how to explain the money to Eleanora. She happily accepted the story Liana had fabricated of a menial job in Naples, with payment in US army rations. The explanation of dollars, which to poor Italians were the equivalent of gold dust, was quite another matter, though, and one which required careful thought. But Liana knew she had to find a plausible explanation soon. Eleanora *must* see a doctor.

She glanced at the clock again. God, the soldier was hanging about! She transferred her attention back to the sweaty body on top of hers, and pulled his penis out of her vagina. Another five minutes and he will twist my breasts off. What does he think I'm made of? Roughly massaging the hot, sticky organ, she flicked its sensitive tip with her fingers until she felt it harden, and warm drops of liquid began spilling. Thank God for that, at last he was ready. Raising her hips, she guided the by now wildly elated GI back into her body.

The wail of an air-raid warning began to filter into the room, the smooth, undulating sound contrasting with the American's animal-like grunts as he ground into the soft flesh beneath him. He was taking longer this time, and his uniform buttons were digging into her. They hurt, and Liana decided he had had long enough. Raising her hips in a rocking motion, she grasped his testicles again and willed him to come once and for all. It worked; gasping frantically for air, his jabbing thrusts gained momentum, finally culminating in one great deep stabbing movement.

As soon as he went slack, Liana slid her body from beneath his with practised ease. She'd given him more than his money's worth. Now she was free.

'Christ almighty! I'll come to you again.' Grinning stupidly, he rolled over on to his back. As if he has performed some miracle, thought Liana scornfully. She reached for her dress, watching him with loathing as he lay there panting, satiated with pleasure.

'There's a raid on. You'd better go.'

The sounds of gunfire and the thudding of bombs finally penetrated his consciousness, and his face paled. 'Why the hell didn't you tell me?'

'You were busy, or don't you remember?' So much for the brave soldier. She laughed. His open fear was pathetic. She pulled her dress over her head, and slid into her pants. 'There's a shelter at the end of the street if you're that worried,' she told him.

'Too damned right I'm worried.' He tried to zip his trousers, then remembered he'd torn them open in his haste to get at her. He cursed, aware that the girl was watching him calmly while he sweated like a pig with raw fear. Damn the trousers, he'd fix them later. Buttoning his jacket across his open flies he crossed to the door. 'Aren't you coming to the shelter?'

'I'll take my chance. I've lived through plenty of raids before.'

'Suit yourself, but I for sure as hell am not taking chances,' he spluttered, adding on a whining note. 'Only landed in this godforsaken place yesterday. Nobody told me we'd be goddamned bombed!'

'Armies have a habit of doing it,' Liana said sarcastically. What did the fool expect? He was in the army; he must know there was a war on. 'Friends or enemies, it makes no difference. They all drop bombs.'

Along with many Italians, Liana had given up long ago wondering which side was doing the bombing. Bombs fell, and people died, although never for one moment did she consider that she could be one of them. She needed to stay alive, because somebody had to look after Eleanora. Other people got killed, but not her.

The GI didn't waste time trying to persuade her. The silly bitch could die if she wanted. He for sure wasn't going to. He pushed through the door which swung open lopsidedly on its broken hinges. Liana watched his dim outline as he fumbled his way down the dark stairway. Good riddance, she thought. He had almost vanished in the gloom when he reappeared abruptly, his figure illuminated by a brilliant orange flash. Everything – the hair on his head, the fine khaki of his uniform, the wooden stairs, the minutest cracks in the walls – all were lit with terrifying clarity by an eery orange glow. A single ceiling lath came down first. Like an avenging sword, it unerringly swerved towards the soldier, piercing him straight through the chest. Liana watched in fascinated horror, as, like a hot knife through butter, the lath slid through his body and emerged from his back. It stuck out like a triumphant flag, unfurling a swathe of crimson flesh. The GI's head jerked back, and he looked straight at Liana. His mouth formed an O of surprise, and he seemed about to speak. But instead of words, a huge pink bubble emerged, like a grotesque balloon of bubble gum, then it burst as he began to vomit his own lungs. His eyes, once brilliant blue and alive, suddenly clouded, becoming fixed and staring in death.

Events followed one another in such quick succession that Liana had no time to be afraid. The building began to fall and a choking blackness descended. Her last thought, as dust and darkness engulfed her, was of the money. She must get the money. With a superhuman effort she reached towards the bed, and her groping fingers found it beneath the pillow. Ramming it into her brassière, she heaved a sigh of relief. Safe, she thought. No-one will get it now. Then she lost consciousness.

*

The first thing Liana noticed was the quietness. It was unnatural. She had never experienced such complete and utter silence before. Then the cold began to seep into her consciousness, and she felt afraid. It was bleak and muted as the grave.

'Am I alive or dead?' In panic she shouted out loud, and her voice echoed, crowding back in on top of her. An overwhelming sense of deliverance washed over her. I'm alive, I'm alive.

29

The moment of euphoria was brief, however, as she suddenly realized she was trapped by solid masonry and wood. Her left arm was completely buried in rubble. By wriggling a little she found that she could move the fingers of that hand. She moved them again, experimentally waving them about. They felt free. Spreading them out wide, some of the fear began to dissipate. The cool night air was blowing on her hand. She was sure of it.

'I must be near the surface. I mustn't panic. Someone will rescue me soon.' Unknowingly, she reasoned aloud, and her voice rebounded once more from the walls of her prison.

Tentatively she began to explore with her free hand, touching, assessing, trying to distinguish the objects around her. The door to the stairway was above her, holding up the rubble from the roof. How much, and how heavy is the stuff above me? Do I try to move or do I stay still? Better to stay still, she decided, for now anyway. A bed – mine I suppose, she thought – lay beneath her, cushioning her body from the broken floorboards. It was the wall beside it which had collapsed, imprisoning her left arm. She carried on with her slow tactile exploration, gaining in confidence. If I keep my head I'll get out, she told herself confidently. Then suddenly her fingers became entwined with another hand. She squeezed it, but there was no answering pressure. These weren't living fingers; they were cold and stiff. A dead hand. 'Share my grave,' it seemed to say.

'No!' she screamed shrilly, twisting her head frantically as a vivid image of the impaled soldier came back to her. Her scalp prickled with horror. It was bad enough sharing a bed with him in life, but to share it with him now, in mutilated death. Shuddering violently, Liana tried to move away.

The movement, although only slight, brought bricks and plaster crashing down, filling her mouth with choking grit, and making her eyes sting. It was then that she realized how small the space was that had saved her life – how small, and, therefore, how little air she had.

'I must keep calm.' Speaking aloud was a comfort. It gave an illusion of somebody else being with her, somebody who could listen.

Forcing herself to go on, she moved her hand past the cold fingers and felt the rough wool of a knitted garment. It was the old woman's shawl. Thank God, it wasn't the soldier, it was the woman. The rest of her body was covered by fallen masonry. The inner wall must have caved in on her. Poor old thing. Liana hoped her end had been quick. She felt less afraid lying beside the dead woman, although logic told her it made no difference, a corpse was a corpse. Nevertheless, she still preferred the old woman for company.

Liana assembled her thoughts and concentrated on the facts. The room she had shared with the old woman had been on the top floor of the tenement building. That was good, she reasoned, because she should be on the top of the pile of rubble. That, and the fact that her left hand was free, surely meant that the rescuers would reach her first. She did not allow herself to think that there might not be any rescuers. Defeatism was not a trait that could ever be levelled at Liana. Subconsciously, she lifted her chin, setting it in a determined line. There would be rescuers, hordes of them, of course there would.

Time passed slowly; she seemed to have been there for hours, and still no-one came. The cold seeped into her bones, slow, insidious and paralysing. Liana wanted to sleep, but knew she must not. She must stay alert to attract the rescuers when they came. She decided to signal with her free hand. It would keep her occupied and she might be seen by someone. The weight of rubble pressing on her arm was hampering the blood supply to her hand, and moving her fingers was difficult and painful. Gritting her teeth in determination, Liana slowly clenched and unclenched her hand. At least, she hoped that was what she was doing, but by now her arm was so numb that she wasn't even sure her hand was actually moving. The pain brought tears to her eyes, but she persevered. Open and close, open and close.

'Please let someone see it,' she whispered.

'Christ! Look, sir. There's a hand sticking out up there, a girl's hand, and it's moving.'

'Where, Charlie? Oh God, yes, I see it. Come on, let's get up there and start digging.'

Liana knew she was crying when she felt a hot wetness run down the icy cold of her cheeks. Men's voices. English voices, and they were just above her now. They are going to get me out. Soon I will be free. She wanted to shout with joy, but did not have the strength. From inside her prison she could hear them grunting with the effort of heaving bricks and planks aside, then suddenly everything moved, sliding inwards, and a shower of suffocating dust almost buried her. Coughing and spitting out particles of dust, she fought for breath. Oh God, I'm going to die before they get to me.

'I can't breathe. Be careful,' she thought she had shouted, but only a faint whisper came from her cracked lips.

31

'Better be careful, sir. We'll have the whole bloody lot down on top of us.'

But at last the night air flowed in through the hole like a river of clear sweet wine, and Liana gulped in grateful breaths. Captain Nicholas Hamilton-Howard and his NCO Charlie Parsons, had taken half an hour to excavate the narrow opening. Now they had to drag the girl out.

'Anyone else in there with you?' Nicholas called out in Italian.

'No-one alive. There's a dead woman and a . . .'

'We're only interested in the living.'

'We'll still have to be careful, sir.' Charlie pointed upwards. By some quirk of fate, a chimney breast, complete with tall terracotta pot had remained intact. It was balanced precariously above them, swaying ominously every now and then.

'The sword of Damocles,' muttered Nicholas. 'Pray God the hair is strong.'

'The hair, sir?'

'Never mind. Just pray!'

'Yes, sir!' What the hell was his captain talking about? Being a practical man Charlie didn't waste time praying. Instead he lay down and inched his way into the hole until he had Liana firmly in his grip.

'I've got her, sir,' he called back. 'You can pull us out now.'

Captain Nicholas Hamilton-Howard did pray, more from habit than anything else, but a prayer none the less. 'Our Father who art in heaven, Hallowed be Thy name.'

The familiar words were comforting, helping to assuage the guilt that Charlie, his subordinate, was taking a greater risk than he. But as Charlie had pointed out, he was much smaller than Nicholas, and only he could get into the hole. This was the sixth body they'd clawed out from the ruins that night. He prayed harder. Let her still be alive, and stay alive. All the rest had been dead or dying.

Charlie emerged, a dark profile against the light of the fires now erupting in the ruins all around them. Tightly clasped in his arms was a tall, slender girl.

'Is she . . .?'

'She's alive, but exhausted.'

Nicholas felt irrationally elated. 'Thank God. At least we've retrieved something living from this hell.'

The grimy trio slithered and stumbled down the ruins of the once tall tenement building to reach the relative safety of the road. More and more fires began to blaze in the ruined buildings surrounding them, illuminating a vista of wanton destruction, and Nicholas realized that the devastation was far worse than he'd first thought. He knew it was illogical, but he felt vaguely responsible. He was part of the occupying forces now, the Allied liberators. It was October, and they'd been in Italy for more than a month. Surely they could have done something to prevent this German raid?

Charlie looked at the apocalyptic scene. 'This won't be the last one,' he said on a note of pessimism, accurately reading his captain's thoughts. 'We haven't got the bloody aircraft to see them off.'

But Nicholas was not listening. He was supporting Liana in his arms as she gradually regained full consciousness, gulping deep draughts of the night air into her oxygen-starved lungs. How lovely she is, he thought in amazement. He looked past the grime and torn clothes, and could see a young woman of incredible grace and beauty.

As soon as she was fully conscious, Charlie fished the ever-present hip flask of brandy from his pocket. Some men lit a cigarette under stress. Charlie always took a swig from his flask. For some illogical reason the habit always irritated Nicholas, but tonight he was grateful that Charlie had it with him, and so was Liana. Silently she took the proffered flask, and, tipping back her head, drank from it.

The two men watched her in silence. She sat before them, surrounded by scenes that might have been from some biblical drama, a thin, strangely calm figure, quite aloof from the turmoil spilling around them. Jet black hair tumbled loosely over her shoulders; a torn dress revealed a neck as long and graceful as any queen's in an Egyptian wall painting; high cheekbones and huge, almond-shaped dark eyes completed the exquisiteness of her features. She turned suddenly and looked her rescuers straight in the eyes. Her bearing was confidently erect now that she had recovered consciousness, and her full mouth curved in a grateful, yet imperious smile.

How is it, wondered Charlie, that she can manage to appear virtuous and innocent, and yet convey sensuous sexuality at the same time? In his book, girls were either one or the other, not both. For his part, Nicholas was beyond consciously analysing the aura she exuded. He was only aware of one thing as he gazed at her. He wanted her. It faintly shocked him that he could even think of sex at such a time, but this girl touched a raw, erotic chord within him in a way he didn't understand. Compassion mixed with lust, a strange combination.

'I imagine she has that effect on a lot of men,' Charlie observed drily.

'Hell!'

Embarrassed, Nicholas tried to push his very obvious erection down behind the rough serge of his trousers. Thank God the girl hadn't noticed. She had turned away from them and was staring up at the steep hills that overlooked Naples. There were fires on the hillsides, too. In their hurry to get back to the safety of the north, the bombers had discharged their loads at random. The fires were where villages had been hit by stray bombs.

'What shall we do with her now?' asked Charlie. 'We can't stay here, and we can't take her with us. I wonder where her family is? Being Italian, she must have a hundred or so relations somewhere.'

'What is your name?' Nicholas asked the question softly. He could see her tensing by the second, and assumed it was delayed shock setting in.

'Eleanora,' she whispered. 'Eleanora.' The flask was clutched against her breast so tightly that her knuckles shone gleaming white through the skin.

'Well, Eleanora,' began Nicholas, 'if you feel well enough to tell . . .'

But she was not listening. Raising the flask hurriedly to her lips, she took a second gulp of the brandy before thrusting the flask in the direction of Charlie. Her dark eyes stared straight through and past them, fixed on the black shadowy hills now blossoming with glittering beacons of fire. Then, before either of them could stop her, she struggled to her feet. For one brief second her slender form swayed, and Nicholas, thinking she was on the point of fainting, put out his arms to catch her. But, steadying herself, she regained her balance.

Liana was unaware now of her rescuers, unaware even that she had whispered Eleanora's name. She was conscious of only one thing. She *had* to get back to the *castello* and Eleanora. She could see that the village of San Angelo was on fire, and knew that the *castello* might have been hit as well. When she first stood, weakness and nausea almost caused her to fall, but, dredging up the hidden reserves of strength which had always driven her on in the past, she willed her legs to run and forced the necessary strength into her body. There was no alternative. Liana knew she had to get there and help Eleanora.

Charlie and Nicholas watched, mouths gaping open in astonishment, as the girl they had thought half dead suddenly began to run. Fleet of foot, she nimbly dodged past the fires and scattered debris. In a few minutes she had disappeared completely, vanishing without trace into the darkness of the night. Not once did she stop and look back.

'Well, I'll be buggered,' said Charlie.

*

It's not really any farther than usual, it just seems it. Liana tried to reassure herself, but the fleetness of foot she had summoned up in the beginning had gone now. Tiredness caused her to stumble, catching her feet in every rut and pothole of the unmade track. Only a little way farther, she told herself. Soon I shall see the village and the *castello* and know for certain.

Already, though, she felt sick with fear. The distinctive sweet perfume of burning olive oil permeated the air around her. That meant the precious communal store in the village was on fire. Rounding the last twist of the path where it divided, one track going to the village, the other up to the *castello*, she stopped and looked up. Her worst fears were realized. The *castello* was on fire, as well as half the village.

'Eleanora,' she screamed, 'I'm coming, I'm coming.'

The ancient building flickered and glowed with a ghastly beauty, its walls clothed in flickering red and gold. In later years Liana would remember that sight, for it imprinted itself indelibly on her mind. But at that moment, her only concern was to find enough strength to get there. Relentlessly urging her numbed limbs forward, she ran up through the huge Roman portals of the gateway and staggered into the courtyard.

Eleanora was leaning over the edge of the well in the centre of the courtyard, struggling to haul up a bucket of water. She was covered in soot and coughing badly, but at least she was alive. From force of habit Liana crossed herself, then felt angry. Why thank God? If there were a God, why did he let the bombs drop in the first place? Why did he ever let there be a war?

'Liana!' Eleanor's pale face lit up at the sight of her. 'I thought, I thought that maybe you had been . . .' She began to laugh and cry at the same time, wiping away the tears with the back of her grimy hand, streaking white lines across her sooty cheeks until she looked like a clown.

'Killed?' Liana laughed. 'What, me? Don't be silly, I'm indestructible. Besides, only the good die young, you know that.'

'And you're not good?'

Liana spun round to face the man who'd spoken. 'Who are you?' Hostility made her voice sharp. 'What are you doing here?'

This was their place, hers and Eleanora's. They did not need or want anyone else to intrude. Her eyes registered everything about him at one glance. He was tall, taller than most Italians, good-looking, with a mop of curly hair, and dressed in what looked like a very ragged uniform. But he had no shoes, she noticed. His feet were bound in dirty rags, padded so that he could walk.

'I'm helping put out the fire,' he said mildly, leaning across and taking the bucket from the edge of the well. 'Any objections?'

'Raul came up from the village to help,' explained Eleanora as soon as he'd disappeared. 'The fire is nearly out now, thanks to him. One incendiary fell in the old servants' quarters.' She followed Liana's gaze to the squat, rectangular tower, the walls of which were still lit with brilliant hues of red and gold. 'That's the reflection from the village fire. The olive oil is burning.'

'I know, I can smell it.' A frown creased Liana's forehead. She was suspicious of this man Raul. 'Are you sure he's from the village? I thought there were only a few old men there. All the young men were taken for soldiers long ago.'

'We don't know much about the village now,' Eleanora pointed out reasonably. She didn't share Liana's suspicions. To her Raul had appeared like a guardian angel. She started to cough. 'We never go there, and Raul says quite a lot of soldiers are returning to the south now.'

'Oh, does he.' Liana was not convinced. She was sure that he had never set foot in the village before.

Raul reappeared and they quickly stopped talking about him. He put a bucket in Liana's hand. 'Hurry up. If we work together we should be able to douse the fire completely within half an hour. I think your friend Eleanora should rest.'

They both looked at Eleanora. She was leaning against the parapet of the well for support, and coughing now as if her lungs would burst.

'Oh God, yes, she must.' Liana hurried over to her. 'Come and lie down,' she said tenderly. 'I'll join you in a minute,' she called back to Raul over her shoulder as she led the exhausted girl away.

'By the way,' he called back, 'I'm not from the village. I'm from Rome, and I'm a deserter from the Italian army. You don't mind, do you?' Raul had seen the open suspicion in her eyes and knew he had to set Liana's mind at rest.

'Just put the fire out!'

Raul grinned. She didn't mind so much that she was going to refuse his offer of help. He shouldered the bucket and swung his tall figure across the courtyard towards the area of the fire. So that was Eleanora's friend, the one who had a cleaning job down in Naples that paid so well with US army rations! His gut reaction towards Liana had been the same as that of the Englishman earlier in the evening. He wanted her in his bed. He'd get her, too. He always got the women he wanted. Liana would be no exception.

'A cleaner indeed!' He laughed out loud at the mere thought.

With a face and body like hers, he knew how she got food. There were only two ways Italians could get army rations, an illegal racket or prostitution. He'd put his money, if he had any, on prostitution. But instinct told him to be careful, not to rush her, not to be too friendly. He had told her the truth about himself, or at least some of it, but he sensed she would still resent his presence at the *castello*. That was something he had to overcome, because he had every intention of staying – for as long as it suited him. It was a good place to hide out until things settled down.

He felt lucky. He was always lucky. He'd fallen on his feet yet again, in spite of all the odds against him. He had picked out the *castello* standing alone on the hillside because it looked abandoned. The bomb was a bonus, falling at just the right time for his purposes. Eleanora had accepted his presence without question when he appeared, only too grateful for his help.

He paused thoughtfully. He'd have to win over Liana quickly. She was a different problem altogether. Not only was she prickly and hostile to his presence, there was something else about her. He sensed a disconcerting steeliness behind her beautiful face, a purposeful resolve that he was sure hid a secret. He smiled slowly. He had a pretty good idea just what that secret was. It hadn't taken long for him to gauge that Eleanora was an innocent, unworldly and devoutly Catholic girl, and he guessed that Liana wouldn't want her to know about her own activities in Naples. Eleanora would be shocked and horrified. He wasn't shocked or horrified, but he *was* sure. Liana was selling the only thing she possessed, her body.

The bucket full, he started off again towards the fire. It was unimportant; he intended to stay anyway, and his curiosity would be satisfied in good time. Liana would tell him. She would tell him everything, and come to his bed with open arms. He had supreme self-confidence where women were concerned. He had never met one yet who could resist his charms. So why should the beautiful Liana be any different?

Chapter Three

December 1943—March 1944

Raul hammered in the last nail, then, standing back, looked at his work with satisfaction. Considering he'd used rusty nails, recovered from some of the bombed village houses, and odd pieces of wood retrieved from the same source, he thought the shutters looked remarkably good.

Pulling them together he fastened them shut with the latch. 'Can you feel any draught?' he called through the closed shutters.

'No, the kitchen feels twice as warm already.'

'Twice as warm as what?'

Inside the big kitchen of the *castello* Eleanora laughed at his teasing. 'You know what I mean.' Throwing another piece of firewood in the *stufa*, she carefully closed the cast-iron doors of the ancient stove.

She was enjoying having Raul Carducci live with them. He made himself useful in so many ways, mending things, collecting wood so that now they were always warm. Why, she could even be extravagant when she felt like it, like now, whereas before, when she and Liana had painstakingly collected firewood, each piece had had to be strictly rationed. And today he had made shutters so that they would keep even warmer. In return she had given him Don Luigi's old shoes and a woollen coat, much to Liana's disapproval.

That was the only blot on her new-found happiness. Liana still resented Raul, in spite of everything he did for them. She had not actually said so, but the only quarrel they had ever had in their lives was when Eleanora had given Raul Don Luigi's old clothes. Normally content to let Liana have the last word in everything, Eleanora had dug her heels in and won the day that time. She couldn't understand Liana's attitude, and Liana refused to talk about it. She noticed that when Raul was with them, Liana always seemed tense, as if she was on her guard, hiding something. But what, or why? They had nothing to hide, but still the feeling persisted, and Eleanora felt uneasy.

Raul opened up the shutters again, allowing the last watery pink ribbons of winter sun to stream into the kitchen. He came in, stamping his feet and blowing on his cold fingers, slamming the door behind him. 'Well, that should please Liana when she returns. If anything I can do will ever please her!' The fact that he hadn't yet won her over irritated him. He wasn't used to stubborn women, and had found to his chagrin that Liana had an iron will.

Eleanora took a bowl of broth from the pot bubbling on the top of the *stufa* and settled herself down on her bed. All three of them slept in the big kitchen now. The icy winds of winter howled up the mountainside with ever-increasing ferocity as each day passed, and the kitchen was the only warm room in the *castello*.

'It will please her, Raul. I know it,' Eleanora assured him.

Liana had gone down into Naples again to her work, another thing that was still a source of mystery to Raul. His inquisitiveness knew no bounds, but even his ingenuity had not yet found a way to satisfy it. These days there was always enough food, and the last time Liana had returned she had even brought back a bar of soap. Eleanora had drooled over it with cries of joy and brought out a fine porcelain soap dish from the back of the cupboard, carefully placing the soap in it. It was a luxury none of them had seen for more than two years, and Eleanora watched over its use with parsimonious solicitude.

Raul watched Eleanora. She was happy and in expansive mood. Now was a good time to talk about Liana.

'Where exactly does Liana work?' He was careful to keep his voice seemingly disinterested and casual. It wouldn't do to let Eleanora know he had already tried to prize the information from Liana herself, without success. The solid wall she'd built between them, a mixture of secrecy and antagonism, had proved impossible to breach, even with his persuasive charm.

'It's none of your business,' was the only response he had provoked.

A spasm of coughing shook Eleanora's sparse frame. Raul poured himself some broth and sat beside her. He watched her objectively. Whatever Liana did to earn the food, and he was sure she did it for Eleanora, she was wasting her time. In his opinion nothing on this earth could save Eleanora; her lungs were riddled with tuberculosis, and soon she would die. He hadn't been in the disastrous Greek campaign in the winter of 1940 for nothing. He'd seen young men, once stronger and fitter than he, succumb in their hundreds to the disease, and he knew that once it got a firm hold in the lungs there was nothing to be done. There was no cure, and now with the wet and cold of winter to be endured, he was sure Eleanora's time with them grew less as each day passed. He said so to Liana the last time she'd been up at the *castello*. Eleanora had been feverish all week, and had hardly eaten so that she had become more emaciated than ever. A terrible cough tore at her lungs from morning until night.

'You do know it is only a matter of time, don't you?'

'A matter of time for what?' Her voice was sharp, as though she didn't understand what he was talking about.

Raul persisted. 'Before Eleanora dies.'

She had turned on him then, her face twisting in desperate fury. He was reminded of a vixen they'd cornered once when he was a boy out hunting. The vixen had turned on the huntsmen, and, regardless of her own safety, had defended her young until the last breath had been beaten from her pulped body. Liana had that same expression, the same wild possessive glitter in her eyes. It was then that Raul realized, with something close to humility, that there was nothing Liana would not do for Eleanora, because she loved her with a fierce, unreasoning, passionate love. It was a love so pure that it seemed to blaze like an awesome spiritual power. But love was not enough. Raul knew nothing could save Eleanora.

'She will *never* die. Not while I'm alive. As soon as she's a little stronger, I'm taking her down into Naples to see a doctor.'

'She'll never be strong enough, and anyway how could you pay? There isn't a doctor in Naples who'll give free treatment.'

'I will pay,' Liana answered quietly. 'I'll do anything to get Eleanora well.' A radiant determination illuminated her face.

Helpless, and infuriated at her refusal to face facts, Raul was harsher than he'd intended. 'It's hopeless, can't you see that? All the money in the world couldn't make her well. Eleanora has advanced tuberculosis and there is no cure.'

'She has a weak chest, that's all.' That was the end of the conversation. Her face closed and shuttered, Liana turned away.

Raul despaired. The cynicism he'd cultivated until it had become an integral part of him had been ripped apart in that brief conversation. His heart faltered in unfamiliar compassion. Shocked and saddened, he wondered how Liana would cope with death when Eleanora's time came.

The coughing spasm over, Eleanora managed a wan smile at the watching Raul. 'Have a sip of broth,' he said gently, dragging his mind back to the present, 'and then tell me about Liana.'

Obediently Eleanora drank some broth, then laid the bowl aside and made herself more comfortable on the bed. 'I thought you knew,' she said innocently. 'Liana is a cleaner in one of the *palazzis* of Naples, used now as offices by the American and English army, although I don't know exactly where.'

'She is very highly paid,' said Raul knowing full well that the civilians working for the army were paid a pittance. Liana was not a cleaner. Women who worked at scrubbing and washing had rough, calloused hands. Liana's hands were soft and her nails beautifully kept.

Eleanora smiled. Confined by her illness to the environs of the *castello*, most of the recent horrors of war had passed her by. She had still managed to retain a childlike innocence. It was reflected now in her proud answer. 'That must be because she is very highly thought of.'

'Yes, I suppose it must.'

The wry tone of Raul's answer was lost on Eleanora. Her mind was on other matters, back in the past. She looked at Raul seriously. 'Do you know that we were starving before Liana went down into Naples and got this work? We ate weeds from the fields, berries, nettles, anything we could find. In the end there were not even any weeds left. We had nothing.'

Raul pulled a sympathetic face. 'You don't have to spell it out for me. I, too, know what it's like to starve.'

'You? But you were in the army.'

'The *Italian* army!' Raul was scornful. 'An army composed of ignorant peasants and run by fools, ordered about by an even bigger fool, Mussolini, the great blustering buffoon. Everything was botched and bungled from beginning to end. Not enough equipment, not enough uniforms and certainly not enough food.'

'But you're not a peasant. Why were you in the army?' Eleanora dared ask the question which had been puzzling the two girls. 'You said once you were at university, so why weren't you exempt like the other students?'

The room rang with a bitter laugh, and Raul turned and put his hands gently either side of her pale face. 'Your memory is too good, little one,' he said. He had hoped that they had forgotten he'd told them he was once a student. It was a fact he hadn't intended to let slip out. Now, he shook his head. 'Many, many evil things have happened since *Il Duce* came to power. One day Eleanora, when this wretched war is over, then perhaps I will tell you. But not now.' He kissed her pale cheeks and adroitly changed the subject. 'How long has it been like this, just the two of you up here? It's strange a *marchesa* and her friend living alone in a ruined *castello*. What happened to your parents and Liana's?'

The ruse worked. Eleanora's mind slid back to poignant memories. 'It was not always like this,' she said softly, 'and we were not always poor. My mother I don't remember very well. She died when I was little. Liana's mother was my nurse, and Liana was my sister, although not my blood sister. My father, the *marchese*, was killed in Spain at the battle of Guadalajara in March 1937.' She looked at Raul defiantly, a little unsure of his reaction. 'He was fervently anti-Fascist and joined the Garibaldi battalion. He died fighting for the Spanish republic,' she paused before adding bitterly, 'killed by his own countrymen, the Italian Fascists.'

'He was not anti-Semitic, then?'

Eleanora shook her head, surprised at the inflexion of relief in Raul's voice. 'Of course not. He hated Mussolini and everything he stood for. That was why, after his death, the Black Shirts came and . . .' her voice faltered, trailing into nothingness.

Suddenly Raul understood the poverty and emptiness of the *castello*. 'The Fascists came and sacked your home?'

Eleanora nodded. 'I remember I couldn't understand why no-one wanted to know us. Liana's mother explained that it was too dangerous. All the servants ran away. We were quite alone except for Liana's mother and Miss Rose, our English governess and teacher. And of course, Don Luigi, our old priest, stayed as well. The Fascists couldn't frighten him. For a while we managed quite well. We had a goat for milk, we grew enough to eat, and some banking friends of my father made sure we had enough money for other necessities, although, of course, they had to help us secretly.

'Then in June nineteen thirty-nine Miss Rose left, too. She decided it was getting too dangerous, and went back to England. She wrote once, and then we had a letter from her brother telling us that she had died of a heart attack.' Eleanora sighed. 'We were very sad. She was here for ten years and we spoke English with her every day. I still miss speaking English, although Liana was always much better than me, much better at everything. Miss Rose used to say that her English accent was nearly perfect, not Italian sounding at all, and that she was very clever, clever enough for university.' She stopped lost in thought.

'And then,' Raul prompted.

Eleanora shrugged expressively. 'And then Italy joined Germany in the war. At the same time, in nineteen forty, the money suddenly stopped coming. That was when everything started to go wrong.'

'You can say that again,' interrupted Raul with feeling. 'The war ruined everything for everyone.'

'Liana's mother was killed in January nineteen forty-two.' Eleanora blinked back impulsive tears at the memory. 'She was raped by some men and then beaten to death.'

'Oh, my God!' Even Raul was jolted out of his customary composure. 'Why?'

'Because she tried to stop them from stealing our food supplies. The men were deserters from the army.' Eleanora shuddered. 'It was terrible, terrible. I thought Liana was going to die, too, when she tried to save her mother. I've never seen anyone like it before. She was so brave. She fought them like a fury. But it was useless. There were too many of them and they were too strong. They just picked her up and threw her to one side like a rag doll and then killed her mother.'

She fought like a fury. Yes, Raul thought, I can well imagine it. That might explain some of Liana's hostility towards him, and he couldn't blame her for that, for, by his own admission, he was a deserter, too. It was an understandable reaction, although he was sure there was more to her animosity than just that, much more, and he needed to find out. No, needed wasn't really the right expression. He didn't *need* to, he wanted to. He wanted to find out what really lay behind that beautiful but inscrutable face. What he had learned so far impressed him. She was certainly different, seeming to possess an emotional strength so powerful it enfolded her, impenetrable, like chain-mail armour.

'At least she had a decent funeral,' said Eleanora, wiping her eyes as she continued the conversation about Liana's mother. 'She lies in my father's family vault down there.' She waved a hand vaguely in the direction of Naples. 'But when Don Luigi died . . .' She shuddered violently.

'What about Don Luigi?' Raul leaned forward eagerly, sensing something unusual.

Raul listened for the most part in silence as the harrowing story unfolded. Don Luigi had died of old age at the end of September 1943, just a month before Raul himself had arrived at the *castello* and when the Germans were retreating back up to Rome. In the mayhem following the Allies' blanket bombing, a funeral had proved impossible to organize. All the villagers, except those too infirm to move, had fled from the continual bombing and gone to hiding places in the hills; there was no-one left to help the two girls.

'We tried to go down into Naples to get help, but turned back when we reached the outskirts. We just couldn't go on. It was so awful.' Eleanora's voice convulsed into momentary silence as she struggled with emotion at the memory. She took a breath, then continued. 'Where tall buildings had once stood there were only mountains of bricks. And everywhere, everywhere we looked there were dead bodies. Some had been run over by tanks, and they were flat. We didn't even realize that they were people until we were actually standing on them, because they were like grotesque mats covering the road. And oh Raul, the flies. I shall never forget the flies, how fat they were, their bodies bloated, shining blue and green in the hot sun. They were feeding on the remains like vultures.'

Raul said nothing for a moment. Eleanora's description evoked powerful memories for him, too. He had been part of such scenes himself, sometimes on the side of the perpetrators of such violent atrocities. He closed his eyes, blotting out memories of Greek villages that the Italians had ravaged. War, how he hated it. The whole thing was a nightmare whichever side you were on.

'So what did you do?' he said at last.

'Liana made me promise not to tell.'

'You're already told me half, so you might as well tell me the rest.'

But Eleanora was distressed now. 'I promised,' she said. 'I can't break my word. It wouldn't be right. I wish I hadn't said anything.'

'But you have, and you might as well finish the story.' He took her hand. 'I promise you faithfully that I shall keep it a secret. We'll never mention it again, and Liana need not know you told me.'

Eleanora took a deep breath, and looked at Raul. She wanted to share the burden of knowledge, he could see that. He smiled encouragingly, and she made up her mind.

'We . . .' she stopped. 'Liana buried him. Out there in the earth by the old chapel. He had no coffin, no service, nothing at all. We did it at night, and I shielded the lantern so that Liana could see. She wouldn't let me touch him, said I needn't sin, but that it didn't matter about her.' Tears slid silently down Eleanora's cheeks. 'Do you think Liana is doomed to eternal damnation?' she asked.

'Of course not,' said Raul, knowing how devoutly religious Eleanora was. 'God understands.' Empty words as far as he was concerned, but ones which comforted the distraught girl.

Wiping her eyes, she continued, 'When Don Luigi lay in the earth, Liana said . . .' She stopped, closing her eyes, reliving the moment.

'What did she say?'

Raul was impressed. He remembered thinking the very first night he'd met Liana that there was a hint of steel in her expression. Now he knew why. He could think of no other woman who could have stomached the task, and got on and done it without help from anyone. He'd always sensed she was a fighter and courageous, but now he knew she could do anything. He imagined her viewing their situation with resolute, clear objectivity. A man needed to be buried, so she did it, refusing to let superfluous emotions stand in her way. Liana was a survivor, like him. She would never flinch from anything that stood in the way of survival. Whatever it was that needed to be done, she would do it.

'She said a strange thing,' continued Eleanora slowly, speaking with her eyes still closed. 'She said, "I loved him when he was a man. But now he has changed into an old black crow. That is what we're burying Eleanora, a dead bird not a man." Then she shovelled the earth on top of him and has never mentioned it from that day to this.'

Raul got up. He prowled around the room restlessly. The story disturbed him – not so much the gruesome facts, because, awful as they were to Eleanora, he'd built a protective shield of immunity from such horrors during his time in the army. What disturbed him was the disconcerting insight it had given him into Liana's character. He shivered suddenly.

'You're cold.' Eleanora was concerned.

Raul shook his head. He was not cold, but felt shivery. Something like fear tightened in an iron band around his heart. He couldn't explain it. He tried to think clearly, to analyse the mental images suddenly flashing before his confused mind, but found he couldn't, because nothing made sense. Why should he be afraid? Was it Liana he was afraid of? No, that was ridiculous. She had nothing to do with his future life. Once he left this place, their paths were hardly likely to cross again. He had ambitions of fame and fortune, and had no intention of hanging around the Naples area any longer than necessary. Whereas Liana, for all her courage and determination, was only a girl. Marriage to some Neapolitan boy was her only hope, if she was lucky. The farthest she'd go would be to her mother-in-law's house. But the feeling of apprehension persisted, a shadowy presage of a price he would pay. She, Liana, would demand it, and the price was shame and bitterness.

How fanciful he was being – too dramatic as usual. He laughed, the disturbing, fragmented thoughts dismissed already. 'No, I'm not cold. A ghost must have walked over my grave,' he teased.

'It's mine they should be walking over, not yours,' said Eleanora quietly. Raul turned and looked at her. She was sitting composed and still, resignation at the knowledge of her impending death clearly written in her eyes. 'Look after Liana for me,' she said suddenly.

'I will,' Raul heard himself promising.

Without realizing it, he had picked up the threads of their lives, his and Liana's, and tangled them together.

*

Eleanora died sooner than even Raul had expected. Liana was back at the *castello* for a few days, and Eleanora was pleased and excited as she always was whenever Liana was with her. It was the middle of December, and the day was unusually warm. There was no hint of the drama to come as Raul watched the two girls walk across the courtyard to the gateway. Eleanora seemed less weary than of late, and the two girls laughed and chattered as if they hadn't a care in the world. When they reached the shelter afforded by the great gate, Liana spread out the blanket and they both settled themselves, soaking up the unexpected warmth of the winter sunshine.

'It's so beautiful here,' said Eleanora softly. 'I think Naples must be the most beautiful place in the whole world.'

The great sweep of the bay spread before them, enfolded protectively by the purple haze of distant mountains. The sea, an ocean of serenity under the sun, shone grape blue, tranquil and enchanted. Naples itself sprawled lazily along the shoreline. The city looked peaceful, distance blurring the jagged outlines and skeletons of the bombed buildings. A soft, blueish, shimmering haze diffused ugly reality into a radiant dream. Only the occasional perpendicular skein of grey smoke, hanging motionless in the still air, denoted that somewhere in the city, a building was burning.

'From here it is,' agreed Liana.

She marvelled at the changes of perception that distance made. It could have been another planet, and yet at the same time it was impossible for her to ignore its existence. Staring down in disbelief, Liana tried to equate the cynical streetwise prostitute with the girl now sitting with Eleanora in the sunny gateway. I am two people she thought, but which one is the *real* me? Turning, she looked at Eleanora, the gentle girl who could not have been closer, even if they had been blood sisters. Eleanora smiled lovingly, and, reaching over, clasped Liana's hand. Suddenly Liana wanted to weep with relief. How could she have ever doubted it? In spite of everything, *this* was her real world, and she would let nothing, *nothing*, spoil it.

'People have looked at this same scene for a thousand years,' remarked Eleanora. She sighed contentedly, stretching a little in the sun.

'And will continue to do so for the next thousand,' said Raul, joining them.

Liana felt irrepressibly happy. For once, thought Raul, she looks as young as her nineteen years. Laughing, she stood up. 'I'll leave you two to your romantic imaginings while I make us some coffee,' she said.

The acorn coffee was almost ready when Liana heard Raul's call. Her feet flew across the uneven cobbles towards the gateway where her friend was sitting.

Eleanora was dying. Liana knew it immediately. The knowledge scarred itself across her brain, and she faltered in her headlong rush. Then she hurried forward, trying to smile cheerfully, and put her arms around her lifelong friend, willing some of her own strength to flow into that frail body. But already it seemed as if Eleanora was physically removed. Her normally pale face was suffused with a surrealistic pink glow from the morning sun, and her eyes were fixed on something only she could see. Something far away, out of Liana's reach. It was as if her soul was walking away from her body; and she's not even looking at *me*, thought Liana despairingly.

'Eleanora, look at me.' She shook her, desperately trying to drag her back, away from that distant place, back into the world they had always shared.

'I don't think she can hear you.' Raul, accustomed to the sudden, brutal death of battle, watched transfixed. The atmosphere of peace surrounding Eleanora was so strong it was almost tangible. He was both awed and frightened. What was it she could see that they couldn't?

'Eleanora, listen to me. Look at me. Don't leave me.' The sound of Liana's voice eddied down the mountainside. There was something so awful in the sound, an intense misery, that the hairs on the back of Raul's neck prickled.

Flinging herself in the dust, Liana held her friend's face between her hands. Look at me, look at me, she willed. Every fibre of her being concentrated on Eleanora. If *only* she would look, then she would not die.

For a wonderful moment she thought she had succeeded; Eleanora's eyes suddenly cleared and focused on Liana. But a sense of chilling bleakness penetrated Liana as she gazed into those eyes. There was no mistaking the shadowy haze of death; it was clearly mirrored. Eleanora smiled gently, the same loving smile Liana had always known, but it was weak and fluttery now, like a butterfly about to fly off to a sweeter flower. A dry, paper-thin hand reached up and clasped Liana's warm, living one. 'I'm sorry Liana, but I have no choice.'

'You have, you have.' It was an angry cry. Liana wasn't ready to let go; she refused to accept the inevitable.

Raul remembered Liana's boast that she would not let Eleanora die. By God, she's going to fight until the very last moment, he thought. He stood a few yards back, leaning helplessly against the wall, unwilling to be drawn into the circle of grief surrounding the two girls.

'I have no choice,' repeated Eleanora faintly but with undeniable conviction. Her hand tightened on Liana's. 'Light a candle and pray for me, a candle before the Madonna. There is no-one to hear my confession, no-one here to absolve my sins. Ask Our Lady to forgive me. Promise me, please.'

'I promise,' Liana heard herself saying gently, her voice in stark contrast to the seething outrage she felt. Absolve her sins! Eleanora had no sins. She had *never* sinned. So why was God punishing her by killing her with this hateful disease? Why did it always have to end the same way?

Eleanora smiled. 'Thank you.' Reaching up she brushed feebly at the tears coursing down Liana's cheeks. 'Don't cry, darling. I shall always be with you for as long as you live. Nothing can separate the indivisible.'

Eleanora turned her gaze back towards the sea. A small sound, like the rustle of dry leaves before the wind, drifted from her lips. Her eyelids drooped and flickered, then finally closed, and Liana knew she was beaten. Death, that formless shadow always dogging her footsteps, had won again. She began to weep.

Raul turned abruptly away and walked down the mountain-side. He was unexpectedly moved by emotions he wanted no part of. He had chosen the *castello* as a place of escape; this is not my tragedy, he reminded himself. He paused to light a cigarette and noticed with disquiet that his hands trembled.

He walked and kept on walking, but Liana's weeping followed him. The piteous sound leaped up at him from every scrubby bush, every rock, every stone. The whole world was drowning in her melancholy keening.

He shivered suddenly. An image of years filled with the sound of weeping flashed through his mind. He drew fiercely on his cigarette. Why should he remember the happenings of a few months of his life, the death of one girl, the grief of another? It was nothing to do with him. In a short while he would leave this place, and all would be forgotten.

*

It took three harrowing days before Liana finally admitted defeat.

An epidemic of smallpox and typhoid was decimating Naples and already spreading to villages in surrounding areas. People were dying in the streets. They lay where they had fallen, studiously avoided by the passers-by who hurried on eyes averted, clutching rags to their noses. A pall of death hung over the city; every street, every square was a glimpse of the portals of hell.

Raul wanted to leave immediately, but Liana was adamant. 'Not until I've made the arrangements. I have the money. Eleanora must have a *proper* funeral.'

Unwilling to leave her alone in the stricken city, Raul stayed on. But for him the final straw came when they chanced upon a group of women dancing to drive the sickness away. He choked in anger. 'Medieval peasants,' he spat. 'Offering up pagan rituals. Can't you see, Liana, you'll not get the coffin or the funeral you want here. You'll have to make your own arrangements.'

'It's not too much to ask.'

But Liana knew it was too much. Why should anyone show any interest in a dead girl called Eleanora? She was just another body. The preoccupation of the inhabitants of Naples, those still well enough, was how to avoid death, not get involved with it.

'Let's get out of here.'

Raul dragged her back up to the *castello*. Liana didn't object. There was no point in fighting the inevitable. She stood for a long time looking down at the dead Eleanora. Why did you leave me? What did I do wrong that you wanted to leave? Oh yes, my dearest love, you didn't deceive me. I know you welcomed death like a familiar friend, more familiar than me. Was there nothing more you required from this earth? Not even me? Do you know that in going you have taken a part of me with you? I will always mourn the void you left for as long as I am bound to this earth. How could you do this to me? How could you?

Liana closed her eyes. She wanted to feel something other than anger and emptiness, but couldn't. Even willing all the good memories to come back failed; there was nothing inside her but a slow, burning anger at the futility of everything. Opening her eyes she looked down at Eleanora once more. In death, her fragile beauty had assumed the brittle delicacy of a porcelain doll's. A faint smile curved her lips. Liana wanted to wipe it away. It seemed a profane mockery. How could she smile in the face of death?

'She looks at peace,' said Raul coming to join her. He thought she had been alone with Eleanora long enough. Everything had a limit, even grieving. In spite of his resolve not to get involved, he wanted to reach out and comfort Liana, to make her understand that Eleanora had embraced death with dignity and relief, that she wouldn't have wanted Liana to mourn or to feel angry and resentful. But the comforting words on his lips died away when faced with the cold stoniness of Liana's eyes.

'We'll bury her tomorrow,' she said harshly, and turned away.

The next morning a bitter cold rain came lashing down in torrents. It swept in from the sea, a grey shroud obliterating everything on the mountainside except the nearest objects.

'Perhaps we should wait,' Raul suggested, not relishing digging in the stubborn, rocky soil on such a day.

'We'll do it today,' Liana said.

Raul bit his lip in exasperation but didn't argue. When Liana made up her mind, no-one could change it. If he didn't help her, he knew she would do it alone. Anyway, he thought sombrely, maybe it is better to get the unpleasant task over and done with.

'I'll light the sanctuary lamp in the chapel.' He knew Liana would not renege on her promise to Eleanora. She would light a candle.

Ten minutes later Liana hurried across the cobbles towards the chapel to fulfil that promise. An old blanket flung over her head and shoulders partially shielded her from the penetrating rain.

At the door of the chapel she paused. The flame of the sanctuary lamp flickered dull red through the dusty glass, illuminating the statue of the Madonna in the alcove. The familiar sight unlatched a door into her memory, and for a brief moment Liana remembered how it had been in those far-off days before the war. Then it had seemed that nothing could threaten the rhythm of their lives. The blue-robed Madonna had been real in those days, a living, breathing person always able to grant the simple wishes of two small and innocent girls. A smile touched her lips as she remembered. 'Light a candle, say a prayer, and everything will be all right.'

Reaching out, Liana tried to hold on to the comforting image, but it receded as rapidly as it had materialized, leaving the merciless reality of the present, the cold grey bleakness of the day, rain penetrating the gaping holes in the roof and forming dirty puddles around the masonry which littered the floor.

Now I see as a woman, she thought, staring with distaste at the puddles, an *old* woman, too old for childish dreams. Too old at nineteen; Liana couldn't decide whether it was funny or sad, or just plain stupid. Whatever it was, she knew it was impossible to go back and find the girl she had once been. So much had happened in the last few years which made the past meaningless. So now, she looked again at the blue-robed Madonna of her childhood, and her critical eyes saw a chipped and faded plaster figure. The brass crown looked cheap and tarnished, bereft of the semi-precious jewels it had once held. Liana remembered them being prised out of their sockets by looters.

She wished she had not come, but she had promised Eleanora, and a promise had to be kept. Skirting the puddles, she made her way over to the Madonna and lit a candle. Oh, it is so cold, she thought, trying to concentrate, cold as the grave we shall soon prepare for Eleanora. Her fingers shook and she had difficulty putting the candle in the rack. It was full of candles burned down to blackened wicks. Eleanora had lit all those, never missing a single day. And much good it did her, Liana thought bitterly. This will be the last time a candle is lit in this chapel.

'This is for Eleanora,' she said loudly, as if daring the statue to contradict. She slid to her knees and tried to pray, but nothing came. I promised and I must do it, she told herself. The familiar words were there, she could hear them jangling painfully in her head, but they were confused and in the wrong order. Getting out her rosary, she slipped the beads through her fingers, hoping for comfort from the familiar shapes. But the beads were no comfort. They were cold as death itself.

'It's no use, I can't do it.' Liana struggled to her feet and stared at the statue. Why have I never noticed the stupidity of that simpering painted smile before, she thought, a terrible hatred welling up inside her. '*There is no God*,' she found herself shouting.

'There is no God, no God, no God.' The words sneered and mocked at her, echo upon echo building up into an earsplitting cacophony. 'No God, no God, no, no, *no* . . .'

Liana turned and ran. At the door, held back by something stronger than her own will, she turned for one last look. The driving rain, penetrating the roof, was dripping down over the statue. The Madonna was weeping, or so it seemed. Tears coursed down her cheeks, streaking a pale path through the dust. In the flickering light from the candle the weeping face came alive. Eleanora's eyes followed Liana, mute and reproachful. The tears that fell streaked down Eleanora's cheeks.

'You're dead. Don't look at me like that.'

With a scream Liana pushed through the door and slammed it behind her. Taking a deep breath, she deliberately raised her face to the drenching, cold rain. Her mind was playing tricks on her. The sooner they buried Eleanora the better. She ran to find Raul.

The next hour was physically hard for both of them; but for Liana, putting Eleanora into the unwelcoming wet earth was the most horrific thing of all. She cringed back, recoiling from what had to be done. Raul hadn't even permitted the use of one of their precious blankets as a shroud.

'We'll need it for ourselves this winter. We have to stay alive. Our need is greater,' he said.

And she knew it was true. What had to be done had to be. But her heart ached at the indignity of it all. At last they were nearly finished, and Raul began to shovel the heavy earth, sodden from the unceasing rain, into the shallow grave.

Liana fell to her knees, oblivious of the mud and rain. Reaching down into the grave, she touched Eleanora's face one last time.

'Forgive me,' she whispered.

She drew her hand away as earth began to cover the face. A clod of earth must have triggered a rigid muscle, for suddenly Eleanora's eyes flicked open, and she stared up into Liana's terrified face. Tears of rain began to streak a pale path down her cheeks. It was just as Liana had seen her in the chapel.

'You're supposed to be dead. Don't look at me like that.' Liana's scream curdled the blood in Raul's veins. Aghast, he watched as, propelled by the floodtide of hysteria, she flung herself into the muddy grave and began clawing away the earth.

'What the hell . . . Liana, have you gone mad?' Raul tried to pull her away from the grave.

Liana fought him like a wild thing. 'She's looking at me. We must get her out. I must . . .' Then there was silence as merciful oblivion descended.

Raul hadn't meant to hit Liana quite so hard, but now he took advantage of the time she was unconscious, and finished filling in the grave. He did it blindly, trying not to look. What an awful freakish trick fate had played on them. The staring eyes unnerved him, too, but he didn't let them deter him, and as soon as the mound of earth was secure, he picked up the still unconscious Liana and carried her back to the *castello*.

He took off her wet clothes, and, wrapping her in a blanket, cradled her, childlike, in his arms. He stayed like that, in front of the warmth of the *stufa*, until she regained consciousness.

'But her eyes,' Liana said.

'You imagined it. You were hysterical. I'm sorry I had to hit you.'

Raul held her close, reasoning that there was no point in telling her the truth, and Liana believed him. She wanted to believe him, telling herself that he was right, her overwrought imagination had run riot. There was nothing to be afraid of, nothing at all. But she clung to him for comfort for the rest of that night. His was a warm, solid body; he was not a figment of her imagination. Her need to be close to another human being was desperate, and Raul was there.

After that day in December, Liana began to like Raul and to trust him little by little. They talked and talked, and gradually she confided in him, and the small bits and pieces that formed the jigsaw puzzle of her life fell into place. Eventually, she openly admitted that all the food and money came from prostitution.

'I don't understand. How could you do it?' Raul was curious. He had seen the sensitive, fastidious side of her character, and the squalid nature of prostitution did not fit her image.

Liana shrugged. 'I had to do it, so I did. I could kill someone if I had to, couldn't you?'

'I've never really been put to the ultimate test,' said Raul reflectively. 'I've always managed to avoid trouble.' It was true, he had. Always running, never staying to fight. His family and friends were all dead, because, foolishly, they had tried to defy the evil powers unleashed by *Il Duce* and Hitler. In his opinion, fighting was for idiots. Only those who either ducked out, or went along with the system, stayed alive, and he was one of them. What would I really do if I was forced into a corner? If someone depended on me? Would I behave differently? Of course, said his conscience soothingly. No, mocked his brain, it would be the same as always. He turned to Liana. 'Did you *have* to become a prostitute? Was there no other way?'

'We needed food,' she replied matter-of-factly. 'I tried to get other work. I even begged.' She gave a desultory half-smile. 'Begging was worse than prostitution. I hated the humiliation of it. But anyway, I was a hopeless beggar. I achieved nothing. Don Luigi and Eleanora were both ill, and the three of us were starving. I was desperate. Then, I suppose you could say the gods smiled on me, because I met Rosetta. She showed me how to get food by letting men use my body. So I let them. It seemed a small price to pay then. Perhaps if I'd known they would both die anyway . . .' her voice trailed away.

'In war-time people do many things they are ashamed of.'

'I am not *ashamed* of it.' Liana's eyes flashed scornfully. 'I would do it again. Now, if it was necessary. I told you before, I could, and would, kill. I'd do *anything*.' She laughed humourlessly. 'I didn't like it, sex, I mean. Why on earth it is called "making love" I cannot imagine. Men seem to enjoy it, but for a woman, pleasure is impossible.'

Her words and demeanour reminded Raul forcibly that she was a survivor. In that respect they were alike. But whereas he survived by devious means, and always for himself, she was different. Liana was motivated by a conviction that her actions were right and by a deep instinctive courage to fight for her life and for those she loved.

'I understand,' he said. 'It was wrong of me to use the word "ashamed". But you are mistaken about one thing.'

'What?'

'Women *can* enjoy making love.'

'Hah!' Liana scoffed. 'You'll never convince me of that.'

Raul remained silent. He could be patient. He had plenty of time to kill and he knew the right moment would come, sooner or later. Then, and only then, would he introduce her to a sensual world as yet unknown to her. He smiled, looking forward to the task of convincing her. And she would be convinced! Until then, he could wait, and in the meantime be her friend and brother.

Liana gave up prostitution after Eleanora's death; her frantic quest for ever more food and money was over now. There was a plentiful supply of food hidden in the *castello*'s kitchen, enough to last them for a few months if managed carefully. Anything else they needed could be bought on the black market with the American dollars also hidden in the kitchen.

There were hundreds more dollars hidden away behind the loose stones in the disused shepherd's hut halfway down the mountain and Eleanora's jewellery hidden beneath the kitchen floor. But Liana hugged that knowledge to herself. It is an insurance for the future, she thought. I will tell Raul when we need to use it.

The American dollars were worth their weight in gold, much better than trying to buy with Italian *lire*. Raul was a quick-witted and skilled negotiator when it came to doing deals. Standing attentively by his side, Liana learned how to haggle, how to be poker-faced, never giving anything away, never, never letting the vendor know that you actually wanted something very badly; instead, feigning indifference, until they became anxious, worrying that perhaps they would not make a sale at all.

Gradually their life took on a pattern, and slowly Liana's grief receded into the background. She enjoyed being with Raul. Whenever it was warm enough they sat together in the pavement cafés now beginning to spring up all over Naples and drank acorn coffee, watching as winter slipped away, melted by the warmth of the soft February sun. Spring always came early to the south; the broadbean-seller reappeared, his cry *'fave fresche'* echoing down the streets, confirming that spring really was just around the corner.

In the middle of February, Raul went down into Naples alone. Sitting in pavement cafés, holding hands and exchanging the occasional chaste kiss were beginning to pall. It might be enough for Liana, but he wanted more. Somehow he had to find a way, do something to make her want to give herself to him. He came back looking triumphant.

'A present,' he said, putting the parcel in Liana's hands with a flourish. He stood back, watching with satisfaction as her beautiful face lit up with childish delight.

'A present. For me?' Liana could hardly believe it. She tried to remember the last time she'd received a present of her very own, but couldn't. And now here was Raul giving her, Liana, a gift. She gazed at him, eyes shining. 'For me?' she whispered again, breathless with wonder.

Raul felt his stomach churn, but suppressed the sexual urge tearing at his guts. Not now, he must wait, and if he played his cards right . . . 'Of course it's for you,' he answered softly. 'There's no-one else here. It *must* be for you.'

At his words Liana began excitedly tearing aside the wrapping paper and quickly extracted the present inside. 'A *pastiera*' she cried, holding it aloft. Then she sniffed at the spring-time cake – a real luxury bought specially for her. 'Oh, Raul, it's wonderful. Smell it. It smells of orange blossom and ripe grain.' She drew in a deep breath, savouring the moment. Her very first present from a man. Suddenly she felt very young and inexperienced and yet at the same time knew what it was to feel like a woman who is cherished. Her very first present. 'Let's eat it now,' she said impulsively, 'and open that bottle of wine we have in the cupboard. Oh, Raul, where did you manage to get it? No, no, never mind, don't tell me, just having it is enough.'

Raul laughed at the flood of words tumbling out in her excitement. He could not have chosen better. For him it was a pleasant moment, leading, he hoped, to more pleasure. He couldn't even begin to guess at the significance the cake held for Liana. For her it was a moment of magical fragility, a moment she would remember for the rest of her life. Streetwise and cynical where men were concerned, she was totally unprepared for the aching tenderness of the emotions now flooding through her.

Later, replete and sleepy from too much wine and cake, it seemed the most natural thing in the world for Liana to slide her arms around Raul's neck and kiss him. She had never kissed a man on the mouth with warmth and love before, nor even thought consciously about it now. But the soft sweetness of her moist lips said more than the words she uttered. 'Thank you, Raul.'

For a moment Raul paused, hungry and calculating. Then he made his decision. Now was the right time.

With an erotic delicacy born of experience, his hands moved slowly down her body, every part of him aware that he had to be careful not to frighten her. Liana responded to his caresses with a sigh of contented submission, parting her lips and kissing him again. Encouraged, Raul began to undress her slowly, kissing her all the time, his mouth moving gradually away from hers down to her nipples and then down over her rib cage to the smooth flatness of her stomach. Finally, when her limbs were sensuously relaxed and she was whispering his name softly, he slid his face down between her thighs and his tongue sought out the spot he'd been longing to touch since he'd first met her. Now he'd make her dissolve with longing. She was already moist, but he waited patiently, tongue probing, circling, nibbling until she screamed in frenzy and her hands grappled with his shoulders, trying to pull him upwards. Then he moved. Hard and controlled, he entered her easily as she spread her legs wide in welcome.

'Now,' he said. 'Now.' Each explosive thrust was tinged with triumph. He possessed her at last.

*

Liana lay in a dreamy sated peace, her breathing matching that of Raul's in an easy, lazy rhythm. She had never been so relaxed, so happy. If there is a paradise, surely this must be it, she thought, this languorous, undemanding harmony of mind and body.

'And to think I thought I could never enjoy making love.'

Raul laughed easily, and ran his fingers lightly along the exquisite shape of Liana's high cheek bones. He settled her more comfortably in the crook of his arm, folding her into the curve of his body. She had never looked more beautiful. Making love had given her a unique glow, a shining halo of beautiful sensuality.

'There are many ways of making love, Liana,' he whispered softly. The needs of his body were growing urgent again; it had been so long since he'd had a woman. He wanted her again and again. 'Touch me,' he murmured, 'and I'll teach you some more.'

Shyly, she reached out, running her fingers over the soft mound of flesh in his groin. Then growing bolder she cupped it in her hand, feeling her own excitement rise as it moved and stirred. Raul wanted her again, and suddenly she knew she wanted him. Her huge dark eyes, cloudy now with desire, looked up into his. A shudder of pleasure quivered through Raul as he kissed her slowly. She was better than he had anticipated. He would enjoy teaching her. Lightly running his tongue along the curve of her lips, he provocatively began to draw out the latent sexuality he knew lay beneath her innocence. For as he had found out to his heightened delight, she was innocent, in spite of her prostitution.

Slowly he led her along the path of sexual exploration, gentle at times, demanding at others, but always giving her pleasure before taking his own. Now she was lying in his arms, her sexuality awakened, and longing for more. As his mouth teased hers, she reached up, pulling his head down hard. He could feel her full breasts, nipples risen and taut rubbing against the mass of hair on his chest. Rotating her hips slowly, she pressed the length of her silken body against his. 'Show me again, Raul. Love me again.'

Three weeks passed in a shimmering, erotic haze of love-making. There had been many other women for Raul, and he taught Liana all the ways he knew of heightening the act of sex until it became a sublime physical gratification. Sometimes it was so wonderful that Liana thought she would die from the intensity of her feelings. More than anything she wanted to please him, and often surprised him by taking the initiative and finding new ways to give him pleasure.

Now she knew what she had been born for. Now there was a purpose to her life. Now, at long last, everything made sense. She was made for Raul, made to love him. Every time she gave him her body it was an act of worship.

'I love you, darling, darling Raul.' Every morning was the same. She awoke early as the first grey fingers of dawn inched under the gap of the kitchen door. Rolling on to her side, she drank in every feature of his beloved face, etching it on her memory to be taken out and looked at whenever they were apart. That didn't happen often, but how she hated those times, no matter how short. Even a few hours was too long, for only when Raul was at her side did she feel truly alive. When he was away half of her withered and died, only to be revived when he returned.

He stirred sleepily. She reached out, stroking the dark reddish curls of his hair, then running her forefinger down the line of his cheekbone until she reached his mouth.

Raul bit her finger. 'Say it again.'

'I love you. I love you.' Liana needed no second bidding to declare her love.

'I love you, too.' The words came easily, empty, meaningless. He had said them many times before, exercising his talent for plausible lies.

He loves me! Liana marvelled at this miracle, nuzzling into him, smiling against his chest. This is my world. This is my fate – to be with Raul for ever and ever. The shimmering fire he has lit in my soul will never go out.

I'll always love him, even if I live to be a hundred. 'I love you.' The words were always on her lips.

Raul's voice interrupted her ecstatic musings. 'If you love me as much as you say, why don't you make me some coffee?'

Laughing, she bent over him, silky dark hair showering across his face and chest, a shining, living blanket. 'You know I'll always do whatever you want.' She kissed him.

'Anything?'

'Anything, darling.' Suddenly Liana became serious. 'I mean it. My life is yours, to do with as you please.'

Raul pushed her dark hair back so that he could see her face. 'Supposing I asked you to do something terrible,' he teased. 'Supposing I asked you to make a great sacrifice, something you didn't want to do.'

'I'd do it.' No hesitation, not even a moment's thought. How could there be? Loving was giving, loving was needing to be needed. And she loved Raul. 'I will do anything for you, Raul. Whatever it is you want out of life, I'll help you get it.'

Raul laughed, pulling at her hair. 'And what can you do? You're only a poor Italian girl!'

She was about to tell him she had money and jewels hidden away, to tell him she had the means for their escape from poverty when the right time came. But her words were silenced by Raul's kisses and soon forgotten completely as her body responded with a familiar thrill of weakness to the touch of his strong hands. Oh, yes, she would do anything for Raul. How had she ever lived without him? How *could* she live without him? The terror and utter bleak desolation of such a prospect was appalling. Her heart almost stopped beating for a moment. Then relief flooded through her. How stupid I am to even think of such a thing. Raul is here, Raul wants me. Now, now! She shuddered as he entered her, loving the feel of his body moving inside hers, slow at first, then gaining momentum, faster and faster until she was lost in a kaleidoscope of oblivion, all thoughts of life without him forgotten.

*

'Darling, we do need more coffee. You know we do. I won't be long – two, three hours at most. I'll be quicker on my own in this weather.'

A cloud of fear crossed her face. 'Raul, don't go. Not today. Leave it until tomorrow.'

It was 19 March 1944, a momentous day for Naples. Vesuvius was erupting. Raul and Liana stood together beneath the portals of the great gate, watching as the huge bulging mass of steam and ash rose higher and higher into the sky until it obliterated the sun, causing a menacing gloom to daub the landscape in darkening colours. Already a hazy film of ash was falling heavily, covering everything in a soft grey blanket.

'You're not afraid, are you?'

'No, of course not.' She was too proud to admit to that. 'But . . .' How could she explain the irrational sense of foreboding which was spreading its tentacles through her, draining her of reason? The sensible part of her mind told her she was being stupid and childish, but she tried to stop him. 'Don't go, Raul. Not today.'

He laughed at her, and kissed her teasingly. 'You worry too much, Liana. This doesn't mean bad luck. Haven't you ever heard about reversing superstitions? This is a good omen.' Impetuously, he scooped up a handful of the fallen ash and scattered it playfully over her. 'See you soon.'

Liana stood in silence, wishing she could laugh at his joking, but the feeling of foreboding was even stronger now. This was a bad day, she *knew* it. Her eyes, following Raul's lithe figure as he ran down the mountainside, filled with ineffable pain. She watched as he leaped and jumped over boulders; he was so full of life. Where would his irrepressible energy take him? Away from you, said her inner voice.

The ash was falling even more heavily now. Giant flakes swirled about his figure like a snowstorm. She stayed in the gateway until his tall form became a mere dot, almost indistinguishable from the flakes of ash falling from an ever-darkening sky, then it disappeared altogether.

Liana turned away then and walked back towards the kitchen, the sound of her lonely footsteps on the cobbles muted by the layer of ash. Behind her lay a trail of scuff marks where she had dragged her feet like a tired old woman.

Chapter Four

19 March 1944

Propelled by his characteristically passionate belief that today would be his lucky day, Raul quickly forgot about Liana and her irrational worries. Not that he had even given them very much attention at the time. Raul was not a long-term worrier. Apart from the occasional irritating pricks of a mostly dormant conscience, the days came and went leaving him untouched by doubts. Every morning he awoke convinced that today must be *his* day, his own, very special day, the day when his fortunes would change and Lady Luck would tap him on the shoulder.

When he had teasingly thrown the ash at Liana he had meant what he said. The terrible majesty of the erupting volcano darkening the sky filled him with a sense of awe and power. On such days as this history was made. It heightened his presentiment that today something special would happen.

Running down the mountain, he flung back his head and whooped with exuberant laughter. 'What a day,' he shouted to nothing and everything. 'What a day!'

Arriving in Naples he found it seething with people, the atmosphere lively, excited, sometimes apprehensive, but full of gossip. The pavement cafés were thick with faded umbrellas, put up so that the clientele could speculate on the outcome of the eruption in relative comfort whilst drinking Marsala and coffee. Raul loved the bustling, busy ambience. He was in his element. This was his world, the city. He loved the cosmopolitan mixture of people rubbing shoulders with one another and could happily ignore the beggars, dirt and disease. Not for him the stultifying peace of the countryside; he needed the vibrant life of a city, even such a broken, battered city as Naples. He longed for the day when he could pick up the threads of his career again and rejoin the world of theatre and film.

It was something he had never told Liana. She thought he was happy in the seclusion of the *castello*, and so he was, for the moment. But not for ever. It could never be for ever. He would die of boredom. As far as Liana was concerned he had been a student in Rome. She had no idea what he had studied, and had never asked. As for his ambitions, Raul kept those to himself. He was beginning to worry that Liana might have fallen in love with him. It would pass, of course. Such emotions always did. They never lasted. Sometimes her smile made him afraid, so absolute and sure was the brightness shining from her eyes. She would find it difficult to let him go, but he knew he could not explain either the compulsion that drew him to the performing arts or the obsessive fear he had of becoming necessary to the life of another human being. Or, much worse, having someone become necessary to him. Anyway, how could he even expect her to begin to understand what he needed from life? In spite of being well versed in the classics, and speaking almost perfect English, she was still an unsophisticated country girl, a girl who had lived all her life halfway up a remote country mountain, and by her own admission, never been inside a theatre or seen a film.

Pushing through the crowds, he suddenly stopped, the last remaining thought of Liana driven from his head. He caught his breath in excitement, and opened his eyes wide with glee. Now he knew his premonition of good luck for today had been well founded, for there, right in front of him, sat Gustavo Simionato, the most illustrious Italian film and theatre director of pre-war days.

Raul recognized him immediately, any student of the theatrical world would have done. In pre-war days, Simionato's photograph had always shared equal prominence with that of his stars. The man was a legend in his own lifetime. Raul had studied the camera and lighting techniques adopted by him as part of his course at Rome University. There was no doubt about it: it was Gustavo Simionato in the flesh.

He was sitting alone at a café drinking coffee. This was the opportunity Raul had been waiting for, the day when Lady Luck reached out and tapped him on the shoulder, and he responded with instant enthusiasm. He didn't hesitate, not even stopping to think of what he might say when confronting the great man. He walked straight across to the café and when he reached Simionato's table the words rolled off his tongue as easily as if he had been rehearsing them for years.

'Signor Simionato, please permit me to buy you some wine.' Raul executed a small bow with a flourish. The same bow from anyone else might well have seemed deferential, but from Raul it was anything but. Rather it served to enhance his self-confident charm.

Simionato looked at the man before him through narrowed eyes. Thirty years in the world of theatre, with all the pretensions and foibles that world encompassed, enabled him to recognize Raul's narcissistic vanity for the professional opportunism it was. He had no intention of making it easy for the young man; let him sweat for whatever it was he wanted.

'Why?' The single, abrupt word was not intended to be encouraging.

Raul was not intimidated; quite the reverse. He relished the challenge, rejoicing in the surge of adrenalin which flowed through him. Simionato noticed that his hair, a mop of dark reddish curls, positively bounced with vitality, and his dark eyes sparkled audaciously. 'Because it will be an honour to buy wine for the greatest artistic director of cinema and stage that Italy has ever known.'

Simionato gave a great roar of genuine laughter. Now he was openly amused at Raul's brazen flattery, and enjoying it, too. 'Red wine,' he said, snapping his fingers to attract the waiter's attention.

Raul felt in his pocket and made a rapid calculation. He hadn't enough *lire* to pay for the wine he'd just invited Simionato to share. He would have to use some of Liana's American money with which he had intended to buy coffee substitute. No matter – wine for this influential man was of more importance at the moment, much more importance. He crossed his fingers, hoping that the café had something decent to drink hidden away in the cellars. He would die of shame if the waiter produced the type of rubbish they always gave to the American GIs. Maybe *they* couldn't tell the difference between good and bad wine, but Simionato was an Italian, a cultured Italian, a nobleman by birth, and he most certainly would be able to make the distinction. Raul sat down opposite Simionato.

'I, too, intend to become a director,' he said, coming straight to the point.

'Films or theatre?' He was bold this one, self-possessed to the point of arrogance.

'Both. I have the talent.' It was a very positive statement of fact.

The wine arrived, and Raul poured two glasses, aware that the older man was eyeing him quizzically, assessing him. He passed a glass to Simionato then took a sip from his own, almost sighing audibly as he realized that not only was the wine drinkable, it was also a good vintage. The waiter must have recognized the famous man and given them a bottle from their secret reserve. Grateful, he tipped the waiter all the remaining lire in his pocket.

Simionato made an appreciative grimace: a good start – a man who knew where to lay his hands on a decent bottle of wine must have something going for him

'It's not easy for a young man to get started,' he said, 'especially in Italy at this particular time.' He took another long sip of wine before adding with slow deliberation. 'Not easy, even for a young man with talent.'

'I agree, of course. It isn't easy. Nothing is easy. But neither is it impossible. Particularly if the young man in question has a good teacher.'

'You have such a teacher?'

'I will have if you take me on.'

In the silence that followed, Raul wondered if, in his eagerness to get what he wanted, he had overstepped the boundaries of impertinence and offended the great man. For a few seconds Simionato stared at Raul, his wily eyes beneath hooded lids keen and searching. Then he tossed back his wine in one gulp and set the glass down on the table with a bang. True to his reputation as a man who always acted on gut instinct, he had made up his mind. 'Do you have any ties here?'

'None.' Raul spoke without hesitation.

'Good. I'm leaving Naples today for Reggio, and thence on to Sicily where I am to start filming. You can come with me as my assistant.'

Raul leaped to his feet, unable to conceal his jubilation. 'You won't regret it.'

'Very true. It won't take me long to find out whether or not you have this great talent you think you possess. If you have, you can stay. If you haven't, then you can go.'

'I'll be staying,' said Raul, his face composed now, his dark eyes determined. And he would. He would show Simionato. The old man had talent, but more importantly he had the experience which brought wisdom; and that was what Raul wanted. Impatient as always, he could not wait to accumulate expertise through years of practice. Much better to learn it from someone else, and give his own superior talent a chance to really blossom. Then he would be a force to be reckoned with in his own right.

Simionato was slightly surprised when Raul said he had no ties. Where he had been living? Not on the streets, surely? He observed Raul more closely. He had a sleek, well-fed air about him, which certainly did not come from living rough. If it had been before the war, Simionato would have thought Raul had had a wealthy, doting benefactress. He was the type – a good-looking young man who would do very well keeping some older woman sexually happy and being well paid for his favours. But were there any such women left in Naples now? Simionato doubted it.

Raul made no mention of family or friends, and never left Simionato's side as they prepared to leave. Over lunch he talked non-stop about his dreams and ambitions before pumping Simionato for every scrap of information about the forthcoming film.

Simionato was pleased with himself. As vain as Raul in his own way, he prided himself on his judgement; during the troubled years of the thirties and forties he'd taken care to swim with the political tide without actually forming an open allegiance. Hence, he had survived the war with a great deal of his personal fortune intact. Now, having recently sold a silver Cellini salt cellar to an American general, he had just enough money available to finance a new film. Lucky for Raul that he had presented himself at precisely the right moment. Simionato had a strong feeling that together, he and this ambitious young man would lead the renaissance in the Italian post-war film and theatre world. He was getting old; he needed a young blood like Raul to stimulate him, a ruthless young man with stomach enough to fight the authorities and gall enough to persuade people to lend money against their better judgement for future projects, and perhaps most importantly, to see artistically with new eyes, fresh and uncluttered by years of experience. Yes, he needed Raul as much as Raul needed him; it would be a symbiotic relationship.

*

The ramshackle truck hired by Simionato lurched southwards out of the city. Its course was of necessity erratic because the road was full of bomb craters. On the outskirts of Naples the truck slowed to walking pace. An enormous fountain blocked most of the road, and had to be negotiated. Blown by a huge blast from its original position in front of the church, it now rested, incongruously intact, complete with marble angels, in the middle of the road.

A row of grimy, underfed *scugnizzi* sat on the rim of the marble basin, dangling their skinny legs over the edge, and watched them. As soon as they could see that the truck's occupants were not American, and there was therefore unlikely to be anything worth stealing, they lost interest. Their black eyes, dull and lethargic from hunger, stared disinterestedly as Simionato wrestled with the steering wheel. 'Poor little devils.' He jerked his head in the direction of the small boys. 'Their war is far from over.'

Suddenly Raul's mind was jerked from its self-satisfied preoccupation with his own rosy future, and he was reminded for the first time of Liana. He tried to banish the thought. Out of sight out of mind, he told himself, but the pang of betrayal could not be denied.

Involuntarily, he turned his head to take one last look back at the *castello*, but ash was still falling like snow from the erupting volcano and blotted out the view. All that was visible through the gloom were streams of molten lava, trickling down the slopes of the distant volcano – the heartbeat of the mountain pulsating in blood red and orange. His own heartbeat quickened for a moment, imitating the tempo, then it stilled in response to the firm disciplining of his thoughts.

He turned back and concentrated on the road ahead. Liana would endure. She was a survivor, like him. The momentary pang of guilty regret was outweighed by the knowledge that it was the right time for him to move on. The chance had come, and he had taken it. There was no choice. An unambitious fool might have been swayed by the thought of the lonely girl, but he was no fool.

He looked at the repugnant *scugnizzi*. 'Yes, it's a pity for them,' he said.

Then he stared straight ahead, wishing he could already see Sicily. There was no point in turning back again. The die was cast. His war was over.

Chapter Five

April 1944

'Early pregnancy, that is the reason for your sickness, young woman.' The doctor delivered the diagnosis abruptly. 'Nothing to worry about.'

He made a quick calculation; if she wanted an abortion, which most of them did, could he do it now? He had six women waiting outside, probably all wanting abortions – he recognized most of them from previous encounters. Mentally ticking off the time it took, he looked at Liana. Yes, I can give her a quick scrape; it's early enough for that.

Liana lay on the couch, her mind reeling in shock. Pregnancy – it was something she had never countenanced, never in a million years. A rush of conflicting emotions exploded within her. A baby, another person, part of herself and Raul – living proof of their love. It had to be Raul. No other man had touched her since Eleanora's death. Then her lips quivered as the nausea which had brought her to the doctor in the first place threatened to overwhelm her. Hot and cold flushes of panic washed over her, leaving her body drenched in perspiration. Oh God, no, no, no! I can't have a baby, not now of all times. For a second, and it was only a second, she thought of abortion. Plenty of girls had it, she knew that. But not me, she thought. It was as if the tiny thing growing inside her had cried out, 'Love me, love me, please,' and in that moment had captured her heart.

She had told Raul she could kill if she had to; but she knew she could never kill the child in her womb, not *their* child. This baby is utterly dependent on me, she thought. The recognition of that fact was devastating her; she felt a fierce outpouring of protectiveness engulf her. 'Don't worry,' she whispered silently to the embryonic form within her, 'I'll look after you. I'll never let anything happen to you.'

Realizing the doctor was watching her curiously, Liana rallied her thoughts with an effort. Her inherent practicality took over. 'Why am I pregnant now?' she demanded.

Dr Porzio paused a moment from a perfunctory washing of his hands in the grimy basin beside the couch. He looked at Liana closely. There was something different about this one. She was a prostitute, of course. Most women were. Their bodies were all they had left to bargain with. But even to his cynical eyes Liana's beauty looked much too refined for prostitution. Unlike most of the population, she gave the illusion of being untouched by the sordidness around her. 'You've survived by prostitution, I suppose,' he said slyly. It was a statement more than a question.

Liana felt a flare of anger at his derisive assumption, but her dark eyes never flinched from his. It is all right for you, she thought, you are a doctor and yet I know you cheat, charge too much, steal drugs and perform illegal operations. She wanted to confront him with all those things, but dared not. For the time being she needed him on her side. Besides, she wanted him to forget her as soon as possible. Experience had taught her to be distrustful. The less anyone knew about her the better.

Taking care to hide the contempt she felt, she merely said quietly, 'Yes, I have. For more than a year. But I've never got pregnant before, so why has it happened now?'

Dr Porzio shrugged, his interest already waning. She would definitely be asking for an abortion now – a pregnant prostitute was an out-of-work prostitute. His only interest lay in gauging how much she could afford.

'Why not before? Probably because you weren't ovulating – common enough these days due to lack of food. Undernourished bodies don't conceive.' He stopped, his eyes flickering with a lecherous sneer as he slowly took in every detail of Liana's finely shaped body. 'You've been too good at your job, young woman, and eaten too well, and now you're paying the price. You're a functioning woman! Have you ever had the curse?' He sniggered as he spoke, and Liana clenched her fists. If only you knew, you *runt*, she thought, how much I want to strangle you with my bare hands.

But she swallowed her anger and answered smoothly, 'I've only had the curse once – this year at the end of February, beginning of March.'

'There you are, then, that's your answer.' Dr Porzio's lips stretched back in an attempt at a smile. He should keep his mouth shut, thought Liana, averting her eyes as a row of rotten stumps was revealed where his teeth should have been. 'Conceived towards the middle of March, sickness now at the beginning of April.' He counted on his fingers. 'The baby is due middle to end of December this year.' He dried his wet hands, wiping them on the front of his dirty white coat, and came across to Liana. 'I can get rid of it now if you like, provided you've got the money, of course.'

His dirty hands, nails bitten to the quick, reached out like evil claws and Liana instantly recoiled in revulsion. 'Get rid of it? Oh, no, I've no intention of doing that,' she said quickly, unable to disguise her contempt any longer.

Dr Porzio was surprised, and then angry at her open display of contempt. Arrogant little bitch. A product of the gutter. Who the hell did she think she was, daring to speak to him, a doctor, in that tone of voice?

'And how will you live?' he sneered. 'The answer, my dear, is that you won't be able to. You won't be able to earn money in the usual way, and what decent Italian man would take you on? A pregnant whore! Go now, but you'll be returning. Only don't leave it too long or I may refuse to do it. I take no responsibility for corpses!'

Liana swung herself down from the examination couch. 'I won't be back,' she said coldly.

Leaving the doctor's surgery, she walked rapidly through the crowded streets of Naples, brushing past people with unseeing eyes. Her mind was racing feverishly ahead, planning, planning, planning. I should never have left it so long, she chastized herself, realizing that she should have done something besides trying to find Raul on her own. I should have got help, confided in someone. The problem is who?

If he were free, he would have returned to the *castello* by now; it was inconceivable that he would have just left her. Why should he? Tears filled her eyes as she remembered their passionate love. How idyllic our lives were. The pain of that sweet memory halted her in her tracks. She stopped, then, straightening her back, strode resolutely ahead. It will be idyllic again, she told herself, determined not to let her resolve waver, because I *shall* find him.

The fact that he had not returned could only mean one of two things. Either he had been taken ill, and someone was caring for him, or he had been wrongly arrested by the Allies. Of the two possibilities she decided wrongful arrest was the most likely. Raul was as strong as an ox, and she just couldn't imagine his succumbing to illness. And even if he had, she was absolutely certain that somehow he would have got a message to her so that she wouldn't worry. Arrest and imprisonment *must* be the answer – it had to be.

She made a decision. She would go to the Allied Field Security office. People were always saying they knew everything that was going on: who had been arrested, and for what crime; who had been injured or killed. She had also heard that they were English and usually kind and helpful. Why hadn't she thought of it before? Of course they would find Raul for her.

Back at the *castello* Liana lit the *stufa*. There was a lot to do, and she couldn't afford to lose any more time. Pregnancy made finding Raul more urgent than ever. Tomorrow she would go down into Naples to the FS office where it was essential she should make a good impression. The more she thought about it, the more convinced she became that Raul must be in the Poggio Reale, the vast prison in Naples. Liana knew, as did all Neapolitans, that it was full of men arrested by the Allies on all manner of trivial offences. I will get you out, Raul, she promised, setting her beautiful mouth in a determined line. I will get you out, and then we will be married, and together we will look after our beautiful baby.

Heating the flat iron on the *stufa*, she carefully ironed one of Eleanora's dresses. It was much better than any of her own. The demure dark blue suited her. It was very late before she went to bed that night, but everything was ready for the morning, her hair washed and glossy, the dress clean and ironed and her shoes shining from the olive oil she had rubbed into the leather. A terrible extravagance, she had thought whilst doing it, but worth every drop of the precious oil, because it was for Raul. Anything was worth it for Raul – and the baby.

Lying in her narrow bed by the side of the *stufa*, Liana tried to sleep. She needed all her wits about her tomorrow because tomorrow, just for the day, she intended to be the Marchesa Eleanora. She opened her eyes, staring blindly into the darkness. You don't mind, do you, Eleanora, she whispered silently. After all, you were the one who said we were indivisible. The darkness of the room, warmed by the fire in the *stufa*, enfolded her comfortingly. No, of course Eleanora would not mind. Closing her eyes, she turned over and began to slip into an exhausted sleep.

It will only be for tomorrow, Eleanora, she thought sleepily, only tomorrow, just to impress the English soldiers with your fancy name. She smiled. Raul would applaud her smart thinking when he knew. It was just the kind of thing he would have done.

Chapter Six

April 1944

'I am the Marchesa Eleanora Anna Maria Baroness San Angelo di Magliano e del Monte, and I want you to find a missing person. His name is Raul Carducci, and I last saw him on March the nineteenth this year.'

Liana's carefully rehearsed speech went exactly as she had planned – well, almost, she thought, listening to herself. Her English accent was impeccably haughty, although nerves made her voice a little husky and the words tumbled out faster than she would have preferred.

A hushed silence reigned in the small office. The only sound came through the window – shrill voices of a group of children shrieking excitedly as they played tag in the sunshine of the *piazza* outside. The two soldiers in the office, the tall blond one at the large central desk and the smaller dark man at the other were both silent.

Uneasy, Liana was aware that they were gazing at her with a strange intensity, as if unable to pull their eyes away. Why do they look at me as if they are seeing a ghost, she thought, clearing her throat nervously. Why are they staring so? Her heart thudded against her ribs, her hands felt clammy. Have they seen through my subterfuge? Surely not, it wasn't possible, and anyway I have not done anything wrong.

The need to find Raul was imperative. Firmly suppressing the rush of nervousness, she stood her ground. Using Eleanora's name was not against any law that she knew of, and it had been the logical thing to do. The wishes of a *marchesa* would carry more weight than those of an ordinary peasant girl, and the need to find Raul overruled all other considerations. Hiding her fear she waited, resolute and dignified. Tall and erect, she gazed unflinchingly at the two men, giving nothing away.

Nicholas was the first to find his voice. 'Eleanora,' he said on a note of incredulous astonishment.

Startled, Liana gazed at the blond man. It was her turn to stare now. He sounded as if he knew her, as if he was pleased to see her. She was puzzled and more than a little apprehensive but she swallowed her fear. Raul, Raul, the beloved name hammered through her brain – she *had* to find him.

The moment the tall, dark girl had walked into the office a door into Nicholas's memory had swung open. Immediately the night of the bombing flickered back, every detail etched with precise clarity. He realized with surprise that his subconscious had stored the memory away, perfect and intact, ready to emerge at the touch of a trigger. And now here she was, and, even more amazingly, speaking English as if she conversed in the language every day of her life. Surprise registered; but so did a brief flicker of premonition. It seemed to Nicholas that his future flashed before him, a mixture of passionate love, conflict and tragedy, all confusingly mixed together. It unnerved him, and for a long moment he remained silent, uncertain of what to do or say next.

He repeated her name, 'Eleanora.' How could he ever forget it? The single word he had heard her utter that terrible October night the previous year. Another long and awkward silence followed and Liana twisted her handbag nervously, clasping it to her chest. Her palpable nervousness helped Nicholas. He had to say something to put the poor girl at her ease. 'I'm so glad you speak such good English, my dear,' he said. 'It makes life easier for me. My Italian is not as good as it should be.'

'I had an English governess,' said Liana, feeling some explanation was needed.

Nicholas saw Charlie staring at him and knew he was thinking they really ought to be getting down to the business of this missing man she had called about. He pulled a sheaf of papers towards him. 'Now, Eleanora,' he said, 'I hope I may call you that, what . . .'

'I am always called Liana.'

The words escaped from her lips before she could stop them. With a muffled gasp she froze, rigid with fear. Oh God, already she had spoiled everything by a moment of stupid carelessness. Why hadn't she kept her mouth shut? Her name was supposed to be Eleanora. Now they would find out who she really was, dismiss her as an impostor, and Raul would never be found.

Lowering her eyes and ostensibly searching in her handbag for a handkerchief, Liana thought rapidly. How could she explain? You can't, said part of her brain, but I must, said another, for the sake of Raul and his child I must think of something. Swallowing hard, she looked up ready to begin a faltering explanation of the slip, but to her amazement the blond officer was smiling broadly.

'Liana,' he said thoughtfully, rolling the name experimentally on his tongue. 'I must say I like it much better than the other mouthful of names you gave us just now. Much easier to remember.' Liana heaved a sigh of relief. It was all right; she was going to find Raul after all. Or to be more precise, this friendly young officer was going to find him for her. Nicholas patted the chair at his side encouragingly, wanting more than ever to put this beautiful young woman at ease. 'Why don't you sit down, Liana? Tell us everything, right from the beginning, and how we can help.'

Charlie said nothing; he sat and watched, silent and curious. So the beautiful young girl they had rescued had turned up again. Somehow he was not in the least bit surprised, although for the life of him he knew he would never be able to explain why. He looked at her carefully. He had forgotten the full impact of her strangely arresting beauty, although he was pretty certain that his captain had not. Yes, there was definitely something uncanny about her appearance at their office, as if it were meant to be. One thing was quite clear, however: although the two men might remember her extremely vividly, it was obvious from her puzzled expression that she did not recall them at all.

Nicholas lost no time in reminding her, and gradually Liana relaxed, her initial worries draining away. 'That is how I knew your name was Eleanora,' he said finally, then added curiously, 'but whatever were you doing in that awful part of town at night, and alone? It is not the sort of place for a girl like you. Why weren't you safely out of harm's way, up in your *castello*?'

A natural question, but one not anticipated by Liana. It threw her into a panic, the muscles in her throat tightening with fright. How could she justify her presence in the slums of Naples? 'Oh, I . . .' How foolish she had been to think that just one lie would be enough. Inevitably one untruth led to another. I must be careful and convincing, she reminded herself as she sought for the right words. It was of vital importance that they should believe her. For a moment she hated herself for lying. She didn't want to lie to this pleasant, fair-haired man before her or to his companion who had helped save her life. But the justification came almost immediately, dispelling all guilt. For Raul's sake, and for the sake of his child, it was necessary. Hesitating only fractionally, Liana began again, surprised at the ease with which the glib words came to her. 'I was taking a little food to a bedridden old woman who once worked for us. The poor thing lived there in the slums; she died that night in the bombing raid. Hers was the body next to mine.'

Compassion showed in the steady gaze of Nicholas's clear grey eyes, and Liana felt her heart contract with another guilty pang. Would he be so understanding if he knew what she had really been doing? I doubt it, she thought. In fact I know he would not. No-one will ever understand.

In the next half-hour, Liana skilfully expanded her capacity for skating near the truth without actually revealing it. Instinct told her to stick as near to the facts as possible, that way she was less likely to make a mistake at a later date. Once she had her nervousness under control, she became aware that she held the two men captive in the palm of her hand. It gave her a heady sense of power, a power she didn't hesitate to make full use of. She gave them a sketchy outline of her fictitious past – most of it, of course, Eleanora's although she managed to weave in parts of her own, too. Her father, she told them, had been killed in Spain before the war, fighting against the Fascists he hated so much.

'Afterwards my mother and I stayed on at the *castello* with Miss Rose, my English governess and teacher, until she, too, left for the safety of England. Then we were quite alone.' She thought it prudent to say nothing at all about Eleanora or Don Luigi, even under the guise of other names. 'Because of my father we were shunned by everyone, for fear of reprisals by the Black Shirts. They did come to the *castello* and took away almost everything of value, but after that they left us in peace.'

'You poor things,' said Nicholas with genuine sympathy. He thought of his mother and her friends. They were safe in the peaceful countryside of southern England. True they had been bombed and there was food rationing, and they grumbled about that. But they had no idea of what it was like to live in a country dominated by a Fascist dictatorship then occupied by a foreign power, and to lose the most basic of freedoms. Please, God, they never would.

'Then in nineteen forty-two my mother was murdered.' There was no need to act; Liana's voice broke with genuine emotion as she recalled her mother's harrowing death. Charlie and Nicholas listened with growing horror as she recounted the events, then Charlie made some coffee and insisted she drink it.

After a while, fortified by the coffee, she went on to tell how she survived alone, starving most of the time. She consoled herself that it was almost the truth – of the three of them left at the *castello* she had survived, and neither Don Luigi nor Eleanora would have lived as long as they had if it had not been for her. Then came the introduction of Raul, the purpose of her visit to the FS office. Raul, she told them, was a distant cousin, and had returned when the tattered remnants of Mussolini's army had finally broken up. Liana had hastily decided it would be wiser to say that Raul was a cousin. It was a much more convincing reason for being so concerned for him. What could be more natural than trying to find one's only living relative?

'When Raul returned, and after the Allies landed, I was lucky enough to sell some jewellery I had managed to hide from the Fascists, and we started to eat a little better.' She hung her head and looked at the two men from beneath a thick fringe of dark lashes, the tremulous smile on her lips expressly designed to melt their hearts. 'I suppose I must confess we bought black-market food. You won't arrest me, will you?'

It was a shrewdly calculated statement. She knew perfectly well that she already had their sympathy. They would not arrest her. But sympathy was not enough. She needed to appeal to them, to persuade them to help her. Confessing everything abjectly, throwing her vulnerable femininity at their mercy would, she hoped, have the desired effect.

The ruse worked perfectly. Nicholas and Charlie exchanged knowing smiles at her innocence. 'If we arrested everyone who bought from the black market, we'd never have enough space in the prisons,' said Nicholas. 'Now let me see what we can do.' He scanned the notes Charlie handed him. Every detail Liana had related was meticulously recorded. 'From what you tell us, I would say the most likely cause for Raul's disappearance is mistaken arrest. There is a lot of confusion, and the language barrier is always a problem. I notice Raul does not speak much English.'

'Hardly any,' said Liana, feeling more hopeful by the minute. The fact that he had echoed her own thoughts was very encouraging. She began to relax; Raul was as good as found.

'We shall check the registers this very afternoon. Come back tomorrow and we should have some news for you.' Nicholas rose and kissed her hand with old-world gallantry as a now beaming Liana departed.

'Do you really want to find this Raul?' asked Charlie pointedly. 'Wouldn't you prefer her to be all alone in the world so that she turned to lean on you?'

Nicholas smiled. It was difficult to hide things from Charlie, the knowing old devil. 'No, I don't want to find him, not really,' he answered. 'I'd much prefer to keep her to myself. However, I can't let her down so I shall do as I promised.'

One week later Liana was almost beside herself with despair, although she was careful not to show her escalating fears to the two men. The knowledge of the baby, which she had promised to protect, had endowed her with an extra sense of pragmatic shrewdness, so when she presented herself at the FS office every day, she always presented a calm, hopeful exterior.

'I know you will find him,' she told Nicholas the last time he had apologized because of the lack of information. 'I have every confidence in you.' Then she had smiled her beautiful gentle smile, which made him feel sick to his stomach because he had achieved absolutely nothing, and left.

Nicholas and Charlie had drawn blanks everywhere. There had been no sign of Raul in the prison register. Nevertheless, they had followed up every lead no matter how insubstantial – all to no avail. There was no sign of Raul Carducci, nor any indication that he had ever existed. Eventually there was no alternative, Nicholas had to decide to call a halt. They both had other work to do and couldn't go on looking for just one man for ever.

'God, Charlie, what shall I do?' Nicholas sifted irritably through the mound of papers on his desk, as if he were hoping a clue would miraculously present itself. 'She has to be told we're going to give up.'

'Well, sir, there's no point in beating about the bush,' said Charlie, practical as usual. 'You'll have to be blunt, and she will have to face up to the truth. Her cousin cannot be found, and what is probably more to the point, will *never* be found.'

That afternoon Charlie slid out of the office when Liana arrived. He rarely shirked his duty, but that afternoon he decided Nicholas could have all the privileges of rank; besides, he didn't want to see the pain in her eyes when she heard their verdict.

'Coward,' muttered Nicholas as Charlie passed Liana in the doorway. She looked more beautiful than ever in a loose-fitting, powder-blue dress which was a little too large for her. Her dark hair was coiled demurely into the nape of her lovely neck. Like a modern madonna, thought Charlie, then cursed himself for letting his thoughts become mawkishly sentimental.

Nicholas had spent the morning practising different ways of broaching the subject but had not found it easy. Which ever way he put them, the words still sounded bald to the point of cruelty. Eventually he had decided that it would be better to get it over and done with as quickly as possible.

Now she had actually arrived, he motioned Liana to sit on the chair by the desk, which she did, sitting with her back ramrod straight, clasping her handbag to her front as if for moral support. Nicholas looked up, intending to give a reassuring smile, but found he could not. He could not bear to look into her dark, imploring eyes, so he gazed instead at the neat pile of papers in front of him on the desk, and steeled himself. Then he said far more brusquely than he had ever intended. 'In my opinion, and that of my colleagues, your cousin Raul Carducci is dead.'

Liana half rose from the chair, her arm raised as if to beat off the words. Dead, dead, DEAD – the words shrieked in her head. She had been worried, she had been afraid, but her fear had been of the endless, time-consuming bureaucracy. Never for one moment had she seriously considered that Raul might be dead. Oh, God! Was the shadow of death really still with her? Liana shuddered, repulsing the thought. No, it could not be – not the Raul she knew, he was always so vital, so alive. He could not be dead; and she would not, *could not* give up, not now – Raul's child was growing day by day and needed a father.

'But you said it was possible for people to get lost in the Poggio Reale. It has happened before. Every day people turn up who are not registered. You said that. You *told* me!'

The bleak note of desperation in her voice chilled Nicholas. This was going to be worse than he had thought. 'If he were there, we would have found him by now,' he said. He carried on quickly before she could interrupt. 'Liana, I don't have to explain to you about the Zona di Camorra or the *camorristi*. You know Naples is a dangerous place.'

'But they are criminals. Raul wasn't involved in crime,' she cried. 'What are you talking about?'

'You don't have to be involved to get killed,' said Nicholas sombrely. 'All it needs is to be in the wrong place at the wrong time. To be in the way. We've been to the *carabinieri*, the *Pubblica Sicurezza*. There is no information.'

He didn't mention that they hadn't pursued the matter too thoroughly from either of those sources. The Allies had no wish to get drawn into the activities of the *camorristi*, and for his own part Nicholas knew with growing certainty, that if he found Raul, then he would lose Liana. The attraction he had felt at the beginning had become an obsession which he had taken care to hide, even from Charlie. He wanted her now more than he'd ever wanted any other woman. He had struggled to reconcile her needs with his own desires, but knew to his shame, that his judgement was clouded.

Liana sat silently in front of the big desk. She knew it was true what Nicholas said about the Zona di Camorra. Those people, the *camorristi*, lived outside the law. Theirs was a secret world with their own warped form of justice and honour. Official enquiries always met a wall of silence because *Omerta*, the code of silence, reigned supreme. Murders were never reported, and bodies only found when it suited some devious purpose to have them dumped in a conspicuous place. She had to accept the dreadful truth that Raul was dead. Her faith in Nicholas was absolute. If Nicholas had not been able to trace him then no-one would. The unthinkable had happened; Raul was dead. Liana remembered those fleeting nightmares she had sometimes had when she and Raul were together, and how she had thought then that without Raul life would be impossible, not worth living. The terrifying, bleak desolation of the nightmares filled her now. She could almost feel her life's blood draining away until she was nothing, nothing but an empty shell masquerading as a living woman. Then she remembered the baby, Raul's child. No, she was not quite dead and neither was he.

'Oh, God, what shall I do now?' Without thinking she had whispered her thoughts out loud.

What should she do now? For a fleeting moment she thought of what other girls would do in her situation – have an abortion, get rid of the child while it was still not too late. But it was only a fleeting moment. She was not like other girls; and they did not carry Raul's child – Raul's child, a stream of obsessive possessiveness surged through her. Raul might be dead, but she had a part of him no-one else had, no-one else could ever have – his child. For Raul's sake a solution had to be found. She could have the baby and try to rear it alone. No, that idea was rejected almost immediately. A woman alone, with no money to speak of and a child to rear – the idea was inconceivable; a life of poverty was not for Raul's child. Briefly she considered returning to prostitution, but dismissed that idea as impracticable on two counts. Who would look after the baby while she worked? Plus the fact that the foreign soldiers, the only ones with any real money, would not be in Italy for ever, and then what? Reluctantly Liana came to the conclusion that only one positive and unpleasant fact was staring her in the face. At the moment, she could see no alternative for the future except a life of abject poverty.

She stared blindly ahead, her surroundings forgotten in her desperate concentration on the future. Nicholas sat and watched her. Suddenly Raul's words sounded in her ears. *Supposing I asked you to do something terrible. Supposing I asked you to make a great sacrifice, something you didn't want to do.* And she remembered, too, her answer. *I'd do it. Anything.*

Well, now that time had come, the time for self-sacrifice. Raul was not there, he was unable to ask for himself, but his unborn child was inside her and in her overwrought imagination she felt the child urging her on. There has to be a way, she told herself, and I will find it. Obsessed still with her passionate love for Raul, and burning with the inner fire he had lit, she made a silent vow. *Whatever life demands of me, wherever the path leads, I will take it, for Raul and his child.* There was no alternative. Raul's child demanded nothing less.

Her beautiful mouth looked stern as she made up her mind. Somehow she would achieve respectability, become a woman people would look up to, and she would be rich. Raul's child would never know what the words 'to want' meant, because the best of everything that money could buy would always be there. But how to achieve such a miracle? That was the immediate problem.

'Liana, my dear. Let me help in whatever way I can.' Nicholas came round from behind his desk to sit beside her. He took her hand in his, and stroked it gently.

Liana looked down at her own slender, olive-skinned hand, held in his enormous fair-skinned one. The blond hairs on the back of his fingers gleamed in the light from the window. It is a strong hand, she thought, an embryonic idea beginning to form in her mind, a strong hand belonging to a strong and good man. Not only was he good and strong, he was also an aristocrat, an English aristocrat. Soon, when the war was over, he would be returning to his beautiful house in England. It was a peaceful place, untouched by war. She knew that because he had told her so. From what he had said it sounded the perfect place in which to bring up a child, her child, hers and Raul's. Yes, a child could be very happy in such a place. The thought slowly calcified as she calculated the possibilities. Prostitution came in many forms, but with just one man, and that man acting as a substitute husband and father, it would not be like prostitution at all. It would be respectable. Here was the solution she had been seeking staring her in the face. A husband, security, and a ready-made father for Raul's baby. Taking a deep breath Liana made up her mind and looked up at Nicholas.

'Would you really?' she whispered, blinking, suddenly aware of how advantageous were the tear drops hovering on the end of her long lashes. 'Would you really help me?'

'Of course. Anything I can do, just ask me, and I'll do it.'

A smile lit his handsome face, his clear grey eyes glinting with enthusiasm, boyish and eager. Uncomplicated himself, he could never have imagined the complexity of thoughts that twisted and turned through Liana's mind or the plans she was already formulating. Although he tried to keep his eager thoughts in check, he could only think of one thing. Part of him was ashamed that he should be thinking in such a way at a time like this, but he could not help it. The image of her long, slender body lying in his arms while he made love to her rose before him time and time again. Lust showed in his eyes, and Liana recognized it.

I'm halfway there already, she thought, and almost laughed out loud in triumph as she bent forward and placed a chaste kiss on his cheek. 'Thank you, Nicholas,' she whispered. 'It's good to know that I have a friend I can count on. I have no-one else in all the world.'

'Count on me,' he said, 'for anything.' Never for one moment did he dream where those words would lead him; or that the years ahead would hold passion, heartbreak and sorrow beyond his wildest imaginings.

Liana walked slowly to the door, acutely aware that time was of the essence. If Nicholas were to marry her and be convinced that it was his own idea, then she had to start executing her half-formed plans now. Each time I see Nicholas I must plant the seed of an idea in his mind – yes, that is how I will do it – until eventually, in a very short while, his desire to help me, propelled by his desire for my body, will inevitably lead to the belief that he wants to marry me. A secret smile touched her lips. She had no doubt whatsoever of her ability to accomplish everything she had in mind in the time she needed. It was almost as good as done.

Nicholas watched her graceful figure as she paused in the doorway. How lovely she was, young, lovely and alone. Then she turned back and smiled a shy, tremulous smile with just the merest hint of latent sexuality. How sweet she is, thought Nicholas firmly squashing the idea that he might be taking advantage of her. She was sweet, and yet at the same time so very desirable. The calculating smile of a siren had the desired effect. Nicholas smiled back and felt as if his guts had turned to water.

'I *will* count on you,' she said softly. 'Perhaps we could have a coffee together tomorrow?'

'Marchesa, I'll organize my life around your needs,' answered Nicholas grinning broadly and sweeping a low bow. 'I'll make sure you are never lonely.'

'Thank you.' Again that strange inexplicably secretive smile that tied his stomach in knots, and then she was gone.

'Getting the beautiful *marchesa* into my bed is my highest priority,' Nicholas later told a sceptical Charlie. He had genuinely meant it when he had said he would help her and that she could count on him. But uncomplicated male that he was, he had never thought beyond the fact that helping her would also get him what he wanted. What might happen to her when he was posted away from Italy had never crossed his mind, because, fascinated though he was by Liana, he was not in love with her.

'Maybe, but is that *her* priority?' Charlie snorted cynically. Somehow he could not see it being that easy. Surely Nicholas must realize that a young woman with the aura of calm dignity that Liana exuded wasn't going to hop into bed with him just because he felt like it!

Nicholas chose to ignore Charlie's comment, and spent the rest of the day in a rosy daydream.

While Nicholas dreamed of nothing else but making love, Liana spent her time mentally rehearsing and preparing herself for the drastic new direction in which she intended to channel her life, a new and very different life without Raul but with his child. There was no point in allowing herself the luxury of dwelling on mournful thoughts of Raul. Now was not the time for sentiment. Liana realized that no matter how real, or painful, her love for Raul was, it had to be put away, packed into a dark recess of her mind. Here and now was of vital importance, that and the future.

However, there was one major flaw in her plan, and that was the fact that Nicholas was unaware, as yet, of the fact that he would be marrying her. It was a problem, but not an insurmountable one. Confident of the power her attraction held for him, Liana thought he should not take too long to persuade. I *can't* afford to take long, she thought. The time factor is very important. She counted up the months on her fingers and for a moment felt afraid. There was so little time. It was imperative that she should be married by the beginning of May. That way it was perfectly feasible that the baby could be thought to be premature, and no-one, especially Nicholas, would be any the wiser.

She undressed, and stood before the only mirror the *castello* possessed. It was cracked and disfigured by patches of damp so that Liana had to turn and twist to examine every aspect of her figure with an objective eye. At last she turned away, satisfied. Her figure was as slender as ever, and there was no hint of pregnancy. Nor must there be before I am married, she thought grimly, although I must take care to eat as much nourishment as possible. The secret would be to eat well, but very, very carefully.

The other problem was the matter of virginity. Nicholas must have a virgin bride if he was never to have the slightest shadow of doubt in his mind. He must be convinced that he was the first man ever to have penetrated her, and, therefore, that the child was his.

Suddenly she laughed and patted her stomach. 'Just imagine, you are going to have an English earl for a father. What do you think of that?'

Although she knew that it was still a microscopic dot, Liana imagined the baby laughing and kicking in glee. Together they would snap their fingers in the face of fate, she and her daughter. It would be a daughter, she was sure of that, a strong and determined survivor like herself, but there would be no shadows to dog *her* footsteps. She would make certain of that.

Casting her mind back to the matter of virginity, Liana decided to visit a Dr Turzo in Naples. She had heard from the other girls who worked the streets that he was good at his job – that of repairing hymens. Apparently 10,000 lire was the going rate. Although she begrudged the thought of spending so much of her hard-earned money, she cheered herself with the conclusion that in reality it was a bargain. Ten thousand lire would buy a secure future for the baby and herself.

Suddenly, and without warning, the momentary euphoria at plans for the future passed and Liana found herself flinching at new thoughts. Pretence, that would be the hardest part of all, the pretence. It was foolish to persuade herself that there would be no deadly echoes from the past; of course there would. Marriage to Nicholas meant sharing his bed. She would have to submit to his sexual needs, and more importantly she would have to convince him that she enjoyed it. He must think her response to him was real, when all the time she would know she was cheating. How could it not be cheating? She didn't love Nicholas and never could. Love for Raul still filled every corner of her being. The fact that he was no longer alive didn't alter her feelings.

When she thought of the irrevocability of the step she was proposing, the courage to go on almost failed her. Wrapping herself in a blanket Liana knelt by the *stufa*, and, leaning her cheek against the cold iron, allowed herself the luxury of remembering. Memories of the times she and Raul had made love beside the stove floated mistily through her mind. How different it had been then. The room had been warm and glowing, with no dark corners, and no lies nor pretence. In her innocence she had mistakenly thought the light which seemingly had filled her life with such purpose would go on and on for ever.

She began to weep softly. Bitter, scalding tears scoured down her cheeks. 'Oh, Raul, Raul,' she sobbed, hiccupping and half choking in her grief, the rigid self-control broken for the moment. 'Why did you show me what love was like? Why did you show me, and then leave? It would have been better if I had never known.'

Even the thought of the child curled inside her womb failed to comfort her. Nothing could sweep away the sense of emptiness and desolation that surrounded her. But the streak of steel in Liana, which was her own special hallmark, told her that, in spite of the sense of desolation, sorrow and weeping achieved nothing. With an almighty effort she reimposed the rigid control which had stood her in good stead many times before. All I need is determination, she thought, and everything will be all right. Pulling the blanket closely around her and clasping her hunched-up knees to her chest, Liana viewed her future with the icy detachment of a general planning a devastating campaign.

*

One week later, however, she was worried. Her carefully planned campaign was not progressing nearly fast enough. Time was running out if she was to preserve her secret and ensure the future of Raul's child. But still her relentless determination sustained her – determination plus desperation. She had no other plan, so this one *had* to succeed. Not once did she let Nicholas ever suspect that anything was worrying her. For him, she always presented the same mysteriously calm and alluring mask. They had progressed from being just friends and would have been lovers if Nicholas had had his way. But, desperate though she was, Liana knew she could not afford to let her guard down. Once he had made love to her, it would be all too easy to discard her and go on his way. He had to want to *marry* her. While Liana worried, Nicholas failed to recognize the steely will behind her dark almond eyes and continued to persuade himself that it was merely a matter of time before she succumbed to his charms.

Liana now decided that the time had come to let him go a little further, make his desire a little more desperate, more difficult to contain. She was playing with fire, she knew that, but it had to be done. It was a warm afternoon, and they were spending the time together walking along the remains of the promenade near the harbour in Naples. The castle ramparts rose above them, glowing and golden in the sun, the azure sea and sky melted into one another. On such perfect days war seemed very far away, and Nicholas felt lighthearted. It was almost like being on holiday. As soon as they reached a sheltered spot, well out of sight of others, he drew her passionately into his arms.

Bending his head, his mouth sought out hers. God, how desirable she was. The thought of her slender body beneath his hands suffused him with heat. Liana responded, raising her head willingly for his kiss. In fact, as she had found out to her surprise, kissing Nicholas was not as unpleasant as she had feared. At least he didn't slobber all over her the way that some of her clients used to. Nevertheless, the ardour she simulated was an emotion she did not possess.

Today she purposely let his hands explore more. Nicholas felt his excitement rise; he was making progress. He felt the outline of her full breasts and even gently teased at her nipples, feeling them rise and harden under his touch. Then, dropping his hands to her hips he began the slow move downwards. It was then that she stopped him.

'No,' she whispered.

'Why not? I want you. I won't hurt you. I'd never do that.' There was a silence, then Nicholas sighed heavily and answered himself. 'No, don't tell me. I know. Nice girls don't.' In the last week his passion had gradually built up, his desire blazing so much that he could hardly control himself when he was with her.

'I'm sorry, darling,' Liana said tenderly, slowly-unwrapping his arms from around her and putting a distance between them. She smiled a slow, tantalizingly serene smile which had the effect of filling Nicholas's head with erotic images.

Still she allowed nothing in her manner to betray the rising tide of panic she was feeling. It was April the fourteenth – a whole week had passed since she had decided Nicholas was the husband of her choice, and still he was only thinking in terms of a casual affair. Would he never regard her as a future wife? But he must, and somehow she would make him. I'll make a pact with the devil himself if it is necessary, she vowed. Nicholas must be chastely seduced until even he understood that marriage would be the only way he could ever be fulfilled.

*

'Hell, Charlie. I must be the only bloody man in the whole of Naples to fall for a goddamned virgin!'

It was later that week, and Charlie and Nicholas were sitting together in a pavement café. He poured himself a tumblerful of the sweet, sticky Marsala, instead of the usual small glass, and slammed the bottle down bad-temperedly on the café table.

Charlie grinned. Unlike Nicholas he had not underestimated Liana at all. At the beginning he had not been certain what she had in mind, but he thought he had a pretty accurate idea now. The old saying was true, he reflected. Still waters did run deep. He had sensed from the beginning that there was a lot more to Liana than met the eye. 'Drowning your sorrows?' he said, eyeing the amount of Marsala.

'Too bloody right. I only wish there were some decent English beer, then I could do the job properly!'

Nicholas was fuming, because for him it had been a particularly frustrating day. He had taken Liana across to Capri, expressly for the purpose of seducing her. On the boat that morning, as it chugged through the pearly mist rolling across the surface of the water, Liana had leaned against him in a way that had almost prevented him from breathing. She was soft and relaxed, her breasts outlined against the thin cotton of her blouse. When we get to Capri, he thought, banking on the island's reputation for drugging its visitors with emotion, she will be mine.

He found a place where they could be alone together, far away from any other human life, high on the cliffs above an ultramarine sea of startling clarity. As they lay on the sweetly scented turf, disturbed only by the occasional bee blundering its way from one clover-head to another, Nicholas had mistakenly thought his moment had come. They were Adam and Eve in the Garden of Eden. He could feel her nipples rise and harden to his touch. He *had* to have her.

'Oh, darling.' With one swift movement he pushed aside her blouse and kissed the velvet flesh of her breast.

Liana sat up abruptly, pushing his hand away. 'I cannot,' she said. 'It is wrong.'

'But, darling, I love you. I want you.

Why doesn't he say something else, thought Liana beginning to feel irritated. Lowering her eyes, she held the irritation in check, merely saying softly, 'I love you too, Nicholas.'

Then she turned towards him, discreetly buttoning up her blouse, and smiled. Nicholas wondered how many women there were in the world who could say no with their lips and yes with their eyes. She reached over and shyly slid her hand inside his shirt.

'Oh, God, Liana, don't do that. Not if you want me to control myself.' Nicholas groaned and pulled her pliant body towards him. 'If you love me, why not? Why can't we, for God's sake?'

Liana hesitated, then decided the time had come to be a little less subtle. It was time to give his mind a push in the direction she wanted him to go.

'Because one day, like all normal girls, I hope to marry; and I want to be a virgin for my husband.' Nicholas opened his mouth to protest, but she put her fingers lightly on his lips. Her touch was a rebuttal, and yet at the same time a caress. 'I must be practical, darling. I do love you, and I know you love me. But we come from different worlds, you and I. You will not be in Italy for ever. Soon you will be posted away, and I'll have to stay here and make my own life. It won't be easy for me; but you, you will return to your life in England and forget all about me.'

'I'll never forget you.' Nicholas was adamant.

'Remembering me won't help me to find a good husband,' said Liana firmly. 'In Italy you *have* to be a virgin. It's an old-fashioned country.'

Nicholas recounted the conversation to Charlie that night as they drank their way through two bottles of Marsala. Liana had returned to the *castello* alone after kissing a fond, but this time, Nicholas thought, a distinctly firm farewell.

'Well, why *don't* you marry her?' said Charlie looking at the morose face before him. 'What is wrong with her? Ask yourself, have you ever been as smitten by any other woman before?'

Nicholas shook his head, a thoughtful expression crossing his face. 'No,' he said slowly. 'I've never felt like this before. All the girls I've ever known were debs I got lumbered with at parties before the war. Most of them had teeth to rival the horses they were all so fond of and were about as sexy as a bale of hay.'

Charlie laughed at the description. 'I've seen pictures of those sorts of girls in *Tatler*.' Nicholas raised his eyebrows. 'Well, a man has to read something in the dentist's waiting room!' Then he added earnestly. 'So, why don't you seriously consider marriage to Liana? I know she's poor, but she has the advantage of blue blood, even if it is Italian!'

Nicholas jerked his head up and stared at Charlie. 'I ought to marry into money,' he said slowly. 'My family is as poor as the proverbial church mouse.'

'Bloody stupid idea,' said Charlie, not bothering to mince his words. 'Money won't make you happy. Thank God I'm not an earl. I married my missus because I loved her and I still do. I can't wait to get back to her. She's no beauty, not like Liana, but I love her, and she'll keep me happy for the rest of my life. We don't need much money, just enough to keep the wolf from the door.'

'I suppose it is bloody stupid,' mused Nicholas. 'Why be unhappy with some horse-faced, sexless heiress when I could be ecstatic with an exquisite Italian *marchesa*?'

'Exactly,' said Charlie.

'I'll ask her,' said Nicholas. He stood up, his face flushed from excitement and the Marsala. 'I'll ask her tomorrow.'

'Well, perhaps you should take a day or two to think about it.' Charlie felt honour-bound to utter some words of caution, but it was too late. The seed of the idea had germinated, taken root and flowered in those few minutes.

'I'll get a ring tonight, and ask her tomorrow. I know a decrepit old prince who is desperate for money. He'll sell me a ring.' Without waiting for Charlie's reply, Nicholas left the café and walked away into the night. Not for one moment did he stop to weigh the balance of love and desire. For him it was one and the same thing. Why hadn't he thought of it before? Of course, it was the perfect answer. He loved Liana, and it was natural to want her. And, of course, she loved him, and wanted him, too. She had told him so many times. Suddenly everything seemed very clear cut and easy. Their future together stretched away before his mind's eye, blissfully serene, just like Liana's smile.

Left on his own, Charlie sat and worried. He lit a cigarette and puffed on it nervously. Why did he have to open his big mouth? He should have let Nicholas work things out for himself. Now he felt responsible.

*

Nicholas paced up and down the office impatiently. He should have been out on the visits he had been scheduled to make by his commanding officer. The black-market trade in penicillin was getting out of hand, and his orders were to track down the source of the pharmicists' supplies. It was an urgent order, one he should have attended to right away. The army hospital itself was running low on the drug, but Nicholas could not concentrate on army orders, not even urgent ones. Everything would have to wait until he had seen Liana, and today of all days, she was late. Meanwhile he was besieged by last-minute doubts followed by wild bursts of elation – doubts when he remembered the wintry remoteness he sometimes glimpsed in her eyes, and then elation at the thought of her voluptuous body and her sensual smile.

'Scoot,' he said to Charlie the moment the tapping of her sandals could be heard coming down the long marble corridor leading up to the office.

Charlie scooted, glad to get out of the way. More than ever he regretted his careless words of the night before. The man was bewitched by the girl! In which case, common sense told Charlie, you had absolutely nothing to do with it. It would have happened sooner or later. You didn't make up his mind for him, he made it up himself. But common sense did not help; he still felt responsible. He crossed his fingers, and gave what he hoped was an encouraging smile to Nicholas. 'Good luck, sir,' he said.

'Hello, Charlie.' Liana passed him in the doorway.

It was particularly warm for the middle of April, and she was wearing a pale, lemon-coloured summer dress, one of Eleanora's. No matter that it was shabby and had been mended many times. The delicate colour gave her skin the look of sculpted ivory and her hair had never looked so black and luxurious.

There was not the slightest shadow of doubt now in Nicholas's mind. Pushing the door shut behind her, he took the heavy tresses of her hair in his hands. Wonderingly he let it fall through his fingers. It was like raw silk. She was the most beautiful woman he had ever seen.

'Will you marry me?' he asked.

She looked up quickly, a question in her dark eyes. Had she really heard correctly? He nodded, and her eyes began to sparkle with pure unadulterated joy. How could I have ever thought you remote, he wondered as she flung herself into his arms.

'Oh, Nicholas, yes, yes, yes.' He felt the softness of her body melt against him as if she was boneless and dissolving into him. 'When? Oh, please, let's make it soon.'

A thrill of wild triumph surged through Liana as she spoke. She had succeeded. Marriage to Nicholas and escape to England was within her grasp. Suddenly the narrow confines of her horizon broke asunder; the future was limitless.

Nicholas was kissing her. 'Oh, yes, darling. Soon, I promise. It will be soon. As soon as I can arrange it.'

His breathing quickened and his hands rose from her waist, sliding upwards until they cupped her breasts, his thumbs spiralling faster and faster around her nipples.

Not yet, not yet. Suddenly she wanted to scream as apprehension spewed sickeningly through her. He wanted her now, but it was too soon for that. She had not had her hymen repaired yet. She began to tremble. Please let me hold him off until then, she prayed silently. I must get to a doctor as soon as possible. I've got to be as pure as driven snow for him. Nothing less than the appearance of perfect virginity will do. Please make him stop.

Nicholas felt the shudder pass through her frame and mistook it for desire as great as his own. His fervour increased, and his mouth sought out hers again. Reason slipped away. All he knew was that he could not get enough of her. His tongue prised her lips apart, filling her mouth as he wanted to fill her body.

Liana let herself go limp, and with grim determination isolated her mind from her body until she was able to think with calm detachment. I'll push him off in a moment. I mustn't appear too unfriendly. Nicholas must think I want to really but . . . Suddenly the memory of the way she had responded to Raul flooded through her mind and the calm detachment disappeared. Oh God, the bitter, bitter anguish. This man holding her, touching her, devouring her almost; this was all so wrong. It should be Raul. If it were Raul she would have surrendered willingly. There would have been no need to think, only to love. But it can't be Raul, not ever again. Raul is dead, dead, *dead*. With a choking, retching sob she pushed Nicholas away.

'I'm sorry, so sorry. But . . . but I can't.'

Nicholas looked at her chalk white face and trembling hands. It's my fault, he thought, guilt washing over him. I've rushed her. I know she wants me, but she's inexperienced and frightened. And when he saw the tears trickling slowly down her cheeks, it confirmed his views. A girl like Liana, brought up all her life to save herself for the sanctity of marriage, would never want to compromise, not even when engaged. He felt ashamed at his lack of control.

'Forgive me, darling,' he said softly, wiping the tears away with his handkerchief. 'I'll wait until our wedding night, and then I'll be gentle, I promise. There's nothing to be afraid of.'

Liana managed a shaky smile. Unwittingly Nicholas was handing her the excuse she needed on a platter, and she grasped it gratefully with both hands.

'Thank you for being so understanding,' she said softly.

When the wedding night comes, she silently promised Nicholas, I will be prepared, mentally *and* physically. Then I will make it up to you.

She let him kiss her hands, and slip the engagement ring on her finger. It was a fire opal, set in gold.

'I'm not superstitious, are you?' Nicholas asked as she looked at the ring gleaming on her finger.

'No, of course not.' But an uneasy shiver ran through her just the same. She remembered having heard that having an opal in the house was said to be like having a spy. It was a charmed eye, which could see into the secrets of one's heart. She held up her hand so that Nicholas could see the ring and the opal caught the light, shooting flashes of milky flame. It would never know *her* secrets. Anyway, only stupid people believed in such nonsense, and she wasn't such a person. 'No, I'm not at all superstitious,' she said. 'Not superstitious at all. It's a beautiful ring.'

Chapter Seven

April 1944

Nicholas was true to his word, he wasted not a single minute. For someone normally irritated by mountains of paperwork, and who always procrastinated whenever possible, he showed a surprising aptitude now he put his mind to the task in hand. He launched himself with gusto into the bureaucratic machinery necessitated by the proposed wedding. Marriages between Allied army personnel and local girls were normally frowned upon by the military, but Nicholas was in a good position to pull a few strings, and had no compunction about pulling them. He used all the influence at his disposal, helped by the fact that in civilian life he was an English earl and Liana an Italian *marchesa*. That fact alone proved more than useful in the initial oiling of the wheels. His commanding officer, an inveterate snob, gave his permission without hesitation.

'Probably the wedding of the year as far as he's concerned,' observed Charlie sourly.

'It will be,' said Nicholas with glee, closing his mind to the fact that all other applications had been refused. That was not his problem.

To Liana's relief the lack of proof of her identity was accepted by the authorities without question. The fact that her home had been looted, bombed and burned was good enough. Obtaining all the necessary replica documentation was easily achieved with a little bribery as was the civil-marriage certificate. Dealing with the Neapolitan authorities was even easier than dealing with the British army. A pocketful of cash could buy anything.

'Christ!' exploded Charlie who went with Nicholas to sort out the necessary paperwork. 'Is there anybody in Naples who is honest?'

'Probably not,' said Nicholas, 'but who cares?'

'I do. It seems so wrong.'

Nicholas laughed. 'That's your English puritan streak speaking. These people are used to it. They don't expect honesty, so they are never disappointed.'

Charlie kept silent. There was nothing he could do, but he wondered whether Liana felt the same way. Did she, too, accept cheating as a way of life? It was not something he could ask Nicholas.

The tiny, run-down church of San Niccolo was specially chosen by Nicholas for the wedding because it was out of the way and had a mere handful of impoverished parishioners. The ancient priest was starving like everyone else, and more than willing to be bribed. Once a handful of money was securely tucked away under his soutane, he assured Nicholas that he would officiate at the ceremony, even though Nicholas was an Anglican.

'All the same in the sight of God,' he mumbled toothlessly, his pious expression turning to avaricious glee as he counted the money.

Nicholas did have a momentary qualm about that. He wondered whether or not his mother had received his letter telling her that he was to be married. He had teased Charlie about his English puritanical streak, but at the same time uncomfortably remembered that his mother had very firm views on the subject of morality and religion. She would have a fit if she knew he was to be married with, what she considered to be, Catholic mumbo jumbo, incense and ringing of bells! Then he grinned as he thought of it. Why worry? She was in England, which, all things considered, was probably just as well. By the time she finally met Liana, she would be his wife, the new Countess of Wessex, and nothing would be able to change that. The wedding service would be history. And as for any other objections, Liana's Italian pedigree was impeccable enough to silence the most class-conscious Englishman or woman, even his mother!

At last everything was arranged. The date of the wedding was set for May. The time, the church, and Liana's wedding dress were all organized. Charlie had arranged the reception and the invitations had been sent out. Nicholas finally relaxed.

'Now,' remarked Charlie on a note of irony, 'perhaps we can both concentrate on what we ought to have been doing, and maybe catch up with some of the army's work.' He passed a sheaf of letters across to Nicholas who grinned unrepentantly.

Nicholas began flicking uninterestedly through the papers, then uttered an expletive. 'Bloody hell! I could do without this.' He flung a typewritten sheet across to Charlie. 'Why couldn't they have given this assignment to somebody else?'

Charlie scanned the piece of paper. 'Down to Bari for a week,' he said pulling a thoughtful face. 'Well, at least you'll be back on April the twenty-eighth, which gives you two days before the wedding. It could be worse.'

*

'Sorry, darling, but an order is an order. I'm lucky they didn't arrange it when we are due to be on our honeymoon.' Nicholas apologized profusely to Liana when next he saw her. He did not want to leave her now, and certainly not for a whole week, but there was nothing he could do about it. He had to go.

Liana nearly fainted with relief. It was the chance she had been waiting for. Nicholas had been so attentive since the engagement she had begun to fear she would never escape from him for long enough to visit Dr Turzo. A whole week without Nicholas. It was more than she had ever dared hope for.

'Don't worry, darling, I understand,' she said, managing to look and sound suitably disappointed and hide her satisfaction at the same time.

'Charlie will see that you lack for nothing.'

'I forbid you to worry about me. I shall be fine. I'll stay up in the *castello* and just laze about in the spring sunshine, dreaming of our wedding day.'

Nicholas departed reluctantly for Bari, but first he made Charlie promise to keep an eye on Liana. She had already gone back to the *castello* after kissing Nicholas a fond farewell.

*

Lazing in the spring sunshine and dreaming. God, that was a laugh! If only they knew; but they didn't, and never would. She tried to think of the sunshine and her future, but the pain frequently blotted out all coherent thought. There was no time for dreaming, only for pain. She had known it would hurt, but never had she imagined that the agony could be anything like this.

Liana lay on a couch, legs up and splayed wide open. Dr Turzo had tied them with tapes to metal bars on either side of the couch to prevent her from moving. Her arms, too, were tied to the sides of the couch to prevent movement, so that there was no escape from the agony of the needle as it plunged in and out. It felt red hot as it pierced the tender flesh, but Liana did not cry out. Her teeth clenched tightly on the rag rope she'd been given to bite, and perspiration poured down her face, soaking the pillow on which her head rested.

'We will have no screaming, please,' said Dr Turzo when he had rammed the rag into her mouth. 'There are other patients waiting outside, and I don't want them put off.'

Not once did a muscle move in her face, and her eyes remained closed. Only her hands betrayed her. The knuckles gleamed so white it seemed the skin would surely split to reveal the bone. How much longer would it take? How much longer could she stand it? The needle kept on coming, in and out, in and out, as the delicate tissue was drawn tautly together.

'Nearly finished. Your new husband should enjoy demolishing this.' He laughed cruelly. Wouldn't mind doing the job myself on this one, he thought, letting his hands wander appreciatively for a moment over the soft skin of her belly. A good-looking girl. His wandering hand reached her breast – lovely and firm. He licked his lips greedily, wishing he had taken her to bed before he'd started the stitching. She was certainly different from most of his clients.

Liana felt his wandering hands, but was past caring. How did he know she was getting married? She hadn't told him. Or had she? She tried to think clearly, but the heaving tide of pain was too much. The suffering was too much; she could bear it no longer.

'I can't go through with it,' she thought she had shouted, but no sound came from her lips. The rag fell from her mouth, and her head lolled to one side as she fainted.

Dr Turzo cursed. 'Bloody women! Always a nuisance.' The last thing he needed was an unconscious woman in his surgery. Hastily, he put in the last three stitches, then slapped her face. 'Wake up. You can't sleep here.'

The voice reverberated round and round inside her head and Liana opened her eyes. It was Dr Turzo. She could see his black-rimmed spectacles swimming in and out of focus. Cold water was splashed on her face and the room stopped revolving. 'Is it finished?' She struggled to sit up.

'Yes.' He untied her arms and then her legs after stuffing a pad in her crutch. 'Put your knickers on. There will be a little bleeding, but not much. Here are some penicillin tablets to prevent infection. Take three a day for five days. If you are ill, don't come back to me. And don't tell anyone I stitched you.'

Liana slid off the operating couch on to a chair at the side. 'When is it safe?' She felt sick and giddy.

Dr Turzo laughed. 'For intercourse? Can't wait, can you?' he sneered. 'A week to ten days should be sufficient. Now, give me the money and get out of here. I'm a busy man.'

Fumbling in her bag, Liana extracted the 15,000 lire he wanted. It was more than she had expected, but that covered the operation and the drugs. 'Here,' she held out the money.

The notes were snatched and rapidly counted. Liana felt weary with disgust. She felt disgusted for them both, herself and the pock-marked little man before her. We are both cheats, she thought numbly. Dr Turzo looked up. The amount of money was to his satisfaction. His thin lips stretched back in an attempt at a smile, a wolf-like leer, revealing sharp, yellowing teeth. I've never met a clean doctor, Liana thought hazily. The only two I've met have both been disgusting.

Unaware of her disapproval, Dr Turzo smiled again. 'Good,' he said. 'Now go, be careful and remember what I said. Don't come back here. I don't want to see you again.'

Liana nodded and left the surgery. Afterwards she wondered how she had managed to walk away, but manage it she did. With grim determination she forced one foot in front of the other until she came to a part of Naples where she knew Charlie would never think of looking for her. Here she was lucky, and was able to rent a clean but spartan room from a widow.

Signora Fazzini took pity on the ashen-faced girl. She assumed that Liana had just had an abortion, and Liana did not bother to enlighten her. The next few days passed in a blur of pain and fever. Liana took the penicillin regularly and tried to eat, and made sure she drank plenty of water for the baby's sake.

By the time the fever left her it was the day before Nicholas was due to return from Bari. She knew this, because she had brought a notebook with her, and had carefully marked off each pain-filled day. There was no room for error in her plans. She had to be ready by the time Nicholas returned. Much to Signora Fazzini's astonishment, she spent her first day out of bed washing her clothes, then washed herself and her long luxuriant hair with a bar of soap she produced from her handbag. In return for the loan of an iron, Liana gave the rest of the precious soap to the widow.

The young woman who stepped out into the street the next day was clean and smart. Her lips glowed pink from a touch of lipstick, and a faint fragrance of perfume lingered in the air as she passed by.

Signora Fazzini leaned far out of the window, nearly knocking her precious pot of geraniums off the ledge in an effort to catch a last glimpse of Liana. Who would have guessed that the girl who looked at death's door a few days ago would walk out today looking like a film star from one of those American magazines? It was only when Liana had disappeared from view that she realized she knew absolutely nothing about her. She had not given a name, nor any indication where she had come from, nor where she was going to. But she was well educated, Signora Fazzini could tell that; she was not slipshod about the endings of her words in the way most Neapolitans were. She hurried down to seek out her neighbours. What she had to tell them was enough to keep the street gossip going for more than a week.

*

Charlie was uneasy and perplexed. Fidgety, he shuffled the pile of papers on his desk, aimlessly moving them from one spot to another, staring with unseeing eyes at a week's work. New orders from the CO, cancellations of previous orders, letters, unfiled reports – all waiting to be done.

'Damn it,' he swore out loud. He'd wasted most of the week trying to find Liana, and now he had this mountain of work and still had not found her. 'If only I'd minded my own business in the first place,' he muttered under his breath.

But he had not, and now he could not put the clock back and pretend he had, no matter how much he wished that he could. What should he say when Nicholas returned later today and asked him if he had seen Liana? Should he tell him the truth, or lie and say he hadn't had time to pay her a visit, and hadn't seen her because she hadn't been down to the office?

He relived the past week, hoping to dredge up a clue that perhaps he had missed. Every day he had visited the empty *castello*, every day, hoping that Liana would be there, every day being disappointed and becoming more and more puzzled and worried.

Plain ordinary curiosity had prompted him to climb up to the lonely building the first time, the day after Nicholas had left. Castles and aristocracy were far removed from his normal everyday life in civvy street. He wanted to see the *castello* for himself; it would be something to tell his wife when he returned to England. In his imagination he had seen Liana surrounded by a beautiful, faded elegance, the kind of house he had seen in films. He knew exactly how it should look.

The reality shocked him. This isn't a home, he thought, staring around him. This derelict place is hardly fit for rats to live in. God, what unbelievable poverty! He almost laughed out loud when he remembered his own home. They wanted to move out of dirty, dusty Clapham into something better. But the semi in Clapham was a palace compared to this place. The memory of the suburban house cluttered with shabby but comfortable furniture flashed before his eyes. In Clapham they had clean linen tablecloths, china and glass, and the house had a lived-in smell of people and food, but here there was only dirt and decay, and a faint, musty animal smell.

Charlie wandered through room after room of the rambling building. Every room was the same – depressingly empty and totally devoid of life. A few flakes of gilt still adhered to some of the doors and window frames, and what had once been rich, flocked wallpaper peeled from mouldy walls. Sometimes there was a lighter patch on a wall, showing where a painting had once hung. In one room there was a broken chair abandoned in a corner, the exquisite ball and claw legs stacked up as if for firewood. The intricately painted backrest had already been chopped up, obviously destined for the stove. But apart from the broken chair, there was nothing at all in the whole of the *castello* except for the kitchen. Only in the kitchen did Charlie find any sign of life. Cold grey ashes spilled out from the bottom of a cast-iron stove. There were three beds and some blankets, a few cooking utensils and a meagre supply of food.

Charlie was not an over-imaginative man, not someone who was easily moved. But on that first day as he gazed around him at the decay and dereliction, he found his throat aching with sorrow for everything that had once been in this place and was now no more. He wondered about the people, their lives and loves. What had happened to those who had once lived in these empty rooms? And gradually he began to get some idea of Liana's desperation to get away. He couldn't blame her; who wouldn't want to leave? There was nothing for the living in this desolation.

But it drew him back, day after day, and not once did he see any sign of Liana, nor any evidence that she had even been there. It wasn't that he wanted to think badly of her, but little by little doubts began to creep into his mind.

Perhaps she has *never* lived in this place! The thought struck him on his last visit. It was the day before Nicholas was due to return. They only had her word for it; no-one had bothered to substantiate it, and he knew

Nicholas had never been to the *castello*. Maybe the truth was that she wasn't a *marchesa* after all, and she had disappeared because she had suddenly got cold feet, and found she couldn't go through with the deception.

Now, awaiting the arrival of Nicholas, he held his aching head in his hands, and groaned. 'God, what a mess.'

'Hello, Charlie. Is Nicholas back yet?' Liana leaned against the door jamb looking as serenely beautiful as ever.

Charlie reacted by exploding into anger. 'Where the hell have you been?'

Take care, take care, Liana thought, a fearsome shiver striking deep into her heart. It had never occurred to her that Charlie would look for her. But she knew now, looking at him, that he had been up to the *castello* and could guess by his reaction what he had found. Taking a deep breath, she chose her words very carefully, and adopted her most radiant smile.

'I've been staying with a friend outside Naples. I was not feeling well, but I'm better now. Why do you ask?' Her tone was innocently questioning. What had Charlie found apart from the empty *castello?* What could he find?

'I went up to the *castello*,' said Charlie, still looking grim. 'And anyway, I thought you said you didn't have any friends.'

Liana's heart sank, but not for one moment did she let her smile waver. She even forced out a gay laugh. 'Oh, Charlie, if only I had known, I would have stayed up there. But once I had sold the furniture there didn't seem much point in staying. So I went to say goodbye to my friend. She is a very, very old lady, crippled with arthritis and cannot leave her house. Once I'm married to Nicholas I'll probably never see her again.'

She hoped it sounded convincing, and prayed Charlie would not pursue the whereabouts of her fictitious friend. He was not entirely convinced, that much was obvious. With her senses now acutely sharpened by potential danger, it was easy for her to detect the flicker of doubt that crossed his face.

'Sold the furniture?'

Liana came to a swift decision. She would have to gamble on when he had made his first visit. 'Yes, I sold everything to some American officers on the very day Nicholas went to Ban. They happened to come by in a jeep and were mad on antiques. It was too good an opportunity to miss, so I got rid of all my old junk. I took the money and they came back with a lorry that night and took the furniture away.' Giving Charlie a conspiratorial smile, she added casually, 'You must have come up the following day. After I'd left.'

'Yes, I did,' said Charlie, but he still sounded doubtful.

Liana could have cried with relief at her deliverance; the gamble had paid off. No-one could possibly dispute her word, and, of course, she would have no idea of any of the Americans' names. Charlie remained silent, looking at Liana reflectively. Galvanized by a wild courage born of desperation, Liana knew she *had* to get him on her side, make him part of her secret. So she fixed her dark eyes on his face, hypnotizing him with their deep, slumbrous depths. 'Can you keep a secret?' she whispered, her lips curving in the most delicious smile Charlie had ever seen.

'Yes.' He found himself whispering back, so bewitched was he by her gaze.

'I've got enough money for that new tractor Nicholas needs so much for his farm in England.' Excitedly, she clapped her hands together like a small child, smiling delightedly at him as she spoke. 'And all the money is in American dollars. But please, please, Charlie, don't tell Nicholas. I want to surprise him myself. But you must come up with us to the *castello*, when I give it to him. It's all hidden up there.'

'I won't breathe a word,' said Charlie, all doubts gone now. He was completely won over.

*

Charlie stood grinning now as he watched Nicholas's astonished face.

'My God, Liana. Where did you . . .? How on earth?' Nicholas stuttered into silence as Liana stuffed bundle after bundle of American dollars into his hands.

'It is my dowry,' said Liana in dulcet tones, bowing her head demurely as she spoke. 'Now you can buy that tractor you said you needed.'

'But how . . .?'

'I sold the furniture', she waved vaguely, indicating the empty rooms surrounding them, 'to some Americans.'

'Oh, Liana, you should have let me do it,' said Nicholas, leafing through the money. 'I could probably have negotiated a much better price for you.'

An awkward silence ensued, broken only by a dry leaf rustling across the floor in the draught. Tactless bugger, thought Charlie angrily, immediately on the defensive for Liana. Poor kid, she did her best. What more does he want? But he need not have worried, Liana could fend for herself.

'It is not enough?' she asked coldly.

The icy tone of voice was matched by an abrupt change in her demeanour. She had changed from a young girl anxious to please into a haughty woman whose eyes flashed dangerously. It would never do for Nicholas to know that the money was really her earnings from prostitution, and blind instinct told her the best way to fend off unwelcome questions was to act the injured party.

Nicholas was overwhelmed with remorse, just as she had intended. 'Darling, I'm sorry. I didn't mean it that way.' He flung his arms around her and hugged her tight. 'Of course it's enough. More than enough. Anyway, I'm not marrying you for your money.'

Liana shrugged, disguising her worry with a show of aloofness. Not for one moment must *anyone* doubt her word. Wriggling free from Nicholas's embrace, she retrieved a wooden box from beneath a loose flagstone in the kitchen floor. The box was chipped and stained with age. Charlie and Nicholas watched in silence as Liana carefully prised it open and flung back the lid.

'Christ almighty!' blasphemed Charlie, expelling the air through his teeth with a long whistle.

Inside the box, on a bed of faded red velvet, lay Eleanora's heirloom, an exquisite set of matching jewellery: amethysts and diamonds set in gold – a pendant necklace, drop earrings and a bracelet. Liana tilted the box to catch the afternoon sunlight, and a blaze of purple and white fire filled the room as the stones caught the light.

'I think you must agree that I come well prepared as a bride.' It was an imperious statement of fact, one that could not be denied.

Nicholas stared at her. She faced him, a challenging glow of triumph seeming to swirl about her, and for a reason he could not pin down, he felt vaguely ill at ease. Then she smiled the slow dark smile that turned his loins into watery fire.

'You will make the most elegant countess in Britain,' he said.

'I will,' said Liana firmly. 'I shall surprise everyone.'

I don't doubt that, thought Charlie, watching her with reflective eyes. She would surprise everyone, probably Nicholas most of all. But would all the surprises be happy ones? Charlie suddenly realized, that, wrapped up as he was with her physical beauty, Nicholas had never stopped to consider the inner strength and shrewdness she possessed. He thought she was all feminine wiles and mischievous quick-wittedness. He had told Charlie as much.

'Sometimes I think she is a delicious child,' he said.

Charlie instinctively knew differently. Liana was not a child, not in any sense of the word, even though she was very young. She was a woman who was destined to go far. He wished he could see into the future. How far would she go, and which direction would she choose?

Chapter Eight

1 May 1944

Raul expertly flicked a cigarette from the packet and, placing it between his lips, lit it. Inhaling deeply he leaned back, soaking up the sun which blazed down from the brilliant blue cloudless Sicilian sky. A sense of smug satisfaction enveloped him. He had played his cards well, with his usual instinctive flair, and life had been good to him since that day in March when he had joined Gustavo Simionato.

He looked around at the village square where the film company was now camped out. It was hot and dusty, and as noon approached the stones throbbed with a white-hot heat. Apart from those being used in the film as extras, the villagers had retired to their small stone cottages to escape the heat and also the clutter of cameras, lights, and miles of cable strewn everywhere. At first glance it looked chaotic, but Raul looked on with pride. It was an ordered chaos, and he had helped to create it. Everything was on schedule, and that fact was due in no small way to Raul's ceaseless work, his fanatical attention to detail, and, what was even more important as far as Simionato was concerned, was that they were well within the confines of the budget. The money raised by the sale of the Cellini salt cellar was proving to be barely enough, but Raul was a careful manager and zealously strict with the crew. Nothing was wasted, no extravagances allowed. He was a hard taskmaster both to the crew and the actors.

Raul knew Simionato was pleased with him. So he should be; there was nothing he could criticize. As soon as the light was right they would begin shooting the film, a film destined to make him famous, of that Raul was certain. In his imagination the film was already finished, and he could visualize his name in large letters, prominent amongst the credits, RAUL LEVI.

'Use your real name, son,' Simionato had said when he had found out that Raul's father was Jewish. 'All the best showbusiness people are Jews; it will be a help, not a hindrance to your career.'

Raul had taken his advice; and now that Mussolini was dead, shot by partisans at Dongo on Lake Como in April of that year, there was even less reason to use his mother's name, Carducci. No-one now in Allied occupied Italy admitted to anti-Semitism or Fascist sympathies, even if, secretly, a few still entertained them.

'Raul,' Simionato called to him. He was ensconced in the director's chair, surrounded by a jungle of snaking cables and wires, a sheaf of papers on his lap. 'Show me once more how you intend to move the extras across the village square.'

Raul was only too eager to oblige. 'See, they come across at this angle towards the two principals. As soon as the fight commences they start to move, at first only two, then three and a group of four, then gradually they all crowd across to form a semicircle. On film it will look like a crowd of spectators at a boxing match, as if they are completely surrounding them, but there will still be room for the cameras to focus on the principals.'

In his mind's eye Raul had angled each camera shot, knowing exactly how it would look. He had taken care setting them up so that each frame picked up the peculiar stark beauty of the Sicilian landscape.

'Good.' Simionato was pleased. 'But you'd better run over it again with those idiots.' He indicated the local Sicilian peasants milling about on the edge of the square. 'Cheap to hire and authentic-looking extras they might be, but I'm not certain about their predictability.'

Raul grinned: his sentiments exactly. 'Leave them to me.'

He leaped to his feet and strode across the square. Small, swarthy, and sullen to a man, the Sicilians watched impassively as the tall northern Italian with a mass of reddish hair came towards them. Raul knew that the film was not of the slightest interest to them, but that did not worry him. All that mattered to them was the handful of lire notes they would pocket at the end of the day, and all that mattered to him was getting a good reel of footage in the can. It was a reasonable working relationship.

Reaching the crowd, Raul paused, then stubbed out the remains of his cigarette and felt in his pocket for a fresh one. He did it quite deliberately. Always vain, he relished dramatic mannerisms, and he was practical enough to know it was a perfect way of gaining attention without saying a word.

Raul placed the cigarette between his lips. Powerfully aware of the expectant silence he had created, he felt an arrogant sense of satisfaction. All these people, waiting for him to speak! He reached for his lighter, savouring the moment. But before he could flick a flame into life, a hand thrust a flaring lighter beneath his nose. Startled, he looked up. A tall dark girl was holding the flaming lighter. The sun, now almost directly overhead, threw her face into shadow, but it burnished the lustre of her thick hair so that it shone like ebony.

'Signor, per favore.'

The unexpected appearance of the girl caught him off balance. Staring wildly at the shadowy face he tried to speak, but no sound came. The confident young man, never at a loss for the right words, was suddenly, struck dumb. Hand trembling, he reached up and loosened the collar of his shirt but a tight band around his throat and chest threatened his breathing. In spite of the intense heat, Raul was aware of cold beads of perspiration prickling across his forehead and upper lip, and the light and shade of the square suddenly fused into one confusing mass. Only the girl remained clearly visible, tall and aloof, her face in shadow. It was then that he realized the past was staring him in the face. It was Liana holding the lighter.

'Raul, get a move on.'

Simionato's voice dragged him back to the present. His breathing reverted to normal, although his heart still thudded uncomfortably; but his vision cleared and the cobbled square swam back into focus. When he looked again he could see there was nothing special about the girl, a Sicilian peasant the same as the others, a little taller perhaps, but that was all. The past confronting the present! How stupid; it was a trick of the light playing on his imagination.

'Thanks.' Hastily he accepted the proffered light but, annoyed, he noticed that he could not stop his hands trembling as they cupped the flame. He pointed to the chalk marks on the cobbles and spoke more brusquely than he had intended to the waiting extras. 'Stay behind these marks, then move across the square shouting, just as you've rehearsed. But not until the two men begin to fight. Do you understand?'

A sea of dark faces stared mutely in his direction. Raul turned away feeling irrationally irritated. He wanted to shout at them, but held his tongue. It wasn't their fault he was edgy. That damned girl had unsettled him.

Why the hell should he think of Liana after all this time? Damn it! It was nearly two months since he had left Naples, and not once since that first day had she ever crossed his mind. He'd been too busy, and anyway it wasn't the first time he'd walked out on a girl and never given her a second thought, so why think of Liana? She wasn't *that* special. And why the hell did he suddenly feel guilty? He'd done nothing wrong. In fact during the time he'd been with Liana he'd been very kind, helped her in every way he could. No, he had nothing, absolutely nothing to feel guilty about. His conscience was clear. After all, he'd never made any commitment. She must have realized that.

He walked back to Simionato, but the jaunty self-confidence was temporarily missing from his stride. I haven't thought of her, and yet she's always been there, he mused. He wondered why, then dismissed the thought as Simionato shouted impatiently. There were more important things to think about.

'Raul, for God's sake get a move on,' roared Simionato. Raul ran into position as Simionato shouted. 'Action.'

The cameras whirred into life and the actors began to speak their lines. From his allotted place Raul worked feverishly, checking the angles, keeping an eye on the extras, watching the lighting. Simionato gave him a thumbs-up sign; he was pleased with the way it was going. Raul grinned; he was pleased too. He would definitely make it to the top of the pile, and in record time, too, if he had anything to do with it.

He looked at his reflection in the back of the camera lens, and stroked his chin thoughtfully. Maybe he should grow a beard. It would make him look older and much more distinguished.

Chapter Nine

1 May 1944

'Everything is over now, thank God.' Nicholas heaved a sigh of relief.
'The wedding, the reception: all that is behind us. No more hurdles to clear
or hoops to jump through.' He was particularly glad the wedding service
was over. To tell the truth he had not felt comfortable during the ceremony,
his long-ingrained Protestantism rebelling at the Catholic rituals. He would
have much preferred to have had a simple service in the Norman church of
his own village. But Europe was still at war, and they were lucky to have
organized the wedding at all.

'Hurdles and hoops?' Liana turned to Nicholas looking puzzled. It was
an English turn of phrase she had never heard used before.

He laughed at her expression. 'I mean the obstacles which were in the
way of our being together, as we are now.' He put his arms around her
tenderly and drew her out on to the tiny balcony of their room. Holding her
close, he leaned back against the open shutters. How soft her perfumed hair
was against his mouth. 'I will tell you now,' he said, 'now that at last we
are really married, that sometimes I despaired. There were days when all
the red tape seemed insurmountable, and I wondered if we would ever be
able to marry.'

'I never doubted it,' said Liana, which was true. Even in her worst
moments, she had always known that somehow, by some means, the
problems which arose daily would be overcome, and she would marry
Nicholas. So great had been her determination, that she had never allowed
herself to think anything else; anyway the alternative was unthinkable.
'Anything is possible if you really want it.'

'Sweet innocent,' whispered Nicholas, smiling as he kissed her hair. 'I
hope you are never disillusioned.'

Never to be disillusioned! Liana turned her head slightly to hide a wry
smile. How impossible that is – I have no illusions! To have illusions one
has to be innocent, and I'm far from being that. I've done whatever I've
had to do, and that's how I shall always be, because I know it is the only
way to survive. Turning back, she looked up at her husband. Poor

Nicholas, it is you who harbour the illusion. That illusion is me, your wife. But I'll work hard so that you can keep your illusion intact. I shall be a good countess, and a good wife. Perhaps then, she thought wistfully, this joyless feeling that fills my soul will be obliterated, the strange empty feeling that even the knowledge of the baby didn't help lessen. But she knew why the feeling existed, why it would always exist. Raul had taken part of her away with him the day he had disappeared, and she had found nothing to fill the void it had left.

'How can I be disillusioned,' she said now. 'I will always be happy with you.' Reaching up she softly touched Nicholas's cheek. 'Tell me again about England.'

'Well, you will live in the house with my mother, the Dowager Countess of Wessex, Lady Margaret. I hope you will like each other, although the house is so large you need never meet if you do not want to.' He paused, then added almost as an afterthought, 'And my brother, William, will probably be at home, too – for a while anyway. Until he manages to sort himself out. He was a pilot in the Battle of Britain and got shot down. He had to have a leg amputated, and needs help to get his life started again. Mother tells me he is depressed.' He hesitated as if about to go on, then stopped. 'Well, that's about it,' he said.

'I'm sure I shall like them both,' said Liana. She was determined to make friends with her mother-in-law and Nicholas's brother, for she shrewdly realized that if her plans for improving the Hamilton-Howards' fortunes were to succeed, she needed allies, not enemies. 'Poor William,' she added softly. 'It must be terrible for a young man to lose a leg.'

'Yes,' said Nicholas, his voice oddly heavy. 'I worry about him. God, I do hope you can get on with him.'

'But of course I will. I will *make* him like me.' But the tone of Nicholas's voice as he spoke of his brother disturbed her and the beginning of doubt gnawed inside her. 'Tell me again about the house,' she said quickly, determined to lighten the mood. Doubts had to be dispelled the moment they appeared. Doubts she could not tolerate, they were not part of her plans, not now, not ever.

'The house is old and is called Broadacres. Parts of the original building date from the early sixteenth century but most of it was rebuilt after a fire in 1650, and that is the house we live in now.' Nicholas sighed. He always felt despondent when he thought of all the responsibilities awaiting his return to England. 'Somehow I've got to raise the money to restore it. Most of the house is dropping to pieces.'

'We'll get the money,' said Liana confidently.

Nicholas laughed. 'We?' He tousled her hair. 'You, my sweet innocent, have no idea of the size of the problem.' He kissed her. 'But we shall be happy, even if the roof does leak.'

Liana returned his kiss, but her mind was elsewhere, in England to be precise. She longed for the day when they could leave Italy and go to England, because only then could she begin to formulate her hazy plans into a more concrete form. She already knew a little of what would be expected of her in her role as the new countess from what Nicholas had told her. She had to be involved and interested in the lives of the people of the estate and the village. You must be a figurehead, Nicholas had said, boring sometimes but necessary.

'And we'll keep your Roman Catholicism quiet,' Nicholas had added.

'I'm not a believer,' said Liana. 'I'll go with you to your church if you want me to, but I don't believe in God. Nothing can make me believe in God.'

So vehement was her statement that Nicholas was momentarily taken aback. Then he comforted himself with the thought that she was young and had survived terrible experiences in the war. She only thought she didn't believe, but of course she did. Everybody did. His own belief was of the comfortable, unquestioning type. He went to church, prayed, and then promptly forgot about it. For him, religion was just there, like daytime and night-time, always the same, always predictable. He shared the opinion of many Englishmen: deep, philosophical probings were not only unnecessary, they were almost indecent.

Wrapped in Nicholas's arms, Liana looked out from the balcony of the tiny pink-washed house in Puzzuoli. Nicholas had rented it for their brief three-day honeymoon. By some miracle of fate, Puzzuoli had escaped the devastation of the rest of the country. The ugliness of the savagely scarred landscape of war existed only a few miles away, and yet here nothing had ravaged these timeless cobbled streets. Here it was warm and peaceful. Fishing boats were tied up at the harbour wall in the same way as they had been for centuries. They bobbed up and down slowly on the swell of the sea. The only sound was the occasional slap of the water against the boats' hulls.

Liana yearned to draw in the peace that surrounded her and wrap it, like a mantle, around her soul. But peace was something that eluded her, and yet she had to achieve some measure of it if she was to suppress all memories of the past. And that was something she *had* to do if she was to retain her sanity.

Hard work and ambition seemed to offer the only salvation. A faint smile played around her mouth. Nicholas was unaware as yet of her decision to make him the richest earl in England. But soon he would find out and stop worrying about the wretched leaking roof, and then she too would find some kind of peace. It could never be perfect. Liana, practical as ever, knew that perfection did not exist on this earth, but she would be rich, so rich she would never have to bow her head in deference to anyone, not even her own husband. Other women might yearn for other things – a husband they loved, his children. But she was not other women. For her, wealth would suffice. She *would* be happy, but it would be a different kind of happiness from that which she had imagined for herself in her childhood.

Much as she would have liked to dismiss it from her mind for ever, Liana acknowledged that she could never forget the agony and joy of her life in Italy. It would always be there, beneath the surface; and soon she would have a very tangible reminder of that short period of joy which had changed her life so drastically. Raul's child would be born in December.

It was time to consummate the marriage. She turned back into the room. 'I'll unpack our things,' she said, adding softly, 'before we go to bed.'

Nicholas felt a dizzy thrill of desire run through him at her words. This was what he had been waiting for, but he had promised to be gentle, and was still determined not to rush her. So he remained where he was, staring with unseeing eyes at the deepening purple of the brief Mediterranean dusk. Give her plenty of time to get undressed and slip into bed. She was bound to be shy.

'Tomorrow we'll go sightseeing,' he said. 'We'll explore this land of ruins and legends. Did you know that Nero is supposed to have murdered his mother here? What was her name?'

'Agrippina,' replied Liana, smiling to herself in the dimness of the room. She was well aware of what Nicholas was thinking. I am lucky, she thought, not for the first time. He is a kind man.

'What a place for a honeymoon.'

Liana laughed softly. 'And what stories we'll have to tell our children in years to come.'

'Our children?' It seemed to Liana's anxious ears that Nicholas's voice was edged with a hint of bitterness, or was it anxiety?

'Why, yes. You do want children, don't you?'

Oh God, she'd never thought of it before. Supposing he didn't want children. What if he intended using a sheath to prevent her conceiving? What would she do?

Nicholas did not answer immediately. He stood quite still, his back towards her, the horizon blurring before his eyes. Children, yes he did want them, but . . . A sudden vision of his father, drunk and in a towering rage, seared his brain; a riding crop was in his hand and Nicholas could feel it crashing down first on his shoulders and then on to William. He took a deep breath, resolutely dispelling images of the past. Life would be different for his own children. He would never raise a hand in anger. They would know only love and peace. Nothing would be allowed to scar their minds.

'Yes,' he said at last, 'I do want children.'

Liana had been holding her breath during the long pause. Now at last she could breathe. 'Oh, so do I, darling. So do I.' The plans for a secure future for Raul's baby were falling into place.

Moonlight began to filter a ribbon of silver across the sea as Nicholas closed the green venetian shutters and turned back into the room.

Liana was not in bed as he had expected. She was standing in the centre of the room, looking at him. Their one small suitcase had been unpacked, and now she stood still and silent. Nicholas thought she was afraid.

'Darling,' he said, and started to move towards her. He was about to tell her not to be frightened of him but she interrupted him.

'Wait.' The word was uttered so softly that Nicholas could not be sure whether she had actually spoken or he had perhaps imagined it.

The moonlight, sliding in between the wooden slats of the blinds, bathed her in a silvery light, turning her into a replica of one of the stone maidens that adorned the ruined temple not far from their villa. Nicholas was aware of a feeling of unreality, a feeling enhanced by her total silence. He watched with incredulous amazement as the girl who had kept him at bay for so long, not even allowing him to slip an exploratory hand into her bra, now began to undress. She took off her clothes slowly, folding them up carefully as she went along. Nicholas remained where he was, watching and drinking in the intriguing mixture of innocence and eroticism.

Finally, Liana was completely naked, and the full impact of her beauty was revealed to Nicholas. She was slim and her legs were long. Even in the cold light of the moon her skin glowed with a warm, golden sheen. Jet black hair streamed down over her back and shoulders, partially screening the fullness of her breasts with their wine-dark nipples. Liana wondered for a moment if Nicholas would notice the darkness of her nipples, a sign of her pregnancy, but she need not have worried. He was too aroused to notice anything clearly.

Proudly tossing back her hair, she walked slowly across to him, and leaning lightly against his chest, she let the fullness of her breasts rest against him for a moment. A quiver ran through his tall frame. Satisfied that he was aroused, Liana began to unbutton his shirt.

Nicholas had thought it impossible to want a woman more than he already wanted Liana, but he was now aware of a new sensation, a force of such enormous dimension that it was frightening in its intensity. He could not remember getting undressed. She had started it, he knew that, but who had finished? It did not matter now; it was unimportant. Suddenly they were on the bed; he on top of her, his face buried between the full, soft mounds of her breasts.

For Nicholas the world ceased to spin on its axis. All that existed in the universe was the wonderful silkiness of her skin, the beautiful, special smell of her body. Even the hair that covered the soft mound between her legs was like silk. He wanted to eat her, drink her. Gasping, he thrust downwards, mouth open, tongue searching, but Liana pulled at his head. Intent on his pleasure, Nicholas resisted, but she persisted.

'Darling,' he protested.

'Shush, darling. Let me,' she whispered, pushing him back gently until he reluctantly rolled over on his back.

Unprepared for his new bride to take any initiative on their wedding night, Nicholas almost drowned in the unexpected pleasure. The perfume from her hair filled his nostrils, as her mouth moved down his body, kissing, biting, teasing, sucking until she reached his penis, already rock hard and erect. Her mouth closed on it, while her tongue flicked and darted and swirled around the soft tip.

A rainbow of inexpressible sensations exploded from his groin into wild ribbons of fire, reaching into the top of his skull. With a terrible cry of wild abandonment, the last vestige of his control broke, and Nicholas rolled Liana over on to her back and plunged into her soft body. Deeper, deeper, deeper he strived to penetrate her very core. In the blood-red mist of his frenzy Nicholas was vaguely aware that his huge, rigid organ was tearing into soft flesh, but nothing in the world could stop him now; all thoughts of gentleness had long since flown as he poured his manhood into her with ever-increasing violence.

Liana screamed out in pain. It hurt, oh God, how it hurt. But she had him. Arching her back, she bucked her hips against his body with a strength that astonished and excited him. Then it was over, the final explosive thrust left him spiralling down, weak and gasping.

Exhausted and drenched in perspiration, they lay still at last, arms and legs entangled in each other and the bedclothes. Liana let out a long, shuddering sigh of satisfaction. Every drop of him was in her, and she knew he had felt her skin tearing. Now the baby's future was safe. She had done it, just as she had planned. A triumphant smile curved her lips. Oh yes, Nicholas, she thought, anything is possible if you want it badly enough.

Her hand stroked the smooth skin of his back. She had promised herself that she would give him a wedding night to remember, and she would. The next time would not be so painful, not now that the recently stitched membranes were ruptured, and the more times they made love, the more convincing would be her immediate conception. With deliberate sensuality, she moved her body beneath his, and reached out to encircle his limp member with gently massaging fingers.

Nicholas could hardly believe it. His only experience of sex before had been quick, fumbling affairs, and he had always ended up feeling that the girls had been doing him a favour. They had let him enter and come, and that had been that. They had never shown any particular enjoyment, and they had never touched him. But Liana was different, oh, so different. She did things to him which drove him mad with wanton delight so that he climaxed again and again. And to his joy, she let him do anything he wanted with her lovely body. Nothing was too intimate, nothing barred. Raul had taught her well, and her own natural sexuality led her the rest of the way.

Finally Nicholas slept. 'I love you,' he mumbled as he pillowed his head against her soft breasts.

Liana lay still, her fingers softly caressing his fine blond hair. I ought to say I love you, too, she thought, but somehow she couldn't bring herself to say those special words, not tonight.

'I'm so glad you do,' she said at last.

Nicholas grunted sleepily. Why was it that tonight of all nights she had not said she loved him? He had said it, time and time again. Then he smiled contentedly, nuzzling like a child into the comfort of her breasts. Of course she loved him; she had told him that by giving him her wonderful, incredibly sensuous body. What more could a man ask for? Of course she loved him; there was no doubt of that.

Liana lay pinned beneath the weight of his body, her hand still idly twisting locks of his hair. The sound of regular breathing eventually told her he was asleep. I have chosen well, she thought. Nicholas had surprised her with his love-making; he had been gentle and sensitive as well as passionate and demanding. She considered her life ahead objectively. Nicholas adored her, and she would make certain she kept it that way. Making love to him was not so bad; pretending was not as difficult as she had imagined it would be. The baby would be born in wedlock. She smiled; there would be no problems. All she had to do was keep memories of Raul at bay.

That, however, *was* a problem. Hour after hour Liana lay in bed, weighted down by the sleeping Nicholas. Her body was exhausted, but her mind refused to be stilled. Making love with Nicholas had unleashed the very memories she sought to suppress. She tried to concentrate on the room, the here and now, and fixed her eyes on the lines of moonlight streaming through the gaps in the blinds.

But as she tried to concentrate, the parallel lines of light disappeared, and Raul stood before her, every beloved feature etched indelibly on her mind. She watched as he turned. He was walking away, down the mountainside. If only she could reach out and touch him, stop him. But he kept on walking; the falling ash from Vesuvius swirled about him, gradually covering his hair, his clothes, everything, until he had disappeared from sight.

The moonlight moved across the room, inch by inch, until it stretched in brilliant stripes across the bed. A bright spear of light glinted on Nicholas's hair, turning the blond into glittering silver. For the first time since she had decided to marry Nicholas, the full enormity of the deception she had embarked upon struck home. For the first time she felt apprehensive, felt a deep-seated and terrible doubt about the rightness of her decision. She had always known she was cheating, but now she realized she was cheating twice over: cheating Nicholas, and cheating her unborn child. But there was no other way, she cried out in anguish, trying to justify it to her newly awakened conscience. If there was, don't you think I would have taken it?

Liana bit her lip and felt tears of self-pity and regret welling up behind her eyelids. Now was not the time to cry; it was too late, much too late for tears. And anyway, she knew only too well that tears achieved nothing, nothing at all. In spite of that, she was helpless to prevent them. Like a rising tide they advanced until, unchecked, they welled up and overflowed, rolling silently down her cheeks and seeping at last into the corners of her mouth until their wetness touched her tongue. If it had been a deadly poison, she knew the taste could not have been more bitter.

'Forgive me, Nicholas,' she whispered. 'I had no choice.'

PART TWO
1944—1961

Chapter Ten

Donald Ramsay laughed, a warm, comfortable chuckle. 'The mice have well and truly ravaged her mink this year!' he said, rolling a cigarette with care. It was a difficult manoeuvre, using the last few precious shreds of his hoard of beloved tobacco. Lovely tobacco this, he thought regretfully, wondering if he would be able to obtain any more this side of Christmas. But although he used it all, it was not enough. The finished cigarette drooped limp and mournful from his mouth, and he singed his bushy grey moustache with the flaring match as he lit it.

Wrinkling her nose distastefully at the smell of burning whiskers, his wife turned and stared at him. 'What *are* you talking about?'

'Lady Margaret's coat.' He nodded towards the lonely figure of a woman waiting at the quayside. 'I wonder if she knows.'

Dorothy Ramsay laughed and glanced briefly at the woman, dwarfed now by the hull of the hospital ship as it slowly drew nearer the busy Southampton dockside. 'I doubt it. Vanity is not a criticism that could ever be levelled at Margaret. I do believe she never looks in a mirror. Poor Margaret, she'll never get another mink coat until rationing ends, and not even then unless her financial position improves.'

As she spoke she tugged self-consciously at the sleeves of her blue summer coat. Perhaps turning the cuffs had not been such a good idea; it showed how faded the jacket had become. She sighed. She had always prided herself on being a smart woman, and clothes rationing was, for her, one of the most frustrating aspects of the war. 'Although I did think that perhaps today, of all days,' Dorothy Ramsay added reflectively, 'she might have taken a little more trouble with her appearance.'

Reaching over to the back seat of the car, she picked up a well-thumbed copy of a June edition of *Tatler*, and flicked it open at an article entitled 'Way of the War'. In the centre of the page was a wedding photograph of Nicholas and Liana outside the church in Naples.

Her husband took it from her and read out loud. '"It is fitting to report, now (June the fourth nineteen forty-four) that Rome has been taken."' He snorted angrily. 'Although what the hell that has got to do with it I don't know. Load of bullshit. Bloody stupid this magazine.'

'Donald!' Dorothy reproved him mildly. 'Mixing with all these American soldiers has definitely not improved your language.'

'Coloured it, though.' Donald laughed, unrepentant.

His wife sighed, reflecting how the war had changed them all. She knew her husband felt a vicarious thrill from mixing with all the American troops who had flooded southern England prior to the Normandy landings the previous June. In August, there were still quite a few waiting to be shipped over to France to carry on with the fight, and now the wounded men were beginning to return, most of them to Southampton, where they were taken by train and ambulance to the Royal Victoria Hospital at Netley.

Too old for the armed services himself, Donald Ramsay felt frustrated with his role of country doctor; he wanted to be on the offensive, at the front tending the wounded – doing something useful, as he always put it. Dorothy smiled at him fondly. Little did he know how much he was loved and needed by all his patients in the villages of Hampshire. Someone had to look after the civilian population, and he did a good job. He delivered the babies, comforted the war widows, jollied along the old folk, sorted out the epidemics of measles and chicken pox which the village children succumbed to at regular intervals, and, with the vicar, was regarded as father confessor and comforter to all.

Her meandering thoughts came to a halt as her husband continued reading. '"To report, now that Rome has been taken, the wedding of the Earl of Wessex to the Marchesa Eleanora Anna Maria, Baroness San Angelo di Magliano e del Monte: Lord Nicholas and his new wife the Lady Liana, as she prefers to be called, will return to England as soon as hostilities permit."'

'They should have put as soon as pregnancy permits,' said Dorothy pertly. She peered over her husband's shoulder to look at the photograph. 'She is a *very* good-looking girl, very good-looking indeed. That's why I thought perhaps Margaret might take some trouble.'

'With her appearance?' Donald Ramsay finished the sentence for his wife, drawing fiercely on the flickering remnant of his cigarette before throwing the stub out of the car window. 'She's too worried to think about anything as trivial as that.'

'About William?'

'About everything. William's out of hospital now, physically patched up as well as can be expected for a man minus a limb, but mentally a wreck. A pity, because he was going through such a good patch before the war. This injury has put him back to square one.' Dr Ramsay contained his exasperation with difficulty. As a country general practitioner, he knew his skills were inadequate to help with William's depression. He wanted him to seek expert help. Indeed he had pleaded with Margaret and William, but they had both stubbornly refused to even acknowledge that such help was needed. 'And now, today she has Nicholas's foreign bride arriving, and I've no doubt she's worrying herself silly about the coming baby.'

Dorothy looked anxious. 'You mean, worrying that the child might turn out to be as difficult as William?'

Donald snorted grumpily.

'Well? Do you think the baby will be all right?'

'There's no reason why the baby should be anything other than healthy in every sense of the word. But I suppose she'll worry; it's in her nature – worry, but keep it under her hat as usual.' He sighed. 'Oh, I do wish she'd act on my sensible advice sometimes.

'And then she's got the added worry of Broadacres going to rack and ruin, although perhaps that wouldn't be happening so fast if she weren't being cheated right left and centre by that fiddling pair, the Catermoles.' He moved restlessly in the cramped confines of the car. 'It's all too much for her. She's a kind and gentle woman, but she has no strength of character. She hasn't even got the courage to sack the Catermoles, although she knows very well that she ought to. Sometimes I think she'll have a nervous breakdown if someone doesn't come along to help her. She seems to have aged so much these last two years. She's an old woman.'

'Well, you can't help her any more than you do, and she is not that old. Good heavens, fifty-three isn't old! She's younger than both of us,' said his wife. 'We'll just have to hope that Nicholas comes home soon and sorts things out.'

With one accord, their heads turned to watch the woman waiting on the quayside. She looked forlorn in the alien world of ships and cranes surrounded by busy little steam engines chuntering along their curving tracks, shunting goods wagons hither and thither. She walked slowly along to the far end of the wharf, eventually being brought to a halt by a mountain of coal piled up ready to feed the ever-hungry steam engines. The top of the pile was painted a startling white; the authorities believed it discouraged thieving. One piece of coal taken, even from the bottom, and the white line slipped, making the theft obvious at once.

'Margaret ought to paint her bloody coal white. *All* of it. Then maybe the bloody Catermoles wouldn't thieve ninety per cent of it.'

'Don't swear, dear,' said his wife automatically, without the faintest hope that he would ever stop.

*

The Dowager Countess of Wessex, Lady Margaret Hamilton-Howard, stood for a moment staring at the coal with unseeing eyes, then looked down at a dog-eared photograph clasped tightly in her hand.

'Liana, Liana,' she repeated the name softly to herself.

Nicholas had said in his letters that she must call her Liana, not Eleanora. He had also said her English was good. Oh, I do hope so, she thought. Her stomach tightened in a sudden knot of fear, the way it did so often these days. I can't seem to get anything done when I give orders in English, so how will I manage to make her understand our way of life if she doesn't speak the language?

But she does. Dispiritedly she tried to reassure herself. Nicholas said so in his letters, and he wouldn't lie to me, not to his own mother. She swallowed the fear. No point in worrying, the girl was almost here now. I'll find out for myself soon enough, she thought with an air of resignation.

Turning, she retraced her footsteps, her thick brogues clumping awkwardly along the concrete quay. She could feel the uncomfortable lisle stockings slipping on her thin legs, and knew that by now they would be hopelessly wrinkled. The girl in the photograph did not look as if her stockings would ever wrinkle. Lady Margaret snatched another surreptitious glance at the photo. Liana looked very glamorous – in fact quite daunting altogether. A warm breeze tugged at the untidy tendrils of her iron-grey hair scraped back into something vaguely resembling a bun, and she felt much too hot in the mink coat. I wish I hadn't worn the damned thing, she thought irritably, but then remembered she could not find anything else in the last-minute rush. All her other coats, all old, either had buttons missing or the hems had come undone. Mrs Catermole had said she would mend one, but of course she had not; and Margaret herself could hardly thread a needle, let alone sew on a button or take up a hem.

'I dunno as how you expect me to do everything, madam,' Mrs Catermole had said sullenly when, summoning up courage, she had tentatively broached the subject the day before. 'I've had no help in the house or kitchen these last two weeks.'

I should have asked her about the two women from the village who were supposed to come in. I gave her the money. Oh, it's no good; I'm absolutely hopeless. I'm getting worse and worse at giving orders and managing money, and the awful thing is the Catermoles know it. The thought made her heart sink; and not for the first time, Lady Margaret wished she had been given a different education, one which would have better equipped her for the life she now had to lead.

The tug pulling the cumbersome troopship into her allotted berth let off a sudden burst of steam and tooted loudly. It was the signal for steel hawsers to snake over the sides, hissing as they made their way from ship to shore, ready to be wound round the sturdy iron bollards on the quayside. Lady Margaret, hastily moving farther back out of harm's way, collided with a pair of American military police who were also awaiting the arrival of the ship.

'I do beg your pardon.' Lady Margaret glared at them as she spoke. Every single one of the silly young girls from the village would have given anything to bump into a pair of 'snowdrops', as the American MPs had been nicknamed. With their white helmets and gaiters they were considered to be very glamorous but as far as she was concerned, they were just another uncomfortable reminder of the war and all the unwelcome changes it had wrought in her life, changes she was increasingly unable to cope with. She glared at the Americans again and then immediately felt ashamed for looking so unfriendly. 'I'm sorry,' she repeated, attempting a tentative smile. I shouldn't be cross, she told herself, they're only boys. Why, they're not even as old as Nicholas, and they are far away from home, too. 'My fault,' she added, and walking away put a good distance between herself and the 'snowdrops'.

'Funny old girl,' remarked one MP to the other. 'My mom dresses better than that, and she lives in the Bronx.'

'So what? Your mom is a Jewish immigrant; she has to look smart. That woman doesn't need to bother. She's probably Lady something,' said the other knowledgeably. 'Just take a good look at her face. Jesus, it's like a horse's. With a face like that, she's gotta be a goddamn Lady. They all are!'

*

122

'A horse,' thought Liana looking down at the waiting woman from her position at the ship's rail. Nicholas's mother looks like a horse.

It had to be her mother-in-law; there was no-one else waiting, and she had written that she would be on the quayside. The baby suddenly kicked violently, and Liana forgot about her mother-in-law as nausea swamped her and she felt violently sick again. Oh, God, how the baby had been kicking this last week! The nearer the ship had drawn towards England the more she had kicked. It was almost as if her daughter – Liana was still sure it was a girl – was saying, 'I don't want to go.'

The solitary figure of the woman on the shore swam out of focus as Liana's nausea increased. For the moment she could think of nothing as she fought for control. Gripping the rail tightly, she gritted her teeth, telling herself fiercely that she hadn't come hundreds of miles to arrive in England and immediately disgrace herself by being sick in front of Nicholas's mother.

The ship's doctor had cast a cursory eye over her during one of her worst bouts of sickness. 'You'll be all right on terra firma,' was his diagnosis before dashing off to see to his other patients. He was too busy to spend time with a pregnant woman who, in his opinion, should never have been allowed on the hospital ship anyway, even if she was a countess. He had enough to do with the wounded American soldiers who were crammed like sardines into every square inch.

By the time Liana felt well enough to open her eyes, the heavy steel hawsers were securely looped around the bollards, and two of the gangplanks had already been lowered.

The ship's captain suddenly materialized at her side and saluted. 'You are free to leave whenever you wish, Your Ladyship,' he said. 'Your luggage is already being removed from the hold. I understand you are being met.'

Liana drew in a deep breath, and, straightening her back, forced a smile to her lips. Although now five months pregnant, her figure was still slim, and the loose summer dress gave no hint of her pregnancy. Which is just as well, she reflected grimly that morning when surveying herself in the cabin mirror, because officially I am only three months into my pregnancy.

'Thank you, Captain Anderson,' she said, extending her hand graciously. 'Thank you for making my journey as pleasant as possible, and please convey my thanks to your crew for taking such good care of me.'

'It was a pleasure for us all, madam.'

He spoke the truth. The beautiful young countess had captured the hearts of all the men. They knew she was pregnant, because that was the reason she was being rushed back to England, and they also knew she had been far from well. But she had never complained, and had always taken the trouble to personally thank anyone who did anything for her, as well as finding time to comfort the wounded. When he had asked them how she had helped, they had all said the same thing; that somehow she radiated a strength, a fierce, shimmering strength, which in turn gave them strength too.

I wonder how old she is, he thought now, eyeing the graceful woman standing before him. Impossible to tell. Her type of beauty was as ageless as time itself. The flawless bone structure, the dark, deep eyes set in heavy, almond-shaped lids ensured that she would look as striking at ninety years as she did now. He caught her gaze and looked away again quickly. Those eyes, so dark and mysterious, and so full of pain. He did not look again because he had an absurd notion that if he looked too hard he would surely drown in their depths. But he would have sworn on oath that it was pain he could see.

'It was a pleasure, madam.' He heard himself repeating the words woodenly and hastily dropped her hand as soon as he realized he was still holding it. 'Please, God, this damned – sorry, I mean *wretched* – war is soon over, and your husband can join you in England.'

'Yes,' said Liana briefly.

She did not echo his 'please, God'. In her opinion God had nothing to do with it. Men had caused the war, and men would finish it when they decided they had had enough of killing each other. *Your husband can join you in England.* The words had a strange, remote sound. *My husband,* Nicholas, my husband! Already in the short time they had been separated his memory had faded. The few weeks they had shared together now seemed unreal; but he is real, she reminded herself, more real than Raul. Despair threatened to engulf her. In spite of her determined efforts to be sensible and realistic, it always did whenever she thought of Raul. It was wrong, she knew it was wrong. Raul was the past, and Nicholas the future. Nicholas should be uppermost in her mind; but Liana had found she was unable to change her emotions – the power of Raul's memory was too intense. Maybe it would lessen after the birth of his child. It was the only faintly comforting thought, and Liana hung on to it with tenacious determination and concentrated on the present.

124

There were more immediate problems to think about, traversing the gangplank being the first. Liana realized after one quick glance that it was precipitously steep, and, although she would have dearly liked a helping hand, she was too proud to ask. Stubbornly bent on starting off in England in the way she intended to continue, she held her head high and swept down the gangplank with a confident air of assurance, as if she did such a thing every day of her life.

As Liana approached, Margaret Hamilton-Howard moved forward, trying to reconcile the conflicting emotions her daughter-in-law immediately aroused within her – intimidation at the sight of the haughty beauty striding down the gangplank, and relief as she realized that although she was foreign, she was a woman of good breeding. Of that, there was not the slightest shadow of doubt in Margaret's mind. Liana's classical bone structure and elegant poise convinced her that she possessed good breeding and a certain strength of character. Thank God. She almost said the words out loud in her relief.

Although she had never for one moment admitted it to anyone, and never would have done because it would have been disloyal to Nicholas, she shared the misgivings of the locals, and those of her own class, who had voiced doubts over the wisdom of Nicholas's marrying a *foreigner*. Clara Maltravers, a long-time acquaintance and neighbour, had summed it up over tea and scones in Winchester only last week, leaving Margaret in no doubt where her opinion lay. 'Foreigners are all right, my dear, in their *own* countries, but they are not quite right for England. After all, they have such mixed blood. I'm afraid this *marchesa* will never fit in.'

But now, watching Liana, Lady Margaret felt reassured. The young woman looked as though she would fit in, fit in very well indeed. She also looked very determined. It was hard to imagine the bitchiness of Clara's tongue causing the new countess any particular consternation: in fact, Liana looked as though she had the capability of frightening Clara Maltravers, and her ilk, to death. The thought gave Margaret a certain amount of malicious pleasure.

Donald and Dorothy Ramsay got out of the car and approached as Liana alighted from the gangplank. Margaret Hamilton-Howard rushed forward, stuttering in her anxiety to get the introductions over.

'Liana – yes, I know I've got to call you that. Nicholas told me. This is Doctor Donald Ramsay and his wife, Dorothy. They very kindly brought me in their car because I have no petrol. It's the rationing, you see. I do get some for the farm, but there never seems to be enough for the car, and the doctor is allowed more.' All this was uttered abruptly without taking a breath. Then she stopped, pale grey eyes anxious, mouth puckered nervously. What should she do next? She held out her hand, wondering whether or not she ought to kiss her new daughter-in-law, then decided against it.

Liana grasped her hand firmly and smiled. She was in no doubt about what was necessary, and, leaning forward, she planted a gentle kiss on the leathery skin of her mother-in-law. 'I'm so happy to meet Nicholas's mother,' she said softly before turning to Dr Ramsay.

Perfect English, Margaret noted with relief, just as Nicholas had written. There was the faintest trace of a foreign accent, but that was all. Of course, she looked Italian. Margaret was very conscious of the striking difference between Liana's dark, olive-skinned beauty and the rather washed-out colouring of the three Anglo-Saxons greeting her. In that respect she *would* stand out; her beauty was quite breath-taking.

Donald Ramsay came forward and smiled. 'My extra petrol is one of the perks of being a country doctor,' he said. 'We were glad to come and welcome you to your new country. This is my wife, Dorothy.' While Margaret saw only her beauty, the doctor's astute eyes were sizing up Liana as the introductions ensued. He could see she needed rest and good, wholesome food. He also deduced that, unless he was very much mistaken, she was more than three months pregnant. 'I'll be delivering your baby when it arrives. Nicholas wrote and told me it is due in February,' he said casually, 'so I'd like to give you a check-up as soon as possible.'

Liana swallowed; it was her own guilty conscience making her go cold. There was no way he could know, no way, no way! 'Thank you, Doctor Ramsay. I'll let you know when I am ready.' The words were flat, expressionless and absolutely final, effectively terminating any conversation concerning her pregnancy.

'Of course. I'll wait to hear from you.' Donald Ramsay held his peace.

Liana's voice might have been expressionless, but Donald Ramsay's practised eye had seen a flicker of something in her face although for the life of him he could not decide what it was. What beautiful eyes, he thought, watching her graciously incline her head towards his wife as she spoke, but what a strange expression he had glimpsed. Was it pain, bitterness, and infinite weariness as well as an extraordinary resoluteness of character? Was it even possible to see all those things in one glance? If it were true that the soul was mirrored in one's eyes, then the new Countess of Wessex had a very complex soul indeed. He shrugged; he was being a silly old fool. Flinging open the doors of the old Austin, he indicated that they should get in ready for the journey back to Longford. What was the matter with him? Was he getting visionary in his old age? Mirror of the soul indeed!

The 1938 Austin Cambridge was hardly big enough for four people. Lady Margaret and Dorothy Ramsay sat in the back. On account of her height, Margaret was forced to fold her long body in half, and now sat with her knees hunched up beneath her chin.

'I will sit in the back,' offered Liana politely, seeing Lady Margaret's discomfort.

'No, no. You sit in the front so that you can have a better view.'

Better view of what, Liana thought, gazing around in amazed horror at the utter devastation they were driving past. In the city of Southampton not one complete building was standing for as far as she could see. Street after street was the same. The road had been repaired, but either side of the highway lay the cavernous black mouths of bomb craters. An attempt at tidiness had been made by stacking the piles of rubble behind makeshift wooden barricades so that every now and then they passed a mountain of broken bricks and concrete.

As usual Donald Ramsay did not miss a thing. His training had taught him not to, and now his discerning eyes noticed her distress at the scenes of destruction. He guessed she was not prepared for such sights in England. 'We were badly bombed in nineteen forty and forty-one,' he said quietly.

Liana shuddered visibly; in spite of her rigid attempt at self-control, she could not help it. She had never imagined that this part of England had also been laid waste by war. London, of course; she knew that. But not here, not southern England. In her mind she had confined devastation on such a scale to Europe, and mostly to her own small world around Naples. Nicholas had never mentioned it, and so she had never even contemplated the fact that she was likely to come face to face with such sights in Hampshire.

I thought I was coming to peace and beauty, she wanted to shout. Suddenly the old familiar panic rose in her throat, the panic she was so sure she had banished. Peace and beauty? In this horrible place? Choking back tears of anger and frustration, she stared silently out of the window. How ironic that the thought which had kept her going was fallacious. She had clung tenaciously to the idea of the peace awaiting her on arrival in England – doggedly, day after day, gritting her teeth and disciplining her mind and body to accept the sickness during the long sea voyage from Naples because in the end she was sure it would be worth it. On the worst days she had lain in her cabin repeating the words out loud, 'Peace, peace, peace,' and drew succour from the mere sound. She forced herself to think about the tranquillity and beauty of the green countryside. Nicholas had described it so vividly it had seemed real. Peace and beauty were what she had expected; and now her disappointment at the reality was too intense, too shattering to attempt to put into words. No-one could possibly understand.

Liana slumped down in the uncomfortable bucket seat of the battered Austin. What a hateful place this was; she could not even see any green. She remembered standing at the ship's rail as they had steamed up Southampton water, anxious for her first close glimpse of her adopted country. Then, as she had looked through the warm heat haze of the Solent, England *had* seemed green and misty. But now, when she was on dry land, she could see only too clearly it was not green at all. The greenness must have been a mirage, mere wishful thinking, because there *was* no green. Grey was the predominant colour. Everything was grey, grey, grey: gaunt, double-decker grey trams rattling along grey and dusty streets; even the people looked grey, their clothes, their faces. Everyone was drab, their expressions unsmiling. Was this really a peaceful land she had come to?

'We've had a bad war, too, my dear,' said Donald Ramsay, apprehensively watching her dark, brooding expression. He cursed Nicholas. Why couldn't he have told her what to expect, damn it? She was disappointed. No, more than disappointed, she was distraught. What was it she had expected, for heaven's sake? 'The countryside is quite different. You'll be living miles away from here,' he said in what he hoped was a firm and comforting voice. 'Wait and see.'

But Liana was hardly listening. Homesickness for Italy was striking at her with a gut-tearing intensity. It was something she had never expected to happen. True, she had looked back with nostalgia at the Amalfi coast as it had receded slowly, first blue and then purple, before finally merging indistinctly with the horizon. Then she had put it out of her mind and thought only of the future. But now she suddenly longed for Italy, and most of all for its colour. Conquered and vanquished, bombed and battered, every inch of soil fought over, Italy had survived, never succumbing to this terrible drab greyness. In the unreliable mists of memory, the dreadful black days were forgotten. Only the vivid blue of the sky remained; and the colour of the sea, the way it was always changing, fluctuating from shades of green to purple; and the bright red, pink and purple of the flowers – always, always the blaze of colour from the hibiscus, geraniums and bougainvillaea, which not even the most persistent bombing could ever totally destroy. But here, in England, it looked as if the Germans had succeeded in extinguishing life. Everything was pale, washed out and exhausted-looking. It all had a terrible, depressing sameness. Liana closed her eyes; she could not bear to look.

*

The crunch of the gravel as the Austin drove in from the road awoke Liana. They drove through the stone triumphal arch, erected by one of Nicholas's forefathers, into an enormous forecourt, the centre of which was dominated by a formal garden of clipped box-yew with a fountain in the middle. Dr Ramsay stopped the engine and cranked up the handbrake.

Liana sat up and stared, hardly able to believe her eyes.

The great square, honey-coloured house shimmered in the warmth of an August evening sunset. It stood, as if planted by some giant hand, firmly amongst a vast expanse of green lawns that swept away down a slight incline towards a distant lake. On either side rose ancient cedar trees, their dark branches stretching protectively towards the house. The house itself was a glowing jewel, a topaz set with a hundred windows surrounded by jade.

'It is the most beautiful house I have ever seen,' Liana whispered.

'This is your new home,' said Donald Ramsay.

Sunlight filtered through the horizontal branches of the cedars, casting long dark shadows on the lawns. The turrets on the wings either side of the house were slowly turning pink as the sun changed from yellow to a glowing red orb, and in the far distance a horse whinnied at the sound of voices. Liana turned and could see a huge chestnut stallion kicking up his heels in the long grass of a field on the far right-hand side of the house, away from the manicured lawns. His whinnying disturbed a barn owl which flapped its wings slowly and majestically as it rose from a hawthorn bush at the edge of the field then, drifting silently, it sailed smoothly in front of the house before disappearing into the dense darkness of the cedar tree on the left.

Lady Margaret carefully unfolded her long legs and got out of the car. 'That field ought to have been cut for hay long ago. Rufus gorges himself on the grass,' she said, looking over to where the horse stood waiting expectantly for his mistress to greet him. She sighed, even her beloved Rufus momentarily forgotten. 'But nobody ever seems to have any time.' Her permanently worried expression deepened as she spoke. 'I've already told William that when Nicholas comes home we shall have to sell the house. We shall never be able to afford to stay on here. It will be an impossibility, the way things are going.'

'Never,' said Liana abruptly, her mouth tightening into a grim line.

Since deciding to make Nicholas one of the richest earls of England, she had often wondered how and where she would start. Now she knew. Suddenly it was so obvious what her first task was to be. Her mission would be to secure the future of Broadacres. Everything else suddenly dwindled into unimportance. There was no point in Nicholas's being wealthy if the family lost Broadacres. That was why she needed to earn money. By the time I've finished, Liana vowed, Broadacres will be the most glorious house in the whole land, even more glorious than it is today. She gazed at the house with a passion so great it was almost a pain. This beautiful house would never be sold, not while she had any breath left in her body. 'Never,' she repeated.

Margaret Hamilton-Howard turned slowly and looked at her daughter-in-law in astonishment. Liana had climbed out of the car and was standing quite still, as if transfixed. She was staring at the house with great intensity. For a moment Margaret felt afraid. The setting sun highlighted Liana's profile, illuminating her indescribable beauty. Fascinated, Margaret watched, for behind that beauty she could almost see Liana marshalling up secret forces of determination. She was really serious. She meant what she had said.

For the first time in months the creases on Margaret's face changed from a frown into a slow, incredulous smile. She began to believe that the house would not be sold, would *never* be sold, and that she would be able to stay there until she died, just as she had always wanted. All this was going to happen because this slender girl standing beside her had said so. With the utterance of those two emphatic words, Liana was guaranteeing that four hundred years of history would not be lost.

'Come into your new home, my dear,' she said, holding out her hand. The sudden rush of warmth she felt for Liana startled her. Resignation had been the emotion uppermost in her mind at the prospect of a daughter-in-law, so the prickly beginnings of affection surprised her.

*

After the shock of her initial disappointment, it now seemed to Liana that she had truly arrived in paradise. Margaret showed her round some of the house while Donald and Dorothy Ramsay bullied Mrs Catermole into producing something reasonably edible for dinner that evening.

'Plenty of time for you to look more closely later,' said Margaret, dragging a speechless Liana after her through room after room and down countless corridors filled with paintings and statuary.

Nicholas had told her that the family was poor, and Liana believed him; but in her mind she had equated a poor English aristocrat with a poor Neapolitan noble. In Naples, it was common enough to find nobility living in empty shells of what had once been beautiful palaces; in reality they possessed very little more, and often not even as much, as the average peasant. Why, even Eleanora's *castello* before it had been looted possessed only a sparse amount of antique furniture and carpets, none of which had been of particularly good quality. Eleanora's beautiful jewels, which Liana had brought with her to England, had been the exception. Now, her mind reeled, first in shock, then in pleasure and astonishment as Margaret casually pointed out the elegant French and English furniture, the seats upholstered in silk and tapestry, the chandeliers, gilded mirrors, fine paintings, Savonnerie and Aubusson carpets and rare Persian rugs. The catalogue of riches went on and on; and Nicholas had said they were poor!

'I don't understand,' said Liana, needing to pause for breath as Lady Margaret galloped on ahead towards a flight of stairs. 'All these beautiful things are worth so much money. Why do you say you must sell the house?'

Her mother-in-law halted. 'All this', she answered with an expressive wave of her arms, 'is worth nothing as it is. It actually costs money to keep it, and that is one of the problems. We have no money in the bank, and the estate makes a loss. Every year I have to sell something to pay our debts. We cannot go on and on like that. Eventually Broadacres will be empty.'

'No, you cannot,' agreed Liana, beginning to understand the extent of the problem. She followed Margaret down a staircase to an empty wing of the house.

Here the walls were scratched and shabby, and the floor bare of carpets. 'This was used for some of the children evacuated from London at the beginning of the war to get them away from the bombs,' Margaret explained, seeing Liana's mystified expression.

'Lucky children,' said Liana, her mind going back to Naples. There the children had had no such refuge. They lived as best they could.

'We had one hundred children in all,' said Margaret wistfully. 'It was a very happy time. Most had never been in the country before, and cows and horses were like zoo animals to them.' She laughed at the memory. 'Oh, they were so enthusiastic. I can see them now coming back from nature expeditions with their jam jars full of tiddlers – those are tiny fish from the river – and the Christmases! They were the best the house has ever known – so full of noise and excitement, hundreds of parcels wrapped up and put beneath the tree at the end of the East Gallery. An old man from the village, George Jones, used to be Father Christmas. What a sight that was! After breakfast on Christmas Day the door would open and there was the Christmas tree, all lit up with coloured lights and by the side George Jones in his fake white beard and red cape. As Father Christmas, he had a present for every child.'

'It sounds lovely,' said Liana, thinking of her own Christmases before the war – not lonely, but always quiet: just her and Eleanora, the *marchese*, Don Luigi, Miss Rose and her mother. After their deaths, and once the war had really started, Christmas had stopped meaning anything at all. She dragged her mind back to the present. 'What happened to all the children?'

'They went back to London when the bombing stopped, and for a while the army used these rooms as offices. But they moved out at the beginning of this year, and now it is empty as you can see.'

'And the furniture and paintings?'

'All stored upstairs,' said Lady Margaret. Then she said abruptly, 'Let's try to find William.'

William was reading in the Arcadian drawing room. He was sitting in a winged armchair by one of the many windows. 'This is Liana, Nicholas's wife,' said his mother.

William did not move to greet them. 'Bring her here,' he said.

Obediently Margaret led Liana across to the chair. Liana saw a tall blond man, very like Nicholas – like and yet unlike. His grey eyes were not as clear, his mouth had bitter lines etched deeply either side and although the curve of his lips was the same, it was not gentle.

'You are tall for an Italian,' he observed, watching her through narrowed eyes.

'Not all Italians are short.' Liana was suddenly wary. There was an innate hostility about him. He made her feel uneasy; she wondered why.

'Well, at least you don't look like a peasant, thank God.' His eyes returned to the book on his lap.

'William!' Margaret made a small, apologetic gesture for her son's rudeness.

'That is because I am not.' Although her voice was bland, a tiny flicker of fear caused her to tremble. It was almost as if he knew something. But he could not. There was no need to feel disturbed.

'So I've been told.' The coldness in his voice disquieted her far more than the actual words. He had already made up his mind. He did not like her.

'Don't worry about William,' Margaret tried to reassure her as they left the room. 'He's not himself at the moment. He's still terribly bitter and moody about his injury.'

'Yes,' said Liana slowly, hoping she had been wrong in her assumption. Perhaps that was the reason for his coldness; it was because he was deeply unhappy. 'It must be very difficult for him.'

'It is. We leave him to himself. Don't worry if you don't see him for days on end. He often doesn't want to talk to anyone.'

'I understand,' said Liana, wishing she did.

Chapter Eleven

Dinner was served in the Grey Room, an enormous room on the western side of the house with windows catching the last rays of the evening light. The long table, set out formally with exquisite china and cutlery, all gleaming with a brilliant lustre, impressed and slightly overawed Liana. None the less she suddenly felt hungry. Donald Ramsay courteously pulled out a chair for her and she sat down looking about her still amazed at the grandeur of the house. She could see that the room looked even larger than it actually was because of the positioning of the ornately carved mirrors on the walls.

'Why is this called the Grey Room?' Liana asked. She could not understand it; there did not seem to be any grey at all. The whole room glowed with colours, all reflected in the mirrors.

William joined them, and Liana noted with relieved surprise that now his attitude seemed benign, the hostility apparently gone. The resemblance to Nicholas was much more marked now, especially when he smiled. She smiled back, but was still a little wary. He was not *quite* like Nicholas. His face lacked the spontaneous openness of Nicholas. There was a certain shuttered atmosphere about William, as if he had deliberately closed the doors on his true self. She watched him cautiously as he spoke. He seemed curiously apart from everyone else in the room, even though he appeared to be at ease and joined in the conversation.

'You may well ask. Why indeed?' he said pleasantly, seating himself beside Liana. 'I'll tell you. It is because what little you can see of the walls between the mirrors is covered with grey silk tapestry.'

'The mirrors are said to have come from the Palace of Versailles,' added Margaret, a nervous smile hovering about her lips. Thank God William had decided to be friendly after all.

'And the Savonnerie carpet was woven on a design by P J Perot in seventeen forty-five,' said William.

'Let the poor girl relax,' said Donald Ramsay, 'and stop giving her a history lesson.' He, too, was pleased to see that William was making an effort to be sociable.

134

Everyone laughed, and Liana, who was still apprehensive, could see the assembled company relaxing. It seemed they were all pleased that William had decided to be friendly.

A sour-faced woman brought in an enormous soup tureen and sullenly dumped it with a loud thud in the middle of the table.

'Thank you, Edith,' said Margaret with a nervous stutter. 'I'll ring when we're ready for the next course.' The woman departed without a backward glance, shutting the door noisily behind her.

The soup was brown and thin and tasted like hot water, and the bread, which was greyish in colour, was dry and tasteless. Liana began to lose her appetite, but she tried to drink a little soup and forced some of the unpalatable bread down her throat. When Margaret rang the bell, Liana hoped the next course would be better. On the long sea voyage to England when she had not been feeling sick she had enjoyed the food on board ship, but it was an American ship; maybe English food was different.

'Toad in the hole,' said Edith Catermole re-entering the room and plonking a large oval dish down in the centre of the table. 'It's the best I could do at such short notice. There is a war on, you know, and I didn't know *everyone* was staying for dinner.' She glowered pointedly at the Ramsays, who equally pointedly ignored her.

'Toad in the hole?' said Liana in a horrified voice. She could hardly believe her ears.

'Sausages in batter, my dear,' said Dorothy Ramsay, stifling a smile at Liana's expression. 'Not *real* toads.'

'And runner beans and potatoes,' added Mrs Catermole, slamming two more dishes on the table with ill grace. 'The stewed rhubarb and jelly for dessert is on the sideboard. Will that be all?' It was not so much a question she asked Lady Margaret, more of a challenge.

'Oh, yes, thank you, Edith. Everything looks very nice,' said Margaret, more nervous than ever. Liana noticed the nervousness and wondered why. Surely her mother-in-law was not afraid of her own servant?

The entire meal was awful. The only decent thing was the bottle of red wine Donald Ramsay produced from his doctor's bag when Mrs Catermole had gone.

'Down to my last five bottles of good claret,' he said, uncorking it carefully. 'We'll have to drink Dorothy's dandelion wine when they've all gone.'

'Makes even Edith's toad in the hole taste quite pleasant,' said William, wrinkling his nose appreciatively as he took a sip.

But not even the good wine changed Liana's opinion. She wondered how the English could be so cheerful about such dreadful food, but as no-one, other than William, made any comment, she assumed they liked it.

Food apart, Liana enjoyed her first evening. There was no mistaking the genuine pleasure they all derived from welcoming her to Broadacres, and that appeared to include William. Later it was William who took her up to her bedroom, the room she would eventually share with Nicholas when he returned to England.

'You will have a beautiful view in the morning,' he said, drawing the heavy damask curtains across the wide windows. 'Right down to the lake and the Palladian bridge.' Then he politely excused himself and left her.

Liana explored curiously. The bedroom was huge. White walls, hung with prints depicting hunting scenes, rose to a sculpted cornice, and painted cherubs sprawled across the ceiling. Either side of the room were doors set in elaborately scrolled and gilded columns. Each door, Liana discovered, led into another two rooms – a dressing room with armchairs, a couch, dressing table and enormous wooden wardrobes; then another door leading into a bathroom. One bathroom was tiled in blue, the other in jade green. Liana could hardly believe such luxury. She and Nicholas each had their own dressing room and bathroom. The dressing room with the blue bathroom obviously belonged to Nicholas because the wardrobe was full of his clothes. She knew they were his; they smelt of him. Sticking her head in the wardrobe she closed her eyes and sniffed, and for a moment felt close to him. But the lure of her very own bathroom was too strong to stay there long. Filling the green enamel bath with warm water, she carefully unwrapped the tablet of soap lying in the porcelain soap dish. To her delight the soap was green too. Everything matched; even the towels in the cupboard by the washbasin were green.

Little did she know, as she lay in the warm water luxuriously soaping herself, of the struggle which had taken place in preparing the bathroom for her.

'A terrible waste,' Edith Catermole had objected.

But for once Lady Margaret had insisted, and the brand new, but pre-war, towels and delicately perfumed soap were extricated from the store cupboard and laid out in readiness for Liana.

After her bath, warm and relaxed, she was ready for bed. But before sliding in between the crisp white sheets, she turned out the lights, and, crossing the room, drew back the curtains and opened the window. The night air was chilly now, and very, very, still.

The lake was invisible in the darkness, but a thick mist glowed a ghostly grey through the darkness, showing where it lay. The smell of rich, damp earth mingled with perfumes of many flowers, and there was a faint smell of farm animals. It was very different from Italy. She was used to the dry, tangy perfume of wild thyme and rosemary, and in autumn the sweet smell of olives. She drew in a deep, appreciative breath. This was quite different, much more rich and varied, and she loved it.

Much more rich. The phrase stayed in her mind when she finally settled down to sleep. Much more rich; that was what she intended to make Nicholas and herself. Idly, she wondered why William had not done something to try to reverse the family fortunes. He enjoyed living at Broadacres, that much was obvious, but he did not seem interested in how things were organized. Nicholas had been more involved than William, even before the war, she knew that. But he had told her that whatever their farm manager did, the estate never seemed to do more than just break even. They desperately needed a new tractor, but there was not the ready cash available. Nicholas loved the country, even though, by his own admission, he was not a particularly efficient farmer. William was different. From his conversation at supper Liana learned that apart from fishing he was not interested in the estate and farm, and spent the rest of his spare time reading. That was good; it cut out potential complications. The future looked good for whatever changes she decided were needed; and common sense told her there had to be some way to make this fertile land viable.

*

August 1944 was a warm, golden month. William was right about the view, and the early morning mists drifting across the waters of the lake on to the velvet green of the lawns surrounding the house never failed to entrance Liana when she looked out from her bedroom window. But by breakfast-time each day the mist had disappeared, snatched up and torn to shreds by the golden rays of the sun. She spent every waking moment outside, methodically walking the estate, the farm and the woodlands. Her keen eyes missed nothing, for she knew that if she were to achieve her goal of restoring the house and making Nicholas the richest earl in England, then she had to know everything there was to know about the estate. It did not take long for Liana to conclude that the estate in itself would not be enough to amass any great fortune and that other avenues for making money would eventually have to be explored. But for the time being, Liana decided to concentrate on the most obvious thing: the estate.

It took a week to learn to find her way around the enormous house and its vast lands. She could see at once that the opportunities were limitless, and time and time again she marvelled at the casual way Nicholas had spoken of his home. He loved it, but the actual fact that he owned the house and all the lands around it seemed more of a burden to him than anything else. Liana thought he was incredible. How could he think of this enchanted, beautiful place as a burden? She was walking beside a cornfield, shimmering rich, ripe and golden in the mellow sunlight, an occasional flash of red where a poppy thrust its impudent head up amongst the ears of corn. Suddenly she threw back her head, and laughed out loud in sheer exultation.

Everything she had dreamed and hoped for had come true after all. She *had* been right to marry Nicholas, for she *had* succeeded in escaping the profanity of war. Not once since arriving at Broadacres had she yearned for Italy. The pain of loving Raul was still there, of course, always waiting to surface the moment she let the mental barriers relax, but miraculously even that, *even that* was not as painful now. The beauty of Broadacres had a healing property. Some of the rawness seemed to have gone. Maybe in time she would forget everything. The revolutionary thought halted her in her tracks. Maybe, *maybe in time* I will even learn to love Nicholas as a wife should love her husband. Goodness knows, Nicholas deserves it. He plucked me from hell and transplanted me to this wonderful place.

She climbed over a stile which led to the grassy chalk uplands. The land rose either side of the valley, and the softly rounded slopes were covered with sheep. They looked naked, still bare from having their fleeces shorn; but the weather was warm and they were not bothered. In perfect unison they marched slowly forward, munching away at the short, sweet-smelling turf. Liana pulled herself up and over the stile.

A shaft of sunlight caught the opal of her engagement ring, momentarily blinding her with flashes of milky flame: the all-seeing eye; the past; the baby; Raul, RAUL! It had the effect of dissipating her euphoric mood in an instant, and she remembered Margaret had asked her to be sure to be in the house this morning when Donald Ramsay called. He wanted to examine her, to check on her pregnancy.

She turned on herself bitterly; she should have known it was impossible to escape. The longing for her homeland might have been replaced by a real love for England and the Itchen Valley but she was foolish to think that Raul could ever be denied, could ever be replaced by Nicholas. Part of Raul was wriggling impatiently inside her now, anxious to be born; and, once born, the child would be an even more tangible reminder. A moment ago she had been happy, now her heart ached. There was no escaping the past – a sombre thought, but one with which she had to live.

Liana sat on the stile considering the immediate practical implications. I ought to go back, her conscience nagged her. Margaret wanted her to; she dithered, uncertain, but the hesitation was only fleeting and then an obdurate look settled on her face. Doctor Ramsay will have to wait; I'm not ready to see him yet. I must prepare myself mentally. The thoughts churned over, slow and deliberate. It would not be easy to fool Donald Ramsay with fictitious dates but he had to believe her, had to be utterly convinced. Somehow she must make him so certain that he would not even consider questioning the dates. Yes, more time was needed; today was not the right day. Having decided that, Liana resolutely shouldered the burden and, putting it temporarily from her mind, continued walking across the downland towards a knoll topped by a dense copper beechwood. This group of ancient trees, she knew, marked the boundary of that part of the Broadacres' estate.

Margaret watched Liana's diligent and single-minded inspection of Broadacres and everything around her with bewildered awe and admiration. Liana was an enigma. Never before had Margaret met a young woman who on the surface was a vulnerable, gentle beauty, the very essence of femininity, but who also possessed such an obvious streak of deeply ruthless determination. She could not help thinking it was almost as if her spine was made of steel instead of bone. So different from me, thought Margaret. But she liked her, and desperately hoped that they would become good friends. It would help fill the void left by her own daughter who now lived in New Zealand, and whom Margaret missed more with each passing year.

Life had not been kind to Margaret. As a young woman she had grown up large-boned and awkward, with a face resembling the horses she loved so much. She knew that she was ugly. How could she not? It was a fact which had been thrown in her face often enough by her disappointed parents. How could they ever marry her off? No eligible man with a penny in his pocket would ever look twice at her. When she was young, girls of her class were expected to marry well, and suitable husbands were ruthlessly hunted during the débutante season.

Even now, so many years later, Margaret shuddered when she remembered that ghastly year, the year of her eighteenth birthday, when she was forced to attend balls and dinners, go to Ascot and Henley, squeezing her raw-boned figure into unsuitable frilly dresses. She hated every moment. Shy and retiring, she had been considered the unqualified failure of the season.

Not a single eligible bachelor had looked at her until the very handsome Viscount Richard Hamilton-Howard, later to become Earl of Wessex, appeared on the scene. Between them, the two sets of parents contrived to hastily marry the pair off. Everyone marvelled that such a handsome young man as Richard should agree to marry a plain girl like Margaret. However, he made no objection, and indeed, seemed indifferent to the arrangement, and the wedding went ahead. A violent, and desperately unhappy marriage followed, only ending when the earl died unexpectedly from a massive stroke in 1935.

The disastrous coupling produced three children. Of the three, only Nicholas, the second-born, had ever given Margaret any lasting joy. She had never understood William, her youngest son, and was afraid of his unpredictable swings of mood.

The eldest, her daughter Anne, four years older than Nicholas, had emigrated to New Zealand in 1937. Margaret loved her dearly, but Anne hated her father and always quarrelled with William. Finally, after a terrible scene, Anne had stormed from the house saying she would never live there again while William remained. In vain had Margaret pleaded, but Anne was adamant. The passage was booked, and she sailed for New Zealand. There she met and married a New Zealand farmer, Richard Chapman, and in January 1941 bore him a son, Peter.

Margaret prayed every day for the good health and happiness of the grandson she had never seen and hoped that one day they would come to England so that she could meet him. It was a forlorn hope. Anne would never return while William was there. And now that it seemed there was no alternative but for William to stay at home for ever because of his injury, the prospect of Anne's return grew more and more remote.

Now Margaret was waiting impatiently in the breakfast room for Liana to join her. She was worried. Yet again Liana had missed her appointment with Dr Ramsay. Donald Ramsay had reassured Margaret, saying there was nothing to worry about; he would catch up with Liana within the next day or two. Her other worry was William. Common sense told her that she should be pleased at his change of mood, the sudden friendliness and willingness to please, the unexpected development of an easy-going nature. But alarm bells were ringing in her head. Was it the lull before the storm? Gut instinct told her that he had successfully pulled the shutters down over his real self. There was another man behind those shutters, one he did not want the world to see. She mentioned her fears to Donald Ramsay, who pooh-poohed them.

'For God's sake be thankful for small mercies,' he said. 'William seems to have settled down at last. Who knows, perhaps the trauma of the war was a blessing in disguise for him.'

'Perhaps.' Margaret was not convinced. If Donald did not believe her about William, he would never believe it if she told him that she often felt Liana was hiding behind shutters, too. Sometimes she caught a glimpse of such sadness that she wanted to fling her arms around Liana and say, tell me about it. But she never did. Her own English reserve and Liana's carefully erected barricades prevented it.

At last Liana joined her at the table, bending first to plant a kiss on her mother-in-law's cheek. 'Good morning, Margaret,' she said softly.

Margaret smiled, William forgotten for the moment. 'Good morning, dear. Did you sleep well?'

'Perfectly.' It was the ritual opening conversation of the day, the same every morning. Liana enjoyed it. She found it had a soothing effect, and gave her a sense of continuity and permanence.

She watched Margaret thoughtfully as she poured the tea. She could sense Margaret's unhappiness, and was certain it had something to do with William although she could not think of any particular reason.

Casting her mind back to Italy, she remembered her grim determination to get on well with Nicholas's mother, whatever the cost. She half smiled now. How easy it had been. In spite of her unfortunate and rather forbidding appearance, it had not taken Liana long to realize that Margaret was a gentle woman who would not hurt a fly and that although she was hopeless at organizing her own life, or anything else for that matter, she was generous and well meaning. Respect had quickly grown into love. Sometimes Liana thought that all the love lying dormant since the death of Eleanora had now been transferred to Margaret. In a strange way, the relationship was very similar. Liana knew she was the strong and dominant personality, and Margaret the one needing help. Yet at the same time, Margaret provided Liana with the firm anchor she needed. Chance had brought them together, two very different women from different worlds; but they each filled an empty space in the life of the other, and from now on fate had ordained that their lives should run in tandem.

Liana brought her mind back to the problem of the estate. Now, she decided, was an opportune moment to steer the direction of their conversation towards the subject of how the estate was managed.

'Nicholas told me the Broadacres estate was "run down", to use his words,' she said. 'At the time, I didn't really understand what he meant because it was such an English expression, but now, I think I do. He meant it was being wasted. I have some ideas which I think could help things to run more smoothly. I'd like to make things easier for Nicholas so that there is not so much for him to do when he comes home, and I think it could help you, too. It must be difficult for you managing everything on your own. Will you allow me to help?' Feminine intuition made her refer to Nicholas; he was after all the nominal, although absent, master of Broadacres. It would never do for her to appear too domineering.

During the day-time, when she had been walking, Liana's mind had accumulated facts like a filing system and in the evenings she had put that information to good use. Broadacres had an enormous library, housed in part of the house always called the Lower Cloisters. Here she had found many books on farm and estate management, animal and fish husbandry, and woodland management. There in the library, surrounded by priceless bookcases and bureaux designed especially for Broadacres by Thomas Chippendale, all relics of Broadacres's illustrious past, Liana sat reading. But it was the future not the past which preoccupied her fertile mind as she gained information from the mountain of books spread out across a mahogany drum table.

Each evening she sat reading, her eyes racing across the pages, learning and absorbing knowledge quickly. It was not long before she realized that, with planning and hard work, and not much capital outlay, many things on the estate could be changed for the better. What puzzled her was why Nicholas or William had never worked this out for themselves. She knew, because Margaret had told her, that their education had been the most privileged available – Winchester College and Oxford University – and yet neither of them had put their knowledge to practical use. It seemed that gentleman farmers, as Margaret always called them, preferred to simply take pleasure from their land, not utilize it. In Liana's opinion, things would have to change. Making money came first, pleasure was a secondary consideration.

Liana's method of accounting was simple and basic – most of Miss Rose's education had tended to concentrate on the classics. Even so, she did not find it difficult at all to assemble facts and figures which clearly showed where mistakes were being made, although the mistakes did not account for everything. Meticulously juggling with lists of crops, available land and potential harvests, Liana calculated that, with a little reorganization, this time next year the estate and the home farm could be making a profit. In fact, the more she read and assimilated, the more she was shocked. The losses Lady Margaret was being forced to accept and pay for were quite scandalous. Something was very wrong; and Liana had a shrewd idea that the estate manager, Sidney Catermole and his wife Edith the housekeeper and cook, had something to do with it. That was one of the first problems to overcome, and one which would need tackling head on.

'Margaret, will you let me help?' she repeated, more firmly this time.

Her mother-in-law regarded her doubtfully, carefully setting down her cup of tea. 'I know I do need help,' she admitted, 'but is it right for you to do anything at the moment? You should be taking care of yourself, not worrying about my problems. The baby is the most important . . .' Her voice trailed off as she realized that, yet again, Liana's orange juice and boiled egg were not on the breakfast table. She picked up the bell from the sideboard and rang it briskly. She never dared disturb Edith Catermole for herself, but for Liana and her unborn grandchild, that was a different matter. She found the courage. 'You must have a proper breakfast. You need that orange juice and egg,' she said firmly. 'Nicholas will never forgive me if I neglect his child.'

His child, Nicholas's child! The familiar spasm of guilt besieged Liana but she gave no indication other than holding herself a little more erect and ramrod stiff. 'I'm perfectly all right, Margaret. I'm well and I'm eating plenty. Anyway I don't want to spend too much time over breakfast, I want to get out and look around the . . .'

Margaret clicked her tongue in disapproval. 'Sometimes I think you forget you are pregnant.'

Forget! Oh, Margaret, if only you knew! How can I forget that I am pregnant with Raul's child? Raul's, and not Nicholas's. Each day I love this place more, each day I learn to love you more, and each day the deception seems worse because of that. No, I cannot forget, and I hate cheating you, although I have no alternative but to keep silent.

Forcing a smile to her lips, Liana said. 'You are wrong. I don't forget, Margaret.'

After long delay, a bad-tempered looking Mrs Catermole eventually entered the breakfast room. 'Yes,' she said, adding 'madam,' and managing to make it sound like an insult rather than a politeness.

'Oh, Edith.' Margaret forced herself to smile in the face of the other woman's hostility. 'You have forgotten Lady Liana's orange juice and boiled egg.'

'We haven't got any – orange juice or eggs.'

'But why not? Doctor Ramsay gave you the ration book and the welfare book for the extra food because of her pregnancy. You had them the week before she arrived. Surely you must have had time to get these things by now? And as for the eggs, we must have some, surely? We keep our own hens for fresh eggs.'

'The hens aren't laying. Sidney reckons it was that doodlebug that landed in their field last month. A doodlebug is a flying bomb Your Ladyship.' Mrs Catermole looked at Liana accusingly, as if she personally were responsible for the bomb.

'I know. I have read about them in the newspapers.' Liana smiled reluctantly, feeling she ought to attempt to defuse the unpleasant atmosphere for Margaret's sake.

Margaret sighed. Whatever she asked for, it was never available, and there was always a plausible excuse for its absence forthcoming from Edith. Without actually checking the hen house herself, which she was afraid to do in case the Catermoles caught her at it, she had to accept her word. 'Well, what about the orange juice, then?'

'I swopped the points. Her Ladyship never said she *wanted* orange juice, and you did say *you* wanted roast beef this Sunday,' intoned Edith with a long-suffering air, as if explaining the facts of life to a simpleton. 'So you'll have your beef but *she*', nodding her head towards Liana, 'won't have her orange juice.'

Liana interrupted, firmly suppressing her rising temper and resisting the temptation to snap at the surly woman. She spoke softly, the tone of her voice unwavering. 'Never mind, Mrs Catermole. I'm sure I shall survive very well without the orange juice.'

She smiled pleasantly, gauging that she could afford to. Little did they know it, but the Catermoles would feel the first of many changes she intended to make. She had instinctively disliked them at their first meeting and since then neither Mr nor Mrs Catermole had done anything to encourage a change of mind.

Carefully hiding the anger surging within her, she watched Edith Catermole. She was sure the woman was taunting Lady Margaret, sneering because she knew very well Margaret's gentle nature would prevent her from answering back. But I'm not gentle, thought Liana, and I will make you pay. Oh, yes, pledged Liana, you will pay, my dear Mrs Catermole, and so will that husband of yours. But not yet.

Intuitively she took care to lull the surly woman into feeling self-confident. Let her feel sure that she had won the day yet again. From beneath half-closed eyelids Liana watched the smug little snigger which tugged at the woman's thin lips and hid her own secret smile. Mrs Catermole had no idea of what lay ahead. The lessons learned on the streets of Naples were well and truly imprinted on Liana's mind; never, never show your hand until what you want is within reach. At that moment she did not know how she was going to deal with the Catermoles but deal with them she would, *and* when they were least expecting it.

'I didn't think you'd be worrying.' Edith sniffed smugly and glowered balefully at Lady Margaret. 'Plenty of oranges where you come from.' She started to leave the room.

'Yes.' Neither the tone of Liana's voice nor her demeanour indicated to either Margaret or the housekeeper that for most of the time the inhabitants of Italy, including herself, were starving, because oranges were only available at inflated prices on the black market.

The black market! Of course, why didn't I think of it before? A germ of an idea was coming, and Liana smiled slowly. 'To save you any more trouble, Mrs Catermole, and because I know how busy you are, I shall be doing the shopping for Lady Margaret, William and myself in future. So I shall be very grateful if you can let me have the three ration books and my welfare book when you have a spare moment.'

There was a sudden silence in the room. Margaret's head came up and she stared at Liana in astonishment. Hold their own ration books! Do their own shopping! The idea was revolutionary as far as she was concerned; the thought had never occurred to her. All her life she had been actively discouraged from thinking for herself, and on the few occasions in her youth when she had shown any signs of initiative, she had been firmly suppressed. Now she was hopelessly out of practice.

Margaret suddenly felt very nervous: this was going rather too far. Did Liana really know what it entailed – going to the village shop in Longford and queueing with everybody else? Margaret had never even set foot in the shop, let alone queued. She opened her mouth to voice a protest but one sharp glance from Liana and she quickly closed it again. The girl had a plan, she could see it in her eyes. Suddenly Margaret felt more confident. Whatever needed to be done Liana would do it, and she, Margaret, would stop being useless and help her.

As for Edith Catermole, it was as if she had been struck by a thunderbolt. She stopped walking mid-stride and turned back. Her usually tightly zipped mouth fell open in astonishment. It hung slackly as she regarded Liana with an uncertain, confused gaze. It was a long time since anyone had had the effect of making her unsure of herself, and she did not like it. And what was more, she did not like the new countess. Edith had small, dark eyes, like black boot buttons Margaret always thought, and now they swivelled towards Liana brimming with malevolence. Liana looked at the gimlet eyes set in the pasty face and disliked her more than ever. Not many people could outstare Edith Catermole, but Liana's inner core of steel shone through her deceptive, doe-like eyes, and it was Edith who dropped her gaze before shuffling awkwardly out of the room.

'Yes, Your Ladyship,' she muttered as she went through the door.

'But I've never shopped for groceries in my life!' said Margaret in a scandalized whisper as soon as Edith had disappeared.

'In Naples I bought and prepared my own food,' said Liana, thinking how horrified Margaret would be if she knew how ruthlessly she had schemed and fought for every scrap of food. 'Don't you have an English saying, "There is a first time for everything"?' Seeing Margaret's dismayed look, she added more gently, 'We'll do it together. I promise you'll enjoy it.' She flashed her such a sweet and confident smile as she spoke that Margaret found herself smiling back and surprised herself by thinking, yes I suppose I might even enjoy it. Yes, I *will* enjoy it.

'Now today,' Liana continued in a businesslike tone of voice, 'I'd like to meet Wally Pragnell and his wife, the tenants of the home farm.'

*

Later that afternoon, sitting in the great glory of organized muddle that was the Pragnells' kitchen, Liana marvelled at the difference she felt.

Whereas nothing but ubiquitous antagonism had emanated from Edith and Sidney Catermole, nothing but cheerful amity surrounded Wally and his wife, Mary. The kitchen itself was enough to raise the spirits of the most depressed soul, and Margaret obviously loved it. An enormous fireplace almost filled one wall and in its recess stood a gleaming black polished kitchen range with wooden seats on either side. A delicious mixture of cooking smells filled the kitchen: warm bread, pastry, meat stew. Liana, rarely hungry, suddenly felt ravenous. Everything was spotlessly clean – crisp red-and-white-checked curtains at the windows, a wooden table scrubbed until it was bleached bone white, every pot and pan sparkling like mirrors.

Mary and Wally Pragnell were both in their early fifties. A life on the land had given them red, weatherbeaten faces, making them look older than their years but their energy was indefatigable. Mary Pragnell bustled about preparing tea for them, her rotund figure darting into cupboards and flitting in and out of the larder with all the nimbleness of a young girl.

'Oh, Mary, you always spoil me. You know I'll do anything for your cooking.' Margaret settled herself happily in a worn leather chair by the window.

The two women chattered on as the table was laid ready with a blue, willow-patterned tea service, Mary's best one, only emerging from the china cabinet when Lady Margaret came. Liana started listening to their conversation, but her attention was distracted by the baby in a pram just outside the window. She guessed it must be about nine months old. It lay in its pram, kicking up fat brown legs in the sunshine, pulling at its toes and chuckling happily. She wondered who it belonged to – certainly not Mary Pragnell, she was too old to be producing babies now; but as no-one mentioned it, she did not like to ask. However, once Mary Pragnell announced that tea was ready, Liana temporarily forgot about the baby.

Since her arrival in England, she had become resigned to the unpalatable food served up by Mrs Catermole and had eaten very little. Margaret had never commented, so Liana had assumed that all English food was the same. Now, as Mary's two daughters, Meg and Dolly, came in with plate after plate of food she knew it was not so. They brought in an enormous, round, crusty brown loaf, still warm to the touch; hot scones with creamy white sides and gleaming golden brown tops; dishes of honey and strawberry jam with whole strawberries the size of large pebbles; clotted cream, thick and lumpy, spilling over from its container; and butter, pale and delicate in colour like newly opened primroses. Meg brought in an apple pie as well, baked in a blue and white enamel dish, the top decorated with pastry roses and leaves, all crunchy and brown with baked sugar. An enormous brown enamel teapot stood ready on the kitchen range, from which Mrs Pragnell poured strong dark tea.

'But what about the rationing?' Liana could not help exclaiming. It was Mrs Catermole's constant plaintive excuse for the lack of fresh food. Even the bread at Broadacres was always hard and stale.

Mrs Pragnell stopped pouring tea and looked surprised. 'Why bless you, Me Lady, that's no problem to us country folk. We grows all we needs. We has our own milk, so we makes our own butter and cream; we has bees in plenty who gives us honey: and as for meat, why, we've got chickens, rabbits, ducks, pigs.' She ticked them off on her fingers one by one. Then she turned to Lady Margaret and smiled, 'And Wally have slaughtered the biggest heifer, haven't you, Wally?' Her husband nodded, smiling broadly, but unable to get a word in edgeways, 'So you'll be getting your bit of beef on Sunday. I had the butcher put it aside for you and told him to make you up some sausages. I told him, not too much bread filling, give Her Ladyship a bit of extra meat in them for a change. I daresay Mrs Catermole will be serving them up to you later in the week.'

'I daresay,' said Margaret on a wry note.

Why, she knows very well she is being cheated. The unexpected realization infuriated Liana. She wanted to say, why can't you stand up to them? Why don't you do something about it? But wisely she kept her own counsel. It was not in Margaret's nature; but no matter, the Catermoles would get their just rewards. She, personally, would see to that.

Finally, Liana had to refuse Mrs Pragnell's offer of yet another scone. 'I really cannot eat another thing,' she said reluctantly. 'I wish I could. This food is truly, truly ambrosia. I mean, food fit for the gods,' she added hastily, seeing the puzzled expressions on the Pragnells' round country faces.

Wally beamed with pride. 'That's our Meg you've got to thank for that,' he said. 'There's not a cook the length and breadth of Hampshire who can touch our Meg.'

It was late by the time Margaret and Liana set off to walk back to the Big House as all the Pragnells called Broadacres. Their way took them down a lane with high banks; the tight-leafed, twisted hedge of hawthorn and hazel on the top of the bank was ridged crimson with the setting sun. As they walked slowly through the warm, scented air, Margaret told Liana about the Pragnell family.

Wally was the farm tenant but had to take his orders from Sidney Catermole who was the estate manager. Mary helped run the farm and should have overseen the selling of farm produce. 'But Edith Catermole always does it now,' said Margaret. 'She took it over when rationing started because she said Mary wasn't businesslike enough.'

'What do you think?' asked Liana.

Margaret looked unhappy. 'Well,' she hesitated. 'I've always been taught not to interfere in the running of the estate. My late husband wouldn't let me. He appointed the Catermoles, so I didn't like to say anything.'

'Your late husband?' queried Liana.

Margaret smiled at Liana's bewilderment. 'It's an English way of saying dead,' she replied.

Suddenly memories of Don Luigi came back. She remembered his saying once that idiomatic English is best left to the English because it is mostly incomprehensible to foreigners. 'Oh, now I understand,' she said. 'But, Margaret, as he is dead, surely you can do whatever you wish?'

'Yes, but I'm not very good at giving orders,' confessed Margaret, looking shamefaced.

'Ah, but between us we could do it,' said Liana with a confidence that immediately cheered Margaret. 'Now tell me some more about the Pragnells.' Although she had not mentioned it to Margaret, it was beginning to become mote and more obvious to Liana that the Catermoles were up to their necks in the black market. It was logical: where there was a shortage, there would be a black market. In that respect she suspected England was not so different from Naples.

Margaret continued with her rambling account of the Pragnells. 'You saw the two daughters.' She shook her head and sighed. 'A burden on their parents, both of them – financially, I mean. Dolly, the eldest, is twenty-three and the reason she said nothing and hid herself at the back of the room is that she's deaf and dumb. But she's not unintelligent and can pick up things very quickly. She's a wonderful needle woman and made that pretty dress Meg was wearing. Give her a magazine, and she can copy any dress in it.'

'I shall get her to make me some clothes when I've got rid of this lump,' said Liana decisively. She patted the now just visible, rounding form of her stomach. 'She should be able to earn money with her needle if she's that good.'

'Yes, but she needs someone with business acumen to help her, and no-one has any time for her.'

Liana stored that piece of information away. I will find time later, she vowed, after I have dealt with the most immediate problems. 'And Meg?' she asked. 'What is wrong with Meg?'

'Ah, yes, Meg. She is just twenty, and beautiful as you must have noticed. Meg's problem is the baby. Did you see the baby in the garden?' Liana nodded as Margaret continued. 'The baby, a boy, is illegitimate. Poor Meg, I doubt she'll get a husband now. Country people are very prudish, and the fact that the child's father is a foreigner only adds to the problem.'

A sudden raw fear guttered through Liana's soul. *Foreigner, illegitimate*: what hateful words. Was the whole world blind and prejudiced? In that instant her heart bled with compassion for Meg, and she felt an immediate kinship. It took a special kind of courage to go on living in the same village, to give birth to a baby and then to keep it without a husband to support mother and child. 'Where is the child's father now?' she asked, her practical nature coming to the fore.

'Oh, he is still here. His name is Bruno Bauer. He is a German prisoner of war working on the estate. He lives in the loft above the stables and reports back to the POW camp outside Longford once a week. That is why they cannot marry. He will be sent back to Germany as soon as the war finishes. If only he could stay here as he wants, they could be married, but the authorities have refused permission. They say he must go back to Germany,' Margaret snorted indignantly, 'although for the life of me I cannot see why. Poor devil, he has nothing to go back to, nothing at all. You see, he comes from Hamburg, and everything, his family, their business, his friends, everything he ever knew, was wiped out on July the twenty-seventh last year. The English had been bombing Hamburg for weeks, but on that night the bombs from England obliterated the city. More than 45,000 people died on that one night alone. They say fireballs rolled across the city and out into the countryside, burning everything.' Margaret's voice trembled with tears at the thought. 'Nothing can justify that,' she added softly.

Liana looked at her mother-in-law with renewed respect. You even care about your enemies, she thought. You really do care. 'You don't hate the Germans then?' she asked. 'You don't think they deserved such a fate?'

'I don't hate anyone,' said Margaret fiercely. 'Wars are caused by politicians not ordinary people. And although I'd like to, I find I cannot even hate the politicians. After all, they are men, too, all made in God's image, or so I try to believe.' She did not add that she found her faith tested to its utmost where her own son William was concerned, a fact which caused her intractable pain.

Men, made in God's image. But did God exist? A debatable point, thought Liana, but she kept the thought to herself, knowing Margaret would be shocked if she knew the extent of Liana's disillusionment. Margaret might not be able to hate, but cynicism had made Liana less charitable. She could hate, and she did. She hated the soldiers who had used her body. She hated the unscrupulous fat cats of Naples who had grown rich on the war from the black market, always exploiting those weaker than themselves. And now she hated the Catermoles for exploiting someone as caring and gentle as Margaret Hamilton-Howard.

Rounding a bend in the lane they disturbed a family of rabbits. Entranced, the two women stood and watched as they fled. The adults were gone in a flash of white tails bobbing through the undergrowth, the babies hanging back, curious for a second look at the two great creatures who had disturbed their nocturnal gathering. It was almost dark now. An enormous harvest moon had risen and hung like a great yellow melon in the sky. It was so beautiful Liana wanted to cry.

Her head went back and she stared fiercely at the moon. I will make changes here. I will ensure that this place will always be peaceful and beautiful, she thought passionately. My daughter, Raul's daughter, is going to grow up in this place, the most beautiful place in the world. Suddenly, she wished everyone could be happy. Everyone, including Meg and Bruno and their baby son. Slowly she smiled triumphantly; she had an idea.

'Don't tell the Catermoles that we've seen the Pragnells today,' she said to Margaret.

Margaret looked puzzled. What was it Liana was thinking? She looked more lovely than ever in the mellow light of the harvest moon, beautiful and strangely mysterious. 'All right,' she said slowly, 'but why?'

Liana's reply was to smile maddeningly and link her arm through her mother-in-law's. The Catermoles are as good as gone, she thought with malicious satisfaction. But she did not take Margaret into her confidence. Instead she treasured a heady sense of reined-in excitement at the thought of the battle ahead. She would enjoy pitting her wits against the Catermoles', but they were small fry. Next came the world. She would enjoy that battle even more. The fact that she was pregnant did not daunt Liana, for she felt fitter now than she had done for the past three or four years. The crystal-clear, pure country air gave her energy. Slipping her hand into the pocket of her dress, her fingers closed around the thin airmail letter she had received from Nicholas that morning. You will be pleased, she told him silently, because Broadacres will be a better place by the time you return. It is the least I can do, for you are fathering another man's child, Raul's child. For a moment the happy thoughts faltered and she wished it were possible to stop loving Raul; but in spite of that Liana knew she was happier now than she had ever dared to hope. Broadacres offered her so much, so much.

They rounded the last bend and the Big House came into view. Its silhouette stood out against the night sky, the planes and angles alternately ivory and ebony in the moonlight. Liana smiled and thoughts of Raul receded. By this time next week the first part of my plan for changing the fortunes of the Hamilton-Howards will be in operation. Having once made up her mind Liana did not believe in wasting time. All I need now is to gather together the appropriate ammunition. She smiled again in the shadowy darkness and squeezed Margaret's arm: the Catermoles would be providing that, albeit unwittingly.

Chapter Twelve

Three weeks later Liana and Lady Margaret sat down to what had now become their normal breakfast. William was in his room. As Margaret had feared, the bout of good humour had not lasted, and he had reverted to his usual moody brooding. His presence always cast a blight over the room, and both women were glad when he chose to remain isolated although neither mentioned it to the other.

Liana drank her orange juice, eyeing the crispy bacon, double-yolked eggs and the loaf of wholemeal bread with a new-found healthy appetite.

'I still find it difficult to believe,' said Margaret, looking with pleasure at the beautifully set-out table, 'so much has happened in such a short time.'

The Catermoles had gone, routed in no uncertain manner by Liana because, just as she had so shrewdly anticipated, they had played right into her hands. The final hour arrived when, on the Sunday following the visit to the Pragnells, lunch-time came but the promised roast beef did not.

'Let down at the last minute,' Edith Catermole said in answer to Margaret's timid query.

Liana did not hesitate. This was the moment she had been waiting for. She went storming into the kitchen, Margaret following, her eyes wide open in awe as she beheld the metamorphosis taking place before her. Gone was the fragile beauty with just a hint of inner strength. In its place was an imperious, haughty woman whose eyes flashed a fire that no-one dared defy. It was the same woman who had confronted Nicholas when threatened, only then she had been on the defensive and fear had been the impetus motivating her. Now she was on the attack, and the feeling of power and anger made a heady combination. Although angry, Liana found she was also enjoying herself. 'The heifer was slaughtered earlier in the week,' said Liana baldly, coming straight to the point, 'so what happened to the meat?'

'What heifer?'

At first Sidney Catermole tried bluffing but Liana quickly demolished each excuse he presented until eventually even his furtive and devious mind ran out of ideas. At her insistence the ration books were produced, and as Liana had long suspected many of the coupons and points were missing.

By now, Edith and Sidney Catermole were apprehensive wrecks. Liana knew they would have given anything to escape from her presence there and then but she had no intention of letting them off the hook quite so easily. She could not forget the way they had ridiculed and cheated Margaret so she reasoned it would not hurt to make them suffer a little themselves. Bullies, she believed, should always have a taste of their own medicine. A good fright would do them no harm at all.

'Lady Margaret, could you telephone the local police station? We have a serious matter of black-marketeering to report,' she said, her voice grim and serious.

'Oh, my dear, do you think we ought?'

'Give me one good reason why we should not.'

There was no answer. The Catermoles stared at Liana, their faces the colour of putty. She smiled slowly, enjoying their fear. It was almost possible to see their shifty little minds rattling about in their heads, looking for a way out. But there is no way out, Liana thought triumphantly. They were scheming cheats, preying on the weakness and goodwill of others, and hatred for all they stood for blazed from her face. It might not be possible to rid the whole world of corruption and greed but she could certainly rid Broadacres of the Catermoles.

Turning abruptly, she walked across to the window, tapping the ration books reflectively against her cheek. She had no intention of involving the police, indeed, did not know how to begin to involve them, but the Catermoles did not know that and never would. What she wanted was to force them to slink away, like beaten dogs, their tails between their legs. What she wanted was to make them so afraid of her that they would never set foot in Hampshire again. Reaching the window, she wheeled round fiercely, watching with a small stab of pleasure as they both jumped nervously.

'Mr and Mrs Catermole,' she said, concentrating on eradicating the faint trace of her Italian accent so that her voice rang out clear, cold and imperious, each word tipped with steel. Margaret watched her with undisguised admiration. 'I have had second thoughts, mainly, I might add, in deference to the inconvenience it will cause Lady Margaret. I will not call the police. But only on one condition, and that is that you pack your belongings and get out of this house and off this estate today and promise never to set foot in Hampshire again. I have plenty of evidence against you which I shall keep. If, in the future, I hear that you are anywhere near this estate, then I shall have no hesitation in using this evidence. Retrospective charges will be brought against you, and without doubt you will both go to prison. Do you understand?'

Liana smiled inwardly at the aghast and yet relieved expressions on the Catermoles's faces as they nodded their agreement to her terms. In fact, there was not much in the way of concrete evidence, and furthermore she had no idea whether or not retrospective charges could even be brought under English law. It was a calculated yet intuitive gamble on her part, and it paid off. The Catermoles could not wait to start packing. By that evening they had gone.

Almost before Margaret had time to draw breath, Liana had put the rest of the plan she had already formulated into operation. Meg had been installed as housekeeper and cook for Broadacres, with Dolly and two part-time women from the village as housemaids. Bruno had taken over the running of the estate under the watchful eye of Wally who had been made overall manager of the estate and home farm, with an appropriate rise in salary to match.

'Do you think we can afford to give him a rise?' asked Margaret, slightly apprehensive about all the lightning changes taking place around her.

'I can afford it,' said Liana firmly. 'I shall use some of the money I brought over with me from Italy. There is no point in its sitting in the bank doing nothing.'

'So you see, mother, you have nothing to worry about,' said William sarcastically. 'Liana obviously has everything worked out down to the last penny!'

He had made no objections to the changes apart from insinuating that such an obsessive interest in value for money as Liana possessed indicated a distinct lack of breeding. Liana remained silent and concealed her scorn. What was the use of having breeding and being penniless? Although William did not seem to realize he *was* practically destitute. He was wildly extravagant, spending money and writing cheques, never giving a thought to their financial circumstances. Liana wondered if he thought money just materialized out of thin air!

'We must humour him until he's better,' said Margaret in answer to one of Liana's shocked protests. She had just been presented with yet another of William's bills. It was for wine and champagne, supposedly in short supply but somehow available to William whenever he went on one of his frequent trips to London. There he apparently consumed vast quantities of alcohol if the bills were anything to go by.

The loss of a leg three years before did not, in Liana's opinion, give him the right to spend the rest of his life living off other people. 'William will have to work; he'll have to do something on the estate,' she told Margaret.

'Yes, yes, dear. But not yet.' Margaret was always agitated at the thought of anyone asking William to do anything.

'Later he will *have* to work. He can't live the rest of his life and do nothing.' But William solved the most immediate problem by being recalled to hospital for two weeks for further fittings of another artificial limb. 'At least in hospital he won't be able to spend money,' said Liana.

'I shouldn't count on it.' Margaret had long ago resigned herself to William's hastening the family bankruptcy. She found it difficult to change to a more positive attitude.

Liana had no such qualms and did not doubt her own ability. She would get William working although she had reluctantly begun to realize that William was more of a problem than she had at first thought. And it was not just the fact that he made no secret that he resented her presence; it was something else. It was more than just plain ordinary dislike. Liana puzzled and wished she had some clue to William's odd behaviour. When Nicholas returns, she resolved, we will tackle the problem of William together. The thought made her pause. Together! With a shock she realized that for the first time since her marriage she was beginning to think of Nicholas as her husband. She was actually beginning to feel married. How strange life was; why should she feel like that now, when Nicholas was far away with the Fifth Army as it slogged its way painfully across northern Europe? It was a good sign, though. All the strenuous physical and mental work was effectively blockading unwanted thoughts of the past. Yes, she must concentrate on Nicholas; he was the future.

Liana took advantage of the two peaceful weeks William was in the orthopaedic hospital to push through the other reforms she had planned. Bruno was paid a salary for the first time; it was put aside each week in a savings account at the bank, ready for collection at the end of the war. As a prisoner of war he was not officially allowed to earn money but Liana did not see why he should work for nothing. She also scandalized the village, and caused a minor uproar with Margaret and the Pragnells, by encouraging Bruno and Meg to live under the same roof as man and wife.

It was more than Lady Margaret and Mary Pragnell could stomach. Radical change which left them gasping was one thing, but this was quite different. It was not the done thing, men and women living openly together. That was her foreignness showing, they told each other as they came together to tackle Liana on the matter. They needed each other for moral support in the face of her determined stance. She listened quietly to their protestations and arguments against the arrangement, then countered it with, what seemed to her, sensible, compassionate logic.

'So they are not married but they love each other and have a child. What is marriage after all? A mere piece of paper.'

'A very important piece of paper,' said Mrs Pragnell. She worried over what the villagers would say. An illegitimate baby was bad enough but living in sin! It was unthinkable.

'And they will *have* that piece of paper, just as soon as the war is over. Bruno will be staying here in England because I intend to see that he does.'

'Well . . .' Mrs Pragnell began to weaken and Liana's instinct was to push her point home and win the day, settle the matter of Meg and Bruno once and for all.

Impulsively flying across to Mary Pragnell, she took the work-roughened hands into her own soft, slender ones. 'Would you deny your beautiful daughter and your adorable grandson this happiness? I think not,' she said softly, shaking her head. Her dark eyes blazed with a fierce light as she tried to explain, tried to cleave a way through years of inbuilt prejudice, tried to make it right for Meg in a way it could never be for herself. 'Meg and Bruno have done nothing wrong. Loving each other is not a sin, and they have both suffered. Why should they suffer any longer when it could be so different?'

'Yes,' said Mary, thinking of Meg alone in her room, weeping night after night. Helpless to change things, she had never mentioned it, and neither had Meg but the sound had torn at Mary's heart. She thought, too, of Bruno tramping his solitary mile-long walks in the woods, a sad, haunted expression on his face. 'Yes,' she repeated slowly, 'they have suffered. Heartbreak and shame is a heavy burden for young shoulders. But for the life of me I cannot see that changing. The villagers will always sneer and never forgive or forget. People will always taunt them.'

'Only some, not all,' said Liana vehemently. 'The mean spirits in the village will always think in a mean-spirited way. But that is *their* problem. They are not important. Good people have charity in their hearts. If you love Meg, truly, truly love her as only a mother can, then give them your blessing. That is all they need.'

Mary looked at Liana. Why was it she had never noticed the deep compassion in Liana's face before? How could she have missed it? It was etched around her mouth and shone in the limpid darkness of her eyes. For a brief moment as Mary Pragnell looked into those eyes she thought she caught a glimpse of a terrible hopelessness and sorrow, something so deep it was far beyond her comprehension. Usually Liana succeeded in tucking the ever-present pain far away at the back of her mind, usually she managed to stamp on it until it was only a dull ache. But today the sorrow of Raul's loss surfaced with renewed vengeance. The thought of Meg's suffering and of wasted lost love reminded her of Raul. The irony was that while there was hope for Meg, there was none for her. Raul was lost to the world and her for ever.

Mary's expression made Liana realize that something of her thoughts must be mirrored in her face. With a discipline born of months of practice, she quickly relegated all thoughts of that beloved face, all thoughts of their few enchanted weeks together, back to where they belonged, so far back that sometimes she could almost fool herself into thinking she had managed to stop feeling anything at all.

'I'll tell them they have my love and support, and Wally's, too,' said Mary slowly. If Lady Liana could suffer for her daughter, the least she could do was to throw away her own prejudice.

'Mine, too,' said Margaret, suddenly wondering why on earth she had thought it wrong in the first place. Liana had summed it up so well – good people did have charity in their hearts. But she still worried. 'Liana, do you really think it will be possible to get permission for Bruno to stay on after the war?'

'Of course. It is merely a question of getting in touch with the right people.'

Such was her aptitude for suave self-assurance that they believed it was as good as official, and Liana let them think it. Of course she had her own private moments of doubt, but never allowed herself to dwell on them. That was being a defeatist, something she had never been. Instead she started a concerted campaign of letter-writing, to their Member of Parliament, to the War Office, to the Society for the Welfare of Prisoners of War, indeed, to anyone who might be remotely interested or who could be influential in obtaining the desired outcome.

As for Meg and Bruno living together out of wedlock, it provided the villagers with an item of gossip for a week or two, then it became accepted as the norm. As Liana had predicted, everyone, save for a few sanctimonious souls, began to link Meg and Bruno's names together as naturally as if they were already married.

As a result of all the changes, which everyone agreed seemed to have occurred with miraculous speed – 'Like magic almost overnight,' as Mary Pragnell was fond of saying – the employees on the estate were content with their lot. Liana gained respect and admiration, and the general consensus of opinion was that although her ways might be a little strange sometimes, there was no doubt that her heart was in the right place. The estate workers were slow, country folk, and to them Liana's impatience to get things done quickly was strange, but then, they told each other, she was a foreigner after all, and what else could be expected. She was bound to be different!

Lady Margaret sometimes felt she ought to pinch herself to make certain it was not some wonderful dream. Her life had changed so dramatically for the better. So much so, she still found it difficult to believe; and it had all happened so quickly. Margaret was inclined to agree with Mary Pragnell: it really did seem like magic, and she felt quite dizzy when she stopped to think about it. If only William would stay away longer, then life would be perfect.

But William returned from his period of hospitalization when the two weeks had passed and seemed to be able to walk more easily on his new leg. Almost immediately he gave Liana a sealed envelope.

'What is this?' Liana was aghast. The envelope contained a bill for a considerable amount of money. Even by William's extravagant standards it was large.

'What does it bloody well look like?' William's voice throbbed with truculent resentment. He hated having to pass it over to Liana and had asked his mother to pay the bill. But for once in her life she had stood her ground and forced him to give it to Liana.

'She is dealing with all the finances now,' she said, 'Liana and Mr Porter, the bank manager.'

Liana stared at the piece of paper in her hand. 'But when did you . . .? I thought you were in hospital.'

'Not all the bloody time. Thank God they let me out for an afternoon occasionally.'

'But how . . .? I mean, I don't understand. All this money! What . . . where is Fortnum & Mason?' That was the name printed in fancy lettering on the top of the bill.

'Fortnum & Mason, my dear sister-in-law, is the finest food store in London. People with class would never dream of shopping anywhere else. But, of course, you wouldn't know that, would you? How could you? You're only an ignorant foreigner!'

Determined not to let him have the satisfaction of making her angry – he was obviously panting for a fight – Liana bit her tongue. She was not going to quarrel with him the first day he was back from hospital and she reminded herself that William had, and probably still was, suffering a lot. 'One hundred and fifty pounds is a lot of money,' she said quietly. 'And we have very little in the bank.'

'Then get an overdraft. Sell a painting, or one of those bloody Chinese vases that litter up the corridors. Do what you damn well like, but just pay the bloody thing.'

Arrogantly indifferent, William strolled out of the room, leaving Liana near to tears with impotent rage. How could he be so irresponsible? But there was nothing she could do, and once again she found herself wishing Nicholas was back in England. Maybe he would be able to exercise some control over his brother. Sighing, she reluctantly wrote out the cheque. A food hamper and six bottles of wine for one hundred and fifty pounds. It was scandalous. Liana made up her mind that after the birth of the baby she would go up to London and visit Fortnum & Mason. She wanted to see for herself what it was that made this shop so special and expensive!

William settled back into Broadacres, quickly resuming his solitary routine of reading and fishing, but Margaret noted with increasing worry that he had acquired a new habit: that of drinking at home. Although she knew from friends that he was often drunk when in London, he had never drunk to excess at Broadacres before. It was a new and worrying development, and one which she feared could end in disaster.

During all this upheaval and reorganization, Liana found it very convenient to continue to fend off Donald Ramsay. And he, being the wise doctor that he was, reassured Margaret, who was getting increasingly agitated, and told her not to worry. He could see for himself that Liana's figure was continuing to round gently and that her cheeks now had a healthy tan from her days in the sun. So he had been patient, knowing that eventually she would have to come to him. Now, in the middle of

September, Liana knew that the time had come. She could no longer put off the visit to Dr Ramsay. So when Margaret suggested it yet again, she agreed to an appointment being made.

*

Liana lay on the couch in Dr Ramsay's surgery ready for his examination. On the way, her usual indomitable courage had sagged and nearly deserted her: the only two previous occasions she had consulted a doctor had scarred her mind. But once there, she felt more at ease. Donald Ramsay's surgery bore no resemblance to those in Naples. He and Dorothy lived in a rambling, comfortable, thatched cottage, surrounded by spacious gardens, on the edge of the village of Longford. It served as a home for the doctor and his wife, and combined a surgery, waiting room and dispensary for his patients. Donald Ramsay had tactfully withdrawn as Liana had undressed, and now she waited for his return, watching through the half-open window.

Fragrant honeysuckle tendrils reached out, pushing at the lace shielding the window, and beyond that Liana could see that the garden was a chaotic riot of colour – roses and lupins competed for space amongst the cabbages, carrots and lettuces. Not an inch of soil was wasted. Next year, that is how the kitchen garden at Broadacres is going to be, thought Liana, as usual her mind racing on ahead with plans. Always so busy planning for the future, sometimes there was hardly time to think about the present.

Donald Ramsay brought her mind back to the present with a jolt, however, as he gently palpated her abdomen. 'Assuming that you conceived on your honeymoon, you are coming up to approximately four and a half months' pregnancy,' he said. He chose his words with care. She was still very small, but his expert hands could feel that the baby was well formed and very active.

'I *did* conceive on our honeymoon,' said Liana quickly.

Donald Ramsay hesitated. He wanted to gain her confidence, make her trust him. If the baby was due earlier, he wanted to know. Indeed, needed to know for her own safety and that of the baby. He was not interested in morality or what others might perceive to be the lack of it. She must understand that and be convinced that he believed moral judgements were outside his province. His work was solely concerned with the welfare of the body.

'You know, of course,' he said, 'that anything you say to your doctor is in the strictest confidence. I would never repeat it to anyone, not even your husband.' There was no answer from the slender figure on the couch. In desperation Dr Ramsay tried another tack. He pointed to the carved ceiling rose, from the centre of which hung the light. 'A double insurance of my silence, "Sub Rosa": anything said under the rose is an honourable secret. You must have seen the symbol of the rose on the confessional box, so you know what it means.' Then he cursed himself for raising the point of her Catholicism; it was something they had all taken care to skirt around. But she did not seem to mind.

'I am a lapsed Catholic, Doctor Ramsay. Didn't you know? And there is nothing I need tell you. Not even "Sub Rosa".'

She raised her head from the pillow on the couch and, fixing her dark eyes on his face, smiled at him. Bewitched, Donald Ramsay found himself smiling back. Satisfied, Liana laid her head down and relaxed. There was nothing to worry about. He believed her. Although he was unaware of it, her smile had the same effect on Donald Ramsay as, on earlier occasions, it had on Charlie. She had hypnotized him into believing her.

Afterwards when he thought about it, Donald Ramsay felt irritated. He realized that he would have sworn black was white if she had asked him to do so, such was the magnetic power of her gaze. No wonder Nicholas succumbed to her charm, he reflected wryly; and no doubt would continue to succumb for the rest of his life! But he kept his own counsel, and did not mention it to either Dorothy or Lady Margaret, not least because he was baffled by his own behaviour. It was strangely out of character, and he could think of no rational explanation. They would laugh at him – an old man beguiled by a pair of dark eyes!

So he merely told them that in his professional judgement, Liana was perfectly fit and healthy, and the baby should arrive some time towards the end of January, beginning of February.

Liana left his surgery promising faithfully to see him for regular check-ups, then arbitrarily dismissed the pregnancy from her mind. It was not from callousness or lack of love for the coming baby that she refused to let herself dwell on it. It was because it was so much easier to keep thoughts of Raul at bay if she concentrated on formulating plans for the future. Raul had gone from her life for ever. She had to be practical; had to stop crying for the moon which had long since passed from her heaven. The sun shone on Broadacres, and that was her future, hers, and Nicholas's and the baby's.

Her aim for the future was to ensure that the following year the whole Broadacres estate and farm would run at a profit. In this respect she was more than aided and abetted by Bruno who had the same courage as Liana when it came to taking a gamble. Reckless sometimes, Wally thought. But whatever his doubts he knew Lady Liana would have him agreeing with her before she had finished.

'How can I not agree with her, Mary?' he asked one night after Liana had persuaded him that it was a good idea to sell the old Fordson tractor, although it was still going well, and buy an older model which Bruno said he could renovate in a couple of days. The surplus money, plus some of her own, would be used to buy a combine harvester. 'She looks at me with those damned great eyes of hers, and I finds myself saying yes every time.'

'Not only can we cut and bind the rest of our own wheat this year,' Liana said enthusiastically, 'but we can hire it out to other farmers.'

'Most farmers hereabouts have nearly finished with harvesting,' Wally had protested. ''Tis nearly the middle of September.'

'I wasn't thinking of hereabouts,' said Liana, laying what she knew was her trump card on the table. 'I was thinking of the Midlands and then further up in the North of England. They harvest much later there, and through the *Farmer's Weekly* I have made contact with several groups of farmers in the North. They are only too anxious to hire our machinery at the right price.'

'Trouble is,' grumbled Wally now to his wife, ''tis all very well in theory, but supposing something goes wrong with the machinery.'

'If you don't agree, then you should have said no,' said Mary, with a noticeable lack of sympathy.

'Haven't noticed you saying no to anything,' returned her husband, feeling slightly aggrieved at her attitude. 'I hear we've got to move the old caravan down to the main road so as you can have a farm shop. Why didn't *you* say no? And who'll be doing the housework here in this house?'

'There's no need to say no when it's a good idea,' replied Mary tartly. She was looking forward to a change from housework. 'And Mrs Larkin is coming in three mornings a week to do for me, so you don't have to worry about the house. Lady Liana is paying her out of my wages from the shop. This winter we'll be selling potatoes, carrots, parsnips and cabbages from the farm. Meg will be making some bread and cakes from estate produce for sale, and then Lady Liana says we can sell our own honey and any extra cakes Meg can make from her own ingredients. We will all be better off. I will get my wages; Meg will get a percentage on what she makes for the estate plus taking all the profit on her own stuff; and we'll take all the profit on our honey.'

'The Lord preserve me from organizing women,' grumbled Wally but it was a good-natured grumble now. Mary was more vivacious and excited than he had seen her for a long time. Quite like a young girl. He grabbed her as she passed. 'Let's go to bed early tonight,' he said. It was good to feel her full breasts squashed against him.

'I think maybe you'd better stop looking into Her Ladyship's eyes,' replied Mary, startled at her husband's unexpected display of randiness.

But later, as they snuggled together like two sleepy dormice in the middle of their billowing feather mattress, she was glad she had not given in to her first impulse and resisted. Everything was looking up since Lady Liana arrived, including it seemed, her own sex life.

September drew to a close. Liana was so busy teaching herself the ways of the land, learning as much as she could from Wally and Bruno and reorganizing practically everything in sight that sometimes Lady Margaret reprimanded her for not resting and eating. 'I worry about her,' she said to Donald for the umpteenth time.

'And I order you to stop worrying,' replied Donald sternly, knowing his words would fall on deaf ears. Margaret was a worrier; nothing would ever change her.

'But she is working so hard.'

'She enjoys work. She loves being busy. Leave her alone.'

It was true, Liana did enjoy it, for two reasons although she could never decide which reason motivated her most. Was she busy because she wanted to start making that fortune she had promised herself she would make for Nicholas? Or was she busy so that there was never time to think? Work was a very effective way of slamming the door shut on the emotional powerhouse within her mind. She had discovered that years ago, after her mother had been murdered, and then later when Raul had disappeared. Then, she knew she had only survived their losses by concentrating her mind on the project in hand to the exclusion of everything else. First it had been caring for Eleanora, and later securing a future for her baby. Only when occupied was it possible to obtain some kind of comfort. Only then did some kind of soothing balm seep over her – when her mind and body were exhausted and she lacked the energy to open the door to pain and torment. So she made certain now that every ounce of energy was used to gain what she had set her heart on, the accumulation of money. And to this end she ruthlessly directed her intelligence and determination.

Her love affair with Broadacres continued unabated. She wanted to know everything. Nothing was too much trouble. She stayed up with Wally one night, watching two of the late summer calves being born.

'She cried,' said Wally when he told Mary. 'You know, sometimes I think she is tougher than any man I've met. But she was woman enough when she saw those new-born calves.' Then he added softly, 'But 'tis always a miracle to see those wobbly little heads feeling for the teats.'

'You're a big softie yourself,' said Mary smiling.

Liana watched spellbound: the colour of the harvested land gradually changed from gold to brown as the earth was ploughed after harvesting. In a sky streaked with the lustrous pinks of autumn, flocks of birds in their impressive V-formations flew south to warmer lands; they could feel the impending chill of winter. The field hedges were trimmed back from their summer wildness and the air was filled with the fragrance of burning greenwood.

Liana remembered her first impressions of England when she had landed in Southampton. Then the memories of Italy had been fresh in her mind. How traumatic those first few hours had been. She had never been back to Southampton. That ugly grey seaport was not the place for her; she loved the countryside with its ever-changing colours. It helped soften the ever-present, underlying sorrow of Raul's loss and soothed away the worries which surfaced every now and then concerning Nicholas's eventual return. The peace of the countryside was a better tonic than anything Donald Ramsay could have prescribed, and Liana relaxed. She was worrying about nothing. There was no need to fear Nicholas's return.

The Broadacres's combine harvester was now far away cutting and binding wheat in the Midlands, and so far, in spite of Wally's doom-laden prophesies, had not broken down. Fat cheques were making their way into the farm account as each group of farmers paid for the hiring. The elderly bank manager was pleased and not a little astonished. After years of mismanagement, it had taken a foreign slip of a girl to size up the situation and do something about it. English to the core and distrustful of anything foreign, he had never crossed the English Channel and had no intention of ever doing so. Nevertheless, he was not immune to her charm and he too fell under Liana's spell.

It pleased Mr Porter to entertain her to tea and biscuits in his office. Not only did she bring a sparkle of glamour into his otherwise rather dull life, she also boosted his ego by listening carefully to everything he said. She took his advice on the various accounting methods he devised and did the accounts herself, under his close supervision at first. It was a source of delight to both of them, watching some of the debts gradually disappear. By Liana's reckoning, with the added income from the shop and the hire of farm machinery, the home farm would be breaking even by December of that year. Unless there was a fire, flood or some other natural disaster. Mr Porter agreed with her.

As the canopy of leaves in the woodlands changed from green to brown, red and gold, and the berries in the hedgerows glistened bright red, they harvested the potatoes and other root crops. At Liana's insistence, and with Bruno's agreement, they sowed more diverse crops than ever before. As well as barley and wheat, they sowed sugar-beet on fields previously left fallow – a new crop for Broadacres.

'We know nowt about beet,' Wally protested.

'Then we will learn, and in a few years' time we will crush our own beet,' Liana informed him. She was quite confident. After spending hours poring over leaflets from the Ministry of Agriculture and the National Farmers' Union she knew the soil was of the right type. She also knew the more they diversified the more money they could make – a bad harvest of one crop would be balanced out by a good harvest of another.

'How can we crush it?' Wally found it difficult to keep up with Liana's mind.

'In our own sugar factory, of course. There will be plenty of vacant land for sale in Southampton after the war and plenty of men looking for work, according to the newspapers. We can build a factory there, and that way we shall control the whole process, from seedtime to harvest to selling.'

Wally just nodded. 'The things she thinks of,' he told Mary in one of his nightly reports. ''Tis quite amazing!'

Everything in the Big House was running smoothly now, thanks to Meg. Dolly was very happy to be useful; and Liana had persuaded the village schoolmistress to give Dolly lessons three evenings a week. She was learning to read and write and astounded her sister and parents with her rapid progress. The teacher told them that soon Dolly would be able to communicate with them by means of simple written notes.

*

On a still October afternoon, when the mist was already stretching eager cold fingers towards Broadacres house, Liana decided to walk to the home farm and join Mary Pragnell for afternoon tea. Margaret was out riding with the Hampshire Hunt. The excited baying of the hounds floated as clear as bells in the still air.

Liana stood and listened, imagining the scene. Once, Dorothy Ramsay had taken her to a meet.

'When you've had the baby, I'll teach you to ride and you can join us,' said Margaret when the meet was assembling, her face flushed from the stirrup cup, the cold and the effort of keeping an over-excited Rufus under control.

'She might not like it,' said Dorothy. 'She might be like me – on the side of the fox.'

'Thank you, Margaret, but no.' Liana declined the offer quickly, adding softly, 'It must be awful to be hunted.'

But Margaret had not stayed to listen. Rufus bucked and, breaking into a sideways gallop, had taken her out of earshot.

Now, as Liana stood listening in the still air, she hoped the fox would be lucky again and escape capture as he had that day. Her eyes strained towards the distant outline of the downs, looking for the tell-tale sign of birds scampering skywards, fluttering like smoke before the wind.

But there were no birds and the sounds of the hunt vanished tantalizingly away up the valley. All was peace and silence once more. A sound from the stables caught her attention. Thinking it was one of the farm dogs accidentally shut in, Liana walked across and opened the main door to the stables.

The smell of whisky hit her as the door swung back. It was William in the stable, not one of the dogs. He had fallen awkwardly, twisting his false leg beneath him.

Not stopping to think, Liana flew across to him. 'William, let me help.'

Her outstretched hands were brushed away with rough impatience and William looked up. It was then that Liana knew for certain that William hated her. It was unmistakable, his eyes glittered with it. She caught her breath in fear and stared. Why, she wanted to ask. Why? What have I done to you? Is it because I try and curb your reckless spending? Should I have been more careful, taking greater account of your terrible injury? Are you in more pain than I know? But all these questions remained unanswered. She had no chance to speak before William lashed out violently at her.

'Don't touch me,' he snarled through slurred, drunken lips. 'Don't touch me, bloody Italian *wop*.'

Liana did not answer. Scrambling to her feet she left him where he was in the straw on the floor. He stared up at her, and, looking into his pale grey eyes, Liana could see that his hatred was all-consuming, illogical and completely beyond reason. Suddenly the unnamed apprehension which had been bothering her ever since she had first met William clicked into place. He did not need a reason. He just hated her and he was dangerous. The cold fingers of fear closed around her and, although the afternoon was still warm, Liana found she was trembling. Of course, she ought to have realized before but stupidly she had allowed the pleasure of living at Broadacres to lull her into a false sense of security. Fool! Broadacres was paradise but she had forgotten paradise had an attendant serpent.

Leaving the stable Liana walked back to the house, the visit to Mary Pragnell forgotten. As she walked, she stared straight ahead, her gaze unwavering, a cold determined light in her eyes as she fought to rally her willpower. It is better that I know all is not perfection, she thought. Now that I know, I am prepared. There is nothing to be afraid of, nothing of substance anyway.

But, even though she told herself she was being completely irrational, she was careful to lock her bedroom door that night. And for the first time since leaving him, she longed for Nicholas, longed for the solid comfort of his warm, protective body at her side. Retrieving all his letters from the bedside cabinet, she sat up late and re-read every one of them. Suddenly his cheerful presence seemed to be with her and Liana realized with surprise that she was beginning to look forward to his return after all. Well, well, perhaps brother William had done something good after all! Liana smiled. How infuriated William would be if he knew.

Chapter Thirteen

'Feeling cold, Your Ladyship? Wishing you were back in sunnier climes no doubt.' William entered the room.

It was late November. A week of hard frosts had robbed the deciduous trees of their remaining colour. Outside sleet hammered like stones at the window panes, and inside the temperature hovered just above freezing. Liana huddled almost inside the enormous open fireplace in a vain attempt to gain some warmth from the two logs smouldering grudgingly on the hearth. It was wasted effort. What little heat the burning wood did generate vanished immediately up the great yawning chimney.

'Yes, I am cold.' Liana ignored his second remark. She was getting used to his jibes and had schooled herself to let them wash over her. To William's face she maintained a pleasant, impersonal front but inside she was wary, ever alert. Totally unpredictable, he could be hateful one moment, then switch on the charm so that he was almost like Nicholas in character, the next – almost but not quite. Liana was never fooled. Nor would she allow herself to become afraid of him, unlike Lady Margaret. Not that Margaret had actually admitted her fear, not specifically in so many words. But Liana knew the fear was there. Margaret's continual excuses for whatever William did, her unwillingness to disagree with him on any subject.

William's drinking was increasing daily, and today his breath reeked even more strongly than usual of the whisky he habitually drank. But he was not obviously drunk. Liana tensed, knowing that alcohol always served to increase his aggressiveness.

'Why don't you go back to Italy where all the wops live? That's where you belong. Not here.' He never lost an opportunity to remind her of her foreignness. But he was crafty, always taking care to wait until they were alone.

'Not any more. I belong here at Broadacres. I married your brother and this is my home.' It was not easy but Liana kept her voice calm, devoid of the anger she always felt rising within her whenever William was in one of his insulting moods.

169

'He must have been bloody mad.'

'A matter of opinion.'

'It's *my* opinion.'

'I'm well aware of that. But luckily Nicholas thinks differently.'

'Maybe he'll change his mind.'

Liana came near to losing her patience. 'William, the sooner you accept the fact that I am here to stay, the better. There is nothing you can do; our marriage is a *fait accompli*.'

Liana turned and left the room. It had been cold and cheerless before William entered and seemed even colder now. There was no point in remaining when he was obviously in such an ugly mood. She would join Meg in the kitchen. At least it was warm there. In fact, it was the only warm place in the whole house because the giant kitchen range was never allowed to go out.

A long Gothic corridor led to the kitchen, stretching down half the side of the house, and to Liana, now heavy with the baby, it seemed never-ending. Between each window, on marble plinths, stood some of the ancient Greek and Roman statuary collected by a pillaging Earl of Wessex during the eighteenth century. The walls and ceiling were finished in grey stucco which was beginning to peel, adding to the overall effect of gloominess of the day.

An extra loud shower of hail against the windows caused Liana to pause for a moment and look out. The wide lawns sloping down to the lake and the Palladian bridge which crossed the far end of the water were almost obliterated by the freezing sleet.

Suddenly her mind reeled and time slipped, plunging Liana backwards. It was Italy, not England, and the cold rain obliterating the landscape was sweeping inland in torrents from the sea, just as it had on the day they had buried Eleanora – she and Raul. Sometimes it seemed to Liana that it had all happened a lifetime ago. Someone else's lifetime, not her own. But then suddenly, without any warning, the painful memories would return sharper and more clear cut than ever. They burned into her now, cleaving her in two. She bent double, face buried in her hands. Was it possible to die from remembered pain? She answered herself: no, of course not. A memory was not a physical thing, it was only in the mind. But if that was so, why did it hurt so much? Why did it feel so real?

It was no good, she could not deny the memories. Unreasoning desolation flooded through her. Raul, darling Raul. I loved you then and I love you now. I'll never stop loving you, never, never, never.

Bleak despair swept over her. Liana stopped fighting and gave in to it, leaning her cheek against the cold window pane and welcoming the pain now with open arms. Oh, the relief, the exquisite relief just to let go, to let her guard down for a few moments, letting a little of the poisonous deceit seep out.

Lady Margaret found her. She was slumped in the window seat, blue with cold, tears pouring down her cheeks. 'Come, my dear,' she said tenderly, wrapping her arms around her.

She wanted to help and to weep with her, too, so dark and bitter were Liana's tears. But she had too much good sense to probe into such deep grief. Instead she gently but firmly led Liana towards the warmth of the kitchen.

*

Much later Liana realized that the kitchen had proved to be her salvation in more ways than one. For there in the warmth she suddenly remembered the *stufa* at the *castello* – how efficient it was in spite of its great age, and how little wood it used. That night she sat up late in the library, planning. The project claiming her attention, having topmost priority now, was 'a warm Broadacres' – or at least some of it – campaign. The English might be content to exist in near arctic conditions but she was not. The kitchen range had given her an idea, and with painstaking efficiency Liana transformed that idea into a concrete plan. The following day she summoned Bruno. If hard work and ambition were to be the only balm against unwelcome memories, then, Liana reasoned, why shouldn't her mind be engaged in bringing a little comfort into all their lives?

Bruno came into her office. He stood politely just inside the door, very conscious of his mucky farm clothes. 'Yes, my Lady.'

Liana looked up, smiling. The tears of yesterday were gone now, as if by magic. In their place was her usual serenely beautiful expression. Bruno marvelled at the mercurial change of mood. She was a different woman from the one he had seen distraught and weeping in the kitchen. But the serenity was a mask donned with difficulty. Only Liana knew the very special dedication it took to confront her sorrow then put it away and pretend to the world at large that she was who they thought her to be.

'Bruno, I understand there is a forge at Elverton.'

'Yes, there is. But nothing on the farm needs repairing.' Bruno was puzzled.

'It's not mending I have in mind, Bruno,' said Liana. 'It's making. Can you take me there now?'

'But I've only got the farm lorry. You can't ride in that.' Bruno was horrified. He usually borrowed the doctor's Austin when Lady Margaret or Liana wanted to go anywhere, which was not often. The yellow Rolls Royce belonging to the Hamilton-Howards had been mothballed for the duration of the war, along with most other civilians' cars.

'Why not the lorry?' Liana laughed outright in genuine amusement at his expression. 'Bruno, please do not make such a disapproving face. As long as I don't have to walk all the way to Elverton, I don't care what I go in.'

As usual, once she had made up her mind, Liana left no stone unturned in order to achieve her goal. The goal now was warmth. She had conceived a plan which she was sure would transform a small part of Broadacres into a warm home instead of the enormous refrigerator it now resembled.

The long hours in the library the previous evening paid off handsomely. Her plans fell into place with lightning speed. She presented drawings and figures to the blacksmith and his mate as if she had meticulously worked them all out months in advance and hid a satisfied smile as she watched the heads of the two men poring over her plans. Little did they know she had sat up half the night, hastily scribbling her ideas on large pieces of paper, before carefully making the drawings and the detailed plans. Fred Blaker and his mate at Elverton Forge, had been making farm machinery and charcoal kilns for more years than they cared to remember, so the log-burning stoves Liana had outlined presented no particular difficulties. And once she had explained in greater detail exactly what she had in mind, it seemed simplicity itself.

'No problem at all, Your Ladyship,' said Fred, scratching his head and wishing he had thought of the idea himself.

'I know, of course, that to begin with we shall need to keep the stoves fairly small in size and number,' Liana said, 'because of the shortage of metal. But as soon as the war is over, we will make larger ones for the downstairs of the house and then move the small ones up to the rest of the bedrooms. After the war we'll aim to have the whole house warm, and ventilation will be no problem because every room in the house, even the bathrooms, has a fireplace. We'll connect the flues for the stoves up into the existing chimneys.'

'My word, Your Ladyship,' said Fred admiringly, 'that's real clever. You think of everything.'

The news soon got around the village. Lady Liana was at it again. She was having heating installed in the Big House. It was Mary Pragnell, of course, who spread the news.

'Fred Blaker, over at Elverton, he have got orders to make five stoves,' she said in her broad Hampshire accent, 'one for the breakfast room, one for the Arcadian room and three others for the bedrooms. Imagine that, warm bedrooms! I'm not sure that's healthy myself, but there you are, that's what she wants.'

There were others who shared her disapproval on that aspect. Heated bedrooms, who ever heard of such a thing! It was natural and healthy to scrape the ice from the inside of the windows in winter. But, of course, it was because Lady Liana was foreign. The English, a hardy race, thrived in cold bedrooms. The villagers were surprised that Lady Margaret had agreed to such a revolutionary idea, little knowing that she could hardly wait for a stove to be installed in her bedroom!

But in the evenings, over the bar of the Mayfly, it was generally agreed that Lady Liana might be foreign but she had her head screwed on the right way. Log-burning stoves, not coal. Why use coal, when everyone knew there were enough logs lying unused on the Broadacres estate to keep five stoves going for several years.

*

Clara Maltravers invited herself over to Broadacres. Village gossip concerning the log stoves inevitably spread across the Itchen Valley and reached her ears. Eventually, as Lady Margaret showed no sign of inviting her, curiosity got the better of her and she manufactured an excuse to come over. She sat now, luxuriating in the warmth of the gold and white Arcadian room, drinking tea and eating one of Meg's feathery light scones.

'Well, my dear, your daughter-in-law might be foreign but I must admit she has certainly proved to be something of an asset, surprising though indeed that is! A warm room, *and* in December. I must ask Fred Blaker at the forge to make me one of these log-burning stoves. I could certainly do with it. The wretched coal ration is used up in no time at all.' She shivered, thinking of the cold Victorian mausoleum of a house waiting for her on the other side of the valley.

'You can put in an order with me if you wish – half the cost payable in advance: Mr Porter, the bank manager, has told Liana to insist on that but I suppose I might be able to persuade her to give you priority treatment.'

'Pardon?' Clara Maltravers's plummy voice ricocheted off the white carved panelling behind her. 'Did I hear you correctly? Put an order in with *you*?'

'Yes.' Margaret tried not to sound too smug, but it was not easy. It was not often she had Clara Maltravers at a disadvantage. 'Liana designed the stoves, and after advice we have put the design up for a patent application and have formed a company for manufacturing them. Elver Forge Industries it's called. Our emblem is a baby eel – that was my idea. It will be stamped on each stove.'

'*You*, going into industry?' Mrs Maltravers was scandalized. 'Farming is one thing, it goes with our class, but industry!' She gave a delicate shudder. 'Why, it's unheard of! Industry is for new money, not for aristocracy.'

'Yes, into industry *and* money,' snapped Margaret, annoyed at Clara's condescending attitude. 'And goodness knows we could do with the money! As Liana says, farming is an industry, too – a different kind of industry, and one we so-called "gentleman farmers" have never been particularly successful at getting organized although here at Broadacres things are beginning to improve, thanks again to Liana; she has so many ideas. But to get back to your stove, I must tell you the order book is already full. It has been quite amazing. As soon as people hear about them, they want one, just like you. But, of course, Fred Blaker can't make as many as needed because of all the shortages although he's busy collecting every suitable piece of scrap metal he can lay his hands on. So, my dear Clara, if you do seriously want one, then please let me know as soon as possible and I'll see what I can do for you. Of course, the moment the war is over and the men come back, we shall be able to take on more labour and Fred will expand the forge. Unfortunately until then we shall have to limit the output. Liana says . . .'

'Talking of Liana, where is she?' interrupted Mrs Maltravers. She felt put out and rather huffy. She was used to bullying Margaret, not being put down! It was difficult coping with this new, confident woman, and slightly worrying. She glanced at her reflection in the mirror opposite and patted the sculptured waves of her tinted hair: rigidly perfect, she noted with relief. Thank God. The sight boosted her deflated morale. Margaret looked as if she had come straight from the stables as usual, which indeed she had. Iron grey hair straggling more untidily than ever, Clara noticed disdainfully, and, of course, wrinkled stockings and low-heeled shoes which made the fashion-conscious Clara shudder but at the same time gave her a smug satisfaction. She warmed to her theme. 'I've only seen Liana once – at the harvest festival service in Longford Parish Church.' Clara was a regular churchgoer and never lost an opportunity to bully the vicar mercilessly. 'As Liana is the new countess,' she now said archly, 'I do think it imperative that she should be seen in the Wessex family pew every Sunday. You should insist that she attends. Remind her that it is her duty.'

'Liana will come, if and when, she wishes,' replied Margaret with an abrupt snort of laughter. The idea of anyone insisting Liana did anything was ludicrous.

'Well, where is she now? Shouldn't she be taking tea with us?'

Margaret sighed. Clara was beginning to sound querulous. She had fixed ideas concerning social etiquette, her small world being rigorously bound by it. Margaret, who had always found the endless round of coffee mornings, tea parties and minor charity works petty and irritating, had opted out of them after the death of the earl and had made no effort to introduce Liana to the meaningless social merry-go-round of county society although she did intend to take her to London later in the year. She knew what they all said – a woman of her social standing should be active in the county – but she did not care and knew Liana was much too busy with the estate to care either. And never in a million years could she imagine Liana having anything in common with women like Clara Maltravers.

'Liana is too busy. She is working. The library in the Lower Cloisters has been converted into an office. It is the most convenient place to store all the books and ledgers, and since the estate telephone has been installed she has everything she needs to work efficiently.'

Realizing she was not going to bludgeon Margaret into summoning Liana, Clara changed the subject. 'Are you going to the Twentieth Ball in aid of Queen Charlotte's? It's at Grosvenor House on December the sixteenth this year. I assume you have been allocated tickets as usual. If you are not going, perhaps you might like to let Sir Funtingdon and his wife have your tickets. I told them you would. They have been left off the list.'

'I was thinking of going and taking Liana.'

'But you *never* go. You *always* just make a donation.'

'There is a first time for everything,' said Margaret tartly, unconsciously echoing Liana. She rose to show that the tea session was over and accompanied a very put-out Clara Maltravers into the cavernous marble entrance hall of Broadacres.

'Being pregnant will pose a dreadful problem for Lady Liana,' sniffed Clara, determined to put a dampener on Margaret's plans. 'She'll never have enough coupons to get an evening dress. I would offer to help, but I've already used up my coupons on my own dress. I've ordered it from Harvey Nichols.'

'We shall manage,' replied Margaret, anxious to get rid of Clara. She had few illusions about the retrospective meaningless offer, knowing very well that Clara would not part with clothing coupons unless she were held at gunpoint. And she saw no point in telling Clara that the problem had already been resolved with spectacular results. Let her find that out on the night of the ball, then her supercilious expression would soon disappear! The thought filled Margaret with unaccustomed glee, tinged with not a little vindictiveness, and she bade Clara an unusually warm farewell.

*

On 16 December 1944 Bruno waited for Lady Margaret and Lady Liana at Winchester railway station; they were due in on the night train from Waterloo. The station was dim, the lights heavily shaded: the blackout was still in operation but the waiting room was cheerful with paper chains strung across the ceiling and a small Christmas tree, lit up with fairy-lights, standing in the corner. Bruno waited and wondered, as did the rest of the staff at Broadacres, how the two women had fared. It had been Liana's introduction to high society.

When the train steamed in, a door from one of the darkened carriages opened and for a moment the light from inside illuminated his two favourite women, next to Meg, of course. Bruno had never seen Lady Margaret brimming with such good spirits or dressed so fashionably. Why, the old girl looked quite presentable. Lady Liana, however, was another matter altogether. She looked like a princess straight from the pages of a Grimm's fairy-tale. If her picture isn't plastered all over the front page of tomorrow's *Daily Express* I'll eat my hat, he thought proudly.

The evening had been an unqualified success, far exceeding Margaret's hopes and aspirations. Both women's dresses had earned them critical acclaim, a fact which pleased Margaret all the more because they had spent very little money. Her own dress was an old ball gown which had long languished unused in a cupboard. With Dolly's skilful help it had been remodelled into the latest fashion. Liana had insisted on doing her hair, and for once it was slightly waved in the front and drawn back into a shining french pleat at the back instead of the usual straggly bun. With her pearl drop earrings, and three-strand pearl choker, she looked every inch the dowager countess.

Liana looked exquisite, so delicately beautiful that Bruno's heart almost burst with pride as he tucked both women up comfortably with the travel rug. Like everyone else at Broadacres, he felt possessive and protective towards Liana. She had brought something special into their lives, and was treasured accordingly. What a woman – clever, hardworking, glamorous. Bruno could not take his eyes off her.

He was not the only man unable to take his eyes off Liana that evening. The new Countess of Wessex had captivated every man at the ball, including Winston Churchill who had insisted she and Lady Margaret sit at his table. Even now, as Liana walked in front of Margaret up the wide stone steps and into the marble entrance hall of Broadacres, Margaret found it difficult to believe that the evening had been so wonderful.

If she had gone with anyone but Liana, Margaret knew she would have passed the time as she usually did on such occasions, stuck at the back of the room, hating every moment and counting the minutes to when she could make her escape. Although she had been determined to launch Liana into society, Margaret had never expected to enjoy it. But in her anxiety to protect her foreign daughter-in-law, her usual tongued-tied shyness had disappeared and she had found herself animatedly discussing a wide variety of subjects. Not that she need have worried for Liana, because she proved that she was more than capable of holding her own. And when the conversation switched to a topic of which she knew nothing, she charmingly acknowledged her ignorance, thus winning the hearts of those around her.

It was Liana's dress, however, that initially caused all heads to turn. Out of the corner of her eye Margaret had seen Clara Maltravers staring open-mouthed, and concealed a smile. By the end of the evening whispers had given rise to a rumour which in turn had become accepted as fact: there was a wonderful new designer in London, a Jewish refugee, a personal find of the countess's, whose clothes were exclusive and wildly expensive.

In fact Liana herself had created the dress. It was fashioned from a spare gold brocade curtain found in one of the store rooms. Liana had drawn the design and Dolly had put her heart into it, making a dress that was daring, elegant and eye-catching. A halter-neck top supported her full breasts, and was cut low enough to be tantalizing but remained just high enough to be decent. To cover her pregnancy the brocade fell straight from her bust into a flaring A line, swirling into a shimmering train at the back. With it she wore the diamond and amethyst jewellery brought with her from Italy. The sparkling jewels set in mellow old gold suited her Nefertiti-like beauty, showing off her flawless olive complexion. She stood out, a cool exotic lily, making the bevy of English roses look slightly overblown in comparison.

As they entered the hall of Broadacres Liana took off the velvet evening cape given her by Margaret and threw it across a *chaise-longue*. Like Margaret, she felt elated and happy. Her first step into English society, and she had made a good impression. What was even more important, although she did not mention it to Margaret, was the fact that she had made some very useful business contacts, contacts which she had every intention of following up. Consciously using the power she knew she possessed, Liana had mesmerized the men with her beauty and intelligence. The verdict had been unanimous. The young Earl of Wessex had got himself a very fine, and unusually intelligent, wife.

'Margaret.' Liana swung round and helped the older woman remove her heavy cloak. 'Thank you for taking me. I have had the most wonderful, time.'

'Oh, so Lady Liana was impressed with the high society set-up.' An unpleasant snigger echoed loudly down the curved staircase.

Startled, both women looked up. William was slouched sideways on the top stair, an empty whisky bottle in his hand. He was very drunk, but not too drunk to talk. He was still capable of that. The light from the single chandelier in the hall cast weird shadows across his face, adding a twisted, slightly unreal dimension to his features. His pale eyes glittered. 'Italian wop meets the English aristocracy,' he sneered. 'How's that for a headline? The gossip columnists will be sharpening their pencils. They can spot a sham a mile off.'

The breath left Liana's body as she gasped. She knew his words were merely an expression of his irrational hatred of her, that they had no basis. It was her own guilt which made her gasp. My own guilt, she reminded herself. William knows nothing, nothing at all. All the same, she wished he had used any other word but sham.

'William! How dare you speak to Liana like that? Apologize at once!'

'Apologize? For what, mother? For speaking the truth? She *is* a wop, and I bet they all shunned her.'

It was not often Margaret found the courage to stand up to William, but now his insults were more than she could tolerate. She started to walk up the staircase towards her son. 'For your information, William, Liana was an enormous success. Winston Churchill himself insisted that we sat at his table all evening.'

'What? Churchill bloody well fraternizing with the enemy?' William's voice spiralled higher and higher as his rage increased. 'All bloody right for him. All he fucking well does is sit in Ten Downing Street issuing bloody silly orders, while people like me go and fight. I've lost a bloody leg because of him.' Grabbing hold of the polished mahogany banister he hauled himself up.

Margaret reached the top of the stairs. 'William,' she said coldly, 'I think you'd better go to bed. We'll talk in the morning when you're sober. *Please* William.' Reaching out, she touched his arm.

'Get out of my way, you silly old cow.' Raising the empty whisky bottle, William lunged towards his mother. Lurching unsteadily on his feet, his befuddled drunken state prevented him from aiming accurately. Even so, he managed to catch her a glancing blow on the side of the head.

Margaret ignored it. 'William, William, *please*.' He's my son, she told herself, desperately trying to gain control of the situation. I *must* be able to reason with him. He's drunk, only drunk. 'Go to bed, dear.' But even as she spoke, she knew how pathetically ineffectual the words were. His mood was too ugly for reason. Instinctively she moved backwards out of his range.

William followed, taking a menacing step towards her. There was no mistaking the murder in his eyes as he raised the bottle again.

Hitching up her skirts, Liana flew up the stairs and, flinging herself at William, hung on to his raised arm. 'Stop it, stop it! Don't hit your mother again,' she screamed.

'I'll do what I bloody well like.' He shook her off as easily as a horse swishes a fly off with its tail, so formidable was his drunken strength. 'Get away from me, you sodding wop.' As he spoke, he pushed her.

Liana staggered and tried to grab the banister but it was impossible to get a grip. Her fingers slipped on the highly polished surface and she fell. As she fell, tumbling over and over, down the entire length of the staircase, she was not aware of pain, only of Margaret's high-pitched scream and William's drunken laughter. A detached portion of her mind registered how convenient this was. The baby was due any day now; that fall would make it seem premature. But I must protect her, she thought, trying to close her arms around her stomach, cushioning the baby from the worst of the knocks. I haven't come all the way to England to let Raul's baby be murdered by William. I haven't gone to hell and back to let that happen. She tried to curl her body into a protective cocoon around the baby, careless of her own safety.

*

The lights from the chandelier were dazzling. They blazed straight into Liana's confused eyes. William's face loomed above her. He was mouthing obscenities but the words were indistinct. Suddenly his voice rang clear, piercing through her semi-conscious state. 'Die, you bitch, die. We don't want any foreigners here. Go on, why don't you do the decent thing? Die, die, die.'

I won't die, thought Liana defiantly, screwing up her eyes against the lights. I won't die, not just to please you.

'Die,' shouted William.

I *won't, I won't* and neither will my baby. She wanted to shout the words at him so that he would know he could never destroy her. But not a sound came from her open mouth. Why *does* he want to kill me? A confusing question. Why is there so much hate? She was afraid. But what was she afraid of? Does he know that Nicholas is not the father of my child? How can he know? He's never even been to Italy.

Her mind whirled faster and faster. Nothing made sense any more. There were so many faces swimming above her now, Margaret, Meg, Bruno and Dr Ramsay. Why were they going round and round? Oh God, why didn't they keep still? They were making her feel sick. She closed her eyes for a moment against the swirling mass. Then opening them again the first face she saw was Eleanora's, Eleanora's dead face with the staring eyes, her sweet face covered with mud and streaked with tears of rain. Liana knew then what she had to do. She had to get Eleanora out of the earth and into a coffin. Why didn't someone help her? It was so hard pulling the weight of the body alone. She could feel the strain tearing at her muscles as she struggled. The pain increased until it became unbearable.

With an almighty effort Liana sat up. 'Help me!' she screamed. Then pain shattered her mind and tore her body into a million pieces.

Chapter Fourteen

'I don't know, Margaret I wish I did, but I just don't *know*!'

Donald Ramsay brushed irritably past the anxious woman. Dear God in heaven, hadn't he quite enough on his plate at the moment, without being pestered with questions he couldn't answer?

'Will Liana be all right? Is the baby damaged?' Margaret persisted, not willing to be brushed aside.

The repetition alone drove him mad. 'I don't know. I don't know,' he repeated.

A girl in premature labour as a result of a fall and an aggressive drunken young man. He felt guilty. Locking William away as he had ordered Bruno to do was hardly a compassionate or scientific solution. Yet what alternative did he have? He knew the answer was none, at least for the time being. Locked away William was safe, presenting no further threat to himself or others. Dealing with a drunk with a homicidal tendency was quite enough for any country GP to manage, but the problem did not stop at that as he well knew. And it was a problem made worse, in his opinion, by Margaret's refusal to face it. On arrival at Broadacres that night he had pleaded with her.

'Margaret, for God's sake let me ring Doctor Burnham. He's the top man at the Ticehurst asylum. Between us we can arrange for William to be admitted now, tonight. If anyone can help and make a definitive diagnosis once and for all, it's Roger Burnham.'

But, stubborn as ever, Margaret fiercely repudiated the suggestion. 'No! I don't want others involved. William is our problem. It's a family matter.'

'You must involve others for William's sake if not for your own. He's mentally ill, surely you must see that.'

Margaret started crying. 'Oh, Donald. Don't start that, not now, I can't bear it. It's bad enough worrying about Liana without having to feel guilty about William.'

'God almighty.' For once Donald lost his temper and swore at her. 'Why the hell should you feel guilty? An illness is an illness.'

'I can't help it, but I do. I feel guilty because he's my son,' sobbed Margaret. 'That's why I don't want to send him away. He must stay here. We can help him more than any doctor.'

'I don't agree. I think you should seek outside help, have the whole damned thing investigated properly, going right back to square one.'

But the most he could get from Margaret was a reluctant agreement to talk to Nicholas about it when he came home, and with that Donald had to be content. He felt cross and exasperated but had no more time to waste arguing over William. There was Liana to consider, and at the moment her need was far greater than William's.

Donald wished Margaret would be quiet now. He could do without being asked questions, the answers to which he was not even allowing himself to consider.

He could not tell Margaret that he was worried sick about Liana. He could not tell anyone because there was nothing tangible he could put his finger on. Her membranes had ruptured, and she was in labour. As far as he could tell, the baby appeared unharmed by her fall: the heartbeat was strong and labour appeared to be progressing normally. It was Liana herself who worried and perplexed him. It was her body pushing out the baby, her uterus contracting so that her stomach taughtened to a peak every few minutes, and yet it seemed to him as if she was strangely indifferent to that pain. There was something abnormal about her labour. It was almost as if she was not there, as if the Liana they all knew was somewhere else, far removed from the labour room. She was suffering, there was no doubt about that, but he could have sworn she was unaware of what was actually happening. His head ached with worry.

Liana was very restless and agitated, grabbing whoever came within reach, pulling and struggling with surprising strength. And why did she keep on repeating her own name? 'Eleanora, Eleanora, help Eleanora?' Didn't she know they *were* helping her as much as they could? It was the most curious thing he had ever encountered, because he was sure she thought she was talking about someone else, not herself. She wasn't, of course, common sense told him that. Nevertheless it was uncanny, and the appalling panic in her voice made him shiver. He cursed under his breath, determinedly trying to shake off the strange helpless feeling which he knew was threatening to warp his professional judgement. Whatever happened he of all people had to keep a cool head.

Of course, the rational explanation was that she was still semi-concussed. She had obviously knocked her head when she fell, that was easy enough to deduce. There was a lump the size of an egg on her forehead, and, of course, that was the reason for her strange behaviour. Logic told him that, just as logic told him not to fret unduly. She was young, she was healthy, there was nothing to worry about. But in spite of logic the bizarre feeling persisted. He sensed that she desperately needed help, a special kind of help, some form of reassurance for a terror beyond his reach and understanding. Donald Ramsay felt fearsomely inadequate and hated himself for it.

'Doctor, can you speak Italian? Can anyone here speak Italian?' The midwife came out of the bedroom. The sound of Liana's raised voice could be heard in the background. 'She seems very upset about something. Jabbering on and on she is, but I can't understand a word of it.'

'I daresay it wouldn't make much sense to us even if she were speaking English,' replied Donald Ramsay wearily. What was Liana talking about? He rang Winchester hospital again. Hell, why did switchboard operators always seem particularly dense at two in the morning when you most needed them to be helpful? 'Yes, yes it *is* Doctor Ramsay again. Yes, I *do* still want to speak to Mr Gilmour, the specialist obstetrician.' He covered the mouthpiece with his hand and turned back to have a word with the midwife, but she had disappeared back into the bedroom.

'Donald.' The cheery voice of John Gilmour at last. 'Still having problems?'

'John, thank God. Have you finished your Caesarean? Because if you have I'd really like . . .' He stopped mid-sentence as a high pitched, piercing yell echoed down the stairway, followed by the hiccupping crying of a baby. The child was born. 'It seems I don't need you after all,' he said abruptly, and, dropping the phone back into its cradle, raced up the stairs, taking them two at a time.

'A girl,' said the midwife as he ran into the room. 'Popped out like a jack-in-the-box. I'm afraid you've got quite a lot of stitching to do, doctor.'

At four o'clock in the morning, an exhausted but jubilant group stood in the kitchen of Broadacres. The honour of popping the corks had been assigned to Donald Ramsay although, as he pointed out, he had been on the telephone at the vital moment, therefore it should be the midwife's honour.

'I'm sure you've had more practice at opening bottles than I have, Doctor Ramsay,' said Nurse Cottle rather primly. 'You open them.'

So Donald proceeded, and the flying corks from two bottles of ten-year-old Dom Perignon hit the kitchen ceiling with resounding bangs. Mary, Wally and Dolly had come over from the home farm and joined Meg, Bruno and Lady Margaret during the waiting hours. Now it was all over they could breathe easily again. Smiling with relief they raised their fizzing glasses to each other.

'To Lady Liana and Lord Nicholas,' said Donald Ramsay solemnly, 'and to the new member of the Hamilton-Howard family. Thank God for the safe delivery of a healthy, if rather small, baby. And God bless both of them, mother and child.'

'God bless both of them,' came the heartfelt echo.

The only person missing was William. He was sound asleep, and Donald Ramsay knew from previous experience he would probably remember nothing when he eventually awoke.

It was 17 December 1944. Donald Ramsay was now quite certain that the baby had arrived on time; but this knowledge he kept to himself. The tiny, squalling female he inspected carefully immediately after the birth was perfectly formed and very lusty. In his opinion the fall had precipitated events by a few days but not much more. After the birth, Liana gradually began to rejoin the real world but her eyes were filled with a misty light which shone with pain. Donald Ramsay felt his heart go out to her. What was this unknown pain? He sensed it was nothing to do with the trauma of birth, just as he also sensed that there was nothing he could do to help. It was something fate decreed she needed to bear alone.

He handed Liana the baby as soon as she had been stitched and made comfortable. 'Here is your daughter,' he said, placing the baby in her arms, smiling gently, glad her physical ordeal was over. 'You were sure it was going to be a girl, weren't you?'

Liana smiled back gratefully. Gradually the pain began to recede. She looked down at the tiny, damp curls on the baby's finely shaped head. They were a dark henna red, exactly the same colour as Raul's hair. Round dark eyes, fringed with incredibly long, silky lashes, stared up at her. A rush of love threatening to choke her welled up at the sight of such beautiful perfection: this was the moment of triumph. This was what she had schemed and fought for, endured agony for, and now she was certain every moment had been worth it – all the cheating, all the lying, even that terrible nightmare she had just had about Eleanora; she recognized it now for the awful fantasy it had been. Yes, every single ghastly moment had been worth it for their precious daughter, hers and Raul's.

Donald opened the door and let a very nervous but excited Margaret enter the room. She crept in silently and they stood side by side, watching as Liana put the baby to her breast. There was no hesitation; the tiny scrap knew exactly what to do. Her pink gums closed firmly around the nipple and she began to suck vigorously. At that moment Liana loved her so much, so fiercely, she thought her heart would explode with joy. If only Raul could see his daughter, she thought passionately. How much he would love her.

'Nicholas will be so proud.' Margaret came and sat on the side of the bed. She reached out gently and softly touched the tiny pink hand now clutching at Liana's breast.

The whispered words startled Liana, cruelly jerking her from triumphant euphoria back to reality. Nicholas! Oh, my God, I have forgotten Nicholas. What was she thinking about? The cheating wasn't finished; it would never be finished; it would have to go on and on. Depression settled itself like a black bird of prey on her shoulders as she realized that the birth of the baby was merely the beginning of yet another lie. Liana felt herself go cold with a rush of guilty panic. Would Nicholas acknowledge the baby as his own? There was no likeness to him, no likeness at all. But that did not mean a thing. Nicholas was sure he had married a virgin, and of course he would love his own daughter. His daughter, Nicholas's daughter, not Raul's.

'Yes,' she whispered, 'I hope Nicholas will be pleased.' She turned her head abruptly to hide the single tear of regret which, in spite of her effort to contain it, slid down her cheek.

Margaret, seeing the tear, misunderstood. 'Don't cry, my dear. Of course Nicholas will be pleased. He has a beautiful daughter to love as well as a beautiful wife. Everything bad is finished now, no more pain or nightmares. Poor Liana, what a terrible time you've just been through. Donald has explained to me how difficult it was, and how brave you were. Thank God the baby, although premature, is absolutely perfect; and you, too, will suffer no lasting damage.' She touched the lump on Liana's forehead. 'I'm so very, very sorry about William. He didn't mean what he said or what he did. It was the drink. It takes over and changes his personality. You do understand that, don't you?'

'Yes,' said Liana, struggling to regain her composure. 'I do understand.'

That at least was true; she did understand, far better than Margaret thought. She was sure now in her own mind that there was something inherently evil in William's character, and it had nothing to do with drink. Alcohol was merely the trigger which released the catch, unleashing his true emotions. Yet how ironic, she thought grimly, watching the baby's jaws working rhythmically as she sucked, that William of all people, should have unwittingly provided the perfect camouflage for the birth. Because of the fall, I need give no explanations. The baby is assumed to be premature; no-one will suppose otherwise. Once again fate had worked in her favour. Welcome relief flooded over her and she relaxed. There was no need to be depressed.

'Had you and Nicholas decided upon any names before you left Italy?' Lady Margaret watched the baby suckling, entranced by the tiny child.

Liana smiled remembering what Nicholas had said. 'If it is a girl, call her what you like, as long as Margaret is one of her names.'

'Yes. Her name will be Eleanora Margaret.'

Margaret beamed, her bony features transformed into a kind of beauty with joy. Her first grandchild was to be named after her. 'The most wonderful Christmas present I've ever had,' she said.

Donald Ramsay, however, felt a sudden shiver run the length of his spine. 'Eleanora?' he said quietly. 'Isn't that your own name?'

Liana looked up quickly. Something in the tone of his voice worried her. For a moment, just a few brief seconds, she thought Donald Ramsay knew her secret. Then she relaxed again. She must learn to stop being ridiculously suspicious; no-one in the world knew except herself. Nicholas was Eleanora's father. She smiled at him, her dark eyes shining, and Donald felt his fears disappearing as he smiled back.

'Of course,' Liana said softly. 'It is my name, but as I never use it, I think it is only right and proper that the baby should have it. It is a family name.' Suddenly the lies came easily again as she slotted herself and the baby back into their allotted roles. 'It has been used for female children in my family for generations.'

Chapter Fifteen

The filming in Sicily finished ahead of schedule at the beginning of December 1944. Raul was pleased to return to the civilization of Rome. The journey back up through Italy by road had been long and uncomfortable, the southern half of Italy still being paralysed by post-war chaos. Simionato's money had virtually run out, and it was difficult to organize funds from the remoteness of Sicily. Their journey back, loaded with the precious cans of film plus all the filming equipment, had been made in a series of totally unreliable pre-war lorries.

'As soon as we get back to Rome, we can get on with the cutting and editing,' Simionato told an impatient Raul, 'and things will look up.'

'And they have.' Raul leaned back in his chair and lit a cigarette, enjoying the expression of amazement on Carmelo's face.

He had met Carmelo Farzinni, an old university acquaintance, on the Spanish Steps the day before, and now they were sitting in a café in the Piazza del Popolo. Carmelo had thought Raul dead, along with the thousands of other Jews who had disappeared from the city. But I should have known better, thought Carmelo wryly, looking at the confident man sitting opposite him. Raul always had a certain air about him, a self-assurance verging on arrogance. To tell the truth, Carmelo had never liked Raul, and found that his opinion had not changed much with the passing of time. Nevertheless, Raul still exerted the same old pull on his contemporary – a grudging admiration for his sheer nerve, and a certain amount of envy in what he had apparently achieved.

'You are actually living with Gustavo Simionato, in his house?' Carmelo was impressed. Everyone in Rome knew where Gustavo Simionato's villa was.

'Yes, now it has been vacated at last by the American general who took it over. I suppose we must be grateful for small mercies. Both the previous tenants, the German and the American, were apparently quite civilized. They took care of the antiques and *objets d'art*, thank God.' Raul flicked the ash from the end of his cigarette with worldly nonchalance. He was enjoying playing the sophisticated man-about-town in front of Carmelo.

'You speak about the place as if it belongs to you.'

'It will one day,' said Raul with authority. 'Simionato has no children, is not even married.' He lit another cigarette and gave one to Carmelo. 'I am like his son.'

He grinned, thinking of Simionato's imposing house near the Vatican City – the circular staircase lit by exquisite Venetian glass chandeliers; the large salons; the imposing library; the smaller salons filled with priceless ceramics; and the cool, walled garden filled with ancient statuary set amongst lush greenery and ornately carved Bernini fountains. The garden and villa were a haven of elegant peace set right in the middle of vibrating Rome. Yes, it would all be his one day. He would see to it.

'What about you?' Carmelo asked. 'Are you married? Do you have children? I am, I got married before I went off into the army. My wife's name is Paola and we have a two-year-old son, Marco.'

Raul laughed, and signalled with an arrogant snap of his fingers for the waiter to bring more *grappa* and coffee.

'You must be mad to marry so young,' he said, the incredulous note in his voice annoying Carmelo. 'No, I'm not married and never will be. If I want a woman, I find one. It's no problem. But a lifetime commitment! To coin an Americanism, "that's strictly for the birds".'

The *grappa* and coffee finished, they went their separate ways, Carmelo to his job in the bank and his ordered, domesticated existence, and Raul to wander around the city looking for a suitable Christmas present for Simionato. He dawdled, breathing in the very essence of the Eternal City. Rome had been spared the bombing which had devastated other cities. As a result it had recovered from the hostilities very quickly and seemed the same now as it had been before the war. It had always excited Raul then, and it did now, filling him with nervous energy. He loved the crowds, the pigeon-filled piazzas, the domes and campaniles, the buildings old and new. He felt that he was a living extension of the city, that his roots, too, were buried deep in twenty-eight centuries of history.

His mind drifted back to the meeting with his old university acquaintance. Truly Carmelo must be mad to allow himself to be tied down by a wife and child. What mattered to Raul was to live life with a captial L, free to do what he wanted when he wanted, to sleep with a different woman every night, free from recriminations and responsibilities, free to pursue his goals in the showbusiness world without the need to think of any person save himself. That was the kind of life he needed and was

189

determined to have, the exciting kind, which was denied to a man if his life included clinging women or children.

He lit another cigarette and wandered slowly through the picturesque Trastevere district then quickened his pace. December 17th, only a few days before Christmas, and the present for Simionato still to be chosen.

He was grinning as he strode off towards a shop he knew of where there was certain to be something suitable for his benefactor. Simionato had to be kept sweet – an unusual present, that would do the trick, keep the old man looking on him with a favourable eye. Raul did not believe in taking chances. Simionato was pleased with his work but Raul wanted more than that. He wanted the old man to look upon him as the son he had never had, if his boast to Carmelo were to come true. He thought of Carmelo again and laughed. 'Do I have any children?' he repeated softly under his breath. 'As if I'd be fool enough. Huh! What a stupid question.'

Chapter Sixteen

'Why, she's beautiful.'

Nicholas, anxious to see the baby the moment he arrived at Broadacres, brushed past Liana and, hurrying into the nursery, bent over the cot. He picked up Eleanora. Liana noticed how fair his hands seemed in comparison to the tiny, olive-skinned six-month-old baby with the thatch of dark henna red hair. Baby Eleanora gurgled and kicked her tiny legs, looking up at Nicholas with dark, sparkling eyes. Then she smiled. At that moment the lingering, niggling qualms Nicholas had been experiencing disappeared. It was true that Donald Ramsay had been very reassuring in answer to his anxious questions, questions he did not want to ask but nevertheless knew he had to. But still, until that moment, the vague doubts had lingered and not even Donald's brusque no-nonsense words could brush them aside.

'Oh, you fathers are all the same,' he had said briskly. 'Always worrying whether or not the child you've sired is a perfect specimen of the human race.'

'Don't tease me, Donald. It's very important to me. You know that.'

'As the family physician I've already given my opinion to your mother, as I'm sure she has already told you. But nevertheless I'll repeat it. You are sane and healthy and so is Liana. There is absolutely no reason why your children should be any different.'

'But there's no guarantee that she'll stay healthy.'

'Life doesn't come with guarantees, Nicholas. If it did it would simplify everything, but unfortunately a child is not like a new watch or a radio, there are no guarantees.'

Nicholas sighed. 'I worried tremendously when I first knew Liana was pregnant. I thought of past times and dreaded the future. But, of course, I didn't mention my worries to Liana. I wanted her to remain as well as possible.'

'And so she was and is.' Donald became exasperated. 'Nicholas if everyone thought like you, viewing the future with dread, as you say, the human race would have fizzled out by now because no-one would have had the courage to have children. But perhaps luckily for all of us the human race is reckless where the future is concerned, and we have survived. For God's sake forget about the past. Your sister Anne has a son, Peter, who by all accounts is a perfectly charming child. Why should your own daughter be any different?'

'I'd forgotten about Anne's son.' Nicholas relaxed. 'Yes, perhaps you are right.'

Donald looked serious. 'I am right, Nicholas,' he said. 'Your daughter is absolutely perfect. She's beautiful, obviously intelligent even at this early age, and has a wonderfully sunny disposition. You have nothing to worry about.'

Now, looking down into her dimpled, smiling face, Nicholas could see for himself. What did it matter that his own father had been moody and violent and that William seemed much the same? This baby was like her parents, Liana and himself. She was serene and happy. Nicholas vowed he would never let one single cloud cast a shadow on her horizon. Every day of her life would be carefree and pleasure-filled. He smiled at baby Eleanora again and was rewarded by a wide, toothless grin in response.

'She knows me,' he said triumphantly, settling her comfortably in the crook of his arm. He turned back to Liana and smiled. 'She's perfect, darling.'

'Yes.' Liana gripped the rail of the cot. Her hands felt icy, the magnitude of her deception overshadowing Nicholas's pleasure. The irrefutable knowledge that Eleanora was not Nicholas's daughter seemed so obvious to her; surely he must see it, too. Sunlight splashed on the baby's head and dark red, tiny corkscrew curls shimmered – Raul's hair, Raul's eyes, Raul's colouring. Nothing like Nicholas, nothing at all.

'Come here.'

Oh God, he knows, *he knows*. 'Why?' Liana tensed even more. What could she say? How could she explain?

'Why? Darling, what a strange thing to say. Why indeed! Because I want my family to be all together with me, that's why.' Liana hesitated then slowly walked around the edge of the cot towards Nicholas. He stretched out a long arm as soon as she was within reach and drew her to him. 'You look worried, darling. Tell me,' he whispered, 'what is it that's worrying you?'

The gentleness in his voice was almost her undoing. It was so utterly wrong to cheat him, and yet there was no alternative, not now. Once on the long road of deceit there was only one way to go, and that was forward, ever onwards. For a brief moment she visualized deceit as a physical thing, like a huge ball rolling along gathering momentum as it gained in size over the years, a chilling vision. Then she pushed it from her mind and tried to concentrate on the present. 'It's nothing,' she muttered in answer to Nicholas's question and stared into Eleanora's round, smiling face.

'Something is worrying you. I know it.'

Liana looked up at Nicholas. 'Well, it's been such a long time. I . . . we were together for such a short time, and I wondered how . . .' It was true she had wondered how their life would be when he returned. Would it be difficult being a wife again? At least it was possible to tell him part of the truth.

Nicholas pulled her head close, pressing her cheek against the roughness of his sweater. 'Don't worry, darling. It will be all right,' he whispered. 'I know we've been parted now for a whole year, but we'll pick up where we left off. Just wait and see. I love you, darling. I've never stopped loving you. I've thought about you every single day, you, and my wonderful daughter. And now at last we are together. I've got you both in my arms.'

Liana felt doubly guilty. Nicholas had thought about her every day, but she had not always thought about him. Sometimes he had been conspicuously absent from her thoughts for days on end. She reached out and caught at Eleanora's grasping starfish of a hand. 'You like her? The baby, I mean.'

'Like her? Darling! She's my *daughter*, of course I like her.'

His daughter; he accepted her. Limp with relief, Liana clung to him. 'I was afraid,' she confessed, skating perilously near the truth. 'I was afraid that you wouldn't like her.' She raised her face to his, eyes bright with unshed tears. Joy, thought Nicholas as he kissed her. Relief, knew Liana, pure, unadulterated relief.

It was their first real kiss since his return. Nicholas wanted to prolong it for ever, but at last, reluctantly, he drew his mouth from hers. She still had the power to send the blood coursing like fire through his veins. It was difficult not to take her to bed there and then. He looked at her thoughtfully, seeing the uncertain tenseness showing in her face. He would have to wait, take his time: ease his way gently back into her life. He looked back down at the baby. 'She's like you, but she has my mother's hair.'

'Your mother's?' Still nervous, Liana wondered why Nicholas should say that. Eleanora's dark red curls could not be more different from Margaret's iron grey wisps. Was he trying to trap her?

Nicholas laughed gently, this time mistaking her nervousness for surprise. 'Why, yes. My mother's hair was red before she turned prematurely grey. A mousy red, it's true but with the addition of your genes we have a daughter with mahogany-coloured hair.' He kissed the top of the baby's head.

Liana relaxed. 'I didn't know.' It was difficult to envisage Margaret with red hair. Reaching up, she drew Nicholas's head down to hers and kissed him with grateful passion. The first hurdle of Nicholas's homecoming had been successfully negotiated. He was convinced the baby was his.

After a moment, Nicholas put Eleanora back in her cot then turned to Liana. Knowing what he wanted, she took his hands, pulling them towards her until they cupped her full breasts. Then, appropriating his mouth, she kissed him, a long, slow, delicious kiss, her tongue slipping between his lips with calculating, consuming ardour. Nicholas felt his penis rise and harden. If she went on kissing him like this he knew he would not be able to wait as he had planned. Liana felt the stirring in his groin. Good, he wanted her! She was about to overcome the second hurdle, the resumption of her role as wife to Nicholas. Pressing her pelvis invitingly against the rock hardness of his now rigid organ, Liana kissed him with increasing fervour. Nicholas held her, marvelling at the way her body became fluid so that it almost melted into his own. Desire overwhelmed him, could not be denied, and, smothering a cry of urgency, he picked her up and carried her into their bedroom. The months apart fell away into nothingness as Liana's beautiful body seduced Nicholas into the timeless realm of unthinking bliss once again.

'I love you,' he breathed, prolonging the moment before at last he entered her, knowing the pleasure of that fleeting ecstasy was almost unbearable. She was his, his, no-one else's, only his. 'I love you, I love you, I love you,' he whispered in time to the increasing urgency of his thrusting body. Then awareness itself disappeared as mindless urgency reigned supreme.

Liana wrapped her sleek legs about him, binding his body to hers. Her husband had returned and claimed her. All was well.

*

Glad to be back in the peace of Broadacres after the horror and turmoil of war, Nicholas was happy. Although at first he was a little surprised to discover that Liana had been transformed into a hard-headed young businesswoman, quite different from the timid, soft creature he thought he had married, it did not bother him. In fact, he admired her purposeful ambition and was amazed at the changes she had achieved at Broadacres in such a short time. Sometimes he wished, for her own sake, that she did not insist on working such long, hard hours but he could see that she enjoyed it, thrived on it in fact, and as each day passed he could see her becoming more and more integrated into the life of Broadacres and its people. So much so, that sometimes even he forgot that she had come from Italy. But in spite of the estate taking up much of her time, work was never allowed to interfere with their married life. Liana was the perfect loving wife.

There was one minor hiccup to begin with. Clara Maltravers, as interfering as ever, raised the subject of a nanny.

'That baby should be taken away from its mother now,' she said, not long after Nicholas had returned to Broadacres. She had come over to take tea and welcome Nicholas home. 'It's high time you advertised for a nanny. The *Lady* is still a very reputable magazine; you should be able to find someone suitable through that.'

'Well, I'm not sure about a nanny just yet,' demurred Lady Margaret. She was enjoying sharing the duties with Meg and Liana as far as baby Eleanora was concerned, a pleasure she had never had with her own children as Nanny, a dragon of a woman selected by her husband, had always been there to take the children away.

'What is a nanny?' Liana was ignorant of the custom of the English upper classes of always farming their children out, first on to a nanny and then into boarding school.

Clara tut-tutted in annoyance at such ignorance. 'Someone who will take that child,' she indicated Eleanora who was sleeping peacefully in Lady Margaret's arms, 'and teach her good manners and all the other essentials needed to turn her into a young lady. Nicholas had a nanny, didn't you?'

'Yes,' said Nicholas with a wry laugh, 'and I hated her.'

Eleanora woke up and began to cry. Margaret cuddled her. 'Hush, hush,' she crooned, and kissed the top of her head. 'She's teething,' she explained to Clara.

'Someone,' said Clara, looking most disapproving, 'who wouldn't spoil the child. No nonsense, such as being picked up when she cries. Babies should be left to cry; it's good for their lungs. A good nanny', she said, warming to her theme, 'is far better than any mother. She always knows what is best for the child.'

'If nannies always know best, why did you hate yours, Nicholas?' Liana asked. 'And why did you have her?'

Nicholas shrugged. 'I didn't have much say in the matter,' he confessed, wishing Clara Maltravers would be quiet. 'It's always been that way. All the Hamilton-Howards have been raised by nannies.'

'Why?' asked Liana.

'Because, my dear,' said Clara, 'it just isn't the done thing for people of our class to raise their own children.'

'Well, it will be now,' said Liana firmly.

'What?' Clara stared at her.

'The done thing.' Margaret recognized the steely calmness in Liana's voice and felt elated. 'My,' she corrected herself, 'our child is not going to be raised by some stranger who will never pick her up when she cries. She is going to be with people who know and love her, and she'll be picked up whenever it is necessary.'

'But you can't,' Clara protested. 'What will people say?'

'I can and I will; and what is more I am quite capable of bringing up my daughter to be a lady and furthermore I could not care in the least what people might say.'

'Nicholas, you must say something,' Clara appealed to him.

'Whatever Liana wants, I want,' said Nicholas, smiling at Liana's determined expression, glad that she did not want a nanny.

195

'And so do I,' echoed Lady Margaret.

And so it was settled. There would be no nanny. Eleanora was to be brought up within the family circle without outside interference.

'Really! That whole family is dominated by the new young countess,' grumbled Clara to friends later. 'They'll rue the time, one of these days, that they ever admitted her to that family. Mark my words!'

*

Inspired by Liana's achievements, Nicholas, too, began to take a much more active interest in the management of the estate. Always keen on things mechanical, he took over the management of the rapidly growing business of hiring out farm machinery and also the day-to-day supervision of Elver Forge Industries. Of all the new ventures, the log-burning stoves had proved to be the biggest single money spinner, and Nicholas decided to try and get William involved. This was for everyone's benefit as well as William's.

Margaret had kept her promise to Donald, and they had discussed William's unpredictable and sometimes violent temper with Nicholas, although she refused to even utter the words 'mental illness'. Difficult, depressed, moody – William, she agreed, was all of those things, but not ill.

It was difficult for Donald. As the family doctor and family friend, he tried to put his point of view as forcibly as possible without causing offence. 'But it's hopeless,' he confessed to Dorothy later. 'They're a couple of ostriches burying their heads in the sand when it comes to William.'

Nicholas had agreed with his mother. 'I know William is difficult and can even be very unpleasant. But we've got to give him a chance. He's had a terrible war – losing a limb, all the pain he's suffered . . .' Nicholas sighed, and continued thoughtfully, 'I suppose he must be full of self-doubt, too, about his ability to function as a man. It's enough to change anyone.'

'But can't you see?' Donald persisted. 'William hasn't *changed*. He's just got worse. He's ill, just as your father was ill.' It was a mistake to say it. As soon as he had uttered the words Donald knew it.

Both Nicholas's and Margaret's mouths tightened. He could almost see them visibly drawing together, closing ranks, shutting out the truth, reinforcing the ingrained pride which made discussing the possibility of William's being ill an act of treachery. The long history of the Hamilton-

Howards was littered with bitter pride. Nothing had changed over the years. Margaret and Nicholas were the same as their ancestors. True they worried, but the same obstinate irrationality persisted when it came to actually taking some positive action. There were some things they would not countenance discussing with anyone. Wearily Donald realized that he was fighting a losing battle and gave up.

However, in spite of defending his brother to Donald Ramsay, Nicholas had quickly sensed the hostility between William and Liana on his return to Broadacres. Although Liana had never mentioned it, it bothered him. He wanted no ill-feeling between them but could understand how Liana must be thinking. She worked as many hours as was humanly possible, whereas William did nothing except sit alone and brood over the unfairness of life. Maybe William's state of mind would improve if he were occupied, and it would certainly increase the family harmony.

'I need a hand at the Elver Forge today. I wondered if you could help me?' Unable to think of a more tactful way of approaching William regarding work, Nicholas decided to plunge straight to the point. He was very careful, however, to phrase it as an invitation rather than an order.

'Why?'

'I told you. I need a hand and there's no-one else I can ask.'

'I'm not cut out for physical work.' William was dismissive of the friendly overture. 'I'm a cripple or has that fact escaped your notice?'

A cripple in more ways than one, thought Nicholas angrily, noting the half-empty whisky bottle at William's elbow. 'It's not physical work I have in mind,' he said equably, keeping his temper with difficulty. No wonder there was an atmosphere between William and Liana. His brother was antagonistic to everything and everyone. For a moment, a brief moment, he considered again Donald Ramsay's words, *seek further medical advice*, but then almost immediately rejected them. What could doctors do? What did they know? No well-meaning stranger could change William's unpleasant character. He was their problem, a problem only the family could cope with. 'It's supervising the men moving some of the cutting machinery into another shed,' he finished.

'Sorry, not interested,' answered William sullenly, flipping through the pages of his book.

'Only interested in this, I suppose!' Exasperated, Nicholas picked up the whisky bottle.

William snatched it back. 'None of your fucking business. I bought this from my own allowance, not from your precious money.'

'And who will pay for the next bottle? Us, I suppose. Liana has shown me the bills the estate pays on your behalf. You never live within your allowance.'

'And for a bloody good reason. Your sodding wife set the allowance too fucking low. It's not enough.'

'Liana said it's what the bank manager recommended as reasonable.'

'Liana said, Liana said,' mimicked William. 'You sound like a bloody parrot. Why don't *you* take charge of the estate and finances, big brother? Then you can ask me to help you.'

Nicholas clenched his fists in anger. William's sneering tone was hard to take, especially when he was speaking of Liana. But he managed to keep his voice calm and quiet. 'You know perfectly well that we run the estate as a team,' he said. 'All of us are involved. Even mother helps and has her own responsibilities. But Liana has the financial flair, something the rest of us lack.'

'So *you* say.' William poured himself another whisky. He raised his glass. 'Fuck off, big brother. I don't need you or your wop of a wife telling me what to do. And I certainly have no intention of working for you.' Involuntarily Nicholas stepped towards him. 'Go on, hit me,' William jeered. 'Hit your poor crippled brother!'

Not trusting himself to speak, Nicholas turned and walked from the room. William could drown in whisky. The sooner the better.

*

Eleanora grew from a small helpless baby into an attractive, dark-haired little girl. As she grew older, where Liana always saw Raul – for a likeness to Raul it most certainly was – Nicholas and Lady Margaret exclaimed over likenesses to distant relatives. They both worshipped Eleanora, and she adored them, basking in their love and returning it in overflowing measure. An open, happy, uncomplicated relationship flourished between the three of them. William ignored the child's existence, but as he was uninterested in everything except his own secretive world, no-one worried. By tacit agreement, although for entirely different reasons, William's presence was almost ignored by the three of them, although the monthly presentation of extravagant bills still continued to irritate Liana.

Her own relationship with the growing Eleanora, however, was different. It was not lack of love which prevented Liana from being as demonstrative as Nicholas or Lady Margaret, rather an excess of it. The powerful emotions which surged through her whenever she even looked at Eleanora were so awesome they frightened her. But alongside love was always fear, the fear of giving herself away. Because Raul shared the space occupied in her heart by Eleanora, Eleanora made her cautious. So she held her emotions in check, always afraid to lower her guard, afraid to show too much love.

Nicholas noticed the restraint and it puzzled and saddened him. Could it be that Liana did not love their daughter as much as he? Sometimes, when she was unaware that he was watching, he would catch a strange mixture of emotions on her face – love and a deep sadness as if she were mourning something. Once he did attempt to find the reason. She had been particularly quiet and withdrawn one day, and he felt he had to confront her, try somehow to coax her worries out into the open.

'What is it, Liana?' he asked gently, not wanting to hurt or frighten her into withdrawing even more.

Immediately her dark eyes grew wary. 'What is what?'

'This unhappiness. Sometimes you are unhappy. Don't deny it, because I know you are. Can't you tell me?'

But Liana was not to be drawn into lowering her guard. She scoffed 'Unhappy? Me? What nonsense you do talk, Nicholas. I'm the happiest woman in the world. And why shouldn't I be?' Smiling broadly she slipped her hand in his. 'Silly man,' she added affectionately.

But Nicholas noticed the smile on her lips did not reach her eyes and he persevered. 'I don't know why. That's why I asked. Can't you tell me?'

'There's nothing to tell,' Liana interrupted quickly, laughing and kissing him at the same time. 'Oh, Nicholas, you have too much imagination.'

'You're sure? There is nothing?'

'Absolutely positive.' Liana was very firm.

The subject was closed, and Nicholas was left knowing that he still had not the faintest idea of what Liana was really thinking. Behind her beautiful dark eyes, her soul lay barred and shuttered to all but herself. Apart from William, it was the only cloud on Nicholas's otherwise perfect life. But he continued to worry because, small girl though she was, Nicholas was sure that Eleanora sensed her mother's restraint when they were together.

'Liana's too intense, that's all it is,' said his mother defensively when he had mentioned his misgivings to her. 'How can you doubt her love for

Eleanora? Look how determined she was not to have a nanny. She wanted to bring her up herself.'

'Yes, I know. I'm not saying she doesn't love her. I know she does. But there is some sort of barrier between them. I know it when I look at her face. I'm sure of it.'

'Don't waste time worrying about it,' advised his mother. 'Liana will be all right in time. She's had a lot of adjusting to do. I think she needs another child to make her feel more secure.'

In spite of himself Nicholas grinned at his mother's very feminine logic. Another child: the panacea to a young woman's problems! 'We'll have another child when Liana conceives, not before,' he said, shrugging his shoulders philosophically, unwilling to admit to his mother that he was also worrying about that. A confused mixture of emotions churned within him whenever he thought about more children, half of him desperately wanting more, preferably a son, and the other half telling himself to be sensible and to be content with the lovely daughter he already had. 'Anyway,' he added, 'Liana has no reason to feel insecure.'

'You don't know much about Liana's life before you met her, do you?' Margaret was not a very worldly woman, but her deep love for Liana provided an almost spiritual insight into the complex character of her daughter-in-law. She, too, was sure that the girl was troubled in some way and only wished she could help.

'I know what she has told me.'

'Exactly. But what *hasn't* she told you? That girl has suffered far more than you or I could probably even begin to imagine. I know suffering when I see it and I can often see it in Liana's face. Oh, I'll admit she keeps it very well hidden, but it is there none the less.'

'You may be right.' Nicholas was reluctant to admit that he sometimes came to the same conclusion; but he was sure it had nothing to do with Eleanora, so why should she reject her? 'But even so I still don't understand why, so often, Liana keeps her own daughter at arm's length, it doesn't make sense. Sometimes I think she is afraid to touch her. Perhaps I should talk to her again. Perhaps I should ask . . .'

'Never,' snapped Margaret emphatically, her voice surprisingly harsh. 'Some things are best left unsaid. You of all people should know that.' Then she smiled, taking the edge off her sharp words. 'Give her another child, my dear, and let her come to terms with her own private grief when the time is right.'

Nicholas sighed. Give her another child. That was proving easier said than done, for Liana showed no signs of conceiving. And although he never ceased to thank God for Eleanora, he knew deep in his heart that more than anything he longed for a son.

Donald Ramsay was confident now that any future children would be as healthy and happy as Eleanora. 'You are a good combination,' he said, 'you and Liana. You've only got to look at Eleanora to see that.'

Nicholas agreed but as much as he loved Eleanora the yearning for a son grew greater, a son to carry on the name, a son to inherit Broadacres, a brother for Eleanora. 'I'll do my best,' he said now to his mother, 'but founding a dynasty isn't as easy as you make it sound!' Then he added with a smile, 'You like Liana a lot, don't you?'

He was glad of that. His mother now had two more people to love, and was loved by them in return. In middle age she had found a new lease of life and was blossoming before his very eyes. Untidy and as scatterbrained as ever, she had lost her permanently worried expression. Her angular face was softened now by love.

'Like!' she snorted. 'You men are such unimaginative creatures. Like is an understatement. I love her. I love Liana for all sorts of reasons and not least because she has changed my life.' She wagged her finger at Nicholas. *'And* I'm looking forward to my next grandchild.' She did not need Donald Ramsay to convince her that any future children of Nicholas's and Liana's would be as perfect as Eleanora; she had already made up her own mind on that score. They would all be lovely, there was no doubt about that.

But there was no sign of another child in spite of their passionate love-making. Nicholas wondered if Liana thought it strange, but it seemed not, for she never mentioned it nor seemed the slightest bit perturbed. In the end Nicholas broached the subject himself, for although he continually told himself that he should be content and that his life was perfect, the longing for another child, a son, was becoming something of an obsession. One evening he could hold his tongue no longer. He waited until they were in bed and Liana was warm and relaxed in his arms.

'I wonder when we'll have another baby,' he said casually. There was no answer, but he immediately felt her go tense, an almost imperceptible movement but just enough for him to notice.

'When nature decides it is the right time, I suppose,' she said, after a long pause.

'You do want more children, don't you?'

'Darling, of course I do.' The unexpectedness of his first question had thrown Liana off balance for a moment but now she was in full command of her senses again. Nicholas was never to know it was the very last thing on earth that she wanted. Not now, not ever. One child was enough, Raul's child. Oh, Raul, Raul. Her heart ached with pain when she thought of him, a pain as fresh and raw as it had been on the day he had disappeared.

A coldly detached portion of her mind knew she must divert Nicholas's thoughts away from the desire for more children and yet at the same time reassure him. Another deception. But by now Liana was adept at suppressing the pinpricks of her conscience. She bent her head, kissing him on the lips then, moving down his body, kissed her way to his penis. As soon as he was hard enough, Liana lowered the softness of her body to enclose the rigid shaft. 'Maybe we'll be lucky this time,' she whispered as Nicholas rose to meet her. He lifted her up and turned so that she was beneath him. Her words passed unheeded. Nicholas was now beyond thinking of another child. He was only conscious of his own rising need to take Liana and make her part of himself.

The ploy had worked. Nicholas had forgotten. Liana smiled in the darkness. There was no need for her to worry: there would not be another child. Confident of the powerful allure of her body, she was sure she could always use it to distract Nicholas whenever necessary.

But for once Liana was wrong. Nicholas had not forgotten, on that night or any other, although he was lulled into believing that she, too, wanted another child. But later, when still no prospect of another baby seemed any nearer to materializing, Nicholas went to Donald Ramsay.

'She's probably working too hard. Stress can sometimes cause a form of infertility,' said Donald, not in the least bit worried. 'Be sensible; there's no rush. She's very young. Give it time, and for God's sake don't mention your concern to her.'

'I've already mentioned it,' admitted Nicholas, 'but she laughed at me. She said it would happen when nature decided.'

'In that respect she's quite right,' agreed Donald, slightly put out that Nicholas had, in his opinion, rushed his fences. 'You can help by trying to persuade her to ease up a little on the work she does but please, Nicholas, do be sensible and learn to be patient yourself.'

Donald Ramsay was too wise to voice his own thoughts on Liana. In his opinion Nicholas needed time to understand the complex woman he had married. Everyone thought Liana an exceptional young woman, and she was. But, unlike others, Donald and his wife Dorothy were not entirely fooled by the steely image she projected. The steeliness of resolve did exist, there was no doubt of that, but it was finely sprung and stretched taut. Donald knew he would be wasting his breath if he tried to explain that to Nicholas now, so he held his tongue.

'One wrong move, and she'll snap like a violin string,' Dorothy had observed to her husband. 'God alone knows what could happen then. Liana needs time to herself, time to reinforce her emotional defences against whatever it was that tore them down in the first place. Something dreadful must have happened to her in the war.'

Donald agreed. It was on the night of Eleanora's birth that he became sure that Liana would never open up her mind and heart, not to him, nor to anyone else. Even in the midst of all her pain she had clung on to whatever it was that tormented her, clasping it to herself tight, and hidden it with a desperate tenaciousness. And Donald's psychology was that if she could not open up and release the pain, there was only one alternative for her, at least for the time being. She needed to build a wall around the emotions she was too afraid to share, a wall so high and so secure that eventually she would be able to relax. One day in the future, for her own sake, Donald fervently hoped that she would be able to unburden herself because only then would an inner peace come to her. But that day was a long, long way off. He knew how much Nicholas adored his wife but sometimes Donald wondered if loving was enough.

While Nicholas was worrying about Liana's inability to conceive, the truth was that long before he had returned to Broadacres Liana had made a decision. There would be no more children. The silent vow she had made on their wedding day to give him a son was forgotten, swept away on a tide of illogical obsession and renewed passion once Eleanora arrived. Her reasoning was simplicity itself. The arrival of Raul's child filled her heart, mind and soul with even more poignant memories of Raul. Even the pain of his loss, and the ever-present ache of knowing she was deceiving Nicholas every minute, every hour of every day could not dull the closeness she felt to Raul every time she looked at Eleanora. She had no need of more children. Raul's child was gift enough. Eleanora filled her heart by keeping Raul alive in a very special way. There was the terrible fear that children from Nicholas would push Raul out of focus, usurp him from the central hidden core of her life where he existed in a fantasy world, the very essence of life to her, not dead at all. Liana was not prepared to risk losing such precious memories so she hardened her heart and deliberately denied Nicholas the son he longed for.

Next to keeping Raul alive in her heart came her almost equally passionate love for Broadacres, and initially she was anxious about its fate. She knew that if Nicholas should die before William, then William would automatically become the next earl. Should that happen she had no doubt that William would lose no time in ejecting her and Eleanora. She could imagine his malicious glee at such a prospect. From Margaret she learned that if Nicholas did not produce an heir in the form of a son, the next male member of the family would inherit the earldom, and if William were not alive the title would go to Peter, the son of Nicholas's sister who lived in New Zealand.

But it was not the inheritance of the title that worried Liana, it was who would have Broadacres. She wanted it for herself and she wanted Eleanora to have it after her. Divine Providence having placed Broadacres and its lands in her lap, she had no intention of losing it. So she waited, picking the moment very carefully, and casually mentioned her fears to Nicholas not long after he had returned to Broadacres.

'Darling, what would happen to Eleanora and me if you should die?'

Nicholas had laughed at first. 'I've just survived a war, darling. I've no intention of dying now!'

But Liana persisted, she had to make him look at it seriously. 'Accidents can happen,' she said solemnly, 'and I know William would be the next earl if you should die, and I also know he doesn't like me. He wouldn't want me here at Broadacres. I'd have to leave.'

'Rubbish,' Nicholas would not listen at first. 'Of course he wouldn't throw his own sister-in-law out.'

'He would, Nicholas, and you know it. In fact, if he were in one of his black moods, he'd probably throw your mother out as well.'

Nicholas thought long and hard and reluctantly faced the fact that Liana was probably right. He thought of William and his black, unpredictable moods, his unreasonable hatred for anything or anyone he took a dislike to; he thought of his mother, and of Liana and baby Eleanora, and realized that it was not something he could leave to chance, hoping that a son and heir would come along quickly. He had to do something now. He made up his mind on a course of action, and in so doing quite unwittingly sealed his own fate where any future children were concerned.

'There is no need for you to worry,' he told Liana. 'William will never be able to force you to leave Broadacres because I shall make a will leaving the house and estate jointly to you and my mother, and then on your deaths it will go to Eleanora or my eldest son if by then we have a son. If I should die before William, he would, of course, still inherit the title Earl of Wessex, but that is all, because although the law decrees that the title must pass on to the nearest male relative, that relative need not of necessity inherit the estate.'

'You're sure?' Liana had already copiously studied papers in the library which indeed had told her that the estate was not entailed in the way many lands of the aristocracy were. She thought she knew, but she was not quite certain what that meant.

Of course I'm sure, darling. Broadacres and its lands are not entailed, thank God. So that means I am free to leave it to whomsoever I choose. And I am going to make arrangements to leave it to you.'

'William won't like that.'

Nicholas smiled wryly. 'No, he won't, and therefore we won't tell him. There's no need to create extra unpleasantness. Apart from the family solicitor, who can be relied upon for complete confidentiality, only you and my mother need know.'

And so it was done. Margaret was relieved when she knew of Nicholas's decision and thought it a prudent move, although as she said, 'I'm quite certain you will live to a ripe old age, my dear, and produce a whole clutch of sons.' But she agreed with Liana, accidents could happen and it was better to be prepared.

Mr Paris, senior partner of Paris, Paris and Blundell, a firm of solicitors established in Winchester for over one hundred and fifty years, approved of Nicholas's plan. He knew William and heartily disliked him, and thought it sensible that the present earl should make provision for his wife and daughter and also for Lady Margaret. Old Mr Paris knew something of the unhappy life Lady Margaret had lived with the former earl and had a great affection and admiration for the gentle, dignified way she had coped with it. It was good that Nicholas was looking after her; he doubted that William would. The will was duly drawn up, signed and witnessed and locked away in the cavernous vaults of Paris, Paris and Blundell.

Once that was done Liana relaxed. She was safe and so was Broadacres. There was no need to produce a son and heir, no need at all. She could concentrate now on restoring Broadacres to its former glory, close her heart around Raul, her secret love, and forget about babies.

Not once did it occur to her that she was being selfish or that she was denying Nicholas, who had given her everything, the greatest gift she could give him. Nor did it occur to her that it was quite irrational, perpetuating the myth of a man long dead to her and the world. Rationality did not enter into it where Raul was concerned. Liana could not accept that Raul was not real whereas Nicholas was. And if sometimes she did see it, then her eyes were quickly averted. She preferred blindness to sight. Blindness was exquisite, it gave her an illicit joy. It meant Raul lived on in her heart and now could stay there for ever. The obsessive, passionate love generated so long ago in the three short weeks she had had as Raul's lover was as intoxicating to her now as ever and Liana determined she would never let it go.

The plans she had made to prevent conception, long before Nicholas had returned to England, could continue uninterrupted. Some months after Eleanora's birth, Liana had gone to London. Knowing that Donald Ramsay would not approve, and, of course, unable to tell him her reasons, she had gone to a private birth control clinic in London. It had not been easy finding out where to go but as usual she had persisted and once she had found the right place she made her visit in secret one day, when ostensibly she was visiting London to look at new clothes. There she had been fitted with a dutch cap which was then carefully hidden away in her own private bathroom at Broadacres. Once Nicholas returned Liana used it punctiliously with clinical detachment. So while Nicholas was praying and trying to wait patiently for Liana to conceive, Liana was carefully ensuring that conception was impossible. In the beginning she did have the grace to feel a little guilty about yet another deception but after a while it became automatic. And once the future of Broadacres was secured, she saw no reason to think of it at all. Apart from a secret six-monthly trip to the clinic for a refitting, she put the matter from her mind. There were so many other things to think of concerning Broadacres, and in the beginning Nicholas appeared content. There was no time to waste pondering on the rightness of her decision. She had made it and that was that.

*

Nicholas watched Liana growing in intellectual stature as each day passed. Her ability to assimilate facts and then to act on them unerringly and instinctively never ceased to amaze him.

Socially, not only was she accepted but fêted wherever they went. She made it her business to gradually nudge the Hamilton-Howards into the forefront of society. With the inbuilt self-confidence of a family who could trace their history back over four hundred years, they had never bothered much about mixing. They lived secluded lives, doing as they pleased without regard for the consequences. Earning money had always been considered a pastime necessary only for the middle and working classes, not the aristocracy. Before the advent of Liana, apart from selling the occasional picture or some valuable piece of porcelain, Nicholas had never considered dedicating any time to actually generating an income. In pre-war days it just was not the done thing and anyway, like his mother, he much preferred the company of dogs and horses to that of people. He considered a day's hunting, up to his ears in mud in the company of local farmers, much more enjoyable than doing the social rounds. But Liana had opened his eyes and made him see that meeting people was an essential part of their life. Their forays into high society were only undertaken if Liana thought someone worth cultivating would be present. Their socializing was mainly with businessmen and politicians, anyone with the potential of being useful to Broadacres in a present or future enterprise. Liana was the driving force behind all such activities, persuading, cajoling, bullying when necessary, and Nicholas usually a willing follower.

'Darling, I know that you'd planned to go riding. But this is important.' Nicholas recognized the steel-like thread running through Liana's deceptively gentle voice. Inevitably it meant that she would get her way. 'And it isn't as if it's the hunting season now,' she continued, demolishing an argument before he had time to present it. 'It's summer.'

Nicholas made a token protest. 'The Hampshire Hunt rides to hounds all year round.'

'You can miss the meet this once.'

Nicholas gave in, as Liana had known he would. 'All right, tell me the worst. What have you got lined up for me? I'll do anything, as long as it's not opening the Longford Village Fête again.'

Liana laughed, remembering the valiant efforts of Nicholas the year before coping with a thunderstorm, a leaking marquee roof and a microphone which did not work. 'Nothing as awful as that, and much more important: a visit to South Wales.'

'Wales! Whatever for?'

'For the opening of an extension to a steelworks. All the top men in the steel industry plus some important politicians will be there.'

'*Socialist* politicians,' grumbled Nicholas. Like most of his contemporaries he was finding it difficult to come to terms with being governed by the Socialists.

Liana was realistic and didn't care which political party was in power as long as they didn't interfere too much with her plans.

'Darling, this is nineteen forty-seven. The Socialists will be in power at least until nineteen fifty and then will probably go on to win the next election if the newspapers are correct. I think it is about time you accepted that fact. Anyway, Socialists, Conservatives or whatever, it's unimportant. The only people who matter are the ones with power. At the moment, the Socialists have it. It is only a matter of time before steel is nationalized, and it's vital that we get in now and make good contacts with management and politicians. Because if we are to succeed with our plans for expanding Elver Forge Industries, we shall need a reliable supply of steel at a good price. So darling, I have graciously accepted on your behalf to open the extension to the Maeglas Steelworks.'

'Oh, God!' Nicholas groaned. 'You know how I hate occasions like that – all pomp and ceremony; everyone fawning around me because I'm an earl.'

'Nasty, but necessary,' said Liana firmly, linking her arms around his neck and kissing him.

'Slave driver!'

'Darling, it's for Broadacres.'

'I know, I was only teasing.' He kissed her back. 'You've done wonders for Broadacres. I don't know how we ever managed without you.'

'Not very well,' Liana reminded him dryly. 'That's why we'll put up with whoever we have to be nice to in Wales. But', she added pulling a face, 'we don't have to like them.'

'God! I never dreamed you were so practical when I married you,' said Nicholas grinning. 'If I had known, I would have asked you sooner.'

Liana hugged him. 'I'll try to make sure our day in Wales isn't too boring.'

'Darling, nothing is ever boring with you.'

Nicholas spoke the truth. Even going to functions he hated, being fawned upon and flattered by hordes of avid social climbers was not so bad if Liana was there. She had a knack of deflecting the worst bores and, although she conformed, Nicholas knew Liana regarded the so-called social niceties with disparaging disdain. Like his mother and himself, she had a healthy disregard for all forms of pretentious nonsense. Her philosophy was simple: if it would help swell the coffers of Broadacres, then it would be done. But the flattery never went to her head and afterwards they would laugh about it. It formed a bond between them, a secret joke.

Clever, hard-working, impatient to be rich, Liana steamed ahead. A juggernaut at full power, Nicholas often thought, albeit an elegant one. When the Hamilton-Howards sallied forth into the world of high society there were no snide remarks now from Clara Maltravers and her cronies, nor anyone else, concerning the business assets of the Hamilton-Howards. Most of them were green with envy.

*

'I can't think how you manage so well.' Clara Maltravers sighed heavily. 'Even my sheep are a disaster this year. The foot rot has cost me a fortune.' She took another scone and piled it high with cream. 'A fortune,' she repeated piteously.

'If you won't pay out for a decent land manager and good shepherds, what else can you expect.' Liana, joining the family in the Grey Room for afternoon tea was annoyed to find an uninvited Clara Maltravers there. She did not like her, thinking Clara affected and snobbish. 'Those sheep of yours should have been moved out before the meadows were flooded, then they wouldn't have got foot rot.'

'And how long have you been an expert on English sheep rearing?' enquired Mrs Maltravers, her plummy voice ominously sweet.

'I'm not. I only know what Wally Pragnell tells me. He's the expert around here where farming is concerned.'

'I must agree with Liana there.' Nicholas hastily tried to fill an awkward pause in the conversation. 'We'd be lost without Wally.'

'There you are, then,' said Clara Maltravers in a tone of triumphant vindication. 'I'm not so fortunate. I don't have anyone like Wally Pragnell. It's not easy to find men willing to work on the land.'

'There are plenty of unemployed men about,' Margaret pointed out.

Clara glared at her. How dare she have a point of view! 'I said willing workers,' she snapped, 'not unemployed men.'

'Workers are only willing if they are paid enough,' observed Liana pointedly.

It was like waving a red rag at a bull as far as Clara Maltravers was concerned. 'Paid enough! I pay my workers what they are worth and usually that's not much. The wretched Socialists have ruined everything with welfare-state hand-outs – paying people to be sick and unemployed! The country is going to the dogs; people don't want to work. Before the war, people were glad enough to do anything, no matter how little they earned. Today, half of them don't know what real work is.'

'Do you know what real work is? And have you ever wondered how those people managed before the war, when they were too sick to work?' Liana was incensed. 'Have you ever known what it's like to be short of money?'

'Really, Nicholas, anyone would think your wife was a Socialist herself, to hear her talk.' Clara sniffed, outraged at the mere idea.

Nicholas smiled politely. 'I don't agree with everything the Government is doing but I do agree with its attempts to raise the living standards of the population as a whole.'

'Milking the upper classes to pay for layabouts, you mean,' said Clara. 'Taxing those of us with old money out of existence.'

'Most of those with old money, as you put it,' said Liana icily, 'have never done a day's work in their lives. They'd probably drop down dead if they even attempted it!'

Clara gasped in anger but gave up the unequal argument and left Broadacres thoroughly convinced that Liana must be a rabid Communist! She told Margaret as much just before she left.

'Nonsense.' Margaret robustly defended her daughter-in-law. 'The trouble with you, Clara, is that you are not used to people being outspoken. The fact of the matter is, you've had your own way for far too long.'

Clara gasped again. It was outrageous, even the Dowager Countess of Wessex had radical ideas! But she was not convinced neither would she contemplate change. She and her friends determinedly hung on to the disintegrating shreds of their old life and envied the Hamilton-Howards as they moved successfully into the hitherto scorned fields of business and commerce.

*

The day after Clara Maltravers's visit, William emerged from the solitude of his room and joined Nicholas and Margaret in the Grey Room for pre-prandial drinks.

'You've heard about the Berlin air lift?' William was more animated than either Nicholas or Margaret had seen him since he had been invalided out of the Air Force.

Almost as if on cue, a plane droned overhead, the noise echoing through the open windows, an uncomfortable reminder that Europe was not as peaceful as rural Hampshire. Russia, having annexed half of Europe immediately after the war, had now, in 1948, besieged Berlin, and an air lift of food and other essential items was under way to the American, French and British-held sections of the city. The ugly cold war between East and West had progressed one worrying step further.

'Of course we have,' said Nicholas, slightly surprised at William's sudden interest in world events. 'The newspapers and radio talk about nothing else.'

'They're desperately short of pilots. I'm off to London tomorrow. I'm volunteering to fly a transport plane.'

'Oh, William!' Margaret could hardly believe her ears. This was the first time he had shown a willingness to do anything. 'I'll be so pleased to have you flying again. But,' she hesitated, not wanting to dampen his enthusiasm, 'have you thought how dangerous it might be? The Russians may start shooting down the planes.'

William laughed; he seemed exhilarated by the very idea. 'I know, but someone has to do it. I'm willing to take my chance.'

Margaret rushed over to him and hugged him. 'You make me very proud,' she said.

Liana, entering the room after settling Eleanora for the night, was just in time to witness this unusual event.

'William is volunteering as a pilot for the Berlin air lift,' explained Nicholas to the mystified Liana.

Liana was surprised but admired his courage. 'It will be dangerous. It's a brave thing to do,' she said.

'I can't wait to get up into the air again. Damn the danger. This is the chance I've been waiting for.'

William left Broadacres by the milk train from Winchester the next morning. Margaret and Nicholas were pleased, and Margaret prayed that it meant William was coming out of his depression. Flying would do him good.

Broadacres was a happier place without William's brooding melancholy, and everyone, including the estate workers, felt their mood lighten although no-one actually said anything, not in so many words: inbuilt English reserve prevented them from giving voice to such sentiments.

All apart from Mary Pragnell who spoke her mind as usual. 'Damn good riddance to he,' she pronounced loudly in the privacy of her kitchen. 'I hopes the Russians keep him.'

'Master William is not so bad.' Wally was more tolerant than his wife.

She snorted derisively. 'I has my own thoughts on *that*!'

Liana wondered but had no idea what Nicholas and Margaret really thought about William. Their thoughts were their own private domain and she would not have dreamed of asking. Personal privacy was an English characteristic which met with her thorough approval. Still plagued with her own guilty thoughts, it was a relief never to be pestered by curious questions concerning her past. She appreciated the privacy. All the same, she was curious about William and often wondered what it was about him that put both Nicholas and his mother on the defensive, always making excuses for him no matter how difficult he was. Sometimes she caught a glance of something that passed between them but could never put a name to it. Was it apprehension? Fear? She could never be sure.

But there was no mistaking their dismay when they heard that William had been rejected by the authorities for flying duties. The dismay was unanimous. The whole estate fell into gloom.

'He'll be very difficult when he returns,' said Margaret unhappily.

A superfluous statement if ever there was one, thought Liana. Everybody on the estate, from the newest herdsman to Wally Pragnell, knew it; Liana knew it; Nicholas knew it. William would be more than difficult.

I wonder *how* difficult, worried Nicholas; but he did not discuss it with Liana. How could he? How could he even begin to discuss something he had not succeeded in finding the courage to face himself? Nicholas did not understand William or the dark corner of the world he inhabited and he did not want to. Whenever he thought of William, guilt slapped him in the face. The pain was almost physical. It was wrong to wish someone dead, wrong to wish that William had been killed when his plane had been shot down. But Nicholas did wish it. It was against God's law, against his own instinct, but still he wished it. Life would have been much simpler if William had been killed.

He was sure his mother felt the same, and sharing their guilty thoughts might have eased the burden but she rarely ventured any opinion on William, never even talked about him unless it could not be avoided. But words were unnecessary – the expression on her face told Nicholas all he needed to know, and he often wanted to weep. She blamed herself for William's behaviour. Nicholas longed to comfort his mother, throw his arms around her and say it's not your fault, not your failure, but he could not. The undemonstrative habits of a lifetime were too ingrained in both of them. Unused to revealing their innermost thoughts, they were helpless. Neither knew how to unlock the gate to the truth.

William returned to Broadacres and, as expected, was moody, hostile, belligerent and more unpredictable than ever. Most worrying of all were the bills which suddenly started flooding into Liana's office. For Liana, the final straw came when four arrived on one day.

She took the accounts with her into dinner that evening. Hating what she was about to do – disrupt the peace of their evening meal – but determined to confront William in front of Nicholas and Margaret, she spread out the four pieces of paper on the table before her.

'Four unpaid bills,' she said, 'for clothes, food, wine and a walking stick.'

'Pay them,' said William, a sneering challenge in his voice. 'There's not much point in bringing them here, into dinner. Unless, of course, you intend transferring your office to the dining room.'

'Totalling nearly one thousand pounds,' said Liana, ignoring William's interruption. 'The estate has already paid out one hundred and seventy pounds this month on another bill from Fortnum & Mason.'

'That was when William was up in London being interviewed,' said Margaret hastily, her gaunt face taking on a pallid hue. Oh dear, it wasn't wise of Liana to oppose William like this.

'All right. But these four latest bills are all since he has been living at Broadacres.' Liana turned back to William. 'You eat and drink here. Why do you need to buy extras such as quails' eggs and champagne?'

'Because there are never any bloody quails' eggs on the menu. Only Meg's good old country cooking. And I happen to *like* quails' eggs and champagne. Do you object?'

'At these prices, yes,' said Liana. 'We are trying to put money aside to renovate the house. How can we do that if you fritter it all away?'

Nicholas reached across and picked up the bills, hoping to defuse the atmosphere. 'The champagne bill is a bit steep, old man,' he said after a moment's pause. 'Try and keep the drinking down a bit.' Liana fumed.

Why didn't he support her? Then he looked at another bill. 'Three hundred quid for a walking stick! I say, now that *is* a bit much.'

'It's a very special walking stick.'

'So it ought to be at that price. What is it? Solid silver?'

'It has a silver knob on top, monogrammed, of course.'

'Couldn't you have got a cheaper one, dear? A wooden one?' suggested Margaret but her voice tailed away as William turned on her.

'I didn't *want* a cheaper one. I wanted the one I bought.' His eyes flashed venom, and Margaret hastily looked down at her plate, crumbling her bread roll between nervous fingers as if her life depended on it.

Nicholas gathered up the bills and stuffed them in his pocket. 'Of course, the estate will honour them,' he said, 'but next month, William, please try and keep inside your allowance.'

'I'll try. But I'm not guaranteeing anything,' said William sullenly.

Liana was furious. God, how I loathe him, she thought. He's doing it on purpose. He has no intention of staying within his allowance. He doesn't care about anything or anybody. Why can't they see it? William was capable of wrecking all her carefully laid plans for the future of Broadacres. She looked at Nicholas and Margaret. You might be willing to put up with him, she thought, but I am not. He *has* to go.

*

Aware of Liana leaving their warm bed, Nicholas struggled to consciousness. Smiling sleepily he slid over to her side, revelling in the warmth and lingering perfume of her body. 'A creature of habit, darling,' he said. 'That's what you are.'

She laughed soundlessly. 'I know.'

It was true. Liana's early morning routine never varied. Before going down to the nursery to give Eleanora her good-morning kiss, she always walked across to the window and looked out – a still moment in the busyness of her life when she drank in the beauty of the scene, imprinting it for the rest of the day on her mind.

Leaning on the window sill, today Liana's eye was drawn to the misty outline of the copper beechwood on the distant skyline. Why hadn't she thought of it before? The answer to the problem of William was staring her in the face. The new Woodland Unit. Of course, it was the perfect solution. William could be put in sole charge. No chance then of his complaining of being ordered about by others; he could make the decisions and give the orders.

She did not allow herself to think of what might happen if he made the wrong decisions; time enough to consider that when it happened. Inarguably it was the consummate solution. The office was a converted cottage on the edge of the beech forest. With his headquarters there, it would ensure he was out of the house all day, an immediate advantage in itself. And she would make certain there was no liquor available. A secret smile curved her full lips as she weighed and counter-weighed the various hypotheses.

Of course, there was always the possibility that William might be very good, enjoy it and work well; in which case the problem of finding a suitable manager and keeping William out of trouble would be solved. Or he might try but not be good, which would pose a fresh dilemma, one which would need to be handled very delicately. Alternatively he might hate it so much that he would leave Broadacres of his own accord. Then no-one would be to blame, for he would have made the decision himself. As far as Liana was concerned, that would indeed be the perfect solution and the one she was gambling on. William in his present frame of mind was unlikely to make a success of anything. But, of course, Nicholas and Lady Margaret need never know what was in her mind; to all intents and purposes she would be extending an olive branch and trying to help poor William.

However, Liana knew it was essential that it should be Nicholas who approached William. If he ever suspected it was her idea, William would dismiss the whole thing without a moment's consideration. Yes, Nicholas must persuade him. He could take him over to the office in the cottage today.

Having made the decision, Liana immediately put all thoughts of William out of her mind. Even William, disruptive as he was, could not be allowed to mar the final moments of her morning pleasure: watching the early morning sun edging its way across dew-sparkling grass. How beautiful Broadacres was.

Nicholas lay and watched her. Why is she still an enigma to me, he wondered. Will I ever understand what goes on behind that beautiful face? And what was the nameless spectre which always slid into his consciousness whenever he tried to analyse Liana? In spite of her extraordinary beauty the uneasiness he felt was not the fear of losing her to another man. That did not worry him at all. Other men could lust after Liana but she was not in the slightest bit interested.

Not that she was unaware of her sensuality and the effect it had on men; quite the contrary, she knew, and exploited it. Nicholas had watched with amusement as she had used it with devastating effect on men when driving home a business deal. Enchanted and bewitched by her dark smiling eyes which could be sensual, beguiling, innocent or vulnerable, whatever she chose, and unused to dealing with a woman in the essentially male-dominated world of business, they would agree to all her demands, usually to find later in the cold light of day that they had made quite outrageous concessions the like of which they would never have contemplated in normal circumstances. But then it was generally agreed dealing with the Countess of Wessex hardly came under the heading of normal circumstances.

'Your wife is like a beautiful butterfly,' one man told Nicholas. 'She flutters before you, so fragile and delicate. It is only later that one finds the wings you thought were merely brushing against you are made of sprung steel and she has wrapped them around so tightly that there is no escape!'

'A good description,' agreed Nicholas.

'How the hell do you control a woman like that?'

Nicholas was honest 'I don't, and I'd be a fool to try. I love her just the way she is. Even if I don't always understand her.'

'And you're happy?' The man was curious.

'Yes.'

But that was not quite the truth. Nicholas was happy, but the nameless spectre was ever-present. And clouding an otherwise perfect relationship was the painful knowledge that she never gave him her whole self. Part of her spirit was firmly anchored elsewhere; but Nicholas had no way of knowing where or why.

Liana stopped daydreaming and ruthlessly switched her mind back to the present. Swinging round to face Nicholas she said, 'About the new Woodland Unit.'

Nicholas caught his breath in a silent sigh of exasperation. Liana and work! Sometimes he fancied she was like a robot, parcelling her life up into watertight compartments: time to look at the view; time to kiss Eleanora; time for business which was always the major part of her life; and today it seemed her mind was clicking into business gear even earlier than usual.

'What about it?'

'We need to get it going. With the Government's building programme well under way, we need to start making furniture now, in order to get our foot on the ladder first. Once we've established a secure home market, it will give us a base from which we can export to Europe. And I've had a good idea. William can run it. It will give him something to do, give him a purpose in life, occupy his mind and give him less time to waste money.'

'For heaven's sake, Liana. Can't you think of anything besides money!'

Liana bit her lip, annoyed at herself for not gauging Nicholas's mood more accurately. I mustn't rush him, she thought, because he has got to persuade William for me.

'But, darling. I was only thinking of William. How to make his life better.' She slid back into bed beside him and ran her hands slowly across his flat stomach. 'Don't be cross with me,' she whispered, brushing her lips against his chest.

'Don't try and seduce me. You won't get round me like that.'

'Oh, Nicholas! How can a wife seduce her own husband?'

'You can, and you damn well know it.'

Nicholas drew her into his arms. He'd think about William later. Much later.

Chapter Seventeen

'Christ, William, you can't live for ever on the backs of other people.'

This was not going to be easy. William had agreed to walk with him to the Woodland Unit office and talk over the proposal. Although walk was hardly the correct word – prowl would be a better description, thought Nicholas. William made him edgy.

'Why not?' William's voice was flat, uninterested.

'You know damn well why not. It's not fair. We all work and pull our weight. Mother does, I do, and Liana . . .'

'Screw Liana.'

'Don't be so bloody crude.'

'Why not? Screw, screw, screw. That's how she gets her way, Italian whore! She's screwed you all right, right into the ground.' William was angry but his voice had an oddly lifeless quality. Surprised, Nicholas realized it was completely devoid of emotion. Anyone else would have shouted those words.

'Shut up, William. For God's sake.'

Sick at heart Nicholas was tempted to walk away there and then. Only the fact that Bruno was riding Hercules, one of the Shire horses, and was right behind them, made him go on. God, why couldn't life be simple? Why is it my family has to be saddled with someone like my brother? He glanced at the now silent William. He was scowling and his limp was more pronounced than ever. Poor sod. But the twinge of pity quickly faded as William slashed viciously at the ferns bordering the woodland path with his new walking stick. The black expression and the vicious lashing only served to add to Nicholas's dislike, for he reminded him of his father. The black moods were the same. He remembered how his mother had suffered for years. Now that his father was dead and she should have had some peace, she was afflicted by William's warped personality and was suffering again. Why *don't* we talk about it, he wondered. We are hypocrites, both of us. But how many people are there who have the courage not to be? How many people in the world possess the courage to

218

face unpleasant truths squarely? On reflection, Nicholas decided hypocrisy was probably a form of salvation. It served as a tenuous link with sanity.

They reached the cottage. 'Do you want me to stay, sir?'

Bruno did not trust William. He had never forgotten the night of Eleanora's birth. There had been murder in William's eyes that night, and it had not been put there by alcohol, whatever Donald Ramsay might say to the contrary. Bruno was no fool; he'd seen enough of life to know that alcohol unleased emotions already there. It didn't create them. But, like everyone else, he kept his opinions to himself; in his case it was because he had been told to by Lady Margaret. And although the thought of disobeying her never entered his head, he was far from happy about it. Now he watched William and waited.

'No thanks, Bruno. Ride on and see if they've started coppicing Boyatt Wood.'

Kicking his heels into the flanks of Hercules, Bruno rode off. The heavy Shire clumped down the path, and disappeared from view.

'Tell them to leave the sodding place as it is. I like it overgrown,' William shouted after him.

'It needs to be coppiced. You know that. You're just being bloody-minded.'

Nicholas unlocked the door of the cottage and led the way in. Everything inside was neatly set out – all Liana's work of course. When she did something she was fanatical about every small detail. The maps on the walls showed the various forestation schemes, and gave proposed dates for felling, pruning and replanting.

William did not reply to Nicholas's comment about the coppicing. He just followed him in and stared moodily at the different charts but remained silent. Nicholas felt the hairs on the back of his neck prickle. *What is it about William this morning that bothers me so much? Why am I feeling like this? Am I getting neurotic, too? God, why on earth did I let Liana talk me into trying to persuade him to work? We should have left him alone.* William's taunt about screwing had left an uncomfortable echo.

Suddenly William broke the silence. 'The time has come,' he said quietly.

Nicholas let his breath out in relief. 'I'm glad you think so.' *Thank God he was going to be reasonable after all.*

'The orders are very clear.'

219

Orders! What was he talking about? 'There are no orders as such, William. The whole idea is that you are free to run the Woodland Unit as you like. I thought I'd made that clear.'

William looked puzzled for a moment then a blank expression slid across, completely shuttering his face. 'I have my orders and I must obey. The trees are very insistent. Yes, very insistent. I must obey or they will shout. I don't want them shouting at me.' He rubbed his forehead briefly as if in pain. 'It hurts my head when they shout.'

Nicholas swallowed. *It hurts my head when they shout!* Trees shout? What the hell was he talking about? Suddenly the magnitude of William's remark struck him forcibly as he realized its awful significance. He stared at his brother, compelled against his will to recognize the fact that William was far, far more removed from normality than he or his mother had ever dreamed. William was living in another world, a separate world, where the trees spoke to him. The ever-present fear he and his mother had suppressed for so long now surfaced with all the force of an erupting volcano gushing over him in devastating waves and Nicholas was forced to acknowledge that his brother was mad, utterly mad . . .

Suddenly he remembered having read somewhere that it was essential not to show fear or scorn when someone really flipped their lid. I must humour him, he thought, trying not to panic. I must keep calm, think clearly, and at all costs I must humour him.

'What do the trees say?' he asked gently as if it were the most normal conversation in the world.

'They say kill.'

Nicholas shivered. How cold the day was. His lips were dry, and he stumbled over the words but knew he had to keep talking. 'Kill? Whom must you kill?' But he already knew the answer.

'You,' said William simply.

William was very, very still; so still, it was the air about him that seemed to move. His eyes, normally so pale, were dark, the irises dilated until they were black holes in his face. Nicholas stared, not daring to move. He watched William slowly unscrew the top of his walking stick and unsheath a vicious-looking sword. Outside sunlight filtered translucent green through the canopy of broad-leaved trees. Wood pigeons crooned throaty chuckles and the air was thick with the hum of insects. The commonplace little things of a July morning in the forest threw into greater contrast the slow drama unfolding inside the cottage.

This is our own fault, thought Nicholas, his mind detached now. We have all ignored him. We clung to the façade we built for him, fooling ourselves and pretending it was real. But the pretence is ended for ever now. Nicholas watched the façade crumbling away before his horrified eyes to reveal the demonic force which had always been there.

I've got to get out of here. But even as he thought of escape, William raised the sword so that its tip was resting just below Nicholas's left nipple. It was very sharp. Nicholas remained motionless. The moment for escape had passed; any movement now might make things worse. He was bleeding. He could feel the warm blood trickling down his chest, soaking the thin cotton of his shirt. William pushed the point in further, and Nicholas caught his breath in pain.

Later Nicholas was never sure whether he heard or felt the vibration of Hercules' solid hoofs as Bruno came back up the path returning from Boyatt Wood. William appeared to hear nothing. Hercules stopped outside the cottage. Bruno, still on his back, had a clear view in through the open door and sized up the situation in seconds. It seemed as if the big Shire also knew something was wrong, for he stood quite still. Not a hoof moved, not a brass on the leather halter jangled as Bruno slid off his back and crept towards the open cottage door. On his way he picked a heavy junk of firewood.

Nicholas knew he must keep talking to William. Somehow he had to distract his attention, anything to delay the final thrust of the needle sharp point. 'Why do the trees tell you to kill me?'

'They don't like you.'

'Why not?'

'Because you've always harmed me.'

'How have I harmed you, William? I don't understand.'

'By being born. I should be the only son. Mother will love me when you are gone.'

'Are you sure?'

William jabbed the sword deeper and Nicholas gritted his teeth, trying to ignore the pain.

'Of course.' He was scornful now. 'The trees never lie to me; they are my friends. Not like people. They say . . .' The walls of the cottage shook as the heavy weight of William's body hit the floor.

'Are you all right, sir?'

William sprawled unconscious on the floor, felled by a karate chop to the back of the neck with the junk still held by Bruno.

'Yes.' Hanging on to the desk for support, Nicholas found it difficult to speak. He could not stop trembling.

'I'd better ring for Doctor Ramsay.' Bruno knelt down and felt for William's pulse. Still beating strongly; he hadn't killed him, thank God.

Nicholas looked at William. God, why did he look so young and vulnerable? It made him want to cry. William's golden hair glinted in the sunlight slanting in through the door. His handsome face was calm now in unconsciousness and his mouth set in a gentle, sad expression. Piteous. That was the only thing Nicholas could think of, piteous. And we have all failed him. He had never felt so weary or dispirited in all his life.

'Yes, you'd better ring for Donald Ramsay,' he said. 'He will know what to do.'

*

No-one seemed particularly perturbed or surprised when William vanished. Nicholas said his brother had decided to leave Broadacres and had gone to live instead with distant relatives in Scotland.

Not mourning his loss, Mary Pragnell sniffed with satisfaction as she broadcast the news across the counter of the home farm shop, now housed in a permanent building with its own car park on the main road leading from the estate. 'Mary's', as it was known locally, was the centre of gossip. The estate workers and villagers all called in for purchases and news at least once a week.

'Good riddance to he,' she said time and time again as she shovelled the glut of fat Broadacres peas into her customers' brown paper bags.

No-one aired contrary opinion. It was a sentiment shared by all who had come into contact with surly William. A few were surprised that he had decided to move so quickly but no great importance was attached to the speed of his disappearance. Only Bruno knew the truth, and loyalty kept his lips tightly sealed.

Of course Liana queried it with Nicholas. 'Was it because he was asked to work?'

'Yes.'

Something in his tone of voice prevented her from asking more. She sensed he was not speaking the truth, or at least, certainly not the whole truth. But on reflection, did it matter? William had gone, and that was what she had wanted. Even so, initially she was a little worried. Margaret and

Nicholas seemed agitated but as time passed she noticed with relief that they both visibly relaxed; whatever had been worrying them had obviously disappeared. So she put thoughts of William from her mind, and got on with the day-to-day task of her chosen mission in life, amassing the Hamilton-Howard fortune.

*

Nicholas wrote to his sister in New Zealand for the first time in years, telling her that he was now married and had a daughter. But the real purpose of his letter, which he left to the very last, was to tell her that William no longer lived at Broadacres and was very unlikely to return. Knowing how much Anne had hated William, he was hoping that now he had gone, she and her husband might be persuaded to come to England for a visit and stay at Broadacres. Nicholas knew it would make his mother's cup of happiness full if only she could see her daughter Anne again and meet her grandson Peter. That, and another grandchild, if only Liana would hurry up and show signs of conceiving.

By tacit agreement William's name was never mentioned within the family circle or to outsiders, and soon it seemed to most people as if he had never been. Time even healed Nicholas's mind, blurring the memory of that terrible day in the wood. Now he felt only a deep, compassionate pity for William, an emotion he had never been able to feel when they were together. Being apart gave a different perspective, made it easier for Nicholas to slot William into another category. He was no longer an irritant and a threat to his family's happiness, he was his sick brother; locked away in a secure mental hospital for his own safety and that of others.

Donald Ramsay had tried, really tried desperately hard to get Nicholas and Margaret to see reason when he had been called in to help on the day William had attacked Nicholas. He had bullied, cajoled and argued but Nicholas and Margaret would not agree to William's being sent to where Donald was convinced he should go, the Ticehurst hospital in Sussex. It was no use telling them that there he could be examined and treated by the most eminent experts in the field of mental illness – in Donald's opinion the most expert in the country at that time. Even when faced with the irrefutable fact that William was mentally ill, their one thought had been to avoid any publicity. They were of the opinion that by admitting him to such a famous hospital, the fact would eventually reach the ears of the press.

'I can just imagine the lurid headlines in one of the less scrupulous Sunday newspapers,' said Nicholas grimly. 'The answer, Donald, is no to Ticehurst.'

'But the doctors and nurses there are discreet. All medical matters are confidential, you know that,' said Donald.

'So they might be, but information can leak out. No, what William needs is to be well away from curious, prying eyes, and that's where he has to be,' replied Nicholas.

Donald was angry. 'For whose sake? His or yours?'

'For all our sakes, Donald. Surely you can see that.' Margaret was distressed but just as determined as Nicholas.

Much against Donald's better judgement he finally gave up the argument and made arrangements for William to be admitted to an obscure mental hospital on the edge of Dartmoor in Devon. It was a comfortable place set in extensive grounds, but in Donald's opinion, the psychiatrists, although kind and well meaning, were old-fashioned and hopelessly out of touch with modern thinking. Most of the patients were poor, simple, mentally subnormal people, not difficult, violent patients like William. He was sure there was no chance of a detailed case history being built up, one which would delve deeply into William's and the family's past; no chance of a realistic prognosis or treatment. But it seemed that was exactly what Nicholas and Lady Margaret wanted.

'They just haven't the desire to find out,' Donald told his wife crossly when he returned home.

'I would say courage, not desire,' said Dorothy perceptively. 'It takes courage to look deeply into something unpleasant.'

On the advice of the psychiatrists at the hospital, Nicholas and his mother did not visit William. Their one and only visit had precipitated an onslaught of such violence that not only William but also Lady Margaret had needed sedating. She had no wish to repeat the ordeal and was glad to have the excuse not to go.

'Stay away until we deem his personality stabilized,' said the psychiatrist, adding pessimistically, 'although it is possible that he may never be cured.'

Nicholas took the advice, stifling the guilty hope that the psychiatrist was right and that William would never be well enough to return to Broadacres. Of course, he told himself, he would do anything to help his brother if it were possible. But the psychiatrists said they could do nothing, and there was no denying that life had a new dimension without him.

Liana still had moments of curiosity, not believing that William was in Scotland with relatives. But as Nicholas never mentioned him, and as her objective – the ousting of William from Broadacres – had been achieved, she kept silent. Why spoil her relationship with Nicholas, which had settled into a loving and stable pattern.

When they were together, Liana and Nicholas made love every night. There was less urgency about Liana these days. In the beginning Nicholas had sometimes felt that she was desperate to please him. He smiled at the thought. She need not have worried, she always pleased him.

Wildly, madly in love with her then as now, just holding her in his arms drove him mad with an almost uncontrollable desire.

'Ah, Nicholas. So you are not yet tired of me?' Liana teased him. 'The same woman, night after night.' She kissed him, tantalizing him with the quick, darting movements of her tongue as her hands flickered softly down his body.

'I'll never tire of you, darling, never,' Nicholas gasped. Her hands were magic. 'I want you *now*.'

He pulled her towards him but, laughing, Liana slipped from his grasp. 'Too impatient, my darling,' she whispered. 'Anticipation is the best part.'

The velvet fingers stroking slowly between his legs were almost too much. Nicholas groaned with pleasure and increasing urgency. 'I can't wait.'

'Just a little while longer, darling.' Liana slid across and mounted Nicholas, expertly guiding him into the warmth of her creamy centre. Bending down, her full breasts cushioned against his chest, her soft lips closed over his as the lush heat of her body enveloped him. 'Now,' she whispered, her voice urgent, too. 'Now, now!'

Nicholas felt the familiar scream of exquisite pleasure explode inside him and he clung to her as if his life depended on it.

'I love you, darling,' he murmured sleepily much later.

Eyes closed, Liana smiled and slid the length of her silky body closer to his. They always made love until they were exhausted, then Nicholas held her tightly in his arms until morning.

It still amazed him that their love-making had never become mechanical or unemotional. Outside the bedroom Liana was a hard-headed businesswoman but inside, she was a fabulous creature made for him and him alone. Nicholas was even more in love with her than when they had first married, and Liana loved him, too. He knew she did. She never looked at another man, never gave him cause for distrust.

Yet in spite of all that, there were two small black clouds always hovering on his horizon. One was caused by the fact that Nicholas could never completely dispel a ridiculous, niggling jealousy. Although on reflection, he knew jealousy was not the exact emotion. It was a kind of mournful resentment he felt, resentment because of that part of herself he knew she always held back. She was, and always would be, an enigma to him: the beautiful, mysterious woman called Liana, his wife.

And the other cloud was the unfulfilled and growing longing for a son and heir. If only, if only she could conceive another child. For a little while, after William had been sent away to hospital, the longing had subsided and Nicholas had poured all his love on to his only child, Eleanora. She was adorable, and he spoilt her dreadfully, telling himself that there was always the possibility that the next child would not be so lovable, and then he would be hopelessly disappointed. Supposing he and Liana did have a son and he developed the way of William, always sullen and withdrawn and eventually having a breakdown. But gradually that fear subsided, and he remembered Donald's words of reassurance long ago. Of course any son of his would be every bit as adorable as Eleanora. Little by little the desire for a son grew and grew. Every time they made love he thought of it until the longing became an obsession and again, in spite of all his good intentions not to mention it, Nicholas broke his promise to Donald Ramsay.

They had attended the christening of Meg and Bruno's second-born, a daughter named Alice. It had been a happy afternoon. Most of the estate workers had gone to the church and attended the christening party afterwards, and Liana and Nicholas were now alone, relaxing with a sherry before dinner in the Grey Room.

'I'm so glad for Meg,' said Liana thoughtfully. 'She and Bruno are so very happy together. Now they have a perfect family, a son and a daughter.' She was thinking only of Meg, unaware of the bitter ironic comparison with themselves.

Nicholas had already made that comparison. During the service in the church he could think of nothing else. 'Yes,' he said now, in a very low, quiet voice. He stood before the ornate marble fireplace looking down at Liana. 'A son *and* a daughter.'

Liana felt her stomach tighten suddenly into a hard knot of defiant guilt as the import of his words sunk in and she cursed her thoughtless remark. But the years had given her plenty of practice at suppressing guilt, and she quashed it now without remorse. Nothing had changed as far as she was concerned. Not even her love for Broadacres or her growing happiness as Nicholas's wife could displace Raul. He was still the centre of her life, and she was fiercely determined to hang on to his precious memory at all costs. Damn the christening; it had set Nicholas's mind back on to the old track of wanting more children. The subject needed to be changed. 'Talking of daughters,' she said brightly, 'I'd better go and see if ours is ready for bed.'

Draining the sherry glass, she set it down with an air of finality. Nicholas knew very well what it signalled. The conversation was at an end. Liana thought the christening had reminded him; little did she know of his constant longing. As she rose and moved to swish past him, he reached out and caught her wrist, pulling her towards him. 'Liana.' His voice was husky with emotion. 'You must know how much I want a son. You do, don't you?'

Oh, God, why did he have to make it so hard? For a moment his plea unleashed a tide of guilt that threatened to overwhelm her, then her steely resolve hardened and the barrier was in place once more. Raul was the barrier, Raul and their daughter Eleanora. I have everything I want, she thought, grimly determined to keep it that way. Another child would only complicate things. 'Babies don't come off conveyor belts, Nicholas. We must wait.'

But Nicholas was impatient. 'Liana, darling, don't you think we've waited long enough for another child? Please, for both our sakes, won't you go and see a gynaecologist?'

See a doctor! Liana hid the sudden onslaught of fear. He had never mentioned anything about seeing doctors before. This was more serious than she had thought. But no matter, she would never change her mind. How could she, when she could feel Raul's presence sometimes so strongly that it was almost a physical thing. Why, oh why, couldn't Nicholas be content to leave things the way they were? But, of course, he had no idea of the persistent shadow at her elbow, constantly anchoring her emotions to the past. It wasn't his fault. He didn't know and could never be told. So she hid her disquiet as best she could and tried to smile as serenely as ever as she answered quietly, 'There is plenty of time, darling. Don't let's be impatient.'

'Impatient! Liana, it's more than five years now since I returned from Europe. Five whole years. There must be something wrong. For my sake, please agree to go.'

Her dark eyes clouded suddenly, and for the first time Nicholas became aware of her very real fear, although of course he completely misunderstood the reasons. Liana's next words served to reinforce his misunderstanding. 'I hate doctors,' she said, her voice faltering with very real distress. 'I'm afraid of them. I'll never, never go willingly but if you insist . . .' Liana let the words trail away into silence. It was partly the truth. She was afraid of doctors, all of them except Donald Ramsay. Nicholas would never know the reason for her fears, but Liana was counting on his finely tuned compassion and his consuming love for her. Surely he would never force her to go against her will?

It was a calculated risk, but it worked. 'Oh, Liana.' Nicholas was immediately stricken with remorse. 'Darling, you know I'll never force you to do anything you don't want. I love you too much.'

He flung his arms around her and held her tight. The subject was dropped and Liana breathed easily once more. But although Nicholas remained silent he still hoped. He prayed, too, every Sunday in Longford's Norman church. Sometimes Liana accompanied Lady Margaret, Eleanora and Nicholas to church but more often than not she found other, more pressing matters to attend to.

'You can pray for me, darling,' she said to Nicholas. 'If there is a God, I'm sure he will listen to you if you put in a good word on my behalf.'

'I wish you could believe.'

It never failed to distress Nicholas when he heard the hard edge to Liana's voice whenever God was mentioned. He just could not bring himself to accept that she was as cynical as she sounded. She was compassionate and caring – he had seen that so many times in the way she dealt with the people who worked for her. But where God was concerned she was stubborn, never admitting that the existence of a being greater than themselves might even be remotely possible.

'I have good reason not to believe,' was the only explanation he ever got, and with that he had to be content. He remembered his mother's advice that some things were best left unsaid and wondered if he had a hope of ever understanding her.

*

Nicholas began to take an interest in the accounts and after dinner he and Liana would often sit in the library office sifting through facts and figures. Eleanora would come down with them and have her bed-time story before Meg or Dolly put her to bed.

'I want this one,' she would announce, climbing up on Nicholas's knee. It was always the same storybook.

'A different story tonight,' said Nicholas one evening, raising his eyebrows in amusement at Liana. 'Well, it will make a change from Rumpelstiltskin!' He read the title, 'The Lord who lost his crown.'

'Daddy, are you a lord?'

'Yes, darling. Who told you?' Eleanora had always been brought up with Meg's son Rolf, and played with the village children who came to the farm. Neither Liana nor Nicholas wanted her to grow up different from other children, divorced from the realities of life.

'Meg. But she said you never go to London with the other lords. Why not? Is it because you've lost your crown?'

Nicholas laughed. 'No, it isn't. I'm not interested in going to London with the other lords. I'd rather stay here with you. Now do you want this story or not?'

'I do,' said Eleanora positively.

'Perhaps you ought to,' said Liana when Eleanora had disappeared off to bed. 'Take your seat in the House of Lords,' she added, seeing Nicholas's puzzled expression.

'Whatever for? Anyway I thought you disapproved of the Lords, I always thought you had Socialist tendencies.'

'Not when they're going to lose the next election,' said Liana practically. 'And there's sure to be one before the end of nineteen fifty-one. The war will see to that.'

Nicholas sighed in agreement. 'Yes, this bloody Korean war! If the experts are right, it's going to bankrupt the country.'

'But not us,' said Liana with determination. 'However, it will bring down the Government, and you'd better join the winning side. You can make agriculture your special political subject.'

'Darling, I'll never make a politician. You should know that.'

Liana pushed back her chair and came round to Nicholas's side of the desk. 'You will, Nicholas,' she said persuasively, smiling one of her most enchanting smiles. 'You can do anything if you put your mind to it.'

Liana's blandishments won the day. In January 1951 Nicholas took his seat in the House of Lords, albeit somewhat reluctantly.

'You don't have to say a lot,' Liana told him. 'Just being there will be enough.'

And Nicholas had to admit it was. With his arrival in the Lords came the all-important social invitations which Liana knew they needed. It was vital to broaden their circle of contacts if they were to expand in the way she had planned.

*

'I'd like to know how they got tickets to the Lord's Taverners' Ball.' Put out and grumpy, Clara Maltravers thrust the front-page photograph of the *Daily Express* under Margaret's nose.

'The Earl and Countess of Wessex merrymaking at the Lord's Taverners' Ball,' read Margaret obligingly, 'in the company of their Royal Highnesses the Princesses Elizabeth and Margaret and the Duke of Edinburgh.' Clara sniffed disapprovingly. 'Doesn't Liana look lovely?' said Margaret. 'And that jewellery of hers always comes out so well in photographs.'

'There were only twelve hundred tickets,' said Clara, determined not to be sidetracked.

'I expect Nicholas got them because he's become active in politics now,' said Margaret comfortably. 'He's very highly thought of, you know.'

'Humph!' Clara still felt aggrieved The fact that she had recently suffered a severe heart attack and could not have attended the ball anyway was immaterial. She changed the subject. 'Is it true you have entered young Eleanora for the Festival of Britain Gymkhana at Taplow?'

Margaret seized on the less contentious subject with alacrity. 'Yes. Why don't you come down with me now to the paddock? I promised Eleanora we'd practise this afternoon when school finishes. I expect Rolf will be with her.'

'You shouldn't let that child go to the village school and spend all her time playing with the servant's children.'

'Oh, Clara, don't be such a snob!' Margaret was exasperated but soon forgot Clara's irritating ways once they arrived at the paddock and found Eleanora already waiting. 'You call Goldie and saddle him up,' she told Eleanora.

At six and a half years, Eleanora was tall for her age and had all the natural grace of her mother.

'Goldie, here. Good boy.' She swung herself over the paddock gate and fished a lemon-drop out of her jodhpur pocket. 'He just loves lemon-drops,' she told Clara.

Margaret fiddled with the latch on the paddock gate, grumbling that it seemed more difficult to open with each passing day.

'Pity you can't jump over the gate like you used to,' observed Clara.

Margaret pulled a face. 'I don't mind getting old but I do mind getting decrepit. We're a pair of old crocks now, Clara, you with your dicky heart and me with my damned arthritis.'

'I wouldn't say I was an old crock!' snapped Clara. Margaret hid a smile. True to form Clara was not ready to be considered old yet.

'Hey, Grandma! Watch me jump.' Eleanora swung herself up on to Goldie's bare back.

'You can't. You mustn't, not without a saddle.'

But Eleanora was not listening. Bending forward she whispered in the pony's ear and set off at a brisk canter. Margaret closed her eyes as the pair approached the jump. Please, God, don't let her fall. Then she opened them again in time to see Eleanora and Goldie sail effortlessly over the poles.

'Why, you look as if you have been doing it for ages,' she gasped.

'I have,' said Eleanora airily. 'Rolf and I have been jumping bare-back for two weeks now. I didn't ask you because I knew you would say no.'

'Like her mother,' observed Clara. 'A determined young woman.'

'Yes,' said Margaret nearly bursting with pride.

*

The Conservatives won the general election of October 1951 and Liana was pleased. The Hamilton-Howards now had half a dozen businesses as well as interests in numerous smaller subsidiary concerns, and she knew Nicholas's being in the House of Lords gave them added access to the City. Diversify as much as possible – that was now her policy. So when the international commodity market re-opened in December 1951, Liana proposed that they invest heavily in equity shares.

Nicholas protested, not because he was worried about losing money – there was not much chance of that. Liana was shrewd enough to have thoroughly investigated all the possibilities first – but because he thought it unnecessary.

'For heaven's sake Liana, do you really have to start on something else? Already we are what most people would term very comfortable. Thanks to you, we have no money worries. Surely you can take life easy and relax a little now? Do we need to watch the share prices every day? We are rich enough.'

'One can never be rich enough,' came the tart answer. 'Anyway, you needn't watch the market, I'll do it. I shall enjoy the challenge.'

And Nicholas knew she would. Liana thrived on the precarious excitement of treading a dangerous, yet carefully measured financial path. An inner fire drove her on; she enjoyed getting the better of situations, of mastering those awkward individuals she encountered. But Nicholas would have been surprised if he had known that, quite apart from her constant dread of having too much time to think, the very real fear of poverty still lingered with her.

Sometimes when she had made a spectacular deal, Liana would sit up late at night in her office, still situated in the library in the Lower Cloisters, and contentedly add up the figures. They were rich, rich, *rich*! The words floated in her head, giving her a sense of intrinsic wellbeing. She had achieved everything she had planned and in a miraculously short space of time.

She had made money not only for the Hamilton-Howard family but for herself too. She was a rich woman in her own right. Unbeknown to Nicholas, she had taken out a loan using the jewellery she had brought from Italy as security to finance the expansion of Elver Forge Industries, a gamble which had paid off handsomely – the loan had long been repaid. The log-burning stoves were being exported now in large numbers to the continent, and she had plans to set up a factory in the United States. The vastness of the American market fascinated her. When I get a slice of that, she thought, then I *will* start to be wealthy. But she could never explain that to Nicholas, never confess that sometimes she thought just the act of making money had become the hub of her existence. Spending it hardly seemed important but making it was. How could Nicholas, who had never known true poverty, ever understand?

That was a basic difference between them which time and circumstance could never change. He had never been so desperately hungry that even weeds seemed like delicacies. The nearest he had ever come to being poor was having to sell one of his paintings in order to keep up the lifestyle to which he had always been accustomed. No, he had no idea of the degradation of true poverty whereas Liana could remember it all too vividly – the humiliation of selling her body in order to eke out a wretched existence. She would never forget that.

Prostitution, Raul and Eleanora – those three memories were there, implacable, physical, inexorably entwined about her, chaining her to the past. Bitter memories but mournfully sweet, too; memories she fought to keep at bay, working until she thought she was too exhausted to think of them, only to find they refused to flee. They were lodged in her brain, stuck fast, always demanding recognition. Exhaustion was never too great, sleep never too deep to completely deaden the past.

But money, Liana found, was a barrier of sorts and a comfort. One could never be too rich. With her account books and bank statements in the peace of the Lower Cloisters, she did find a form of contentment.

*

Clara Maltravers died suddenly in January 1952, and her house and land came on to the market. Much to Margaret's surprise, her daughter Anne wrote to say that she and her husband, Richard Chapman, were flying over from New Zealand with a view to buying it. With them would come their son Peter, who was eleven years old.

'How did they know about it?' She was delighted at the prospect. Peter was a grandson she had never thought to see. 'I'll have to buy another pony. Maybe, though, I should get a gelding. How many hands do you think? How tall is Peter?'

Nicholas grinned. 'They know because I wrote and told them; and I don't know how tall Peter is.' He was glad his mother was pleased.

Liana smiled at Margaret's typical response. A grandson visiting – buy another horse. 'Perhaps you should wait,' she cautioned. 'Maybe Anne and her husband won't buy the farm or maybe Peter will be like me, and not be a horse-lover.'

'Rubbish,' Margaret snorted indignantly at the very idea. 'He's bound to live on a horse. All the Hamilton-Howards do. Look at Eleanora.'

'Of course he will like horses,' echoed Eleanora, mischievously mimicking her grandmother's voice. Then she switched to an uncanny impersonation of her mother's measured tones. 'And if he does not, he shall be banished from Broadacres for not following in the family footsteps.'

Nicholas laughed. 'You are far too cheeky, young lady, and I don't know where on earth you get your acting ability from. That's certainly not in the family.' He turned to his mother. 'Go on, buy a gelding that should suit him. He's sure to ride.'

'Yes, I suppose loving horses is a family trait.' Liana said what was expected of her but as usual she felt herself go cold at the mere mention of family likenesses. Why did it still happen? There was no reason now to feel the same breathless guilt. Everyone attributed Eleanora's characteristics to the Hamilton-Howard family genes. No-one had ever suspected.

'I expect that's why you are different, Mummy,' said Eleanora, unconsciously compounding the lie. 'You're not really one of us.'

Liana winced. God, if only she knew! 'Perhaps,' she said.

Margaret, ever quick to sense the dormant sadness in Liana but always misunderstanding the reasons, took her arm. 'My dear girl, I wouldn't have you any other way and neither would Nicholas. It doesn't matter a jot that you don't like riding. You have so many talents we haven't. For a start you're much more intelligent. Eleanora is lucky to have such a mother.'

'And lucky to have such a doting grandmother,' answered Liana with genuine fondness. And I'm lucky myself to have such a mother-in-law; she often thought it, a thousand times. Sometimes she allowed herself to fantasize, thinking that even if Margaret knew the truth it would not dim her love for herself and Eleanora. But that was something she could only guess at and would never know for certain because the burden of the secret was hers and hers alone. Margaret's love would never be put to the ultimate test.

*

'They've arrived.' Arthritis forgotten, Margaret leaped out of her chair and raced into the entrance hall of Broadacres.

'It might not be them, Grandma.' Eleanora pounded after her, followed at a more leisurely pace by Liana and Nicholas.

It was. The family Rolls Royce, now back in regular use, crunched to a halt in the gravel before the main steps to the house.

'Anne!' Half laughing, half crying, Margaret nearly stumbled in her haste to get down the steps. Flinging her thin arms around her daughter she hugged her. 'I thought I'd never see you again.'

Anne, perilously close to tears herself, hugged her mother back. The two women were very alike in appearance, both tall and slightly uncoordinated, both untidy. Anne's hair was wispy, too, and tied back in a bun almost identical to Margaret's. The only difference was the colour. Margaret's hair was grey, Anne's a faded blonde. Liana liked the look of her. She looked gentle, like Margaret.

'Oh, it's so good to be home,' said Anne, and then did burst into tears.

Nicholas grinned and raised his eyebrows at his new brother-in-law, Richard Chapman. 'Women!' he said. 'They always cry when they're happy.'

Richard gave a long, slow smile. 'They baffle me,' he said.

Liana was reminded of Wally Pragnell's geniality. Richard Chapman had the ruddy complexion of a farmer and an open, candid face. He looked an easy man to get along with.

Nicholas led the way into the house and up into the Arcadian Room where Meg was waiting to serve afternoon tea. He made the formal introductions but when it came to Eleanora's turn she took matters into her own hands.

'I'm Eleanora,' she announced. 'I'm eight years and two months old. I can ride a horse, *and* I can jump bare-back.' She turned to Peter, throwing her head back so that she could look up into his eyes, every inch of her athletic frame tense with challenge. 'Bet you can't jump bare-back.'

'How much do you want to bet?'

'Oh.' Eleanora was disconcerted. She had not thought of that.

Richard Chapman laughed. 'You'd better be careful, young lady. Everyone in New Zealand rides; it's the only way to get about. Your cousin Peter was practically born in the saddle.'

'You mean you can ride bare-back?'

'I always do.'

Eleanora was impressed. Peter went up several notches in her estimation. 'How about roller-skating?'

Peter shook his head. 'I've never tried.'

'Come on, then. I've got spare skates.'

'Darling, Peter must be tired after the long journey.' But Liana's words went unheeded.

The pair ran giggling from the room, Eleanora's dark, shining curls contrasting sharply with Peter's fine, straight, blond hair.

'Looks as if those two have taken a shine to each other.' Richard Chapman beamed at his wife.

'Oh, Anne, I do hope you will buy Clara's old place. It would be so lovely to have you near. And Eleanora and Peter would be such company for each other.' Margaret's voice rang with longing.

'William really has gone for good?' Anne looked at Nicholas.

'Yes, I think it is safe to assume that he has.'

Liana looked up quickly. How did Nicholas *know* that William might not decide one day to return from Scotland? But Nicholas was smiling confidently; it seemed he was sure. He was thinking of his secret meeting with William's psychiatrist the week before.

'No chance of recovery,' the doctor said.

'Not a hope in hell?'

'I suppose you could put it like that.' The psychiatrist was mildly disapproving.

Margaret sighed. 'I know I shouldn't say it, Anne, but life is so much easier with William in . . .' she hesitated fractionally then said, 'Scotland.'

'I'm sure it is,' said Anne quietly. She reached across and grasped her mother's hand. 'If Richard likes the farm, we will be staying.'

'What's the land like for rearing sheep?' asked Richard. 'Because that's what I'm best at.'

'Excellent,' said Liana decisively; she wanted the Chapmans to stay. 'I'll ask Wally Pragnell, our estate manager, to show you round. He'll be able to answer any questions you have.'

Chapter Eighteen

Anne and Richard Chapman bought the house and land and four months later moved their belongings from New Zealand to England to settle permanently.

As Richard Chapman had remarked on the first day, Peter and Eleanora had taken a shine to each other. But it was more than just a casual friendship. From that very first day it was obvious that theirs would be a deep and lasting friendship. A mutual respect and affection flowered in a surprisingly short time to an almost adult intimacy. Not that the two children were yet aware of the deeper implications of their friendship. Now they just took pleasure in each other's company and enjoyed the passing moments.

The peace and quiet of Broadacres, always shattered whenever Eleanora was about, was now doubly shattered. An astonishing breathless turmoil surrounded the pair as they roller-skated down the long corridors of Broadacres, screaming with excited laughter and putting the life of any hapless adult who happened to be there in imminent danger. If not pursuing that pastime, they were urging their ponies over hair-raisingly high jumps in the paddocks, aided and abetted by Rolf and his friends from the village. Suddenly Broadacres was full of children; just what Margaret had always wanted. She could not have been happier.

When Anne first returned, Margaret was a little shocked to find that her daughter had converted to Richard's religion and was now a Roman Catholic. But it was something she had to accept, and, with William out of the way, she achieved a rapport with her daughter which his presence had always denied them.

Like Eleanora, she adored Peter from the first moment she saw him. It was easy to love him, he was such a lovable boy always laughing and such fun, but kind and gentle and considerate to others as well.

Nevertheless for such a young boy Margaret did think that perhaps he was too devout a Catholic. He seemed to have an understanding beyond his years. That did worry Margaret a little, although she never mentioned it. She had the ingrained Church of England prejudice against the Church of

Rome. She liked her religion simple, and the mysteries within the Catholic Church made her nervous. But she kept silent. Of course Peter always went with his parents to Mass on Sundays, while Eleanora attended Longford Parish Church with Nicholas and her grandmother. However, a small hiatus occurred later that year when Eleanora suddenly announced that in future she intended to go to Mass on a Sunday morning with Peter instead of accompanying her father and grandmother to the parish church.

'But you always come with us. Longford is your church.' Margaret protested.

'I want to go to Mass with Peter.' Eleanora was stubborn.

Not getting much parental support from Nicholas, Margaret appealed to Liana. 'Liana, please will you persuade her?'

'Margaret, dear, what can I do? I don't even believe in God!' Liana was as stubborn as Eleanora and refused to get drawn into the conflict.

To Margaret's great relief the phase did not last long. Eleanora, never very patient, complained that the Catholic service was too long, there was too much ringing of bells and the incense made her sneeze.

'If I have to go to church,' she told her grandmother, 'I'll come with you to the short service because then I can have a ride before lunch.' Then she asked anxiously, 'Is it true that Mummy is a Catholic?'

'Well, dear, she was reared as one,' said Margaret cautiously, not sure where the conversation was leading, 'but she has decided to let her faith lapse.'

'Oh,' said Eleanora, not sure what 'lapse' meant. 'Then I'm not a Catholic. Peter says I am.'

'Peter is wrong,' said Margaret firmly. One Catholic grandchild was quite enough. 'You are Church of England like your father and me.'

'Good,' said Eleanora, glad that the matter was settled. 'Then I shall ride Goldie while Peter is still praying!'

Richard Chapman, a bluff, no-nonsense New Zealander, had very successfully raised sheep in the South Island near Christchurch, and he now set about converting the long under-used land of Clara Maltravers into a haven for fat, thick-cream-coated sheep. He was assured of a ready market for his high quality wool, Liana had seen to that. Never missing an opportunity to diversify she had already recruited two young graduates from Winchester Art College to work on designs for exclusive woollen coats and evening cloaks. They were to be woven and made up in two old established mills in Yorkshire and the finished garments sold through her Knightsbridge fashion store.

'It really will be a "Lady Liana World",' said Nicholas when he heard of the plans. Often he wished he had Liana's ability. She could see all the possibilities, tie all the loose ends together until they formed one compact, viable business.

'Lady Liana World' was the label under which Liana sold Dolly's exclusive designs. From initially running up dresses for Lady Margaret and Liana, a business with a turnover of thousands of pounds had been established. A whole army of local girls now made dresses in the Old Mission Hall at Shawford, the next village along from Longford; every dress was destined for the Sloane Street boutique, where they were snapped up by the fashion-starved society women of London. It amused Liana to charge exorbitant prices. Whatever she asked, the clientele paid. Nicholas protested that she was charging too much.

'Some of them are sisters of chaps I went to school with. We should let them have a special rate.'

'Nonsense. That would be bad business practice. If they are foolish enough to waste their money, that is their problem,' was Liana's quick reply. She had no time for the breed of woman whose only thought was of her appearance. Now, as usual, her thoughts were racing, and Nicholas's faint sarcasm at her expense was lost on her. There were more important things to think about. 'I won't be able to use Richard's wool for the coronation fashions; we'll need to buy in some. It's lucky Richard and Anne have plenty of good contacts in New Zealand and Australia, because I shall need excellent quality wool for what I have in mind.'

Nicholas stared at Liana. She was remorseless, like a machine, her mind always flying on ahead. 'God almighty, Liana, the King is only just dead! No-one has mentioned the date of the coronation yet.'

Liana shrugged, his implied criticism washing over her like water off a duck's back. 'It will be next year. Already Fleet Street is buzzing with rumours that it will probably be in June fifty-three. There will be parties and balls in the spring, then there will be test matches, Wimbledon, Ascot, Henley, Cowdray Park,' Liana ticked off the events on her fingers. 'Then, of course, there will be the Spithead Review. I think I'll get some special waterproof jackets made up for that, very chic with an anchor motif. Women will buy them even if they have no intention of going anywhere near the sea.'

'I suppose it's too much to hope that you will have time for me and Eleanora between now and the coronation?'

Liana laughed at Nicholas's gloomy expression. 'I do believe you are jealous.'

'Yes.' Nicholas admitted it. 'Sometimes I think you don't need me at all.' But he knew jealous was the wrong word. He was envious, and at the same time anxious about Liana's increasing involvement in the world of commerce. Although physically as close as ever, Nicholas often had the uneasy feeling that she was moving further and further away from him.

Liana linked her arms behind his neck and kissed him. 'Darling, how can you say that? I adore our daughter. I'm always there when she needs me, although I must say she seems to prefer her newly found cousin Peter, her grandmother, or a horse to my company! And am I not always here whenever you want me?' She kissed him again.

Nicholas sighed, a mixture of exasperation and affection. There was no argument against that. She was always there when he wanted her.

'Yes, you're always here,' he said. He kissed her back, feeling the familiar stirring in his loins.

*

The coronation of Queen Elizabeth the Second took place on 22 June 1953. Nicholas and Liana as a peer and peeress of the realm were there, although at one point Nicholas had despairingly thought Liana would never have time to get herself organized and to attend. But, of course, she did, managing everything with her usual efficiency and sweeping into the Royal Garden Party on the Friday prior to the coronation, causing heads to turn and cameras to click.

Fashion editors from all over the world were there, eyeing the assembled nobility and even the most eminent of British designers, who had been working flat out for the past few months, waited anxiously for their verdicts. Would their design be voted the best outfit? Of course the top names, Norman Hartnell and Victor Steibel were all serene smiles as they sailed into the Royal Garden Party, but they, too, knew the power of the press. Fortunes could be made or lost at such an occasion. Would the Marquess of Queensbury do justice to her outfit? Would the Duchess of Bedford outshine the Duchess of Kent? No, the unanimous opinion was that the Duchess of Kent was by far the best-dressed woman. Her hat alone was the biggest, an enormous tip-tilted cartwheel of pink with the underside of the brim faced in white.

Nicholas and Liana arrived late. Liana had insisted on finalizing an American deal concerning Elver Forge Industries. Nicholas thought the transatlantic telephone call would never end.

'With this out of the way, darling, I can enjoy the next few days of festivities,' she said, waving a hand at him, shushing him out of the library office.

'If we ever get to London.'

'We will, we will. Just let me finish this 'phone call.'

Their late arrival caused a flurry of attention. Glancing down at Liana, Nicholas felt a familiar surge of pride. She was so beautiful, so perfect, almost unreal; and she was his wife. Fashion editors and journalists, about to pack up and trudge on weary, swollen feet back to Fleet Street, felt a new lease of life billow through them. Pages of half-written copy for the following day's newspapers and magazines were torn up. The word spread. One woman stood out, streets ahead of any other at the Royal Garden Party. It was The Countess of Wessex, and no British or international designer could take the credit for her outfit. The champagne-coloured silk dress and picture hat lined with finely pleated olive-green silk were both her own design.

'Crumbs, Mummy has done it again,' was Eleanora's irreverent verdict when the next day's newspapers arrived at Broadacres.

Peter gave a wolf whistle. 'Yes, your mother looks lovely,' he agreed. They were poring over the newspapers spread out in the kitchen of Broadacres with Rolf and some friends. Meg and Dolly were looking over their shoulders, Dolly pointing and making the little squeaking noises she always did when excited. 'I wish my mother looked like yours,' Peter added.

'She only looks like that because she's Italian,' said Eleanora dismissively. 'And your mother can ride a horse. Mine can't.' At nine years old Eleanora considered that a far more important achievement. And besides she liked her Aunt Anne a lot; she was comfortable, like her grandmother. Too young to rationalize, Eleanora had nevertheless always sensed that her mother demanded perfection. Weakness or tears were not to be indulged before her, but with grandmother it was different. She had never needed to pretend, and now with Peter's mother it was the same. Privately, Eleanora wished her mother were more like them but loyalty prevented her from ever mentioning such a thing.

'I still wish my mother looked like yours. Well, a little bit anyway,' said Peter. 'Of course,' he added, being scrupulously fair, 'I know my mother is beautiful on the inside; it's just that it doesn't show.'

Peter was quieter and more studious than Eleanora, and noticed things that she took for granted. He saw beauty in people and objects, whereas Eleanora, always so energetic, never seemed to have time to stop and stare and wonder. He could see that his own mother was cast in the same mould as Lady Margaret. Slightly better looking and with much more strength of character, but just as careless with her appearance, caring more for the company of animals than people. A pair of jodhpurs and a shirt in summer, the same topped with a sweater in winter were almost the sum total of her wardrobe.

'Would you like to go upstairs to the sewing room and see your mother's dress for the coronation?' asked Meg. 'Dolly is just going to sew on the last few pearls.'

'Yes,' said Peter immediately. He slipped his hand into Dolly's. 'You are so clever,' he said, smiling up at her. It was typical of his caring, thoughtful nature. He never forgot silent Dolly always in the background, unable to contribute to the conversation. She smiled back at Peter. At twelve he already showed signs of the charming man he would later become; his smile made women feel special. Dolly was no exception.

'Boys aren't supposed to be interested in dresses,' said Eleanora grumpily. She was anxious to get out into the paddock.

'This boy is,' said Peter, and that settled it. Quiet though he was, he led and Eleanora followed. If Peter wanted to see the dress, that was good enough. Eleanora would go, too.

*

'Oh, if only it were in colour,' sighed Dorothy Ramsay. She sat on the settee, feet up, eyes glued to the television. 'I wish I were there.'

'You can see more on TV,' said Donald, 'and it's more comfortable at home.' Like everybody else who was not actually in London, they had organized their day around the coronation. A cold spread, prepared by Dorothy the day before, was on the trolley beside them and a bottle of champagne was in the ice bucket, ready to be opened the moment Queen Elizabeth the Second was crowned.

The cameras swept over the interior of the abbey. Members of the Royal Family were already seated in the Royal Gallery, and down below in the South Transept were the peers in their ermine-trimmed, crimson robes.

'I can see Nicholas.' Dorothy leaned forward excitedly. The camera changed shots and showed the peeresses sitting in a dazzling cluster in the North Transept opposite the peers. 'And there is Liana,' said Dorothy triumphantly picking her out.

Liana looked lovely in a sheath-like cream satin dress encrusted with gold embroidery, golden drop pearls and tiny golden and amethyst diamanté. She wore her amethyst and diamond jewellery and on her head, perched on top of her elegantly swept-up hair, was a delicate tiara made up of matching diamonds and amethysts. It was Nicholas's present to her for the coronation. Over her dazzling dress, she wore the traditional peeresses robe of crimson pure silk velvet, banded with ermine.

'Oh, Lord, I wish it were in colour.' Mary Pragnell unconsciously echoed Dorothy Ramsay's wish. 'Oh, Dolly, you should be so proud. Don't Lady Liana look lovely? I wish everyone could see what a beautiful colour that dress is.'

'Well, they can, in the abbey,' said Meg.

'I mean the whole world.'

'Since when have you worried about what the world thinks?' Wally asked with some amusement.

'Since my Dolly's dress is up there being seen to be just as good as, no better than, all those fancy designers' dresses. Give me a Dolly Pragnell dress any day; hers is much better than that Norman Hartnell's gowns. Stuffy, his clothes is. I can't think why the Royal Family always choose him.' Everyone laughed at Mary's passionate outburst but they agreed. Dolly's dress, which she had designed and made for Liana herself, outshone them all.

The Pragnell family had come over to Broadacres for the day to join Meg, Bruno, their son Rolf, now a sturdy nine-year-old, and his sister, three-year-old Alice. Everything that could have been done the day before had been done. Now they could sit back and enjoy the pomp and ceremony taking place in London.

Upstairs in Broadacres, the furniture had been grouped around the television in the newly decorated Arcadian drawing room. From records Liana had unearthed in the library, the room had been renovated, faithfully reproducing the original Inigo Jones' designs. Always a beautiful room, the walls now shone with a warm, creamy white, and the carving from the dado to the cornice was enriched with gold leaf. The Thomas Chippendale settees and chairs had been repaired and reupholstered in red velvet and the

William Kent tables, resting on the ornately carved animal pedestals had been french polished until they reflected almost as much as the gilded mirrors on the walls.

'Peter and I want to go downstairs to the kitchen,' announced Eleanora after being told by her grandmother to keep her feet on the floor where they belonged.

'You'll stay up here today with the rest of the family,' said Margaret. It was not often she was strict with Eleanora but today she felt they should all be together to watch the coronation and hopefully catch a glimpse of Nicholas and Liana.

'It would hurt Meg's feelings if you went downstairs,' said Anne, trying to pour oil on troubled water. 'Look at the lovely cold buffet she has left for us. She has gone to so much trouble to make sure we have everything we need.' She smiled at Eleanora, sympathizing at her restlessness. The elegance and beauty of the newly decorated room made her feel slightly uncomfortable, too; but she understood Margaret's point. It was a fitting place from which to view such a historic occasion. She added a little bribe. 'When the queen has been crowned, you and Peter can have a glass of champagne.'

'Really?' Eleanora was delighted at the thought of forbidden fruit.

'Really,' said Anne firmly, ignoring her mother who was vigorously shaking her head behind Eleanora's back.

Even Eleanora was quiet and watched intently as Dr Geoffrey Fisher, the Lord Archbishop of Canterbury, raised the sacred crown of St Edward. High, high the crown rose in the archbishop's hands before he gently lowered it on to the young Queen's head. Then there was a rustling, a sudden breathless sigh stirring through the ancient grey stone abbey as a thousand noblemen and their ladies lifted their coronets. In the North Transept a sea of waterlilies bloomed, rose in the air and gently subsided – the ermine-clad arms of the peeresses putting on their coronets.

Then a great sound: 'God save the Queen.' It was echoed in the Arcadian Room at Broadacres.

'The words come from the heart of the nation,' said Margaret, becoming unexpectedly poetic, and with tears running down her face. The trumpets in the abbey shrilled, the guns outside boomed across the city of London, bells pealed from a thousand belfries. It was high noon. 'No-one has eyes for anyone save the Queen,' she said through her tears.

'Except Daddy. *He* isn't looking at the Queen; he is looking at Mummy,' said Eleanora, peering closely at the television. 'I think he loves her more than the queen.'

Richard Chapman set about opening the champagne. 'I think he probably does, darling,' said Margaret with a half-laugh, hastily wiping away her tears.

'More than me, too, do you think?' Eleanora asked jealously.

'Of course not. He loves you both.'

In their thatched cottage Donald Ramsay was opening their champagne. 'Look at Nicholas,' he said. 'Even during such a historic occasion as a coronation he can't take his eyes off his wife.'

'He loves her,' said Dorothy comfortably.

'Love or obsession? I wonder, I wonder.' He poured out the champagne. 'He's too intense.'

'Stop pontificating and give me my drink.'

They clinked glasses. 'To Her Majesty. God save the Queen.'

But Donald worried about Nicholas. He had put Liana up on a high pedestal. How would he react if one day she disappointed him? If one day he found she had feet of clay like every other human being? Being the pragmatist that he was, Donald Ramsay had no doubt that Liana had feet of clay. Each man and woman on earth was created with inbuilt imperfections. In spite of Nicholas's adoration, Liana could be no exception.

Chapter Nineteen

Gustavo Simionato had gone on ahead to Coco Chanel's villa in the south of France, leaving Raul to finish editing their latest film, *Bambina*. Raul was pleased. Simionato had let him have an entirely free hand with this latest film, and his name would share equal billing on the credits. Not only that, the previous year, 1952, Raul had directed an opera, *The Italian Girl in Algiers*, at La Scala, Milan. It had been a great artistic success and Antonio Ghiringhelli, the manager of La Scala, had asked Raul to direct *La Traviata* the following autumn. Rehearsals started in September, a month's time. Raul Levi was becoming a name to be reckoned with in Italy, and now he had his sights set on France. It was merely a question of finding the right play; which was the reason he had agreed to go to Chanel's house party.

The editing finished, Raul set off in his newly acquired red MG sports car for the drive to Chanel's villa, La Pausa. By right, Simionato's name should not be on the credits at all for this latest film, thought Raul, feeling slightly resentful, but the villa in Rome was not his yet, and he wanted it. Simionato was an old man now and had recently suffered two strokes and had a heart murmur. Raul consoled himself with the thought that he should not have to wait too long.

Heads turned as the open-topped red car roared through the hot June countryside of Italy. From Rome he took the route to the coast, enjoying dawdling his way along the Tuscan coastline, then through Liguria up to the Riviera di Levante, past Genova and on to the Riviera di Ponente, past Ventimiglia into Monaco, finally arriving at his destination on Cap d'Antibes.

He found a large party assembled around the villa's swimming pool – mostly French and Italian film and theatre people. Raul quickly noted those he thought might be useful to him – he would seek them out for private conversation later – the rest were of no importance. There was also an American family, an elderly, balding man with gold-rimmed glasses, his much younger blonde wife, possessed of abundant breasts which flowed in all directions out of her two-piece swimsuit and a daughter who showed signs of eventually possessing breasts as large as her mother. They looked and sounded out of place. At least I'll be able to practise my English, thought Raul; directing in London was out of the question until he had mastered the English language, a task he was pursuing with vigour.

Having been shown to his room and unpacked, Raul donned swimming trunks and joined the others around the pool. The television was on; they were waiting for the film of the coronation of the Queen of England to start.

While they waited Coco was flicking through a magazine showing photographs of the various events in London leading up to the coronation. 'Of course, the English have never known how to dress,' she screeched. 'How can they? All their clothes are made by men! Men who have no idea how a woman feels, how a woman moves.'

She held up the magazine. The page showed a photograph of the Royal Garden Party on 29 May. The women all wore the latest fashion – nipped-in waists, voluminous long skirts and incredibly high heels; on their heads, most wore cartwheel hats.

'Gee, he's a real dishy man,' said the American woman pointing at the opposite page. She leaned forward to get a closer look. Raul thought her breasts would surely fall out.

Her husband obviously thought so, too. 'Emmy Lou!' he growled.

Emmy Lou giggled, saw Raul watching her and hitched her bosom back into the swimsuit top with a distinctly provocative movement. She's ready for bedding, thought Raul feeling stirrings of interest. He had been busy. It had been at least two weeks since he had had a woman, and celibacy was not the norm for him. He observed Emmy Lou with lustful eyes.

'The Earl of Wessex,' said Emmy Lou reading the caption at the bottom of the page. 'Now, I'd sure like to meet him.'

'Ridiculous clothes,' sneered Chanel, ignoring the American woman's interruption, her voice rising higher on a note of vindictiveness. 'But as Napoleon said, what can you expect from a nation of shopkeepers!'

'I didn't know Napoleon was interested in fashion.' The assembled company laughed at Simionato's joke.

Coco Chanel sniffed and flicked the pages over, then stopped and looked. 'Well, at least here is one woman who looks chic. The Countess of Wessex. Hah!' she exclaimed triumphantly after a moment's silence while she read. 'But why does she look chic? I'll tell you, because she designed her own outfit; it says so here. She wasn't dressed by some man, living out his fantasies of being a woman by dressing women!'

Torn between looking down Emmy Lou's cleavage or the curling black hairs of her bush protruding from the legs of her swimsuit, Raul glanced at the magazine Chanel was waving. He could see what she meant. The Countess of Wessex did look different. Tall, slender, and dressed with cool simplicity, the kind of clothes Chanel herself would have designed. He looked away and then looked back again, drawn by a feeling of familiarity. He looked closer but all he saw was a very aristocratic woman, a haughty woman, one born into the good things of life; and at her side her equally aristocratic husband. They were a handsome couple, the Earl and Countess of Wessex. Suddenly he felt irritated, assailed by a vague sense of unease.

He looked back at Emmy Lou. 'Well, I think she looks real plain,' she drawled. 'I like the other clothes better.'

'That woman looks real smart. And that's how you're gonna look Emmy Lou, or my name ain't Abe Appleton. Coco here is gonna design you some outfits that are gonna make you look like a lady. Every one of them will be unique. No woman in the United States of America will look like Emmy Lou Appleton.'

'I can believe that,' said Raul, an edge of irony to his voice. He wondered how on earth Chanel would cope with such a voluptuous figure. Her clothes were usually designed for, and modelled by, gamine girls who looked as if they had been starved for a year. Emmy Lou simpered, mistaking his remark for a compliment. Silly bitch, thought Raul, but it did not diminish his lust.

'Anyway, Coco, you shouldn't be so vitriolic. It doesn't suit you,' said Simionato.

'Why not? I hate the English. They insulted me when I gave my first show after the war. I could have been ruined.'

'But you are not ruined. The Americans love you. If this is being ruined,' he waved his hands at the wonderful surroundings, 'then I wouldn't mind being ruined, too.'

'Poof! You have got plenty of money, everybody knows that. But yes, the Americans do love me,' Chanel conceded, then, 'quiet everybody, the film is starting'.

Raul lazed back on his sun lounger. He thought the coronation film long and tedious and soon his attention wandered. Yes, the Americans must like Chanel, he thought. The villa was marvellous. Built of grey stone on a promontory looking out to sea, on a site that had once been an olive grove, the architect had achieved miracles. Not a single tree appeared to have been felled; instead the villa had been designed around the ancient, gnarled trunks so that it twisted and turned, having rooms in unexpected places. The ground, richly carpeted with wild lavender, filled the air with aromatic perfume. This was the life, no doubt about it. The place reeked of money. Artistic success had not yet brought Raul the kind of money needed for such a villa, but he knew he must not be impatient. Already he was earning far more than most of his contemporaries. He was not poor, and he would be rich soon enough. Simionato had told him he had named him as his heir; it was just a matter of time.

Raul felt restless: the coronation was boring. How typical of the English to do everything so slowly. And he still felt strangely uneasy instead of relaxed. God, I must need a woman more badly then I thought. A swim was the answer. He would go for a swim. Levering himself up from the sun lounger, he paused just long enough for Emmy Lou to be able to appreciate his tall, muscular figure. Abe Appleton might be a millionaire but he also had a bald pate and a paunch. Raul knew Emmy Lou needed more than money! Satisfied that she had noted the virile bulge in his swimming trunks, he set off down the steep slope that led to the private beach. He was not surprised, half an hour later, to see Emmy Lou sliding precipitously down the steep shingle beach towards the water.

He flipped over and slid through the water to join her on the shingle. 'You don't want this on.' With a quick movement he undid her swimsuit top and threw it aside. Her breasts flowed upwards and outwards. They were lovely. So firm, thought Raul as he fondled them, they might almost have been pumped up.

'Say,' Emmy Lou smacked his hand playfully, 'you Italians don't hang about, do you?'

'No,' said Raul, pushing her on to her back and putting his hand inside her bathingsuit bottom. He found her clitoris easily; that was huge, too. He rubbed it, and she shuddered.

'I haven't said I want to.' She made a token protest.

'You don't have to say anything,' answered Raul. 'Just open up.' He could not wait and, before Emmy Lou could draw another breath, he released his rigid shaft through the leg of his swimming trunks and, pulling aside the soft material of her swimsuit bottom, thrust it inside her. 'There, I told you not to say anything,' he said as she reared up in pleasure.

They were both desperate; foreplay was not necessary; they climaxed together, violent and gasping.

'Gee, that was great.'

'Only the beginning,' said Raul, sucking at a nipple. It was big and hard, like a pebble in his mouth.

'We can't stay here on the beach. Someone might see us. Abe would kill me.'

'He thinks you are faithful to him?'

'Let's just say, honey, he doesn't know for certain that I'm not. And that sure is the way I wanna keep it.'

Raul laughed. 'In the sea then.'

He dragged her, squeakily protesting, into the sea, and together they swam out around a projecting rock until they were entirely hidden from the land by an overhang of the cliff. The water was waist-deep but there was no beach.

'Gee, what did you say your name was?'

'Raul.'

'Gee, Raul, this is impossible. There's nowhere to lay down.'

'Nothing is impossible if you want it badly enough. And I want you.' As he spoke Raul took off his trunks and wedged them on a small ledge, then, reaching down, he slid off Emmy Lou's as well and put them with his. 'Put your arms around my neck.'

Emmy Lou obeyed and Raul began to kiss her, pushing his fingers up inside her, massaging her clitoris with his thumb at the same time. 'Ooh,' she groaned and wrapped her legs around him. Raul entered her but took his time, leaving it until she was jerking spasmodically, thrashing the water into a foam. They stayed in the water an hour and in that hour Emmy Lou learned everything there was to know about different ways of making love in the sea. They staggered back to the villa, limp and glutted.

Chanel spied them coming. 'My God, where have you been?' she screamed.

'Jesus, has Abe missed me?' Emmy Lou was terrified.

'Abe? Abe?' Chanel looked as if she had never heard the name before.

'Yes, Abe Appleton my husband. Has he?'

'Gustavo's had a heart attack.' Chanel rushed down the slope and grabbed at Raul's arm. 'He has been asking for you. Come quick. He is dying, I think. It may be too late already.'

It was. Gustavo Simionato died exactly three minutes before Raul reached his bedside. Kneeling, he took the brittle, paper-thin hand in his, a mass of conflicting emotions teeming in his head and heart. For in spite of his shallowness with women, Raul had become genuinely fond of Simionato over the years. It was not just for his money he loved the old man, but for his humour, compassion and, above all, his prodigious talent. Raul bowed his head in homage, silently acknowledging that the man who now lay lifeless before him was undoubtedly the greatest single figure in his entire life. There would never be another Simionato.

The following day, Raul left. He was to follow Simionato's body in the ornate hearse Chanel had hired. They were to drive without a stop to Rome where Simionato would be buried with full civic honours.

'Raul.' Raul turned; it was Emmy Lou, following him out to his car. 'When will I see you again?'

He frowned, his eyes blank. 'See me?'

Without another word she made a small, hopeless gesture with her hands and turned back to the villa. It was humiliating to realize that the man who yesterday had spent an hour making passionate love to her had already forgotten who she was.

*

Simionato had been true to his word. Everything had been left to Raul. He was now a rich man, rich enough to choose the work he wanted to do, rich enough to wait until the right film, play or opera was offered to him. He chose to do nothing until they started rehearsals for *La Traviata* at La Scala.

With Luigi, his assistant, Raul set about designing the sets and lighting.

'But Umberto usually does the lighting,' protested Ghiringhelli. 'He knows *Traviata* backwards.'

'Exactly, that is why I do everything', said Raul imperiously, '*my way.*'

When Ghiringhelli saw the subtle atmospheric lighting Raul had designed and his imaginative use of sparse sets, he had to approve. He had given the chorus much more room and transformed the whole opera. Under Raul's direction it would seem like a new work.

'This is the new breed of director we must always be looking for,' he told everyone, 'a man who can do everything, see the production as a whole concept from the very beginning.'

He let Raul have a free hand, even to the extent of dismissing some of the elderly chorus, unheard of at La Scala. While they had breath enough to sing, they always remained. But when Raul was faced on the first morning of rehearsal by a stage full of overweight, elderly men and extremely bosomy, equally elderly ladies, he decided to make changes.

'The union will never let you,' forecast Luigi.

'Nothing is impossible,' was Raul's reply. And it seemed that nothing was. By the use of his considerable charm and slightly devious explanations that it would, *probably*, only be for the duration of the performance of *Traviata*, Raul persuaded half the chorus to step down. He knew full well that many of them would never come back to the stage once they had left it; they were too old. He sent them away with their heads full of dreams of returning for the rest of the season. They would find out later, when the younger chorus refused to budge. That was not his problem; he had achieved what he wanted – a considerably revamped chorus.

One Friday morning Raul strode into La Scala. He was auditioning that morning for the remaining three places in the chorus – one soprano and two tenors. He was in an exceptionally good mood. His new mistress, Maria, had proved astoundingly accommodating in bed. Every night for a whole week Raul had been able to indulge in every erotic whim he fancied. It amused him to use and sometimes abuse her body for his own pleasure. Shocking her gave him a vicarious thrill – he knew she would never protest. Maria was a young soprano playing at Piccola Scala, an offshoot of the main theatre designed for nurturing new talent. As he indulged himself with her young body, he was well aware that she was hoping it would land her a leading role in one of his operas. He did not tell her that he thought her voice weak and uncontrolled and that she would never be good enough for anything he directed. When she found that out, she would leave him, but in the meantime he had every night to look forward to.

Luigi handed him a long list of names. 'Christ, couldn't you have cut it down a bit?' Luigi looked worried then smiled as Raul grinned. 'Let's hope some of them are good.'

They sat in the darkened auditorium, Raul with his feet up on the back of the seat in front, leaning back, smoking one of his interminable cigarettes. 'First tenor on, please,' shouted Luigi.

The young tenor walked nervously into the centre spot, lit by a single lime; then the next; and the next. Raul made no comment except to shout, 'Thank you,' when he had heard enough. The decision was not difficult; all the tenors were good but two were much better than the others. He needed two and they were the obvious ones. Raul scribbled their names on the back of an old cigarette packet and gave it to Luigi who had the pleasant task of informing the chosen two, and the not-so-pleasant task of informing those rejected.

'Sopranos next,' shouted Raul, not waiting for Luigi to return.

He was listening to the fourth girl when Luigi slid into the seat next to him. 'Any good?' he whispered.

'Fucking awful,' swore Raul. 'Not one of the bitches can manage a full-blooded top C.'

Luigi sank down in his seat. Even in the darkness of the auditorium he could see Raul's previous good mood had rapidly dissipated. 'Oh,' he muttered disconsolately. He knew Raul's standards: he was never satisfied with anything less than perfection. Even if it was only for a chorus.

The twelfth girl stepped nervously on to the stage and began to sing. Luigi tensed, waiting for the top C. When it came she only just managed to scrape up to the note before wavering off it completely. Raul exploded. 'For Christ's sake,' he shouted, 'it's only a fucking top C. Hasn't your singing teacher taught you that in order to sing C you must be able to get a good E? Get out of my sight and stop wasting my time.'

The girl erupted into noisy tears and had to be led from the stage. Luigi sank lower in his seat. 'This is the last girl,' he said, 'number thirteen.' He hoped it was not an ill omen. God help her if she could not reach the top note.

'Last one, number thirteen,' bellowed Raul.

A tall, slender girl walked on to centre stage. The harsh light of the lime cruelly emphasized the shabbiness of her clothes. But nothing, not even the most piercing light, could find fault with the beauty of her face or the unconscious grace with which she held herself. She began to sing, hesitant at first, then gaining in confidence. It was the voice of a true coloratura, pure silver, soaring effortlessly to the top notes.

But Raul was not listening properly. He half stood as she came into the limelight, gripping hold of the back of the seat in front of him, his hands tense. Now he knew the cause of his vague sense of unease ever since that day at Chanel's villa. He had not realized it then, but now he knew. The picture of the English countess had started it off; she had a vague resemblance to Liana. Long-dormant memories had begun to stir. He looked again at the girl on stage at La Scala: she could have been Liana ten years ago. Hauntingly beautiful, thin, vulnerable, the emotion pouring forth in her voice, she reminded him uncomfortably of the unstinting emotion

Liana had poured over him – over him and everyone she had loved. The top C echoing around the vast auditorium ricocheted and rebounded in Raul's mind and became Liana's wailing cry echoing down the mountainside the day Eleanora had died. He shivered violently, although it was a warm day, and shook his head. For the first time in his life guilt swamped Raul, and the sudden, unexpected birth of a conscience was traumatic. For the first time in years he felt uncertain. What should he do?

Luigi was excited. The number thirteen had not been unlucky after all. 'We're in luck. This girl can sing like an angel. There's no doubt. She's the one. I'll hire her, OK? OK?'

Raul turned, startled. The bleak mountainside disappeared. He was back in La Scala, Luigi's enthusiastic words finally sinking in.

He looked at the girl on stage. She had finished singing and was waiting. But he could not possibly work with someone who reminded him of Liana every day, too damned uncomfortable. 'Get rid of her,' he said harshly.

'But she's the best, she . . .'

'Get rid of her. Do it!' he shouted as Luigi hesitated, unable to believe his ears. 'Hire the first girl we heard.'

Luigi stared after Raul as he walked from the theatre. Where the hell was he going? And what the hell was the matter with him?

Raul did not think about it. If anyone had asked him where he was going, he would not have been able to say. Invisible strings were pulling him, and he had no control, no say in his immediate destiny. The red MG roared down the *autostrada*, across the flat plain of Lombardy, past the rice fields and poplars. Piacenza, Parma, Modena, Bologna: the familiar names flashed past as he drove hour after hour across the viaducts and through the tunnels of the *Autostrada del Sole* on to Firenze, then through Tuscany on to Rome. It never even occurred to him to stop at Rome and stay the night in his villa. It was already late evening and his bones were beginning to ache but the relentless force which had started him on the journey was too strong for him to stop. He drove on and on, past the ruins of the once magnificent monastery of Monte Casino and finally into Naples itself and on up to the *castello*.

It was pitch dark now. The brief Mediterranean dusk had long since given way to night. The car pitched and rolled on the final ascent up the unmade track to the *castello* but Raul drove on heedless of the damage the sharp stones might be doing to the tyres. At last he was there. He stopped the car in the gateway and, switching off the engine, lay back and looked up at the solid black mass of stone surrounding him – the ancient Roman portals, silent witnesses to so many human activities. Completely exhausted now, he slumped back in his seat. The lights of modern Naples twinkled below him and swam out of focus. Raul slept but although fatigued almost beyond endurance, it was a shadowy, disturbed sleep. He awoke continually, every time thinking, why the hell have I come here?

He woke at first light to an eery feeling that time had stood still. It was as if he had never been away – the same mountainside, the same smell of wild thyme and rosemary, the same vast, curving expanse of dark blue sea, shot pink and purple now by the first rays of the rising sun. Slowly he walked to the *castello*. The building had not changed either, the thick stone walls withstanding the ravages of time as they had done for so many centuries. Inside it was empty, a home now for bats and other wild creatures. In the kitchen, lying in a corner, half buried beneath dried rubbish, he found a coffee pot and recognized it at once. It was the one Liana had used.

He sat down on the stone steps of the kitchen and looked out across the cobbled courtyard to the well. He could almost taste the coffee. It had seemed like nectar in those days, the American coffee Liana had earned on the streets of Naples or even the acorn coffee they were forced to drink when real coffee ran out. Where was she now? It was obvious no-one had been to the *castello* for years.

He walked back along the track and made his way to the village. An old crone served him breakfast in the village square – fresh bread and strong black espresso coffee. She remembered Liana and Eleanora.

'Did you get your funeral for the *marchesa* in the end?'

Raul tried not to shudder at her words. He had not banked on anyone's remembering that. 'Yes,' he said briefly. Now was not the time to elaborate. 'You remember me?' he asked cautiously.

She gave a toothless grin. 'I am the only one here who does. God must have sent you to me because I am the only one alive who can answer your questions. Everyone has left this place. Just twenty people live here now, and all, except me, are foreigners! I ask you, what is the world coming to?'

'It's a sad world, *signora*. Where do the other villagers come from?'

'Foreigners from the next village.' She spat in the dust. 'You never could trust those Calitresi, and now look! They have taken over the entire village. Me, the only native left.'

'Do you know what happened to Liana, the friend of the *marchesa*?

'Dead,' said the crone. 'She went down into Naples and then there were bombs, bombs, many bombs. She didn't come back.' She crossed herself piously. 'I pray she had a decent Christian burial. So many didn't, you know.'

'I know,' said Raul slowly. An unwanted mantle of guilt settled on his shoulders. 'It was a terrible time.' He paid for the bread and coffee and went back to the *castello*.

What had he rushed down here for? What on earth had he hoped to find? Liana alive and well, still waiting for him? He had acted on impulse, something foreign to him unless it concerned his own future well-being. His mind ached, his step was heavy.

The sun was high in the sky by the time he reached the *castello*. Brilliant and dazzling, the light should have dispersed any ghosts that might have been left; but it seemed to Raul that the reverse was true. Whereas before in the half-light of early morning he had felt the place to be deserted and empty, now it was full of rustles and sighs. He turned sharply, sure he could hear Liana's laughter, and then he could smell the orange-fresh smell of the springtime *pastiera* cake, the one he had given her the first time they had made love. Suddenly the warmth of the sun faded and he shivered. He could see the sunshine, brilliant as ever, but his skin felt the icy wetness of winter rain, penetrating and cold as it swept in from the sea, and the air was rent with the wail of a soul in torment. He put his hands over his ears to blot out the sound and found that it was coming from his own throat. He was the one who was screaming.

Shaking from the effort of controlling himself, he sank down on to the kitchen steps. They felt warm to his touch. Reassured, he spread his hands on the stone, trying to soak up the warmth. 'God, I must be going mad!' he whispered.

She was dead. There was nothing he could have done; just as there had been nothing he could have done for Eleanora all those years ago. He walked across to the place where he knew she was buried, past the ruined chapel. There was no sign now of the rough wooden cross he had stuck in the earth but the grave looked undisturbed. Grass and a few stubby bushes of thyme were growing on the mound. He breathed a sigh of relief; at least Eleanora slept in peace. He looked down at Naples, shimmering now in the noonday sun, high-rise buildings dominating the bombed ruins of the city. But Raul saw it as it had been in 1944.

Slowly an idea formed in his mind. Two girls had lived and loved in this place, and now there was nothing left to show for their brief lives. No-one except him and the old woman, who would soon be no longer, even knew they had once existed. It did not seem right.

He went back and sat down again on the kitchen steps and, taking a notepad and pencil from his pocket, began to write. He would give them their memorial. It would be a film, a story of pain and suffering and self-sacrifice: Liana's story, a love story, a story of true love that stopped at nothing, not even self-sacrifice. His own sexual affair with Liana was unimportant, it was her extraordinary love for Eleanora that he would write about.

The more he thought about it, the more he realized what a commercial story it was. When he found the right writer to make it into a screenplay, he would make the film. Raul smiled, Liana's unhappy death receding from his conscience. If he could get the story into Hollywood that would really ensure his international recognition. Yes, he would definitely send it to Hollywood just as soon as he could find the right contact.

Chapter Twenty

'God, how I hate boarding school.' It was Christmas 1959 and Eleanora was back at Broadacres for the holidays. Perching on the edge of her mother's desk in the Lower Cloisters office, she bad-temperedly swung a booted foot. She was clothed in what Liana sometimes thought of as the Hamilton-Howards' uniform, jodhpurs and a sweater. 'And now the bloody Government is going to raise the school leaving age. I'll be fifteen in a few days' time; I could have left school at Easter and now I won't be able to.' Pulling her features into a blackly rebellious expression, she kicked out at the walnut marquetry table standing against the wall.

'Eleanora, watch your language, and do keep your feet down, that table is priceless.' Liana sighed in exasperation; why was it her daughter was always so difficult? 'Peter is a boarder at St John's College,' she said, 'and he loves it.'

'Exactly. He loves St John's College. But I'm not *there*, am I? I wouldn't mind being a boarder there; it's an exciting school. They do some fantastic things.' She saw her mother's expression. 'All right, all right I know it's only for boys *and* it's Catholic and I can't go. But I still *hate* St Swithuns. It's a bore and I *hate* it.'

Liana felt confused the way she always did when she was with Eleanora. Her love for Eleanora had not decreased – it was still the most powerful force in her life, that and her memories of Raul – but in spite of her love, she still found it impossible to feel close to her. Nicholas was close to Eleanora; they always laughed a lot together, sharing private, silly little jokes the way people do who are completely at ease with one another. And Margaret, she was close to her daughter, too, perhaps closest of all. Their mutual love of animals, particularly dogs and horses, forged an inseparable bond between them. Liana half smiled now, thinking of the pair of them. How incongruous they looked when together. Margaret was craggier than ever in old age, her poor hands bent and twisted now with arthritis. She had had her hair permed for the coronation and now had it done regularly because it was easier to manage than a bun. Unfortunately the result resembled a walking scouring pad.

By her side Eleanora looked like a young goddess; but the years between them disappeared when they were together. They were never happier than when mucking out the stables, riding to hounds or walking the dogs. Liana knew they both regularly smuggled their dogs up to their bedrooms; dogs were forbidden beyond the lower ground floor now that the house had been completely renovated. But Liana never had the heart to remonstrate with them, knowing how attached they were to their beloved creatures.

Perhaps that's partly the problem, she thought now. I appear to be English, even feel English most of the time, but I shall never become as besotted about animals as the English are. Even the Pragnells had their homes filled with an assortment of animals, and Meg's and Bruno's children had rabbits, hamsters and guinea-pigs as well as the farm animals. At lambing time there were always a couple of orphans being hand-reared on a baby's bottle in the kitchen, and it was the same now with the Chapmans. To them, animals were an extension of their family, but to Liana they were animals. She could never have been cruel to any living creature but was still afraid of horses and did not like the boisterousness of the dogs. And the farm cats always seemed so supercilious; they were an independent lot who preferred the stables to the house.

But although she tried convincing herself that it was these differences which mattered, Liana never succeeded in fooling that deep inner self of the subconscious, that part within her which always saw the truth, no matter how unpalatable, no matter how hard she tried to suppress it. If she had been religious, she would perhaps have called it her soul but she was not religious and because of that did her best to deny its existence. Even so, she knew those superficial matters were not the reasons for the coolness that existed between herself and her daughter. It was not as if Eleanora did not need a confidante or warm, loving approval; she did, like any adolescent girl. But Liana knew she could not be the one to give it, was incapable of giving it, and the reason was that Eleanora looked more and more like Raul with every passing day.

Her dark, henna-red hair was now waist length, a riot of waves and curls, and her black eyes sparkled wickedly in the beauty of her face. Every feature was Raul's – the wide, smiling mouth, firm jawline and sensuously full lips.

When she looked at her, the ghost of Raul looked back through Eleanora's eyes and Liana's heart tightened with pain every time. Even now, nearly sixteen years later, she still wanted to weep when she thought of her lost love. She had thought, even prayed a little sometimes to a God she did not believe in, that the passing of time would make the controlling of her emotion easier. But it had not. Her eyes still blurred with unshed tears, her heart still felt leaden. Why was it that Raul was dead to the whole world but so very much alive to her? As alive and vibrant as he had been the last day she had seen him. She knew the answer. It looked her in the face every time she looked at her. It was Eleanora.

Oh, Eleanora, if only you knew, if only I could tell you why I look away from you, why I keep my own daughter at arm's length. It is because I am afraid that if I look too long and too hard my heart will break. We should have been so close, you and I, but the shadow of Raul drives a wedge between us, and there is nothing I can do to prevent it. I *do* love you, I *do* want to be close, but the monumental wilderness which is my consuming love for Raul, your true father, encircles and encloses me every day. He holds my heart fast, even from the grave.

The words she longed to say remained unspoken, and Liana looked at Eleanora helplessly.

'Bloody boarding school! Why can't I be a day girl?'

'Don't swear,' said Liana almost automatically. She was always saying 'Don't swear,' and Eleanora was always swearing. 'Girls of your class always go to boarding school. You know Daddy agrees with me. It is supposed to be turning you into a young lady.'

'If I didn't go to that bloody school, I could have gone to the Hunt Ball.' Eleanora sighed dramatically. 'First time it's ever been held at Broadacres, and where was I? At that bloody school, stuck in there with a lot of silly little bitches, that's where.'

'Eleanora!' Liana lost her patience. 'Even if you had been here, you wouldn't have gone. You are too young for Hunt Balls. You will stay at that school until you are eighteen, and then we shall see.'

'Then I shall be an opera singer.'

Liana looked up, startled. 'An opera singer! This is a new idea! I thought you were only interested in horses.'

'Nothing new about it. You know I like music,' said Eleanora airily. 'And I can play the piano well enough. Apart from singing, that is all I need to get into the Guildhall School of Music.'

She was indeed a very accomplished pianist although she never bothered to practise much because music always came so easily to her. 'You can play the piano, yes,' agreed Liana, 'but I've never heard you sing. I didn't know you were even interested in singing.'

'There's a lot you don't know about me, Mummy.' Liana mentally winced. Eleanora blurted out the truth, and it hurt. 'Peter says I've got a very good voice. He's got lots of opera records and he knows. Miss Harris, the music teacher at school, says so, too. She's going to arrange for me to have special singing lessons with a teacher from London.'

'I see. Well, I've no objection to the extra lessons if you're willing to work, and I'm sure your father will be pleased. But surely that is all the more reason for staying at school?'

'Yes, but I could be a *day* girl, not a boarder,' said Eleanora, returning to her original theme. Liana failed to recognize the familiar streak of determination, the same steeliness of resolve that she herself possessed.

'You will be a boarder,' said Liana firmly, determined not to give in.

'You never went to boarding school.'

'My life was quite different from yours.'

'Yes, I know. You lived in a castle in Italy and were taught by an English governess. Daddy told me. What was it like? Why don't we go to your castle? I'm the only girl at school with an Italian mother and I can't tell them anything about you, because you never tell *me* anything.'

'There's nothing much to tell,' said Liana curtly.

'But I want to know.'

'And I don't want to talk about it.' Her voice was far harsher than she had intended, for Eleanora's words tore open the old wounds and there was no way she could explain. She looked up at her daughter. 'I'm sorry,' she added on a softer note, 'but I really can't talk about it.'

As her mother looked up, Eleanora glimpsed something that caught at her throat. The serene, impassive mask slipped, just for a second, but it was enough to momentarily halt her in her tracks and stop her impetuous chatter. It stopped her saying that she was planning to persuade her father to take her to Italy the following summer so that she could see for herself the place where her mother had once lived. Instead, she looked down quickly and said, 'Then it's all right about the singing lessons?'

'Yes, it's all right,' said Liana, glad to get back on to safe territory.

*

In view of her mother's very obvious antipathy towards Italy, Eleanora modified her demands and asked to be taken to Europe the following summer, carefully omitting any mention of Italy. However, she met with considerable resistance on that front also, but stubbornly persisted. That Nicholas eventually agreed to Eleanora's insistent demands was due in no small part to Donald and Dorothy Ramsay. Donald, partly retired now, had taken on an energetic young doctor to assist him in the practice. It gave him more time for riding and so he saw much more of Margaret. When not out hunting, they often rode miles together. Donald always enjoyed Margaret's company; with her he could talk horses. 'Galloping over the downs like a pair of elderly lunatics,' said Dorothy good-humouredly.

It was from Margaret that Donald Ramsay learned that Nicholas's desire for another child was becoming an unhealthy obsession – so much so that he and Liana were increasingly quarrelling concerning her refusal to be examined by a doctor. At Margaret's suggestion he persuaded Nicholas to have a sperm count. Personally, although he was careful to keep this to himself, he hoped the result would be low. Then the matter would be settled once and for all, and Nicholas could stop blaming Liana.

When the result did come, it was perfectly normal. 'Damn,' he said coming into the kitchen and waving the pathology slip at Dorothy. 'Nicholas could father a dozen or more children.'

'I'm not surprised,' replied Dorothy. She was bottling raspberries and had two enormous pans stacked with Kilner jars filled with the luscious red fruit. 'You know, last year I had another two jars of raspberries. It's too bad. Those pesky blackbirds have beaten me to it this year. That cat Eleanora gave me is not doing his job.' The cat in question lay flat on his back on the window sill, exposing an enormous ginger underbelly to the sun. His four paws drooped inwards in blissful relaxation. Originally a half-wild ginger tom from Broadacres, he had very quickly decided that life with the Ramsays was much better and now spent most of his time sleeping or eating.

'You feed him too much,' grumbled Donald. 'Why should he bother to catch birds? What shall I do about this?' He waved the pathology slip again.

'Why, tell Nicholas of course,' said Dorothy tartly. 'As his doctor you will have to tell him. Here, sit down and top and tail these gooseberries; they have to be bottled next.' She thrust a pair of kitchen scissors into his hands.

Donald sat down and began to snip half-heartedly at the prickly gooseberries. 'This means, of course, that there is something wrong with Liana.'

'So?'

'Nicholas will try to pressure her into seeing a gynaecologist.'

'And you must stop him,' said Dorothy firmly.

Donald sighed. 'I'm in an impossible position. I know Nicholas desperately wants more children before it is too late, and yet I don't want to push Liana into something she doesn't want. On the other hand, as a doctor, I know the reason for her not conceiving might be some very small thing, something that could easily be put right. Perhaps I should speak to Liana privately before I tell Nicholas the results, try and persuade her to go for an examination of her own accord.'

'You'll do no such thing.' Dorothy sat down abruptly at the kitchen table and put her raspberry-stained hands over his. 'You might be a doctor but you are also a man, and as a man, you have no idea of how women feel about these things. We are happily married but we have no children. The worst time in my life, and the time when at one point I seriously considered leaving you, was when I was being investigated for infertility.'

Donald started in surprise. 'But you never mentioned it.'

'You never asked me! But I'll tell you now. I found it undignified and humiliating to be pushed and pulled about and peered into as if I were a carcass on the butcher's slab.' She held up her hand to stop Donald who was about to protest. 'Yes, I know you doctors don't think of us as women when you are examining us – that is the way you are trained. But many doctors – especially, in my experience, the specialists – are inclined to forget we are human beings as well! And on top of that, having to take my temperature for weeks on end, then having to make love to order when the temperature was right in the vain hope of conceiving.' She shuddered at the memory. 'I sometimes wonder how I retained my sanity.'

Donald gazed at her, his jaw dropping open in astonishment. This was a Dorothy he had never seen before. 'I never guessed,' he muttered.

He looked so shamefaced that Dorothy relented and gently patted his hand. 'That's all behind us now. But back to Liana. In spite of all her energy, strength and resolve, I still have the feeling that it only needs some trigger to break her. There is something about her, as if something haunts her. God knows what happened to her before she came here. So for her sake, don't force her to go through what I went through; it could destroy her. Nicholas has one child, a daughter he adores. He should be grateful for that. Make him see that another child isn't so important, but retaining the love of his wife is.'

263

Donald ached with pain for his wife. All these years she had borne this and not told him. 'I'll persuade Nicholas to let sleeping dogs lie,' he said. And he did.

At first Nicholas was reluctant to accept the advice but when Donald told him how Dorothy had reacted and he understood the very real possibility of losing Liana's love he changed his mind. He could live without another child but he knew he could not live without Liana.

'Take a holiday,' Donald said. 'Take Liana somewhere nice.'

Nicholas pulled a wry face. 'You should know I can never prise Liana away from Broadacres; she sticks to the place faster than a limpet. She never wants to travel, and anyway, the gardens are being opened to the public for the first time this year. She'll be buzzing around like a bluebottle, making certain that everything is perfect.'

Donald smiled. 'Yes, I know about the gardens. Margaret has cut down on her riding in order to supervise the renaissance of the knot garden. Whenever I ring her, all she can talk about is the problem she is having with her linear patterns of box and teucrium! I haven't the faintest idea of what she is talking about.'

'Then you see my problem,' said Nicholas.

Donald agreed. 'Leave Liana at Broadacres. I know you are right about her never wanting to leave it.' He paused, remembering the time he had brought the war-weary Liana to Broadacres that August evening. 'I wish you could have been there then,' he said, 'the first time Liana saw the house. I'll never forget her expression. She fell in love with it there and then, and has never stopped loving it since.' He turned his attention back to Nicholas. 'But you need a holiday. So, if you can't take your wife, take that daughter of yours. I have heard rumours she wants to tour Europe.' He raised his eyebrows and Nicholas grinned.

It was common knowledge that Eleanora was boring the Pragnells, Meg and Bruno, the Ramsays, Margaret, in fact anyone who would listen to her, with her plans for the summer of 1960. She had the route all mapped out: through France to Belgium, to Luxemburg, on to Germany and Switzerland and back. Italy was never mentioned, but like mother like daughter, she had made up her mind. Her resolve to get her own way was absolute. Once on European soil the route could be changed and Italy would be on the agenda.

*

'You don't mind, darling?' Nicholas buried his face in the warm hollow of Liana's shoulder.

Liana thought for a moment. Did she mind? She knew Eleanora was wanting to go to Europe, the rumours had of course permeated to her ears. But Italy was not included on the itinerary, thank God. Although why she should want to deny her daughter sight of her own country she did not know. What was there to be afraid of? Eleanora would never know; nobody knew. It was time to stop being afraid of wispy shadows. In fact the time was long overdue, but still the dread remained. She felt the warmth of Nicholas's arms around her, the strength of his long body lying alongside hers. He had been good to her, this man whom she had so coldly and deliberately chosen as the father for her daughter. It was ridiculous to feel jealous of the closeness of his relationship with Eleanora. It was not his fault she was unable to get close to her own daughter. I must be glad, she thought, glad that he wants to show Eleanora Europe, a place I never want to set foot in again as long as I live. I must be glad he is braver than me.

Not once had they ever talked about the war, since living in England, but Liana knew Nicholas had been exposed to horrifying things, too. There must be some places he did not want to see. The last few weeks of the war when he had been in Germany, he had once confessed to his mother, had been 'hellish'. Now he was contemplating going back there on holiday – to the places he had once fought in, and all because Eleanora wanted to go.

'Of course not,' she said smiling up at him.

He kissed her gently, his tongue sliding into her mouth with easy familiarity. Liana gave herself up to the pleasure of his mouth on hers. These days she found herself wanting him. Wrapping her legs around him, she let him slide into her and involuntarily tightened her muscles, wanting to hold on to his organ, to prolong the slow, easy pleasure. It was at such moments that she thought she did love Nicholas. They gently rocked together towards a climax and she forgot everything else but her sensual need for Nicholas.

It was only afterwards she puzzled about it, about the growing conflict in her mind, the difficulty in separating Raul and Nicholas, the difficulty in setting out her emotions clearly. But always, something deep within her eventually forced her back to the same conclusion. What she felt for Nicholas was grateful affection and a kind of physical love. But true love, real love was what she felt for Raul. He was her man, the one and only love of her life. Nothing could, or ever would, change that.

*

'Of course, if she could have got the Queen it would have been different!' observed Eleanora with a touch of acerbity. She was referring to Liana's decision to open the gardens of Broadacres herself rather than to import a celebrity.

'Don't turn into a bitch, my dear,' reproved her grandmother. 'That is something your mother has never been. She is above that. She is always the perfect wife and mother.'

'Perfect everything,' said Eleanora mutinously. Sometimes she had the strangest feeling of wanting to smash her mother's perfection, smash it and find out what lay beneath. But, of course, that was impossible to explain to her grandmother who would not have had the faintest idea of what she was talking about. Anyway, she hated Margaret's being cross or disapproving and, seeing the frown on her face now, reached over and kissed her. 'Sorry, Gran,' she said. 'I'm feeling grumpy: all those exams and everything at school. I need a holiday.'

'Only a few weeks and you will be having one,' answered her grandmother, 'so help your mother and be a good girl.'

Eleanora hugged herself with glee at the thought. Yes, only a couple of weeks. Soon she could start counting the days and then she would be off on the adventure of a lifetime. Yes, she could afford to be generous and help her mother. Besides, she loved Broadacres, too, and felt proud of the lovely grounds and gardens. In June everything was at its best, not only the formal gardens but the estate as well. The hedgerows buzzed with insects burrowing amidst the riot of wild flowers, and in the pastures sleek horses lazily flicked their tails while wading through a sea of yellow buttercups.

'Nowhere in the world is more beautiful than southern England in early summer,' said Liana in her opening speech. And for once, Eleanora agreed wholeheartedly with every word she said.

All the local dignitaries came to the opening, plus, of course, carefully selected people from the world of commerce and finance. Meg, Dolly and Mary Pragnell, plus helpers from the village, were rushing about serving strawberries and champagne under brightly coloured umbrellas in a spotless stable courtyard. Terracotta pots spilling over with miniature red roses completed the transformation of the yard. Opening day was an unqualified success, and now in July the paying visitors were increasing every day. Like everything else Liana organized, it was proving to be a money-spinner, everything running as smoothly as well-oiled clockwork. Margaret was pleased and proud, and thankful, too, because, apart from a weekly round with a pair of sharp secateurs, her contribution, the knot garden, looked after itself. The rest of the gardens were looked after by three expert gardeners assisted by local boys in their spare time.

Nicholas did not feel guilty about leaving. Liana was happy and wanted to stay.

'I can't leave Broadacres now, not in its first open season.' She linked arms with Nicholas as they walked the estate late one evening. 'Besides, I've got my eye on some property in London. We must invest the money from the garden in something, and this is a real bargain.'

Nicholas immediately felt doubtful about leaving. 'Darling, will I ever be able to persuade you to stop work? It doesn't seem right for me to go gallivanting off if you are about to embark on something new.'

'Rubbish. It isn't work, not if I enjoy it, which I do. Anyway, escorting Eleanora across Europe won't be exactly restful! Have you seen the list she's made? She wants to see every tourist attraction, large and small, on the entire route.'

'I know.' Nicholas laughed. 'She takes after you. When she does something she does it thoroughly.'

Eleanora and Nicholas departed with Liana's blessing and Margaret's dire warning about foreign drivers. 'They all drive like maniacs, *and* on the wrong side of the road!'

*

'I think perhaps it would be wiser not to mention that we're going on into Italy,' said Nicholas.

Eleanora looked up from her postcard-writing. 'What shall I say, then?'

'Don't say anything much. Just say we are here at Nyon, near Geneva; the weather is lovely; the hotel is good. You know, all the usual things. We can send another postcard when we get back into France or Switzerland.'

Eleanora grinned. It had been surprisingly easy to persuade her father to go on down to Italy and revisit the *castello*. Unbeknown to her, he had been longing to do just that anyway.

'Do you think Mummy will be furious?'

'No,' said Nicholas, wishing he felt as confident as he sounded.

But he forgot Liana's possible displeasure as he and Eleanora drove on down through Italy, eventually arriving in Naples. They booked into a hotel overlooking the castle and the harbour. Memories came flooding back to Nicholas. He had forgotten the breathtaking beauty of the spectacular coastline and the bay of Naples.

'How can Mummy never want to come back here?' asked Eleanora, echoing Nicholas's unspoken thought. She leaned over the edge of the restaurant terrace, a glass of *spremuta al limone* in her hand. 'Even the drinks are deliciously different.' Then she stopped and gazed around her. The sea was slowly changing – purple to deep navy blue in the evening light – and the mountains darkened with the cloak of night. 'It's magic,' she said softly and turned back to her father. 'Do you know something, it's strange, but I feel almost as if I've come home. I'd like to learn Italian; I don't want to be only English. I ought to be proud of my Italian half as well. You don't mind, do you?'

Nicholas smiled gently; he had been thinking how well she blended in with her surroundings. She fitted in with the brilliance of the colours and now, seeing her beside the Neapolitans in the hotel, Nicholas realized for the first time how very Italian Eleanora looked. 'Of course I don't mind. Why should I? You *are* half Italian, so why deny it? I'm very glad we came.'

'Oh, so am I.' Eleanora turned back to the sea. 'And I can't wait until tomorrow when at last I shall see the *castello*.'

'It's going to be in ruins,' warned Nicholas, 'so don't be disappointed.'

He looked at the sheaf of papers in his hand. They had stopped off at the local authority's modern offices in Naples. Nicholas thought it prudent to try and find out the fate of the *castello*. He wanted it to be just the two of them when they got there, just himself and Eleanora. The thought that someone else might have moved in and taken it over worried him, and he wanted that matter settled and out of the way. So, while Eleanora zoomed in and out of souvenir shops buying up junk jewellery, he took himself off to the local authority records office. As far as the records showed – and being Neapolitan they were slightly chaotic, masses of yellowing documents stacked higgledy-piggledy in an old box file – no-one had ever laid claim to the *castello* and the authorities were certain it was still empty. With the aid of his marriage certificate and Liana's birth certificate, it had not been difficult to register the building as now belonging to the Countess of Wessex, formerly the Marchesa Eleanora Anna Maria, Baroness San Angelo di Magliano e del Monte. God, he had forgotten how long her name was! Nicholas grinned: of course, the fifty pounds in cash had helped oil the wheels of bureaucracy. Naples had not changed!

As he walked through the Roman portals of the gateway the next day, Nicholas sensed a shadowy doubt. Had they been right to come? Liana would not have wanted it. In opening the doors to the past, would he in some way get more than he had bargained for? But within a moment the doubts had gone as Eleanora darted about the courtyard, exclaiming with little cries of delight and wonder. The *castello* had hardly changed at all. Apart from being overgrown with ivy and brilliant yellow broom which had taken root in crevices in the walls, it looked much the same. He showed Eleanora the flagstone in the kitchen where Liana had hidden the jewels, and she lifted it up and peered inside.

'When you met her, she lived here in this huge place all alone?'

'Quite alone. All her relatives had been murdered.'

'Why did you marry her? Did you feel sorry for her?'

'I married her because I fell in love with her. And no, my darling,' he ruffled Eleanora's dark hair, 'I didn't feel sorry for her. Your mother was very proud. She didn't feel sorry for herself, or if she did, she never showed it. And she would not have liked it either if I had shown pity.'

Eleanora walked across to the gateway and stood looking out across the curve of the bay of Naples. She sniffed. 'It's so different from home,' she said. 'It smells so dry. And all those wild herbs! Meg would go mad with delight. I must take some back for her. In England we have doves and wood pigeons cooing; here its cicadas. You'd think they'd get tired of scraping their back legs together, wouldn't you!' She wheeled round abruptly. 'This place is crying out to be restored. Can't you feel it? Oh, Daddy, say we have enough money to restore it. I don't mean all of it, at least, not in the beginning. Only part of it. Then we could come here for holidays, and maybe even Mummy would come, too.'

'We have the money, but . . .' Nicholas hesitated. 'The decision isn't really mine to make. We must ask your mother. After all the building does belong to her. The decision must be hers.'

*

'But Mummy why not?'

'Because I say not.'

'That is not a good enough reason.'

'It is the only reason I intend to give.'

'Go on, clam up the way you always do when you don't want to do something. You put on that hateful superior expression and refuse to discuss it.'

'Eleanora, don't shout at your mother like that.' Nicholas was torn between the two women he loved most in the world.

'I will shout. Why shouldn't I? Everything has to be done *her* way. You never complain, Daddy. I don't know why not. Is it because you are henpecked? Yes, that's it, isn't it? Henpecked, henpecked, *henpecked*?' Eleanora was hysterical with rage.

'Eleanora!' Liana stood up, her face dark with anger. 'Leave the room and apologize for your behaviour before you go.'

'I will not apologize, not unless you say we can restore the *castello*.'

Liana's voice was low but a terrible anger trembled through it. 'You might as well know now, Eleanora, that I will never agree to it. As far as I am concerned it can fall down, stone by stone. I never intend to return to Italy as long as I live, and I have no intention of letting any of the money I have worked so hard to earn for this family be wasted on such a project.'

'You are denying me my birthright. Do you know that? I'm half Italian, too. When you die the *castello* will belong to me, and I want to be able to live there if I wish.'

Liana sank down on to the nearest settee and buried her head in her hands. She had never envisaged it would come to this, quarrelling with Eleanora about the *castello*. Half Italian indeed.' If only she knew. Oh, god, if only she knew. It was more than she could bear. 'I'm not dead yet, Eleanora,' she said, the words half muffled by her hands, 'and you will have to wait until I am before you can touch the *castello*.'

Eleanora stormed from the room. But Nicholas knew the battle was not yet over. He felt helpless. Two strong-minded women, locked in combat – a head-on collision of wills.

*

Later that night in the relative calm of their bedroom, Nicholas tried to heal the rift.

'Would it really be so bad if you agreed to have the *castello* restored? You need never go there. I can understand that memories, particularly the death of your mother, must be painful. But Eleanora is not haunted by such memories; she loves Italy. She loved Naples. She felt she belonged there, and, of course, in a way she does. She is our child, conceived there on our honeymoon. Remember?'

But Liana could not bear to remember and did not answer. Crossing to her dressing room she flung off her clothes and put on a bathrobe, then entering the bathroom turned the bath taps full on: anything to keep herself occupied; anything to keep memories at bay; anything to put off answering Nicholas. His words had snared her emotions like a savage flick from barbed wire.

Nicholas, thinking she was still angry with Eleanora, followed her into the bathroom, and standing behind her gently put his hands on her shoulders.

'Remember?' he repeated softly. 'Remember our wedding night?'

'Nicholas, don't!' Liana shrugged her shoulders away.

Suddenly she felt very frightened, sick with fear. Remember? How could she forget? God, how guilty she felt. All the long years of fighting, of keeping it at bay, and then suddenly, just when she thought she was safe, without warning it was there again: the ugly truth staring her in the face; the deceit. If only Nicholas knew the deceit. Nicholas, dear, gentle Nicholas who thought he was Eleanora's father, who thought his wife loved him, and she never had. Never had! Not in the way he deserved to be. She wanted to weep, to seek relief in confession. But that was not possible. There was no-one to trust, no-one in the world she could talk to. Oh, God, if only there were someone. But there was not; she faced an empty void and in her fear took refuge in anger, turning on Nicholas, bitter words spilling out.

'Isn't it bad enough that you betray me by going there without telling me? Don't ask me to remember and then try to tell me what I ought to do for Eleanora's sake. The answer is still no. No, no and it will always be no!'

Twisting away Liana turned off the bath taps with trembling fingers. Sight blurred with fear and unshed tears, she fumbled in the cupboard for a clean towel, and finding one jerked it from the shelf. Too late she saw the small box pulled out with the towel, saw it falling. Clattering across the floor it spilled its contents which came to rest against the wainscot.

Nicholas bent and retrieved first the box and then the object it had contained. He stared down at the smooth round rubber object he held in one hand. Liana caught her breath. It was her dutch cap, the latest in a long line of contraceptive devices she had hidden so carefully all the years of their marriage at Broadacres.

'What is this?' he said, his voice careful and quiet.

'Well . . . er, it's a . . .' Liana flushed, and for the first time Nicholas could ever remember she was at a loss for words.

'Is this the reason you've never conceived?'

No amount of lies or intricate fabrication could alter the evidence he held in his hand. 'Yes,' she said.

'Why?' His voice was ominously low.

'Because.' The world she had so carefully nurtured, and which was already showing signs of cracking, cartwheeled crazily through her head and she realized the very real danger of losing everything, *everything*. How could she say to Nicholas *because I only ever wanted Raul's children, and if I couldn't have his, then I didn't want anybody else's*? How could she say this to the man who thought he was Eleanora's father? 'Because I was afraid,' she said at last. 'I couldn't bear the thought of having another baby. Donald Ramsay must have told you what a bad time I had.' It was not the truth but it would have to do.

'Why didn't you tell me?'

'I couldn't, I . . .'

'It was easier, I suppose, to let me go on longing, hoping for a son and heir, while all the time you made damned certain I'd never have one. Christ, Liana, don't talk to me about betrayal!' Nicholas's voice rose in anger.

Liana stood and faced him. Slipping her arms around his neck, she tried to work the old magic, anything to distract him. 'Nicholas, I . . .'

'You've used me.' Nicholas's voice broke with emotion and with a savage push he thrust her away from him. Liana turned and fled into the bedroom. What could she do? What could she say? In her haste and agitation she stumbled and fell across the bed.

'Nicholas, listen to me. I . . .'

'Used me!' Nicholas repeated, standing towering over her.

'No! Nicholas, I didn't mean to. Please let me explain,' Liana whimpered, trying to scramble backwards off the bed. 'Please, Nicholas. No!'

But it was not the Nicholas she knew who bent over her body, violently ripping away her bathrobe in one vicious movement. It was a stranger, a man hell-bent on revenge.

'Christ! You bitch, you *bitch*.' Resentment hit Nicholas with blood-red violence. He felt sick. How dare she deny him his rights as a man, as a father. *How dare she?* His brain exploded with anger and he flung himself down on top of her writhing, struggling body, pinning her down. 'A dutch cap. A sodding dutch cap! All these bloody years!'

Liana fought, desperately trying to get away. 'Nicholas, wait, listen. Don't spoil what we . . .' She screamed in fear and pain.

Impervious to her screams and her scratching hands, Nicholas brutally prised her legs apart and rammed his body into hers.

'Deceiving bloody bitch. Deceiving bloody, bloody . . . bitch.' He sobbed as he ground himself into her in an unthinking frenzy.

Finally it stopped, and Nicholas rolled over on to his back. Liana could feel warm liquid trickling down the inside of her thighs and knew it was blood. In his blind rage he had torn her. Neither moved nor spoke. They lay, silent and still, side by side, two strangers, each battling to emerge from a hideous darkness.

Chapter Twenty-One

Staring at the square of moonlight and starlit sky that was the window, Liana shivered. Then, knowing that she must, or surely perish, she began to reassemble the dismembered pieces of her life. The bruised and aching body stretched out rigid on the bed was nothing compared to the shattered mess of her mind.

She did not consciously begin anywhere in particular. At first random words and isolated snatches of memory battered aimlessly about inside her skull, bluebottles in a closed room, frantically throwing themselves against the window pane in a vain attempt to escape. But gradually things began to accumulate in a more ordered manner and her existence slid into focus.

She remembered the time in Nicholas's office in Naples. She could hear his voice telling her that he was certain Raul was dead. It was so clear it might have been yesterday, and Liana remembered, too, the vow she had made that day. No matter what happened, or wherever the path led, she would follow it for the sake of Raul's child. The child would never know the meaning of the word 'want'.

And I did it, she told herself, I kept faith with that vow. I did whatever needed to be done, no matter how sordid, no matter how painful or unpleasant. And I succeeded in forging a new life for myself and for my child. I achieved everything and more that I set out to achieve. *And* I made Nicholas happy. Even though I deceived him, he was happy. It was a kind of justification, a fact she always clung on to in moments of doubt. It was a comfort to know that she *had* made Nicholas happy. And he would have gone on being happy but for that disastrous discovery. But fate, cruel, quirky fate, had intervened in her life yet again, violently disrupting the illusion so carefully constructed over the years. Never, never in Liana's wildest imaginings, had she thought it possible that a quarrel with her own daughter would lead to the violent and ugly disintegration of her relationship with Nicholas.

It was no use logic's hammering away inside her head, telling her that she was to blame, that she had deceived Nicholas enough by presenting him with a daughter who was not his, without cruelly adding to the deception by denying him a child of his own. Cold, unremitting logic told her that; but she didn't need telling, she knew, had always known, but had for ever turned her face away from the knowledge. Grown bleak with remorseless practice by continually ignoring the cries from within herself, Liana had become almost immune, persuading herself that her path was morally defensible, that the pursuit of her goals, no matter the cost to others, was justified – almost persuading, almost, but never entirely. Every now and then guilt stabbed a little deeper than usual, causing an instinctive flinch of contrition, but it was only a temporary affliction because she had made her choice many years before, and had no intention of deviating from that chosen path. Her eyes were closed and her ears shut to cries of logic and fairness.

The rationale was her unreasoning but unshakeable love for Raul. To her it seemed so simple: it was Raul, always Raul. At times he receded, fading into an insubstantial shadow, but he always came back as if to remind her she would never be free. Liana could not imagine life without Raul superimposed over every living moment. Convinced that each day without him would be intolerable, she clung desperately to his memory, pushing Nicholas away when he threatened to get too close or claim her affection. Whatever the cost Raul had to stay alive for her. He had to be safe and real in the separate world he inhabited, the secret world she was free to float into whenever she wanted. In her innermost heart she knew it was absurd, a madness, to go on idolizing a dead man but the adoration was beyond her control; he was the most precious thing of all. Nothing, not another baby, not even Eleanora, could be allowed to get in his way.

The thought startled her. *Not even Eleanora*. For the first time Liana faced up to the fact that her love for Eleanora and Raul had become hopelessly muddled. Often suspected, never acknowledged, that night she faced it for the first time. A pure, single love was no longer the bright shining beacon which in the past had always led her onwards to success. Everything she had achieved, she thought had been for one single all-consuming love; love for Eleanora and Raul. But now uncertainty struck at the very core of her soul. The beacon was dim, its place taken by murky confusion. Instead of one love, two loves struggled for supremacy, and Liana realized she was faced with a choice: love the daughter or love the father. For long seconds her world stopped turning, then, keeling over, disintegrated into a heap of fragmented emotions.

Eleanora had done that. Eleanora had destroyed her world. Eleanora, when she had demanded the restoration of the *castello*, had forced the issue. By demanding attention for herself she had trespassed in the place sacred to Raul, and in doing so had blurred his image. Appalled at the path down which her thoughts were travelling, Liana tried to shut them out. But the need to keep Raul's memory close twisted at her heart with a tearing pain. Eleanora could not be allowed to blot him out; she needed him. It was wrong, she knew it was wrong, but Liana wanted Raul intact. No-one, not even Eleanora, could be allowed to get in the way.

Despairing, she turned to look at Nicholas. In the past, he had always been her anchor, the constant factor which fed her sanity and kept her in the world of today, the here and now. She looked at the familiar outline of his body. He was the other dimension to her life, the man who had given her Broadacres. There were two things she could not, no, *would not* give up: Raul and Broadacres. Or was it Broadacres and Raul? Oh, God, she didn't know, wasn't even sure about that!

Suddenly her mood changed and a furious, raging anger consumed her. Nicholas and Eleanora had come back from Italy and between them had succeeded in turning everything on its head, making a complete nonsense of her life.

She looked at the still figure for a long time. It was difficult to equate the sleeping Nicholas with the stranger who had violated her body. Shuddering she turned away and took refuge again with the square of silver moonlight. The unimaginable had happened. This man beside her was Nicholas, the quiet, gentle man she had thought she knew inside out, who, because he adored her, would do anything to please her. Yet this man was the same man who had plunged into her, tearing her flesh until it bled. He had degraded and abused her in the most terrible way a man could abuse a woman. Even her deceit did not justify such terrible revenge.

Because of him another door to the past, which of late remained closed most of the time, had been brutally forced open. In a matter of seconds the present had dissolved into the past. How long had Nicholas taken to rape her? It seemed like hours, although in fact it must all have been over in a matter of minutes. But, oh, God, how evil and repulsive that short time had been. In those minutes Nicholas had metamorphosed into the soldiers of Naples, becoming every single hated one of them: the buttons of his jacket had been the buttons of their uniforms pressing into her soft flesh; his grunts had been theirs as they took their pleasure; and the pain, too, had been the same. Liana had forgotten the terrible pain of a huge and rigid penis rasping into a bone-dry vagina. With that single, violent act, Nicholas had dragged the sordidness of Naples from the past and planted it firmly in the haven which had been Broadacres. Nothing would ever be the same again.

Finally, in the darkest hour of night, the hour before the sky begins to turn leaden with the first grey light of dawn, Liana turned her face into the pillow, and began to weep.

*

The morning dawned the same as any other morning. Liana rose and went across to the window and looked out while Nicholas remained in bed. Nothing was said. Of course, they both knew it was not the same and never could be but to all intents and purposes their marriage was wearing its usual face. Nicholas was desperate to talk but was afraid to, and anyway, what the hell can I possibly say, he thought. If Liana doesn't want to speak then I can't. But, oh, God, Liana, if only you knew how much I'd give to be able to erase the past twenty-four hours. You deceived me, true, but what I did – Nicholas closed his eyes – he could not bear to even begin to think about it. Then a terrible thought struck him. She might leave him. He could not blame her. But how would he live? Life without Liana would be unbearable.

Lying there motionless on the bed, it seemed to Nicholas that the room hummed with their thoughts, random signals jostling to get into some sort of order; and without either of them saying a word they came to an agreement. Life would go on as usual, on the surface. That was how it would be. But will I, will either of us, be able to sustain it, wondered Nicholas. It will be like walking on eggshells. What was Liana really thinking? Her studied composure gave absolutely nothing away.

She continued looking out of the window. Don't speak, Nicholas, not yet, she prayed, don't say a thing. I can't cope yet. Maybe some time in the future I will be able to. I don't know. But at the moment I don't want to speak to you, I don't want to touch you and I never, *never* want to have sex with you again. That part of our life is finished for ever.

But she said nothing, just stared out of the window with unseeing eyes, the pearly beauty of the early morning mist unheeded for the first time since she had arrived at Broadacres. We *will* survive, she told herself, gripping the edge of the window sill, fingers taut, skin stretched over knuckles. Somehow we will survive because there is no alternative –

whatever the cost, wherever the path led: that had been her vow. There was no going back. And anyway she could never leave Broadacres, *never*! But it was better not to talk. Some things were too terrible to talk about. Much better to pretend it had never happened, and then perhaps in time it would become unreal. Perhaps in time, it would be as if it never *had* happened. She latched on to that faint hope.

*

Six weeks later Liana made an appointment to see Donald Ramsay's partner, Dr McCallum. His examination was competently brisk, professional and distant.

'I can confirm that you are about six weeks pregnant,' he said. He looked at her speculatively, wondering why on earth she had not gone to see his partner. Donald Ramsay was like part of the Hamilton-Howard family, always over at Broadacres riding with Lady Margaret. It would have been logical to have seen him. 'Does your husband know?'

'Not yet. I wanted confirmation before I told him.'

Dr McCallum looked at Liana's sparse medical notes. She had never been ill, or if she had, she had never consulted Donald Ramsay. The notes merely consisted of a record of her first pregnancy and the delivery in December 1944. He did a quick calculation. Her daughter would be sixteen and she would be thirty-five by the time she had this baby.

'It's a long gap,' he said. 'But don't worry. Modern obstetric practice has come a long way since 1944. As you will be thirty-five by the time the baby arrives, I will book you into Winchester Hospital for the delivery.'

Liana picked up her handbag and rose, indicating that the consultation was over. 'That won't be necessary,' she said crisply. 'I shall have the child at Broadacres, with a midwife in attendance.'

'Too risky,' said Dr McCallum. 'You could lose the child.'

'Risky or not, that is what I want,' said Liana.

It was quite clear there was to be no more discussion. Dr McCallum flushed; he felt like a schoolboy. Liana had put him firmly in his place. He was surprised. He had not met her before and everyone had raved about the Countess of Wessex. Couldn't meet a nicer woman, they said. He looked at her now, her face set in a determinedly arrogant expression, daring him to contradict her. Haughty bitch, he thought angrily; but if she insisted on putting her own life and that of the child's at risk, there was very little he could do about it.

*

It was the week before Christmas. Broadacres was already festive with decorations. The Christmas tree had been delivered the day before and stood as usual in the East Gallery, ready for Eleanora and Peter to decorate it as they did every year. Logs crackled cheerily in the open fireplace of the breakfast room lit by the pale winter sunshine which flooded in.

Liana carefully buttered a slice of toast and spread it with honey. They all had to be told. Now was as good a time as any. She took a breath, hesitated a moment, then said, 'I am expecting another child. It will be born late July next year, nineteen sixty-one.'

Careful to avoid looking at Nicholas, she smiled at Margaret, sure in the knowledge that she would be pleased. At least, she prayed her expression resembled a smile but it was difficult pretending to be pleased when inside she was seething with a mixture of fear and anger: fear at the prospect of having another baby – even now, sixteen years later, she could recall the pain of Eleanora's birth and, as Dr McCallum had pointed out, she was not young from the point of view of childbirth; and anger directed at Nicholas. With that one violent act, he had succeeded in smashing all the years of careful contraception, all the years she had spent maintaining Raul secure in his place in her firmament as the father of her only child. She hated Nicholas for that most of all.

The moment she uttered the words Nicholas knew why she would not look at him, would not even glance in his direction. God, how he knew! Pregnant! Just what she had been trying to avoid for the past sixteen years. How she must hate him. A child, a permanent reminder of the terrible way he had forced himself on her. But in spite of everything he could not stop the little flicker of pleasure at the thought of another child – a son, he hoped. Then almost immediately he cursed himself for his selfishness. How could he be pleased that a child resulted from that disastrous union? A terrible fear surged through him: supposing he were punished and there was something wrong with the child? He would never, never forgive himself, and neither would Liana. No, God was not cruel; it was not the coming child's fault he had been conceived in violence.

He looked at Liana. What was she thinking? Impossible to tell from her face, but he knew well enough why she had chosen this particular time to make her announcement. It was not so difficult to follow her reasoning. With all the family present, private conversation was impossible, and that was what she wanted to avoid. She could not bear to talk to him. He turned towards her, knowing full well what was expected of him. Like Liana, he, too, had his part to play in the charade that nowadays passed for their marriage.

Pandemonium broke out at the breakfast table, and Nicholas took advantage of it to kiss Liana. 'Darling, what wonderful news.' How hollow the words sounded in his ears; surely everyone must know something was wrong.

'I thought you'd be pleased.' Liana looked up then and stared him full in the face for a second, her black eyes cold and wintry. 'You've waited long enough,' she said.

Nicholas quailed before the withering hatred of her glance. She was never going to forgive him.

Eleanora leaped up shrieking, impulsively pushing her father aside to fling her arms around her mother's neck. She was ecstatic. 'Great, great,' she yelled. 'I've always wanted a brother or sister. But I'd prefer a brother. Oh, I do hope you have a boy, Mummy.' She kissed Liana then quietened down and giggled. 'Wait until I tell the girls at school. It proves you can still have sex when you're over thirty!'

'Eleanora!' reproved Margaret, but she burst out laughing. 'That is not the kind of remark you should make to your mother.'

Liana and Nicholas forced themselves to join in the laughter, and their awkwardness passed unnoticed.

'I shall have to take over this new property company you've just set up,' said Nicholas smiling, determinedly playing his part as the happy father-to-be. 'I'm sure Donald Ramsay told you to take life easy.'

'Dr McCallum is my physician, not Donald Ramsay, and no, he did not tell me to take life easy.' Liana frowned at the thought. 'I shall continue as normal. Now is not the time to hand over the reins to anyone else.'

'But I'm not anyone else. I'm your husband.'

'I *know* who you are,' said Liana icily. Then seeing Margaret gazing at them open-mouthed and realizing they were both letting their guard down, she softened her tone. 'But you have to admit I am better at financial matters than you. With the bank rate rising and the new credit restrictions imposed by the chancellor, we can't afford to make any mistakes with the new company. I'd be grateful if you and Margaret would take over the tourist administration for Broadacres next year: that would leave me free to concentrate on building up the property company.'

She had offered a sop to his pride and also to maintaining their façade. Nicholas took it gratefully. There was no other choice.

The news travelled with lightning speed throughout the estate. Eleanora and Lady Margaret saw to that. Everyone at Broadacres fussed over Liana. Although they had to do it in a surreptitious way. 'Lady Liana's stubborn,' said Mary Pragnell to her daughter Meg, 'but she needs looking after just the same.'

'I know that, Mum. I'm not daft. I've been working here now for over sixteen years.'

Mary Pragnell sat, fat legs straddled comfortably apart. Sixteen years had not made a great deal of difference to her appearance – a few more pounds added on to her ample figure but her face was unwrinkled, and as smooth and rosy as one of the Broadacres apples.

'I forgets, you know,' she said in her broad Hampshire accent. 'Time passes so quick. But you're right. More than sixteen years, and we've a lot to thank her for. Comfortable lives we've all had because of her, and now your Rolf has a job on the estate, too. He's a good lad. He will be able to take over the home farm when Wally and me retires. Lady Liana has it all arranged. I doubt Lord Nicholas could have organized it as well.'

Liana knew very well that everyone was keeping an eye on her, and in spite of her stubbornness and her refusal to ease up on anything, in her heart she was grateful. They were good people. She was lucky to have them around her, especially now that everyday life was so difficult. Sometimes she thought that she could not go on pretending everything was fine; it was such an effort. But somehow she did, they both did. She and Nicholas existed side by side, everything appearing perfectly normal. But in reality they were completely alone, in separate but parallel furrows of unhappiness. Liana often sensed that Nicholas wanted to reach across and bridge the chasm between them. But she had made up her mind to hate him, and so she always rigidly withheld herself, aware of the danger of softening, the danger of forgiveness. She was not going to even think about changing her mind. Why should she? It was a question she asked herself time and time again. Why should I? The answer was always the same. Let him suffer and go on suffering. Just as I am.

Desperately unhappy, hating the fact that her body was growing heavier and heavier with child, his child, the child she had never wanted, she refused to give him an opening. Yet at the same time, she was as terrified as he of breaking the flimsy thread which still held them together. Emotion, affection was clamped down upon and shut away. And yet there was something she could not conceal from her inner self – the curious knowledge that she still needed him. Liana could not understand her own conflicting mass of emotions, but she knew he needed her, too.

Nicholas was sure that if only they could be open with each other, discuss their life and problems without losing their tempers, they might stand a chance of redeeming something. But there was no way of opening up the conversation. Liana was polite but distant, very, very distant, and Nicholas never summoned the courage to try; he was too afraid of her reaction.

They remained aloof and separate in unhappy silence, treading warily around each other. On bloody eggshells, thought Nicholas, often angry, but powerless to change anything.

Liana continued working at her normal pace, driving herself up and down to London, tramping around Knightsbridge and Kensington, buying up properties and personally supervising the lettings until finally Dr McCallum became worried. It was the beginning of July. The baby was due at the end of the month and her blood pressure was high.

'What the hell can I do?' he asked Donald Ramsay. 'I've explained to her the dangers of toxaemia. I've told her that she could lose the child, and maybe even her own life. But she takes no notice.'

'Perhaps she doesn't care,' mused Donald.

The tension between Liana and Nicholas had not gone unnoticed by either Dorothy or himself although to his amazement none of the rest of the family seemed to have noticed it. Donald worried about it. What on earth had gone wrong?

'That is something I have thought myself,' confessed Peter McCallum reluctantly.

'Confront her with it,' said Donald briskly.

'You know her better. Wouldn't it be easier if you said something?'

'Much better coming from a comparative stranger. Might shock her into taking notice.'

'I suppose so,' said Peter, privately thinking that in fact Donald was ducking an unpleasant task. But he was a good doctor. He did not shirk it, and tackled Liana head on at the next opportunity. 'I'm ordering you into hospital,' he said after the routine examination. 'Your diastolic blood pressure is a hundred and you've got protein in your urine. From now until the baby is born you must be under observation and have rest.'

'Doctor McCallum, don't be ridiculous. I'm far too busy.'

'Lady Liana, are you intent on murdering this child?'

Her head jerked up. He had shocked her. She drew in a sharp breath. 'How dare you say such a thing to me?'

'I can draw no other conclusion if you refuse to take my advice.'

Liana was silent. All through the months of pregnancy she had refused to let herself think of the child as a human being. Refused, in fact, to think of it having anything to do with her. Now she was suddenly confronted with the idea that she could kill it. Without actually doing anything, she could kill it. Be rid of it. She had never wanted another child. It would be no loss.

The baby kicked suddenly, as if to remind her of its presence, and she knew without hesitation that she could never do such a terrible thing. She remembered telling Raul that she could kill if she had to. But she had meant killing to protect someone she loved, or to save her own life. No matter how much she wished she was not pregnant, Liana could not take an unborn child's life. There was nothing in her make-up that could cause her to consciously harm the baby. She felt a sudden, unexpected rush of pity. Poor little scrap of humanity. It had not asked to be conceived. There was no way her conscience would allow her to condemn an innocent child to death.

She looked at Peter McCallum, and smiled. It was the first time he had seen her smile, and he knew then how she had won the hearts of all who knew her. There was a flash of warmth and beauty that touched him, and something else as well. He searched for the right words to describe it, then found them, *a resigned melancholy*. Yes, that was it, a resigned melancholy, as if she were well used to the burden of sorrow.

'All right, Doctor McCallum,' she said. 'You win. Book me into Winchester Hospital.'

*

Apart from Margaret who came as often as she could and worried herself sick throughout the entire visit, Eleanora also spent all her spare time with her mother during the three weeks she was in hospital. Peter often came with her. They laughed a lot and even made Liana laugh, which surprised her. It was not so long ago she had thought she would never laugh again. But it was difficult not to laugh with them, the two young people were so very happy together. Liana watched them thoughtfully and wondered. Were they falling in love? Peter had matured nicely into a handsome, self-reliant young man of nineteen and was already at university reading English. His quiet studiousness complimented Eleanora's noisy, impetuous nature.

To Liana's relief neither the *castello* nor Italy were ever mentioned by Eleanora. She has forgotten, she thought with relief. Slowly she relaxed, enjoying the unexpected closeness that showed signs of developing between herself and her daughter. Eleanora was so excited about the baby and could not wait for the arrival of her brother. She was convinced it was going to be a boy; nothing could persuade her otherwise. A quirk of fate again, thought Liana wryly. After all these years, it seemed that at last her relationship with her daughter was beginning to come right, and all because of a child who had been conceived in violence and rage.

But Liana was wrong in one respect. Eleanora had not forgotten. Italy and the *castello* were still vivid in her memory, but only to Peter did she confess her longing to return. And he, mindful of the fact that Nicholas had warned Eleanora never to mention it again to her mother, urged caution.

'There's plenty of time to go back later,' he said. 'You know the *castello* is officially registered now in the family name. It has withstood the passage of centuries. Don't you think it can wait a few more years, until the time is right?'

'But how shall I know?' demanded Eleanora, impatient as ever. 'When *will* the time be right?'

'Something will happen, and then you will know. Forget about it until then.'

'I suppose you might be right.' Eleanora was not entirely convinced, and it was against her nature to leave anything open-ended. She liked to have things neatly tied up, organized and planned.

Peter knew that and grinned at her mutinous expression. She was like her mother in so many ways, but there was absolutely no point in mentioning it. Both Liana and Eleanora would have hotly denied there was a shred of similarity between them. He often puzzled over their perverseness. What was it that made mother and daughter so anxious to deny their deep affection or the similarity that existed? Mercilessly they retained their own separate identities. He had seen it repeatedly. They would reach out and then draw back as if self-conscious or maybe even a little afraid.

He thought he understood Eleanora's reasons. She had been rebuffed so often by Liana when younger, she had built up a bright and breezy wall of apparent self-reliance, persuading herself she did not need her mother. But Liana herself was different; she was afraid, he was sure of it, and he wondered why. But now he was happy for them both. He sat back and delighted in watching their new relationship blossom and gain in strength.

He might not have felt so relaxed and contented if he had known that Eleanora had decided to take his advice concerning the *castello* for the time being, and the time being only. Unbeknown to the rest of the family, she was busily learning Italian. From her point of view, discussion on the renovation of the *castello* was merely postponed but far from forgotten. It had temporarily taken a back seat. Other matters took precedence at the moment.

One very important matter was the rapidly burgeoning adult love between herself and Peter. Innocent childish kisses had given way to fumbling adolescent embraces, heightened by a growing awareness of their bodies. Eleanora often felt dizzy with a beautiful, nameless excitement which happened more and more often when they kissed. It made her long to go on, beyond mere kissing. She looked at Peter, and he smiled at her. She felt the now familiar prickle of excitement and lowered her lashes, afraid that her mother might see and interpret her emotions. He loved her. He had said so last night.

She switched her thoughts to the coming baby. 'If it's a boy, what will you call him?'

'I haven't thought about it,' said Liana truthfully.

Gradually, in spite of everything, Eleanora's enthusiasm was beginning to affect her, and she realized that now she was actually looking forward to the arrival of the baby. More importantly, the enforced idleness of the weeks in hospital had forced her to think, to come to terms with life as it was, not as she wished it could be. She had discovered that nothing was for ever, not even hate. A slow forgiveness and understanding for Nicholas edged its way into her heart.

Nicholas entered the private hospital room just in time to hear Eleanora's question and Liana's answer. She looked up at the sound of the door opening. For a second their gazes met and then Liana quickly looked down. Nicholas stood quite still, hardly daring to believe what he had seen. After so many years of marriage she could not hide everything from him, no more than he could from her, and he saw enough to give him hope. The icy look of winter had gone and in its place was not exactly love, but there was a warmth. And surely something more: a plea perhaps? She was ready to meet him halfway.

Sitting down on the side of the bed he took her hand in his and looked down at the delicate lattice-work of veins showing through the skin. Then he raised it to his lips. 'What do you want to call him if it is a boy?'

'You choose,' said Liana, her eyes still downcast. 'It's your son.'

'No, he is ours,' said Nicholas.

'Ours,' said Liana slowly, as if trying out the word. 'Our son.' She looked up and Nicholas saw her eyes were shining with tears. 'I'm sorry he's been so long in coming.'

'I'm sorry, too, that I . . .'

'You still haven't got around to a name!' Eleanora's voice reminded them that they were not alone.

Liana laughed shakily. 'How about James? I always think it sounds so English.'

Suddenly Nicholas reached out for her, and without another thought Liana slid gratefully into his arms. The hate dissipated as if by magic. At last their mutual nightmare was over. It was my fault as much as yours. She wanted to say it but suddenly there seemed no need. The nightmare had been self-imposed, by both of them. Through a mist of tears Liana looked at Nicholas. I need him, she thought wonderingly. There was no denying it. Suddenly her eyes were opened and she could see that she needed Nicholas as much as she still needed the memories of Raul. Her need for both of them was different. There was no comparison, could never be a comparison, but it did not seem to matter. For the first time in her life Liana began to feel things were slipping into their proper place. She felt Nicholas's strong arms holding her and knew that was the main difference. Nicholas is here, she thought with a sudden burst of unexpected happiness. He is warm, I can touch him, and he's holding me safe. Burying her face in his shoulder, she sighed a deeply contented sigh. Oh, he smelled so good.

'Come on,' said Peter to Eleanora, tugging at her arm.

'Why? Oh, yes. Yes, we'd better go.'

Her parents did not hear them leave. Nicholas's tears mingled with Liana's. 'Say you forgive me,' he said, his hand cradling the back of her head, pressing her face close to his. 'And promise me that no matter what happens we'll never stop talking to each other again.'

'I promise,' said Liana. The promise would be broken, of course it would, promises always are, but at that moment she meant it.

Nicholas took a deep breath. He felt as if he were breathing clean, fresh air for the first time in months. The great weight of guilt which had been crushing him these last eight months slid away. The relief was physical. He felt liberated. Liana, love of his life, life of his life, had forgiven him. Suddenly he *knew* the baby would be a boy, a beautiful, healthy, intelligent boy and the most loved son in the whole of England. There was not a shred of doubt in his mind. Their son was destined to draw the two of them together. They would be closer in mind and spirit than they had ever been all the years of their marriage. Nicholas had never believed in mysticism but it did seem to him now as if some mysterious voice were speaking to him, pointing the way to a future filled with happiness.

He looked down at Liana and stroked her cheek gently. 'Everything is going to be all right,' he said.

'I know,' whispered Liana. 'Yes, darling, I know.'

'Well, fancy that,' said Eleanora with a backward glance at the two in the room. 'They're quite lovey dovey!'

Peter put his arm around her. 'And why not?' he asked. 'Love is not exclusive to the young, and anyway your parents are not old.'

'No, I suppose not. It's just that they seem old to me.'

'Ah, that is because you are still a baby,' he teased, kissing the tip of her nose.

'Not that much of a baby.' Eleanora pulled him into the lift that led to the lower floors and the exit from the hospital. As soon as the doors closed she kissed him passionately and he kissed her back.

'Too young, though, to break it to the family,' said Peter seriously as they broke apart when the lift doors slid open. 'They just wouldn't understand. We must keep our love affair a secret for a few more years.'

'Oh hell, yes,' said Eleanora inelegantly, then giggled at Peter's disapproving expression. 'Yes, darling,' she said more seriously. 'I agree. We don't want anyone spoiling it for us. And anyway a secret is much more fun. Just so long as you promise never to stop loving me.'

'That's an easy promise to keep,' said Peter.

'And only for two years, then I'll be in London at the Guildhall School of Music, and we'll be free to do as we please. The only thing is,' she paused, looking at Peter reflectively while he unlocked the door to his battered old estate car, 'you said "love affair" a moment ago, and it's not exactly that, is it? An "affair" is when you make love, and we haven't.'

Peter stared at her. She stood there laughing at him, dark hair blowing in the breeze, eyes passionate, daring, challenging. 'Pre-marital sex is a sin in the eyes of the Church,' he said slowly.

'Oh, damn the Church, *your* Church. Do you want to?'

'Yes,' said Peter.

Eleanora climbed into the car, and waited until Peter sat in the driving seat. Then she slid her arms around his neck and they began to kiss. Opening her mouth a little she pushed her tongue against Peter's lips. She had read books about it and knew it was supposed to be exciting, arousing. It was. At the touch of her tongue, something snapped inside Peter and he groaned. His mouth opened, too. Excitedly they explored each other's mouths with their tongues locked in a drenching kiss. Then, trembling, they drew apart.

'Let's go to the tithe barn down by the old Itchen Navigation,' Eleanora whispered.

It was an invitation Peter could not refuse. Without a word he put the car in gear and drove off. Eleanora slipped her hand between his thighs and smiled up at him.

The medieval barn, the only remaining building of a once thriving abbey destroyed in the fifteenth century, was off the beaten track. The old Itchen Navigation, once a busy canal leading down to Southampton, was now a slumbering backwater. The banks, unused for a hundred years, were overgrown with reeds, and the only sign of life was the domestic activity of moorhens and coots.

'Are you sure no-one will come?' Peter hesitated.

'The barn has still got last year's hay stored in it. No-one is going to come for that today, and it will make a lovely bed.' Eleanora led the way into the ancient timber-framed building.

Once inside they were both nervous. 'You're sure you want to?' asked Peter.

Eleanora looked at him, her dark eyes serious now. 'I'm sure,' she whispered. 'I want to know what it's like, and I want it to be with you. I don't want it with anyone else. I love you.'

Undressing each other between kisses, they were shy at first, but Eleanora led the way, giving him her nipples to kiss and guiding his fingers to her clitoris.

'I think you've read more books than me,' confessed Peter, surprised at her sureness. He was erect and hard and wondered how long he could wait and whether or not he should withdraw before ejaculating.

'We read them at school all the time. That's the only advantage of being a boarder.' Peter rubbed harder with his fingers and Eleanora shuddered. Spreading her legs wide, she pulled his head down to hers. 'Don't wait,' she whispered. 'I want you inside me.'

Peter slid inside. Afraid of hurting her, he went in slowly. The sensation was exquisite. He could not believe how wonderful it felt; and then he knew he should withdraw, it was going to happen. But he could not get out. Wave after wave of pleasure swept over him. It was all over too quickly. They lay still afterwards. Eleanora wrapped her legs around him so that he could not escape.

'Did I hurt you?'

'No. I thought you would. In all the books it says it hurts a bit the first time but it didn't. It was nice. Especially when you came right inside me.' She kissed him. 'I could feel you. It was lovely to feel you moving about inside me.' She let out a long, satisfied sigh. 'It was nice, so nice.'

'I should have come out. You might get pregnant.'

'I won't. This is my safe time of the month. That's why I suggested it today.'

Peter raised himself up on his elbows and looked down at her. Flushed, her hair tousled with pieces of hay stuck in it, she looked bewitching. She smiled slowly back at him and he grinned. 'You set me up,' he said.

'Yes. Do you mind?'

He kissed her slowly. 'I'm very glad you did. Next time, I want to make it good for you, too.'

'You mean for me to have an orgasm, like in the books?'

'Like in the books,' said Peter, sliding down her body until his face was level with the curling black triangle of her bush. He knew it was good from the way she shuddered and jerked, little gasps of pleasure coming from her lips. He felt himself rising again and she rose to meet him as he entered her. They climaxed together, both of them crying out loud in joy.

Lying there afterwards in the softness of the hay, stroking her breasts, Peter kissed her. 'I love you,' he said. 'I shall always love you, no matter what happens.'

'I love you, too. And do you know what?' she raised herself on one elbow.

'What?'

'I think I'm very sexy. I must be.'

Peter laughed. 'I agree, of course. But whatever makes you say so?'

Eleanora lay back down beside him with a contented sigh. 'Because it was much, much better than in the books. Something as heavenly as that can't possibly be wrong. And now I've had it, I don't want to live without it. Do you?'

'No,' admitted Peter. 'I don't. But the safe time of the month is so short, and you mustn't get pregnant.'

'I won't.' Eleanora was airily confident. 'I'll get myself fixed up with something, then we can do it all the time.' She stretched luxuriously at the thought, then turned towards him. 'I suppose you'll go to confession because it's a sin.'

Peter thought for a moment. 'I don't feel guilty because I love you. But yes, I will go. Do you mind?'

'No, I knew you would. That wretched Church of yours. But don't go to that scruffy little Irish priest in the village. Everyone knows he blabs when he's had a drop or two of the hard stuff.'

'I had in mind to go when I'm in London, and be quite anonymous.'

'Good idea.' Eleanora was greatly relieved. She did not fancy Father O'Malley knowing. She began to caress Peter again. 'Shall we do it once more before we go home?'

'I'm not sure that I'll be able to. Eleanora! What are you doing?'

'This is something I read in a book, too!' The words were muffled as she bent over him.

*

James Hamilton-Howard, the new viscount, entered the world on 31 July 1961. He made July by the skin of his teeth, being born exactly two minutes to midnight. In spite of Dr McCallum, the hospital obstetrician Mr Maudsley and Donald Ramsay all worrying themselves over Liana's raised blood pressure and her age, the birth was effortless and straightforward.

'There, I told you there was nothing to worry about. Second babies are always as easy as shucking peas!' said Donald Ramsay, looking at a radiant Liana holding a contented-looking son and heir.

'First time I've heard you mention it,' answered a slightly disgruntled Peter McCallum. He was exhausted and felt that his own blood pressure must have gone up by several degrees during the past few hours. 'I'm going home to get some sleep.'

'Yes, good lad. You do that. I'll take over here.'

There was nothing to take over; the hospital had an on-duty obstetrician, paediatrician and midwife, but Peter refrained from saying so! Donald Ramsay was a good sort, and at his age eccentricities had to be allowed for. Peter McCallum went home to bed, happy at last. Everything was fine; Liana had proved him wrong. 'That woman is as strong as a horse,' he told his wife as he tumbled into bed. Next moment he was asleep.

At one o'clock in the morning Liana was sitting up in bed drinking champagne. The hospital room was filled to overflowing with flowers and family.

'I really must insist, sir. Doctor McCallum and Mr Maudsley said . . .' The midwife was flustered. It was all very well for the doctors to tell her to get rid of the relatives but what did one do when they just ignored the request? 'I must insist, sir,' she repeated to Nicholas, 'that everyone except you leaves the room.'

A gale of laughter swept around the room. No-one was paying the slightest attention to the agitated midwife. Even Dr Ramsay was there, she noticed, feeling cross. He of all people ought to have known better! But Donald Ramsay had already downed three glasses of champagne on an empty stomach and was more than a little merry. 'As I toasted the last one,' he said, 'I may as well do the honours again. To baby James.' He raised his glass. 'May he have a long and happy life.'

'To baby James.'

In the silence that ensued while the champagne was drunk, the midwife jumped in with another ultimatum. 'You must all leave now. Everyone except Lord Nicholas. *Please!*' She was beginning to feel desperate. The noise from Liana's room had woken some of the babies in the next-door nursery. Now wide awake, they all bawled lustily. 'Listen to that,' she said more cross than ever, 'you've woken them, and they automatically think it's time for a feed.'

'Goodness, what a racket those babies are making.' Eleanora pulled a disapproving face. 'I shall want quiet babies like James.' She looked at her new brother tenderly and put her finger against his hand. Automatically the little starfish hand opened, grasping her finger, holding it tight. 'Look, he's holding my hand,' she said in delight.

James lay in the crook of Liana's arm; his white blond hair, still damp from the birth, stuck up in little spikes.

'They all do that. It's a reflex action,' said her grandmother matter-of-factly. Eleanora looked disappointed. 'And as for your own babies, well, you'll have whatever kind of baby the good Lord gives you, young lady. But first you have to find someone willing to marry you!'

Eleanora laughed. 'Oh, that shouldn't be too difficult.' Behind her back she reached out, and Peter caught her hand and squeezed it in his.

'Darling,' he whispered, smiling. Mad, impetuous Eleanora. He found it difficult to imagine her with babies of any kind.

The midwife planted herself firmly in the middle of the room and glowered. Nicholas finally got the message. 'You must all go.' He shushed them, protesting, out of the room. 'Thank you for coming. I'll see you later.'

Margaret was the last to leave. Leaning forward she brushed some ruffled hair back from Liana's forehead in a tender gesture. 'I'm so glad, my dear.' Emotion made her more awkward than usual, and she mumbled so that Liana had to strain to hear. 'Everything is all right now, isn't it? I have been very worried.'

Impulsively Liana reached up and caught Margaret's hand in hers and pressed it to her lips. 'Yes, everything is all right now,' she answered, smiling into the craggy face, puckered a little now with anxiety. 'I'll be home soon.'

'It can't be soon enough for me.' Margaret paused, then added quickly, 'You're sure? You and Nicholas?'

'I'm sure. We are all right. Don't worry.'

Margaret let out a long sigh of relief and, giving Liana's hand a final squeeze, went across to the door. At the door she paused and sniffing loudly searched in her pockets. Unable to find a handkerchief, she wiped away a tear with the back of her hand, then gave them both a beaming smile before departing.

'We were foolish to think we could hide our troubles from everyone,' Liana said as Nicholas closed the door behind his mother. 'Margaret knew something was wrong between us.'

'Yes, but not the truth, thank God,' said Nicholas. 'I'd hate her to know that.'

'She never will. It's all water under the bridge now.'

Alone at last, they sat in companionable silence. Far from being tired after the birth, Liana felt wonderful and could hardly believe such happiness had fallen into her lap. The dark shadows that had always been there flickering on the edge of her life had suddenly disappeared. Even Raul had faded into the background. He was still there, of course; she knew that he always would be, but his memory was no longer dominant. Baby James had achieved the seemingly impossible. He had ousted Raul. The new life cradled in her arms had magically transported her from the turbulent edge of the storm into the centre, the very core of life, where it is always calm.

Nicholas sat silent. He, too, was occupied with his own thoughts. They had taken a perilous journey, he and Liana, and somehow, by a miracle he did not understand, they had survived. Each of them had battled on, struggling along separately, lonely and often in despair. But suddenly their routes had converged, and now they had arrived in the same place. They were blessed, truly blessed.

This happiness must be because I have no guilt this time, thought Liana, looking down at the small, flaxen head. There were no secrets between herself and Nicholas where James was concerned. His conception had been stormy but now they had moved into calm waters, sharing a mutual, uncomplicated love for a tiny child.

James opened his eyes and stared up at her. She knew he was too young to focus but his blue eyes fixed on her with an unwavering gaze. They seemed serene and full of love. Bending her head, Liana laid her cheek against the downy crown of his head. It was warm and soft, perfumed with his own dulcet baby smell. She felt herself melting with love. It was not a fierce and triumphant love the way it had been at Eleanora's birth. This love was sweet with an aura of almost sublime motherliness. She felt so quiet and comfortable. Raising her head she looked down at him again. His round eyes were still fixed on her, brilliant and unblinking. 'His eyes are going to be blue,' she said softly.

'Aren't babies' eyes always blue?' Nicholas bent over to look at James. 'They may change.'

'Not when they are as blue as his. He is going to look just like you, except that your eyes are grey.' She smiled up at Nicholas, a slow, tender smile. 'Just as handsome as you,' she repeated.

Nicholas held her tight. He knew he should leave his wife and newborn son to get their rest but he did not want to break the spell of quietness and new-found faith. Liana instinctively knew what he was feeling and wanted to preserve the preciousness of the moment, too. It would be too easy, she thought with a sudden pang of apprehension, for all this to disappear with the ease of a shadow when the sun goes in. She shivered, and Nicholas held her closer. 'Cold?' he asked.

'No, I . . .' then she stopped, because it would be silly to tell him she was afraid of losing their newly acquired happiness. 'Just hold me for a little while,' she said.

Liana relaxed in Nicholas's arms. There was nothing to fear. The birth of James had put right the wrongs. Life stretched ahead as far as she could see, day after day, serene and untroubled.

PART THREE
1961—1966

Chapter Twenty-Two

The whole family's life changed tempo when Liana brought James home to Broadacres. There was no need for a nanny with so many willing hands anxious to cuddle, kiss, play with and spoil him. Liana still worked at her papers in the library office but only did what was absolutely necessary. The supervision of the estate was left to Nicholas, with Wally and Bruno as managers, and they were more than capable. Rolf was their willing assistant, and between them they hired and fired the casual labour they needed for harvesting and took on regulars when needed. Unlike some estates, Broadacres never had any difficulty in recruiting casual labour. Word soon got around the pool of manual workers who moved from farm to farm in the Home Counties. They were fair, the folk at Broadacres; they told a man how long he would be needed and they paid him right up till the last day, even if the job were already finished.

As August rolled into September, so the combine harvesters rolled through the golden sea of wheat, spewing a plume of grain into the accompanying lorries at their sides and tossing the neatly baled straw into rows from the back on to the stubble. The sugar-beet was lifted after the grain and crushed in the Broadacres factory. Then it was the turn of the fat glossy potatoes to be harvested and sold. The sheds, next door to the dairy at the home farm, were full of frisky young calves, kicking up their heels and eager to suck at a finger, or anything remotely resembling a teat.

Normally Eleanora would have lived in the saddle, eager to put her sleek, summer-fed horses over the highest jumps possible; not wanting to waste a moment indoors before she went back to school. But this year was different. She religiously exercised the horses, having been too well trained by Margaret as a horsewoman to neglect them, but the moment she had finished, she was back with James.

Liana complained to Nicholas but her expression told him not to take her words too seriously. 'I have difficulty in getting near my own son. If I don't have to beat off Eleanora or Margaret, it is Mary Pragnell or Meg. Wally and Bruno are almost as bad. Whenever they ride or drive past, they drop into Broadacres kitchen for a cup of tea, or so they say. But I know it's James they have really come to see.'

Nicholas laughed. 'You should be thankful my sister and her husband live on the other side of the valley and are busy with their sheep, otherwise you'd be adding their names to the list.'

'I should have added Peter's name, though,' said Liana thoughtfully. She sensed a greater maturity in Eleanora and Peter. The thought struck her that they could be lovers, then she dismissed it as nonsensical. Eleanora was at school, still a child. Not even seventeen until next Christmas. But still she wondered, and tentatively broached the subject with Nicholas. 'Peter and Eleanora seem very fond of one another.'

'They always have been.' Nicholas was not paying attention, being much more interested in letting James exercise his leg muscles by bouncing on his lap.

'I mean, fond enough to fall in love.'

She had his attention now. Nicholas looked up quickly, drawing in a sharp breath and frowning. 'Don't be ridiculous. They are cousins.'

'Cousins can fall in love.'

'They are children, both of them. A few more weeks and they will be back at their studies. They won't be seeing each other then until Christmas.'

'You sound as if you don't like the idea. Would it be so dreadful if they did fall in love? I should have thought you would be pleased. It would ensure your family would always be around you.'

'I'm not against the idea,' said Nicholas abruptly and rather too loudly. 'But you are wrong. Quite wrong. They are like brother and sister,' he added.

It was as if he were trying to convince himself, and it puzzled Liana. Nicholas *was* against such a liaison, she was sure of it, even though he had just denied it. But why, for heaven's sake? For the life of her she could not understand the reason for his opposition. She would have asked him, but James distracted her by holding out his plump arms and making demanding grunts. Liana gathered him into her arms, nuzzling his neck, revelling in his delicious baby smell. And Eleanora and Peter were forgotten.

*

Eleanora caught the tube from Waterloo to Westminster. It was a gorgeous November day. The plane trees along the Embankment were still festooned with brilliant yellow leaves; reluctant to lose them, they let them drop slowly one by one. Like miniature kites they eddied down, following the gentle air currents, eventually adding to the already thick yellow carpet spread across the ground.

Eleanora walked briskly, swinging her overnight bag, scuffing up the dry leaves exuberantly, leaving a clear trail behind her. Life was perfect. A level studies were easy for her quick mind; her music was progressing well; and her singing improving daily. A place at the Guildhall School of Music for the following year was almost in the bag. But best of all, she thought, giving her bag an extra swing and charging through a pile of leaves carefully swept into a neat heap by a park keeper, was the fact that sixth formers at St Swithuns were allowed out at weekends. Eleanora went 'home' most weekends – to Broadacres the staff at St Swithuns thought in their innocence but 'home' was a flat rented by Peter in Dolphin Square on the Thames Embankment.

Peter waited outside the Tate Gallery. They would walk the last part of the way to Dolphin Square together. Sometimes he worried about the deception, knowing neither set of parents would approve, but he cared less now. He went less and less often to confession. He was beginning to agree with Eleanora that it was a waste of time. He could not truthfully be penitent and say he would not sin again, because he knew he would. The moment he saw Eleanora any resolution made in good faith not to make love to her would be broken. His life existed of great barren patches, only coming alive when he was with Eleanora. There was no way he could deny what she meant to him. He needed her physically and mentally. When they were together they were both whole and life was perfection itself. Such perfection could not possibly be wrong.

He turned to watch for her and saw her coming, long dark hair streaming behind her as she started to run towards him. Then she was in his arms, breathless and laughing.

'Why can't the year be made up of weekends?' she asked between kisses.

'We'd get bored if it were,' he teased. 'You'd get tired of me.'

'Never, never!' Eleanora was emphatic. 'When we are married, which will be as soon as I'm twenty-one, because then we won't have the bother of needing to ask anyone's permission, it *will* be weekends all the time. And I dare you to get bored!'

Peter laughed. They linked arms and started off towards Dolphin Square and their cosy, tucked-away flat. 'By the time you are twenty-one,' he said,

'I aim to have had at least one play as a West End success, and a book published.'

'And I shall have finished studying and be singing minor roles in Covent Garden.'

'What a successful pair we shall be.'

'Successful *and* happy,' said Eleanora. 'The happy bit is the most important.'

'It doesn't worry me, having to ask permission,' said Peter thinking ahead to their marriage. 'In fact I'd rather. Waiting until you are twenty-one is such a long time. Why don't we do it on New Year's Eve? Not this New Year but the next one. By then you will be eighteen, quite a respectable age to get engaged.'

Impulsive as always, she flung her arms around him and hugged him hard. Loving him so much, she wanted to deny him nothing. 'If you must,' she said, 'if you must.'

It was agreed. In the meantime, Eleanora was happy in the knowledge that they had a whole year and a bit to keep their secret. They would be safe. No-one could touch them for more than a year. It was the strangest thing, and something Eleanora never, never mentioned to Peter, but sometimes she was sure that if anyone else knew of their love it would be destroyed. It was irrational, and she, being practical to the core and not given to fantasizing, did not allow herself to dwell on it. But the thought was there none the less, a niggling little worry that marred an otherwise perfect life.

*

At five months, James was too young to understand and enjoy Christmas in 1961 but he gurgled and chuckled at the lights on the Christmas tree and put every new toy showered on him by family and friends into his mouth, giving them all an experimental chew.

'I can't wait for next Christmas,' said Eleanora. 'We'll take him to Winchester Cathedral on Christmas Eve for the Blessing of the Crib.'

'He won't understand it. He'll still only be a year and a half.' Margaret laughed indulgently at Eleanora's plans.

'He'll love the music and the candles. Oh, Mummy, say yes. Please, please.' Eleanora, aware that her mother avoided church-going whenever possible, was determined to get her permission well in advance.

Liana smiled. Sometimes she thought she understood her daughter. Sometimes. Certainly now she recognized the determined streak in her.

She wanted to exact a promise a year in advance, and would then hold her to it. 'I don't see why not. As you say, he probably would enjoy the music and candles.'

The year flew past, full of the usual activities. Broadacres opened to the public at Easter and closed in October. Part of the house was open now as well as the gardens and brought in a sizeable revenue. Liana skilfully sectioned off the part of the house they hardly used, plus one or two rooms they did use in winter so that the public got the feeling of intimacy with the family. Nicholas wrote the history of the family and also the stories behind the paintings and furniture the public could view. Liana hand-picked the guides and grilled them in their duties. Like everything she organized, it was well run, efficient and financially successful.

Apart from continuing to buy properties whenever she heard of one going at what she considered a knock-down price, Liana reined back on other business interests, content for the first time to leave the management to Nicholas and others. James was her priority. She enjoyed him as she had never enjoyed Eleanora's babyhood, playing with him, marvelling at every new experience, happy watching Eleanora with her brother. Here was a new and different Eleanora with James, showing an infinite patience Liana had never even guessed she possessed.

The rest of the family, too, clustered around James. He grew up permanently chuckling, a happy, contented child. There was always someone on hand to amuse him.

'That child has brought a kind of bloom to the whole Hamilton-Howard family,' said Donald Ramsay. 'Liana is happier now than she has ever been, and closer to Eleanora, too.'

'Yes, it's slightly disturbing,' said Dorothy.

'Disturbing?' Sometimes his wife came out with the strangest things. After thirty odd years of marriage she could still surprise him.

It was mid-November, time to make a Christmas cake again, and Dorothy was mixing the heavy sticky mass in the enormous mixing bowl she kept for that one purpose. She gasped with the effort and, grasping the wooden spoon with both hands, gave a determined stir then rested, leaning on the spoon. 'Yes, disturbing,' she repeated slowly. 'The whole family's happiness revolves around James. Liana and Eleanora's new relationship *depends* on James. What would they do if something happened to him?'

Donald snorted with annoyance. 'What is likely to happen, I ask you?' Yet behind his words was a shadowy doubt. What *would* they do? 'We have immunization for all the childhood diseases now,' he said as much to reassure himself as Dorothy. 'Those were what snatched away the youngsters in days gone by. But no more. No more.' He lit a cigarette and puffed at it furiously.

'You are right, of course,' said Dorothy, emptying the mixture into a baking tin. 'I was being silly.' She put the tin into the oven and carefully closed the door. 'It's just that he is such a *precious* child,' she said softly. 'I suppose the truth is I envy them.'

Donald was at her side in an instant. He saw the unshed tears before she could blink them away. He put his arms tenderly around her. 'You are grieving for all those children we never had,' he said.

'Yes.' Dorothy sighed. 'I suppose that's it.'

*

Liana kept her word made the year before, and all the family, including James, went to Winchester Cathedral on Christmas Eve 1962 for Evensong and the Blessing of the Crib. The service held at five-thirty was especially for children and was not long. Even so, some of the children were restive. But not James. His brilliant blue eyes sparkled with lively interest as he sat on Liana's lap. She was glad she had come. Not that the religious part of the service held any meaning for her, she had not changed her views on that one iota. Long ago she had learned the hard way that life was what you made of it. God, a mystical figure invented by men for men, contributed nothing.

Seated up by the high altar, Liana looked down the long nave of the cathedral. It was easy to believe in a God on High in the presence of such stupendous beauty: the soaring columns to the vaulted roof, ringing now with the sweet pure voices of the choirboys dressed in red gowns with snow-white frilled collars beneath young innocent faces, each one illuminated by the candle before him; the intricately carved wooden choir stalls, all loving works of art carved by long-dead craftsmen; and then beyond, more carving in wood and stone. A vast treasure house of architectural and ecclesiastical glory, dedicated by man to God for nearly one thousand years: the main nave, dimly lit now, so that the glory of the Christmas tree, standing beneath the great West window ablaze with a thousand white lights, could light the way; the spirit of Christmas, the light of the world.

Yes, it was easy to see how men and women deluded themselves. Such beauty was seductive, beguiling. But Liana was not persuaded. She held

303

James close and tried not to remember the time when she, too, had believed and had prayed. But the memories were not to be denied. The red glow of the sanctuary lamp flickered in her mind's eye, and before the statue of the Virgin she could see two girls kneeling, heads bowed, minds locked in prayer, prayers that had been tossed back in their faces, for one was to die a slow and painful death, the other to live in the hideous underworld of prostitution. Then there was Raul. He had come to her without the help of prayers or God, and then he had gone. Liana glanced at Eleanora sitting beside her, now as tall as herself. If a God did exist, he would not have left her alone and pregnant in a hostile world. It was no thanks to God that she had found a father for Eleanora and brought herself and her child to England and a new life.

When the congregation stood and faced the high altar to recite the Apostles' Creed, Eleanora noticed that her mother was silent, her mouth firmly shut in a thin, determined line.

*

They drove back from Winchester through a black, white and silver landscape. It had been very cold for weeks and was now freezing hard. The moon shone from a clear black sky, and already a hoary frost sparkled from every blade of grass and gave every twisted tree the beauty and delicacy of a ballet dancer.

'A magic night,' sighed Eleanora happily. She had James now. He was asleep on her lap, his blond head lolling with the movement of the car.

She turned and smiled at Peter, who had been given permission to attend the service with them. He smiled back and squeezed her arm. Eleanora was eighteen now, and after Christmas, on New Year's Eve, they intended to announce their engagement. Eleanora had wanted to surprise everyone with the announcement, but had given in to Peter's demands that he should ask her father first. A compromise had been reached. Nicholas would be approached just before the New Year's Eve party, he would be in a good mood and certain to say yes.

They were back at Broadacres just after six thirty in the evening. Bruno had lit a fire in the enormous Carrara marble fireplace in the East Gallery. Not that it was really necessary as nowadays the whole house was warm, thanks to the strategically placed log-burning stoves, supplemented by discreet oil-fired central heating; but the flickering flames gave a cosy glow to the Gallery and enhanced the fairy-lights on the Christmas tree.

It had been a tradition ever since Nicholas had returned from the war for the family and staff from the house and the estate to gather together in the East Gallery on Christmas Eve. Meg had prepared plates of hot mince pies and her own special recipe of traditional Christmas bread, which was golden crusted and spiced with cinnamon. There were melt-in-the-mouth sausage rolls, bowls of hot steaming punch and plenty of sherry.

Nicholas had also revived the old tradition of the yule-log, and now Bruno handed him it. It was ash, which was quick burning; to ensure that it did not smoulder and go out, it had been carefully dried in the barn for the past year. Nicholas placed it in the centre of the hearth, and as the housekeeper, Meg ceremoniously threw on a crust of stale bread. As the ash and the bread flared up in flames, glasses were raised in toast.

'We shall have warmth and bread the whole year long,' said Mary Pragnell as she helped Meg pile up fragrant prunings from the apple and cherry-tree wood around the yule-log.

'Superstitious nonsense,' answered Meg, then grinned at her mother's disgruntled expression, 'but a nice tradition just the same.'

''Tis more than a tradition,' said Mary firmly. Her roots were buried deep in the yeoman ancestry of the countryside. Superstition was part and parcel of her life, and neither Meg nor modern-day life would ever budge it.

The chatter and laughter rose several decibels as glass after glass of punch and sherry rapidly disappeared down the company's throats and the piles of food began to diminish.

Nicholas and Liana worked their way round, talking to everyone, careful not to miss a single employee. James was with Eleanora, playing on the floor. She let him rummage through the packages under the Christmas tree. Excited, he held them up, shaking them, his tiny fingers trying to prise off the wrappings before Eleanora deftly removed them.

'Time for bed now, darling,' Eleanora said as James, flushed and by now over-tired, began to whimper. 'Can Peter and I take him up, Mummy?'

'Of course.' Liana kissed James. 'I'll be up in a moment to settle him down.'

Peter and Eleanora bore James off upstairs to his nursery as Liana and Nicholas continued circulating with their guests.

'This is what I missed most in New Zealand,' said Anne to her mother. She and Lady Margaret were standing with Richard watching the merry party. 'I could never get used to Christmas in midsummer.'

Richard laughed. 'Yes midsummer, and we all sent Christmas cards with snow scenes on them. I must admit, even though I am a New Zealander, that this is my idea of the way Christmas should be: the smell of burning wood from an open fire; the scent of pine needles from the Christmas tree; hot punch with cinnamon; and a cold and frosty night outside.' He looked out of the window. 'It's snowing. This year we shall have a white Christmas.'

Anne and Margaret pressed their faces to the window pane. The East Gallery windows looked out on to the gravel forecourt in front of the house, and from the light of the lanterns either side of the front entrance it was possible to see the huge soft flakes of snow swirling down from a now pitch-black sky. The moon had disappeared behind the snow clouds. Margaret pressed her face closer. She could just make out the dark shapes of the clipped box hedge of the formal gardens and the fountain. Beyond that was the large stone arch which led out on to the main road. The snow was falling heavily, settling quickly on the ground, which was iron hard after a week of frost. A white Christmas! Margaret smiled. How lovely. She turned away from the window back into the room. As she did so she thought she saw a movement out of the corner of her eye. She turned back, pressing her face closer to the pane, straining her eyes. She had not been mistaken. There *was* a movement beneath the arch. As she watched, a figure emerged and began to walk through the snow towards the lighted front entrance.

'Someone is coming,' Margaret said, her breath misting up the window as she spoke.

Anne peered with her, rubbing a hole in the condensation in order to see through the glass more clearly.

'My God, it's William,' she said.

Chapter Twenty-Three

By the time James was bathed and ready for bed, which took a considerable time as it involved launching a fleet the size of the British Navy into the bath, more than an hour had passed. Not that Peter or Eleanora noticed at first. They, too, were absorbed with mock sea battles, accompanied by much laughter and splashing. However, eventually and with great reluctance, James was persuaded to leave the bath and be ensconced in his cot. He sat there, pink, shining and smelling sweetly of baby powder. It was then that they realized it was very late.

'Heavens, it's over an hour since we left the East Gallery!' said Peter checking his watch. 'I wonder where on earth your mother is?'

'Still talking, I expect,' said Eleanora. 'I'll get her.'

She left the nursery, careering down the long corridor at her usual breakneck speed. Peter watching her departure grinned; how on earth the sculptures and priceless oriental vases which lined every corridor in the house survived, he did not know. Eleanora took a short cut down the back stairs towards the East Gallery which passed the room used by her father as a study. As she passed she was surprised to see the door half open and to hear her father's voice. Curious, she stopped. It was obvious he was speaking on the telephone.

'I see, thank you,' he said. There was an ominous tension in his voice which froze Eleanora to the spot. She heard the click as he put down the receiver. Then there was a long silence. I ought to go, thought Eleanora, but she did not. She stayed where she was and heard her father clear his throat. He sounded distressed, as if it were difficult to speak. 'Apparently he was discharged from hospital some months ago. Doctor Solly understood he was coming straight here, but I suppose he must have changed his mind and gone somewhere else first. But now, obviously, he has decided to come back to Broadacres.'

'What shall we do?' It was her grandmother's whispered voice.

'There is nothing we *can* do, dammit. We can't tell him to leave. This is his home after all, and he has nowhere else to go. Whether we like it or not, Mother, this is where he has to be, at least for the time being.'

Nicholas sighed. Eleanora worried. Why did her father sound so strangely sad and defeated?

'Yes, yes, I suppose so.' Her grandmother's voice was the same – agitated and worried. 'Of course, I know you are right, but I do worry so. Anne doesn't like him, will never like him, and Liana surely must wonder about him. Does she know where he went after . . .?'

Like Nicholas, Margaret was torn in two, half of her wanting to accept her son, give him succour and shelter, the other half wanting to reject him, not wanting to admit, even to herself, that she was still afraid of him, afraid of what he might do.

'Liana knows nothing. She has never asked because, like Anne, she doesn't much like him either and wasn't sorry to see him go. But it is Christmas, so we must try and make him feel welcome. All of us. The spirit of goodwill ought to prevail, don't you think? Don't worry about Liana. I'll persuade her that he must stay, for Christmas at least, and then we'll sort out something afterwards. And you must persuade Anne. Anyway,' Nicholas's voice rose in an obvious attempt at cheerfulness. 'I'm sure there's nothing to worry about. We've got Doctor Solly's word for it. He is perfectly well now. That's official. So cheer up.'

Eleanora heard them move; they were coming towards the door. Quickly she slipped past and hurried on down the stairs. Who were they talking about? Why didn't anyone like this mystery man? She wanted to find out. She arrived in the East Gallery to find the party guests had gone. Only Meg, Dolly and Mary Pragnell remained, collecting up the plates and dishes and loading empty glasses on to trays. Mary Pragnell was glowering, and even Meg and Dolly appeared to have mislaid their Christmas spirit.

Around the fireplace stood a small group, her mother, Anne and Richard Chapman, and a tall, blond, rather good-looking stranger. Eleanora could see at once that her mother and the Chapmans were tense; it was the way their shoulders were hunched and the brittleness of their smiles. The blond man, on the contrary, seemed perfectly relaxed. He was leaning with one elbow on the mantelpiece of the fireplace, a glass of wine in his hand.

At the sound of her feet on the polished pine flooring, they all turned towards her. It was then Eleanora knew who the unwelcome visitor was. It was her father's brother, her Uncle William. She knew him at once; he was so like her father in appearance, and anyway she had seen photographs. What on earth was all the fuss about? She knew all about him. He had been ill for ages and had then gone to relatives in Scotland. He was the one who had been a pilot and got himself shot down in the battle of Britain. His history seemed rather glamorous to Eleanora; maybe her father was jealous! She did not wait to be introduced but went straight to the group around the fireplace.

'Hello, I'm Eleanora, your niece. I don't really remember you as I was only a baby when you left Broadacres. But I do know about you. You are William, the pilot, the one who got shot down and lost a leg.' Impulsive to the core and never a girl to suffer from shyness, she flung her arms around his neck and gave him an affectionate kiss on the cheek.

William looked slightly startled at the enthusiastic greeting, so different from that of the rest of the family, then smiled warily. 'Well, I must say the grown-up version of Eleanora is a great improvement on the baby I left behind,' he said.

Eleanora laughed delightedly at the compliment. 'I should hope so. Oh, speaking of babies, don't forget James is still waiting for you, Mummy.'

Liana gasped and put a hand to her mouth. 'Oh, dear, I had forgotten. He should have been asleep hours ago.' She bolted down the Gallery towards the back stairs Eleanora had just emerged from.

'James?' queried William. He looked puzzled.

'My baby brother,' said Eleanora. She held out her hand. 'Come on William – may I call you that? Let's sit here by the fire. We've got a lot of catching up to do. I suppose my family have been rotten communicators; they must have been if you don't know about James.'

'You could say that,' said William abruptly. He allowed Eleanora to lead him to a settee near the fire. 'You're not a bit like any of the Hamilton-Howards,' he said, eyeing her dark beauty.

Eleanora laughed unself-consciously. She was used to people making that comment. 'Wait until you see James; he more than makes up for me. He's blond like you and Daddy, has the same features, too. But don't be mistaken about me, I may not *look* like your side of the family, but I've inherited all the family characteristics. I'm not the tiniest bit like my mother. Do you know,' she lowered her voice dramatically, 'she doesn't even like horses!'

William smiled slowly. 'I seem to remember that,' he said.

'Do you ride?'

William shook his head. 'I haven't sat on a horse for years. But now I'm back, perhaps I will start again.'

'As soon as it stops snowing,' said Eleanora, 'I'll take you up on that. We'll ride together. All the horses will be frantic for exercise. How long will you be staying?'

'I'm not sure,' said William.

'Thank God for Eleanora,' muttered Richard Chapman under his breath. Nicholas and Lady Margaret came down the stairs and into the Gallery, closely followed by Peter. 'There are two unopened bottles of champagne here,' Richard called, anxious to maintain and enhance the atmosphere of congeniality introduced by Eleanora. 'Shall I open them?'

'Of course,' said Eleanora cheekily, grinning at her father's startled expression. 'We ought to be celebrating William's return with something special, and champagne is just the thing. Much better than pench.' Still holding William's hand, she squeezed it unselfconsciously. 'It's nice to have a grown-up uncle,' she said.

*

That William was absorbed with relative ease into the family circle on Christmas Eve was entirely due to Eleanora, ably aided and abetted by Peter who immediately sensed the frigid atmosphere. William helped, too, by seeming anxious to please. He was friendly and affable. From the stiff suspiciousness that greeted his arrival, gradually the family began to relax, one by one. Margaret and Nicholas were the first to unwind. It seemed to them that William really was different. Dr Solly had been right about William's health. He *was* better.

Eleanora managed to take Peter aside and hastily recounted the conversation she had overheard. 'I can't think why they are all so against him,' she finally said. 'The poor man has been in hospital. I suppose he is still having treatment for that leg. I think they are being horribly mean.'

Peter could not help but agree. 'It's certainly strange, and I can't understand it either. I know my mother never got on with him. She let it slip out once that she had a brother called William, but then said "the less said about him the better," and that was the end of that! But you know what families can be like. They have a terrible row and then they all remember it for ever afterwards, carry a grudge and never forgive each other.'

'Our family will never be like that,' said Eleanora firmly. 'We shall never row with our children, and I shall never allow them to quarrel with each other.'

Peter laughed affectionately. 'It's a problem we don't need to worry about just yet.'

'I mean it, though.' Eleanora was serious. 'I want a happy family. In the meantime let's be extra nice to William, make certain he really feels one of us.'

Christmas was the time for family traditions, and usually the family went to Midnight Mass at Longford Parish Church. But the snow was falling more heavily than ever when the time came to leave and, after considering the weather, they stayed at home. Even Peter and his parents decided not to go to the little Catholic church in the village for the midnight service.

'It will be the first time we have ever missed the Mass since Peter was born,' said Anne, very reluctant to give it up. 'I think we should go. A little snow shouldn't put us off.'

Richard, however, was more practical. 'I'm no expert on the English weather,' he said, looking out of the window at the blizzard which had now set in, 'but this seems more than just a little snow to me.'

Nicholas agreed. 'If you venture out now you'd probably get stuck somewhere. The roads must be well-nigh impassable; you'd probably end up spending Christmas night in a snowdrift.'

That settled it, even for Anne. 'Oh, I should hate that,' she said shivering at the thought. 'A white Christmas is wonderful when viewed from inside a warm house but the discomfort of being stuck outside, actually in the snow, is quite another matter.'

The news on television was that worse weather was to come. The whole of Europe was frozen solid, temperatures plummeting to unheard-of levels and heavy snowfalls predicted throughout the entire continent.

'You arrived at Broadacres just in time, my dear,' Margaret said to William. 'Another few hours and you would have been stranded somewhere else.' She quickly stifled the uncharitable thought of how nice it would have been if he had been delayed. This was Christmas, she reminded herself, a time for loving, a time for forgiving.

'Yes, Mother, I know,' said William giving a slow smile. 'I knew I had to get here tonight. Something told me to hurry.'

The words were innocent enough but had a horribly familiar ring. Nicholas felt a barb of uneasiness catch in his throat. He turned to look at William, searching his face, afraid of what he might see. 'Who told you?' he did not want to ask, did not want to hear the answer; but he had to.

For a long moment, or so it seemed to Nicholas, William looked at him but the planes and angles of his face were in shadow, masking his expression. 'Who?' he queried, then laughing he turned away and looked into the flames licking up around a new log someone had thrown on the fire. 'I heard the weather forecast,' he said.

Nicholas let out his breath in an inaudible sigh of relief. What was he worrying about? His imagination was working overtime. Of course, William must have heard the weather forecast; it would have been hard for anyone to have missed it. The newscasters had been talking of nothing else but the freakish cold weather for the past week.

Because of the snow, Peter and his parents were easily persuaded to stay the night. The bitter freezing weather of the previous two weeks had necessitated the sheep being rounded up and penned in the sheds already, something normally done after Christmas. So there was no problem with the animals. Daniel, the head shepherd, could easily feed and water the animals with the help of his lad.

Richard went off to telephone him. 'Daniel says there's enough feed to last for nearly a week,' he said on returning. 'After that, we'll need to go down to the barn in the bottom pasture. Let's hope the snow has gone by then.'

In a way the snow is a blessing, thought Margaret, listening to the conversation as it became less and less stilted, more relaxed and friendly. Everyone was making an effort to welcome William. Even Liana, once she had got over the initial shock of seeing him again, felt that William was no longer the threat he had once seemed. He was different. The time away had changed him for the better.

Christmas Day passed as it always did, the only difference being that instead of a pre-luncheon walk down to the lake to feed the ducks crusts from the previous night's party, this year they stayed in. Any possibility of walking was ruled out – the snow was still falling, the sky dark and heavy, burdened with even more snow yet to fall. The lights in the house needed to be on all day. Nicholas and Richard Chapman went out briefly with Wally and Bruno, making certain that all the livestock were fed, warm and sheltered.

'Wally has got the snow-plough ready,' said Nicholas when they returned. 'He reckons we'll be needing it soon.'

'Snowed in,' said Eleanora to Peter. They had sought refuge from the others and were alone for a few moments in the Grey Room. 'How romantic it would be if we were snowed up all alone.' She slipped her arms around his neck and kissed him. 'Not long now before we tell my father.'

'*Ask* your father,' corrected Peter, always a stickler for accuracy.

'Ask, tell, it's all the same,' said Eleanora. She rubbed herself sensuously against him. 'Isn't it hell being under the same roof and in different beds?'

Peter untangled her arms from around his neck. 'Not nearly as much hell as it would be if they found out we were already lovers!'

'Oh, why are people so stuffy?' she said irritably. 'Girls used to be married at the age of twelve in the Middle Ages. I don't see why we should have to pretend.'

'Oh, Eleanora, you know very well why. Don't be difficult. They will think you are too young, and besides you are still living at home. And what is more, this is not the Middle Ages. This is the twentieth century.'

'OK. OK. You win, darling. You always do. Officially engaged this year, to get married later at a date as yet unspecified. I agree to that. But I'm telling you this. I'm moving in with you when I come up to London next September, and don't try to put me off.'

'Who said I was going to?' Peter laughed at her furious expression and pulled her into his arms. He nuzzled the satin smooth skin of her neck and felt himself weakening. 'Maybe I'll try to sneak along to your room tonight. You are *very* difficult to resist!'

*

It snowed for three whole days and three whole nights. Europe was in chaos, Britain more so than anywhere else. Power lines were down, telephones out of order, roads blocked, trains stranded and the temperature consistently plunged downwards. On the fourth day it stopped snowing, the sun shone, the sky was a brilliant azure blue and the temperature started to creep up. Long icicles formed, hanging like frozen fingers from the roofs of all the buildings. The snow, pristine and blindingly white, sparkled and glistened in the sun.

Eleanora and Peter went out before breakfast and cleared a narrow path down to the lake then came back demanding bags of grain and bread to scatter on the edge of the frozen lake for the hungry birds.

'Never mind the birds,' said Nicholas. 'You will have to come with us. We'll need every able-bodied man and woman we have on the estate today. We must move the animal feed from the central store down to the barns nearer the house. If we have more snow, the cattle will starve.'

'But we can't let the birds starve,' protested Eleanora.

'Don't worry. I'll feed them,' said Liana. 'I'll be able to take James down now that you've cleared a path. We'll go after breakfast. He can do with some exercise.' She looked fondly at James, covered in strawberry jam from ear to ear, pushing a woolly donkey on wheels around the breakfast room at breakneck speed. 'He's bursting with energy.'

Nicholas and Richard gulped down a hasty breakfast and set out first, following Wally who was driving the snow-plough. 'We'll be gone all day,' he told Margaret and Liana, the only two women besides Meg remaining behind. 'When we've cleared the roads in Broadacres, we are going on over to Richard's place.'

The rest of the family left soon afterwards, taking flasks of hot coffee laced with brandy, meat pies and sandwiches all prepared for them by Meg.

'They will need it all,' said Meg. The three women stood together on the steps, Liana, holding James, Lady Margaret and Meg, watching as the party set off through the path cleared by the snow-plough. Everyone went, even Meg's youngest, Alice, who was only twelve.

'Mind you stay with someone all the time,' Margaret admonished Alice, who was prancing about like a young pony, excited to be included. 'We don't want to lose you in a snowdrift.'

'I'll look after her,' Eleanora shouted, fashioning a snowball and hurling it at the watching group. 'Don't worry, we shall be quite safe.'

Margaret snorted with affectionate laughter as the three in the doorway scattered to avoid the missile. 'How is it Eleanora can manage to look like an elegant young lady, have some very sensible and mature ideas, yet persist in acting as if she were only six years old?'

'I don't know.' They turned to go back into the house, Meg to her kitchen, Liana and Lady Margaret back to the Arcadian drawing room. 'Sometimes,' said Liana, 'I think I don't know my own daughter at all. She only allows me to see the part of her she wants me to see.'

'Like mother, like daughter,' said Margaret dryly but Liana did not hear. She was too busy pointing out the icicles dripping and glistening in the morning sun. 'If you are going to feed the birds, you'd better go now while it is thawing a little. Once the sun goes in, it will start to freeze again.'

Liana took her advice. Wrapping James up in so many layers of clothing that he looked like a tiny Eskimo, they set off together into the wonderful new white world. Broadacres had suddenly assumed a new dimension – the familiar shapes had changed into mysterious mounds softened by the fleecy white blanket spread across the land. Silence was all-enveloping. The snow deadened all noise, soaking up sound like a sponge. Liana made for the Palladian bridge, intending to go to the far side where the punt they used in summer was moored in a boat house. At the side of the boat house was a culvert where the overflow water from the lake drained into a stream. It was there, in a little patch of ice-free water stretching out into the lake, that the birds always congregated in winter.

James ran on ahead, his sturdy little legs remarkably steady for his age. Screaming with delight, he picked up handfuls of snow, laughing as the sunlight caught the snow crystals on his woollen mittens. Turning his hands this way and that, he held them up so that they sparkled as if covered with a thousand diamonds. Darling joy of my heart, thought Liana watching him. She put down the heavy bags of grain and bread to rest her arms for a moment, and James, seeing her stop, scampered back chuckling with happy glee. His fair hair had escaped from beneath his bobble hat, fringing his rosy cheeks in soft waves. Liana always put off getting it cut; it was such beautiful hair. He held up his pink cheek for a kiss, and she willingly complied before he dashed off again.

All the brightness of the sun seemed to stream around his small form, enclosing him as if he were the most precious thing in the whole universe. And he was. Because of him there was a completely new reason for Liana's existence, and it had nothing to do with the previous relentless quest for money and power. Instead a key had been placed in her hands, a key to emotions she had despairingly thought would elude her for ever – peace of mind and real happiness. For the past year and a half she had trodden Elysian fields, saturated to overflowing with a glowing love that surpassed anything she had ever dared dream of.

James had brought all that love into the world with him, and yet he had not been a love child. A quirk of fate again, always the unexpected, taking her down yet another road of life. But this time, this was the final road. Liana was sure, she felt it in her bones. In spite of the past, in spite of cheating with Eleanora, even in spite of Raul's still having a special place in her heart, she was supremely happy with her husband and family. And Nicholas was happy too. The whole pace of their life had changed. Their love-making now was different, more mature, not so erotic, but much more tender. They were gentle with each other, and that satisfied her. It felt right, and she knew Nicholas felt the same. By giving birth to James she had repaid her debt and in return gained peace of mind.

James had brought Eleanora closer, too, something Liana had always longed for but had never been able to achieve. James had been the unexpected catalyst, helping them to reach out to one another. Liana knew they were still miles apart in many respects but they were both trying and that was something. That is my fault, thought Liana now, picking up the bags of bird food again and trudging on towards the bridge, following in her son's footsteps. However, instead of feeling depressed about the gap that still existed between herself and Eleanora, now she felt hopeful, sure in the knowledge that with the help of James she would be able to bridge the remaining gap. And it has to be me, she thought, because the gap is my guilt.

The last few yards sloped down to the lake, and Liana hurried after James who was rapidly disappearing from view. He had just discovered how to slide. Whooping with excitement, his rotund figure slithered helter-skelter down the path at ever-increasing speed. As they hurried their breath hung like incense in the frosty air.

Passing in the shadow of the Palladian bridge across to where the punt was moored, a dank, cold chill struck. Liana shivered; Margaret was right, the moment the sun went in it would freeze even harder.

The birds were there, hundreds of them, and they greeted the arrival of Liana and James with a cacophony of squawks and screeches. Surging forward, they tumbled over one another in their eagerness to gobble up the grain and dry bread. James gurgled and babbled baby talk, delighted when the ducks took bread from his hands. Soon the waterfowl were joined by hungry birds of the field. Liana had never seen so many together in one spot, finches, tits, blackbirds, thrushes, robins and tiny wrens. Daring in their hunger, the smaller birds even snatched grain from beneath the very beaks of the majestic swans. Liana let the happiness of the moment take possession of her, squatting besides James, blissfully watching his pleasure, careful not to let him run out on to the ice.

'I see you have kept your word. That's good.'

Startled, Liana looked up. William was walking across the ice. She realized that he must have started from the far side because he was in the middle. He had a boat hook with him and was leaning on it for support. Suddenly the sun went in, covered by billowing clouds racing in from the north-east, clouds with an ominous sulphurous tinge of colour. Another snowfall was imminent.

Afraid of being caught out of doors in a snowstorm Liana stood up. 'It's time for us to go.' She reached for James's hand.

'Don't go. I've only just arrived. Hey, James,' William called, and before Liana could stop him James ran out across the solid ice to where William was standing.

'James, come here.'

The loudness of her cry startled the birds. They swept, screaming harshly, up into the air, circling against the darkening sky. Running out across the ice Liana tried to catch James, but stumbled and slid to her knees. Giggling with naughtiness James ran on, and Liana watched, powerless to prevent William picking him up. As he did so, he looked straight into her eyes and smiled, and, looking up at him from her knees on the ice, Liana saw something which made her heart shrivel into a dead cold stone in her chest. The affability of the past few days was a cultivated front. He had fooled them all, for beneath the pleasant smile and friendly voice, and now openly revealed to her, lay the ugliness of spirit she had seen all those years ago in the stable.

'I've been travelling,' he said conversationally, as if they were sitting comfortably at afternoon tea. The very ordinariness of his voice was terrifying. The whole scene was unreal, the frozen lake the mournful cries of the birds, the dirty yellowish clouds overhead; it all took on the substance of a nightmare. Except that Liana knew there could be no awakening. 'I went to Italy,' William continued in the same tone of voice. 'I went to your *castello*. It wasn't difficult to find, and then I went to the village of San Angelo below.'

Liana clambered to her feet. She heard William's words but they hardly registered. Her attention was focused on James, her son. He was the most important thing, and William had him. She had to get James.

'I'll take him now,' she said, smiling pleasantly. I must try to act as if everything is normal she told herself, keep steady. Reaching out she tried to grasp the giggling baby. His fat arms were clasped tightly around William's neck and his bobble hat had slipped sideways.

But William anticipated her move and evaded her, stepping smartly aside, keeping his balance with the aid of the boat hook.

'I took an interpreter,' William continued, as if she had not spoken, 'and we found an old woman in the village who remembered the young *marchesa*. She said she was a very small, weakly girl and she died of consumption at the end of the war. She also told us that the *marchesa* had a friend, a tall peasant girl, whose name was Liana.'

Liana shivered. How cold the wind was now. How difficult it was to breathe; she had to fight to drag the frosty air into her lungs. The impossible had happened; she had been found out. But why now, she wanted to cry out. Why now? She clenched her fists, and faced William, I have to keep calm. I must. For James's sake I must deny it. The thought of James gave her courage. Whatever deception there had been in the past, her son was not part of it. He was the one perfect thing she had given Nicholas, a child who was totally innocent. Nothing must be allowed to harm him. James was without blemish because he had no part in the past.

Facing William, she scornfully denied his words. 'There must be some mistake. The old woman was probably senile.' Her voice was harsh, defensive.

'There is no mistake. You are a fraud. A *peasant*.' William spat out the word with soft venom.

'I am not. How dare you insult me.' Deny it, deny it, she thought grimly. Keep on denying it. His word against yours. No-one will ever believe him.

'Not only a peasant,' he sneered, 'but a common prostitute.' He did not miss the sudden sharp intake of Liana's breath, and laughed. 'Oh yes, my fine lady. A gutter prostitute, passing herself off as a *marchesa*.'

How did he know? Oh, God, how did he know? Keep on denying it, instructed her subconscious, don't let him frighten you.

'You are making this up.' Liana forced herself to keep calm.

'Oh no? The old woman knew well enough. You went down into Naples and returned with food. The villagers didn't have food. And there was only one way a girl could get food in Naples – prostitution.'

'You are being quite ridiculous.' White-faced and trembling, Liana still stood her ground.

'Oh, no.' The words were so low she could hardly hear him. 'You fucked them to get what you wanted, and you fucked my brother to become a countess. It's the same thing.'

'You are disgusting.' But even as she spoke, the truth seared into her mind, burning, scarring; a branding iron plunging into her soul. PROSTITUTE. FRAUD. PEASANT. Mind reeling in shock and confusion, she was suddenly aware again of James chuckling as he played with William's scarf. James; he should not be here. He did not belong in this sordid scenario. Why did William have him?

William began to laugh. 'You should see your face. If ever I needed proof, you've just given it to me.' Then he stopped laughing and became deadly serious. 'But strangely enough I don't care about all that. What I do care about is the way that you have taken over Broadacres, you and your two brats.' His voice rose sharply and he shook James with a sudden vicious movement.

The sharp movement hurt James and he began to cry, sensing that something was wrong. 'Mum, mum, mum,' he babbled, holding out his arms now towards Liana.

Instinctively Liana moved towards the baby but William lashed out at her with the boat hook, keeping her at bay. Then he walked towards the bridge nearer the culvert where the ice was thinner. 'Eventually,' he said matter-of-factly, 'I shall get rid of you all, even my brother. But as his son is here, we might as well start with him, the dear little son and heir, Viscount Hamilton-Howard.'

With one swift movement he plunged the boat hook with crashing force into the thin ice. It made a hole the size of a small window. For a moment, Liana could not imagine the full horror of his intention, but as he lifted James high in the air, she knew with a terrible certainty what he was going to do. With a scream that almost tore her throat out, she flung herself forward. But it was too late. William dropped the baby through the hole.

Liana screamed and screamed and screamed, retching and choking, hardly aware that she was screaming, and pleading with William, asking him to kill her, to do anything, *anything*, but please save James. 'My son, *my son*!' Unable to tear her eyes away from the ghastly sight, she watched her beloved son, her love, her life, float out beneath the ice. His hat was off, the long blond hair floating around his face like an angelic halo; his mitten-clad hands pressed up to the frozen surface as he stared through, his blue eyes open wide; a tiny angel in a stained-glass window.

With a terrible cry of vengeance, pain, and anger Liana launched herself at the hole in the ice. Whatever the cost she *had* to get James. William lashed out with the pole again, preventing her from reaching the life-saving hole. Through the long-distant years, Liana heard her own voice saying, 'I could kill if I had to,' and she knew that now the time had come. With William alive, she would never get near James.

Suddenly she was imbued with all the ruthlessness and the calculating cunning of a born killer. She must get William off balance. She feigned a movement towards him, and he swung at her again with the boat hook, but she had made sure she was too far away so that in trying to reach her he lost his balance. The artificial limb twisted beneath him, and before he could recover, Liana flung herself on top of him and wrenched the boat hook from his hands.

Superhuman strength flowed through her body. She knew what to do and how to do it. She would break his neck with the pole, kill him the way she had seen Wally kill the farmyard chickens. William was frightened now, she could see that, and it spurred her on. Death is too good for you, she thought, ramming the pole up under his chin, forcing his head back. He started to choke. Liana pushed the pole down harder, wanting to hear his neck snap. Struggling they slid across the ice towards the hole, and suddenly William's head went back over the edge and into the black icy water. He thrashed and struggled, arms flailing, hands tearing at her clothes, but she held on to the pole, pushing harder, harder, harder. Then it was all over, he gurgled and choked, his limbs gave a few spasmodic jerks then were still. Exhausted, Liana let go of the pole, and William's lifeless body slid into the hole and down into the darkness of the water.

Liana's attention turned back to James. He was still visible. Down into the water she plunged, smashing frantically at the edge of the ice in a vain endeavour to clear a channel through to him. The edge of the frozen lake was as sharp as glass and cut her hands and face. Great crimson blotches stained the ice. Unaware that she was bleeding, Liana beat at the ice in desperation, trying to break a way through. But the ice was too thick. He was floating away, farther and farther out into the middle of the lake.

'James, *James*!' The harrowing cry was heard up at the house.

Without a second thought Liana took a breath and dived downwards into the dark water. Eyes open, she swam beneath the ice, drawn onwards by the sight of James's hair. It was so beautiful, like golden seaweed. My darling, darling son, my beautiful son, don't be afraid now. Everything will be all right; your mother is here. She reached him. At last she held him in her arms, blue eyes open wide and unwinking, baby mouth curved in a smile. His beauty was exquisite, absolute perfection. Perfection.

When they hauled them from the lake, it was Liana's face that had the look of death.

*

'I am the resurrection and the life, saith the Lord: he that believeth in me, though he were dead, yet he shall live: and whosoever liveth and believeth in me shall never die.'

The words fell like pebbles into a pool, rippling outwards in a sigh of sorrow through the grieving congregation packed into Longford Parish Church. 'Shall never die.' No-one believes that, thought the young priest sadly. Why are they putting themselves through the agony of another funeral service, when I could have officiated at a double one? But there had been no question of a double service. As soon as the coroner had formally released the bodies for burial and set a date for the resumption of the full inquest, the Earl of Wessex had summoned him to Broadacres and made the necessary arrangements. He had been absolutely adamant. His brother's funeral service would be two days before that of his son. His brother was to be interred in the family vault; but his son was to be buried separately, outside in the churchyard.

'We want James to be able to see the sky, feel the sun,' he said.

The vicar, new to the parish, did not understand. Neither did he understand why so few people had come to William's funeral, except for the press who trampled through the snow eager to photograph the family of the Earl and Countess of Wessex. The tragedy of the double drowning had made front-page news. He looked down across the bowed massed heads of the mourners. How different it was today. Everyone who could had come. The difficulties encountered by roads blocked with snow counted for nothing. All those who could possibly reach the little Norman church at Longford had come to the funeral of James, Viscount Hamilton-Howard; and the grief filling the church was so real the vicar felt it should be visible. The brilliant, sparkling sunlight slanting through the narrow windows was an intrusion, an intrusion of the outside world into the grim pool of mourning inside the church.

His gaze switched to the family sitting immediately below him in the front pews. Their faces resembled the marble effigies of their ancestors buried in the churchyard. Hamilton-Howards had worshipped, married, grieved and been buried in this place for centuries. 'In the midst of life we are in death.' How true that was. But each grief was new and hard to bear, and the death of a young child was always the most harrowing for those left behind. The young priest bowed his head, knowing the familiar words of the burial service were of no comfort to them. He wished he could help but he had no words of his own either. They would endure their pain, each in their own way. Only the youngest daughter was openly showing her grief, weeping, weeping, silently weeping, the tears coursing non-stop down her cheeks. The mother, the countess, looked like the Angel of Death herself, black clothes, black hair, black eyes in a white, expressionless face. What was she thinking? Why didn't she respond when her daughter laid her hand upon her arm?

The truth was Liana did not feel Eleanora's hand, did not hear the words of the service. She was conscious of only one thing, the small white coffin with the tiny cross of freshly picked snowdrops on the top. Inside lay James, dead, quite dead, his constant laughter silent now for ever.

She would get used to it. Of course she would. Death was no stranger; loved ones had been snatched away from her grasp before and she had survived. But this time, this time, she had been so *sure*, so certain that the light of life would shine for ever. But then, she remembered, she had been sure before. sure that Eleanora would live; sure that Raul would be with her for always. But death, treacherous death, always held the trump card. The shadowy figure invariably outwitted her just when she relaxed, thinking she was safe. Fleetingly, in the days since James's death, she had thought of confronting the spectre of death herself, face to face. Better perhaps to join those she loved in everlasting darkness. But her courage failed her. Fear of the unknown prevented her from going on. At least she *knew* the darkness of this world, and perhaps that was how it was meant to be, a living death. To be bound by life to a world without light was the same as dying.

Nicholas took her arm as Bruno and Wally carried the small white coffin aloft through the carved Norman arch of the north porch and out into the churchyard. A mêlée of photographers clambered over gravestones in their eagerness to get pictures, brash, intrusive, impervious to the anguish around them; intent only on getting a picture worthy of the front page. Vultures picking over a carcass, thought Nicholas in revulsion. He squeezed Liana's arm comfortingly but she did not notice the photographers or Nicholas. Her eyes were fastened all the time on the casket carrying the body of her son, their son, hers and Nicholas's. In slow procession they followed the coffin to the south side of the churchyard. Winter sunlight glistened on the snow, stretching long fingers of light through the black branches of the ancient yew, planted by their Saxon forebears a thousand years before.

Eleanora shivered and hung on to Peter for support. She hated the photographers and wanted to scream at them to go away. Why couldn't they leave them alone? But like the others she ignored them. The years of training as an English aristocrat had taught even impetuous Eleanora that in times of great emotion, the face one presented to the world was impassive. Even so, she could not be completely impassive, could not stop the bitter, scalding tears still cascading down her cheeks.

They came at last to the freshly dug grave, a black, gaping mouth against the stark whiteness of the snow. To Eleanora it seemed obscenely hungry. Unable to watch the coffin being swallowed up by the ugly black hole, she watched her mother. Every fibre of her being longed to reach out, to cling and touch, ask her mother for the comfort she needed so desperately. She wanted to say I love you, and I need you, too. She wanted to cry with her mother in anguish at the injustice that had taken James from them. But she dare not; nor, she knew, did her father. Liana was unapproachable. She stood there, completely still and beautiful, but terrible to behold, as if carved out of ice herself. Only her eyes moved, following the tiny coffin as it was lowered out of sight for ever into the darkness of the grave.

'Why won't she look at me?' Eleanora whispered to Peter.

Margaret overheard her. Shrunken and aged twenty years overnight with grief, her eyes swimming with unshed tears, she fumbled for Eleanora's hand. Finding it she held it tight, willing what little strength she still possessed to flow through her into her granddaughter's soul. Comfort her, dear God, she prayed, comfort her until her mother can turn to her once more.

'She will, my dear,' she said. 'She will. Give her time.'

'Earth to earth, ashes to ashes, dust to dust.'

Nicholas dropped the ritual handful of earth into the grave. Frozen hard, it fell with a heavy finality on to the coffin. The rest of the family followed suit as custom demanded, but not Liana. Nothing could persuade her to scatter hideous black earth on to her beloved son, even though she knew he would soon be hidden from human eyes by the mound of black earth at the side of the grave. The gravediggers were already waiting, standing back at a discreet distance, leaning against the flint wall of the churchyard.

It snowed hard again that night. Next morning there was no sign of the new grave. All was covered in a fresh white blanket. Liana walked alone to the churchyard. The family protested she ought to have someone with her.

'Let her go,' said Donald Ramsay. He and Dorothy had temporarily moved into Broadacres since the deaths of James and William. 'Let her go. Grief is not pretty when it finally erupts. It can be ugly, gut-tearing, but that is just what she needs. Maybe if she is alone she will be able to let it loose . . . maybe.' He was not hopeful, but it was worth a try.

When Liana reached the churchyard, she stood for half an hour just looking. It seemed significant there should be no sign of James now, no sign at all. But she knew he was there. He was sleeping peacefully now beneath the snow-white blanket and would sleep on for ever, gone from their world, requiring nothing more from anyone, not even from his mother. A single tear slid down her cheek. *Not even from me*, flesh of my flesh, blood of my blood. I can give you nothing now, so sleep, sleep, darling James.

Perhaps it was true, the saying that only the good die young. There was Raul, taken at the prime of his youthful manhood; he had been good to her; and Eleanora, too, so kind and gentle, endowed with a spiritual saintliness. Both too good to be allowed to live. And now James. James was an angel, too young to even think of sin let alone commit it; too perfect for this imperfect earth. The sun slid behind a rumbling snow cloud, causing sunbeams to reach down to the earth like the spokes of a wheel.

'The souls of innocent babes ride the sunbeams. It is their own special route to heaven.'

Without warning her mother's voice came to her across the years. How long was it since she had thought of her mother? She could not remember. What superstitious nonsense her mother had believed. But it was a comforting thought, a special route to heaven, only comforting, though, to those who could believe in such things. For the first time in more than twenty years, Liana found herself wishing she had faith. But she did not, and nothing could retrieve it.

For her there was only one road to any kind of salvation. She had to get on with the business of living and working; and that meant work, work, work. On the way back to the house, her step was brisker and she looked straight ahead. She knew what she had to do. She had done it before. Drowning in grief herself, she was incapable of pity or compassion for others. Nicholas, Eleanora, Margaret, all of them, they would have to survive this agony as best they could, God help them. *God help them*! What a meaningless expression. How much good was their God to them now? But she, Liana, could do without God. There was plenty to occupy her mind. She would lose herself in work. It was the only way she knew to combat grief.

*

When the full inquest on the drownings was resumed by the coroner three weeks later, Winchester City Guild Hall was full. The whole

Hamilton-Howard family attended, many of the estate workers and a large contingent of the press.

'I hopes they're not thinking they'll be getting a juicy front-page story out of this,' muttered Mary Pragnell to Wally, glowering at the press corps. In common with many others on the estate who had known William for years, she wondered whether in fact it had all been an accident.

But she need not have worried. The story that emerged was one of heart-rending tragedy.

The pathologist's report was quite straightforward: death by drowning. William's body had been bruised on the arms and neck, obviously where he had attempted to free himself from the thick ice. Lady Liana herself had suffered bruising and cuts for the same reason. But baby James, being so small, had suffered no bruising. Because of his age and size, unconsciousness caused by the freezing temperature of the water was almost immediate. He had no time to struggle.

The coroner asked as few questions as possible, mindful of the family's great loss. The village policeman, PC Thomas, took the stand. He read slowly and laboriously from his notes.

'By the time I arrived at the scene, sir, the family, who had heard the countess screaming as they returned from feeding their cattle, had got the bodies out of the lake and were taking them back to the house. Doctor Ramsay then arrived and informed me that The Honorable William Hamilton-Howard and Viscount James Hamilton-Howard were both dead, but that the Countess of Wessex, although still unconscious, was alive. I went to the scene of the drownings and took a piece of bloodstained ice. Forensic tests showed the blood to be of the same type as that of the Countess of Wessex, and as you know, sir, she was badly cut on the hands.'

'That was very resourceful of you, Constable. Have you anything else to add?'

'No, sir. Nothing to add.'

The coroner then questioned Nicholas, Richard and Donald Ramsay. But no-one had witnessed the actual drownings except Liana. A hush fell in the Guild Hall as Liana was called forward. She walked slowly, a tall, erect figure dressed entirely in black.

'Do you remember anything?' The coroner, a kindly man, doubted it. He noted the pallor of her face and the fact that her eyes stared straight through him. She looked as if she had been walking and sleeping with death.

'Do you remember anything, my dear?'

'Yes, I remember, I remember . . .' Liana's voice faded away.

'Yes?' The coroner prompted, hating what he had to do.

Liana started again. 'I remember the sun, the birds; James and I feeding them; William, and then James running out on to the ice.' Her voice rose on a note of hysteria and she stopped, raising imploring, agonized eyes to the coroner.

'And then?'

'And then James was in the water, through the broken ice, and William, he . . . oh, God!' With a sob Liana broke down, covering her face with her hands. Why were they making her live it all again? Wasn't it enough that James was dead?

The coroner made up his mind. The evidence was clear. The child had run out on to the ice, the adults had followed and their combined weight had broken the ice. He nodded, and Nicholas came forward and led Liana back to her place with the family. The coroner gave the verdict. 'Accidental death.' As far as the world was concerned, the final chapter in the lives of William and James had been written.

Chapter Twenty-Four

'They say time heals everything,' said Eleanora to Peter. 'Three years; it ought to be long enough.' It was Christmas 1965 and they were packing up ready to go back to Hampshire for the holiday. Eleanora had her own flat now, an apartment in Kensington paid for by her parents, but unbeknown to all the folks at home she and Peter lived together, spending most of the time in his flat. 'But it's not true,' she continued, 'certainly not for my mother anyway.'

'It certainly seems like that,' Peter agreed sombrely. He looked at Eleanora. Had time healed everything for her? He doubted that it had, but knew she would never admit it.

'I believe in living life to the full,' was Eleanora's stock answer whenever anyone commented on the pace at which she lived. She worked harder, laughed louder, and played harder than all her contemporaries with the result that, in the intervening years since James's death, her achievements had been phenomenal.

Emerging now, at the end of her studies, with a beautiful mezzo-soprano voice and the distinction of being awarded the prize for the best overall student at the Guildhall School of Music, Eleanora certainly had reason to be proud of herself. Peter was proud, too, but often wondered whether all the hard work was an effort to contain and bury the grief she was still suffering at the loss of James.

'What are your plans, now that you've finished at the Guildhall?' he asked.

Eleanora looked surprised. 'Plans?' she asked. 'To go to as many auditions and get as many parts as I can fit in, of course. What else did you think?'

'Oh, I thought maybe, you might take a short holiday, stay at home with your mother for a bit.'

'Never!' Eleanora was adamant. 'I can't afford to waste my voice, and I can't afford to waste time. Anyway, I want to be here in London with you, not stuck down in Broadacres where about the most exciting thing likely to happen is the arrival of a new calf!'

Peter laughed. 'You were a country girl once,' he reminded her.

'Not any more.'

In some ways it was true, she thrived in the cultural ambience of the city. Eleanora had developed into a sophisticated beauty like her mother, except that she did not resemble her mother at all in features. But Peter noticed they had identical steely expressions when their hearts were set on achieving something. And because of that same steely determination Eleanora was already getting regular recital work, chorus work in operas, and the occasional small solo part. She was as ambitious as she was determined, and Peter was sure she would succeed. But he also knew the sophistication was a thin veneer. Beneath it lay the same impetuous, hot-headed girl he had first met, as emotionally vulnerable now as she had been at eighteen. Like Liana, she hardly ever mentioned the tragedy of the drowning, and only Peter could even guess at how much she was still mourning the loss of her baby brother. But it was more than that – although it would have taken the Devil himself to have dragged it out of her – she was mourning the loss of her mother as well. For the death of James had been a vicious, two-edged sword, severing the life of a child and ending the delicate flowering of affection between mother and daughter.

'I wish we could help your mother.' Peter got up and drew the curtains, closing in the warmth of the room and shutting out the lights of Chelsea bounded by the leaden grey River Thames. 'Emotionally she has closed a door, shut herself in an empty room and locked everyone else outside.'

Eleanora smiled faintly. 'Only someone like you, a writer, would put it like that. To everyone else she's turned into a hard bitch.'

Peter protested. 'Oh, no, not to everyone. Only to the outside world. I know she has acquired a reputation over the last couple of years for complete and utter ruthlessness in business, but the people at Broadacres know she's the same inside. Anyway, personally, I don't think she is that ruthless. She is just very, very good at whatever she does. A lot of people are jealous.'

'Try telling that to my father. If she's the same, why the hell is he hitting the bottle? And don't tell me he isn't, because I damn well know he is. I think he's ashamed of her. He hardly ever comes up to the House of Lords now; can't face some of his fellow peers I shouldn't wonder, especially not the ones my dear mother has ruined financially. Her property business is the scandal of the city; she's making an absolute killing. That's why I don't call myself Hamilton-Howard any longer; my professional name is Eleanora Howard. I don't want people to know who my mother is.'

'I haven't noticed you declining the money she lavishes upon you,' said Peter mildly.

His reward was an outraged gasp then a sulky reply. 'I don't want her money.'

'Then do without it!'

'You know damn well I can't. How could I pay for my singing lessons? You said yourself I've got real talent and I'm proving it. I'm just beginning to make it in the world of opera. I can't give up now.'

'Why don't you come right out and admit it? You are as selfish and hard as you say your mother is. Sneer at her if you like. Sneer at her ruthlessness, her apparent love of money at any price, *any price*! But don't you understand the price she has paid, *is* paying, every day? Your mother is dying inside and no-one can help her. God alone knows I'd help her if I could, so would your father, your grandmother and everyone else at Broadacres. They still love her and they all know why she acts the way she does, *and* why your father drinks a little too much nowadays.'

'Oh, Peter. I'm sorry; I'm so sorry.' Eleanora flung herself sobbing into his arms. 'You're right, of course, but then you always are. I know I'm being selfish but I'm not hard. I loved James, too, but I can't mourn for ever.'

'I know you loved him. You don't have to wear sackcloth and ashes to prove that.' He pulled her into his arms, stroking her hair, soothing her like a small child.

'Oh, Peter, I've waited patiently just as you asked, because I knew then you were right. I've not told anyone we are in love and want to marry. I've not disturbed their grief. But how much longer?' she raised a tear-stained face to his. 'You said there would be a right time to tell them; that we must wait. But it's been so long now, I'm beginning to think there never *will* be a right time.'

'Well,' Peter kissed her gently. 'I think the time has almost come. I've got a surprise for you. I've been waiting for you to come back from your singing lesson so that I could tell you.' He tipped her from his lap and retrieved a sheaf of papers from the cluttered chaos of his desk. 'Read the top letter.'

Eleanora scanned it quickly, then squealed with excitement. 'Your new play is booked for a season at the Haymarket Theatre, and Richard Burton has agreed to play the lead.' She looked up, eyes shining with pride.

'Read on,' said Peter grinning.

'A Charity Gala Performance will be held in the presence of Her Majesty Queen Elizabeth the Second and His Royal Highness the Duke of Edinburgh on February the sixth nineteen sixty-six.' She gasped. 'But that's next February, only a few weeks away!'

'And the perfect evening to break the news of our engagement to your mother and father and my own parents. We don't need to ask anyone's permission. I'm nearly twenty-five, and you will soon be twenty-one. We'll ask for their blessing, but not their permission.'

'Oh, I can see it now.' Eleanora sprang up and curtseyed deeply, inclining her head theatrically and murmuring, 'Your Majesty.' She looked up, smiling wickedly. 'Elizabeth Taylor is bound to be there. Should I curtsey to her, too?'

Peter laughed. 'Idiot,' he said fondly.

In a moment Eleanora had it all planned. 'We'll get the whole family up to London; book them into the Ritz; and after the show, have dinner and an engagement party.' She flopped back down beside him on the settee. 'This Christmas won't be so gloomy after all. At least we can talk about your play and the gala performance.'

'And your recent performance in *Dido and Aeneas*. Don't forget that.'

'Oh, yes.' Eleanora giggled, her good humour restored. 'My interpretation of the second witch. It might not have got a mention in the reviews, but that new Italian director, Levi, certainly noticed me. As a matter of fact I think he quite fancied me. He said if I wanted to sing at La Scala he'd find a place for me.'

'Yes, in bed most likely,' said Peter sharply. He had heard of the Italian director's reputation with women.

Eleanora chuckled. 'Don't sound so jealous. You've got nothing to worry about. He's old enough to be my father!'

'I know, but that wouldn't stop him.'

It was true, the Italian director Levi was old enough to be her father, but even so he had unsettled her in a strange and exciting way. Eleanora had not mentioned it to Peter. What could she say? She was not capable of analysing the feeling even to herself, let alone to anyone else. But there was definitely something about the Italian. Even when not looking directly at him, Eleanora was aware that he was there. The air seemed to hum with an electric current. Levi possessed a blatant animal magnetism and Eleanora had breathed a sigh of relief when he had eventually left London. For the first time since falling in love with Peter, she had been tempted by prurient thoughts of another man. With a shiver, Eleanora now firmly propelled her thoughts back into the present.

'Wasn't it lovely, seeing Daddy and Gran at the last performance of *Dido*? Although I wish Mummy had come as well,' she added wistfully.

Peter hugged her. 'She'll come to your next performance,' he said. 'You wait and see.' And she damn well will, he vowed silently, determined to try and bring mother and daughter together again, even if he had to drag Liana there.

*

Liana paused a moment, and put down her pen. It was late at night. Everyone else had gone to bed but she was still working in the library office. She let out her breath in a soft sigh. Nineteen sixty-five and Christmas again already. Tomorrow Eleanora would be coming back to Broadacres. Soon it would be the third anniversary of James's death. And William's too, her subconscious reminded her. William! Even now a spasm of pure hatred made her shudder. The fact that she had murdered him caused her no bother. He had murdered James, and for that he deserved to die. She only vaguely remembered the coroner's inquest. Accidental death by drowning had been the verdict. But Liana had not cared about the verdict. If the police had bothered to ask her, she would have told them what had happened. What would it have mattered if she had been charged with murder? James was dead, everything else was trivial in comparison. But very few questions had been asked, and Liana had been left alone with her grief. The only small measure of comfort at that time was Donald Ramsay repeatedly assuring her that James would have known nothing. Freezing cold water caused almost instant unconsciousness in small children. He had known nothing; she clutched on to that. James had been asleep all the time.

She looked around at the office; everything looked the same. Three years – how was it possible for time to pass so quickly and yet stand still at the same time? She did not know. But she did know she had hardly paused for breath during those past three years.

Grief did not alter her meticulous efficiency. If anything, it enhanced it. The first task Liana had set herself after the funeral of James was to find

331

out whether or not William's story had been true. Was there really an old woman still alive in the village of San Angelo who remembered her? She paid a visit to her lawyer in London to engage the services of a reliable detective.

'I need someone whose discretion will be absolute,' she said, 'someone who can speak several foreign languages, preferably French, German and Italian.' She saw no point in letting him know she was, in fact, only interested in Italy.

Her lawyer, Jason Penrose, used to working for her and knowing she never took anyone into her confidence unless it could not be avoided, refrained from asking questions. He was curious, though. Which international company was she thinking of bidding for now? And how could she come straight back into business after such a terrible family tragedy? It would have knocked most men sideways, let alone a woman. 'This firm should suit you,' he said passing her a card.

'Thank you.' She took it, gave it a brief glance, then slipped it into her handbag.

He cleared his throat uncomfortably. 'All of us here in the firm offer you and the earl our sincere condolences.'

'Thank you,' said Liana in exactly the same tone of voice she had used when accepting the card. She rose to go. 'Good morning, Jason.'

'My God, what a hard bitch,' he said to his secretary when Liana had gone. 'She showed no emotion at all.'

'Perhaps she dare not,' answered the secretary, who like most women had more sensitivity and insight than the man who was her boss.

But the 'hard bitch' tag stuck. Jason Penrose never disclosed her business moves; he was too shrewd for that, and besides she paid well for his loyalty. But he was a member of all the right London clubs, a world that a woman, no matter how successful, was never allowed to enter. Seated in deep leather armchairs, and over numerous brandies, the businessmen of London deemed the Countess of Wessex to be a hard-hearted bitch. The fact that she was running financial circles around most of them in deals they wished they had thought up themselves, of course had nothing to do with it. The tough world of business was no place for a woman anyway, not unless she was as hard as nails, which, of course, the Countess of Wessex was. Chaps were different; they had loyalties to school or regiment which, of course, always influenced their decisions, and rightly so. They played the game as only men could. The Countess of Wessex had no such rules, and no allegiance to the Establishment. She saw what she wanted and went after it.

Liana soon heard of her reputation as a hard woman and cared nothing about it. Let them think what they wanted, Jason Penrose and his friends, all of them two-faced snobs. She had other more pressing business. Her first priority was to sort out the matter of the old woman in Italy. She planned it carefully, first choosing a young man from the recommended agency, a Martin Pope, then sending him off first to Paris to investigate the financial standing of a company there, and then on to Bonn for some *bona fide* business with a German company of which Liana was a director. It was something which Liana could have easily dealt with herself, but sending him across Europe was a good cover. Finally she asked him to perform the real purpose of his engagement: to find out if there was anyone living in the village of San Angelo who still remembered the young *marchesa*.

'If there is, then they must be very old by now, because everyone was elderly when I left. They were all poor, and I'd like to help them in their last days, make their life a little easier.' Liana explained. 'But please don't mention this to anyone. I want to make an anonymous gift.'

She put off thinking what she would need to do if William's story were true. First things first. She needed to find out, then she would decide.

Martin Pope returned, and Liana interviewed him in the small private office she used when working in London.

'Well, Mr Pope?' Nervous, she sounded abrupt, impatient.

The brusqueness of her tone made Martin Pope nervous, too, and he stuttered as he began his report. Liana hid her irritation with difficulty. For God's sake get on with it: the words were on the tip of her tongue but she kept silent.

'My investigation into Valmy Internationale in Paris showed their credit base to be anything but sound. Added to that the president of the company, Monsieur Lacroix, has a very dubious track record, and I have papers here to prove he . . .'

Liana leaned forward and took the papers, giving them a cursory glance before laying them down on the desk. 'I'll read them later. Thank you, Mr Pope. Please proceed.'

Slightly disconcerted at the speed with which the interview was progressing, he continued, 'I concluded the business arrangements in

Germany as you instructed, and I have here a personal letter for you from the director in Bonn, Herr Fink.'

'Thank you.' Liana took the letter and laid it aside without reading it. Martin Pope was disappointed; he'd been hoping Herr Fink had praised his work. 'And now,' said Liana, 'the other matter in Italy.' She was not entirely successful in her effort to conceal the tremble in her voice. She hoped Martin Pope had not noticed.

'Ah, yes, Italy.' He fished in his capacious briefcase and withdrew a sheaf of notes. 'I'm afraid I have bad news concerning Italy.'

Liana tensed. Bad news? What did he mean? 'What exactly do you mean by bad news?' She leaned forward, her dark eyes fixed on him.

At last the young man felt gratified. He had her attention now, and about time, too, considering all the leg work he had put in. His tone took on an officious air as he read from his notes.

'"Account of visit to village of San Angelo, March the twenty-seventh nineteen sixty-three. After exhaustive enquiries and with the aid of an interpreter—" I couldn't understand the dialect. I'm afraid that cost extra.'

'Yes, yes, that's all right. Go on,' said Liana.

'"After exhaustive enquiries and with the aid of an interpreter, I ascertained that none of the original villagers were still alive. The people now inhabiting San Angelo all come from the neighbouring village of Caltresi, which they left when the water supply failed. They told me there had been an old woman, one of the original inhabitants who could have remembered the people from the *castello* but unfortunately she died in the severe weather of last winter."' He looked up from his notes. 'So I'm afraid you are too late. There is no-one left for you to help.'

Stifling her sigh of relief, Liana rose to her feet. 'Thank you, Mr Pope. I'm glad I know, even though it is too late.' She took the sheaf of papers from him and put them with the others on her desk. 'The cheque for your services is already with your agency. Please ask them to invoice me for any additional expenses you incurred, such as the interpreter.'

The startled Martin Pope was dismissed, out of the office and on his way almost before he had time to catch his breath.

Once he had gone, Liana read the report for herself, before carefully filing it away. She was safe, and more importantly, so was Eleanora.

But still a tormenting thought constantly plagued her. It was in her mind now as she sat alone in the library office. What if she hadn't so zealously guarded the deception, the lie that was her life? What if she hadn't denied

William's accusations vehemently, but instead had acknowledged the truth and asked him for mercy? Would James still be alive? But it was too late for such questions. What was done was done. There was no way of knowing what might have been. Just as there was no alternative but to go on living, day after long day.

Liana shifted restlessly at her desk. The text on the papers before her swam disjointedly in front of her tired eyes. Where had the last three years gone? Am I really a living, breathing human being, she wondered dispiritedly, or is it all an illusion? Unable to concentrate on the work before her, her mind drifted to Nicholas, no longer her husband in the accepted sense of the word.

They still shared the same bedroom, but never made love now. Sitting alone in the darkened office, lit only by the pool of light cast by the reading lamp, she remembered the last time they had tried to make love. Shuddering, she tried to push the memory of that unmitigated disaster from her mind. But as so often, it refused to budge. Nicholas's voice echoed in her head as clearly now as it had two years before.

He had pulled her into his arms as if she were the lifeline to his existence. No tenderness, just desperation. 'Darling, I need you. God, how I need you. I want to make love to you, to hold you, to touch every inch of you. To forget.'

Liana resisted. 'Nicholas, no. I can't, not yet. Sex won't help me to forget. Nothing will make me forget James. Nothing, nothing.' The anguish of grief was still so raw she could not bear to think of making love.

He kissed her bare shoulders. Blind to everything at that moment except his own sorrow, he needed the comfort of her warm body, the closeness of another human being. 'I don't mean that we should forget James for ever, darling. How could we? But while we make love at least we'll forget for a little while.' He began to kiss her breasts. 'Please, darling, please.'

Liana capitulated. Why not, she thought. If it helps him, I suppose I can do it. What does it matter anyway? What does anything matter? 'All right,' she whispered.

It was a mistake. She knew it as soon as she began to touch him. It was wrong. How could he find pleasure in her body? How could he find pleasure in anything? She wanted to remain as she was, sealed up in the sterile capsule of her own making, insulated against the worst excesses of grief. Why couldn't he understand? She tried to push him away.

But the familiar feel of her body had aroused Nicholas. 'I need you,' he whispered feverishly, 'God, how I need you.' His hands moved across her body, feeling, touching, intimately exploring.

Liana lay beneath him, her mind cold and dead. I've come full circle, she thought feeling her flesh creep with revulsion. Now I'm a prostitute again.

Her coldness communicated itself to Nicholas. Her lips beneath his were unresponsive but still she pulled him in towards her and wrapped her legs around him.

Entering her, Nicholas closed his mind, shut everything out, and waited for the pleasure of the explosive release of tension. But nothing happened. The tension drained away becoming instead a dull frustrating ache.

'Come on!' whispered Liana, rocking her hips, anxious to get the sexual act over and finished.

It was the note of desperation in her voice that finished Nicholas. 'Christ! I can't, I can't. I want to, but I can't.' Limp and pitiful his penis shrivelled and slid out of her body. Groaning, Nicholas rolled away from her. 'I can't,' he repeated dully. 'I can't.'

I ought to put my arms around him and comfort him, thought Liana. But she did not. 'It will be all right next time,' she said.

The words, meant to be consoling, sounded as empty and hollow as they were in reality. She did not mean them, and they both knew it. Since that disastrous night they had both led celibate lives.

Which was one of the reasons for always working so late. Liana put off going up to bed because she knew as soon as she lay by the side of Nicholas, memories of Raul would come creeping out of the darkness, and that made her feel even more guilty about the loneliness of Nicholas's life. In the past she had always striven to keep memories of Raul at bay but now she welcomed them. By reliving the past, remembering those golden weeks with Raul, the laughter and the happiness took on a magical form and gave a small measure of comfort and strength. Feeble echo though it was of the real thing, it lightened the long dark nights, and was better than nothing. It was all she had.

She sighed and pulled a huge pile of files towards her. Problems, problems, economic and world business problems. Liana knew she must concentrate on the here and now. In trying to solve the problems before her, she could forget her own troubles, at least for a little while. Rhodesia had declared independence and the British government under Harold Wilson as Prime Minister was imposing economic sanctions. Liana believed her advisers who told her it was only a matter of time before all trade with Rhodesia would be banned. Now was the time to divest herself of interests in those companies which were likely to be worst affected and channel the money into other more profitable areas. At last, losing herself in the world of facts and figures, Liana worked on until the early hours of the morning.

A tap at the door startled her. It was Margaret in her dressing gown. She leaned heavily on her stick which she needed to use most of the time these days. Her former gangling figure and long straight legs were bent and crooked now. The cold, wet winters sorely tried her rheumatism and arthritis. Liana could only guess at the pain, as Margaret was a stoic of the first order and very rarely complained; but the twisted limbs and swollen hands and feet spoke for themselves. However, she still determinedly hoisted herself on to a horse whenever she could. She and Donald Ramsay rode together most days.

'Can I join you?'

Liana glanced at the clock. It was 2.00 a.m., an unusual time for Margaret to be up and about. 'But of course, if you want,' she answered involuntarily, although surprised. 'I thought you were asleep,' she added.

'I was.'

Margaret motioned behind her and Meg emerged from the shadows carrying a tray. Clearing a space amongst Liana's ledgers and the mountain of paperwork, she put it down. On it was a decanter of whisky, some wholemeal biscuits and cheese.

'She needs a bit of company, does Her Ladyship,' said Meg under her breath.

'There's no need to whisper, Meg,' said Margaret tartly. 'My legs might have given up on me but my ears are as good as ever.'

Liana smiled at the sharpness of the reply and Meg grinned back. Knowing Lady Margaret as well as she did, she had not taken offence.

'Why, then, do you need company?' Liana asked, pouring out two glasses of whisky as Meg left the room. She passed Margaret one and took a sip herself. 'Laphroaig,' she said appreciatively, letting the smoky, peaty taste of the malt whisky linger on her tongue.

'Donald's had a massive stroke. He's been taken into Winchester Hospital. Dorothy has just telephoned and told me.' The gnarled hand that held the glass trembled slightly.

'Oh, my dear.' Liana was at her side in an instant. She knew how much Donald and Dorothy Ramsay meant to Margaret. 'Do you want me to drive you to the hospital now? I'll get a car out ready and wait, while you change into something warm.'

'No point,' said Margaret. She took a sip of whisky. 'He's not dying. Not yet anyway. But he's totally paralysed at the moment. Dorothy says they've hooked him up to a breathing tube and put up drips. Now it's a question of wait and see.' She looked at Liana, her pale eyes watering. 'I know he wouldn't want me to see him like that, trussed up like a chicken with tubes and pipes protruding from every orifice. No dignity in that. Dorothy wants him home as soon as possible, tubes and all.'

Liana understood at once. They wanted her to lean on the authorities. Her response was immediate and decisive. 'Don't worry, Margaret. I'll arrange that. He can have a private nurse at home. There's no need for him to stay in an alien, antiseptic place like a hospital, especially if he is going to die. Knowing Donald, I know he'd prefer to be allowed to get on with it at home in his own good time.'

Margaret sighed. 'Dorothy and I knew you would understand.'

Liana kissed the wrinkled cheek gently. 'I'll get on to it first thing tomorrow.' Of all the people at Broadacres, Liana loved Margaret most. The affection which had flourished between the two women in Liana's first few weeks in England had never wavered, not for one single instant. It just shows how unimportant blood ties are, thought Liana, watching Margaret's tired face tenderly. She is my spiritual mother and always will be.

Liana shared out the biscuits and cheese, and they sat together in silence, eating. Only the regular tick, tick of the French ormolu clock on the mantelpiece disturbed the quietness.

'This will be the first time Donald will have to miss the Boxing Day Meet,' said Margaret suddenly. 'He will hate that, especially as we are having it here.'

Liana thought of death and old age, the tailing-off, the gradual curtailing of all one's abilities. Which was worse, sudden death in youth or slow death little by little? 'Yes,' she said, 'he will.'

Margaret's thoughts were running along similar lines. 'I hope he either gets better or doesn't linger, helpless and dependent on others. Come to that, I hope I don't linger either. I want to be snuffed out like a candle, the minute I can't get on a horse.'

'We can none of us choose,' said Liana slowly. For a moment she reflected bitterly on the past. 'No, we cannot choose,' she repeated. 'Not for ourselves, nor for those we love more than life itself. Death strikes when *he* chooses; it is never *our* choice.'

'You are thinking of James.'

Liana bowed her head. 'I never stop thinking about him,' she confessed.

'There are others who need your thoughts as well; don't forget them.' Margaret's voice was slightly sharp, but kind as well. 'Nothing can make reparation for your loss, *our* loss. Do you think we, too, do not mourn? There is no such thing as perfect happiness,' she said, almost as if talking to herself. 'Oh, it comes sometimes and seems perfect, but alas it is always fleeting. I know that, my dear, far better than you may ever guess.' Margaret shuffled her chair forward across the thick carpet and took Liana's hand in hers. 'You haven't lost James, you know. Not completely. Because he'll always be there, laughing and chuckling in his baby way. But his allotted time on this earth was short, and because of that he'll never grow old, never suffer, never be unhappy. Be thankful for that, and remember that although his candle has gone out in this world, his light still burns in your heart and always will.'

Liana shook her head. 'I wish I could think that,' she said, her voice breaking suddenly with unshed tears, 'but I can't.'

'You must try,' said Margaret gently. 'Now,' her voice took on a firmer note, 'you and Nicholas have a beautiful and talented daughter. And *she* needs your attention now. Do you ever think of her struggling in London?'

'Struggling?' Liana looked up in surprise. 'She has everything she wants: a beautiful flat in Kensington, plenty of money. She doesn't need to struggle.'

Margaret shook her head in a slight gesture of exasperation. Liana had missed the point.

'I mean artistic struggle. The world of opera is a profession existing entirely of highly-strung temperaments, combined with technique, musicianship, intelligence plus a lot of hard work. It is to Eleanora's credit that she has mastered this difficult world. Already, although young, she is beginning to be noticed. She has achieved a great deal in a short time. She not only deserves your interest but your physical support sometimes, when she is singing in London. You have never been to hear her. Nicholas and I have. How I wish you could have seen him. He was so proud of his daughter, you would have thought she was singing the lead instead of merely the second witch.' She laughed at the memory. 'You should be proud, too, and tell her so. She desperately wants your praise and approval.'

Nicholas's daughter. *His* pride thinking she was flesh of *his* flesh, blood of *his* blood. The guilt of deception had not decreased over the years and now, on hearing Margaret's words, it seemed worse. But strangely enough the words also had another effect. A door opened just enough to let a crack of enlightenment through. If they loved her daughter, why not put the futile guilt away and enjoy Eleanora's success and talent with them? Margaret was right, she had not thought enough about Eleanora; indeed, she had not thought of anyone else at all, only herself and her own griefs. There and then Liana resolved to try and put matters right. She owed it to Eleanora as well as to Margaret and Nicholas. In future she would be stronger, more positive, and if guilt reared its ugly head and threatened to spoil things, she would sit on it very firmly. I ought to be able to do that, she thought wryly. After all I've had nearly twenty-two years of practice.

'All right, Margaret,' she said. 'I promise I'll go to her very next performance, and I suppose I'd better educate myself a little regarding opera. It's an unknown world to me.'

'Good,' said Margaret, pleased that she had achieved something. 'And you won't forget about Donald in the morning, will you?'

Liana helped Margaret on her painful way upstairs to bed. 'I won't forget,' she promised.

On the way back to the bedroom she shared with Nicholas, she passed the nursery. A light shone under the door. It was not necessary to open it; she knew who was in there, but she opened it nevertheless. Nicholas was sitting by the cot where once James had frolicked so joyfully. James's favourite fluffy toy, Blue-blue, a large blue bear, was propped up against the pillow. Nicholas was staring at it, an empty whisky bottle in his hand. Pity tugged at her heart. I was wrong, wrong to shut everyone out, particularly Nicholas. She remembered Margaret's words about James, that his light was still burning. Maybe I'll never be able to see the flame, she thought, but perhaps I can help Nicholas to find it. Maybe I can ease his sorrow.

She took the empty bottle from his hand and placed it on the floor. 'Come to bed, Nicholas,' she said gently, and started to lead him upstairs.

Confused by the whisky he had consumed, he clung to her like a small bewildered child. 'Liana,' he whispered, hardly able to believe that at last she had reached out to him.

Chapter Twenty-Five

'Well, *that* wasn't so bad after all.'

The family standing close together on the Broadacres top step waved goodbye. Eleanora waved back and Peter swung the car round on the semi-circle of gravel before driving under the triumphal Arch and out into the main road. Goodbyes over and done with, Eleanora immediately kicked off her shoes and relaxed, stretching out her long legs, pushing the seat back as far as it would go. Liana was tall but Eleanora was already an inch taller, and now fervently praying she would not grow any more.

'Not bad at all,' Peter agreed. 'Thank God, your parents seem to be well on the way towards a normality of sorts.'

'Well on the way!' Eleanora snorted with indignation. 'I thought everything *was* back to normal. Daddy hardly drank at all and Mummy was asking me things about opera as if she really wanted to know. In fact I think she *did* want to know. She actually said she was sorry she had missed *Dido and Aeneas*, and would definitely come the next time I sang. She was quite impressed when I told her that the Italian director had offered me a place at La Scala.' She laughed at the recollection. 'Although I told her that I'd only go to La Scala if he offered me a lead.'

'Oh, darling, don't rush into judgements on the basis of the way things *appear* to be with your parents,' warned Peter. 'Everything is not all well, not yet.' Sometimes Eleanora worried him; she was ingenuous in the extreme. Everything was either wonderful or terrible. There were no in-between times for Eleanora, and that made it so easy for her to get hurt.

'I don't want to hear a deep philosophical psychological argument, or whatever else you choose to call it,' she said now, stubborn as ever. 'As far as I'm concerned things are back to normal. Or as normal as they ever will be with baby James gone and now poor old Donald Ramsay having had a stroke.'

Peter gave up. Knowing Eleanora as well as he did, he knew she could not be forced to see things she did not want to see. But it would have taken more than a few smiles and pleasantly bantering conversation to fool him. They were trying just that little bit too hard, and Peter sensed that Nicholas and Liana were coping, but only just. It was an ordeal for both of them but it was also their only hope of salvation, and he prayed that they would succeed. He thought of John Bunyan's words, 'The name of the slough was Despond.' No-one else could help them; somehow they had to drag themselves from their own particular slough.

All he could do was pray, and that he did every day. His mind, finely tuned and disciplined, was perceptive to the senses of others, always seeing past the obvious outward appearances. It was that faculty which had made him the fine writer he was. His plays were successful because the emotion in them was real, and because he often wrapped up hard-hitting social comment in an acceptable package. The audiences went home thinking, which was just what he always intended.

He changed the subject. 'It was good to see that Dorothy managed to get Donald Ramsay to the meet, even if he did have to sit in the car.'

'Yes and no,' said Eleanora, unusually seriously for her. 'It broke Gran's heart, you know, his not being able to hunt with her. They've always ridden together before but now it seems that era has come to an end.'

'Things change,' said Peter, 'nothing stays the same. It's something we all have to accept sooner or later. But look on the bright side. At least he's got his speech back and the use of his hands. According to Doctor McCallum that's a miracle in such a short space of time. He only had the stroke the day before we came down from London.'

'But he's still partially paralysed; his legs are useless.' Eleanora shuddered. She hated thinking of old age and illness. 'The live-in nurse Mummy has organized to help Dorothy is very nice, but poor old Donald, he isn't the boss any more. Having to be helped to go to the lavatory and being washed: it must make him feel like a baby.'

'Give him credit. I think he's coping better than you think. He's remarkably cheerful, and babies don't knock back the amount of stirrup cup that he did on Boxing Day!'

Eleanora grinned at the recollection. 'Yes, he enjoyed that part of it.' She could visualize it vividly now in her mind's eye; hounds and horses milling around the Ramsays' car; Donald propped up, half in and half out of it, one hand determinedly holding his stick, the other sneaking out and taking a glass from the tray of stirrup cup every time it came within reach. 'And then Gran nearly finished him off for good and all. That new horse of hers has a wicked streak; he's not called Diabolus for nothing. I'm not so sure Donald enjoyed getting kicked!'

Peter laughed as he remembered. 'He enjoyed all of it, and he managed to wack Diabolus a good one with his stick. No, he's not sorry for himself, and he would hate it if he thought you were.'

'Lecturing me again?'

'No, just trying to cheer you up.'

Eleanora put her head on his shoulder and snuggled up against him. 'I know, darling. I don't know what I'd do without you. You are my guide and mentor.'

'I thought I was your lover, soon to be your husband!'

'Oh, that, too!' Eleanora sat up and turned to face him, her eyes glowing with excitement. 'I can't wait until February the sixth. Won't everyone be surprised?'

*

Liana was glad the whole family had all come to Peter's moment of triumph. She loved him dearly. In fact, although she was loathe to admit it, even to herself, she often felt that she was closer to him than she had ever been to Eleanora. It was not because of what they said to each other; it was nothing as simple as that. A much deeper emotion, which she did not really understand, drew her to him. He and Margaret were the same kind of people, both compassionate, both understanding. They did not need to be told things, they instinctively seemed to understand.

'My goodness, we are in celebrated company tonight.' Anne Chapman, for once out of her jodhpurs and shirt and into an evening dress looked around at the assembled company. The foyer was filled with elegantly gowned and bejewelled women and equally elegant men. But as always on such occasions it was the women who glittered and sparkled, and glitter they certainly did. 'I'm glad I took your advice over what to wear,' she whispered to Liana. 'At least I don't look too much of a country bumpkin.'

'I should hope not.' Richard ran a finger round inside his stiff collar. Damn thing, it was uncomfortable and was already rubbing his neck. He looked at his attractively gowned wife. 'Country bumpkin indeed! After what I paid for that dress?'

'Richard!' Anne was embarrassed. It was one of Liana's gowns, designed exclusively for her alone.

Liana was amused, not offended. She was quite used to both Richard and Nicholas forever being scandalized by the price of her clothes. 'Ah, but Richard, remember I threw in the wool cloak free,' she said, 'and you didn't give me the wool! I paid you a good price for it.'

Richard opened his mouth then shut it. The foyer suddenly swarmed with security men and a path was cut like a swathe through the crowd.

'It must be Her Majesty,' whispered Margaret, edging forward to get a better view.

'Hell's teeth,' said Nicholas inelegantly under his breath as Elizabeth Taylor swept past.

She might just as well have been royalty, judging by the entourage surrounding her. Suddenly all the glittering jewellery of the other women faded, seeming mere pinpricks of light in comparison with the diamonds flashing on Elizabeth Taylor. They smothered her neck, ears, hair, arms, fingers and dress. Photographers crawled on the floor, scaled the foyer pillars and clambered over guests, feverishly popping their flashlights, all anxious to get *the* picture. The crowd in the foyer, equally enthralled, gasped and surged forward.

'She'd fall down with the weight if she wore any more jewellery,' murmured Liana.

Anne giggled nervously. She felt overawed in the presence of such a famous film star, especially one who oozed such flamboyant self-assurance. 'It's not often you are sarcastic, Liana.'

'Over the top for my taste,' was Liana's disparaging verdict.

'I agree.' Nicholas and Richard spoke simultaneously, and the five of them started to laugh.

It was at that moment Eleanora spied them. 'What is so funny?' she asked, pushing her way through the seething crowd to get at them. But she did not wait for an answer. The Queen and Duke of Edinburgh were due to arrive at any minute, and she wanted her family comfortably installed in their box before that so that they could get a good view. 'Come on, there's not much time. Peter has managed to get hold of some really good Sancerre; it's on ice in your box, ready and waiting for you.'

Eleanora was excited, her usually rather pale olive skin flushed and her eyes sparkling. 'Anyone would think *you* had written this play, not your cousin,' teased her grandmother.

'I feel as if I have,' confessed Eleanora. Once they were installed in the box, she plonked a quick kiss on Margaret's cheek before dashing off. 'There's not really room for me in here with all of you; I'll be watching from the wings.'

The truth was she wanted to be with Peter, sharing his excitement and apprehension. He was nervous; the preview audiences had received the play well but this audience was different. Not only had they handed over considerable sums of money for the privilege of attending, but many of them were also actors, actresses, writers and directors. They were bound to be more critical.

Richard Burton was not nervous at all; he was supremely confident. 'Don't worry, boyo,' he boomed, his enormous Welsh voice filling the backstage area. '*Black Valley* is set to become a classic, and if that lot out there don't appreciate it, then they should bloody well be ashamed, and I'll tell them so myself!'

'And he would too,' said Eleanora after he had gone. 'Oh, don't worry, Peter. I just know this play is the one which will really make your name and put you in the big league. I've got a gut feeling. You wait and see. They'll love it.'

This was going to be a wonderful evening in more ways than one, Eleanora was sure of it. Excited anticipation bubbled up inside her at the thought of their forthcoming announcement. Being secret lovers had been fun in the beginning, but now she was grown up the fun had gone and she was tired of it. Now she wanted the world to know, and soon they would.

The evening was an unqualified success, the play receiving rapturous acclaim. The glittering, star-studded audience rose to their feet in a standing ovation, and the chant of 'Author, author,' filled the theatre. Eventually a shy-looking Peter was dragged on stage to take his bows.

After the final curtain call, the whole company assembled into orderly lines on stage, ready to be presented to the Queen. Eleanora brought the party from Broadacres down to the stage area through a narrow passageway that wound from front of house to backstage.

'This is used by the electricians when they need to go up on to the gantry to adjust the lighting or sort out any other technical problems with the electrics,' said Eleanora, eager to tell them everything she knew.

'That girl is almost exploding with excitement,' said Margaret.

Liana nodded. 'I know.' She had noticed it herself and wondered why. Surely it could not just be the success of Peter's play? 'But you've made a mistake, Margaret, in calling her a girl. She's a mature young woman now.' She smiled. 'Time has caught up with us without our realizing it. I've been watching her. Eleanora merges in with the theatrical crowd very well, very well indeed. This is obviously her *métier*.'

The assembled company arranged themselves as directed by the security men who were now swarming about the stage. The Hamilton-Howard family were to stand directly behind Peter and Eleanora and await the arrival of the royal party.

The Queen arrived, smiling and looking genuinely delighted at the prospect of meeting the company. The Duke of Edinburgh, looking very handsome in evening dress, was at her side. The gala organizer introduced Peter first. 'Your Majesty, Peter Chapman, the author of the play.'

Peter bowed and everyone nearby strained to catch the words of praise from the Queen and Duke. Then Peter brought Eleanora forward. 'Your Majesty, may I present my fiancée Lady Eleanora Hamilton-Howard.'

Liana smiled, so she hadn't been wrong after all! And Nicholas had poohed-poohed the idea that it was even possible the young cousins might be in love. She was pleased for her daughter and wished her happiness, and now at last recognized the reason for Eleanora's barely suppressed excitement. Turning to Nicholas, intending to gently reprimand him about his lack of intuition, the eager words of pleasure suddenly died on her lips. She stared. Nicholas looked stricken. His face was chalk white, all the life gone out of it. Then Liana looked at Margaret. She, too, looked shattered, worried to death. Anne and Richard Chapman were almost as bad, holding on to each other, Anne looking wide-eyed and horrified.

'We should have seen it coming,' Anne said in a low whisper. 'Then we could have prevented it.'

The royal party moved on down the row. 'What on earth is the matter?' Liana whispered to Nicholas. 'Why this bizarre reaction to the news of an engagement?'

'I can't tell you here.' Nicholas's voice was sharp and tightly abrupt. 'It will have to wait until we all get back to the Ritz.'

In the event it had to wait even longer as Peter and Eleanora had invited several members of the cast as well as the theatre manager to join them at dinner, which promptly turned from a meal into a party. Nicholas felt increasingly distraught, thinking that the evening would go on for ever. Champagne, lobster, strawberries, more champagne: the banquet was never-ending. The toasts were to Peter and Eleanora, and even when the meal was over the guests showed no signs of leaving; in fact other people began to arrive and the partying became more frantic.

Liana, acutely aware of the rest of the family's increasing distress, wished Eleanora and Peter would notice, too. She was beginning to get impatient. Whatever was wrong would have to come out into the open soon. But the newly engaged couple continued to be blissfully unaware of anyone but themselves as they toasted each other, failing to observe that their own family raised their glasses with a noticeable lack of enthusiasm. So much champagne had been poured down their throats with reckless regard for the after-effects that Liana despairingly realized they were incapable of noticing anything. They were swimming in an alcoholic haze on cloud nine.

'I'm going to have hundreds of children,' Eleanora announced loudly to all and sundry.

'I think perhaps you should lower your voice a little,' whispered Liana, very worried now. Nicholas's face was becoming bleaker and more desolate by the minute.

The moment it was possible to do so, Nicholas extricated Eleanora and Peter on the flimsy excuse that, as the father of the bride to be, he wanted to speak to them alone for a few moments. He led the way upstairs to the suite reserved for himself and Liana.

Liana followed, determined to find out what was wrong, looking back puzzled because Margaret, Anne and Richard stayed behind. They looked unhappy, embarrassed, and stubbornly determined, as if they wanted to distance themselves from whatever it was Nicholas had to say.

'Won't be long, folks,' shouted Peter, raising his voice above the din of the party. 'Help yourself to more booze.' He waved his hands in the direction of the champagne buckets, already refilled with bottles, the condensation sparkling on the green glass.

Upstairs, Nicholas led them into the suite and, shutting the door behind him, leaned against it, closing his eyes. God, what a mess. A few split seconds, that's all it would take him to smash the fabric of all their lives, a few moments in which he would destroy the blissful happiness of his only daughter and break the fragile bond which he and Liana had only just succeeded in re-establishing. He was in no doubt about that: their new-found relationship would disintegrate like smoke before the wind. With an effort, Nicholas took a deep breath, steadied his voice, and began.

'There is something I must say.'

'Daddy, I hope you are not going to be difficult about Peter and me.' Eleanora was slightly annoyed at being dragged away from the party. 'I know we really should have told you before, but we just couldn't resist springing the news on everyone in the theatre. We thought you'd appreciate the occasion. And if you are thinking of playing the heavy father and objecting, although I can't think why you should, forget it. Peter and I are both above the age of consent.'

'Eleanora, darling, be quiet.' Peter put a hand on her shoulder, his face serious. For the first time that evening he gave Nicholas his full attention. Why hadn't he noticed before? Nicholas looked terrible, absolutely ghastly. 'Eleanora,' he said again, pulling her down to sit beside him on a nearby settee. 'We've both had rather too much to drink. So much so in fact, that we haven't perceived all is not well.'

'But I don't understand.'

'Eleanora, neither do I.' Liana's nerve cracked and she finally lost her patience. 'Please be quiet so that we can listen to whatever it is your father has to say.'

'Marriage is out of the question for you,' said Nicholas baldly. He held up his hand to silence Eleanora who reared up from the settee ready to object. 'I'm not being difficult; of course, there is a reason, a dreadful reason. It's something that has never been openly discussed within the family, something we've always kept hidden, trying to pretend, I suppose, that it didn't really exist, that it would go away of its own accord, as well it might in time, but not if you marry and have children.'

'If *what* would go away? If *what* exists? For God's sake . . .' Eleanora exploded into anger.

'Hush, darling. Can't you see how difficult this is for your father?' Peter put his hand over hers. 'Be patient.' He sounded calm but it was difficult; he was worried, too. What was Nicholas talking about?

'I can see now, now it's too late, how wrong we were. If only we'd been more frank, if only you had known . . .'

'Known *what*?' Eleanora interrupted impatiently again. 'For goodness sake, Daddy. Tell us!'

'The Hamilton-Howards have an illness which runs in the family. Doctors don't know, even today, precisely how it is transmitted. Some doctors now say that it is not hereditary but many believe that it is. The illness is called dementia praecox, more commonly known as schizophrenia. It was diagnosed in our family in the late nineteenth century. Several cousins and one of your grandparents were diagnosed as schizophrenic; three of them ended their days in asylums. There is still no known cure.

'Both William and my father suffered from it. When William was away from here, he wasn't in Scotland with relatives as we said, he was in a secure mental hospital because he was a danger to himself and others.' Nicholas hesitated. The memories were painful but there was no going back. He had to continue.

'Before it became necessary for him to go away for treatment, William had always appeared normal, although he'd never been an easy person to get on with, not even as a child, and after adolescence he was inclined to bouts of depression. But that was all, and he was very clever, with above-average intelligence. None of us could believe that he, too, had inherited the illness, until he had a violent mental breakdown.'

'Are you trying to tell us William was mad?' Eleanora's voice was disbelieving. 'How could he have been? He flew planes. He must have passed a medical of some sort to have been a pilot in the war.'

'I told you, he seemed all right then. Medicals were not carried out in great depth in those days. None of us thought of his bad moods; after all, moodiness isn't a mental illness. Lots of people are bad-tempered and moody. And to be honest, I have to admit that none of us wanted to think of that. Even when he'd gone through a particularly bad bout of depression we couldn't bring ourselves to recognize it for what it might be.'

'But what about Doctor Ramsay?' asked Peter. 'Did he not feel he ought to do something?'

Nicholas paused. 'Donald Ramsay has always doubted the earlier diagnosis given to the family, although as he pointed out one can never be sure. Originally he was of the opinion that William suffered from a form of melancholia, and that my father, who drank very heavily, suffered from alcoholic psychosis. He was always urging us to take more advice from a specialist in the field of mental illness. But naturally we refused.'

'Naturally! Why on earth did you refuse?' Peter's voice was quiet.

'I should have thought that was perfectly obvious. No-one wants to broadcast the fact that there is insanity in the family. We're no different from anyone else. We didn't want the stigma of madness attached to our name.'

'That's a ridiculous attitude in this day and age. It's not called madness any more; it's an illness. And an illness is nothing to be ashamed of.'

Nicholas ignored Peter's exclamation and carried on. 'Anyway events proved Donald wrong; they both had the disease. My father, in a violent outburst of aggression, tried to murder my mother by strangulation. Luckily I was there and fought to protect my mother. He was not a well man; he suffered from high blood pressure brought on by his heavy drinking, and the struggle with me proved too much for him. He suffered a massive cerebral haemorrhage from which he died three days later, thank God! Perhaps you think I should be sorry that my own father died after fighting with me, but I was not, and I'm still not. It was a blessing that he died of natural causes, because it meant there was no scandal. Donald Ramsay remained silent about the attack on my mother; he thought she'd suffered quite enough without any additional unpleasant publicity.'

'And William? What proved Donald wrong about him?' Peter quietly persisted. They had to know it all, no matter how bad it might be.

'William heard voices, apparently a common delusion in the illness. His voices told him to kill me, and he very nearly succeeded. I wouldn't be here now had it not been for Bruno who knocked William unconscious. After that we knew there was no alternative but to commit William into the care of psychiatrists in a mental hospital. He was sent far away to an isolated hospital on the edge of Dartmoor in Devon, far away from prying eyes, and he remained there until they deemed him well enough to return to us.'

'And he returned for Christmas nineteen sixty-two.' Liana spoke for the first time, her voice so low it was barely audible.

Neither Peter nor Eleanora heard her. But Nicholas did, and a horrible, numbing coldness settled like a lead weight in his chest. Christmas 1962, the Christmas James and William were drowned.

William and the grandfather she had never met were not pertinent to Eleanora: all that was in the past. 'But you're not ill, Aunt Anne isn't ill, and Peter and I are both perfectly healthy. So what is the problem?' She was becoming more and more impatient.

'Oh, Eleanora, can't you see? It's because we're first cousins.' Peter turned to her, grasping her hands. 'I don't know much about this illness, but I do know that the closer an individual's relationship to a person with a possible hereditary illness, then the greater is the risk of that illness being passed on to their children. As first cousins, our children would bear an abnormally high risk.'

Eleanora snatched her hands away. 'I don't want to hear such rubbish; using horrible words like *abnormally high risk*! We're perfectly all right, both of us.' She turned on Nicholas. 'And if all this is true, why did you have me? Why did Peter's parents have him? Why was it all right for you to have children? Weren't you worried that I'd be mad?'

351

Nicholas swallowed hard. God, this was awful. How *could* he justify his own actions? Seen through Eleanora's eyes it must seem irresponsible. 'I did worry, of course I did. But when you were conceived I didn't know then, not for certain, that William had the illness, too. And later Donald Ramsay reassured me. Your mother and I are not related in any way and he was sure you'd be all right. And he was right, thank God, you are. But believe me, if your mother had been my cousin I don't think I would have dared to have children. The risk would have been too great.'

'There you are then.' Eleanora pounced on his words. 'You're not related to Mummy, Peter's parents are not related, and Peter and I are the sanest two people here. So there is no problem, no problem at all. I can't think why you are getting into such a terrible state.'

'But, Eleanora,' Nicholas desperately tried to hammer the facts home to her. 'That is the whole point. I'm afraid Peter is right: it is because you are first cousins. Your great, great grandparents were first cousins, also your great grandparents. It was done to keep the estate and monies intact. The more recent Hamilton-Howards have paid a heavy price for their greed, because the illness has occurred with greater frequency.'

Eleanora still refused to listen. 'A load of rubbish,' was her obstinate comment.

Peter tried to explain. 'Listen, darling, if this illness really is hereditary, then your father and my mother still carry the genes, or whatever it is that transmits it from one member of the family to another, and therefore so must we. I don't agree with your father that marriage is out of the question, but I do think we must take advice before deciding to have children.' Although terribly shocked, he doggedly remained reasonable, desperately trying to assess the matter carefully, logically. 'We must go together and talk to a psychiatrist, someone who is an expert in these matters.'

But Eleanora, not possessing the power of reason and logic, always jumping into everything feet first and thinking afterwards, typically flew into a rage, and the word psychiatrist was the last straw. 'Psychiatrist! Go and see a psychiatrist? You must be mad to even suggest such a thing! Make up your mind, Peter, it's marriage and children, or nothing. Take me as I am, without going to some damned quack and asking for his stupid advice, or forget all about me.'

'Eleanora, *please.*'

'I mean it, Peter. You're so damned careful, always weighing up this and that. I really wonder sometimes how you ever dare breathe!'

'Eleanora!'

'How many times do I have to tell you? I'll never agree to see anyone, not anyone. Marriage and kids without a bloody inquisition from some so-called expert!'

'And what if I don't agree?'

'Then you can forget it.' Leaping up from the settee she raced across to the door and flung it open. 'I'm going back down to the party to get bloody drunk. What a pity you haven't yet given me a ring. I'd have loved throwing it back in your face.'

The door banged behind her and the room was silent.

'It seems you have achieved your objective.' Peter's voice was bitter as he turned to Nicholas.

'It's for the best. Believe me. I know your own mother and father think the same. You can't know how thankful we've all been that neither you nor Eleanora have suffered from the illness.' Nicholas tried to sound positive. 'It's not the end of the world. You will find someone else. You both will.'

'There will *never* be anyone else for me. I love Eleanora, even though sometimes I long to shake some sense into her. I know what she's just said, but I'm not leaving it there. I *am* going to seek expert advice, because I'm certainly not prepared to take the opinion of some nineteenth-century physician even if you apparently are.' He sighed. 'I'd better go back down to the party, too, although I can't say I feel much like it now.'

He closed the door softly behind him, in complete contrast to Eleanora's noisy exit.

The room was silent, and yet it seemed to Liana that it was filled with little whispered cries, grief, bewilderment, shame, sorrow and then anger.

'The sins of the fathers,' said Liana harshly. She felt as if she was suffocating with anger. Always thinking that she had paid with *her* guilt, now she knew it was not so. It was Nicholas's guilt, his silence about William which had forfeited the life of James.

An anger built up inside her with such intensity it was frightening. She could feel it flooding over her in bitter recrimination. Three deaths she had suffered and mourned, and now all the pain came back tenfold. But worse, worst of all, was the fact that now she knew the death of James could have been avoided. If only she had *known* William was mad. Everything she had ever suspected, every word William had ever uttered, every question Nicholas had avoided answering now assumed a blinding significance.

James need not have died. She turned on Nicholas. The burning accusation in her voice made him feel sick.

'You let William come home that Christmas, and yet you *knew* he was mad. You *knew* he was dangerous.'

Suddenly, ghastly comprehension split Nicholas's mind asunder. The death of James had not been an accident. William was involved. Had he drowned James and then drowned himself? Nicholas closed his eyes to shut out the hideous images. Oh, God, what the hell did it matter? James was dead and it was his fault. Now he knew he had lost whatever right he had had to Liana's love for ever. How she must have suffered. But why, in God's name, had she kept silent? Was it for his sake? Because William was his brother? Jesus Christ, what a mess. He sank down in the nearest chair, his head between his hands.

'The doctors said William was better. That it was all right for him to come home,' he said. 'And I believed them.'

'He was mad,' Liana whispered fiercely. 'He was mad, mad!' She stood up and pacing over to the window, stared out with unseeing eyes over the panorama of lights that was London.

A timid knock on the door heralded the entrance of Margaret, Richard and Anne. 'You've told them?' It was Anne who asked.

'Yes.' Nicholas did not raise his head. He was still trying to come to terms with the torment in his mind. What was the connection between the deaths of James and William?

Liana turned towards them briefly, her eyes glittering. 'I know now what you all knew, what you should have told me that terrible Christmas. William was mad, quite *mad*.' She turned back to the window again, her breath coming in ragged gasps.

'Liana, what are you trying to say?' Anne spoke, her voice hesitant, fearful.

Wheeling round so violently that she almost fell, Liana stared at them. Stunned and outraged she was also possessed with a terrible, searing anger. She would never, *never* forgive them. They had all connived to keep the secret. That meant they were all guilty of murdering James.

Well, let *them* suffer now. Oh, they would never suffer the way she had suffered, but she would make sure they carried the guilt to their graves. Let them know William murdered her son, her only son. She began to cry, then laugh, hysterical now. She was glad, glad, GLAD that she had murdered William, only regretting that it was not possible to commit the same murder over and over again, making it worse each time, making him suffer more each time. William did not deserve a scrap of sympathy, and he would get none, because she had no intention of telling them the manner of his death. Let them think his death was an accident.

'Yes,' she said, her voice harsh and brutal. 'I've kept a dreadful secret, too. But I'll tell you now, now that at last it makes some kind of obscene sense. William murdered my son. *He murdered him*! Do you understand that? Murdered! He snatched James from me and walked out on to the thin ice, where he deliberately smashed a hole with the boat hook. Then he dropped James in the hole.' A gasp of horror rippled through the silence of the room. 'I tried to get James out, and William tried to stop me. We both ended up in the water. You know the rest of the story, or perhaps you'd like a graphic description of the scene, minute by ghastly minute.'

A chilling silence swirled around the assembled company and Liana stood quite still watching the mental carnage taking place before her. Like a spreading pool of blood it seeped into every corner of the room until they choked as the full impact of her words sank in.

'Oh, my God. Poor little James. Darling, darling James.' Margaret broke down, sobbing bitterly.

'Yes, darling, darling James. Who is now six feet under, thanks to your mad murderer of a son.'

Richard Chapman got to his feet, moving awkwardly in his unaccustomed evening dress. 'Don't blame Margaret,' he said firmly, turning to Liana. 'She thought William was well enough to be home. We all did. No-one could have foreseen such a terrible tragedy, and harsh words can't change what has happened. Our duty now is to think of those who are living and how best we can help *them*, your daughter and our son. They are innocent victims of this madness, too.'

Liana did not answer. She felt angry and confused, and could only think of James. But thinking was so hard, thoughts hurt, how they hurt. No, no, I can't bear it: I don't want to think! But powerless to stop them the thoughts crowded in just the same. I could have saved James's life. If only I had acted on my intuition. If only I had trusted myself and not others. Why wasn't I more careful? It was my fault. I should never have let go of his hand. I should have picked him up and gone back to the house the moment William appeared. Absorbed in her own tormented thoughts, she did not hear the door open quietly and see Peter help Eleanora into the room. From her unsteady gait it was clear she was very much the worse for drink.

355

'All the party guests have gone now, thank God,' said Peter.

Margaret rushed towards her beloved granddaughter, and, taking her hands, sat with her on the settee. Anne and Peter sat the other side, Anne hastily whispering, relaying the cruel truth of the drowning of James and William.

Tears slid down Eleanora's cheeks. It was all more than she could bear, one hateful thing after another.

'Liana?' Richard's hand was on her shoulder. 'Please help Eleanora, she needs you.'

But Liana remained silent, incapable of thinking of anything other than the death of James.

'Don't you see, she can't.' Eleanora began to cry, noisy hiccupping, gut-tearing sobs. 'She can't think of anyone except James.' Pushing aside Margaret's and Anne's restraining hands, she went across to her mother. 'You always loved James more than me, always. Didn't you?' Taking her mother's shoulders in her hands, she shook her. *'Didn't you?'* She screamed the last words.

'Yes I did, I did,' Liana heard herself screaming back. 'I always loved him more. In a different way from you.'

Sobbing wildly Eleanora rushed from the room. 'Go after her,' said Richard sharply to Nicholas. 'Calm her down and take her back to her own flat. We'll talk it through with her in the morning.' He turned to Liana. 'Did you have to say that?' he asked wearily. 'Have you no thought for the shattering blow life has just dealt her? She cannot marry the man she loves.'

Liana did not answer. She went and sat in the spindly-legged chair by the window and looked out into the darkness of the night. It began to rain. She sat watching the drops slide down the window pane, her eyes dry. Surely there were enough tears already in the world without the sky joining in.

Vaguely aware of the urgent conversations taking place in the room, she sat still and silent, trying to cope with the turmoil in her head. Her heart was dead and cold, yet her mind burned with a fever. James's death had been preventable, but no-one, not even me, she agonized, did anything to stop its happening.

But you can help your other child. You can save Eleanora, cried her teeming brain. What need is there for her to suffer? You know there is no reason why she should not marry Peter, because she carries not a drop of

Hamilton-Howard blood in her veins. This is within your power. Tell the truth and help your daughter.

Liana drew in a sharp breath as the thought hammered inside her head. The reality of the dilemma facing her momentarily banished thoughts of James. Help Eleanora – but to help meant telling the truth. The stark reality of the choice stared remorsely at her. Tell the truth and wreck her own world as she now knew it, or remain silent and wreck Eleanora's world.

How important was the love between Peter and Eleanora? Was it *that* important? Everyone she had ever loved was dead, only Broadacres and her businesses meant anything to her now. Was it important enough to tell the truth and in doing so throw away the only things left for her to care about, Broadacres and wealth. Was it really *that* important?

Since the death of James the emptiness of her spirit had given Broadacres and the accruing of wealth an even greater meaning than before. Those things were *real*. They had succeeded in sustaining her when nothing else had. I need Broadacres as much as a drowning man needs a lifebelt. What other reason do I have for living?

Reasoned out like that it seemed simple and clear cut, a black and white decision. So why, then, was her mind frantically scurrying round in circles? Should she give it all up, give up her very existence for Eleanora's love affair? Yes, yes, of course you must, cried her conscience. Don't be a fool, don't act in haste, wait and see, urged the cold logic in her head. Why should you? Why throw away everything for a love affair?

Liana thought of Broadacres, the house standing square and proud amidst the wide green lawns; of spring, when a thousand daffodils rose from the dark earth year after year without fail to lift their yellow trumpets to the pale watery sun; of summer, heavy with the fragrance of roses; of the colours of autumn and the acrid smell of woodsmoke. Broadacres could endure anything, and while she stayed there so could she.

So where was the dilemma? There was not one. Slowly Liana began to make up her mind. She could not risk losing all she had left by telling the truth of Eleanora's birth.

Inexorably the mental process of tightening the screws of self-justification began. There was no conflict between truth and deceit, because the original deception was now the reality: a fact of life accepted by everyone. It was the way fate had intended it should be. The thought was comforting in a vague, opaque way.

With that thought in place, the tattered remnants of her conscience subsided, collapsing beneath the sheer force of the devastating logic. History had spelled out her damnation many years before. Truth would wreck her own life; silence was wrecking Eleanora's. Broadacres and her own survival merged into one, assuming the same identity. She could not, *would* not tell the truth. Nothing was more important than keeping Broadacres.

PART FOUR
1966

Chapter Twenty-Six

'If you are sure this is what you want.'

'Quite sure. I've already written to Levi, the Italian director. I know he is directing *Euridice* in Florence this summer. It's an open-air performance in the Boboli Gardens, so hundreds of singers will be needed.'

'And after that?'

'After that, I shall move from Florence to Milan, find myself a good singing teacher and hopefully get work during the winter season at La Scala.' Eleanora paced up and down the cloister library, her dark eyes darting aimlessly about from the Waterford chandeliers to the Chippendale bureau and bookcases, anything rather than look at her mother. God, the sooner she could shake the dust of England and Broadacres off her feet, the better.

'I've never heard of this opera *Euridice*. Is it popular?'

Liana made a determined effort to sound friendly and relaxed, all the time wishing that Eleanora would at least look at her. In a way she felt that raging anger would be preferable and easier to cope with. It would certainly be more normal. She could not deal with this enigma, this tightly controlled and cold young woman pacing so restlessly up and down with all the latent aggression of a caged lioness. What Liana was quite incapable of seeing was the fact that it was an exact reflection of herself; blind to her own instinctive characteristics, she could not see that Eleanora was reacting in exactly the same way as she always had in times of crisis – pulling up the emotional drawbridge, compensating the void by immediate action, meticulous planning and making certain that life was full and busy.

Eleanora would not have admitted that she was running away. The truth was she had not even thought about it. Not stopping to analyse her impulses, she was acting instinctively in leaving Broadacres, not consciously realizing that her planning had one single aim, and that was to fill all day every day, so that not even a few spare seconds in which to think were left free. So close in temperament and spirit, but unable to acknowledge it, mother and daughter now faced each other as strangers.

Eleanora looked at her mother with profound irritation. Why was she wasting time pretending to be interested in opera? She doesn't give a damn about the opera or me, she thought angrily. But careful, good-mannered civilities had to be observed, and she answered her mother's question.

'It's not performed often, so can hardly be called popular. Actually it's claimed to be the first full stage opera ever performed. Jacopo Peri wrote it to celebrate the marriage of Maria de Medici and the French Dauphin in sixteen hundred. The Boboli Gardens are the gardens of the original Medici Palace, so it's very logical to perform it there.' She rattled off the facts like a schoolteacher lecturing a backward student.

Liana swallowed hard but took the snub without comment. Although she wished with all her heart it were otherwise, there was no alternative but to recognize that the chasm now yawning between them was as wide as the universe. Eleanora was making that perfectly plain.

'Does Peter know what you are intending to do?'

Liana did not want to ask about Peter, did not want to be reminded of that appalling night two weeks ago when she had been forced to make yet another harsh decision. An unceasing cycle of lies, that is my life. She flinched away from the thought, the guilt absolved by the certainty she was clinging on to that she had had no choice.

Her mind flickered briefly on to Nicholas. Ironic that he, too, had been hiding dark secrets. She hardened her heart. *His* secret had killed. But mine never will; it haunts me and me alone, and will never harm anyone. She had convinced herself of that over the past two weeks, firmly cementing it into her mind, and now nothing would shake that conviction.

Eleanora was hurt now, but she would survive. Whatever she might think to the contrary in moments of high emotion, she won't die of a broken heart as a result of my silence. And she is not like me when I lost Raul, poor, friendless and pregnant. And her character is different from mine. She will bounce back and find someone else and fall in love again. What I did was right. There was no other choice, the course of action was crystal clear.

Liana looked now at her daughter as she mentally justified her action yet again. She had not kept silent only for herself, but for Eleanora, too. The reasoning was simple. The truth would deprive Eleanora of all those things which she now possessed by right of birth and which were essential to her well-being – a family, a home, a father, wealth, privilege and almost certainly Peter's affection as well. Would he, if he knew the truth, still want to marry the illegitimate daughter of an Italian peasant? Liana doubted it.

Eleanora swung round to face her mother. 'Do you actually care whether or not Peter knows? Or even whether or not he is important to me any longer?'

'Darling, of course I care. I want what is best for you. Even now when everything seems so hopeless. You must believe that.' It was true, she did. But telling the truth will not achieve that, she reminded herself. Eleanora's dark eyes bored into her as if searching the darkest corners of her mind. Liana tried to smile reassuringly but failed miserably. How was it possible to find talking to one's own daughter so difficult?

'Really!' Eleanora's tone was disbelieving and disparaging, and Liana knew she was still hugging the pain of their quarrel. Another relic of that dreadful night. How Liana wished she could take back those hurtful words, words spoken in haste and without measured thought. But like everything else, it was too late. Why was it nothing could ever be undone as easily as it was done? Richard Chapman had been right. Dear, sensible Richard. Why hadn't she listened to him, instead of lashing out blindly in her pain? Why had she actually admitted the fact that she had always loved James more than Eleanora? It was the truth, but had served no purpose. Words could not bring James back. All she had succeeded in doing was to hurt Eleanora deeply. Liana understood why her daughter looked at her so coldly now and could not forgive her. Even so, she looked for a glimmer of hope but then turned away, unable to face the rejection in Eleanora's eyes. Perhaps in time, Liana thought forlornly, perhaps in time I'll find some way of making it up to her. It was only a tiny speck of light on the horizon, but Liana clung to it.

'Well, since you ask, Mummy. Yes, he does know. I've written and told him, and I've also told him that I don't want to see him again, at least not for a while. There's no point in prolonging the agony. Besides, I've decided that perhaps we were too hasty in thinking we were in love, really in love with a capital L. It was a first girlfriend-boyfriend affair for both of us and probably wouldn't have lasted. I've advised him to see other girls. For my part, I certainly intend to see other men. Of course, I hope that we shall remain friends. I made that plain in my letter. We are cousins after all, and it's inevitable that our paths will cross at various family gatherings.'

'That is very wise. Your father will be pleased you have been so sensible,' Liana heard herself replying but it was a stranger's voice, stiff and stilted. The right words, but without any real meaning.

'Oh, you *are* communicating with him, then! I thought you had sent him permanently to Coventry this time. That's your usual reaction, isn't it, whenever things go wrong? Don't speak to Daddy, the poor sod!'

'Eleanora!' The word rapped out in anger, then Liana bit her lip. It was no good, she and Eleanora were bringing out the worst in each other. If they were not careful they would end up having another row, and then God only knew what either of them might end up saying. The sooner this conversation was over the better. She reached for a file and pulled it towards her. 'I'll put five thousand pounds in your bank account today. I will also have a bank draft for another five thousand made out for a bank in Italy. You will have access to plenty of money in either country. Thereafter, a regular amount will be paid into both accounts on a monthly basis. If you find it is not enough, please let me know and it will be increased.'

'Thank you.' Eleanora turned to go, then paused at the door and looked back at her mother. In a small quiet voice she said. 'I'm sorry that I lived and James died. But that's the way it turned out. There's no justice in this world, is there?'

'Oh, Eleanora, I didn't mean . . .'

'I'll be writing to Daddy. If you want to know where I am, you can ask him.' Eleanora closed the door and was gone.

The silence of the library, which normally Liana found so comforting, now seemed alien. It rustled and whispered, full of lonely echoes of what might have been. Elbows on the desk, her fingers in a steeple, she rested her chin on her hands and closed her eyes. So this was what it had finally come to. The child she had sacrificed so much for had now, in womanhood, turned away from her. How did it all go so wrong? 'I'll be writing to Daddy,' those were her words, but they meant I want nothing from you. Nothing except my money, thought Liana with sudden bitterness, the money I've mortgaged my soul to the devil to get. Yet I did it all for you, Eleanora, because I wanted the best for you, my daughter. Only the best that money could buy. And you've always had that, and will go on having it, just as I promised so many years ago before you were even born.

Before Eleanora was born. Her mind went back to those days. Next month would be March 1966. On 19 March it would be exactly twenty-two years since she had last seen Raul. Yet his memory was still agonizingly vivid, his presence still close. It seemed nothing could eradicate the past. Although at times fading, becoming less important, always in times of unhappiness Raul came back and Liana drew comfort from the only truly unsullied memories she possessed, the memory of the first love of her life.

And now I'm in limbo yet again, Liana thought. I can't stop loving a man who has been dead for more than twenty years. I gave birth to his daughter, but because I can't acknowledge him as her father I've lost her. I am married to a man who I know loves me, and yet we cannot communicate. Or more to the point – the acknowledgement was reluctant – I don't want to communicate. But why should he expect it when he was instrumental in the murder of my son? *Our* son, her conscience prodded her. But, stubborn as ever, she ignored the inner voice, not wishing to concede Nicholas's pain. Nicholas would have to survive alone as best he could. She could not cope with any more emotion. This was the end of the road, the final convoluted twist to the lie told so many years before.

God, what a mess! Even work provided no distraction; her mind kept wandering. Would I have gone on, she wondered miserably, if I could have foreseen it would end like this? There was no answer. There never *was* any answer. Neither was there any respite because lies, once started, were like life, a steam engine at full throttle just forging on and on and on.

Outside it started to rain, the drops pattering loudly against the window panes. She looked out. Grey, drizzling rain was sweeping across the bleak February landscape. She decided to go out; the melancholy weather suited her mood. A raincoat and wellington boots were always kept in the cupboard by the door. She put them on and let herself out into the cold February day. February was the one month she disliked, a miserable month, everything dead.

Alone in the Arcadian Room Nicholas watched the solitary figure battling against the wind and rain, and his heart bled. Bent almost double in the effort of pushing against the howling wind, the figure walked quickly up the sloping hillside. Now in winter the grassy slopes were bereft of sheep and cattle, the landscape depressingly empty. He watched until Liana disappeared into the beech wood. The bare, skeletal arms of the ancient trees seemed to reach out and wrap around her, then she was gone. He longed to run after her, sweep her up in his arms and carry her back to the warmth and safety of the house, but he did not. There was no point. These days she hardly looked at him, let alone spoke. And when their eyes did meet, he found himself looking away. The stark accusation he saw was more than he could bear. Nicholas poured himself a stiff Scotch and tossed it back in one gulp. He felt utterly helpless. Where the hell did they go from here?

*

Raul read the letter slowly. His spoken English was good now, but he still found reading a little difficult and had to concentrate. When he reached the last page his lips curved in a smile. Eleanora Howard, yes, of course he remembered her. How could he forget her? It was a long time since he had met a woman who had so aroused him at first glance. Oh, yes, he remembered her well, very well. There had been something else about her, too, something strange. She was young and English, and yet there was something about her which seemed vaguely familiar. But maybe it was just the latent sensuality he sensed she possessed; perhaps she was a conglomerate of all those things he desired most in a woman – sexy, intelligent and artistic. Of course he remembered inviting her to La Scala, but at the time she had laughed and turned away as if indifferent. It seemed she was not so indifferent after all. Now she did want to come to Italy. Would do anything she wrote. Well, he would wait and see if she meant what she said. Anything was a big word.

His German secretary watched him. Monika Muller's rather butch appearance was misleading. Everyone who knew him assumed that Raul had engaged her not only because she was ruthlessly efficient when it came to organizing his life, but also because she was without sexual temptation and therefore no competition to the many other women who flitted through his life. In that respect they could not have been further from the truth. Monika Muller was earthily sexy. Her face and figure may not have turned any heads but Raul knew from experience that she was capable of transforming any man into an abject creature of desire once she had him in bed. His affairs with women were numerous but after every one he always returned to Monika, knowing that she would reward his return with some new eroticism. They were both completely and utterly amoral, both dedicated to the sybaritic life, and their on/off relationship suited them very well. While Raul seduced young women, Monika specialized in seducing equally young men. It amused them to compare notes afterwards. No-one, not even Luigi, Raul's assistant of many years, suspected their carnal relationship.

He tossed her the letter. 'Write and tell her to come and see me here at my Rome house before Easter. Tell her I'll give her an audition.'

'In singing?' She raised her eyebrows.

Raul grinned, a shimmer of eroticism lighting his eyes. 'Of course,' he said reaching for his cigarettes. 'To begin with.'

*

The moment he received Eleanora's letter telling him she had decided to go to Italy and accept Levi's offer of finding her work, Peter sought her out. Knowing her so well, he also knew she would not be thinking straight and would almost certainly hurtle headlong into whatever happened to come into her head first – anything to be occupied, anything to put off rational thought. Finally confronting her in her London flat, he urgently tried to persuade her to wait a while.

'Rushing off like this is being ridiculous, and you know it,' he said. 'Before either of us does anything, we should seek further medical opinion. It's always possible it might not be as bad as your father thinks.'

'It is you who is being ridiculous, clutching at straws in the wind. I'm being realistic. I've asked Donald Ramsay, and he has confirmed everything Daddy told us. The disease was diagnosed years ago.'

'Exactly, years ago, and even Donald isn't entirely convinced by the diagnosis. Plus the fact that he's an old man now and is the first to admit that he isn't an expert on psychiatric illness. Things are changing all the time: new drugs, new forms of treatment, new knowledge in the field of genetics.'

Eleanora's face took on a stubborn expression. 'Donald Ramsay is a doctor, and that's good enough for me. What's more he's known our family for years and there's no disputing the fact that it's hereditary. Some of our ancestors have been very odd indeed.'

'Odd maybe. But that doesn't necessarily mean insane, or even that it's hereditary. No-one has ever had the courage to find out for certain. It's something we've got to do, Eleanora. We must find out.'

Eleanora shuddered with distaste. 'I know all I want to know, and believe me, after what I've already found out about the Hamilton-Howards I don't want anything more to do with you. It's finished between us, Peter. Over and done with.'

'Eleanora, you can't just stamp on love.'

'I can, and I have,' was her uncompromising reply.

Peter despaired. It was so typical of Eleanora to react in this totally illogical, impetuous way. But surely she must see how cruel she was being? By running away, she was condemning those left behind at Broadacres to even greater unhappiness.

'Have you thought for one single moment of anyone but yourself? What about your grandmother? Does she deserve to lose you as well as James?'

'I'm not going to die like James. I shall still be around, but not at Broadacres.'

'And what about your father? Have you thought how terrible he must feel?'

Eleanora shrugged. 'As far as I can see he's reasonably happy so long as he's got a whisky bottle close by.'

'Eleanora! How can you be so bloody unfeeling?' Peter's frustration boiled over into anger.

Eleanora flared back. 'Unfeeling! It's you who are being unfeeling, trying to persuade me to stay. Can't you see I can't bear it? It's an impossible situation.'

Peter gave up. It was hopeless. He knew Eleanora and her stubbornness too well. It was useless trying to persuade her now. He would have to wait and choose the right moment. 'Well, go if you must,' he said sadly. 'Goodbye, Eleanora.' He turned and let himself out of the flat.

Eleanora stared after him, contrarily wanting him to return and be more persuasive. Suddenly, Italy seemed very far away.

If only Peter had known then just how near to capitulating she was, how close to throwing herself into his arms, he would have stayed. But he did not; her voice and demeanour gave no hint of indecisiveness.

*

'Well, Peter, at least you were right about one thing.'

Walking slowly around the courtyard surveying her domain, Eleanora spoke aloud, then entering the *castello*, picked up her suitcase and taking it outside stowed it in the car parked just by the stone gateway.

He had said once that she would know when the time was right to go back to the *castello*, and she had. She looked around, still hardly able to believe her eyes. It was amazing how quickly the work had been completed. Her rather stilted Italian had proved more than useful, as had the fact that she was young, feminine and beautiful. Unaware of how like her mother she was, once Eleanora had decided to use the month and a half she had free before the audition with Raul Levi to renovate part of the *castello*, she had set to work like a demon. With a combination of femininity and steely determination she had bludgeoned her way through red tape to get what she wanted. The money, given by her mother, proved indispensable. Slipping a few thousand lire into an eager hand here and there ensured that the work she had in mind actually commenced and, more importantly, was finished.

As a result she was now ready to leave for Rome and her audition. The kitchen and three other rooms in the *castello* had been restored, furnished, and made secure. Eleanora was pleased with them. The outside walls had been stripped of ivy and the courtyard cleared of weeds. Terracotta urns filled with brilliant red geraniums now stood glowing with colour around the well and a purple bougainvillaea planted by the side of the kitchen door was already sending colourful shoots up along the wall. A young woman from the village of San Angelo had promised to come up and water the plants in her absence and dust inside the *castello* once a week. She was satisfied. Everything had been taken care of; there were no loose ends. Or were there? Withdrawing a sealed envelope from her skirt pocket, Eleanora tapped it thoughtfully against her chin. Ought she to have told her father what she had done? Not that he would mind that she had not asked permission, but her mother! That was a different matter altogether. No, much better to leave the letter just as it was, with only the sketchiest of details. She would write again, if she got a part in *Euridice* and settled herself in Florence. But even then, the *castello* could stay her secret, for the time being at least.

It was time to drive to Rome. A tingle of excitement mixed with apprehension flickered in the pit of her stomach. Rome, an audition, a new life, a step into the unknown. Eleanora paused in the gateway and looked back at the courtyard for the last time before leaving. How different now from when she had arrived; how pretty the profusion of crimson geraniums. Outside the ancient walls cicadas were chirruping merrily in the umbrella pines and the dusty smell of wild thyme, sage and rosemary filled her nostrils.

Suddenly her mood switched and inexplicable fears about the future loomed. But if I ever need it, here is my bolt hole, she reminded herself, a place where no-one will find me or even think of looking, a place where I can escape from the world and seek seclusion. Turning away from the courtyard, her gaze swept out through the gateway and down the mountainside towards the city below. It was early April and the harsh glare of the sun hurt her eyes. It was hot, burning hot. A haze blurred the view of Naples, the hillside shimmering and undulating in the heat.

Suddenly, quite without warning a vision of Broadacres burst in upon her mind. It was so clear even the smell of damp river valley earth enveloped her. A smile curved her lips. The horses would be out in the paddocks now, trampling the brilliant yellow celandines underfoot, greedily snatching at tufts of sweet spring grass. A soft green haze would be lighting the landscape with the translucent glow of spring.

The words of a poem she had thought long forgotten sprang unbidden into her head.

Oh, to be in England
Now that April's there,
And whoever wakes in England
Sees, some morning, unaware,
That the lowest boughs and the brushwood sheaf
Round the elm-tree bole are in tiny leaf,
While the chaffinch sings on the orchard bough
In England – now!

How strange that she, who had never paid much attention to poetry during English lessons and in fact always thought it sentimentally slushy, should remember a poem by Robert Browning. It was no use pretending that Italy was her country. It was fascinating, and she liked it, but her roots were in England. The links which tied her to Broadacres were too deep and passionate to be denied. I will go back, she thought, but not yet, I dare not yet. First I must find myself, then I will have the strength to go back. If she went now, she knew she might never tear herself away. She wondered if the horses and dogs missed her. Was Gran still able to ride Diabolus? And had Donald Ramsay recovered enough from his stroke to be able to ride?

Her melancholy mood evaporated as quickly as it had appeared. Blinking back tears and reminding herself that the future was the important thing, she rammed the car in gear and started out on the drive to Rome and Raul Levi's villa.

*

It was not difficult to find the villa in the centre of Rome, and when she arrived the great Levi was at home. An elderly manservant told her to wait in the hall while he went upstairs to fetch his master.

Raul came down almost immediately. 'You left it almost too late,' he said, 'I am leaving for Florence the day after tomorrow to start work on *Euridice*.'

'I know that. I timed it this way. I've been busy.'

Raul looked at her curiously, but Eleanora did not enlighten him. The *castello* near Naples was nothing to do with him.

'Well, now you're here come upstairs and we'll see what sort of voice you have.'

'I'm a mezzo.'

'I know that; it's your range and quality I'm interested in.'

Eleanora followed Raul up the stairs to the music room, looking around curiously as they went. It was a beautiful building, furnished with fabulous antiques. He certainly lived well and was not short of a penny or two by the look of things. She admired the way he strode up the stairs two at a time. He was tall, athletically built, and she estimated about the same age as her father. Meeting him again it struck her forcibly once more what an attractive air there was about him although his face hardly came into the category of good-looking. He must have been once though, Eleanora decided; very good-looking. But now his face had what Peter would have called a 'lived-in' look. Peter! The thought jolted her. Peter. No, I must not think of Peter; think about this man instead. This man was far more interesting.

Suddenly Raul turned and flashed her a smile. Eleanora tried to smile back but found herself blushing instead. His eyes gave out such raw, animal-like sexual signals that against her will she felt herself shuddering in answering excitement. He turned back and continued on up the curving staircase. Eleanora eyed his back speculatively. His reputation with women was legendary; he was a philanderer of the first order and, therefore, eminently suitable to provide her with the diversion she needed at the moment. A lover with no emotional strings attached – a perfect and painless springboard into the future.

Monika Muller was in the room setting out some music. She turned and looked Eleanora up and down. For a moment Eleanora felt uncomfortable; it was almost as if Monika were aware that Eleanora was mentally sizing up Raul Levi as a potential lover. Then she shrugged the feeling off. So what? Monika must be used to it. Eleanora was pretty certain that she had seen many young women throwing themselves at Raul Levi with a view to landing a part in one of his productions. Except that I'm different, Eleanora told herself. I don't need the aid of the casting couch. Any part I get will be because of talent, nothing else. Eleanora stared back at Monika, her gaze hostile. What business was it of hers anyway? She only worked for Raul. What he did in his private life had nothing to do with her. And if I decide to take Raul Levi as a lover, it is my affair and mine alone. Suddenly she felt very grown up and sophisticated to be making decisions about taking a lover; a woman of the world at last. Raul Levi, you don't stand a chance, she thought. If I want you I shall have you!

'Monika, this is Eleanora Howard, the English girl I told you about. Eleanora, this is Monika Muller, my right-hand woman. She organizes my life and speaks half a dozen languages. Without her I'd be lost.'

Monika inclined her head stiffly. Superciliously, thought Eleanora. 'I'm pleased to meet you,' she said in perfect English.

Because she was still a little nervous, Eleanora moved her head slightly with an arrogant toss of her hair. It was a habit she had had since childhood. It was also the self-same movement Raul always employed whenever his composure was threatened. Monika Muller stared. She had sensed right from the beginning when he had first mentioned Eleanora Howard that he was more drawn to the English girl than he cared to admit. Now she thought she knew why. Well aware of Raul's faults, she was acquainted with his vanity. He had always been inclined to narcissism, and this girl was the feminine version of himself, except, of course, he would never see that. But it did account for the unusual attraction that Monika sensed existed between them.

As for himself, Raul had not bothered to analyse his feelings although her name, Eleanora, had succeeded in jolting his memory and he had retrieved the story he had written long ago about the two girls. He had a contact in Hollywood now, a Milton Hyam. He'd get Monika to translate the story and send it off. But for the moment his thoughts were concentrated on the girl standing before him. She was very tall and her beauty, although sensual, had an almost boyish air about it, which added an illicit degree of eroticism. Yes, the attraction he had sensed at their first meeting was still there. A strong chemistry existed between them, and he was certain she could feel it, too. Yet at the same time he was aware of another feeling lurking beneath the surface, a bizarre reflection of times long past. He felt unsettled, and then Eleanora smiled at him, her eyes flickering a blatant sexual challenge. He forgot the strange unsettling feelings as a raging fire spread through his loins. He wanted her, and knew he was going to get her.

Sitting down at the piano, he played an arpeggio. 'Sing,' he commanded.

Monika Muller left as Eleanora's rich mezzo-soprano voice began to echo around the music room. It was time for her to pluck a ripe young man for her amusement. She knew the signs. Raul was going to be occupied with this young woman for some time to come.

*

'Would you like dinner, or . . .?'

The audition was finished. Eleanora had got her part in the chorus of *Euridice* and was content, knowing that Raul had been impressed with her vocal ability. And now, a long Roman evening stretched ahead.

'Or what?' She barely recognized her own voice, it was so husky, so seductive, as if another woman had taken over her mind and body. She shivered, intensely excited and yet a little afraid, knowing full well she was stepping across a border into another world.

'Whatever you want,' Raul answered.

Eleanora stared at him, her dark eyes open wide. Raul looked at her and, never taking his gaze from hers for one single instant, walked across to her. He ran his hands down from her shoulders, letting them rest on her breasts with sensuous deliberation. For the first time in her life Eleanora knew what it was like to be filled with nothing but raw, naked lust. It took her breath away and she gasped.

'I don't want dinner.'

Raul took her there on the floor by the grand piano, clothes miraculously shed in a matter of seconds. Hands, mouths, bodies gasped and slithered in a timeless, chaotic, dark ecstasy. Finally, exhausted and sated they lay still.

Hell, thought Raul, still reeling in faint astonishment at Eleanora's uninhibited response. Who seduced who?

'Whoever said the English were cold?' he said, kissing the long line of her neck and working his way down to her breasts. How many times had they both climaxed? He could not remember. He loved the febrile way Eleanora ground herself against him, frantic for the pleasure of an orgasm. Now the first frenzy had abated, they were beginning another exploration of each other's bodies, this time slow and tactile.

Eleanora debated whether or not to tell him she was half Italian, then decided against it. It was more exciting to let him think she was a hot-blooded English woman. 'The English enjoy fucking as much as anyone else,' she said. 'It's only our weather which is cold.'

'How many lovers have you had?'

'Only one,' Eleanora answered truthfully.

'Did he know a lot of games?'

Eleanora laughed. 'I have a feeling you know many more.'

Her longing for Peter seemed far distant, the time spent with him unreal. Raul engendered a raw sexual excitement which was new and enthralling. She forgot the tenderness of her love-making with Peter and revelled instead in the overpowering carnal greed now burning within her like a fever.

Raul stood up and pulled her to her feet. 'Let's walk naked in the garden,' he said. 'You can be Eve to my Adam.'

It was 2.00 a.m.; the city traffic was as busy as ever. The noise of Rome washed over the high walls into the garden. It was hot, the garden heavily perfumed with gardenias and jasmine. Eleanora hung back. 'Suppose someone should see us?' she said, looking up at the neighbouring buildings, some of which overlooked the walled garden.

'Do you care? I don't.'

Raul looked dark and mysterious in the dim light of the garden, and very exciting. He made Eleanora feel reckless. 'No, I don't care,' she said and, skipping on ahead, jumped into one of the fountains. Posing seductively against the falling water, she called, 'Do I look like a Bernini statue?'

'Exactly like one,' said Raul.

He climbed over the edge of the fountain and Eleanora saw that he was fully erect. His penis was enormous, and glistening with drops of water. '*You* look like one of those rude Greek statues,' she said, then gasped.

Without any formalities he took her again, there and then, slamming her hard against the rough stone of the fountain. The tone of their affair was set – no tenderness, just raw, obsessive sexuality holding them both in thrall. Raul had never felt such a compulsive hunger for just one woman before. He wondered if he could be falling in love. Eleanora knew she was not in love. She knew what love was like; she had loved Peter, and the feeling she had for Raul was not love. But in a way it was more exciting.

Two days later they moved up to Florence where Raul became absorbed in directing *Euridice*. Monika was left behind in Rome, much to Eleanora's relief. She had an uncanny knack of making Eleanora feel that all her thoughts were transparent; that she knew every little detail of the affair with Raul. In Florence, with Monika out of the way, Eleanora was able to relax and enjoy her small role in the chorus. Life was exciting; every day there were new people to meet. The pain of losing Peter receded until she began to wonder if what she had felt for him had been real lasting love at all. Maybe her own words to her mother about the boyfriend–girlfriend relationship had been true.

In Florence, Eleanora did not bother to rent an apartment of her own but shared one with Raul overlooking the Pitti Palace. The sophisticated life of the Florentines suited her extrovert personality. She revelled in every waking moment with a kind of fierce enjoyment and firmly sat on her conscience whenever it showed signs of attempting to rear its head, convincing herself that at last she was really living life as it should be lived.

*

'I've heard from Eleanora.' Margaret waved the letter under Nicholas's nose. 'She is in the chorus of some opera which I've never heard of and living in Florence.'

'I know.' Nicholas sounded anything but happy.

'She says she's having a great time and not missing England at all.' A flicker of sadness passed over her face. 'Do you think that's true?'

Nicholas shrugged. 'I suppose so.' He did not tell Margaret that he had heard, too, and that in his letter Eleanora had said her love life was blooming. The news distressed him. It was much too soon. Feeling sick with worry he prayed that Eleanora had not plunged into some disastrous liaison. He had to tell someone, but not his mother. He searched out Liana and found her in the office. She listened in silence while he read out the whole letter.

'So! In the chorus now, and an understudy part in *Così Fan Tutte* at La Scala in the winter. And in love again! Well, it seems she is doing well and is happy.'

'But falling in love again, so soon after Peter.'

'Young people,' said Liana, signing letters while she was speaking, 'they're all the same these days if the papers are to be believed. In and out of love like yo-yos.'

'Maybe.' Nicholas still was not happy. 'I wish I could talk to her, but she says she won't be home until next year.'

'She also says, "If you feel like coming over to Florence this summer, do come." If I remember correctly. So why don't you? I can't go, of course, but I will write to her.'

Nicholas folded the letter carefully and sat down opposite Liana. 'Are you telling me that you really think everything has suddenly been resolved? All the unhappiness forgotten, gone away?'

'Why not? She's young, she's resilient. She sounds happy. That's good enough for me. I've got other things to think about.'

Liana had no intention of allowing herself to think anything else. Eleanora was happy; therefore, her guilt was purged. Time had proved her right and once again patience had paid off. Thank goodness she had not been panicked into blurting out the truth that night at the Ritz. What a waste of time that would have been, a futile squandering of everything she had accomplished at Broadacres.

Broadacres filled her life these days. Broadacres and its people – the wooded valley brimming with golden sunlight; the dew on the fresh long grass of the meadows in early morning; the crystal-clear chalk streams feeding the broad River Itchen. It was this she loved, this which gave her life purpose. Broadacres was the reason she still schemed and strived, pursuing the many skeins of her business interests with a fanatical devotion. The money was for one thing and one thing only, to maintain Broadacres and its way of life in perpetuity.

'I wonder if she really *is* happy.' Nicholas fidgeted with the letter.

'Why should she say she is if she isn't?' Liana said sharply. She did not want Nicholas to start doubting Eleanora's words.

'To help ease our feelings,' answered Nicholas slowly.

'I don't think so.' Liana was very positive. 'It's not in Eleanora's nature to do that. She has always blurted out the truth, usually regardless of the consequences. If she says she is happy, believe her. Take comfort from that. At least things haven't turned out to be a complete disaster for Eleanora; and Peter must be reasonably happy as well, otherwise surely he couldn't be such a prolific writer? Books, plays, and now film scripts. Hardly a day goes past without his name being mentioned in the newspapers – always some article about his latest success.'

'I suppose you are right,' said Nicholas. 'Anne tells me Peter is going to Hollywood next week to do another film.'

'There you are then. You have nothing to worry about.'

Liana returned to her papers, wishing Nicholas would leave. Eleanora and Peter might be happy, but he was not, and she could not bear looking into his eyes and seeing the perplexed pain and suffering. Like herself, he could not fully comprehend the disaster which had overtaken them. Then suddenly, as it often did these days, her mood swung violently from something near to compassion to a sudden terrible rage. Oh, God, why did he always remind her so of James? The same old questions ricocheted round inside her head, always the same questions, but never any answers. Why had he let William stay that fateful Christmas? Why had he not warned her of his brother's madness? Her hand gripped the pen tightly, and the familiar mantle of bitterness wrapped its coldness around her. She did not care how much pain he was suffering, it was nothing, nothing compared to hers.

'I worry about us, Liana. God, I worry about us.'

Somehow Nicholas scraped together the courage to tackle Liana head on. Since his confession that night at the Ritz, she had withdrawn from him completely, shutting herself away in a high tower of bitterness. The bad patches their marriage had gone through at other times paled into insignificance now. Liana had turned into a stranger, a cold, unpitying woman he could not reach. She blamed him for the death of James, just as he, too, blamed himself. But it was not *all* his fault, surely she could see that?

His cry did touch Liana's heart. Like a bedraggled bird the tiny spark of pity flew in from the darkness, begging her compassion, but before she could respond, it flew out again. There was nothing she could do.

'Stop worrying. We are surviving,' said Liana, not raising her eyes from the papers before her.

'I don't want to just survive. I want to live again, be your husband.' Even their nights were spent apart now. Liana had moved his things into a bedroom along the corridor.

'Sex will not solve anything.'

Nicholas lost his temper. 'Christ! Do you think I don't know that? I'm not talking about sex. I'm talking about talking. I'm talking about sharing our grief, about coming to terms with it.'

Liana looked up and Nicholas wished he had never broached the subject. For a few seconds he saw through the windows of her eyes into the terrible bleak bereavement of her soul, a living hell of doubt and torment. And behind it all, flickering like so many ghosts, brief snatches of what life might have been if only, if only . . .

Nicholas turned and left in despair. Fool! He rounded on himself bitterly. There is nothing you can do. There is nothing in this world that you can do to make reparation for the death of James. He could visualize his future so clearly. It lay before him – long, long years, all bleak and barren. The only spark of hope was Eleanora, his beloved daughter. He would go to Florence. Liana did not want him here.

Chapter Twenty-Seven

Dorothy Ramsay carried the tea tray out into the garden and through into the summer house. The paper-thin bone china cups shone translucent in the sunlight. A large cake plate was piled precariously high with fresh crusty scones and at the side were two bowls, one of clotted cream and the other of strawberry jam.

'This is a lovely surprise,' she said, 'and you've timed it perfectly. Just in time to sample the first strawberry jam of the season.'

'I could smell your cooking from the other side of the valley,' said Peter smiling. 'That's why I came.'

'Well, now you *are* here, Peter, perhaps you can talk some sense into my silly old husband. Try persuading him not to drive that pony and trap until he's got more strength in his hands.'

'Good heavens, woman. I'll never get more strength unless I use them. Anyway, Pegasus has got more sense than most humans. I hardly need to use the reins. He knows exactly where to go.'

Peter ignored their good-natured bickering. 'I'm afraid you're out of luck,' he told Dorothy. 'You'll not get me on your side. I agree with Donald; he'll be perfectly all right. That old horse is as good as a nursemaid any day.'

'Men,' snorted Dorothy. She sounded annoyed but Peter could see a glimmer of a smile. She knew when she was beaten. 'You always stick together.' She began to pour out the tea. 'How long do you think it will be before Margaret and Nicholas arrive?'

'Ten minutes or so. They left a long time before me. Nicholas wanted Diabolus to have a good gallop, and Margaret is exercising', he hesitated, only momentarily it was true, but long enough for the Ramsays to notice, 'Eleanora's mare.'

'Margaret tells me Beauty is off her feed.'

Peter sighed. 'Yes, the vet thinks she's pining.'

Donald grunted irritably. 'Damned stupid girl. Always was too headstrong. Absolutely no need to go rushing off like that. Beauty is not the only one who is pining. Margaret and Nicholas both miss her terribly;

and I daresay even Liana does, always supposing someone could chip their way through that icy shield she has erected and get her to admit it.'

'Donald!' Dorothy frowned. How could he forget that Peter must be missing Eleanora more than anyone?

He knew what she was thinking. 'No, I haven't forgotten Peter. Which reminds me. How did you get on with Doctor Zuckermann? What did he have to say?'

'Much the same as you, Donald. He doubted that an accurate diagnosis was possible so many years ago, although he admitted there may have been some congenital nervous defect which had been compounded by intermarriage. However, as far as Eleanora and I are concerned, his advice was to marry. In his opinion the chance of any of our children being ill is no greater than that of any other couple. He confirmed my own thoughts: the fear of mental illness is often exaggerated out of all proportion.'

'But William *was* mentally ill,' interrupted Dorothy. 'Surely that cannot be denied.'

'Of course not. And almost certainly he had some form of schizophrenia. But it doesn't necessarily mean that anyone else is going to suffer from it.'

Donald snorted. 'There you are. Just what I tried to tell Eleanora, but the damned girl wouldn't listen. She only wanted confirmation that illness had existed in the family and that there'd been a few eccentric ancestors. Once she'd heard that, she shut her ears.' He leaned forward towards Peter. 'You must talk to her again, Peter. Then she'll come back.'

'No, she'll not come back. Not now. Eleanora has already fallen in love with someone else. Nicholas showed me a letter from her when I arrived back from the USA.' Peter managed a weak smile. 'So you see the whole question is now academic. We can forget it.'

There was silence, and Dorothy hurriedly passed him a cup of tea. Peter sipped it, leaning back in the garden wickerwork chair. Tea, he thought wryly, that so English of drinks, the panacea everyone turns to in a crisis. But it was comforting sitting here with two old people in an English country garden. Last week he had been in California where everyone drank Martinis and the gardens were brilliant with hibiscus and oleanders, and shaded by date palms.

Here in the Ramsays' garden, the summer house was shaded by a rambling rose so ancient that its stock was about six inches in diameter and the branches gnarled and moss-grown. But every year, without fail, it produced an abundance of strongly perfumed off-white roses with delicate, tea-coloured centres. They were at full glory now and the lawn was carpeted with the velvet petals of the blown blooms. The rest of the garden was a riot of soft colours, lupins, foxgloves, cornflowers, Canterbury bells, all jostling for space, backed by banks of fragrant wild honeysuckle which had crept into the garden from the copse behind.

Peter thought about Eleanora's letter. It had been a shock. He found it difficult to believe that she could have so easily forgotten the long years of love they had shared. True, they had been hardly more than children when it started, but the love was real, and he had dreamed of their life together when they would conquer the world, he with his writing, she with her singing. How could she switch her affection to another man so quickly, so easily? That was not like the Eleanora he had known since childhood. Impetuous she had always been, but loyalty was another of her qualities. Had she really lost that?

'I don't believe it.' Dorothy's mind was running along the same lines as Peter's. She put her teacup back in its saucer with a loud rattle. 'Eleanora in love with someone else. Rubbish! People don't change overnight.'

'It's hardly overnight,' Peter said. 'It's been four and a half months since we've seen each other. A lot can happen in that time.'

'Overnight,' repeated Dorothy determinedly. 'I think she jumped into bed with the first available man and is now trying to convince herself that she has fallen in love. Forgetting of course, that sex and love are not necessarily compatible.'

Donald raised his eyebrows at Dorothy's outspoken comments but had to agree. 'My main regret is that Nicholas didn't discuss it with me before blurting out the family history that night in London. I'm sure with a little forethought, we could have made it less traumatic.'

'The fact is, Eleanora and I precipitated the event ourselves by springing the news of our engagement.' Dorothy thought how very low and depressed Peter seemed as he spoke. 'It was meant to be a wonderful surprise but it backfired.' Peter leaned back in the chair, closing his eyes against the sun. 'Perhaps it is fate and was always meant to be. You see, the first time Eleanora and I planned to ask permission to become engaged was at the New Year's Eve party of nineteen sixty-two. But by the time New Year's Eve came, James and William had been drowned and, well, you know the rest.'

'What a mess.' Donald sighed. 'I feel terribly guilty myself.'

'Guilty about what?' Immersed in their conversation, the three in the summer house had not heard Nicholas and Margaret cross the lawn. 'Guilty about what?' Margaret repeated.

'What do you think? About never mentioning your damned family secret, of course. As your doctor I should have had more sense. I should have counselled you more wisely.'

Margaret shook her head. 'Don't blame yourself, Donald. You know we wouldn't have listened because we didn't want to. We all share the blame, every single one of us, myself, Nicholas, Anne, and now we are paying the price of years of silence, knowing nothing can ever put right the terrible wrongs we caused by that silence.'

'I don't totally agree.' Dorothy busied herself pouring more tea and topping scones with cream and jam. 'The accident with James could easily have happened anyway. Every year such terrible things *do* happen to other families and those families have to learn to live with the loss somehow.' She gave Nicholas his tea and smiled a gentle, compassionate smile, willing some warmth into the tortured spirit she could see in his clear grey eyes. 'Liana isn't thinking straight at the moment, but she will eventually. Of course, your lives will never be the same. No-one can lose a child and pretend it never happened. But you will learn to live with the memory, both of you, perhaps even to reflect how sublimely happy his short life was. James never knew pain, was never deceived, never disappointed. His whole life was a song of love.'

She paused. The circle of faces watched her intently. Aware of each one reaching out to her for some crumb of comfort, even Donald, whom she had always thought so strong, now doubted the wisdom of his actions. It was as if they were all bleeding to death with unhappiness. Someone has to attempt to staunch the wounds and it has to be me, thought Dorothy, because there is no-one else.

'And as for Eleanora and Peter,' she continued, 'is it really such an intractable problem; is it really too late? I just cannot believe that she is in love with another man. Once she knows there is no good reason why she and Peter should not marry, she'll return, and you can start to pick up the threads of your lives once more.'

Margaret gave a short bitter laugh. 'Not completely,' she said. 'You're forgetting that William murdered James. Things would have been different if James . . .' She stopped seeing the expression on Nicholas's face, then continued slowly. 'But there can be no happy ending for that story, so we must face facts as they are.' She turned to Nicholas. 'Eleanora invited you to Florence. I think you should go and take a good look at this man she says she has fallen in love with. Find out what her true feelings are. Has she really fallen out of love with Peter? Tell her what Peter has found out. In fact, I think it would be a good idea if Peter went as well. She might be ready to listen now that a little time has elapsed. Doctor Zuckermann's opinion might make all the difference, especially if it came from you, Peter.'

'Impossible for me to go, I'm afraid. I'm due back in Hollywood next week. I've signed a contract to work on a new film and I can't get out of that. Anyway, at the moment I'm sure she doesn't want to see me.' Peter knew Eleanora better than all of them. He knew the stubbornness behind which she had always hidden her vulnerability. He had no doubt that she had done a very good job of convincing herself that she was having, as she had put it in her letter, 'a great time'. It was too soon to convince her otherwise. Besides it was something she had to find out for herself. He struggled out of the deeply cushioned chair and stood ready to leave. 'Another point to remember is that Eleanora might very well consider that marriage to me is still too risky. Eleanora is no different from many other people. She has her own inbuilt prejudices and fears and, knowing her, I think they'll be difficult to budge. She has to work things out for herself.'

The group in the summer house watched his lonely figure walk across the lawn. He let himself out through the side gate, and a few moments later they heard the distinctive whine of his sports car as he drove rapidly away down the lane.

Margaret frowned. 'I still think you should go to Florence', she said to Nicholas, 'and find out what is going on.'

*

Eleanora pushed her way through the crowd thronging the enormous railway station of Florence. It was always crowded, night and day. Foreign tourists, easily distinguishable by their clothes and luggage, wandered about consulting timetables and guidebooks, trying to read the signs and find their way. The Italians, inveterate travellers themselves, imbued the place with throbbing life: swarthy peasant families from the south; children trailing after their parents in seemingly never-ending hordes, each one carrying their own bag of food for the journey containing a lump of bread and some salami; the prematurely aged mothers, always laden with the latest baby and luggage, looking harassed, while the men stood grouped together, flat caps on the backs of their heads, smoking, drinking, joking and laughing and eyeing every pretty girl who passed; it never ceased to amaze Eleanora that the station always seemed to be overflowing with monks and nuns, too.

'Where do they all come from, and where are they all going?' she had once asked Raul.

'God knows,' he shrugged his shoulders. 'Don't ask me about the Catholic Church. I'm Jewish. All I know is that Florence is a huge railway junction, and to get almost anywhere in Italy by train you have to come into Florence.'

In her surprise Eleanora forgot about the surfeit of religious brothers and sisters. 'I didn't know you were Jewish. Are you a practising Jew?'

'I thought you knew. Levi is a Jewish name, but no, I'm not a practising Jew. In the same way you are not a practising Christian.'

'Well, I was,' Eleanora found herself saying defensively. 'What I mean is, we always went to church every Sunday. It was expected, so we went. People noticed if our pew was empty.'

It was Raul's turn to look surprised. 'A pew is a seat, isn't it?' Eleanora nodded. 'Why on earth should you be expected to sit in the same seat every Sunday?'

Eleanora hesitated. She had never mentioned to him or anyone else in Italy that her father was an English earl, and that her title was Lady Hamilton-Howard. The fact that she was living with Raul and had walked into the coveted part of a principal understudy in *Così Fan Tutte* had caused enough jealousy. If the rest of the company knew she was a wealthy, titled lady, Eleanora had a shrewd idea her life would not be worth living.

'I told you. I come from a small country village in Hampshire. People are very old-fashioned in the country.'

Raul laughed. 'The same the world over,' he said, and forgot the conversation.

Eleanora had not forgotten. Now, struggling through the crowd, trying to find her father who should have just disembarked from the Milan train, she reminded herself to tell him. Nicholas, the Earl of Wessex, would have to stay behind in England; here in Florence he was plain Mr Nicholas Howard. A hotel room near the Santa Trinità bridge had been booked for him in that name.

Suddenly she saw him – a tall, fair-haired man, standing a good head and shoulders above everyone else – and her heart leaped with joy. She had been so busy telling herself that she was not missing England or anyone from Broadacres that she had come to believe it. But when she saw him, her father, her own little bit of England who had come all the way just to see her, she knew it was not true.

'Daddy,' she yelled, pitching her powerful voice above the level of noise, leaping up and down, waving frantically.

Nicholas heard her and turned. For the first time in months he smiled, a real smile that ended in a warm feeling inside him. She was beautiful, his daughter, and he felt so proud – young, beautiful, vibrant and obviously happy to see him. Elbowing his way through the crowds he reached her in a few strides and gathered her to him in a great bear hug.

'Eleanora, darling. I can't tell you how glad I am to see you. I've missed you. We've all missed you.'

'Even Mummy?' It was said with a flippant laugh, but Nicholas caught the serious undercurrent.

'Yes, of course. Even your mother. But you know what she's like. She would never admit it.'

He picked up his case and Eleanora linked her arm through his. She looked sideways at her father. He looked tired. There were lines at the side of his mouth she never remembered seeing before. He looked more than tired, she decided: he looked sad and weary. She stopped a moment and drew his hand up to rest against her cheek. 'Mummy is giving you a hard time, isn't she?' she said.

'No, she, I . . .' Nicholas groped for the right words. 'We are both finding life hard at the moment. And somehow it seems even harder without you and Peter popping up every now and then. Everyone misses you. Your grandmother wishes you were back to give that wicked Diabolus some really hard exercise. He's getting too much of a handful for her now, although she still rides him. And Beauty misses you.'

'Maybe I'll come back for a weekend at the end of the summer. Then I'll give both horses a run for their money. I'll tire them out for a month.'

She loaded his luggage into her tiny Fiat 500, then they both squeezed into it. 'My God, this is like getting into a sardine can,' said Nicholas inching his long body into the minuscule car with difficulty.

'Except that you are the size of a salmon!'

They both laughed. Nicholas sat back, watching Eleanora coax the little car through the busy streets of Florence, using the horn extensively and taking as many reckless chances as the rest of the Italian drivers.

'You seem very much at home here.'

'Oh, I am. As I told you in my letter, I'm not missing England at all.' She would die rather than admit to the feelings that had swept over her at the sight of her father. That would only make him blame himself, and she knew he had done plenty of that already. 'And from what I read, it seems Peter isn't missing England either.'

'What do you mean?'

She nodded briskly over her shoulder at a half-opened newspaper lying on the back seat. Nicholas stretched over and retrieved it.

'Peter Chapman, the latest whizzkid to hit Hollywood,' Eleanora translated for him. 'Out on the town with Universal Studio's hottest female property.' She snorted derisively. 'A blonde bombshell! And has probably got a brain the size of a pea! I wouldn't have thought she was Peter's type at all. But I'm glad for him anyway. It confirms the conclusion I came to some time ago.'

'Oh?' Nicholas remained non-committal. He remembered Peter's unhappy face when they took tea in the Ramsays' garden. The photo was almost certainly a publicity stunt. Surely Eleanora must realize that? He watched her hands on the steering wheel doggedly nudging the little car through the chaotic traffic. The knuckles were clenched a little too tightly. She did care. But he knew it would be the devil's own job to get her to admit it. She was like her mother, proud and stubborn, regarding the necessity of admitting the need for other people as a weakness. 'Tell me, what *was* your conclusion?' he asked.

'Oh, that.' The Fiat screeched to a squeaky halt outside the Hotel Tosca. She turned and looked at her father, smiling gaily. 'Nothing new, only what I said in my letter. You did us both a favour when you told the truth. We *were* too young to really be in love. I've found another man and Peter has found another woman. That proves it.' Shrugging her shoulders expressively, she climbed out of the car, adding, 'So, as Shakespeare said, "All's well that ends well". I'm sure Peter thinks the same. Don't you agree?'

Nicholas did not answer immediately. Now was not the time to argue the point, not now when she was struggling to find her way, rudderless in an unfamiliar sea of emotions. Better to let the matter drop. The time to argue and to help would come later. Nicholas prayed that not only would he recognize the time but that he would be given the wisdom to know what to do when it arrived. 'You are probably right,' he said quietly.

'I *am* right.' Eleanora was adamant. The hotel porter came out for the luggage. 'Oh, by the way, Daddy, I hope you don't mind, but I have checked you in as plain Mr Nicholas Howard. There is a good reason,' she went on hastily. 'And that is, everyone here thinks my name is Eleanora Howard. No-one knows my full name or that my father is an earl. I have to put up with quite a bit of jealousy as it is because I'm English and I've landed an understudy part. It would only make matters worse if they knew I was a *Lady*. They would think I had been pulling rank with the director!'

'And have you?' Nicholas quizzed her.

'Of course not. Not even *he* knows.'

It was the emphasis on the word he, that gave the game away. Nicholas guessed the director was the fantastic man she had fallen for. He followed the porter and Eleanora up to his room on the third floor. It was large and elegantly furnished and had a beautiful view of the Ponte Vecchio. After tipping the porter Nicholas closed the door and walked over to join his daughter out on the balcony. 'I couldn't have chosen a better room myself,' he said. Should he ask her about this man now or would she tell him?

Eleanora was wondering the self-same thing. Would her father be shocked to know she was living with Raul? No-one had ever known that she and Peter had lived together for years and she presumed everyone at Broadacres thought they were a couple of virginal innocents. She smiled wryly at the thought. Even if she had been, she was certainly no innocent now. Raul had initiated her into ways of eroticism she had never even dreamed possible. Sometimes she had doubts and dissented a little. Were they not too lascivious? But Raul had a peculiar hold over her that she could never fully comprehend. He did not bully her but she was afraid to say no in case he turned away from her. And anyway in the end she never wanted to refuse him because he always managed to persuade her by arousing her physically until she begged him to take her body and do with it what he would. The end result was always the same, a physical gratification so intense that the right or wrong of the act faded into irrelevance, almost into irrelevance, not entirely. Sometimes Eleanora suspected that she was being drawn into a web of corruption but she always pushed such thoughts from her mind, dismissing them as fanciful nonsense. She was in the big wide world now, not in the narrow confines of Broadacres.

She decided to tell him. 'Daddy,' she leaned on the balcony, and studiously kept her eyes on the view, 'I might as well tell you now, before you meet him, that I am living with Raul Levi, the director. He is the man I told you about. He is older than me and he is Jewish, but that doesn't make any difference. I love him, and we are very happy.'

Nicholas tried to swallow his doubts. Instinct told him all was not well. 'Being happy, darling – that is the most important thing,' he said. 'I look forward to meeting him.' Eleanora continued leaning on the balustrade of the balcony, staring straight ahead at the Ponte Vecchio. He touched her arm anxiously. 'Are you happy, darling? I mean really happy? You'll never know how terrible I feel because I destroyed your hopes and dreams of the life you and Peter had planned together. To hurt someone you love is the worst pain of all, and I do love you. So very much.'

Eleanora turned towards him. 'I know you do, but I'm happy now, happy, *happy*. How many times have I got to tell you not to worry?'

She flung her arms around him and closed her eyes. It was ridiculous but suddenly she wanted to weep. Why? I *am* happy, she told herself, life with Raul is different, exciting and fulfilling. *I am happy*. Why, then, did she feel like a child who has had something precious snatched away? She held on to her father, buried her face in his shoulder and fiercely blinked away the tears.

The hot July sun of Tuscany beat down on her bare shoulders. It would not be so hot at Broadacres – the fields of wheat would be just turning from green to gold now and the blackberry bushes would be in full flower, much to the delight of the silver-washed fritillary butterflies. The leaves of the oak trees would be the distinctive brilliant green that only English oaks have, and beneath the copper beeches the shade would spread a tinge of purple on the moss. That was where she and Beauty always enjoyed a slow saunter after a mad gallop up the downs.

She wished she were a child again, when everything had been so simple, when a hurt could easily be put right by her father's taking her into the stables to feed a carrot to each friendly, snuffling horse. Why was it such simple things lost their pleasure when one grew up? Is it, she wondered, because we all become greedy? She and Raul were greedy. Lustful and greedy, they both took but did not give. Their affair was nothing at all like the innocent, loving pleasure she and Peter had found in each other. But that is because I'm grown up now, my needs are different. She persuaded herself that was the reason: it was all part of growing up. But why, then, did it often feel so unsatisfactory? She could find no answer to that.

Nicholas hugged her, holding her tightly. On edge and unhappy himself, he could sense some part of her doubts and longings. Although formless, wordless and intangible, they were there, and his heart bled for her. He held her close as he had when she had been a child, knowing part of her would always be a child to him, no matter how old she might be. Even when she was a mother herself, she would still be his child. The pity of it was he had lost the power of a father to always make things right; the simplicity of childhood had disappeared. Now he could only hope. My only beloved daughter, he prayed, pressing his face against the sweet perfume of her hair. I hope this man is good to her. Please, God, let her be truly happy.

*

Raul was on the telephone to Monika in Rome when Eleanora finally returned to their apartment. She caught the tail end of their conversation.

'What? Oh, yes, good. Then there's nothing to be done until we start rehearsals at La Scala in September. No, no I don't need you here. As usual your organization has taken care of everything. What?' he looked at Eleanora, and his black eyes sparkled wickedly. Holding out his free arm he beckoned to her to come over to him. She obeyed the summons and he pulled her close. 'Monika is asking whether or not you are still with me.'

Eleanora took the telephone from his hand. She still could not analyse her feelings towards Monika Muller although she had wasted enough time trying – antagonism, uneasy dislike or plain simple jealousy at her closeness to Raul, she could never decide. 'Yes, Raul and I are still together, Monika,' she said coolly. 'We seem to suit each other very well.'

'I had a feeling you would.' Eleanora could hear the knowing smile in Monika's voice. 'I look forward to seeing you in Milan at the start of the season. Goodbye.'

'Goodbye.' Eleanora handed the 'phone back to Raul. *She* was not looking forward to seeing Monika in Milan.

'Oh, Monika.' Raul had thought of one last thing. 'When you come back from your holiday would you do a translation for me? It's that story that has been languishing in my top left-hand drawer for years. Yes, *The Two Girls*, that's the one. Into English, please. A friend of mine in Hollywood has told me he thinks he has found a good screenwriter for me. I'm going to send it off to him.'

'A film?' Eleanora was curious.

'Perhaps, if my luck holds. Nothing to do with singing, and no part in it for you, my dear. Now,' he changed the subject, 'what are we going to do with this old father of yours this evening after the performance?'

Eleanora ran her fingers through his dark curly hair, as curly as her own but lavishly streaked with silver. 'He's not so old. About the same age as you in fact.' Raul made a face and Eleanora laughed. 'Don't worry, I warned him. He's not expecting a youthful Adonis. Anyway, back to this evening. I've booked a table at that lovely open-air restaurant near the baptistry. I thought we could all walk there after the performance. It will be cool enough to walk then.'

But after the performance Eleanora and Nicholas walked alone. Something went wrong with the lighting during the opera and Raul remained behind to supervise the repairs. 'He never trusts the workmen,' said Eleanora. 'It would be utter hell for everyone if we turned up tomorrow and they went wrong again.'

Nicholas privately wondered if Raul was putting off the meeting but said nothing. 'I enjoyed the opera,' he said, which was partially true. He had been impressed with the awe-inspiring setting but the actual music, played on ancient wooden and reed instruments, left him cold as did much of the singing.

Eleanora laughed, tucking her arm through his as they strode through the busy streets. She knew her father was no opera buff and only suffered it for her sake. 'All of it?' she demanded.

'Well, some of it.' Aware that she could not be fooled, he decided to be honest. 'The best parts were when I was able to pick you out. You looked very lovely, but then, you always do.'

They reached the restaurant, and at the sight of Eleanora the proprietor rushed over and solicitously showed them to a discreetly screened corner table.

'He probably thinks you are my new lover,' said Eleanora with a chuckle as she scanned the menu.

'Good God! What, at my age?'

She looked up frowning. For the first time Eleanora mentally placed Raul alongside her father. She had always realized they were much the same age. But if she was completely honest, she had to admit that Raul probably looked older. His face was rugged and lined and had a slightly rapacious expression which sometimes she found fascinating and other times a little frightening. She looked at Nicholas. His fair hair was greying but amidst the blond it hardly showed; his grey eyes were clear and honest; and his mouth was gentle. She knew some people thought her father weak, and in comparison to someone like Raul, he was. He was not a pushy, grasping man but in her eyes his weakness was a virtue. He would never harm a fly, let alone a person. He was a man who could be relied upon. He was so typically English, the kind of man always described in books as an officer and a gentleman, which he most certainly was. Suddenly she felt nervous. Her father was not going to like Raul.

'Raul is two years younger than you,' she said.

'But you said he was a *little* older!'

She could tell her father was scandalized from the tone of his voice. Hastily summoning the waiter she ordered a bottle of wine so that they could have a drink while ordering the meal. 'It feels that way to me,' she said. 'Honestly, Daddy, I haven't even thought about it before.' She waved the menu at him. 'Come on, let's order. I'm starving. What do you want? I know what Raul likes.'

'Oh, you choose,' said Nicholas.

Suddenly he did not feel hungry. His beautiful daughter involved with a man old enough to be her father. What a waste! He had always imagined her coming to Broadacres with a young husband, and lots of grandchildren, who would all keep their ponies there and be forever visiting. He had imagined the old house being given a new lease of life, being full of young people, love and carefree laughter. But it seemed that was not to be.

She had fallen in love with an old man who was hardly likely to want the bother of a young family. Nicholas was tempted to test this new love, tell her what Peter had heard from Dr Zuckermann, but then decided against it. Now was not the right time. He must be patient and wait and pray that this new love affair would not last. But she seemed so confident and happy, and an even more worrying thought was that this man was part of a world she loved, the world of opera.

Unable to meet Eleanora's eyes, Nicholas looked around the restaurant. Any other time he would have found it enchanting. Out in the open air of a piazza, an ancient vine formed the roof, the ripening grapes hanging in glistening fat bunches. The red-and-white checked tablecloths were each lit by a single candle in a glass holder. It was busy, the food smelt delicious and the atmosphere was vivacious and happy.

He looked towards the area where the restaurant opened out on to the piazza. A tall man was entering, his face craggy, and he had a large beaky nose. Nicholas eyed him with disdain. A vain peacock of a man, dressed too flamboyantly for his age. His open-necked shirt exposed a dark hairy chest, festooned with gold chains and medallions. He looked flashy and slightly seedy. Nicholas watched in distaste; it was obvious he revelled in attention. he stopped at almost every table, shaking the men's hands and kissing the women. Nicholas reached over to point him out to Eleanora, about to laugh and say, mutton dressed up as lamb, when suddenly she stood up.

'Raul,' she called waving her hand. 'We are here.'

My God! How could she fall for this man? Couldn't she see what he was? In a blinding haze of bewilderment mixed with fury, Nicholas stood up and extended his hand. So this middle-aged Lothario was Raul Levi! He wanted to weep. How could she? How could she say she loved this self-centred, arrogant and vain man? How could she not see what was written all over his face? Nicholas wanted to shake Eleanora, to shout at her, 'What can you see in a man like this? How can he take Peter's place?' But he did not voice the words out loud. He sat down and wished he were anywhere on earth but in Florence.

The evening was a consummate disaster. Nicholas hardly said a word, only answering in monosyllables when he absolutely had to. As soon as the meal was over, he rose to his feet and kissed Eleanora goodbye.

'I'm sure you and Raul want to be together,' he said, 'and I feel like a brisk walk. No, don't come with me.' He raised his hand to stop her. 'I'm quite happy to be alone.' Without waiting for her reply he left.

'So the English Papa doesn't approve,' said Raul, lighting a cigarette and watching Nicholas stride out through the restaurant and into the piazza. 'Too bad.'

'I wish he had.' Eleanora was miserable.

'Why? You are a free agent. You don't need your parents' approval for what you do.'

'But I love them. I want them to approve. Especially Daddy.'

'Love,' Raul scoffed. 'Substitute the word bondage for love, then you've got it about right. Be a free spirit, my dear, like me. Then life is one long string of pleasures.' He ran his finger sensuously down her arm. 'We have had our pleasures haven't we?'

'Well, yes, but . . .'

'And you didn't need Papa's approval. You just went right ahead and enjoyed yourself. Come on.' He paid the bill. 'I feel in need of a little pleasure now. Let's go home.'

It was no use Eleanora protesting. 'No, Raul. I don't feel like it tonight.'

Raul insisted. 'What rubbish, you *always* feel like it.'

Later, at home, when Eleanora did not immediately respond, he grew rough. Her indifference inflamed him with passion, his fingers pried painfully and his teeth pulled on her nipples until they bled. Eventually, in spite of herself, Eleanora coiled her limbs around his and did as he wanted. They made love time and time again, Raul high on a tide of lustful ecstasy. But it was not like that for Eleanora. She found herself wishing it were over, although she took care to hide it from Raul. He was well pleased and once he had finished with her, fell asleep immediately.

When sure he would not awaken, Eleanora slid out from beneath his suffocating embrace and, creeping across to the window, leaned on the balcony. Looking out across the misty twinkling vista of Florence, she could see in the far distance the Apennines standing out darkly against the sky. It was very beautiful, but she felt sick and unhappy. So this is what it's like to feel homesick, she thought, wishing it were possible to press a button and be back in her own room in Broadacres. There, one of the dogs would be snoring noisily at the foot of her bed and the stuffed toys of her childhood would still be sitting in a row on the top of the bookshelf. Peter would be asleep in his house across the sheep-strewn valley and before breakfast they would ride together in the early morning mist.

But no, she pulled herself up with a jerk. None of that was possible. She could go home but it would never be the same. The clock could never go back, only forwards. Peter was in Hollywood, and she was not the same, not the girl she had been. Peter would not approve of me now. He would not approve of my affair with Raul. Somehow the thought of that was the hardest thing of all to bear.

She looked back at Raul, spread out in sleep on the bed. Even in sleep he looked in command of himself. Most people looked vulnerable, softer in sleep, but not Raul. He looked the same, arrogant and self-assured. What was the saying? 'When you have made your bed, you must lie on it.' Eleanora climbed back into bed and lay down. I have made mine, she thought miserably, and now I'm lying on it. She felt like a child, lost and frightened. She remembered getting lost on Waterloo station in London once and feeling the same way, only then her mother had been a few yards away, hidden by a timetable hoarding. Now there was no-one near. This time she had to find the way on her own.

Not far from Raul and Eleanora's apartment overlooking the Pitti Palace, Nicholas sat on the balcony of his room in the Hotel Tosca, staring with unseeing eyes at the Ponte Vecchio. Coherent thought was an impossibility. He had tried but had given up in despair and was now halfway through the duty-free whisky he had intended as a present for Eleanora.

Gut instinct told him that Eleanora desperately needed help, even if she were unaware of it. If he had been a more religious man, he would perhaps have understood his fear and said her mortal soul was in danger from a man like Raul Levi. As it was, confused by unhappiness and bemused by the whisky, his muddled thoughts stumbled blindly along. He had to do something, but what? He thought of Liana. She is strong, much stronger than I am or ever will be. He felt no shame in the thought, it had always been so, something he had accepted. Now their daughter needed her strength. She must do something. Between them they must do something. Between them they would get Eleanora away from Italy and out of the clutches of Raul Levi.

Chapter Twenty-Eight

Everyone on the Broadacres estate was well aware of the fact that His Lordship and Her Ladyship were hardly speaking. The estate and its workers had been welded by Liana to form one big family, and like all families they gossiped and worried. What was wrong up at the Big House? What on earth was going on now?

They had watched the love affair between Eleanora and Peter blossom over the years, and been proud and pleased for the young couple. Now it was over, finished quite suddenly, and no-one from the Big House, or the Ramsays, so much as breathing a word. Why was Miss Eleanora in Italy while Master Peter was on the other side of the world in Hollywood?

'It's Lady Margaret I'm most sorry for, Mum,' said Meg. 'She's so lonely. She still misses James and now Eleanora has gone. Donald Ramsay is still incapacitated from his stroke and her rheumatism's so bad she can barely haul herself up on to a horse. I know she still rides but it must be agony for her. And Lady Liana's no help; she's pretty poor company these days.'

Mary Pragnell, true to form, was exasperated and wanted to shake some sense into Lady Liana. 'It beats me, it do really. She's so clever at some things, and yet she can't see that Lady Margaret and Lord Nicholas are as upset as she is. It's not for us to ask what happened between Miss Eleanora and Master Peter, but it don't help one little bit her not talking to anyone. It's not our place, I know, but someone ought to shake some sense into her.'

'Oh, Mum,' sighed Meg. Her years of working closely with Liana had given her and Dolly, although she could not properly express herself, a deeper insight into the complexities of Liana's character than most. The two sisters sensed a long-term, far deeper sadness in Liana than the tragedy of James's accident warranted. Although Lord knows, Meg thought often enough, that in itself was more than most people could bear. And now Miss Eleanora had disappeared off to Italy without even saying goodbye, and Peter, too. It was so out of character for them both. To say Meg was puzzled would have been an understatement. She returned to the subject of

Liana. 'Mum,' she repeated, 'I think it is a question of waiting. You can't shake sense into someone who has turned to ice. She would shatter into a million pieces.'

'Good Lord, Meg! Turned to ice indeed. You read far too many books these days.' Mary's imagination did not run to such flights of fancy. 'What I'd like to know is, what have started all this misery off again. Things seemed to be picking up nicely, then all of a sudden it's back to square one.' Mary sighed heavily. The effort of putting her thoughts into words was onerous. 'Sometimes I'm thinking she don't love His Lordship at all.'

'Oh, I think she loves him,' said Meg softly, 'but she has lost her way. It needs something to happen, something to open her eyes and point her in the right direction.'

Mary Pragnell gave up. Life was uncomplicated and clear cut to her. You either knew something or you did not know it. You loved, or you did not love. All this complex reasoning gave her a headache. But that did not stop her from loving Liana like a daughter. She would never forget her kindness to Meg and Bruno those many years ago or all the other little kindnesses over the years. 'The trouble is, I'm simple Meg, I just don't understand,' she said. 'A plain and simple woman, that's me.'

'A good woman, that's you,' said Meg affectionately. 'But don't worry about them up at the Big House, something will turn up. You wait and see.'

But in spite of their opinions and varying notions on what should be done, it was left to Donald Ramsay to actually say something. He purchased a new trap admitting at last that he would never ride again. It was more secure and better sprung, and he invited Liana for a ride.

'Why not,' she said. 'If you want to test out the springs, we could drive over to the new crayfish ponds.'

Donald smiled. 'I was hoping you'd say that,' he said. Which was true. The ponds were off the beaten track, which meant he would succeed in getting her out of the office and have her to himself for a while.

Together they drove down towards the river, then took the track across the water meadows towards two large ponds. Broadacres's latest farming enterprise was the breeding of freshwater crayfish. Arriving at the ponds, Liana introduced Donald to Dick Kent, the man she had put in charge of the operation. Dick pulled up a trap full of struggling, brown, lobster-like creatures for Donald's inspection.

Donald was fascinated. He knew freshwater crayfish lived in the chalk streams of Hampshire, but had never seen them, his main interest being in flyfishing for trout and salmon and the odd day of floatfishing for grayling in the coarse season. 'How on earth do they all get into these ponds?' He poked in an exploratory finger, hastily withdrawing it as a vicious-looking brown claw snapped.

'I've collected them from the river and the chalk stream tributaries in the valley,' Dick explained. 'They will breed better here because these ponds are fed by water from boreholes twenty feet deep, not river water. It's much more pure and clear. They'll thrive in that.' He picked up a particularly large specimen. 'This one is about five years old. We'll let him breed for a year and sell him for the table next year.'

'They fetch a very high price in London and Paris,' said Liana. 'That's what made me decide to start breeding.'

'Can't let them get too big in a confined space, though,' said Dick plopping the struggling crayfish back into the pond, 'they're a fearsome, cannibalistic lot.'

'Of course,' said Liana as the trap bumped back over the molehills of the water meadows, 'there won't be much of a profit for the first four years, but after that, Dick Kent will more than earn his keep. He is also an expert on rivers and pollution, and I want him to keep an eye on things now that all these new artificial fertilizers are coming on to the market. I'm inclined to agree with Wally, go slowly, and stick to the tried and trusted ways if possible.'

'What does Nicholas think about all this, the crayfish farming and the fertilizers?'

Liana immediately stiffened, her relaxed manner evaporating in an instant. There was a long pause, then she said. 'I've been very busy. Nicholas is away at the moment. There hasn't been time to talk.'

Donald came straight to the crux of the matter. 'Always supposing you actually want to talk to him at all.'

'Of course I do.' Liana stared straight ahead, screwing up her eyes against the brilliance of the light reflected from the broad river. But she knew she had not deceived him. It was not easy to hide things from Donald. Why waste time in the futility of pretence? She turned to him. 'No, I don't talk, not if I can help it,' she admitted, then added fiercely, 'don't tell me I should, because I can't, I just can't. Every time I look at him I think of James and the fact that he might still be with us if only Nicholas had not let William stay.'

Donald sighed and reined Pegasus to a halt. The horse blew out noisily through his nostrils and, bending his head, began munching at the sweet meadow grass.

'Liana, my dear. You are an intelligent woman. You must know deep inside you somewhere that it is wrong to go on blaming *everything* on Nicholas. It was not all his fault; we are all partly to blame. If it were possible to see all the pieces of the jigsaw that comprise our lives, do you think we would knowingly fit them together if we knew the final picture would be one of sorrow? Of course not. Nicholas made a mistake in keeping William's illness from you, a mistake, Liana, a tragic mistake. But none of us is perfect, not even you, my dear.' There was silence. Donald waited hopefully but Liana gazed stonily into the distance. He tried again. 'If you can't bring yourself to be a wife to him, then at least be a friend, and talk to him. God alone knows he needs one! And so, my dear, unless I'm very much mistaken, do you.'

'I can't.'

'Can't what? Be a wife? Be a friend? Talk to him?'

'I can't *be* anything. I can't do anything. Don't you understand, Donald? *I can't do anything.*'

'God almighty, but you're stubborn, Liana. I don't understand . . .'

'That's just it, Donald. You don't understand. No-one does. No-one ever can.' It was a deep, wretched lament from the depths of her being, a fusion of guilt and sorrow which Donald knew nothing about.

'But, Liana, you must . . .'

'I should have known you weren't really interested in crayfish,' said Liana harshly, 'you just wanted to lecture me.' Seizing the reins from his hands she gave them a sharp flick.

Pegasus, startled by the unexpected sting on his rump, broke into an indignant gallop.

Donald took the reins from her and gentled him down to a trot. 'Take your temper out on me, not my horse,' he said sharply.

The trap rattled and bumped along, and Liana remained silent. Why couldn't she be left in peace? Burning tears threatened to spill down her cheeks, but she grimly held them back and concentrated instead on the beauty of the water meadows. But Donald Ramsay, damn him, had spoilt it all.

Liana was out of the trap the moment it entered the Broadacres courtyard, not even waiting for it to stop before leaping out, fleeing without a backward glance to the sanctuary of her office. Collapsing at her desk, she let her rigid control go at last and dissolved into a violent paroxysm of weeping.

How could she go on with all this guilt and pain? Time passing had made no difference, for no sooner than one pain began to recede, a new burden appeared. How could she tell Donald Ramsay that James's death, and William's madness were not the only crosses she had to bear? She had additional ones of deceit, deceit and more deceit. In her deepest moments of depression, when she was honest, she knew that blaming Nicholas was a deliberate ploy. It took her mind off her precarious hold on sanity. But she could not tell anyone that, not even Donald Ramsay.

The violent weeping died away. Exhausted, Liana wiped her eyes and once more looked to the future. She would cope. Hadn't she always? In time she would even learn to face Nicholas again but not yet. The worst thing was the longing to confide in another human being and knowing that it was impossible. That was the worst thing, the emptiness.

*

Nicholas, hoping against hope for a warmer greeting from Liana on his return from Italy, was disappointed although not entirely surprised. Liana, her mind in a turmoil of confusion and guilt, a legacy of the morning spent with Donald Ramsay, seemed colder and more remote than ever.

This much was soon plain when Nicholas sought her out in the library office. 'Eleanora sends her love,' he said. Not perhaps strictly true, but a good way of introducing the important subject of their daughter.

'She is well?' Liana didn't even raise her head, keeping her eyes fixed on the file she had before her.

Nicholas resisted the impulse to snatch the file away with difficulty. Why the hell couldn't she look at him? 'Do you bloody well care?' But the words on the tip of his tongue were never uttered. What was the point of sowing the seeds of an even greater alienation? He said instead. 'Yes, she's very well.'

'Good.' Liana felt genuinely relieved. At least Eleanora appeared to have sorted herself out more or less satisfactorily. That was because she was fully occupied. Nicholas ought to keep more busy. It would stop him forever reaching back into the past. She ignored the voice telling her that it would also remove him from her presence, thus preventing shadows of the past touching her quite so often. 'Don't you think you ought to go up to the Lords? The Prices and Incomes Bill is going through parliament.'

Nicholas shrugged disinterestedly. So Liana was anxious to be rid of him again already. 'I've never had that much enthusiasm for politics,' he said. 'You know that, and now the Conservatives are in opposition, what can I do?'

'You can vote on any sensible amendments there might be to the bill,' snapped Liana, 'and at least try and limit the potential danger.'

'What danger?'

In recent years, Nicholas had hardly paid any attention to current politics. He had spent his days fishing and riding; it was his way of finding solace. Whereas Liana, who read voraciously anything and everything she could lay her hands on, knew exactly what was happening. Although her interest in politics was solely motivated by how Broadacres and its diverse businesses might be affected.

'The danger of the devaluation of sterling, of course,' she said now sharply.

'I'll go to bloody London if that's what you want.' Wheeling round abruptly Nicholas left the office, slamming the door violently behind him.

He had wanted to tell Liana about this man Raul Levi, about the disastrous relationship Eleanora had become involved in. But he had not because Liana made sure there was no opening for anything like normal conversation. God, it was useless! How could they ever help Eleanora, when the two of them were on some crazy emotional merry-go-round from which it seemed they could never get off.

'No, Nicholas, don't go. I don't want . . .' But what did she want? Swamped with guilt, she answered her own question. She wanted the impossible. These days she thought of Raul more and more. He had made her laugh. When had she last laughed? So long ago, a lifetime ago.

It was all right for Donald Ramsay to preach, telling her to be a friend to Nicholas, to help him as well as herself. But she needed a strong man, someone who would support her, someone to whom she could confess everything, even the duplicity of Eleanora's birth, knowing that he would still be there and stand by her. But Nicholas was not that man. Liana ached with loneliness. It was the utter desolation of that loneliness which forced her to think again of Nicholas. Donald Ramsay was right, of course; he always damned well was! What brutal, cold-blooded side of her nature was forcing her to condemn Nicholas to even greater wretchedness than was necessary? I must try and talk to him, she decided. I *will* try. I owe him that.

But Nicholas had already left Broadacres and stayed up in London for the remainder of July, regularly attending sessions in the House of Lords until it rose for the summer recess. Then, instead of returning to Broadacres, he moved into his club in St James. Liana toyed with the idea of going up to London and seeking him out, but then decided against it. It would be better for both of them if they met again on home ground at Broadacres. Anyway, in spite of her good intentions, she still had not worked out what to say or even how to begin to approach him. They had been estranged for so long now, it would be like approaching a stranger.

Nicholas, in London, thought of returning to Broadacres every day, and every day he put it off, unable to face Liana's coldness and his mother's growing dejection at the continuing absence of Eleanora. Sooner or later he knew he would have to tell them both about the man Eleanora was now living with, Raul Levi. But not yet. He would wait. Choose the right moment.

The moment came. But it was not of his choosing.

'A telephone call for Your Lordship.' The elderly waiter creaked on his way after delivering the message. 'I've had it put through to the corner table.'

'Thank you, Jenkins.' Nicholas rose and settled himself into the relative privacy of the corner and picked up the telephone.

'Nicholas, is that you?' It was his mother, and she sounded very upset.

'Yes. What is the matter?' A host of worrying possibilities ran through his mind.

'Why didn't you tell me Eleanora was *living* with this director person, this Italian man?'

Nicholas tried to make light of it, calm his mother down. 'Mother, this is nineteen sixty-six. Young people these days do live with each other. I didn't think it that important.'

'Of course it's important. I was hoping that she and Peter . . .' she stopped and Nicholas could hear her sniffing, 'that she would soon miss Peter and then come back. But I've had a letter, and she writes as if she is going to stay with this, this *other* man for good. As if it's a permanent thing.' Nicholas's heart sank; his mother did sound very upset.

'Look, Mother,' he began.

'And now I find you don't even think it's important. I told Liana about this man Levi, and all she said was that she was glad Eleanora was happy.' There was a long pause, then she said. 'Eleanora *is* happy, isn't she?'

Nicholas chose his words with care. 'She appeared to be,' he said carefully.

Another long silence followed, and Nicholas visualized his mother's face with painful clarity. 'I wonder if I'll ever see her again,' she said softly. And he knew she was crying.

'Don't be silly. Of course you will. Whatever makes you say a thing like that?'

'It's the second part of her letter. It's so . . . so . . .' Margaret gave up any attempt at disguising her emotion. 'It's so final,' she said at last. 'She writes as if she's never coming back, almost as if she's afraid of something.'

'Nonsense. She'll be back,' said Nicholas with more conviction than he felt. 'And so will I. I'll come down to Broadacres tomorrow. Stop worrying, I'll get Eleanora back to Broadacres.'

*

Nicholas read the letter his mother handed him. She was right. It did sound final. Suddenly he felt afraid. Had he waited too long before making a move? The scrappy little letter from Eleanora worried him. She wrote that soon the Florence season would finish and she would be moving up to Milan, where she had already rented an apartment in the Via Sforza, right in the centre of Milan. She enquired briefly after the dogs, horses, Meg, and Bruno, and had Broadacres had a good season? And finally a brief sentence about Peter, saying that she could not fail to notice how well he was doing; if the Italian newspapers took notice of an English writer then it was a sure sign of success.

Nicholas drew a different conclusion from that of his mother but said nothing. In his opinion it was the letter of a homesick girl who wanted to come home but was too proud to actually take the plunge and come. A way had to be found so that she could come with her pride still intact.

'I'll speak to Liana,' he said.

'When?' His mother was anxious.

'After dinner.'

After dinner he followed Liana into the office where as usual she had some paperwork she intended dealing with. From past experience Nicholas knew it would probably occupy her far into the night. He felt strong and determined. No matter how much of a mess they had made of their own lives, they both had to work together for Eleanora's happiness. He would *make* Liana listen.

Liana looked slightly surprised as he perched himself firmly on the edge of her desk and passed her Eleanora's letter. 'The director she refers to as her live-in lover,' he said once Liana had finished reading, 'is the opera director, an Italian Jew, called Levi.'

'Is it because he is Jewish that you are against him?' Liana asked, as usual tackling the obvious head-on.

Nicholas had not actually said he was against the liaison, or even that he disliked the man in question. He had intended bringing up those points gradually. But Liana had guessed and jumped the gun. Hell, he never had been good at disguising his emotions!

'No! Of course not.' Nicholas felt irritated. How could she be so calm? 'Do you really know so little about me that you can think that? The fact that the man is a Jew has nothing to do with it. It's the man himself. He's a . . .' He searched for the right words to describe Raul. 'He is a rake, a philanderer, a womanizer of the first degree, and he will only bring Eleanora unhappiness. I'm certain of that, and remember, I've met him, you haven't.'

'But Eleanora evidently sees him through different eyes,' said Liana slowly.

She did not sound nearly as perturbed as Nicholas thought she ought to be. She had to be shaken out of her complacency. He took the plunge, voicing at last what he had often thought.

'Look, I know you and Eleanora have never been the closest mother and daughter. And in spite of those terrible things you said to her that night at the Ritz, she loves you very much. In fact, more than perhaps you deserve.' Liana flinched, but Nicholas continued. 'Because of that, I think you have a better chance than most of persuading her that not only is this man far too old for her, but also that there's no chance of lasting happiness for her with him.' He leaned forward and grasped her hands. 'Liana, *please* help her. I beg you.'

She looked up, and Nicholas's heart lurched. However cold she might be towards him, there was something in her dark eyes which had a hold over his heart nothing could destroy. He still loved her in every sense of the word; and knew that whatever she offered, no matter how little, he would take and be grateful. But right now, his concern was for Eleanora. What would she offer *her*?

Liana smiled sadly. Eleanora did love her; she knew it. Just as she knew she herself had never been able to push aside the tangled shreds of memory long enough to show Eleanora an open, loving affection. The longing had always been there, but so, too, had the ever-present memories. And just when everything was beginning to fall into place, James had . . . she closed her eyes against the memory of his death. Dear, darling James. But it was Eleanora she must think of now. She reached out and briefly touched Nicholas's hand. 'I do care about Eleanora, you know,' she said slowly. 'I love her. I always have. I know I've never been very good at showing it, but I really do love her.'

Nicholas breathed a silent sigh of relief. She was going to help, thank God. 'Then you go to Italy and talk to her. You see this man and persuade him to leave her alone,' he said.

Liana immediately drew back, the faint smile gone. How could she tell him she could not go? That she could never go back to Italy, not even to Florence which was miles from Naples? Despairing, she realized that Nicholas had no way of knowing the enormity of what he was asking, because, of course, he could not see the shadowy figure of Raul at her elbow, the man from the past who was always with her, day and night. She dare not risk going back to the country of her birth and making him more real than he already was.

But there was also another reason, one which had haunted her intermittently ever since William's revelations about her past. She had told herself again and again not to even waste time thinking about it because it was an impossibility. But, nevertheless, the lurking fear was never completely eliminated. In Italy someone, somehow, might find out she was not a real *marchesa*. In England she was safe; but she was afraid to risk going back to Italy. But how to refuse Nicholas without seeming hard-hearted? How to give convincing reasons? Her mind raced ahead, feverish, anxious.

'But, Nicholas, I can't go charging off to Italy at a moment's notice.' Inspiration struck and she pushed a copy of the *Financial Times* towards him. 'You know sterling is under severe pressure. Things have gone from bad to worse recently, literally in days. Sterling is at its lowest for nearly two years against the dollar, even Stock Exchange War Loan stock has slumped. Now the government has announced a massive deflationary package which is going to hit us all. I'm not even going to be able to move money abroad for Eleanora so easily in the future: they've slapped a fifty pound-a-year limit on overseas holidays, and I'm waiting to hear what the limit is for students abroad.'

'Perhaps that will make her come home.' Nicholas grasped eagerly at straws. 'Eleanora will hate being short of money.'

'I doubt it.' Liana smiled grimly. 'Eleanora possesses a streak of stubbornness. If anything, it will make her stick it out. However, money is not an immediate problem. She won't be hard up by any manner of means; she already has plenty of money in her Italian bank account. No, the real problem is here, at Broadacres. Unless I move swiftly to protect our interests, we stand to lose much of what we've gained since the war. At the moment Broadacres must be our priority.'

'*Your* priority,' said Nicholas, exploding into uncontrollable anger. He levered himself off the desk and stormed towards the door. 'At the moment, I don't care whether we keep Broadacres or not. There seems to be no point.'

'Of course there's a point,' Liana cried passionately, wanting to make him appreciate the urgency. 'I don't understand you. How can you not care about this place? One of the most beautiful parts of England, and you don't care whether or not we keep it.'

Wheeling round Nicholas said coldly. 'That seems to be the fundamental difference between us. You care about a place and I care about people, especially the people I love. Our daughter, for example.'

Liana flinched at the harshness of his words. 'That's not true. I *do* care about people.' She slumped down at the desk, head between her hands. 'Broadacres and people are all one to me, all mixed up together. I can't separate them.'

'Eleanora needs your help,' Nicholas persisted. Even at the risk of alienating Liana for the rest of his life, he had to try to help Eleanora.

'Nicholas.' Liana's voice was very quiet, her head still clasped between her hands, her eyes lowered. 'It was an excuse, I admit it. But I can't go back to Italy. Not even for Eleanora. There are too many memories there, bad memories, things I have never told you and never can.' There, she had said it, part of it anyway. She prayed that he would not probe and start asking too many questions.

There were no questions, only silence. Nicholas remembered his mother's saying years before that she was sure Liana had suffered more than they could ever imagine. For the first time in all their years of marriage she was admitting that there were things in her past he knew nothing about. Unless she *wanted* to tell him, he knew he would never know. Voicelessly he prayed that she would take him into her confidence. If she did, it would bring them closer and, perhaps, he could even help lay the ghosts of the past. But out of the silence, he heard his mother's voice, 'Some things are best left unsaid.'

Let them stay unsaid if that was what she wanted. All he wanted was her peace of mind. He walked back slowly and took her beloved, stubborn, strong, agonized face between his hands, lifting her head so that she was forced to look at him. 'Why didn't you say that in the first place?' he said gently. 'Then I would never have forced the issue.'

Liana reached up, holding on to his wrists as if to draw strength from him, her dark eyes unnaturally bright. 'You are a good man, Nicholas,' she said. 'Much too good for me. I have never been the wife you ought to have had.' And I can never love you the way you deserve to be loved, but those were words she added silently.

Nicholas continued looking at her for a long time. 'You are all I want,' he said. Then he smiled. 'So, now we must think of another way to help Eleanora.'

'I'll write to her,' said Liana decisively. 'I'll invite them both here. I'll suggest a weekend. She can't say no to a short weekend. Then I can talk to them both and see for myself what this man is like. And if he is as you say he is, then surely she will see that he doesn't fit in with her life. And when I write, Nicholas, I will apologize, and I will tell her how much I do love her.' It was the best scheme she could think of. Although what on earth she would say when they did come, she had no idea. That would have to wait until they arrived.

'Yes, I suppose that is the best way,' Nicholas reluctantly agreed. The sooner he could separate Eleanora and that damned man Levi, the better as far as he was concerned. 'Suggest they come in September. There must be a gap between finishing one opera and starting rehearsals for the next.' Perhaps it would work out. Once Eleanora was on home ground, the situation might be easier to manage. He leaned forward and gently planted a brief kiss on her cheek. 'I'll leave you to write that letter,' he said.

Liana sat for a moment, then her mouth softened into a faint smile. Miraculously, she and Nicholas had taken a few tentative steps towards each other, and she was glad. They had miles and miles of difficult terrain yet to cover but at least they had started. She pulled a sheet of notepaper towards her and began to write to Eleanora.

A tap at the door disturbed her. It was Margaret. 'I just had to come,' she said, breathless from the effort of the long walk down the passage. 'But Nicholas tells me you are inviting Eleanora and that . . . that . . .' words failed her.

'Her lover?' said Liana, hiding a smile at Margaret's old-fashioned embarrassment.

'Yes, *him*,' said Margaret, managing to endow the word him with all kinds of evil connotations. 'Tell her that I'm longing to see her and that we'll have a party.' She paused. 'I suppose you'd better say a party for them both. We don't want her to think we're not keen on this Italian fellow. It's a pity that Peter will still be in America. If only she could see them side by side, she might change her mind.'

'From what I've heard,' said Liana, 'Peter has been out with other girls in America. Perhaps he's fallen in love with someone else by now.'

'Stuff and nonsense.' Margaret banged her stick on the floor for emphasis. 'Peter is a one-woman man. If he can't have Eleanora, he'll remain alone.'

Liana was silent. There was nothing to say because deep inside she knew it to be the truth. Peter would never change. He would write, be successful, but he would not switch to another woman. In that respect he was very similar to Nicholas. They were both steadfast. Perhaps if Eleanora knew there was now a different medical opinion . . . perhaps. But no, there was nothing she could do. Whatever she did now would be wrong; because she had gone so far Liana was desperately afraid that the truth might slip out, and that would be like removing one domino from a carefully constructed pile – the whole lot would come tumbling down. There was nothing for it, the *status quo* had to be preserved.

She started to write, hoping Eleanora would accept the invitation to Broadacres. Whether or not it would solve the problem with Peter was in the lap of the gods, but it might help to get her away from the man Nicholas disliked so much.

Chapter Twenty-Nine

In California it was always sunny. The citrus trees in the garden of Peter's rented house hung heavy with enormous, vividly coloured oranges and lemons. The swimming pool, shaded by oleanders, glinted turquoise in the sun and the lawn was a smooth, even green, a colour achieved by the rows of well camouflaged, strategically placed, sprinklers. But perversely Peter longed for rain, the soft summer rain of England, the misty drizzle which was a pleasure to walk in, and which fed the vast, verdant, undulating valley of some of the richest pastureland in England – the place he loved best, the Itchen Valley in Hampshire.

He thought of Eleanora. More than six thousand miles of land and ocean separated them but he could see her as clearly as if she were standing beside him. Why had she run away; why hadn't she waited just a little while, been just a little more patient? But he knew why. She was rash, impetuous, never stopping to think things through. I should have been firmer, should have made her stop and think. Useless recriminations, he thought wretchedly. But he knew he could not accept that she was in love with someone else, no matter what he had said to the folks at Broadacres. It was too soon, she *could not* be in love again. He wondered what the man in question was like. Was he good and kind? Did he understand how vulnerable Eleanora was in spite of her superficially brash exterior? Peter hoped so.

With an effort he looked at the work on his desk. If he worked hard, he estimated that he could finish the screen adaption he was writing in about five to six months, and then he could go home. Then, and only then, he decided, would he seek out Eleanora and try to salvage something of their previous relationship. I must be patient, he told himself.

He settled down to work. The office looked out on to the garden and the sliding glass doors were permanently open. In England, Peter knew he would be constantly distracted if he looked out into the garden of his home, either by the antics of the dogs or by a flock of starlings strutting self-importantly about. But here, he found it easy to ignore the exotic garden, so perfect it looked like a film-set rather than a real garden.

'The post, Mr Chapman.' The Chinese maid, who came with the rented house, entered the room. 'And a package by courier from Milton Hyam of Twentieth Century Fox. He said you were expecting it.'

'Thank you, Lin Din.'

Peter took the post and the package. He zipped through the post. Nothing of importance. Every day he hoped for a letter or postcard from Eleanora but was always disappointed. He turned to the package and silently cursed Milton Hyam. I should have said no, he thought irritably, and forced Milton to get someone else to look at his friend's script.

But that had not proved easy. 'Gee, Pete,' said Milton in the familiar way he had which Peter hated. 'I told this Italian guy that I'd get the best scriptwriter I've got to read it. And, Pete, old buddy, you are the best.'

'I'll look at it,' Peter said reluctantly.

'Great, Pete. I knew you wouldn't let me down. And while you're at it, just draft out a rough sketch of how you see it on the screen.'

'Only if it's any good,' said Peter, thinking how unlikely that was. He knew it was the first thing the author had written; it was probably pathetic.

'Sure, sure,' said Milton. 'But it'll be good. This guy's got talent. Besides I owe him a favour.'

Well, at least it's not too thick, thought Peter, resentfully eyeing the package Lin Din had dumped on his desk. It shouldn't take too long to flick through. Heaving a sigh, Peter decided to get the wretched project out of the way before going on with his own work. Opening it, he read the title page. *The Two Girls* – hardly a gripping or even a very original title. That did not bode well. Uninterestedly, he turned to the first page and began to read.

Two hours later Lin Din came in with his luncheon tray. Peter looked up at the sound of her footsteps, his face ashen.

'Mr Chapman, sir. Is something wrong?'

'What?' Peter shook his head, trying to clear it, then attempted to drag his mind back to the present and the worried Lin Din standing before him. 'No, no. Everything is OK. Thanks, Lin Din, you can go now.'

She went, but not without a backward glance. Everything was not OK. That was quite obvious.

Peter sat quite still, the luncheon tray untouched. His grey eyes, fixed with intensity on the vivid red of the hibiscus flowers tumbling over on to the patio outside the window, did not see them. All he could see were the words of the manuscript dancing before his eyes.

The Two Girls, a true story, or so the author had written. The storyline was good – a chronicle of passion and tragedy, and unusual, too, because it concerned the selfless, devoted love between two young girls, both of whom were doomed to die, one from tuberculosis brought on by malnutrition, and the other eventually being obliterated by German bombs. A good story, well worth considering as a film script.

He looked down again at the manuscript on his desk then put it together neatly so that the title page was on top again. There it was in black and white, scrawled in the unknown author's handwriting at the top of the title page: 'I have felt able to use the true names of the girls concerned as they are both dead. Also this is their only memorial. Both lie in unmarked graves.'

True names! That was not possible. The author, whoever he was, must be lying. But if he were lying why, out of all the names in the world, did he choose those names?

With trembling hands, Peter opened the manuscript again and began to read for a second time. He felt sickened, unwilling to believe, but still he read on, retracing the lives of two girls who had lived in Naples more than twenty years ago.

A peasant girl called Liana. She was the one who had made the greatest sacrifice, working as a prostitute on the streets of Naples; selling her body for food, in the vain hope that her dearest friend might live. Her clients were soldiers who paid her with American dollars and tins of army food. Liana had been killed in one of the last bombing raids on Naples and, according to the story, her body had never been recovered. Like many others it lay in a mass grave beneath a mountain of rubble which covered vast tracts of Naples. The other girl, Liana's friend, was a *marchesa*, the marchesa Eleanora Anna Maria, Baroness San Angelo di Magliano e del Monte, and she had died in December 1943 of tuberculosis. Her body was buried somewhere on a hillside near the village of San Angelo in the bare earth, with nothing to mark the spot.

Peter tried to think clearly. But now, when he most needed his writer's analytical mind, he found it almost impossible to concentrate. Two names filled his head to the exclusion of everything else. Eleanora and Liana, Eleanora and Liana, the repetition hammered in his ears. Why these two names? Why were the girls in the story named after the two women who, in their different ways, were so important in his life? He pondered again on the identity of the author and his claim of truth. Loyalty and love to the

411

women he knew made him reject the claim. It was too absurd. But in spite of that, a deeper gut instinct sensed a grain of truth. The writer had used the name and the place where his own aunt, Lady Liana, had originally lived, and her full name and title had also been used. Idly he wrote down the two names, Eleanora and Liana, then crossed out the name Eleanora. The girl he loved could not possibly be implicated in the story; she had not even been born in 1943. But Liana – thoughtfully he ringed round the name in pencil – she was alive, and she had been there in the *castello* near San Angelo. He thought of the *marchesa*'s name, Liana's name; strange that the exact name had been used and surely an impossibility that anyone else, apart from Liana, should be called that. But Liana was not dead; she was very much alive. It was always possible, of course, that the writer might have used the name thinking that the *marchesa* had perished in the war; but something else bothered Peter, something he had never thought to question before, but now the story forced him to do so. Why was it that Liana had always insisted on being called Liana, and never by her real name Eleanora? Why did she use the name of the peasant girl in the story? And why was the girl he loved called Eleanora, the name of the *marchesa*? Liana and Eleanora. Much as he hated himself for even entertaining such thoughts, Peter began to feel suspicious. He had to find out more.

Reaching for the 'phone, he dialled Milton Hyam's number.

'Milton?' He cut short the other man's effusive greetings. 'Hello, this is Peter Chapman. I've read that story you sent me. Yes, yes, it's not bad, not bad at all.' The receiver almost slid out of his hand; he was slippery with perspiration. What an effort it was trying to sound casual, when his mind was reeling with unanswered questions! 'What I want to know is, who actually wrote it? You only told me he was an Italian, and there's no name on the manuscript.'

'Who wrote it? Oh, a guy called Levi, Raul Levi. You must have heard of him, he's made a name for himself staging all those weird operas and some pretty fancy Shakespeare as well. He's a great guy, and as I said before I owe him a favour, that's why I asked you to read it. Boy! If you are ever in Rome and need a woman, Levi is the guy for you. He can . . .'

'I want to talk to him.'

Peter abruptly interrupted Milton's enthusiastic flow of information. He did not like the man, and only tolerated him because they saw eye to eye artistically. On a personal level, Peter considered him to be an unscrupulous lecher, and wanted nothing to do with him socially. The moment Milton Hyam said Levi he understood why they were friends. From all accounts they were two of a kind.

Levi, he had directed *Dido and Aeneas* in London! He suddenly felt afraid, and shivered. Levi, Levi, what was he doing now? Good God! Peter remembered. He was directing *Euridice* in Florence this summer and Eleanora was there singing in the chorus. The breath caught in his throat. Like one of his own plays the inevitable was unfolding. But what? That was the worst part – he did not know what it was.

'You wanna talk with him? Is there a problem?'

The feeling of alarm made Peter's voice sharp and abrupt. 'If you want me to write a film-script for this, then I need to talk to the author. And as I'm a very busy man, it will have to be as soon as possible. Do you have a number where I can reach him?'

'Sure, Pete, hang on.' Milton Hyam put down the 'phone and fished out his diary. A stuffed shirt of an Englishman, that's what Peter Chapman was. He grinned suddenly, maliciously gleeful. Peter Chapman and Levi would not get on. Oh, no, they would not get on at all. Those two would mix about as well as oil and water! But, hell, if a good film-script came out of it, who would be complaining? He put on his friendly, I'm-your-buddy-type voice. 'Hey, Pete, I've got a couple of numbers for you. One is his office in Rome, manned by a woman called Monika Muller, and the other is his temporary number in Florence. I'd try the Florence number first.'

'Thank you.' Peter made a note of both numbers then put the 'phone down.

He longed to 'phone immediately, but forced himself to wait. It was infuriating having to hang around because of the time-band difference but Peter had to contain his curiosity until he judged the time suitable. Then he put the call through. He was in luck. The 'phone was answered first time.

'*Pronto.*' It was a man's voice at the other end of the line.

Peter spoke in English. 'I wish to speak to Raul Levi.'

'This is Levi.'

Peter hesitated. Now he had him on the telephone what should he say? Certainly he could not blurt out that he was related to a woman who bore the name of the *marchesa* in Levi's story. A degree of subtlety was necessary and Peter decided to get Levi to tell him as much as possible without too many questions from himself, and to keep it on a strictly business level.

'I'm ringing from Hollywood. I'm a writer with Twentieth Century Fox, and Milton Hyam gave me a story of yours to look at, *The Two Girls*. You remember the one?'

In Italy, Raul sat up and paid attention. 'Of course I remember. You like it?'

'It's very interesting and I think has great possibilities.' As Peter spoke, he tried to visualize Levi. He had never actually met him, and had only seen him once, very briefly, when he had gone to pick up Eleanora from a rehearsal. Peter remembered him as being tall and very dark, but that was about all. He wished now he had paid more attention. It was difficult concentrating on the conversation, but vital to find out more. 'Indeed it has all the ingredients for a good film, and that is why I'm calling. I need to know if the story is true in its entirety and that you've omitted nothing. As you say it is a true story, we must be certain that there is no likelihood of anyone left alive who might contradict you or even worse sue you or the studio. The studio's lawyers are very hot on this sort of thing.'

'I assure you, it is true. Every word is true.'

In Florence Raul pulled an expressive face as he spoke. Most of it was true: only the ending was fabricated to suit his own purposes. And there was no-one left alive to disprove what he said.

'How, then,' Peter chose his words with great care, 'did *you* come to know of this story? Both girls are dead, you say, lying in unmarked graves. So who told you about them?'

For five minutes Raul spoke without interruption. At the end of that time Peter was convinced that, for the most part, Raul was speaking the truth.

Raul explained how, after he had deserted the army, he had sheltered in the *castello* with the two girls for almost a year. During that time, in spite of Liana's sacrifice of her own body in order to get food, Eleanora had died and he and Liana had buried the body on the mountainside. And then Liana herself had been killed in Naples. After that he had left and eventually had met and teamed up with Simionato. Raul explained to Peter that his part in the affair was the only part he had changed. He was, in fact, the unnamed village boy who had helped the two girls. Otherwise it was as it had happened.

But Peter knew it was not the *whole* truth; one did not need to be endowed with a sixth sense to realize that. There was more to be told, and Peter was certain that only Liana, Countess of Wessex, could do that. He sat holding the 'phone against his ear, hardly conscious of the voice at the other end still talking. Something was wrong, very wrong, and he must speak to Liana as soon as possible. There was no alternative but to show her the story and ask her if she knew of an explanation.

Of course, it was perfectly possible that there was an answer, a very simple one, something he had overlooked. Maybe, because he was a writer, he automatically looked for dramatic, complicated reasoning behind any storyline, and maybe because Levi was in the theatre world, too, he had taken small grains of truth and concocted them into fantasy. It was easy enough to do, and Levi would have no reason to suppose anyone in Hollywood would be likely to challenge his story. No-one other than Peter would have thought twice about it, and why should they? It was pure coincidence which had landed the manuscript in Peter's lap, the only man in Twentieth Century Fox with the background knowledge enabling him to recognize the names.

'Does that give you all the answers you want?'

Peter flinched. He had forgotten Levi on the other end of the line. He thought of Eleanora in Florence and almost asked Levi how she was getting along. But he kept silent. With a chorus of a hundred or more it was unlikely that he would know what each individual chorus member was doing. Anyway, now was not the time to speak of Eleanora, particularly in view of her name. Nothing must be allowed to alert Raul Levi that the story's validity might be questioned.

'Yes, thank you for explaining your part in the story.' Peter hoped his voice was suitably smooth in spite of the fact that his head was buzzing with unanswered questions. 'I'll be in touch again when I have drafted the film-script. Then we can talk further.'

*

In his apartment in Florence Raul put the 'phone down and suddenly realized he had not the slightest idea of the name of the man he had just been talking to. He shrugged. No matter. He said he would be in touch, and Milton Hyam would know anyway. Pure luck, though, that he had telephoned this morning. A few hours later and he would have been on the way to Milan. Eleanora had already gone on ahead. He frowned now, thinking of her. Why the hell did she decide she had to be so damned independent all of a sudden? Renting her own separate apartment in Milan, against his wishes. An utter waste of money when she would be spending all the time in his, as he had forcibly pointed out.

'But I might want to be alone sometimes,' she said, 'or have my mother and father over. They couldn't stay with you.'

'They could stay in a hotel.'

'If either of them do come, I want them to stay with me,' Eleanora said stubbornly and refused to discuss it further.

She did not add that lately she had begun to have doubts about their relationship. Mesmerized as she was by Raul, sometimes she even thought she loved him, indeed was almost sure of it. But then something would happen which made her recoil from his presence, and she wanted to leave. Although the strength of will to make a final break was always lacking. Adding to her doubts was the fact that every now and then, in spite of trying not to, she thought of Peter. Those were her lowest moments when she found that she missed him so much it was a physical pain. Those were the moments when she needed to be alone, the moments when Peter and thoughts of Broadacres flooded her with homesickness. At those times, Raul was an intruder, and she needed a place of her own.

Raul had no idea that Eleanora ever had doubts; to him she was just the same as the first day he had met her. Just thinking of Eleanora made him desire her. Damn it! If she had been here they would have made love right here on the floor, the way they always did whenever the mood took them. But no, obstinate and determined, she had gone on to Milan before him. No other woman in the past had defied him, and if one had, then he would have summarily dispensed with her services in no uncertain manner. Women like that were a nuisance. If there was one thing Raul could not tolerate, it was not getting his own way. But for some reason he could not explain, he wanted to hang on to Eleanora. Even now, after their terrible row – and what a row that had been! – the weekend after the end of *Euridice*.

'Where the hell do you think you've been? A whole weekend away. Not a word, not a 'phone call.'

'You don't own me, Raul. I'm a free agent. Just as you are.'

'Have you been with another man? If you have, I'll kill you.' Grabbing her arm roughly, Raul swung her round to face him.

And face him she did, with not a trace of fear. 'Kill me? How melodramatic, how very Victorian! I didn't know you rated fidelity high on your list of priorities. It must be a recent addition!'

'I'll throw your belongings out on the street. I'm not having a two-timing bitch living with me.'

Eleanora shook herself free. 'Don't waste your energy, my dear. I'm going anyway. I can't live with a man who thinks he owns me twenty-four hours a day, seven days a week. Bondage, Raul, bondage, that's what it is. You told me you were free and proud of it, and I agreed. Now I find out the freedom is only for you, not me!'

She began to run up the stairs. 'Eleanora, no, don't go. Just tell me where you've been.' Raul could hardly believe it was himself speaking.

Eleanora paused, looking back down the curve of the staircase. 'I go where I want when I want,' she said fiercely. 'Take me the way I am or let me go.'

He took her the way she was and they ended up making passionate love, and Raul never found out where she had been.

Now he made himself a coffee and lit a cigarette. What was I thinking of, letting her get away with it? I must be going soft in the head! But he grinned at the memory, anger dimmed now, only admiration left for the ferocious way she had stood her ground. Dark hair flying, black eyes flashing, she had matched him word for word, not intimidated in the slightest, and not giving an inch. Eleanora was very impressive when she was at the height of anger.

*

In Milan, Eleanora let herself into the apartment on the Via Sforza. It was small, just one bedroom, a tiny kitchen and bathroom and a living room with a balcony which looked out on to the busy street. Even with the windows closed the noise of the traffic filled the apartment. But it would do. It could be her Milan bolt hole when there was not enough time to fly down to the *castello* near Naples.

She thought of the row with Raul. Why hadn't she told him where she had been? It was quite simple and innocent. Filled with a sudden longing to be alone she had gone to the *castello*. After buying coffee, bread, wine, oil and tomatoes on the way down, she had not moved from the enclosing confines of the old walls. The weekend had been spent just idling away the time, sitting in the sun, relaxing and letting her mind empty of all thoughts. Raul, of course, thought she had been with another man. But she did not want any other man.

Not unless it is Peter, said an inner voice. A vision of Peter came into her mind, sudden and unprompted, his fair hair burnished by the sun, his clear grey eyes honest and tender. She closed her eyes in pain for a moment, then resolutely made herself stop thinking of him. Anyway, Peter had not been the reason for not telling Raul of the partially restored *castello* which was her hideaway. No-one knew, and Eleanora hugged the secret to herself. All her life, she had loved the excitement of keeping a secret, but the *castello* was more than just a secret. It was somewhere of her own, but it was more than merely a place to hide. Eleanora searched and failed to find the words which could convey what she felt. It was almost as if the *castello* itself had a role of its own to play, a role which would be revealed when the time came. But for now, it was important that it should remain a secret.

She had made it up with Raul, of course. She needed him and she knew he needed her. There was a tie between them which was difficult to explain. Something was holding them together and it was more than just sex, although it was not a tender love or affection. What she felt when with Raul could not be compared to the way she had felt with Peter. With Raul, it was a flawed, obsessional attraction, something which neither of them had the power to end. Raul had not said so, not in actual words, but Eleanora knew that she was the first woman to stand up to him and get away with it. Just as she knew that whenever they might part in anger, he would come back to her, as she would go to him, albeit unwillingly. Eleanora felt depressed; she felt imprisoned, stifled. It would take a thunderbolt from heaven to cleave them apart.

Opening the window which led on to the balcony, she wandered out and sat down in the decrepit cane chair which obviously stood outside winter and summer. Paper crackled in the deep pocket of her dress as she sat, and suddenly Eleanora remembered the letter. In the rush of leaving Florence, she had picked it up, stuffed it in her pocket and then forgotten it.

Now she took it out, recognizing her mother's neat handwriting on the envelope. It was faint but she could just make out the circular stamp of Longford Post Office on the envelope. Miss Martin of the thick grey cardigan, winter or summer, and the half-moon spectacles, would have stamped that, banging it down as if her life depended on it and holding the letter up to the light to see if she could glean anything of the contents. The rattle and roar of the trams and cars of Milan faded, and Eleanora smiled. She could hear the sound of a tractor chugging slowly up the incline past the long flintstone wall leading to the lych-gate of the church near the post office. Many, many times she had sat in the shade of the lych-gate, eating an ice cream purchased from the post office, watching Wally driving the tractor slowly through the village trailing a load of sweet-smelling hay.

Yes, that would be about the only sound in the late afternoon of Longford. She sighed wistfully and slit open the letter.

My dearest Eleanora

I hardly know how to begin this letter when I remember the last words you spoke to me. And I remember them very well because I should never have let you think them, let alone say them. 'I'm sorry that I lived and James died.' I am the one who should be sorry. My thoughtless words caused you to think this, and they can never be unsaid. But I ask you now to forgive me, and I tell you that I do love you, have always loved you, and always will.

But I must be honest, too. My love for you was *different from the love I had for James, and I will tell you some of the reasons why. You were born during the war, not long after I had left Italy for England. When you were a baby I was still haunted by bad memories of the war (memories I can't talk about even now) and I realize, looking back, that it affected the way I treated you more than I ever imagined at the time. I was never carefree in those first few years, the years when you were growing up. I know that you sensed it and turned to Margaret for the kind of comfort I should have been able to give but couldn't. I can't tell you how glad I am that you had Margaret for a grandmother. She is my best friend and something like a mother to me as well, and I am thankful she gave you so much love. I loved you, too, but always held back.*

With James it was different. I cannot pretend that everything was a bed of roses before he was born. It wasn't. Your father and I have had some very bad patches in our marriage, but somehow we emerged in one piece, and after James was born was one of the happiest times of my life. That is why my love for him was different. It was carefree. And it wasn't only me. We all loved him, and I know it was our happiest time together as a family. But tragedy struck and we lost him. And then, I'm afraid, I thought only of myself. I didn't comfort you or Daddy or Margaret. I only thought of me, of my loss, when all the time it was our loss. I must have a very selfish streak in me because whenever things go wrong I only ever think of myself and shut everyone else out. I'm not trying to excuse my behaviour, only to explain it.

I know now I should not have let you go rushing off alone when you were so unhappy. I should have made you stay and talk about yourself and Peter. But I was being selfish again. I couldn't see then, that you, my living daughter, were more important than my dead son. But I know now. Just as

I know that I cannot blame your father for hiding the secret of the family illness. I know, too, that happiness is always fleeting. It is not a gift given to us to hold in perpetuity. We have it for a short while, and then it is gone. It is always possible that the happiness you and Peter had may not have lasted, even without your father's unhappy revelations.

Liana had thought long and hard about this sentence. And put it in partly as a sop to her own badly strained conscience. But in spite of her conscience she was still sure her silence was right. The opportunity for truth had come and gone; all she would achieve by speaking out now, would be to inflict even more sorrow on the whole family.

Eleanora read slowly and turned to the final page. For the first time in her life she felt she had progressed a little. She was beginning to understand some part of her mother's character.

I wish you would come home. Not for ever. I know that if you wish to continue with singing you will always be travelling. But come home sometimes and see us all. We want to keep in touch with you, and your friends in opera, so why don't you come for a long weekend? I suggest that, because I know you will soon be starting rehearsals in Milan. But surely you must have a weekend free? Come home, and bring the new man in your life and introduce him to us. If you are fond of him, then we have all got to get to know him so that we can like him, too. Do persuade him to come, and both come home for a weekend. Please say yes.

Your loving Mother.

PS Your grandmother is waiting with bated breath for your reply.

When Raul arrived in Milan, Eleanora read him the last page of her mother's letter. 'Well, what do you think?' she asked. 'Would you like to come to England with me?'

Raul put his arms around her and looked down into her face. He smiled into the dark eyes looking up into his. Her face seemed as familiar to him as his own. I am besotted by her! It was an admission he had never thought to make where any woman was concerned. But Eleanora was different. She stirred a multitude of feelings within him, emotions he had never experienced before.

'I'll come,' he said. 'Let's make it the middle of September.'

*

Peter flew into Heathrow the first week of September. The manuscript of *The Two Girls* was in his briefcase. One thing after another had conspired to prevent him from returning to England earlier; even now Milton Hyam was unhappy.

'Gee, Pete, I thought you were staying here for six months or however long it took. That was the agreement.'

'This is essential family business,' was all Peter would give as an explanation. 'As far as the agreement is concerned, you'll have your scripts on time. I'll take them with me and work on them while I'm away.'

Milton accepted with ill grace. 'How long will you be?'

'Not long.' Peter crossed his fingers as he spoke. The truth was he did not have the faintest idea.

In fact, as he collected his luggage from the carousel in the teeming airport he wondered how on earth he was going to approach Liana without offending her. How could one ask questions about such a mysterious coincidence of names?

But he did make a plan of sorts as he drove himself down from London past the fields and villages of Sussex and into Hampshire. He decided that it would be best if Liana remained ignorant of the author's identity. That way there would be no obvious slant to the story. He would present it to her as a tale purporting to be the truth, ask her to read it, and await her reaction. There must be a better way of doing it, he thought irritably, but for the life of him he could not think of it.

It was late by the time he turned in through the majestic iron gates that led to the Chapmans' residence. His mother had hardly changed the garden since Clara Maltravers's day. Roses still dominated the formal garden, and Peter sniffed appreciatively at their perfume. It always seemed to him that the last flurry of blooms in September smelled the sweetest, as if they were demanding to be appreciated before they retired into winter hibernation. The dark purple of the late lavender flared in the light of his headlights. All was silent now but in the morning the garden would be dominated by the busy hum of bees feverishly gathering nectar before the onset of winter.

His mother came out on to the porch to greet him. She kissed him. 'This visit is unexpected,' she said, noting how tired he looked, as if he had not slept properly for a week. 'But all the more appreciated because of it.'

Peter kissed her back. He had not given any reason for coming, and could not think of one plausible enough to satisfy his mother. But at least he was here, and now he must be patient. And hope Liana would supply all the answers. Everything depended on Liana; only she could expose Raul Levi's story for the fraud it must surely be.

He had a late supper, then sat with his parents in the drawing room. On the other side of the valley, towards Broadacres, a field flared orange in the darkness. They were stubble-burning. His father put a glass of malt whisky in his hand.

'You haven't adopted the American habit, ice with everything, I hope?'

Peter let the soft tang of the ten-year-old whisky soak into his palate. 'I wouldn't insult the whisky,' he said.

Richard Chapman looked at his wife and raised his eyebrows. She nodded, understanding the unspoken question. Peter would have to be told sooner or later. Better to be told now, before he came face to face with Eleanora and her Italian lover.

'Eleanora's coming to Broadacres at the end of the week. Just for the weekend.' Peter sat up, his expression suddenly showing signs of animation. Richard hated saying what had to be said but forced himself to carry on. 'I don't know whether you are aware of the latest developments, but she is living with an Italian man, apparently old enough to be her father, and he is coming with her.'

Peter sank back down in his chair, his grey eyes sad. 'Oh,' he said. Then. 'What is his name?' He asked more out of the need to say something to fill the awkward silence than any particular desire to actually know.

'His name is Levi. Apparently he is the director of the operas she is involved with.'

'*Levi!*' The name hit Peter like a thunderbolt. 'Oh, my God.'

Richard and Anne looked at their son helplessly. What was wrong with him? Ashen-faced, whisky glass trembling in his hand, he looked as if he had seen a ghost. In truth Peter was buffeted by a mass of conflicting emotions. Liana and Eleanora, the two girls in the story by Levi; Eleanora living with Levi. What a ghastly coincidence. But the overwhelming emotion was a sense of premonition. When he wrote a play he always felt as if he were gathering together tangible threads as the characters he had created were eventually linked together for good or evil. He had the same feeling now but with one frightening difference. He was one of the threads, they all were, and an unseen hand was linking them together.

'You know this man, Peter?' Anne asked quietly.

Peter looked at his mother. Beyond her through the window he could see the uneven flickers of yellow and orange as the last of the stubble burned out. I must be going mad. What is the matter with me? Sternly he reined in his thoughts. Premonition; threads being gathered together: what rot! How could Levi have anything to do with life in this peaceful Hampshire valley? He was an unprincipled man with women; it stood to reason he would be equally unprincipled with the truth. It was obvious – he had gone to San Angelo for some reason, heard gossip from the villagers about the *marchesa* and the peasant girl disappearing, then made up a totally fictional story, never dreaming that the *marchesa* in question had married an Englishman and gone to live in England. Almost certainly that was it. Liana would sort it all out tomorrow; there was nothing to worry about. Nothing to worry about! Except that his beloved Eleanora was living with Levi. How could she? But even as he asked himself he knew exactly how. Impulsive as always she had jumped in at the deep end, without asking herself questions. He had always told her that one day that impulsiveness would be her downfall. But surely she didn't really love him?

'Well?' Richard Chapman grew tired of waiting for an answer. 'Do you know this Levi chap?'

'I only know of him,' Peter answered slowly. 'He is a womanizer of the first order. It would have been easy for him to seduce someone like Eleanora.'

'I thought as much,' Anne said unhappily.

'You never know. Perhaps this affair will die a natural death,' said his father, feeling that someone had to say something faintly hopeful.

'Perhaps.' Peter did not want to talk about it. He felt shattered, unable to think straight. 'I'm going to bed,' he announced abruptly and disappeared up to his room.

But sleep was fitful, punctuated by Liana and Eleanora drifting in and out of his dreams like ghosts. Sometimes they were as now, dressed in present-day clothes; sometimes much younger, ragged and thin, two starving waifs caring for each other. And always in the background was the tall, dark figure of the man Levi.

Chapter Thirty

Liana was in the home-farm orchard with Meg. The mellow warmth of an Indian summer sun filtered between branches laden with fruit. Bees buzzed busily around a huge clump of self-seeded Michaelmas daisies glowing mauve and yellow by the lopsided wooden gate. All was peaceful, the fruit harvested at leisure. This was not the commercial orchard: the fruit here was for the consumption of the inmates of Broadacres and the rest of the estate workers.

Peter walked towards the two women, disturbing hordes of Red Admiral butterflies feeding on the fallen, over-ripe pears. Living jewels, they fluttered up before him, heralding his presence.

'Peter! What a lovely surprise.' Liana came over and kissed him. 'Meg and I are trying to decide how much fruit to freeze before we throw the orchard open to all comers. Buying those big freezers has proved to be a boon. No more bottling these days. You really ought to persuade Anne to buy one.'

'Liana,' Peter interrupted her. 'May I speak to you? It is important.'

Meg caught the troubled look on Peter's face. Poor boy – she still thought of him as a boy – something is troubling him. 'There's no need to stay, Your Ladyship,' she told Liana. 'Alice is coming to help me as soon as she's finished exercising her pony and mother will probably come down as well. We'll pick and store all the fruit necessary.'

Liana was reluctant to leave. She loved the orchard in September. Although she had nothing to do with the actual growing of the fruit, she always felt proud and satisfied when surveying the red, shiny apples, the plums smudgy with bloom and the pears, luscious green and gold teardrops hanging from the branches. She smiled at Meg's tactfulness. 'I know you don't really need me, Meg. But picking fruit is one of the few manual tasks I really do enjoy. Never mind,' she linked her arm through Peter's, 'there is always tomorrow. Come, Peter. We'll go to the library.'

Once in the library Peter thrust the package containing the manuscript into Liana's hands. On the way over to Broadacres he had rehearsed half a dozen different speeches, all perfectly lucid and sensible, telling her roughly what was in the story and asking her to read it for herself and then give him her reaction. Of course, he had also planned a carefully worded form of reassurance; Liana was not to worry. All she had to do was to rubbish the story, preferably with some concrete form of evidence to back up her word, and that would be the end of that.

But now there was an added urgency, and one which Peter had not foreseen when he had left America to return to Britain, the imminent arrival of Eleanora with Raul Levi, the author of the damned story! He dithered, should he tell Liana the name of the author? No! He decided against it. Better that she did not know.

If Liana were able to prove the story a fabrication, Peter reasoned, it would provide him with a good opportunity for him to confront Levi and threaten him with legal action if he attempted publication. That in itself could prove a very effective wedge between Eleanora and Raul Levi, and one which, if given the opportunity, Peter intended to hammer home as hard as he could. It would be better if he could do it alone without the knowledge of others. The last thing he wanted was Eleanora flying impulsively to Raul's defence. All is fair in love and war, Peter thought grimly, and one way or another I must defeat Raul Levi.

But now, face to face with Liana in the library office, he found all his carefully rehearsed words frozen into silence. Instead, his brain rocked emptily in time with the ticking of the ormolu clock. Strange, he found himself thinking, why is it I've never noticed how loud it is before? With an effort he forced his brain back into gear and found some words, not the right ones, but at least he regained the power of speech.

'Would you read this,' he said abruptly, indicating the manuscript Liana now held in her hand, 'and let me have your reaction as soon as possible?'

Then filled with shame at his complete and utter cowardice, he turned and bolted from the library. Liana stood holding the package, surprised at Peter's rapid departure. She could hear his footsteps echoing through the stone cloisters as he made his way swiftly towards the spacious Gothic hall which led out into the gardens near one of the cedar trees. It is better that she should read it alone, Peter told himself as he hurried along, without my influencing her in any way.

What he could not bring himself to freely admit, and what had caused his precipitate flight, was a thought which had been haunting him intermittently ever since he had first read the manuscript; that enough of the story might be true to imply that Liana was not who she said she was.

That she was Italian was not in doubt; that she was married to Nicholas and had a daughter Eleanora also was not in doubt; but was she the *marchesa* she had always claimed to be? Peter felt disloyal even allowing the thought to creep into his brain but found he was incapable of preventing it.

Left alone, Liana opened the package, extracted the manuscript and read the title, *The Two Girls*. Then she noticed the handwritten note at the top, 'a true story'! How odd. Why was Peter giving her a manuscript to read? She had nothing to do with the world of literature and knew very little about it. Why was he asking her opinion? Curiosity aroused, she sat down at her desk and prepared to read it. But as her hand reached to turn the first page, the telephone rang. It was Jason Penrose, now not only her London lawyer but her general manager as well, whose task it was to oversee all her international companies.

'Lady Liana.' He came straight to the point, knowing from past experience Liana could get very impatient if he skated round a subject. 'We have run into problems with the French subsidiary of Elver Forge industries. An all-out strike at the factory in Lyons is threatened, and I don't need to tell you how damaging that would be to the overall position of the company. We desperately need foreign revenue as the pound may yet be devalued, in spite of what Wilson says.'

The manuscript was forgotten. Liana's mind switched on to business matters. 'I agree about devaluation, Jason. Personally I've never trusted that damned prime minister. Freezing wages and prices is never going to work. But our own problem in France: what do you suggest I do?'

'You must come up to London so that I can brief you properly, and then I think we should fly out to Lyons together and have direct talks with the management and workers. In my opinion it's the only way to defuse the situation.'

Liana did not hesitate. 'Right. I'll get myself organized; it won't take long, and I'll be up on the next train from Winchester to London. Book a flight, tonight if possible, and please be sure that I can get back to Broadacres by Friday night. My daughter is coming for the weekend, and I don't want to miss any of her visit.'

Once she had made up her mind, Liana never wasted time. She worked quickly, methodically pulling out the papers in the Lyons file, putting them in her briefcase before dashing upstairs. There she just as methodically selected the few clothes she would need for the three and a half days she would be away and neatly packed a small case. After checking that her passport was in her handbag, she flew downstairs and out to the stables where she knew Nicholas would be. Margaret's horse, Diabolus, had been limping, and Nicholas had called in the vet.

He turned in surprise as Liana rushed in, noticing with faint alarm that she was wearing one of her city suits and was carrying her briefcase and a small suitcase. 'You're going up to town?'

He felt hurt that she had not told him. Since their conversation about Eleanora they had slowly, day by day, moved a little closer to each other. Still not living as man and wife, they had nevertheless managed to gently ease their relationship on to a more stable footing. Talking was becoming easier, and even the silences were no longer quite so tense and awkward. So now, when he saw her obviously ready to leave without having said a word to him, he felt hurt and worried. Maybe she was on the point of withdrawing into herself again.

Liana heard it in his voice and knew he felt aggrieved. On an impulse she crossed the space between them and, reaching up, kissed his cheek. It was the first time she had voluntarily touched him since the traumatic night at the Ritz when William's illness had been revealed.

'I'm sorry, but I didn't know myself until ten minutes ago,' she explained. 'Jason Penrose has been on the 'phone. We have a crisis at the Lyons factory. I have to go there and sort it out before it gets any worse. I'm afraid there's no alternative.'

'But Eleanora is coming on Friday. That is only three days away.'

Liana smiled and Nicholas's heart suddenly lightened. It was almost like one of her old smiles, dark, mysterious, and he was sure he sensed tenderness. 'I haven't forgotten,' she said softly. 'I know how important it is, and I shall be here. I've instructed Jason to get me a flight back so that I'll be here for dinner on Friday evening at the very latest. I may even be back Friday morning.'

Nicholas heaved a sigh of relief. 'Good,' he said. 'Eleanora and I need you here.' Then, taking courage from her smile, he bent forward and kissed her gently on the lips. He felt her soft mouth tentatively respond beneath his before he drew back. They stood a moment, both smiling, suddenly as shy and awkward as a pair of teenagers, both instinctively knowing that the brief kiss had been a giant step towards mending the ravages of their fractured relationship.

'I must go.' Liana crossed to the stable door then stopped. 'Oh, Nicholas, I've just remembered something. I've left my office window wide open.

Will you remind someone to shut it? There are loose papers all over my desk.'

It was late that evening, after dinner, before Nicholas remembered the open window in Liana's office. He went down to shut it himself. The breeze through the open window had scattered papers from the desk all over the floor, and Nicholas collected them together. Having nothing better to do, he sat down and began sorting them into order. Liana was always fanatically neat; she would hate it if she came back to find everything in a muddle. The manuscript did not need sorting; it was all neatly stapled together. He put that to one side, then looked at the title page curiously. *The Two Girls*, apparently a true story if the note at the top was anything to go by. What was Liana doing with a manuscript? Surely she wasn't thinking of going into publishing!

He flicked open the first page and began to read.

*

The silvery chimes of the French ormolu clock on the marble mantelpiece struck twelve as Nicholas finally closed the manuscript and left the office. His footsteps were leaden, each movement an effort as he walked through the stone cloisters along which Peter had fled so precipitously earlier that day. The clocks throughout the house began to chime midnight, one after the other, the way they always did, none of them ever quite in time. It was a good five minutes before the last echo died away. Normally, the sound comforted Nicholas, giving him a feeling of permanence; he had been used to the sound of clocks chiming out of sequence since childhood.

Now, far from comforting, the sound was irritating, intensifying the feeling that his own life was out of sequence. The words he had just read swam crazily through his head. Taken as a whole, none of the chronicle made sense. And yet passages rang so true that Nicholas's heart had faltered, missing a beat, as he had read: the description of the bombed and broken-down *castello*; the half-burnt village of San Angelo; the life of Eleanora and the death of her father before the war in Spain; the looting of the *castello* by Mussolini's Black Shirts; the departure of Miss Rose, the Englishwoman, just before the outbreak of hostilities. All that was familiar to Nicholas. Liana, his own wife, had told him of her father's death and the looting, and he had been to the *castello* and the village during the war himself, and it was exactly as described.

But then came the puzzles, one after another: the presence of another girl, a peasant girl called Liana, the very same name that his wife had always said she had been called. But the Liana of the story had been a prostitute on the streets of Naples and her mother had been raped and murdered by deserters from the Italian army. That did not fit with the truth as Nicholas knew it, for it had been the *marchesa*'s mother, his wife's mother, who had been so brutally murdered. After that, the story twisted and turned and became totally unfamiliar. It told of an old priest, Don Luigi, who lived with the two girls until his death and subsequent crude burial at night on the mountainside. But Liana had never mentioned anything about a priest. And the death of the Marchesa Eleanora in December 1943. That, of course, was absolute nonsense. The *marchesa* was alive and well. He should know, he was married to her.

The whole thing was a fabrication masquerading under the banner of truth – it had to be. There was no other answer. It was extraordinary, though, the coincidence of the names, Liana and Eleanora. Extraordinary and worrying. Why had the author chosen those *two* names? It might have been credible if one had been used, even the full and correct title of the *marchesa*, but to use the two names which his own wife laid claim to seemed more than merely coincidental. Why did Liana insist she was always called Liana and not by her baptismal name of Eleanora?

Nicholas relived the moments he had first seen the young woman destined to become his wife. And for the first time he began to have doubts about her reasons for being in that part of Naples. Had Liana really been telling the truth when she had said she had been delivering food to an old woman that night, the night of the bombing raid, the night he and Charlie had dug her out of the ruins of a slum tenement? Why deliver food at night? Night in the slums of Naples was not the usual place to meet a *marchesa*. A prostitute yes, but not a *marchesa*.

Unable to sleep Nicholas sat in his room, staring out across the darkened lawns, a decanter of whisky by his side, a glass in his hand. Question after question tumbled through his head, and each spawned yet another and another and another, each equally unanswerable. Or were they?

The pearly mist of an early autumn dawn crept across the lawns. A fox made his way along the edge of the lake, leaving a trail of footprints in the silvery dewed grass. He was blatantly sure of himself as he trotted back to his lair after a night's hunting, and stopped for a moment, staring up at the house as if looking at the lonely figure still sitting motionless in a chair by the window. Nicholas watched him but the world of Broadacres waking to another day seemed unreal and far away. The splintered, nightmare world of Naples in 1943 felt much closer.

Eventually he reluctantly became convinced that it was impossible to dismiss the story as just empty words. It had to be more than that. But who had written it, and why? Surely not Liana. But why was it on her desk? Nicholas sighed, his head ached; those questions would have to wait until she returned. In the meantime he decided that he must try to analyse it piece by piece.

He took as his starting point the death of the Marchesa Eleanora. The description of her death, the other girl's grief and the final, harrowing ordeal of her burial rang so true. Surely whoever wrote it could not have made it up? So, assuming the real *marchesa* had died, by fitting together the jigsaw of pieces he knew to be true plus pieces from his own memory, Nicholas came at last to two possibilities. Neither were pleasant as the same painful fact stood out, stark and accusing, in each: Liana, his wife, the Countess of Wessex, was an impostor.

He considered the differing possibilities. A girl from the district, knowing the real Liana and Eleanora had both died, had assumed the mantle of the *marchesa*. There would have been nothing to stop her. Times were chaotic, most of the villagers had been killed or had fled from the bombing; no-one would have known. Then she had come down into Naples armed with a story about looking for her cousin Raul Carducci, a product of her imagination and an excuse to meet an eligible English officer. Nicholas baulked at the thought but then forced himself to face it. It was common enough knowledge that many Italian girls had been desperate to marry English or American soldiers, anything to get away from their own starving, poverty-stricken country. A lost cousin and the title of *marchesa* were a perfect introduction. As indeed, reflected Nicholas, they had been.

But there were serious flaws in that line of reasoning. Only someone very close to the two girls could have known the family history or have access to the money and jewellery. Also, how would an ordinary girl from that district have been so well educated? She certainly would not have been fluent in English or so well versed in the classics. And finally, why insist on calling herself Liana? Why not stick to the correct name of the *marchesa* Eleanora?

Dismissing that theory, Nicholas reflected on the second possibility which was that his wife Liana was the Liana of the story. It would account for the fact that she still preferred the name Liana. But the story was wrong in as much as she had not been killed as stated. Instead she had lived and had assumed the identity of her dead friend. With that identity she had married an Englishman and had escaped from Italy to England.

Suddenly Nicholas felt the raging anger of betrayal. Whichever way he looked at it there was no escaping one fact. Liana had married him because of what he was, an Englishman, and not because she loved him. Perhaps she had laid her plans to marry him in much the same ruthless way he had seen her laying her business plans. It was a sobering thought, realizing he had been cold-bloodedly used by a woman to further her ambition. It was an even more sobering thought to know that he had loved her then, and still did now, even if she had manipulated him. And surely she must have loved him? In the earlier days of their marriage, before everything had gone so disastrously wrong, Liana had always been so loving and tender. It must have meant something to her. It could not *all* have been make-believe.

He remembered their courtship in Italy, the way she had always resisted his advances. She could have let him get her pregnant and then blackmailed him into marriage, but she hadn't. She had waited. He remembered her saying once that he would leave Italy and forget her. Then she would marry an Italian, and in Italy to get a good husband a girl had to be a virgin.

It struck him like a thunderbolt from heaven. Good God! Why hadn't he thought of it before? There was the fatal flaw to this line of reasoning, too. The peasant girl Liana in the story had been a prostitute, selling her body regularly on the streets of Naples for much-needed money and food.

Nicholas almost wept with relief. What a fool he was not to have realized it before. Whatever the answer was to this strange tale which appeared to weave together fiction and truth, his Liana was not, and could not have been, the Liana in the story. He had experienced the indisputable evidence that she could not have been a prostitute, for his bride had come to him still a virgin on their wedding night. Nicholas remembered how he had tried to curb his eagerness so as not to hurt her, but failed, and in his haste had been unable to prevent himself from tearing her. He remembered, too, how she had cried out in pain although she had selflessly welcomed his body; and later, the following morning, he had seen the proof with his own eyes, the bedsheets stained with her blood, the blood of a virgin.

Oh, God, what a relief! What the hell did that stupid story matter? Why on earth had he even wasted a moment just thinking of it? Standing up, he flung open the window and leaned out. The sun has risen now. He drew in a deep, ecstatic breath. It was going to be another hot September day. A bumble bee droned laboriously past, almost blundering into his nose. Nicholas smiled, remembering Donald Ramsay's saying once that evolution had been unkind to the bumble bee. 'Threw all thoughts of aerodynamics out of the window when that insect was designed,' he had said.

He felt almost light-headed with cheerfulness. Whatever the origin of the story on Liana's desk, it was obviously libellous, which was probably why she had it. He felt a faint twinge of pity for the author who had been so foolish as to use her names, having no doubt that Liana would be merciless when she instructed Jason Penrose to act on her behalf. He would ask her about it as soon as she returned from France.

He looked at his watch. 'Damn!'

It was much too early for breakfast to be served. Meg was training a new maid, and she was proving to be a slow learner, so these days breakfast had been appearing even later than usual. Ravenously hungry and bursting with happiness, Nicholas did not feel inclined to wait. He went down into the kitchen and made himself a pot of tea and some toast.

Meg came in just as he was leaving the kitchen to carry it upstairs. 'You should have called me, sir,' she said. 'I've been up for ages. Two of the cows calved last night, and I went down to see them. One of them is a real beauty. Bruno thinks you have a champion Friesian bull in the making.'

'I'll be down to see him later,' said Nicholas, 'after I've had a couple of hours' sleep.' Meg looked puzzled. 'I had a disturbed night,' he said grinning widely.

Meg wondered why, but did not ask. She looked at Nicholas closely; he did look tired but relaxed and for once, very happy. She breathed a sigh of relief. Perhaps because her own marriage to Bruno was so blissfully happy and uneventful, she always felt acutely distressed when the relationship between Liana and Nicholas fell apart as it seemed to have done so often of late. The last few years had been difficult and her tender heart had bled for them, particularly as there was nothing she could do. But things were looking more hopeful now, with Eleanora coming back at last, even if it was only for a short visit. Perhaps their lives would change for the better. Meg hoped so.

'It will be lovely to see Miss Eleanora again,' she said. 'I was wondering about dinner on Friday night. Shall I do roast beef and Yorkshire pudding? It was always one of her favourites, and I daresay she could do with a decent meal after living in Italy.'

Nicholas smiled. Meg never ventured further than the county towns of Winchester and Salisbury, and like most country folk was certain that anyone living abroad must be dreadfully deprived of anything worth eating. Nothing could be more terrible than not being able to eat good plain English fare.

'She'd love that,' he said. He paused at the kitchen door and turned back. 'I'll ask Lady Margaret to invite the Chapmans and the Ramsays to dinner, and we'll make it a splendid occasion.'

'In the Waterford Room, Your Lordship?' asked Meg hopefully. She loved setting out the table in the Waterford Room because it was so gloriously opulent. The family hardly ever used it; it was much too large and grand for ordinary occasions.

'Yes, Meg, why not?' said Nicholas slowly. 'It will certainly impress Eleanora's guest. Yes, we'll definitely dine in the Waterford Room, with the best silver and crystal and the Coalport dinner service.'

A slightly malicious thought struck him. With any luck the grandeur might even intimidate that strutting peacock of a man, Levi; that, plus a room full of Eleanora's disapproving English relations! Nicholas knew that Anne and Richard disapproved of Levi as a partner for Eleanora, and not just because he had taken Peter's place. The age-difference alone made him unsuitable in their eyes. As for his mother, although she had maintained a surprisingly discreet silence when informed that Eleanora and the new man in her life were coming to stay at Broadacres, he guessed she had probably discussed it at length with the Ramsays. Margaret was always fair, and he knew she would reserve making her final judgement until she had met the man himself. But once she had decided that Levi was unsuitable for her dearest and only granddaughter, Nicholas counted on her doing everything within her power to unravel the liaison.

Wednesday and Thursday slipped by rapidly. Nicholas, busy helping with the harvest, almost forgot about the strange story still lying on Liana's desk. An unexpectedly fine warm spell had settled over most of England and farmers everywhere were working long hours, desperate to get in the grain harvest before the weather broke. Bags of dry grain meant a handsome profit. Broadacres had just invested in one of the latest hi-tech combine harvesters, and the smaller farmers, who still hired their equipment from the estate, were panting to get their hands on it.

'Not till we've got our own harvest in,' said Wally firmly. 'Just you remember that, Rolf, my lad. After this harvest, when I'm retired, it'll be your door they will come a knocking at, and don't you let them have it until you're good and ready.'

Rolf grinned. 'I'm not daft, Grandad.'

Nicholas overheard. 'He certainly isn't, Wally. You've got nothing to worry about, the home farm will be in good hands.'

By Friday they were nearly finished. 'Only the barley in Inkpen Acre to get in,' said Rolf. 'We ought to finish that by tomorrow.'

'Tomorrow!' Wally was indignant. 'With this new-fangled piece of machinery, we'll get that barley in by tonight. You mark my words.'

Nicholas had his doubts. Inkpen Acre was a misnomer, being far more than an acre. The field was enormous and covered several hundred acres of difficult, sloping terrain. But by early evening, when the sunset burnished the sky with an autumnal lustre, they were halfway to finishing. It seemed a pity to stop, so they carried on. Nicholas glanced at his watch. Eleanora had telephoned the previous day and left a message with Margaret. She and Levi were due to arrive at seven in the evening. Liana should have already arrived; she was due back at Broadacres in the middle of the afternoon.

'I must leave by seven-thirty this evening at the very latest,' he told Wally. 'We have a dinner party at eight-thirty. I shall need time to get ready.'

'Don't you worry, Your Lordship. We shall finish up here using the headlights if necessary. There's not a bit of dampness in the air this evening. We'll get the last ear of barley in, no trouble.'

Nicholas wondered if he would have time to talk to Liana about the story before dinner. He hoped so, but was not unduly worried; there was always tomorrow. Then he forgot about it as they all concentrated on manoeuvring the efficient, but cumbersome piece of machinery up along the steepest part of the Inkpen ridge where the barley had yet to be cut.

*

Back at Broadacres, Meg, with Alice helping her, was setting out the dining table in the Waterford Room. Melanie, the new maid, had been relegated to the kitchen for the night to peel the vegetables. She accepted this change of duties with sublime fatalism. She knew she was clumsy, and the mere sight of all that sheer, sparkling Waterford crystal and the paper-thin bone china plates made her hands shake with nerves. No, she would much rather stay in the delicious-smelling kitchen with Dolly and Mary Pragnell supervising her, and where a dropped potato was not a crime of catastrophic proportions.

Margaret was in her room on the telephone to Dorothy Ramsay. 'What do you think? I've not told Nicholas that Peter is over from the States, and that I've invited him to dinner tonight along with his parents.'

'I can't see what you are worrying about.' Dorothy was trying, without much success, to be reassuring.

'But Peter will meet Eleanora's new lover.' Margaret forced herself to say the word although old-fashioned, ingrained prejudices made it difficult.

'Well, my dear, it has got to happen sooner or later. I think in a way, it will probably be easier for him with all the family present.'

'I only hope you're right.' Margaret was not entirely convinced. 'If Liana were here, I'd ask her, and if necessary put Peter off. But she hasn't arrived yet. Her flight back from France is late, so I can't. Oh, how I wish you and Donald were coming tonight.' There was a pause, then she said, 'Why aren't you?'

Dorothy laughed. Margaret had become a trifle forgetful in her old age. 'Because it is a family dinner party, and also because you haven't asked us.'

'Well, I'm asking you now. In fact, now I remember it, Nicholas did tell me to. Don't know why on earth I didn't. You and Donald are as good as family. There's not a single skeleton in our cupboards not already well known to you both so you might as well come and see the latest one. Come and tell me what *you* think of this wretched new man of Eleanora's.'

'Hold on, I'll have to ask Donald. He might not feel like coming out tonight. Although he is walking a little now, it is still such a struggle for him.'

Margaret snorted unsympathetically. 'I won't take that for an excuse. If I can get around on the withered knobbly things that pass as my legs these days, he can certainly come over here this evening.' Then she added plaintively. 'I need you, both of you.'

'One minute.' Dorothy would not commit herself.

To Margaret's joy the answer was yes. 'Bruno will come over and get you in the Rolls,' she said. 'Eight for eighty-thirty.'

*

Liana was feeling very irritated. There had been absolutely nothing in Lyons which could not have been sorted out by the local management if they had only possessed more guts and initiative. Men, she thought impatiently. Why are they so often afraid of a confrontation when it comes to words? I should have let them fight it out in a physical brawl, then they would have been satisfied! Jason Penrose had felt the sharp lash of her tongue on the homeward journey, and wished he had gone across to Lyons first and found out the lie of the land. The final straw was the flight delay because of engine trouble. It was not Jason's fault, although he ended up feeling as if it were.

Now she jumped from the train at Winchester, marched briskly along the platform and out through the exit just in time to see the last taxi disappearing down the hill into the city.

'Should be another one along in a minute, Your Ladyship,' said the station porter who knew Liana by sight.

'What do you call a minute? One, two three or ten?' came the snapping answer.

'Well, I don't rightly know. 'T ain't easy to say,' he answered in his soft Hampshire drawl.

Liana felt ashamed at herself for snapping his head off. He was doing his best and trying to be helpful. 'I know that.' She sighed. 'I'm sorry to be so impatient but I am in rather a hurry.'

The porter disappeared, leaving Liana waiting disconsolately, wishing she had rung Bruno from Waterloo asking him to meet this train. But it was a little late to think of it now; she would have to wait. The porter suddenly reappeared wreathed in smiles. He pointed to the road junction at the bottom of the hill. 'I've got old Jock for you. There he is now, on his way up.'

A black taxi was coming up the hill. 'How did you do it?' Liana was delighted and pressed a one-pound note into his hand.

'Easy, I 'phoned the transport café from the station master's office.' He grinned conspiratorially. 'He's gone off duty.'

The net result was that instead of arriving back at Broadacres rushed and in a bad mood, Liana was able to relax, knowing that she would have time for a bath before dressing for dinner. I might even have time to read that story Peter left with me, she mused. I ought to try and do it. He did ask for my reaction as soon as possible, and that was several days ago.

On arrival at Broadacres Liana found everything well organized and under control. She was a little surprised to see that they were using the Waterford Room, but congratulated Meg on the table-setting which looked magnificent.

'I see we have an extra large party for dinner,' she said, noting the place numbers.

'The Chapmans and Ramsays are coming. I think Lady Margaret wanted them to see Miss Eleanora's new young man.'

Liana pulled a wry expression. 'I haven't met him myself but I understand he is not all that young. So don't look too surprised when you meet him!'

'Forewarned is forearmed as they say, Your Ladyship,' said Meg, wondering how old he actually was. 'Shall I call you when Miss Eleanora arrives?'

Liana looked at her watch. 'Did Lord Nicholas arrange for drinks at eight?' Meg nodded, and Liana made a quick mental calculation. There was still time to catch up on the reading for Peter before dinner. 'No, don't call me. I'm going to bathe and dress for dinner then work in my office for a little while. I'll meet everyone in the Grey Room for drinks.'

Liana chose her outfit for the evening with care, a simple dark green velvet evening dress which clung to her still youthful figure before flaring out into soft folds around her feet – a skilful blend of glamour without being too stark. An hour later she made her way down to the office. As they were dining in the Waterford Room, she wore the amethyst and diamond jewellery brought over with her from Italy; a room of such elegant beauty deserved the best. She fingered the necklace as she walked. Strange that she should be thinking of Eleanora tonight with such clarity. Her mind, in spite of her rigorous attempts at disciplining it to forget, did still dwell on the past, but although Raul's image always remained clear, Eleanora's had gradually faded with the passing of time. But tonight it was as if Eleanora were there with her, and she fancied she felt the touch of her hand and heard the last whispered words her friend had ever spoken. *'Don't cry, darling. I shall always be with you for as long as you live. Nothing can separate the indivisible.'* Liana shivered. That had been in December 1943 and this was September 1966, almost twenty-three years ago, a lifetime away and yet it could still touch her enough to make her want to weep.

But her life was here now. And there was plenty to do. Resolutely pushing the memories back to where they belonged, she straightened her shoulders and quickened her pace. The present was the important part of her life, not the past.

The sound of tyres crunching on the gravel filtered down the cloister corridor from the front of the house. Liana paused and listened. The sound of voices, greetings, Eleanora's laugh. It was Eleanora and Levi arriving. Good, they had plenty of time to change for dinner, and she had plenty of time to read.

*

Before driving round to the front steps, Eleanora had stopped the hired car under the triumphal archway which led into the forecourt in front of Broadacres. 'I suppose I had better tell you now,' she said.

'Tell me what?' Raul was staring at the imposing edifice before them. The house was lit by the last glow of a fast-fading sunset, the faint purple of dusk blurring the edges of everything in sight. But nothing could blur the magnificence of the scene before him: the great square house; the manicured lawns; the huge cedars of Lebanon standing guard either side of the house; the lake and the Palladian bridge in the distance. The foreground was just as impressive, the boxed hedge of the formal garden with the fountain playing in the middle, every leaf of the hedge looking as if it had been carefully trimmed with nail scissors. Although Raul had worked in England, he had never been out of London; but he had no difficulty in recognizing a stately home when he saw one. The houses of the English aristocracy were always in Italian magazines. He turned towards Eleanora and smiled. Silly girl, she was going to apologize because her parents were servants here. 'Tell me what?' he said again.

'That my father is the Earl of Wessex and my full name is Lady Eleanora Hamilton-Howard.'

It took a few seconds for the information to penetrate Raul's brain but then he began to laugh. 'Oh, Eleanora,' he said at last, 'why do you sound apologetic? And I thought you were going to tell me your father was a servant here.'

'You are not put off? A lot of people think families like ours are snobbish, but we're not.'

'It would take more than a snobbish family to put me off you.' Raul caressed her neck, then let his hand wander down to cup her breast. He rubbed her nipple with his thumb. 'Just think, I've been screwing English nobility all this time without knowing it!' His voice roughened and he slipped his hand inside her blouse and bra, releasing a breast. Bending his head he took the nipple in his mouth, biting it almost savagely. 'I can't wait to screw you again, My Lady,' he said.

'Raul! Not here.' Eleanora pushed him aside and edged away irritably. 'Promise me you will behave properly. And you can forget that.' She pushed Raul away as he attempted to caress her again. 'There won't be time for making love before dinner. As it is we'll just about have time to bathe and change before eight, when we all meet in the Grey Room for drinks.'

'You sound like an Englishwoman already.' Raul was annoyed at her very obvious reflex movement away from him.

'Perhaps that is because I am!' said Eleanora sharply. She buttoned up her blouse primly before driving the car around the semi-circular gravel drive.

Raul slumped back in his seat feeling bad-tempered. This weekend looked as if it was going to be a complete and utter bore: Eleanora being snootily prim and English; no sex! And even worse, he would be stuck with all her relations, no doubt the ultimate in English stuffiness. It was going to be one long yawn.

*

Outside it was almost dark but it was warm. The sound of the combine harvester still working up on Inkpen Acre echoed down through the valley. Liana smiled, pulling the manuscript towards her, ready to read. The last of the grain harvest would soon be in, and not a single field flattened by rain this year. Broadacres would make a good profit with their top-quality grain.

She started reading. The bright light of the desk lamp spilled out over the page, illuminating the neatly typed words. But gradually as Liana read on they ceased to be words. Instead the pages became a series of vivid images, images of the past, exact images of her own life in Italy during the war and after the Allied occupation. Everything was there: the early years before the war, starting with Eleanora's father, the *Marchese*, being killed in Spain; the flight of Miss Rose; the dreadful death of her mother and her ineffectual fight to save her; her own life carefully documented; the steps that led her into eventual prostitution in the desperate effort to keep herself and Eleanora alive; the death of Don Luigi and his lonely burial; and lastly the tragic death of Eleanora. Even the account of her ghastly burial on that cold wet day in December 1943 was there, nothing omitted, nothing at all. Except that instead of Raul's helping the young Liana, it was an unknown young man from the village of San Angelo. That was the only difference, that and the fact that the writer wrongly stated that Liana had been killed during a bombing raid on Naples. Apart from those minor deviations, everything else was exactly as it had happened.

Liana turned the last page and quietly closed the manuscript. Now she knew why Peter wanted her to read it. Not only because of the coincidence of the names, but because the descriptions of the pain and suffering, of the brief moments of happiness before the final tragedy were so vivid and had the ring of truth. But what Peter could not know was that only one person in the world knew such intimate details. That person was Raul Carducci. Was it possible that he was still alive and had written this story? Or had he told it to someone else, who had then written it down?

Sitting completely still, as if carved out of stone, Liana stared straight ahead. Looking through the pool of light from the desk lamp, out through the open window to where the headlights of the harvester were moving slowly along the hillside, her eyes saw not the present, but the past. On and on went the vision tunnelling backwards through time until finally she was there, alone on the barren, arid hillside above Naples, the fragrance of wild thyme and rosemary and the sweet smell of ripe olives in her nostrils. The past had caught up with and overtaken the present.

How long she sat, enmeshed in a warp of time, she did not know. But slowly Liana realized that it was possible the impossible had happened. Conflicting emotions caused her heart to beat unsteadily, fluttering like a bird one moment, thumping heavily like a lump of lead the next. One moment she was reeling under the impact of a joy so great she could scarcely breathe; Raul was still alive, and he had written the story in the belief that she was dead. But why had he not written about their beautiful love affair? Why had he not told of his love for her? Why substitute an unknown man from the village as her companion in the final days at the *castello*? Then, just as suddenly, the joy was replaced with the familiar, bitter anguish. Raul was dead, but by a quirk of fate, the same fate which had always dogged her life, the story had lived on through some unknown person. Now written down, although not the complete story, there was enough to give Peter, and anyone else who might read it, the insight to be able to guess at the truth – not the whole truth, Eleanora's parentage was still safe, but she, Liana was not.

She closed her eyes. All the years, such a heavy, heavy burden she had carried – a strange burden, a mixture of pain and grief plus the bitter-sweet joy of her daughter. But the secret of her own identity, Liana had always thought to carry with her to the grave, and now it was a secret no longer. For here it was, lying on the desk in front of her, written out in story form. And Peter had read it.

Upstairs in the hall, Alice was given the task of banging the gong to signal the drinks were ready in the Grey Room. She gave two hefty bangs, just as her mother had told her, then made her way, smart in her new parlour maid's uniform, into the Grey Room, ready to serve the drinks.

The vibrating resonance of the gong echoed down, drifting along the stone cloisters into the library office. It roused Liana out of the half-dreaming state she had fallen into. She sat up abruptly. Joy at the possibility that Raul was still alive and fear of discovery jostled for supremacy in her mind, both emotions pressing in on her until it was almost unbearable. But as she stood, ready to make her way to the Grey Room, Liana knew what she must do: the same as she had always done – give nothing away. For the time being she would wait. Facts, hard facts, those were what she needed, and the first one was to find out the name of whoever had penned the manuscript.

Making her way along the cloisters and up the stairs, she paced herself in slow, measured steps. Breathing slowly, she regained some control of the erratic beat of her heart. If Raul were dead and someone else had written the story, then her secret was still safe. For nothing, except the joy of being held once more in Raul's arms, would persuade her to admit the truth, and Liana had no doubt of her ability to successfully refute the story if it should prove necessary. Only for Raul would she confess, for nothing less could possibly make up for the loss of Broadacres and everything that went with it. It was Raul or Broadacres, a simple choice.

At the door of the Grey Room she paused. It seemed she was the last to arrive. The murmur of voices and the occasional burst of laughter percolated through the door. Holding her head high, she opened the door and swept in. Alice bobbed forward, a gin and tonic already prepared for her on a silver salver.

'Thank you, Alice.' Liana smiled at Meg's young daughter. 'You do look nice tonight. I'm glad I chose that blue for you instead of black; it brings out the colour of your eyes.'

Alice blushed prettily. 'Thank you,' she said shyly, and retreated across to the sideboard.

Liana turned to greet the other guests. She smiled at Peter. I wonder if she's read the manuscript, he thought. There was nothing about her assured appearance to suggest she had, or if she had, was in the slightest bit perturbed. Her smiling gaze swept past Donald, Dorothy and Margaret, all sitting on the largest of the Chippendale settees. Richard and Anne Chapman were standing by the white marble chimney piece with Nicholas. Richard smiled and raised his glass in a half-salute which she returned. Out of the corner of her eye she could see Eleanora and a tall, slightly balding man, standing by one of the windows. They had their backs to the room, and Eleanora was pointing out of the window into the darkness. Nicholas came across to meet Liana.

Kissing her on the cheek, he turned and called to Eleanora. 'Darling, come and say hello to your mother, and bring your guest.'

At his words the two at the window turned back into the room. Suddenly Liana felt the solid floor slipping away into nothingness beneath her feet.

Eleanora was coming towards her. She was smiling, speaking, saying something but Liana could not hear. Her eyes were fixed on the man beside Eleanora: father and daughter walking together. It was Raul. The passage of years had changed him, coarsened his features, but not so much that she could not recognize him. There was no mistaking the man she had dreamed of for the past twenty-three years, the father of her daughter.

Her gaze switched to Eleanora. She was clinging on to Raul's arm, laughing. Father and daughter! Lovers! Oh, my God! What malicious power had conspired to twist their lives and bring them together in this fashion? A choking nausea overcame her. Father and daughter, Raul and Eleanora. Oh, God!

With a crash the glass dropped from her nerveless fingers and shattered on the floor.

Chapter Thirty-One

Downstairs in the vast kitchen of Broadacres, Mary Pragnell was extolling the virture of good, plain cooking.

'Now, if Lady Liana had fainted and there had been soufflé on the menu, a right pickle we'd have been in and no mistake. But as it is, nothing will spoil by waiting a few minutes. Turn the gas down under that soup, Melanie, there's a good girl.'

Melanie did as she was told. 'Do you think it *will* only be a few minutes? Alice said she went out like a light.'

'Of course.' Mary was comfortably positive. 'Her Ladyship is no weakling. Been overdoing it, that's what. Dashing off to France, and then dashing back here, working in her office right until the last minute and then dashing straight up to dinner. Anyone would faint! A little lie down and she'll be all right.'

But Liana did not want to lie down. 'No, Donald, I am perfectly all right.' She struggled to an upright position and saw that someone – it must have been Nicholas because he was there with Donald – had carried her into the little anteroom, next door to the Grey Room. She was on the Victorian day-bed which stood against the wall.

'But, darling, you must be exhausted. That's why you fainted.' Concerned, Nicholas knelt at her side.

Liana looked at him, then trembling looked quickly away. The gentle compassion in his voice only emphasized the tortuous, guilt-ridden emotion now tearing her to pieces. The blindness, which she had so steadfastly cultivated was swept away in a sudden blaze of simple perception; what right had she ever had to blame him for anything? Her own shameful burden was so much greater. Never knowingly would he have allowed William to harm James; whereas every single deception she had practised had been planned. Put into perspective, the family secret of William's illness was understandable. Her own deception was quite another matter. True, it had always seemed justified. Or to be more honest she had always succeeded in persuading herself that it was justified. Until tonight. Now the flimsy veil of absolution had been torn to shreds, life had

443

turned its full nightmarish circle, revealing the truth in an ugliness she had never dreamed possible. Nicholas was still kneeling at her side, and Liana turned towards him wanting to speak, but no words came. The dreadful enormity of what she knew she must do robbed her of speech. And the worst thing of all was the knowledge that she would be robbing Nicholas yet again. He had lost his only son, and soon, through her revelations, would lose his daughter.

For the first time, she allowed herself to concede that his grief at the loss of James equalled hers and that she had compounded it by turning away from him. By not sharing the sorrow, she had made it worse. Now he was about to lose the daughter he had loved so dearly for the past twenty-two years. He did not deserve to be so badly hurt. Without warning, long-buried memories of her wedding day came back, and Liana remembered how she had thought then that she had married a good man with integrity who would never let her down. And if she was absolutely honest, she knew he never had.

She remembered, too, the vow she had made to herself at her wedding. She had vowed to make him happy, vowed that he would never know the truth and would never regret marrying her. For a time she had succeeded, they *had* been happy. But even during the bad times of their marriage, she had always persuaded herself it was never so bad for him. She was the one who suffered, not Nicholas. If anyone had prophesied that a day would come when Nicholas would have to pay the price of *her* deception, Liana knew she would never have believed them. Now that day had come. But, of course, I should have known, I should have guessed! The thought filled her with misery. Why hadn't she foreseen the obvious? All her life fate had twisted events in unexpected directions, always with the same end result, unhappiness.

'Liana?' Nicholas said again.

'I'm all right,' she repeated, unable to think of anything else to say.

'Liana, why not give dinner tonight a miss? Eleanora will be here for the whole weekend. So we can always have another dinner party tomorrow. Meg would love the excuse to plan two on the trot, you know she would. I'll explain to everyone that you have been overdoing things and are tired, and you go up and go to bed and rest.' It was unlikely that she would listen, Nicholas knew that. But it was worth a try. He watched her face thoughtfully, tightly closed and shuttered now, devoid of emotion. He knew Liana had had a shock, and that in some way Raul Levi was connected with it. Momentarily, he wondered if Levi was tied up with the story he had read in her office but then almost immediately dismissed the idea. That was impossible, the man had only just arrived. Besides he was a famous man of the theatre. What connection could he have with the two impoverished young girls who had lived years ago?

'No!' The word rapped out, sharp and emphatic. Donald Ramsay looked at Liana curiously. Was it his imagination, or did she sound desperate?

He probed gently. 'Why not, my dear? A dinner party is not so important, is it?'

His voice seemed to have a calming effect, for she turned to him and forced a smile. 'No, it's not so important.' Then turning back to Nicholas, she apologized. 'I'm sorry, Nicholas, I don't know why I snapped so bad-temperedly. I shouldn't have. I do understand that your only concern is for me but you know how I hate fuss. I am all right. Really I am.' She held out her arm towards Donald. 'Take my pulse, please, and tell Nicholas that I'm all right.'

Obediently Donald took her pulse. There was not much point in saying that her pulse was racing like a mad thing because he knew she had every intention of going in to dinner. Nothing that he could say would stop her. So he said, 'Don't worry, Nicholas. The pulse is perfectly normal and Liana is the best judge of how she feels.'

'Which is like my pulse, perfectly normal,' Liana said firmly, getting up and smoothing down her dress. 'I'll tell you why I fainted. I've just remembered, I've had nothing to eat since my coffee and croissants in Lyons this morning. I'm absolutely starving.' A quick glance at her appearance in the gilded mirror above the fireplace to tuck a few stray wisps of hair back into the upswept french pleat of her coiffure, and she was ready. Turning back towards the two men, she smiled enchantingly, as only Liana knew how, and held out her arms. 'Come, my dears, I shall have two escorts into dinner.'

Involuntarily both Nicholas and Donald smiled back at her, reacting as usual to the mysterious magic of her dark eyes. Then they looked at each other; Donald raised his eyebrows, and Nicholas gave a faint, helpless smile. Liana was a stubborn woman, there was nothing they could do that would make her change her mind. There was no point in arguing any longer. So together, the three walked to the Waterford Room to join the rest of the company for dinner. But as they walked, with Liana talking in her usual knowledgeable way about this year's good harvest, as if that were the only thing in her thoughts, both men knew that her mind was not on her inconsequential chatter. Nor had she fainted through hunger. Something was very wrong. They both felt an ominous sense of unease and, unbeknown to each other, they had each drawn the same conclusion. The unease stemmed from the arrival of Raul Levi, the man Eleanora had brought with her from Italy.

Donald, of course, knew nothing of the story lying on the desk in Liana's office. He also knew nothing of a Raul in her past, the lost cousin and the search for him that had eventually led to her meeting with Nicholas. His feelings were based not on knowledge but on sheer gut reaction. He had seen the multitude of conflicting expressions in Liana's eyes when she had first turned towards Raul Levi. He was certain that she knew him. If he had been a betting man he would have put money on it. But more than that, he could not imagine what significance he held for her.

Nicholas, however, was like a dog worrying at a bone. Reluctant, but unable to prevent himself, he was slowly fitting the pieces together. The story on her desk. His first meeting with Liana. Then the second, when she had been searching for her cousin, Raul Carducci. Raul Levi and Raul Carducci. Was it possible that they could be one and the same person? Was that why she had fainted? And if so, who was she, this woman walking so sedately at his side, the woman who had been his wife for nearly twenty-three years? He glanced down at her. She hid her distress well; she *was* distressed, he was positive of that. Her head was held high, the familiar classical features were to all intents and purposes serene and untroubled. The years had been kind to Liana. At the age of forty-one, she could easily have passed for thirty-one. Her skin was unlined and her hair as luxuriant and dark as ever, not a grey hair in sight. The slender, feminine elegance of her figure was the envy of many, much younger women.

On reaching the door, Nicholas and Donald stood back, allowing Liana to precede them into the Waterford Room. She walked before them, beautiful and regal. Every inch a countess, thought Nicholas, feeling the familiar surge of pride he always felt at her appearance on grand occasions. What rubbish he had been guilty of thinking! There was no way she could be the girl Liana in the story, no way she could have been a common prostitute. There *was* an answer to the mysterious story, and he was sure Raul Levi had something to do with it, and after dinner, he would damn well make it his business to find out. But not now, not in front of the

Ramsays and his sister and brother-in-law. No, it would have to wait. He hoped that dinner would not be too prolonged an affair.

It was a hope shared by more than one person at the dinner table that night.

*

The polished mahogany of the long rectangular dining table gleamed a warm red in the light shed by the three elaborate silver candelabra spaced at intervals down the centre. The fine points of the crystal glasses and the overhead crystal chandeliers for which the room was famous caught the light from the candles and, acting like prisms, cast a rainbow glow on the mass of silver cutlery placed with infinite precision at the place settings. Meg and Alice moved amongst the diners with polished efficiency, serving the first course, a Broadacres home-produced pâté with melba toast. Meg had set out the food on the plates with exquisite artistry, decorating the slivers of pâté and toast with parsley leaves and wedges of lemon.

'Very pretty, my dear,' whispered Dorothy as Meg paused by her place.

'Thank you.'

But Meg was disappointed. She had a horrible feeling that all her hard work was going to be wasted. First Lady Liana had fainted, an unheard of phenomenon, and now the atmosphere at the dining table was so tense that Meg felt as if she were physically battling her way through it. What was going on? She mentioned nothing to her mother who was in the kitchen rushing around, red in the face, making certain everything was ready to be conveyed upstairs the moment it was needed. Her mother was busy enough, and anyway, Meg knew she would tell her to stop imagining things. But she knew it was not her imagination.

Even Alice mentioned it as they were loading the dumb waiter with the first pile of used plates and cutlery. 'Funny sort of feeling in there tonight, Mum. They all seem kind of uptight and on edge. They're not really talking properly. Have you noticed?'

Meg closed the doors, gave the pulley a hefty yank and the dumb waiter trundled down the shaft into the kitchen where Mary Pragnell was waiting to remove the dirty plates and load on the soup tureen of fish bisque.

'Yes, I've noticed,' said Meg. 'Perhaps none of them like that Italian chap Miss Eleanora has brought home with her.'

'*I don't,*' said Alice with the uncompromising positiveness of the very young. 'I think he's a horrible old man. What can she see in him? I wouldn't have anything to do with him.'

The bell rang signalling the dumb waiter was on its way up. 'That's as may be. But just you keep your thoughts to yourself. It is none of our business,' said Meg severely, thinking at the same time how right the child was. What on earth must Lord Nicholas and Lady Liana have thought when they first saw him?

Raul was confused, uncomfortable and apprehensive. He was not sure what his initial emotions had been when he had first seen Liana. The shock of meeting her face to face was still reeling through his brain. That it had been a shock to her as well as himself was not in doubt. He knew very well, even if no-one else in the room did, why she had fainted. Like him, she could never have expected their paths to cross again after all these years, especially as she had moved away from Italy and into a completely different world.

Her eyes flickered across to him now, haughty, imperious and cold as death. Words were not necessary. Raul shivered and looked away, knowing that she was blaming him for the manner in which he had left her alone as a young girl. The sparkling lights of the room dimmed momentarily as he remembered her worried young face peering at him through the murky gloom of the falling ash on that March day. Then his black eyes hardened with self-justification and he looked back at her defiantly. What had she got to look so bloody superior about? Christ, he thought viciously, not only is she still bloody well alive, but she is also an English countess.

It would have been better if she had not been Eleanora's mother. That was unfortunate but it could not be helped. Anyway it wouldn't make a damned bit of difference as far as he was concerned. Why should it? She and her snooty husband could be as hostile as they liked but they wouldn't get Eleanora away from him.

'When exactly did you meet our daughter?'

Nicholas glanced at Liana as she spoke to Raul Levi. A perfectly ordinary question, and yet her voice had a strange ring to it.

'Initially during rehearsals for *Dido and Aeneas*, in London.'

'I see. And when did you start living together?'

'Mummy!' Eleanora was embarrassed. 'Please!'

'I'm sorry, darling. I just wanted to know how long this . . .' she hesitated, 'this liaison has been going on.'

'Since I met Raul again in Florence. And please could we not discuss it at the dinner table.' Eleanora was acutely aware of the embarrassed silence around the table and the disapproving stares of Meg and Alice.

Nicholas looked at Liana curiously. It was unlike her to discuss such personal matters on such a public occasion. He tried to change the subject. 'I understand you've had a very unusual career in films and theatre,' he said.

'Yes, you could say that.' Raul wished the conversation would switch away from him.

'A rags to riches story?' Liana enquired, her voice honey smooth.

'Yes,' said Raul.

He watched Liana curiously. Every inch of her manner and carriage oozed English nobility, and he was forced to acknowledge a certain grudging admiration. There was no doubt she carried the role off well, as if she had been born into the life, instead of into a peasant family, her mother a servant. Of course, the education she had shared with Eleanora had given her an advantage, and he remembered now that the young Liana had always had a slightly superior manner; but how the hell had she managed to catch herself an earl? Not from her trade as-a prostitute, he thought grimly. He would wager his life that the snooty Earl of Wessex knew nothing of that! A rags to riches story she had said. Was she warning him to keep quiet? Well, she had nothing to fear, he would not betray her.

His mind moved on to the problem of the damned story he had written. Thank God at least the manuscript of *The Two Girls* was still in Hollywood with Milton Hyam's writer friend. That would need to be retrieved at the earliest possible moment. Hell! Milton might prove difficult, especially if he was thinking he could make money from a film of the story; but no matter what objections Milton might raise, Raul knew without a shadow of doubt that he must get it back.

He looked down the row of aristocratic faces sitting either side of the table, their hostility towards him barely concealed beneath smilingly conducted polite chit-chat. He smiled grimly: a lynching mob if ever he saw one. They would hang, draw and quarter him if he dared to publish. The fact that the countess had once been a prostitute might be the truth but one look at Liana's face opposite him, as haughty and disdainful as the rest, and Raul was certain she would deny it. She had already given him a veiled warning anyway, that remark about rags to riches. It must have been a warning. No, much better burn it, cut his losses and forget the whole thing, and get away from Broadacres as soon as possible.

Of course, it wasn't going to be easy persuading Eleanora to leave early; but there was no way he was going to stick out the whole damned weekend. He slid a sideways glance at her sitting beside him. Funny, Eleanora didn't look like her mother at all, and, although Liana was still beautiful, Raul didn't feel attracted to her sexually. Strange, he thought, it was always the same, once he had finished with a woman, that was it. He lost interest. Only Monika Muller had the power to draw him back time after time. He looked at Eleanora again. Yes, he was still attracted to her. It would wear off eventually, he was almost certain of that. But for the time being he still wanted her. But perhaps because of her mother there was a certain air of familiarity, and it was that fact which had attracted him in the first place. At the moment, though, he felt annoyed. She was distancing herself from him, and he knew why. The moment they had entered the Waterford Room and he had seen how grand it was, he had felt out of place. He wasn't dressed correctly, and he blamed Eleanora.

'Why the hell didn't you warn me that this was going to be a formal dinner, damn you!' he hissed at her in a low voice, very conscious of the other men's dinner jackets and black ties, while he was wearing an informal cream jacket and open-necked shirt with the usual array of gold medallions resting on the thick hair of his chest.

'I did say it was *dinner*,' Eleanora emphasized the word, 'with drinks beforehand. I assumed you understood. When I saw the way you were dressed, I presumed you preferred the theatrical director appearance rather than the formal look.'

Raul tightened his lips at the faint undercurrent of sarcasm in her voice. Little bitch, she was being as snooty as the rest of them. 'You could have been a little more explicit.'

'By the time I saw what you were wearing it was too late for you to change. Oh, yes, thank you, Meg, I will have some of the Chablis.'

Quite suddenly Raul felt strangely depressed, an unusual mood for him. He told himself it was because Eleanora was quite different here. She had changed towards him the moment they had driven in through that damned stone arch. But that was the least of his worries. The sooner he got himself out of this situation the better. Once he had Eleanora back in Italy, she would be his again and all this would be forgotten.

'White wine with the fish bisque, sir?' Meg's chilly voice interrupted his train of thought.

'Oh, yes, thank you.' God! Even the damned servants were condescending. He wondered where the nearest 'phone was which he could use without being overheard. He would ring the States that very evening and leave a message on Milton's answer machine if necessary. The sooner the manuscript of *The Two Girls* was put under wraps, the better.

Peter, torn between staring, without its appearing too obvious, at Liana and then Raul, was finding polite conversation almost an impossibility. Nevertheless he persevered, partly from habit and partly because he was at a loss as to what else to do. The moment before Liana had fainted he had caught a glimpse of her face, and in that instant he was sure of two things. Liana knew Raul Levi, and she had read the story. The sight of Raul standing before her in her own house had shocked her. No, no, he thought, casting his mind back to the expression he had glimpsed, shocked was not the right word. Disbelief, that was her first fleeting emotion, then Peter remembered how her gaze had flickered from Eleanora to Raul and back again. That was when she was horrified, utterly horrified and very frightened. He felt sick, sure now that her reaction could only mean one thing. Part of the story *was* true. But which part? Oh, God, let it not be that Liana was the peasant girl of the story, the prostitute. But even as he said the silent prayer, Peter was sure in his own mind that it was a vain hope. She *must* be the Liana in the story. What would she do? What could he do to help her? His writer's analytical mind delved into the possibilities. Slowly, he began to formulate an idea.

The soup bowls were cleared away and Alice laid fresh plates then returned with Meg to serve the meat course.

'Claret with your roast beef?' Meg paused by Peter, claret bottle poised over a wine glass. Peter stared down at his plate, oblivious to everything around him, his mind busy. 'Master Peter,' Meg hissed, 'do you want some claret?'

'Oh!' Peter jumped. 'Sorry, Meg, I was miles away. What did you say?' He saw the claret bottle in her hand. 'Oh, yes, yes, I'd love some claret, and the roast beef looks perfect.'

'Thank you,' said Meg, 'I'll tell my mother. She did the cooking tonight.' You haven't even noticed it, and I doubt that you will taste it either, thought Meg, watching Peter's expression. He was right when he had said his mind was miles away. It was. What on earth was the matter with the family tonight? Surely it couldn't all be due to one unwelcome visitor?

Peter sipped his claret and ate the roast beef but, as Meg had suspected, he might as well have been eating sawdust for all the enjoyment he gained. With every mouthful, the plan he eventually formulated began to seem more and more plausible. He took the facts as he thought them to be. Apart from himself and Liana, no-one else had read the story Raul had written. He glanced across at Raul who had decided to hell with the lot of them and switched on his famous charm which never failed to work. He was chatting to a stony-faced Lady Margaret.

'You know, you should be proud. Your granddaughter Eleanora has a great talent.'

'Yes, I do know. I've heard her sing.'

'She should go far.'

'She will. But of course it is essential that she mixes with the *right* people!'

Raul gave up; the charm was wasted. She didn't like him either. It was quite obvious she didn't regard him as one of the *right* people.

Peter's mind went back to his plan. It should be relatively easy once Liana knew that he, Peter, could be trusted never to reveal her secret. Between them, they would threaten a libel action against Raul, pointing out that it would be his word against theirs. If necessary, they could threaten that the entire force of the Hamilton-Howards would be launched against him, although Peter fervently hoped it would not be necessary to involve any other member of the family. Once his mind was made up Peter became impatient and found the long drawn-out formalities of dinner, something he normally enjoyed, beginning to pall. He wondered what Liana was thinking. The expression on her face gave not the slightest hint.

Eleanora, sitting beside Raul, found herself comparing him unfavourably with Peter and her own father. At first, when her mother had fainted, she had thought that perhaps they had known each other. It was not an impossibility. They were both Italian and could have met before the war. But Raul had said nothing other than to exclaim like everyone else at her mother's fainting fit, and when she had returned to the room Liana had said nothing either. The only odd thing was her mother's strange and embarrassing remarks about her living with Raul. Eleanora could accept that she did not like it, but somehow there seemed to be more than just disapproval in her voice.

She glanced across at Liana now and felt the familiar twinge of irritation she often felt when looking at her mother. Why is it, she wondered, that I can never even guess at what she is thinking? She watched Liana incline her head gracefully towards Donald Ramsay who was expounding on some topic. She was smiling and nodding her head and looked incredibly beautiful.

Eleanora watched her for a few moments. My mother must be one of the most beautiful women in the world, she thought, and here she is, surrounded by friends and family, and yet to me she seems alone. Eleanora had never tried to put her feelings into words before but now she realized what it was that was so different about her mother, apart from her beauty. It was that she was surrounded by an aura of loneliness. But why should that be? She was never lonely. Everyone adored her. Eleanora gave up; it was too difficult trying to puzzle out why.

She switched her attention to Raul. He had given up talking to Lady Margaret and was now talking to Dorothy Ramsay. But she noticed that, however the conversation started and whatever topic originated it, they invariably ended up with the talk centred on Raul, on *his* doings, on *his* successes. How is it that I've never seen how egocentric he is before, she wondered with amazement. Raul was interested in nothing and no-one except himself. Politics, world affairs, science, ideas and beliefs, things which Eleanora had always been used to hearing discussed avidly at mealtimes, were of absolutely no interest to him. Unless it was something he had personally experienced or something that could be of some use to him in the furtherance of his career, Raul did not want to discuss it.

An uncomfortable thought which had been lurking at the back of her mind for some time finally emerged and she acknowledged it. The only thing we have in common is sex! She felt ashamed. Looking up, she caught Peter's grey eyes looking at her, and hastily lowered her own. She wished he still loved her. But that was impossible; she had betrayed his love. If only I had not been so hot-headed. If only I had listened and taken further advice. If only I had not met Raul, if only, if only. *Ah, but you searched Raul out, you know you did!* Her conscience would not be stilled. *You had every intention of taking Raul as a lover, and you succeeded.* Yes, I succeeded, she acknowledged miserably, knowing that leaving Raul would not be easy. His hold over her was strong and possessive. Indubitably he would not willingly give her up. Eleanora stared down at her plate; there seemed to be no way out of the mess she had got herself into.

The conversation at the dinner table swirled, for the most part, in meaningless, unformed patterns about Liana. Sitting in the beautiful room, playing the part of the gracious hostess, she was suddenly forcibly reminded of her feelings on her wedding day. How hard she had needed to concentrate then to control the near hysteria she had felt. But I was much younger then, she reminded herself, and inexperienced in deceit. If I could get through the marriage service on that day, I can surely get through this dinner party now.

Donald Ramsay interrupted her flow of thought. 'I take it from your earlier remarks that you do not particularly approve of your daughter's rather elderly boyfriend,' he said quietly.

Liana made a small grimace. 'I cannot say that I am happy about it,' she replied. Oh, God, what an understatement that was!

The distress in her eyes as she spoke made Donald want to reach out and comfort her. But he did not. Old age had made him much more humble. Now he acknowledged that he was powerless to change peoples' lives, much as he might wish to. It was only now and then that he was given an opportunity to gently push someone in the right direction, and then he took it.

But these circumstances were quite different. Because he, too, had been partly instrumental in the damage which had been done, the guilt was shared. Cursing the hereditary illness and the obsessional secrecy of the Hamilton-Howard family, to which he had always acquiesced, he speculated how differently events might have evolved if the truth had been properly aired. Then the traumatic evening at the Ritz would never have happened and Eleanora would not have flown off to Italy on an impulse, where, desperate and unhappy, she had ended up with an entirely unsuitable older man.

Donald tried to tell himself that it was Raul's age which put him against the man, but deep down he knew it was much more than that. He did not like him, and it was not just a question of mild disapproval. The man might be clever artistically, but Donald Ramsay recognized corruption when he saw it. Raul Levi was immoral and amoral, totally corrupted by ambition and the pursuit of pleasure.

I was too proud, he thought, I was so sure that I knew what was best, but I should have forced the family to take further advice. With hindsight it was easy to see that honesty would have been the better policy.

'Stilton, Donald?' Nicholas passed him the enormous Stilton cheese dish.

'Why, yes, thank you. Although to tell the truth I've already eaten far too much for a man of my age.'

He tried to sound cheerful. Nicholas certainly looked as if he could do with a little cheering, and no wonder. Cutting a sliver from the Stilton he passed it on. Hindsight! Such an easy faculty to acquire, but always too late. It was never possible to go back, only forward. The past could not be altered. If only he could think straight perhaps there was a way to unravel the mess they had all contributed to, but he could not think. I'm getting too old, Donald decided unhappily. My powers of reasoning are deserting me.

'Thank you.' He took the port bottle, poured himself a generous measure and passed it on.

Liana was smiling automatically at whatever anyone said until her cheeks ached from the effort but her thoughts were still in the past. Yes, it *had* been difficult, her wedding day, and yet in a way it had been made easy because she had been fired by the driving force of desperate necessity, the need to provide for the coming child. Now she had no driving force. She felt spent, completely tired and spent. Her eyes flickered yet again across to Raul. Where had he gone that day? Why had he gone? But even those questions seemed irrelevant and unimportant in the light of what she now knew. Preposterous, hideously unthinkable! His own daughter!

Depressed beyond measure, Liana looked back on so many futile years wasted in dreaming; all the time holding back, turning away the man who loved her. And for what? For a man existing solely in her imagination. Covertly watching Raul and listening to his conversation, it was impossible to equate the self-centred man at the dinner table with the gentle Raul of her dreams. The handsome, once sensitive face, was coarsened by self-indulgence, and she felt a surge of revulsion. What did Eleanora see in him? What had attracted her to a man so different from Peter? But that, too, was unimportant. Whatever it was, she, Liana, now had to finish the cruel obscenity of the affair.

It was easy to understand now why Nicholas had disliked him on sight. The two men were so different. Nicholas was a gentle, considerate man, a man who had always put the happiness of others before his own. Ironic that it had taken her twenty-three years to realize that, only understanding now, too late, that what she had derisorily dismissed as a weakness had in fact been a form of strength through love. He lacked ambition but ambition was not a strength, it was merely another name for greed. Nicholas possessed a far greater quality, compassion. He was a man who would never walk away from a stray dog, leaving it alone and friendless on a barren hillside. Raul had walked away from a young girl.

If it had not been for Lady Margaret and Dorothy Ramsay, together with Richard and Anne Chapman, conversation during dinner might easily have petered out and died away all together. All sensed the tension, but in the absence of anything more tangible, they rose to the occasion and true to their inbred good manners, the conversation never flagged. Nevertheless, no-one was sorry when Meg and Alice took away the port and Stilton and brought round the coffee cups and liqueur glasses.

Liana looked down the table. The vivid rich blue and gold of the Coalport china coffee service caught the light. How beautiful it looks, she found herself thinking. How beautiful everything is. Everything and everyone, all so dear to her and so well loved. With a conscious effort she tried to imprint the scene on her memory. After tonight, everything she loved so much, the beautiful house full of wondrous things, the estate, all the people on the estate and the people surrounding her now at the dinner table, all would be lost to her. But it was the people nearest to her that mattered most, the people whose lives she was about to shatter for ever.

Meg and Alice finished pouring the coffee and liqueurs. 'Leave the coffee pot, Meg. We will help ourselves to more if necessary. If we need anything else, I will ring.'

'Yes, Your Ladyship.' Meg put the coffee pot on the silver salver in the centre of the table and motioned Alice ahead of her out of the Waterford Room.

Liana tapped the side of her cup with the tiny silver spoon. The tinkling sound halted the faint hum of conversation. She stood, straightened her back and collected what reserves of strength she had left to get the better of her sudden breathlessness. 'There is a story which I must tell you,' she said quietly.

The poignant, hopeless quality of her voice touched all those listening. Distressed, Peter realized what she was about to do. He had to speak.

He stood, too, so that his eyes were level with hers. 'There is no need for the story,' he said equally quietly, willing her to understand what was in his mind. 'It can be resolved.'

Suddenly, Liana was aware that her hand was being clasped. She looked down. Nicholas was looking up at her, his eyes blazing with compassion. He was certain now that at least part of the story must be true, and she was about to confess it. 'I, too, have read *The Two Girls*,' he said. 'I came across it by accident in your office. Sit down, darling; it is of no consequence to anyone but ourselves. As Peter so rightly says, it can be resolved.'

Raul took a hasty gulp of coffee, scalding his throat in the process. Jesus Christ! Nicholas and Peter had read the story! How the hell did they get their hands on it? Why wasn't it still with Milton Hyam in Hollywood? Then he remembered Eleanora telling him that her cousin Peter was a writer, and that he had a contract in Hollywood. Bloody hell! That must be it. What sodding bad luck! Of all the people Milton could have given it to, he must have chosen Peter Chapman, the only man who would recognize the names. Raul opened his mouth to ask if his guess were true, then closed it. He would wait, see what Liana had to say for herself. He put the coffee cup back in the saucer but found to his annoyance that his hand was shaking so much the cup rattled noisily.

Eleanora turned and looked at him. Raul looked nervous. She wondered why.

In the moment that Nicholas spoke, Liana knew what had eluded her ever since the day of her marriage. She realized that it was not just his good qualities she admired. She loved him. Like a great beating of wings, all the love she had spent so many years denying flooded through her. Too late, too late sneered her mind cruelly, ruthlessly logical. And, of course, it was true. She was impotent now to change the course of events. The new-born love foundered and was stilled, her heart turning into cold stone. Once he knew the truth, the *whole* truth, he would turn away from her for ever. Any man would. It was inevitable.

'The story you read, Nicholas, is incomplete,' she whispered. Then her voice gained in strength as her resolve hardened. For Eleanora's sake, she had to go through with it. 'There is a final chapter which must be told. And I am the only one who can tell it.'

Chapter Thirty-Two

Liana closed her eyes. There was no escaping the truth; it had to be told. But she could not bear to watch the hurt in their faces as one by one, they realized the extent to which she had betrayed their love and trust. That would be more than she could endure. And so she closed her eyes.

The sound of the combine harvester working up on Inkpen Acre drifted in through the open window, carried on the still warm air of the September evening. Night-scented stocks outside in the garden filled the room with fragrance. There was no sound or movement in the room, and yet Liana felt the air vibrating with a feeling so intense that she knew that if she did not speak soon, it would stifle her.

She began the story at the beginning, from her earliest memories as a small child before the war, when her mother had been a servant and she had been chosen to be the young Marchesa Eleanora's companion. She told it all, scrupulously careful to leave nothing out. She told how gradually, innocent childhood happiness had been replaced by misery after misery, first by the death of Eleanora's father then by the nightmare of war, starvation, and the murder of her own mother. There was a faint hissing intake of breath. Liana guessed it to be Eleanora, but it did not cause her to shrink from continuing the harrowing sequence of events which eventually led to her becoming a prostitute in order to survive. Neither did she shrink from telling how innocence, of necessity, gave way to hardened cynicism. How she became used to selling her body for money and food and grabbing with both hands whatever else she could get, legally or illegally. Survival, and getting her beloved Eleanora well were the motives, but Liana did not offer them as an excuse, merely stated the facts.

The lush smell of the Itchen Valley had long since gone for Liana. Now her nostrils were filled with different, less pleasant perfumes – the heat and dust of the arid hillside outside Naples; the stench of the city after bombing: how well she remembered that acrid, all-pervading smell of burning buildings and bodies. Long-suppressed images of the past filled her mind, becoming more real than the reality around her as she spoke: the death of the old priest; his makeshift burial at night by the light of a single lantern; the bombing raid after her evening's work as a prostitute; Nicholas and Charlie Parsons digging her out; and her subsequent flight back to the *castello* which was burning. She caught her breath at the memory. Oh, the terrible beauty of that sight, the vivid red and gold, the walls shimmering like living velvet in the fire. She could see it, smell it, almost touch it. Her heart pounded as it had on that night so many years before. Then she told of her first meeting with Raul Carducci on that night. How they fought the fire together.

Only then as she spoke, did the irony of it strike her. The two men who were destined to chart the pattern of the future years for her had both entered her life on the same night. One was to betray her, the other to be betrayed. But these thoughts she kept to herself. The story had to go on; only when it was finished would the picture be clear.

When she got to the death of Eleanora, her voice faltered and she stopped. Raul, thinking she would stop there, breathed a sigh of relief. Thank God, she was going to leave out his part in the story. As it was, she had spared him involvement by carefully adhering to the name she had known him by at that time, Raul Carducci. Of all the people in the room, only *she* knew Raul Carducci was now Raul Levi. So the years had not changed her that much after all. Underneath that steely exterior she was still soft-hearted, still thought of others; but she was a fool, too, he thought wryly. If only she had kept silent, something could have been worked out. After all, he was not such an unprincipled bastard that he would have purposely wrecked the life she had made for herself. Why the hell was she blurting it all out now? He could only suppose she had panicked on realizing that Nicholas and Peter knew part of the story, thinking they would put two and two together and come to the conclusion that she was the Liana in the story. Pity, he thought. I could have sworn it was fiction; but if she chooses to sacrifice herself on the altar of truth, how can I stop her?

Curious, he wondered how the family would take to the fact that she had admitted being a prostitute, and glanced at the faces around him. Were they shocked, horrified? No, he decided, none of them seemed to be registering those emotions. Disbelief was the expression he saw written across their faces, sheer, utter disbelief. He was surprised. He had expected the strait-laced English to be shocked. But, on reflection, perhaps they were *so* strait-laced, they just couldn't believe what she was saying! What Raul did not and could not know was that Liana had passed herself off as the Marchesa

Eleanora, and for the other occupants in the room it was a double revelation. Not only were they trying to come to grips with the fact that she had formerly been a prostitute, but also that she was not the *marchesa* they had always thought her to be.

His smug self-satisfaction was shattered a few seconds later, and his eyes flew back to Liana. She was continuing the narrative.

'After Eleanora's death,' said Liana softly, 'I thought my spirit would never emerge from the sorrow which smothered it. I never went back to prostitution. I had enough money saved, and anyway in those first few weeks whether I lived or died was unimportant to me. But the young man Raul, Raul Carducci, whom I had distrusted so much at first, gave me strength and showed me kindness. Slowly, little by little, I fell in love with him, and eventually we became lovers. My life was transformed. We had enough to eat, not a lot, but enough because Raul was clever at manipulating the thriving black market of Naples. For me it was a magical time. I left the horror and sorrow of the past behind me and stepped into a world full of love and beauty which, foolishly, I thought would last for ever. But, of course, it didn't. It ended very abruptly. On the nineteenth of March nineteen forty-four, to be precise, for that was the last day I saw Raul Carducci.

'My last sight of him is imprinted on my memory along with the date. It was the day Vesuvius erupted, and I last saw his figure disappearing into the ash, which by then was falling like snow, as he walked down the mountainside into Naples. I thought he would return some hours later with the coffee he'd gone to buy, but he did not come back. Two weeks later I found out that I was pregnant.'

Liana paused again. The hardest part was yet to come, but soon it would be over. She opened her eyes briefly. The audience watching her was so still it seemed they were hardly breathing. The only movement was the flicker of light from the guttering candles. The candles in the silver candelabra had almost burned out. Like me, thought Liana sadly, by the time their light is out, mine will be, too. Eyes closed again, she continued. This time she came to the fateful meeting again with Nicholas in his office, when, in order to impress him, and hoping to find Raul, she had introduced herself as the *marchesa*.

'At the time, I thought it would only be necessary to play the part of my friend, the *marchesa*, for a few days. Just until Raul was found. But Raul was never found, not a trace. He had just disappeared. The days dragged by, and eventually Nicholas told me that he was sure Raul must be dead. Of course, I believed him. There was no reason not to. Many people just disappeared in those days, killed in bombing raids or murdered. Once I was convinced that Raul had gone from my life for ever, it seemed logical to go on with the pretence.'

Leaving nothing to her listeners' imagination, Liana told how, knowing that Nicholas was already attracted to her, she made up her mind to make Nicholas love her enough to want to marry her. He thought she was a *marchesa*, and she knew he was an English earl. The American dollars, the proceeds of prostitution, would be her dowry, buying her and the coming child, another life far away from Italy. She also had Eleanora's jewels, no use to a dead girl, but essential now to her in the role of a *marchesa*. Shrinking from nothing, Liana explained that in Naples it was possible to find doctors, who, for a price, would stitch up a girl's hymen. The sordid details of the operation and aftermath described with stark reality, caused her audience to shudder. It was necessary, Liana explained carefully, that her hymen be stitched, so that Nicholas would think her a virgin on their wedding night.

She paused, and opened her eyes. Raul, sitting opposite, was staring, but Liana could see the full impact of her story had not yet sunk in. 'I succeeded in my subterfuge. Nicholas did think me a virgin. But Eleanora, born on December the seventeenth nineteen forty-four and thought by everyone at Broadacres to be premature, was in fact a full-term baby. Because I was two months' pregnant on my wedding night.'

Raul gasped. What was she saying? That Eleanora was *his* daughter? No, surely not. Liana wasn't pregnant when he left. She *must* have slept with someone else. She *must* have gone back to prostitution after he left. It had to be.

'But that means . . .' Eleanora's horrified voice broke into Liana's narrative.

Liana turned towards her. 'It means two things. First, the man you've always called Daddy, Nicholas, Earl of Wessex, is not your father. Raul Carducci is, and . . .'

'But Raul Carducci is dead,' interrupted Peter quietly. His heart was bleeding for Liana. God, how he wished for her sake that he had never set eyes on the story. But another person was involved, the girl he loved and would always love, and for Eleanora's sake, he had to know for certain what he already suspected. 'Why have you told us the truth now? Why did you not leave Eleanora and Nicholas in ignorance? What further harm would that have done?'

Liana inclined her head in his direction. The movement, untypically, lacked grace, seeming like that of an old woman. 'I think you already know the answer, Peter,' she said wearily. 'But will you tell me something first? Do you know the author of *The Two Girls*?'

'Raul Levi,' said Peter.

'Raul Levi!' Nicholas's voice broke with disbelieving emotion. 'Oh, God, Liana, tell me what I'm thinking isn't true, please.'

With a tremendous effort of will, Liana denied the tears which were longing to be spilled. The pain in his voice, the despair! And all put there by me, she thought. I'll never be able to make reparation.

'I only wish I could, Nicholas,' she said, her voice low and steady. It had to be that way. The last few ugly facts had to be spelled out quietly, clearly, so that not a doubt, not a shred of misunderstanding was left in the mind of anyone. She lifted her head and looked straight at Raul. 'Raul Levi is the Raul Carducci in the story of my life. They are one and the same man, only the name is different. Raul Levi is the father of my daughter, Eleanora.'

There was silence, broken eventually by Eleanora's horrified whisper. 'Raul Levi is my father?' She turned her head from side to side, frightened and confused.

Liana could not answer for a moment. Outside, the low rumble from the combine harvester stopped abruptly: the barley harvest was gathered in. In the silence that followed, an owl hooted, mournful, lonely. The long, drawn-out cry emphasized the stunned silence in the room.

'Yes, Raul Levi, is the man I knew as Raul Carducci, and he is your real father. I did truly think he was dead. I'm not telling you this and trying to excuse myself. There is no excuse, I know that. But I hope perhaps you will understand the reason for my deception. I vowed you would never know, that *no-one* would ever know. I thought, mistakenly, that the deception could harm no-one, that only I would suffer by never knowing peace of mind. But it seems that the saying is correct, and that true life really is stranger than fiction. Of all the men in the world you could have met and fallen in love with, fate ordained that you should meet the man who is your real father, and fall in love with him. Believe me, not for *any* *other* reason would I have told the truth.' Liana's voice took on a ring of defiance. 'I intended to deceive until the day I died. But circumstances have forced the truth out of me. So now at last you know.'

Liana looked around at the faces staring at her. 'Not only is Eleanora not Nicholas's daughter, but neither she nor I have a single drop of aristocratic blood in our veins. We spring from peasant stock, both of us.' At last she looked down towards Nicholas sitting silently by her side, but still she could not bring herself to look into his eyes. 'I ask only one thing of you, Nicholas, and that is, please don't blame Eleanora. None of this was her fault. I, and I alone made the decision to deceive you before she was even born. And to her you are her father. She has always loved you as her real father, and I know her love for you will never die. I beg you, if you can, please go on loving her as your daughter. I am the only one to be blamed. My whole life, since the day I met you, has been one long lie.'

Nicholas half rose as if to speak. But Liana put up her hand and stilled the words. 'There is one other sin to which I must confess, but which I must admit seems unimportant to me now. However, you may wish to do something about it. I suppose criminal charges could be brought against me; I leave that decision to you. It concerns William. It is true that he murdered James, but equally it is true that I, in turn, quite deliberately, murdered him. After he had dropped James through the ice, I pushed his head back into the water with the boat pole, and held it there until he drowned.' It was the only time her composure faltered. With a half-strangled sob at the memory, she said. '*That* is a sin I do not repent. I would do it again if necessary.'

Liana turned and walked to the door. There was nothing more to say; she had said it all. Now there were no more secrets. The room was dim; most of the candles had burned out. She switched on the lights and the magnificent Waterford chandeliers sprang into brilliance as a thin ribbon of smoke drifted up from the last candle. Pausing a moment, she turned to look at the family seated at the table, imprinting their dearly loved faces on her memory, but careful to avoid looking into their eyes. Then silently she opened the door and left the room.

*

'Well, that was one hell of a story,' said Donald Ramsay slowly. He was filled with admiration for Liana.

So was Dorothy. 'What a terrible life she had. The poor, poor girl,' she whispered.

'What a terrible life *she* had! Where do you think that leaves me?' Eleanora was near to hysteria. 'Suddenly she springs it on me that I am the bastard daughter of . . .' Turning and looking at Raul with an expression of revulsion on her face, she pulled her chair away from his with a violent movement. 'Oh, God, I've been sleeping with my own father! It makes my flesh crawl!' she said, clasping her hands to her mouth as if she was likely to be sick at any moment. 'I'll never, never forgive her for this. What has she done to me?' Her voice rose higher and higher on a thin wail of frenzied hysteria.

'To *us*,' shouted Raul, equally angry. 'Why the hell did she keep quiet all these years? I admit being into a lot of things, but incest is not one of them! Liana forced me into *that*.'

'If you hadn't deserted her when she was pregnant, you would have *known* your own daughter.' Peter was angry, too, angry at Raul, angry with Eleanora. Why couldn't they see it was an accident of fate? Why couldn't they stop thinking of themselves and think about Liana and Nicholas whose lives had just disintegrated, piece by piece, with every word she had spoken?

'I didn't know she *was* bloody well pregnant.'

'And would it have made any difference if you had?' Nicholas asked, his quiet voice contrasting with the raised tones of the others.

'I doubt it,' Peter answered for Raul. Everyone at the table looked at him. He was working himself up into a towering rage, something totally out of character for Peter. 'Everyone in the entertainment world knows of Raul Levi's reputation,' he said passionately. 'He is a ruthless womanizer, a ruthless manipulator, a man who has only one real interest in life, *himself.* I doubt that he was so very different in nineteen forty-four. Poor Liana, how well he took her in. Young, unhappy, vulnerable, she was easy prey for a man like Raul Levi to use and then discard when it suited him.' He leaned forward across the table, fist clenched in anger. Instinctively Raul moved back, afraid that Peter intended to smash the fist into his face. But he had no such intention. 'This is purely academic now that so many years have elapsed,' said Peter. 'But why *did* you not return to Liana on that day in March? And why the different name?'

Raul hesitated then shrugged his shoulders. What was the point of getting angry? What was done was done. He glanced down at the weeping Eleanora. Pity about her. He had gained a daughter, the last bloody thing he had ever wanted, and lost a lover! Monika would be surprised when he told her. Having got over the initial shock of the knowledge that he had been sleeping with his own daughter, Raul was no longer appalled. His complacency had been jolted badly, but that was all. And although he hated acknowledging it, he had known in some mysterious way that Eleanora had been lost to him from the moment Broadacres had come into view. Bloody ironic, he thought savagely, her hysterical weeping beginning to annoy him. She feels so much part of all this but she doesn't belong at all. Her bloodline doesn't make her one of this snotty-nosed aristocratic crowd, even if she does behave like one! Suddenly he longed for the earthiness of Monika Muller. They were two of a kind, and he knew where he stood with her. The sooner he left this damn place the better.

'Why did I not go back? Because I met Gustavo Simionato in a pavement café in Naples,' he said baldly, 'and he offered me a job on condition that I went with him that day to Sicily.'

'So you went?' said Nicholas with damning accusation.

'Of course I bloody well went.' Raul's full mouth twisted into a sneer. 'Why not? I had my career to think of.'

'And left a nineteen-year-old girl alone, in wartime, to fend for herself.'

'Christ almighty! She'd been fending all right for herself before I met her. She did very well as a prostitute, and now I hear that she had money and jewels hidden away, much more money than she ever let me know about. Oh, she could fend for herself all right. Or have you forgotten where her dowry came from? Jesus Christ! What a hypocrite you are.'

'Don't blaspheme at my dinner table,' snapped Lady Margaret leaning across and glowering at Raul, 'and answer Peter's other question. Why did you change your name?'

'I didn't change it. I just never told Liana my real name. I used my mother's name, Carducci. She was Italian, and my father Jewish. It wasn't good to have a Jewish name in nineteen forty-three – there was still plenty of anti-Semitism in Italy – so I played safe and used the name Carducci.'

'A prostitute,' wailed Eleanora loudly, ignoring Raul. 'My own mother a prostitute. How disgusting, how immoral. How could she? Oh, God, a prostitute!'

'Only because she had to be,' rapped Nicholas. 'Just you remember that, my girl, and for God's sake stop that weeping and wailing. You're giving me a headache.' Eleanora's sobbing subsided to a snuffle. 'Yes, a prostitute,' said Nicholas quietly. 'Difficult for you to understand, but then you've never known what it is to starve. And I do mean *really* starve. It was terrible in Naples in the last years of the war. We, the soldiers, had our rations brought on ships from England and America, but the Italians had nothing. Everything had been destroyed, their crops, their animals. People were reduced to eating earthworms and nettles if they were lucky enough to find them, and they boiled empty shells from the beach just to make fishy-tasting water, which they called soup! Your mother didn't sell her body from choice; she didn't even do it for herself; she did it to try to save her friend. But you, *you*,' his voice filled with scorn, 'you, who have never known what it is to want for anything, *anything*! You *chose* to be immoral. So don't flaunt your sanctimonious values in front of me, pretending to be better than your mother. You will never be half the woman she is. No-one forced you to live with Raul Levi,' Nicholas couldn't bring himself to say 'your father'. 'No, you chose to do it, out of your own free will. So don't condemn your mother for lack of morals, when your own appear to be non-existent!'

Eleanora gasped. 'How dare you say that to me? Comparing me with *her*. I don't know how you can bear to stand up for her after what she has done to you.' Agitated, she banged her fist on the table. 'I don't understand how anyone could . . .'

'Eleanora! Be quiet.' For once Lady Margaret's voice rang with unaccustomed authority. She struggled painfully to her feet, her knobbly, arthritic hands pushing back her chair with difficulty. Hastily rising, Richard Chapman hurried round, helped ease the chair back, and, fetching her sticks from where they rested against the wall, handed them to her. 'Thank you, Richard.'

'Oh, Margaret.' Richard's face was stricken with a mixture of bewilderment and sorrow. 'What can we say? What can we do?'

'Say? Do?' Margaret snorted with a short, sudden laugh. She turned slowly, taking care to get her balance evenly distributed on her sticks so that her twisted legs and painful feet supported her better. 'Say? Do?' she repeated in ringing tones. 'Before anyone *says* or *does* anything more, I would advise you to remember the words of our Lord, as told in the gospel of St John. "He that is without sin among you, let him cast the first stone at her."'

'Well said, Margaret,' whispered Dorothy, her eyes shining with unshed tears. 'Come, Donald, we'll go with Margaret. These young people have a lot of thinking and talking to do.'

The remaining occupants of the room sat mute, watching the three old people depart. Lady Margaret's words left an uncomfortable echo.

*

'Grandmother is right.' Eleanora spoke first, her voice muffled now by ragged sobs, low and hesitant as she struggled to come to terms with cognizance of the unacceptable facets of her own character. 'Who am I to judge her? It's quite true, I haven't got too much to be proud of.' Turning, she looked at Raul, aware of the scales falling from her eyes and with them the power of his superficial charm; now she saw him clearly. She knew, too, that she was looking at him for the last time. 'Neither of us have much to be proud of, have we?' she said with painful but forthright honesty, heedless that Nicholas, Peter and his parents were listening. 'Our affair was based on one thing, and one thing only, lust. And even if you were not my father it still wouldn't have been right. Lust is no substitute for love.'

'Christ!' Raul smashed both fists angrily down on the table, rattling the delicate coffee cups in their saucers. 'For God's sake stop being so damned self-righteous. It's not my fault I'm your damned father. And stop going on about lust! love! What the hell is the difference?'

'If you don't know now, then you never will,' said Peter.

'Shut up,' snarled Raul, a raw line of colour slashing his cheeks as his rage built up. 'There is only one goddamned thing that concerns me, and that is I find I've been sleeping with my own bloody daughter! I don't like that. As I said before, I'm not into incest. But just get this straight. It isn't my fault it happened. None of this is my fault. It's Liana's fault for bringing Eleanora up as the daughter of another man.'

He looked at Eleanora and saw the mixture of fear and dislike in her eyes. For a second, just a few split seconds, it flashed across his mind how different it might have been if he had been a different kind of man. A different man might have questioned the attraction he had instinctively felt for Eleanora. A different man might have felt a paternal affection towards a talented young girl. A different man would not have walked out on Liana. But he was Raul Levi, a man who had always regarded every woman as a sexual object, and because of that the attraction had irrevocably drawn him into a sexual relationship. Self-gratification, the basis of his life, had destroyed any chance there might have been of ever knowing his daughter as a daughter.

But the moment came and went in the time it took to draw a breath, and Raul banished it from his mind. He did not believe in wasting time on what might have been, only on what was. 'I'm going,' he said harshly. 'I shall never see any of you again.' He turned towards Eleanora. 'Especially you. You are not, never have been and never will be my daughter. I want to forget that any of this ever happened.'

With three swift strides he was at the door, but Nicholas was there before him. 'The story,' he said. 'What are you going to do with the story?'

Raul gave a short laugh. 'What the hell do you think? I'm going to burn it, of course. How you sort yourselves out is up to you. But I don't want my name dragged into the headlines for a bloody story. Professionally, things are going well for me, and that is exactly the way I intend to keep it.' He opened the door then paused and said, 'Ironic, isn't it? Originally I wrote that story thinking to exorcise ghosts of the past. And all I've succeeded in doing is creating a whole lot more!'

Nicholas looked at him. He could see quite clearly the shadow of a loss which Raul was incapable of seeing. Perhaps one day, he thought, in years to come, when he is an old man, Raul will realize that when he denied his daughter, he lost more than anyone here tonight. Nicholas knew from experience that broken pieces could in some miraculous way be stuck together. It would take time, but somehow he and the family would do it, and they would be whole again one day and that would include Eleanora. Whereas Raul would be alone with his ghosts.

'We are all haunted by the past,' he said. To Raul's surprise his voice was gentle. 'And we can never undo what has been done. Only learn to live with it.' He was thinking of the tangled web of deceit they had spun between them, he and Liana, ending in the death of James and the destruction of Eleanora's world as she had always known it.

Raul, knowing nothing of this, did not understand and wanted nothing from Nicholas. Least of all his pity. 'I shall not be haunted,' he said abruptly and opened the door to leave.

'Before you go,' Nicholas suddenly became very businesslike. 'I would like you to sign a document to the effect that you will never reveal the story my wife told us tonight; and that you will never publish any part of the story you wrote or anything else that you might know appertaining to any of the characters involved. Also I would like delivered into my hands all copies of the story, *The Two Girls*.'

Raul shrugged. 'I'll sign whatever you want if it will keep you happy.'

'It will,' said Nicholas. 'And the story?'

'There are only two copies, one of which I understand is here. The other I will send to you.'

Nicholas turned to Peter. 'Will you go with Raul to my study and draft a statement? I know I can trust you to make sure it's watertight.' He nodded towards Eleanora, who had left the table and was now standing staring out of the window into the darkness. 'I want to speak with Eleanora alone.'

Peter glanced across at Eleanora. Her shoulders were hunched with unhappiness. She looked so young – a child again, a small, bewildered, lost child. Liana's story had cast her adrift, broken all the ties of security she knew and loved. The vulnerability which Peter knew had always been there under the surface, just beneath her impetuous, bubbling vivacity, was now etched in every line of her body. He smiled sadly at Nicholas. 'Yes,' he said. 'She needs you.'

He could not help wishing that she needed him, but knew it was not yet his time. She had to come to terms with the new knowledge of herself. And more importantly, come to terms with the knowledge of who her real father was and what he had been to her. That would be difficult. He could almost feel her pain and revulsion from the tense lines of her body. I must be patient, Peter told himself. I must wait and help her when, and if, she asks for it. My time will come again eventually. But now she needs Nicholas to allay her fears and provide an anchor from which to fix her life once more. He followed Raul out of the room.

'We'll go, too.' Richard Chapman shepherded his wife Anne towards the door.

Anne hesitated. She wanted to say something comforting to Eleanora but everything she had heard, everything which had happened, was so far outside her range of experience, she was still finding it difficult to comprehend. Her own life was well ordered. She was not given to impulses, and imagination was not her strong point. But Eleanora's desperate unhappiness now and Liana's harrowing story earlier in the evening had upset her ordered world. It was that fact which touched her most. Order meant security, and security to Anne meant happiness. When she had fled from Broadacres, she had found the security and happiness she had needed with Richard Chapman. Now she wished it was within her power to endow Eleanora with a similar happiness.

Crossing to Eleanora she touched her arm. 'Don't worry too much, my dear. The time will come when you will be able to look back on tonight without pain or recrimination. Life works out in some very strange ways.'

'And none stranger than mine,' said Eleanora with a sad, wry smile.

'Oh, my poor darling, I didn't mean it like that. You know I didn't.' For once Anne threw caution to the winds and grabbed hold of Eleanora, hugging her tightly. 'I meant that one day you will be happy again, and all of this will seem unimportant. It will, it will, I promise.'

Eleanora hugged her back, grateful for the unexpected show of affection. 'Thank you, Anne,' she said. 'I can only hope you are right.'

'I am,' said Anne firmly. Richard was at the door, signalling frantically with his eyebrows that they should leave. She gave Eleanora a quick kiss on the cheek and followed him from the room.

Eleanora turned to Nicholas. She felt stiff and awkward, as if he were a stranger. 'People are surprising,' she said at last. 'Anne was the last person I thought would forgive my behaviour. I know what strict moral views she has, and I've hardly been a model young woman. I should think she must be very glad that Peter and I are finished.'

Nicholas ignored the remark about Peter. He wondered if, in all the chaos, anyone besides himself had realized the obvious. There was absolutely no impediment whatsoever now to Eleanora and Peter marrying if they wanted to, because they were not related in any way. Of course, Peter must have realized it, but in the aftermath of confusion, while everyone's minds were still occupied with Liana's astounding revelations, no-one else appeared to have even thought of it, least of all Eleanora. But that could be sorted out later. First of all, Nicholas wanted mother and daughter reconciled, reunited and able to look into each other's faces without bitterness or memories of the past standing in their way.

'I'm glad you think your grandmother was right,' he said quietly. 'And you must know that what she has learned tonight will not change her love for your mother. She and Liana became close friends before you were born, and nothing can shake the foundations of that. I'd like to think that in time you, too, will have some understanding.'

'She deceived you for me, her unborn child,' said Eleanora. 'I know that. I knew it even when I was screaming at her.' There was a long silence, then Eleanora said slowly. 'Tell me some more about what it was like in Italy when you first met Mummy.'

Nicholas was glad to oblige. He had wondered what he was going to say to Eleanora, how to comfort her. Talking about, and adding to the already graphic story Liana had told, helped him, too. When at last he had finished he said, almost to himself. 'But she was wrong about one thing. She didn't make me fall in love with her. I was a very, very willing suitor.'

He smiled at Eleanora. 'You may find it difficult to understand, but I think I fell in love with your mother the year before, when we first met so briefly in autumn nineteen forty-three. Yes, that was when I fell in love, on that October night, when Charlie Parsons and I pulled her from the bombed tenement building. Although like you, when I was young I had difficulty in differentiating between love and lust.' Eleanora flushed, but Nicholas, lost in his own thoughts, continued. 'I thought then that I wanted her physically because she was so beautiful, but now I know it was far more than that. The memory of her face never left me, and when she turned up in my office six months later, I knew I didn't want to let her go. I did look for Raul, but I must admit that for my own selfish reasons, I always hoped we would never find him. I always sensed that if we did, I'd lose her again. As you now know, we never did find Raul, and I married Liana.'

'Oh, Daddy, you really do love her, don't you? You don't blame her, even though she . . .' Suddenly Eleanora gasped, put her hand to her mouth and burst into tears. '*Daddy*, oh God, I forgot! I can't say that any more, can I?'

Gently, Nicholas took her hand in his. She trembles like a frightened bird, he thought tenderly. 'Look at me, Eleanora,' he said. She looked and saw a face glowing with warmth and the eyes of a compassionate, loving father. Her noisy tears quietened into soft crying. 'I *am* your father. I always have been and always will be. The ties of blood are not as strong as the ties of true love. Always remember that, Eleanora, and never doubt me, whatever people may say, now, or in the future.'

'I'll remember,' she whispered. Reaching up she softly touched his face then flung herself into his arms, holding him so tightly he thought he must suffocate. 'I'll remember,' she repeated, slowly letting go her tight hold. Wiping her eyes with the back of her hand, as a child might have done, she managed a shaky smile. 'I love you, Daddy,' she said, 'and I've never felt so loved and cared for as I did a moment ago when your strong arms were around me.'

Nicholas smiled. 'I've got my daughter back,' he said softly. 'And as for the past. Your affair with Raul Levi . . .'

Eleanora shuddered and backed away. 'I feel so ashamed,' she whispered. 'I know I shall feel dirty for the rest of my life.'

'As for your affair with Raul Levi,' Nicholas continued in a firm voice. 'I'm telling you now, as your father, forget it. It's finished, it's history. Water under the bridge.'

'Muddy water,' said Eleanora.

Nicholas smiled. 'We all muddy the water from time to time, my dear. That was what your grandmother meant about casting the first stone. None of us are innocent. Now you must be brave and go forward without looking over your shoulder.'

'It won't be easy.'

'Life very rarely is. But we must still try and go on. And you will, won't you, darling?'

'Yes, I'll try.'

'Good girl.' He kissed her tear-stained cheek. 'Now, get some rest. I'll see you tomorrow.'

Eleanora kissed him back and left the room. Nicholas watched her go. She looked so young, but so weary and dispirited, all her effervescent life extinguished. But youth was on her side. God willing, she would recover soon.

Now Nicholas knew he must go to Liana. They must talk, and this time there would be nothing between them, no ghosts of the past to blur and distort. Neither of them had any skeletons left in their cupboards now. This evening Liana had finally stripped away the remaining lies and deceptions and they were free to face each other and make a new start. It was what he wanted more than anything in the world.

As eager as a young boy going for an assignation with his first love, he ran up the stairs and along the long corridors towards Liana's bedroom, sure that she would be there. He knew his Liana. She would be sitting looking at the view she loved so much, the sweeping lawns of Broadacres unfolding away up to the downs on the edge of the valley. Moonlight shone in regular square patches through the windows on to the rose-red Wilton carpet of the corridor which led to the bedrooms.

'The corridor always looks so cold,' she said before commissioning the factory at Wilton to weave the carpet in one continuous piece in the colour of her choosing.

Nicholas smiled. She had been right, of course. She always was. Now, even in the moonlight, the corridor glowed with all the warmth of a summer rose.

'Liana I . . .' impatient, he began speaking, hardly waiting for the door into her bedroom to open.

The door swung back, revealing the large room brilliant with moonlight. But it was empty, quite empty. Nicholas stopped. He had been so sure, so certain that at last they could go forward together, all the shadows put behind them. Surely Liana knew he loved her no matter what had happened in the past? Then the devastating thought struck him. Perhaps she did not love him, perhaps in spite of everything she still loved Raul. It was quite possible. His own love for her had no reason, no logic. Not for one moment had he ever stopped to consider whether or not Liana was worth it. Love was something that existed beyond the power of reason.

He tried to think back. Had she intimated her feelings towards Raul by any word or intonation? Despairing, he sank down on the bed amidst the scattered, discarded clothes. She must have been in a terrible hurry to leave. His mind was numb, incapable now of lucid thought. A future without Liana was inconceivable.

PART FIVE
1966—1968

Chapter Thirty-Three

The flowers appeared regularly, once a month, without fail – always poppies, not the large cultivated ones but small wild flowers, delicate in colour and shape. They came from an expensive florist in Knightsbridge and were driven down to the churchyard at Longford by a man in a van. The van driver, apart from the fact that he was to put them on baby James's grave, knew nothing. Neither did anyone in the shop in Knightsbridge. They were ordered and paid for by post; the florist merely followed the instructions. There was no card, no message, nothing to intimate who they came from, but their presence eased the loneliness in Nicholas's life and helped keep hope alive during the next two years. They had to be from Liana. Before disappearing she had often picked wild poppies and placed them on James's grave.

'Poppies are for sleep,' she said. 'I want him to sleep in peace.'

When he looked at each month's fresh flowers Nicholas could hear her voice as clearly as if she were standing beside him. And on the first anniversary of James's death, after Liana's disappearance, a cross of snowdrops came. Then he was certain. Liana *was* sending them. But finding her proved an impossibility.

She was not with Raul. It had not taken Nicholas long to ascertain that fact. He was now living quite openly with Monika Muller and it was even rumoured that they might marry. But where was Liana? She still cared about Broadacres, that much he knew. The business affairs of the Broadacres estate and all subsidiary firms continued to run smoothly, and in fact they were making more money than ever before. Nicholas told Jason Penrose to do exactly as Liana instructed him. Jason was receiving his orders from Liana by letter, always posted in London, and was communicating with her through a box number. Nicholas wrote to the same box number, but his letters were returned unopened. He could not understand it. Why had she gone? Why did she want nothing more to do with *him*? Had she really found living with him so hateful?

Lady Margaret understood, or thought she did. In her opinion, Liana had finally realized what Margaret had been certain of all along: she loved

Nicholas. And it was because she loved him that she had fled. Unable to live with the hurt she had brought him, she had fled in the mistaken belief that he would be better off without her, not realizing that she was hurting him far more by staying away. There was Eleanora to think of as well. Margaret could only guess at the ghastly added guilt Liana felt by knowing her deceit had ended with father and daughter living together as lovers. How Margaret longed to be able to find Liana and tell her these things.

She agreed wholeheartedly with Donald when he said, 'The longer Liana puts off facing her daughter and husband, the harder it will be for all of them.'

But she did not tell Nicholas that. He was depressed enough already without her adding to it. He needed reassurance, so she said, 'It will be all right. Eventually she will understand that you still love her and that nothing can change that. And she must long to see Eleanora, too. When she finds out that Eleanora is back, living here, then she will return to Broadacres.'

She sounded so positive, Nicholas wished she were right but was not so sure. However, there was nothing he could do but hope, so he got on with life at Broadacres where there was always plenty to be done. Besides, there was Eleanora who needed him at her side with the constant reassurance of his love.

Christmas 1966 was desolate without Liana. To Nicholas the celebrations seemed pointless, but he followed the traditions just the same. The party was held as usual in the East Gallery. But it was a lack-lustre affair. No-one mentioned the disappearance of Lady Liana, but, of course, Nicholas knew the estate workers gossiped amongst themselves. It was inevitable. He wondered what conclusions they had drawn, because apart from Dorothy and Donald Ramsay, no-one outside the family knew the truth. He supposed they were thinking that he and Liana would eventually have a divorce. It was very noticeable. No-one even mentioned Liana's name.

It was a strain for everyone, and Meg observed that there was far less alcohol consumed than usual.

'They are all afraid that after one drink too many, they might blurt out a question,' she said to her mother.

'As well they might,' Mary Pragnell agreed. She and Wally had discussed Liana's disappearance at length. 'Some say as how they had a row and he packed her off. But I can't believe Lord Nicholas sent her away,' said Mary. 'You've only got to watch him, wandering around the place like a lost dog. No, he never sent her away. But then, I can't believe either that Lady Liana would go of her own free will. She always loved it here so much. Broadacres was her life.'

'And I'm certain she loved Lord Nicholas, too,' said Meg.

'Seems like you was wrong,' was Wally's gloomy verdict.

But such was the loyalty of everyone on the estate that apart from mulling over Liana's disappearance with their respective spouses, it was never a subject for discussion at work or social occasions. By tacit agreement, each and every one of them kept their own counsel.

At Eleanora's insistence, Nicholas went with her to Winchester Cathedral for the Blessing of the Crib before the Christmas Eve party. He had not wanted to go, at first refusing point blank to even countenance it, but eventually Peter persuaded him.

'It's all part of the healing process,' he told Nicholas, 'for you as well as Eleanora. I know the last time we went was with James and you don't want to be reminded. But it is because of that, because it was such a happy occasion, that you must go. We must all remember the happy times, and strive to keep those memories vivid and alive. Human beings spend far too much time remembering bad things, forgetting that the important thing is to treasure the good memories. Each moment spent polishing a good memory keeps it fresh in our hearts. Of course, we can never completely banish bad memories, nor should we even attempt to, but we can keep them in perspective, overshadowed by the light of happier times.'

'Sometimes I think you should have been a priest, Peter. You have a wisdom far beyond your years. You would make a good counsellor.'

Peter pulled a face. 'I have not the vocation,' he said wryly. 'I can't pretend I don't want a woman in my life. I want marriage and children, not the emptiness of celibacy.'

'Marriage to Eleanora?'

It was something Nicholas had not asked before. Neither Eleanora nor Peter had mentioned it, and Nicholas had noticed that Eleanora made no effort to seek Peter out. If anything it was the reverse. She melted away into the shadows on the few occasions Peter had visited them. They appeared friendly on the surface, but as far as Nicholas knew, she had never been alone with Peter since her return to Broadacres. A week after Liana's disappearance, Peter, of necessity, returned to Hollywood to work, only now flying back to England for Christmas, intending to stay two weeks before returning to California for another three or four months. In the meantime, although she continued with her singing, and went to London once a week for a lesson, Eleanora showed no signs of wanting to resume her singing career. Grateful to have her presence at Broadacres because she eased his own loneliness, Nicholas made no attempt to persuade her to go back to the theatre. And she seemed happy to pick up her old life of riding and hunting. Nicholas was glad of company in the saddle. Neither his mother nor Donald Ramsay would ever sit astride a horse again, and he missed their lively camaraderie.

'Yes, marriage to Eleanora,' said Peter in answer to his question. 'There is no-one else for me. Never will be. Not being related simplifies things. We have nothing to fear now about having children.'

'What does Eleanora say?'

Peter shook his head. 'I haven't mentioned it to her. She's not ready yet. At the moment she is still consumed with guilt over her affair with Raul Levi. She has to get over that first. But I can be patient. Sooner or later she will realize that she needs me as much as I need her.'

But although he sounded and felt confident that Christmas of 1966, Peter began to feel impatient as time passed and still there was no sign of Eleanora turning towards him. She took to spending much spare time with the Pragnells, now happily retired from the home farm and living in a small cottage in Longford village. To Eleanora they seemed like the passing seasons of the year, certain and predictable. Their conversation was undemanding. They never asked difficult questions, never asking what she was going to do with her life, never even asked after her mother, although she guessed they must often have wanted to. Instead of wasting time talking, Mary Pragnell taught her how to cook the traditional country dishes: pike in cider in the coarse-fishing season; squab pie after a good pigeon shoot; cakes; pastries; and bread. It was bread Eleanora enjoyed making most. It was such hard physical work kneading the dough, good therapy for her to vent her growing frustration.

For as time went by she did desperately long to speak to Peter, to ask his forgiveness, and to find out whether or not he still cared for her. If he had given her some indication that to him she was more than just an old friend, she might have plucked up courage and spoken long ago. But he did not. Instead he seemed content to resume the previous uncomplicated relationship of their childhood. He wanted her as a friend, nothing more, and so precious to her was the friendship that did remain, that Eleanora never dared to speak in case she broke the fragile thread.

On the day before Christmas Eve 1967, Eleanora went for a morning gallop on Diabolus. Peter had just come back to Hampshire from his London flat, and he joined her. Together, they flew like the wind over the downs in the pale winter sunshine, horses' hooves drumming into the hard, frosty ground, their breath billowing like smoke in the cold air. When the horses were reined in on reaching the top of the ridge, steam rose from their lathering flanks.

'They'll need a good rub-down as soon as we get back,' said Peter, rubbing the neck of his big bay. The horse snickered with pleasure at his touch. Eleanora watched in envy. How she longed for the affectionate touch of his hand, to feel Peter's arms around her, to be held close. What did he think of her? She looked for a sign, but there was nothing. Her affair with Raul had poisoned that kind of love. Suddenly she wanted to weep. Peter started to trot briskly down the other side of the ridge. 'Let's take the long way back,' he shouted over his shoulder. 'It will be just like the old days.'

'It will *never* be like the old days,' said Eleanora abruptly, and took Diabolus down the steep slope at breakneck speed. Her eyes were filled with tears, and it was just as well Diabolus knew the route so well; it was only due to his skill that he did not break a leg or she her neck. But when they reached the bottom, he arched his neck and turned to nip at her riding boots, a gesture of reprimand. 'Sorry, old boy,' Eleanora patted his neck, remorseful now. 'I know I shouldn't have been so reckless.' Then, without waiting for Peter, she dug in her heels. Diabolus responded enthusiastically. He didn't mind now they were on the flat. He thundered along on the track back towards the stables at Broadacres.

Peter descended at a safer, more leisurely pace, his eyes reflective. Eleanora had sounded upset. Perhaps the waiting was over. Maybe now, at long last, they could begin talking and hopefully put their lives in order.

Back at Broadacres, Eleanora gave Diabolus a vigorous rub-down and covered him with a warm blanket. Sensing her distress, he nuzzled her, wrinkling his velvety nose, nipping affectionately at her hair and blowing out noisily through his nostrils. In spite of her misery, Eleanora smiled. 'You're getting to be a big softie in your old age,' she told him, giving him a carrot.

Leaving him contentedly crunching, she leaped on the ramshackle bike always kept in the stables, and cycled over to the Pragnells' cottage.

The kitchen smelled like a brewery. Mary had just mixed some fresh yeast with sugar and warm water ready to make the Christmas bread for the next day's party. 'You're just in time,' she told Eleanora, 'if you want to make the cinnamon bread.'

Eleanora poked at the yeast. It was good and fresh and was sponging up nicely. 'Yes, I do,' she said, 'I feel like pounding the living daylights out of something.'

'Kneading is what dough wants, not pounding,' said Mary severely. But she noticed the look of unhappiness on Eleanora's face, and as Wally was not there to stop her she decided to break her silence and say something. 'Is Master Peter back from London yet?' she asked casually.

'Yes, he's back.' Eleanora was non-committal. Then anger got the better of her. 'Why do you call him "Master Peter" as if he's a child? He isn't. He's a man, and I'm a woman.'

''Tis habit,' said Mary, eyeing her curiously. 'But I knows full well you're grown up.'

'Oh, Mary,' wailed Eleanora. 'I don't feel grown up. Not any more. I'm treated like a child. Everyone is so *careful*. We don't talk to each other, not properly, and I don't know what they are thinking, what Peter's thinking. And I miss Peter terribly, and, oh Mary, everything is such a *mess*.'

If Mary was surprised by this outburst, she did not show it. Wiping her floury hands on the front of her apron she said firmly, 'Then 'tis about time you did grow up, my girl. I'm not family, so it wouldn't be right for me to interfere, especially as I don't know all the ins and outs. But I'm telling you now, get on that bike of yours and go and find your father and start talking. Say whatever you've got to say, and then see what happens.'

'I don't know whether I can.'

'Thought you told me just now you was a woman,' said Mary scornfully.

Eleanora cycled back to Broadacres thoughtfully. She found her father struggling with the farm accounts in the library office. He looked up, smiling, as she entered, glad of the interruption.

It's now or never, thought Eleanora, and plunged head first into the conversation before she lost her nerve. 'Daddy, what would you think, I mean, how would you feel about me if you were Peter?'

Nicholas was startled. 'If I were Peter?' he repeated.

'Yes.' Oh dear, this was difficult, but once started Eleanora knew she had to go on. 'I mean, about me sleeping with, with . . .'

'Raul Levi?'

Eleanora nodded. 'Yes. Except that he wasn't just a man called Raul Levi, he was my own father. Would you . . . could you love someone who'd been guilty of incest?' Eleanora's voice sank to a whisper.

'If I loved her, it wouldn't make any difference.'

'But I wonder what Peter thinks. He's so distant.'

'Do you love Peter?' Nicholas asked slowly.

'Oh, yes. I've never stopped. I tried to pretend to myself that I had, that was why I . . .' her voice petered out.

'Water under the bridge,' Nicholas interrupted, 'remember?'

'Yes, I remember. But it's not so easy.'

'I told you that I didn't think it would be,' said Nicholas gently. 'But you can't let one mistake ruin the rest of your life. Learn from it. Learn not to be impulsive, learn to consider others. Let something good come from it, and get on with your life.'

'I know what you say is right and sensible, but I'm not sure how to go on.'

'You said a moment ago that you had never stopped loving Peter.'

'Yes, but . . .'

'Then you must tell him. He's not a mind-reader. He doesn't know how you feel.'

'But I can't just go up to him and blurt it out.'

'Why not? No point in pussy-footing around. You've wasted enough time as it is.'

'You sound just like Gran does sometimes,' said Eleanora, a wisp of a smile crossing her face.

Nicholas noticed the smile and was relieved. 'I take that as the supreme compliment,' he said.

Bullied by Nicholas, Eleanora remounted the bicycle and rode across the valley towards the Chapmans' house. Peter saw her coming in through the iron gates into the drive. She swept through, pedalling quite fast, but as the house came nearer gradually her legs slowed down. She was pedalling more slowly now, seeming to hesitate. Afraid that she might change her mind, Peter flung open the huge Gothic front door, leaping down the four steps with one bound, racing down the drive to meet her, finishing standing square in front of her, blocking her path.

'Peter, I've got to talk to you.' They weren't the words Eleanora had planned to say, but no matter. She had said something.

'I know,' he said. He was breathless even though he had only run a short way.

Eleanora dismounted and Peter took the bicycle, propping it carelessly against the withered wintry branches of the roses. He took her hand in his, and in silence they walked into the house, through the hall and into the library where a log fire burned brightly in the stone fireplace. The bicycle stayed where it had been so abruptly abandoned. It was there for a long time, perched drunkenly between a rose and a lavender bush.

It was all so much easier than either of them had ever dreamed or hoped that it could be. At first hesitant, then firmer as she remembered her father's advice, Eleanora said, 'Peter, I want you to know that I still love you. It's something I have to tell you, although it doesn't mean that I expect anything from you. I expect nothing, because I know I deserve nothing. Running off and jumping into bed with Raul Levi was stupid and wrong, and I'm ashamed of myself. I would still be ashamed, even if he hadn't turned out to be my own father.'

Peter put his fingers up to her lips to stop the words, then drew her down so that they were kneeling on the rug before the open fire. 'Didn't I always tell you that your recklessness would lead you into trouble?' he said, but Eleanora knew from his gentle smile that what had seemed so dreadful only seconds ago was suddenly quite unimportant. 'But nothing you have done or might do,' said Peter softly, 'will ever stop my loving you.'

'You still love me?'

'Always, my darling, always.'

Peter leaned back against the old leather chesterfield and pulled Eleanora into his arms. With a sigh of relief she fitted her head into the hollow of his shoulder. 'I feel as though I've come home at last,' she whispered, afraid to speak too loudly in case she broke the spell.

'And so you have, almost.'

'Almost?' Eleanora twisted so that she could look up at him.

'Yes, *really* home will be after we're married.'

'Yes, I suppose it will.' She was dying to ask him when he thought that might happen, but kept her peace. Peter would lead and she would follow. Slowly Eleanora reached up and touched his face in a feather-light caress. 'I'll marry you, Peter, whenever you say and wherever you say. I leave it to you, and afterwards I will follow you to the ends of the earth if necessary.'

They kissed, a long, slow, gentle kiss, full of passion, and yet at the same time strangely chaste. So much had happened since their last kiss. They had both changed. Now, reaching out to each other, it was with a new maturity. Eleanora was aware of a humility and tenderness she had never possessed before. She savoured the rediscovery of their love, praying that they would succeed in keeping it sweet and pure.

'It won't be necessary to go to the ends of the earth,' whispered Peter at last, into a warm corner of her mouth. 'Only to London for a while, and then later we'll move back to Broadacres. I'll ask your father if we can have a wing of the house.'

The thought was idyllic. By the time they had finished talking, it was much too dark and late for Eleanora to ride back to Broadacres on her bicycle, so Peter took her and the bike in the estate car. Contented, they drove slowly across the winding river valley towards the big, honey-coloured house that would soon be their home. Neither had hidden anything in their hours of talking. Peter made Eleanora see that she had nothing to be afraid of by telling the truth so she had poured out her heart, all her doubts, her fears and the subsequent growing shame of the life she and Raul had led. She found that the truth, once out in the open, could be dealt with. And how easy it proved to be with someone like Peter to help her. She understood, too, when Peter said he did not want to make love until they were married. It seemed right. Between them they had wiped the slate clean. Now they could look forward to their wedding day. And it would be a very special day.

'Something we will both remember for as long as we live,' said Peter. 'The day we make a commitment to each other before God.'

Eleanora smiled, her new-found sensitivity enabling her to accept how important Peter's religion was to him. The old resentment had gone. Although she still did not completely understand, she knew it important because it was an integral part of Peter's being and could not be separated. And now she knew she did not even want it to be. It made him what he was, the good, gentle, but emotionally strong man she loved.

As the estate car turned in under the triumphal stone arch of Broadacres, Eleanora glanced up at Peter's profile. Already the memory of the time spent with Raul had faded. Now it was less of a nightmare, more like a bad dream. How could I have ever for a single moment doubted my love for Peter, she wondered. How could I have been so stupid?

They found Nicholas and Lady Margaret comfortably settled by the fire in the Grey Room.

'Have a whisky.' Nicholas jumped up the moment they entered the room and moved across to the tantalus on the sideboard.

Eleanora sensed he was nervous. 'It's all right, Daddy,' she whispered. Her eyes shining.

Wheeling round, an unstoppered decanter in his hand, he said. 'You mean . . .?'

'Yes, Eleanora has agreed to marry me,' said Peter. 'In a Catholic church, sir. I hope you won't object.'

'Why should I? I was married in a Catholic church myself. May the first nineteen forty-four, in a tiny little church in Naples.'

Margaret banged her stick on the floor. 'As long as you have a blessing here in Longford Parish Church, so that I can come and have a new hat, you can get married in the same blessed church in Naples for all I care. But don't waste any more time. I'd like some great-grandchildren before I move on to the next life.'

'Oh, Gran,' said Eleanora laughing. 'Give us time!'

'A toast,' said Nicholas, pouring enormous measures of whisky. 'To Eleanora and Peter.'

'To Eleanora and Peter,' echoed Margaret.

A long silence followed. The happy mood suddenly blighted as they all thought of Liana. 'Oh, how I wish Mummy were here,' said Eleanora.

*

Lady Margaret longed to throw away her sticks. The porter at Waterloo was very kind. He had seen her at once as she struggled off the train, sticks getting mixed up with the handles of her luggage, and had taken her cases and put them on a trolly.

'I'll take them over to the taxi rank for you, luv,' he said. He knew it had to be the taxi rank. The old girl would never manage the escalator and tube.

But he was walking much too fast. The taxis at the far end of the Waterloo concourse seemed miles away to Margaret's painful feet and legs. I wish someone had warned me old age would be so damned painful, she thought resentfully, and began to wish she had not come up to London. Probably a waste of time anyway, common sense told her. There was no guarantee that Liana would turn up.

The porter loaded the cases into the taxi and accepted the tip Lady Margaret pressed into his hand. Five pounds! The old girl was generous. 'Thank you,' he said, tipping his cap.

'The Waldorf, please.' The taxi sped forward. Margaret leaned back and looked out of the window. She had forgotten how lovely London looked on an April day in the sunshine. Now that the weight was off her feet she felt excited, sure that her course of action was right. Somebody had to do *something*.

The lilac was in full bloom in the Embankment Gardens, pushed on to flower ahead of country lilac by the heat of the city. The heavy flower heads on the bushes drooped in a gorgeous disarray of pale and deep purple, throwing the serried ranks of scarlet tulips in the flower beds before them into greater contrast. Margaret smiled. The tulips looked like miniature guardsmen, bright scarlet and black, all standing upright and still in perfectly straight rows. They had a few beds like that at Broadacres – people expected some formal flower displays – but on the whole, under Liana's guidance, they had gradually reverted to the old-fashioned flowers, planted in clumps not rows. Liana, Liana, she sighed. Always her thoughts returned to Liana. Would she come?

*

'I've already ordered tea, my dear. Salmon and cucumber sandwiches and fruit cake. I hope that is all right.' The pianist tinkled away on the grand piano, a medley of half-recognizable, instantly forgettable tunes.

Liana sat down opposite Lady Margaret. 'You were very sure that I would come.'

'Not sure at all,' Margaret admitted, 'but hopeful.'

'You got at me in a very sneaky way, putting an open letter in the middle of papers I had to read.' Liana smiled hesitantly. 'I thought I was the one with the devious mind! How did you persuade Jason Penrose to do it? I'd left very strict instructions that I was not to be contacted by anyone.'

The tea arrived and Margaret poured them both a cup. 'I decided that at my age it was about time I did a little bullying. So I bullied him, and he succumbed.' She reached into the depths of her voluminous handbag and pulled out a sealed letter. 'This is for you.'

Liana looked at it. Half of her hoped it would be Nicholas's writing on the envelope – she was regretting sending back his letters unopened – but it was not. She recognized Lady Margaret's hand. 'Why this?' she asked, waving the envelope, 'Now that we are together we can talk. I don't need letters.'

'Do you read *The Times*?' Margaret ignored the reference to the envelope.

'Only the Financial Section.'

Margaret nodded. 'I thought as much.' So she was right. Liana had not seen the announcement of Eleanora's engagement to Peter. She waited a moment, then asked abruptly, 'Are you happy?'

There was a long silence. The tinkling piano intruded into the thoughts of the two women. Margaret's spirits plunged. She suddenly felt terribly depressed. Perhaps she was being a silly old woman and had got it all wrong. Maybe Liana *was* happier to be left alone. Perhaps she had even met another man. But no, she dismissed that thought as foolish. Liana loved Nicholas, she was sure of it, and she certainly loved her daughter. She must miss them both.

'Happy,' said Liana at last, her voice soft and reflective. 'I'm not sure I know what happiness is. Or even if I ever did. One thing is certain, I've gone so far from that emotion that I'm not sure I could remember how to be happy.' She looked at Margaret, who saw that her dark eyes were as beautiful as ever, but not impenetrable as before, not as remote. Now they were sad. 'But I am at peace,' Liana said at last.

'You make it sound as if you were dead,' remarked Margaret wryly, briskly passing over a plate of sandwiches.

The tiny brown triangles of bread reminded Liana with vivid, startling clarity, of the first tea she had eaten with Margaret at Broadacres when the sandwiches had been made with Mrs Catermole's stale bread. A vision of the house, with the two cedars standing sentinel flashed before her. Then one after another came other visions, all kept at bay for so long, now released by meeting Margaret. Nicholas and Eleanora on their horses; the mêlée of the meet with hounds and horses everywhere; the gardens; the river; the home farm. Her eyelids pricked with unshed tears. She missed everything about Broadacres and she longed to see Nicholas and Eleanora, to know what they were doing. But she had promised herself she would not ask, and she did not.

'In a way, I suppose I *am* dead,' she answered sombrely.

'You don't have to be. Nicholas loves you. He misses you very much. If you had read his letters you would know that.'

'I wish I could believe you, Margaret. But I cannot; and I don't want his pity, I couldn't bear that. And it must be pity, not love, because he has no reason to love me. Indeed, he has every reason not to.'

'When did reason ever enter into loving?' asked Margaret crossly. 'Donald warned me that you would be awkward.'

'How are Donald and Dorothy?' In spite of her resolve not to ask anything, the words popped out of their own accord.

'Getting older like me,' said Margaret, 'and not willing to sit around any longer watching you young people mess up your lives. As Donald keeps reminding me, we don't know how much longer we shall be here. "Our tenancy on this life is nearly up. The Landlord will be calling in the lease any day." That is what he says.'

Liana looked distressed: a world without Margaret, Dorothy and Donald was unthinkable. 'Tell him from me not to be so morbid,' she said.

'It would be better coming from your own lips.' Margaret stopped, the stubborn look she knew of old was on Liana's face. 'Determined to suffer, aren't you? Determined to take *all* the blame. Not willing to be a little generous and ease the lives of others by allowing them some guilt.'

'Oh, Margaret, now you are being ridiculous. How can I possibly ease the lives of others by allowing *them* guilt?'

Margaret did not answer the question. Instead she pointed to the envelope, now lying on the table. 'Put that in your handbag,' she said. 'There is a date written in the top left-hand corner of the envelope and a time. That is when you must open it.'

'Why the mystery?' Liana was surprised. When she had met Margaret at the Waldorf, the last thing she had expected was a cloak and dagger operation.

'Now,' said Margaret fishing in her handbag again and eventually retrieving another envelope which she passed to Liana. 'You must open this tomorrow. When you have read it, you can either use what is inside or tear it up. For all our sakes, I pray that you will use it.'

'You make it sound almost ominous,' Liana said slowly, turning the envelope over and over in her hands.

Margaret smiled suddenly. 'The last time I saw you, we heard what you called the final chapter of your story. But you missed something, the last paragraph.' She tapped the envelope. 'This is the last paragraph of the final chapter,' she said, 'and you should be part of it.' She reached across the low table, and grasped Liana's slender hand in her own wrinkled, mis-shapened one. 'I love you', she said, 'like a daughter. Remember that.'

Chapter Thirty-Four

Now she was here it drew her like a magnet, the craggy building standing atop the hillside. Everything looked just the same, and yet at the same time strangely different. What was it? Then Liana realized. Coming back after twenty-four years she was viewing the scene with adult eyes. When she had left, she had been little more than a child, so her parting view was that of the child who had grown up here, as were her memories. In those far-off days, it had always seemed to Liana that the *castello* was at the peak of a mountain; now she had a better perspective. In comparison to the towering mountains in the background, the *castello* was on a hill, a very large hill, but a hill none the less.

She paused halfway up to take a breath; it was a very steep hill, the sun of the first morning in May burned her bare arms. Being away for so many years, she had forgotten how hot the southern Italian sun could be at this time of year. England in May was usually blessed with a gentle, damp warmth. Here it was hot and dry. When she stopped, the familiar aromas and sounds of her childhood permeated her senses: wild thyme and rosemary; the hum of a thousand insects on the hillside and the harsh sawing sound of the cicadas hidden away in the branches of the silver-grey olive trees, and umbrella pines. What had once been a track up the hillside to the village of San Angelo was now a road surfaced with tarmacadam. Hardly surprising, considering the last time Liana had walked this way was twenty-four years ago. But on reaching the fork, she was surprised. The track leading up to the *castello*, which she had fully expected to find overgrown and neglected, was also surfaced with newly laid tarmacadam. It was not often used, that much was evident from the weeds which were beginning to grow at the edges, but nevertheless she could see the dusty marks of tyres on the road. Someone had come this way recently.

A delicious smell of fresh coffee, mixed with that of tomatoes and garlic being cooked in oil drifted along from the direction of the village of San Angelo. Liana was tempted to stop and see if the taverna in the village square still existed. During the war it had closed from lack of food, but perhaps now it sold coffee. Then she looked at her watch. There was no time, not if she was to follow the instructions given her by Margaret in the first letter, and she was a whole day late as it was.

Her initial reaction on opening the letter as instructed after leaving Margaret at the Waldorf, had been a stubborn, no. How could Margaret ask her to do such a thing? Especially now, when she knew the full story. No, Liana had decided, she could not possibly do what was asked of her. So she had put the letter away and did the usual thing, sought refuge in work. Jason Penrose was inundated with instructions and Broadacre Estates made a killing on the gold market owing to Liana's prudent buying before the gold panic in March 1968. But all the time the words of Margaret's letter kept intruding, displacing the printing of every page she tried to read. Eventually Liana gave in, and, getting it out, read the letter one more time. It was signed by Margaret, with a PS at the bottom from Donald and Dorothy.

My dear Liana

I'm sorry for the subterfuge, but knowing you as I do I was sure that if I just spoke, you would argue (successfully) against me. So I am writing my words down in black and white. This way, they are not fleeting, they won't disappear on puffs of my aged breath. This way my thoughts will stay on the paper and (unless you choose to burn the letter immediately) they can be read more than one time.

When I look back on the last twenty-four years, I can clearly see the thread of tragedy running through all our lives. But make no mistake, it was not put there by you alone; you were only a part of it. But as well as tragedy, I see much happiness and many good things. Don't forget these things, Liana. Remember the bright days as well as the dark ones.

Perhaps it was all meant to be. I don't know. But whatever the reason, we must learn from our mistakes. If we don't learn something in this life, what point is there in even being born? We have all made mistakes, you, Nicholas, me, Eleanora, Anne and Richard. Only Peter seems to have managed not to have blundered; although perhaps he should have hung on to Eleanora more tightly, and not have let her go rushing off to Italy. Or should he?

You see, my dear, when I discussed all this with Donald and Dorothy, we all came to the same conclusion. In a strange way, it was a good thing that Eleanora met up with Raul and brought him home, because their relationship was the trigger to the truth. If you are thinking that only more unhappiness has come from that knowledge, then you are very much mistaken. One very positive and good thing has emerged. We all know now that there is nothing to prevent Eleanora and Peter from marrying, and they do *intend to marry – very soon. If* they *have been able to come to terms with the past, (and you must be sensitive enough to know how difficult that has been for Eleanora) then surely* you *can do the same!*

I can't promise the paradise of eternal happiness, but surely it is worth trying *to pick up the threads of your former life? The past is the past. What is done is done. It only bears a relevance to the future if you let it.*

So I ask you to go back to Italy, because I think Donald Ramsay is right. He says you must go back to your roots, and then you will see that the past twenty-four years count for far more than the life you led before. You are a different person now. You are a woman of forty-three years, and you came to England as a young girl of nineteen. Donald says that only after you have returned to Italy and finally laid the ghosts of the past to rest by yourself, can you ever hope to accept them for what they really are: links, in the chain which is your life, links which are an integral part of you, but not in any destructive sense. You are the continuation of everything which has gone before, love and *sorrow. Only when you can see this will you truly belong to us.*

There, my dear, I have admitted it – belong to us. It isn't only for your sake that I am trying to help. I am being a selfish old woman. It is for my sake. I want you back. Everyone at Broadacres wants you back.

Use the air ticket and fly to Naples. Open the second envelope when you are at your former home, the castello *near San Angelo. Don't think I am being dramatic and silly, please,* please, *open it on the date and at the time on the envelope – not before, and not after. This is* very *important.*

I am praying that you will do as I ask.

Your loving mother, Margaret.

Then in Dorothy's handwriting:

PS 'Years steal

Fire from the mind as vigour from the limb:

And life's enchanted cup but sparkles near the brim.'

Donald says to tell you, Byron knew what he was talking about. So don't waste time! Love, Dorothy and Donald.

Liana knew now, as she climbed the last few steps of the way up to the Roman gateway into the *castello*, that Donald was right. He knew more than most just what the years could steal, although it could never steal fire from *his* mind. The letter had forced her to look objectively at what lay ahead, and she saw year after year of bleak loneliness if she pursued her solitary path. Margaret and the Ramsays were right; it was worth a try, coming back. It would be futile ending up a lonely old woman, not even knowing whether or not an alternative had ever been possible.

She reached the gateway and crossed the courtyard. It looked far prettier than she had ever seen it. No weeds between the cobbles, brilliant pink and red geraniums in terracotta urns and stone troughs against the walls and around the well, purple bougainvillaea spreading its way up and over the door which led into the kitchen area. Liana stopped, it all seemed so welcoming, not in the least how she had expected to find it. A large key was sticking out of the kitchen-door lock, obviously meant for her to turn. She turned it and opening the door stepped inside. Part of the *castello* had been separated off from the ruins and beautifully restored. There were no unhappy ghosts in these sun-filled rooms. Everything was clean and smelled of fresh polish, the furniture was pine and copies of Etruscan pottery hung on the newly plastered walls. It *felt* happy.

A vase of freshly picked mimosa stood on the pine table in the centre of the kitchen, the small, brilliant yellow bobble flowers seeming to add an even more cheerful light to the room. Liana sat down at the table and opened the second envelope. Glancing at the time, she saw she was a little late. I must hurry, she thought, hastily unfolding the single page of paper.

After scanning it quickly she smiled. So, Eleanora had disobeyed her after all and had restored the *castello*. Her anger all those years ago now seemed ridiculous. Her daughter had been right, and she had been wrong.

She heard the laughter of the other Eleanora, the young girl of her childhood, her dearest friend, and knew she was there in the *castello* with her. Eleanora's voice echoed across the years, tender and overflowing with love. '*I shall always be with you for as long as you live. Nothing can separate the indivisible.*' No hint of sadness now as past and present merged together.

'And you are.' Liana spoke aloud, but she was smiling through her tears. 'You are with me. You were right, and I was wrong. You had faith and I didn't. I can see it now. Part of you has a new flowering in Eleanora. New and completely different, but linked back to the past by love. You are, and always have been, a link in the chain of my life. Just as they have all been. Even Raul and baby James, they are links, too, part of the whole me.'

Suddenly she realized she was standing in the middle of the kitchen, speaking in a loud voice, half laughing, half crying. Just as well the place is empty. What a fool I must sound, she thought. She fished a handkerchief from her bag and wiped her eyes, then looked at her watch.

'I must hurry. I shall be late.'

A shower of pollen from the mimosa floated down, sparkling golden dust in the sunlight as the kitchen door slammed. Liana had left the *castello*.

*

The door to the tiny ancient church creaked protestingly at being opened. The congregation, four people whom Liana had never seen before, turned and stared, but the three people standing before the priest at the altar rail did not move.

'I call upon these persons here present to witness that I, Eleanora Margaret Hamilton-Howard do take thee, Peter Richard Chapman, to be my lawful wedded husband, to have and to hold from this day forward, for better for worse, for richer for poorer, in sickness and in health, to love and to cherish, till death do us part.'

'Do you think that's the mother? The Countess of Wessex?' The British vice-consul's wife, always curious, hissed the question at her husband.

Her husband did not hear her, but the consul, her husband's immediate superior, did. He looked disapproving, and made a point of ostentatiously turning back to face the altar. 'It is no business of ours,' he said. 'We have merely been asked to witness this marriage.'

Unabashed, the vice-consul's wife continued to watch the elegant woman who was slowly making her way down the narrow central aisle. 'I think it is,' she said.

Father Kevin Brophy looked up and glared. Was it not bad enough that he had been dragged out of retirement to conduct a service in English, without its being continually interrupted by doors opening and people whispering! 'Sssh,' he hissed loudly.

Liana hurried the last few steps and stood just behind Nicholas.

The moment her footsteps stopped, he turned. His grey eyes lightened as he smiled. 'You came,' he said simply.

'Sssh!' Father Brophy hissed so loudly he started coughing. He took a large sip of wine from the communion chalice. The wine had come in useful after all. He took another large sip. Might as well finish it; they were not taking communion. In fact, if he had known the bride was not a Catholic he would never have agreed to the ceremony; but the powers that be had kept it from him. He paused, resumed his mantle of dignity and continued. 'You have declared your consent before the Church. May the

Lord in his goodness strengthen your consent and fill you both with his blessings. What God has joined together, let no man put asunder.'

'Amen,' the congregation and the newly weds said together.

Eleanora and Peter turned. Liana caught her breath. How beautiful Eleanora looked. She was radiant, dressed in a cream linen suit, a spray of white orchids in her hand. Liana's fashion-conscious eye spotted Dolly Pragnell's unerring instinct for the right outfit for the occasion. She smiled tentatively. Would they accept her presence? Peter and Eleanora halted by the side of Liana. Words were not necessary. Their loving smiles told her all she needed to know. They were glad she was there, and it was right. She was the mother of the bride. Proudly she watched them walk ahead down the aisle.

Nicholas followed, but he paused and waited for Liana to fall into step beside him. It was so easy, so natural. Together they followed Eleanora and Peter outside into the sunlight, the father and mother of the bride behind the new husband and wife.

We made the same vow here on the same day in the same church, twenty-four long years ago. Liana looked at Nicholas. Was he thinking the same as herself?

'Nearly a quarter of a century,' he said picking up her thoughts. 'Time now, I think, to close the door on the past.'

Liana nodded. The words she was struggling to find were smothered by Eleanora flinging her arms around her the moment they got outside and hugging her until she could hardly breathe. But I must remember to tell him we have to leave the door ajar, she thought. We must never close it completely. Every link in our past is important because it forges the future.

And there was a future. She remembered Byron's words, 'And life's enchanted cup but sparkles near the brim.' They had the time. Life's enchanted cup could still sparkle for them.

Printed in Great Britain
by Amazon

65694750R00293